BLACK CROSS

GREG ILES

BLACK CROSS

A DUTTON BOOK

DUTTON
Published by the Penguin Group
Penguin Books USA Inc., 375 Hudson Street,
New York, New York 10014, U.S.A.
Penguin Books Ltd, 27 Wrights Lane,
London W8 5TZ, England
Penguin Books Australia Ltd, Ringwood,
Victoria, Australia
Penguin Books Canada Ltd, 10 Alcorn Avenue,
Toronto, Ontario, Canada M4V 3B2
Penguin Books (N.Z.) Ltd, 182–190 Wairau Road,
Auckland 10, New Zealand

Penguin Books Ltd, Registered Offices:
Harmondsworth, Middlesex, England

First published by Dutton, an imprint of Dutton Signet,
a division of Penguin Books USA Inc.

Distributed in Canada by McClelland & Stewart Inc.

First Printing, January, 1995
10 9 8 7 6 5 4 3 2 1

 REGISTERED TRADEMARK—MARCA REGISTRADA

LIBRARY OF CONGRESS CATALOGING-IN-PUBLICATION DATA

Iles, Greg.
    Black cross / Greg Iles.
      p.   cm.
    ISBN 0-525-93829-X
    1. World War, 1939–1945—Secret service—Great Britain—Fiction. 2. World War,
1939–1945—Germany—Fiction. 3. Holocaust, Jewish (1939–1945)—Fiction. 4. Zionists—
Fiction. I. Title
PS3559.L47B53 1995
813'.54—dc20   94-34642
                                                                              CIP

Printed in the United States of America
Set in Sabon
Designed by Julian Hamer

PUBLISHER'S NOTE

For
Betty Thornhill Iles
AND
Every man and woman
who sacrificed their lives
in the Allied cause.

ACKNOWLEDGMENTS

Many thanks to Natasha Kern, a superagent in the true sense of the word.

Many thanks to Elaine Koster, a publisher with the guts to let her authors break the rules.

Special thanks to John Grisham.

To Edward Stackler, fine editor and master of POV!

For research assistance: Scotland, Colin Maclean and Beryl Austin; London, Folly Marland, Stuart Hamilton, and at the Imperial War Museum, Peter Simkins; Washington, D.C., David Kasmier; Portland, OR, Oriana Green; Novato, CA, Dale Wilson

Medical advisors: Jerry Iles, M.D., Michael Bourland, M.D., Noah Archer, M.D., Barry Tillman, M.D., David Steckler, M.D.

Electrical engineering: Marlon Copeland, Howard Wooten

Languages: Toos S. Nooijen, Jean-Claude Coulerez, Susan Callon, Christof Schauwecker, Gloria Glickstein Brame

8th Air Force: Austin Ingels, Donald Toye

Judaica: Jerry Gross, Louis DeVries, Ronald E. Stackler

Matters Scottish: Diana Gabaldon <g>

Special thanks to Jeff Walker for devious plot insights.

Special thanks to Geoff Iles for brotherly advice.

Kudos to all the pros at Dutton/Signet.

Readers: Betty Iles, Courtney Aldridge, Mary Lou England

Putting Up With My Obsession Committee: Carrie and Madeline.

All mistakes are mine.

There is a mysterious cycle in human events.
To some generations much is given.
Of other generations much is expected.
This generation has a rendezvous with destiny.

—Franklin Delano Roosevelt

It's odd how death often marks a beginning rather than an end. We know someone for ten years, twenty years, longer. We see them in the course of daily life. We speak, laugh, exchange harsh words; we think we have some notion of who they are.

And then they die.

In death, the fluid impressions formed over a lifetime begin to assume definite shape. The picture comes into focus. New facts emerge. Safes are opened, wills read. With finality, and with distance, we often discover that the people we thought we knew were actually quite different than we imagined. And the closer we were to them, the more shocking this surprise is.

So it was with my grandfather. He died violently, and quite publicly, in circumstances so extraordinary that they got thirty seconds of airtime on the national evening news. It happened last Tuesday, in a MedStar helicopter ambulance en route from Fairplay, Georgia—the small town in which I was born and raised—to Emory University Hospital in Atlanta, where I work as an emergency physician. While making his rounds at Fairplay's local hospital, my grandfather collapsed at a nurses' station. Fighting to ignore the terrible pain in his lower back, he had a nurse take his blood pressure. When he heard the figures, he correctly diagnosed a leaking abdominal aortic aneurysm and realized that without immediate emergency surgery he would die.

With two nurses supporting him, he spoke on a telephone just long enough to summon the MedStar from Atlanta, forty miles away. My grandmother insisted on remaining by his side in the chopper, and the pilot reluctantly agreed. They don't usually allow that, but damn near everybody in the Georgia medical community knew or knew of my grandfather—a quiet but eminently respected lung specialist. Besides, my grandmother wasn't the kind of woman that men talked back to. Ever.

The MedStar crashed twenty minutes later on a quiet street in the suburbs of Atlanta. That was four days ago, and as yet no one has determined the cause of the crash. Just one of those freak things, I guess. Pilot error, they like to call it. I don't really care whose fault it was. I'm not looking to sue. We're not—or *weren't*—that kind of family.

My grandparents' deaths hit me especially hard, because they raised me from the age of five. My parents died in a car crash in 1970. I've seen more than my share of tragedy, I suppose. I still do. It sweeps through my emergency room every day and night, trailing blood and cocaine and whiskey-breath and burnt skin and dead kids. Such is life. The reason I'm writing this down is because of what happened at the burial—or rather, who I *met* at the burial. Because it was there, in a place of death, that my grandfather's secret life revealed itself at last.

The cemetery crowd—a large one for our town, and predominantly Protestant—had already drifted back toward the long line of sedate Lincolns and brighter Japanese imports. I was standing at the green edge of the graves, two side-by-side holes smelling of freshly turned earth. A pair of gravediggers waited to cover the gleaming silver caskets. They seemed in no particular hurry; both had been patients of my grandfather at one time or another. One—a wiry fellow named Crenshaw—had even been brought into the world by him, or so he said.

"They don't make docs like your grandpa anymore, Mark," he declared. "Or *Doctor,* I should say," he added, smiling. "I can't quite get used to that title. No offense, but I still remember catching you out here at midnight with that Clark girl."

I smiled back. That was a good memory. I can't quite get used to the title either, as a matter of fact. *Doctor* McConnell. I know I *am* a doctor—a damn good one—but when I stand, or stood, beside my grandfather, I always felt more like an apprentice, a bright but inexperienced student in the shadow of a master. That was what I was thinking when someone tugged at my jacket sleeve from behind.

"Afternoon, Rabbi," said the gravedigger, nodding past me.

"*Shalom,* Mr. Crenshaw," said a deep, much-traveled voice.

I turned. Behind me stooped an avuncular old man with snow-white hair and a yarmulke. His twinkling eyes settled on me and gave me a thorough going-over. "The spitting image," he said quietly. "Though you're a little heavier-boned than Mac was."

"My grandmother's genes," I said, a little embarrassed to be at a disadvantage.

"Quite right," said the old man. "Quite right. And a beautiful woman she was, too."

Suddenly I placed him. "Rabbi Leibovitz, isn't it?"

The old man smiled. "You have a good memory, Doctor. It's been a long time since you've seen me up close."

The old man's voice had a low, musical quality to it, as if all its edges had been worn away by years of soothing, reasonable speech. I nodded again. The gravediggers shuffled their feet.

"Well," I said, "I guess it's about time—"

"I'll take that shovel," Rabbi Leibovitz told Crenshaw.

"But Rabbi, you shouldn't be doing heavy work."

The rabbi took the shovel from the amazed gravedigger and spaded it into the soft pile of dirt. "This is work for a man's friends and family," he said. "Doctor?" He looked up at me.

I took the other shovel from the second man and followed his example.

"Afternoon, Mark," muttered Crenshaw, a little put out. He and his partner shambled off toward a battered pickup that waited at a discreet distance.

I shoveled earth steadily into my grandmother's grave while Rabbi Leibovitz worked on the other. It was hot—Georgia summer hot—and soon I was pouring sweat. As the backfill rose toward my feet, I was a little surprised to find that the shoveling felt better than anything I had done since I first heard the news of my grandparents' deaths, and far better than anything anyone had said to console me. When I checked the old man's progress, I was surprised to find him only a little behind me in his work. I went back to mine with a will.

When I finished filling my grandmother's grave, I walked around to help Rabbi Leibovitz. Together we finished filling my grandfather's in a couple of minutes. The rabbi laid his shovel on the ground behind him, then turned back to the grave and began praying quietly. I stood holding my shovel in silence until he had fin-

ished. Then, as if by mutual consent, we started walking to the narrow asphalt lane where I had parked my black Saab.

I saw no other cars nearby. The cemetery was a good mile and
a half from the center of town. "Did you walk all the way out here,
Rabbi?" I asked.

"I caught a ride from a good Christian," he said. "I was hoping
to ride back with you."

The request caught me off guard, but I said, "Sure, glad to do
it."

I opened the passenger door for him, then went around and
got behind the wheel. The Swedish-built engine revved smoothly.
"Where to?" I asked. "You still live across from the synagogue?"

"Yes. But I thought we might visit your grandparents' house.
Are you staying there while you're in town?"

"Yes," I admitted. "Yes, I am." I looked at him curiously. Then
I felt a familiar sense of recognition. I had seen these situations before. Some people don't feel comfortable confronting serious medical symptoms in a physician's office. "Is there something you need
to tell me, Rabbi?" I asked slowly. "Are you in need of medical
attention?"

"No, no. I'm quite well for my age, thank God. But there is
something I'd like to talk to you about, Mark. Something I think
your grandfather meant to discuss with you . . . eventually. But
somehow I don't think he ever made the time."

"What are you talking about?"

"About what your grandfather did in the war, Mark. Did he
ever talk to you about that?"

I felt myself flush a little. "No. He never got past 'I did my duty
when it was required.' "

"That sounds like Mac."

"He never talked to my grandmother about it either," I confided, surprising myself. "She told me that, and . . . it hurt her. It
was kind of like a hole in our lives. Small, maybe, but there all the
same. A dark place, you know?"

Rabbi Leibovitz nodded. "A very dark place, Mark. And I think
it's about time someone shed a little light on it for you."

Fifteen minutes later we were standing in the study of my grandparents' house. Three generations of doctors had grown up in this

rambling country clapboard. We were looking down at the steel fire-safe where my grandfather had always kept his personal papers.

"Do you know the combination?" the rabbi asked.

I shook my head. He reached into his back pocket, withdrew his wallet, and dug around inside until he found what he was looking for—a small white card of introduction, one of my grandfather's. He read some numbers off the back, then looked at me expectantly.

"Listen, Rabbi," I said, beginning to grow uncomfortable. "I'm not exactly sure why we're here. I mean, I know you and my grandfather were acquaintances, but I never knew you were close. Frankly, I don't see how anything in that safe could be any business of yours." I paused. "Unless . . . he left the synagogue a bequest in his will. Is that it?"

Leibovitz chuckled. "You're a suspicious man, Mark, just like your grandfather. No, this has nothing to do with money. I doubt if Mac had much left, to tell you the truth. Except for the insurance, which was only around fifty thousand, I think. He gave most of his money away."

I shot him a sidelong glance. "How do you know all that?"

"Your grandfather and I were more than acquaintances, Mark. We were fast friends. I know about his money because he gave a lot of it to the synagogue. Once you made it through medical school, he figured you could take care of yourself, and your grandmother too, if he happened to die first. He owned this house, of course. You'll get that. As far as the money he gave me, I was to use it to help persecuted Jews who were trying to reach Israel." Leibovitz turned his callused palms upward. "This all goes back to the war, Mark. What Mac did during the war. If you open that safe for me, everything will become much clearer."

That reasonable, forthright voice was hard to refuse. "All right," I agreed, knowing I was being manipulated, but strangely unable to resist. "Read the combination again."

As Leibovitz read, I worked the dial on the safe until I heard a *click,* then pulled open the heavy door. The first thing I saw was a stack of papers. Just what I had expected. They looked like legal documents—titles to the two family cars, the house, an ancient mortgage.

"Do you see a box?" the rabbi asked. "It would be nearly flat, and not too large."

Carefully I dug through the papers. Sure enough, near the bottom of the stack my fingers touched a flat wooden box. I removed it from the safe. It was made of plain pine, about six inches square. I had never seen it before.

"Open it," Leibovitz commanded.

I looked over my shoulder at him, then turned back and lifted the lid off the box. The glint of polished metal flickered in the light.

"What is that?" I asked.

"The Victoria Cross. The most coveted decoration in the British Empire. Have you heard of it?"

"The Victoria Cross. . . . Isn't that what Michael Caine won in *Zulu*?"

Leibovitz shook his head sadly. "Television," he muttered. "Yes, the Victoria Cross was awarded to a handful of Englishmen who repulsed an overwhelming Zulu army at Rorke's Drift in South Africa."

I lifted the cross gingerly and examined it in the light. It was bronze, and hung from a crimson ribbon. The center of the cross bore a lion standing upon a crown. Engraved on a scroll beneath the crown were the words: *FOR VALOUR*.

Rabbi Leibovitz spoke as if addressing a small congregation. "The list of recipients of the V.C. constitutes the most revered roll in English military history, Mark. As far as the public knows, only thirteen hundred and fifty have been awarded since the decoration was instituted by Queen Victoria in 1856. But there is another list—a much smaller list—that is known to no one but the monarch and the prime minister. It is the Secret List, and upon it are inscribed the names of those who have performed unparalleled acts of valor and devotion in the face of the enemy, but of such a sensitive nature that they can never be revealed." He took a deep breath, then said: "Your grandfather's name is on that list, Mark."

My head snapped up in astonishment. "You must be joking. He never mentioned anything like that to me."

The old rabbi smiled patiently. "That was the charge that came with the award. The decoration can never be worn in public. I suppose the secret cross was given so that in the dark of night, long after glory had passed, men like your grandfather would have something to remind them that their . . . sacrifices were appreciated."

Leibovitz looked thoughtful. "Still, it takes a special kind of man to hide that kind of glory."

"Granddad was no egomaniac," I conceded, "but he wasn't especially modest either. He didn't hide honors he deserved."

Leibovitz sighed sadly. "Mac deserved this honor, but he wasn't proud of what he had *done* to deserve it. He began the war as a conscientious objector, you know."

"I didn't know that."

"Mark, long ago your grandfather sought me out to discuss something that troubled him deeply. He'd spoken to his Christian pastor about it, but said the fellow hadn't really understood what he was talking about. The pastor told Mac he was a hero, that he had no reason to be ashamed of what he'd done. Mac struggled along on his own for a while, then finally came to me."

"Why you?"

"Because I'm a Jew. He thought perhaps I could give him special insight into his problem, that I might be able to help him to unburden his soul."

I swallowed. "Did you?"

"I tried my best. I truly did. Over a period of years, in fact. And he was grateful for the effort. But I never really succeeded. Your grandfather carried his burden with him to the grave."

"Well, damn it, you've got to tell me now. What did he do that was so terrible? And when did he do it? He told me that he spent the war in England."

Leibovitz's eyes settled on some neutral point in space. "He spent *most* of the war in England, that's true—doing research at Oxford. But for two short weeks, your grandfather traveled quite a bit. And his travels ultimately led him to a place that must have been very close to hell on earth."

"Where was that?"

Leibovitz's face hardened. "A place called Totenhausen, on the Recknitz River in northern Germany. As to when Mac was there, if you turn over the cross it will tell you."

I turned the cross over. Engraved on its back were the words:

Mark Cameron McConnell, M.D.

15 February 1944

"That's the date that the act of valor took place," Leibovitz mur- mured. "Fifty years ago, your grandfather did something so strategi- cally important, so singularly heroic that he was awarded an honor only one other non-British subject has ever received. That other recip- ient was also an American."

"Who was it?"

The rabbi straightened up with difficulty, his spine stiff as a ramrod. "The Unknown Soldier."

I felt a lump in my throat. "I can't believe this," I said hoarsely. "This is the most extraordinary thing I've ever heard. Or seen," I added, holding up the ribbon and cross. It seemed somehow heavier in my hands.

"You're about to see something still more extraordinary," Leib- ovitz said. "Something unique."

I swallowed in anticipation.

"Look under the padding in the box. It should still be there."

I handed the cross to Rabbi Leibovitz, then gingerly lifted the linen cloth that lined the bottom of the pine box. Beneath it I found a frayed swatch of woolen cloth, a Scottish tartan pattern. I looked up questioningly.

"Keep going," Leibovitz said.

Beneath the tartan I found a photograph. It was black-and- white, with contrasts so stark it looked like one of the old Dust Bowl photographs from *Life* magazine. It showed a young woman from the waist up. She wore a simple cotton dress, her slender body posed rather formally against a background of dark wooden planks. Her shoulder-length hair was blond and straight, and seemed to glow against the unfinished wood. Her face, though worn by care lines around the mouth, was set off by eyes as dark as the wood be- hind her. I guessed her age at thirty.

"Who is this?" I asked. "She's . . . I don't know. Not beautiful exactly, but . . . *alive*. Is it my grandmother? When she was younger, I mean?"

Rabbi Leibovitz waved his hand impatiently. "All in good time. Look beneath the photograph."

I did. A meticulously folded piece of notepaper lay there, wrin- kled and yellowed with age. I lifted it out and started to unfold it.

"Careful," he warned.

"Is this the citation for the award?" I asked, working delicately at the paper.

"Something else altogether."

I had it open now. The handwritten blue letters had almost completely faded, as if the note had been put through a washing machine by mistake, but the few words were still legible. I read them with a strange sense of puzzlement.

On my head be these deaths.
W

"I can barely read it. What does it mean? Who is 'W'?"

"You can barely read the writing, Mark, because it was nearly washed away by the freezing waters of the Recknitz River in 1944. What the note *means* can only be explained by telling you a rather involved and shocking story. And 'W'—as the author of that note so cryptically described himself—was Winston Churchill."

"Churchill!"

"Yes." The old rabbi smiled mischievously. "And thereby hangs a tale."

"My God," I said.

"Would you have any brandy about?" asked Leibovitz.

I went to fetch a bottle.

"I lay it all at Churchill's door."

The old rabbi had ensconced himself in a leather wing chair with a crocheted comforter around his knees and the brandy glass in his hand. "You know, of course, that Mac first went to England as a Rhodes scholar. That was 1930, the year after the Crash. He stayed two years, then was asked to stay a third and matriculate. Quite an honor. When he graduated and returned to the U.S., I'm sure he thought his 'English period' was finished. But it wasn't.

"He graduated medical school in thirty-eight, somehow squeezing in a masters in chemical engineering during his internship. By then it was 1940. He entered general practice with a friend of his father's, but he'd hardly settled in when a phone call came from Oxford. His old tutor told him that one of Churchill's scientific advisors had been impressed by some monographs he'd done on chemical warfare in World War One. They wanted him to join a

British team working on poison gases. America wasn't in the war yet, but Mac understood what was at stake. England was hanging by a thread."

"I do remember that much," I said. "He agreed to go on the condition that he would only work in a defensive capacity. Right?"

"Yes. Rather naively, if I may say so. Anyway, he took your grandmother with him to England, just in time for the Battle of Britain. It took some doing, but he talked Susan into going back to the States. Hitler never did invade England, but by then it was too late. They were separated for the duration.

"Fifty years," Leibovitz said softly. He paused as though he had lost his train of thought. "I suppose that seems an age to you, but try to picture the time. Dead of winter, January, 1944. The whole world—including the Germans—knew the Allies would invade Europe in the spring. The only question was where the blow would fall. Eisenhower had just been named Supreme Commander of OVERLORD. Churchill—"

"Excuse me, Rabbi," I interrupted. "No disrespect intended, but I get the feeling you're giving me the long version of this story."

He smiled with a forbearance learned at the sides of impatient children. "You have somewhere to go?"

"No. But I'm curious about my grandfather, not Churchill and Eisenhower."

"Mark, if I simply told you the end of this story, you would not believe me. I mean that. You cannot absorb what I am going to say unless you know what led to it. Do you understand?"

I nodded, trying to mask my impatience.

"No," Leibovitz said forcefully. "You don't. The worst thing you have ever seen in your life, all the worst things put together— child abuse, rape, even murder—these are as nothing compared to what I am about to tell you. It is a tale of cruelty beyond imagining, of men and women whose heroism has never been equaled." He raised a crooked finger and his voice went very low. "After hearing this story, your life will *never be the same.*"

"That's a lot of buildup, Rabbi."

He took a gulp of brandy. "I have no children, Doctor. Do you know why?"

"Well . . . I assume you never wanted any. Or that you or your wife were sterile."

"I am sterile," Leibovitz confirmed. "When I was sixteen, I was invited by some German doctors to sit in a booth and fill out a form that would take fifteen minutes to complete. During those fifteen minutes, high-intensity X-rays were passed through my testicles from three sides. Two weeks later, a Jewish surgeon and his wife saved my life by castrating me in their kitchen."

My hands felt suddenly cold. "Were you . . . in the camps?"

"No. I escaped to Sweden, along with the surgeon and his wife. But you see, I left my unborn children behind."

I didn't know what to say.

"That's the first time I've ever told that to a Christian," Leibovitz said.

"I'm not a Christian, Rabbi."

His eyes narrowed. "Do you know something I don't? You're not Jewish."

"I'm not anything. An agnostic, I guess. A professional doubter."

Leibovitz studied me for a long time, his face lined by emotions I could not interpret. "You say that so easily for one who has lived through so little."

"I've seen my share of suffering. And alleviated some, too."

He waved his hand in a European gesture that seemed to say many things at once. "Doctor, you have not even peered over the edge of the abyss."

Laying his hand across his eyes, Leibovitz sat motionless for nearly a minute. He seemed to be deciding if he had the strength to tell his story after all. Just as I was about to speak, he removed his hand and said, "Now are you ready to listen, Mark? Or would you prefer to leave things as they are?"

I looked down at the Victoria Cross, the faded note, the Scottish tartan and the photograph of the woman. "You've hooked me," I said. "But wait here a minute."

I went back to my grandfather's bedroom and got the small tape recorder he had used for dictating medical charts, and a thin box of Sony microcassettes. "Do you mind if I tape this?" I asked, setting up the recorder. "If the story is that important, perhaps it should be documented."

"It should have been told years ago," Leibovitz said. "But Mac would have none of it. He said knowing or not knowing about it wouldn't change human history by one whit. I disagreed with him. It's long past time to bring this story into the light."

I glanced at the window. "The light's almost gone, Rabbi."

He sighed indifferently. "Then we'll make a night of it."

"Can I give you a bit of advice? Editorially speaking?"

"Ah. You're an editor now?"

I shrugged. "I've written a few journal articles. Actually, I've been toying with writing a novel on my off weekends. A medical thriller. But perhaps I've found a new story to tell. Anyway, here's my advice—you can take it or leave it. That 'picture the scene' and 'I suppose' business? Drop all that. Just tell the story like you think it happened. Like you were a fly on the wall."

After a few moments, Leibovitz nodded. "I think I can do that," he said. He poured himself another brandy, then settled back into the leather wing chair and held up his glass in a toast.

"To the bravest man I ever knew."

2

OXFORD UNIVERSITY, ENGLAND, 1944

Mark McConnell quietly lifted the long steering pole out of the Cherwell River and slapped it back down. A spray of water and ice drenched the leather-jacketed back of his brother, who perched on the forward seat of the narrow wooden punt.

"You goddamn shitbird!" David whirled around, almost upsetting the boat in the process. He dug his gloved right hand into the river and shot back a volley of water and ice.

"Hold it!" Mark cried. "You'll sink us!"

"You surrendering?" David dipped his hand into the water again.

"Declaring a temporary cease-fire. For medical reasons."

"Chickenshit."

Mark wiggled the pole. "I've got the firepower."

"Okay, truce." David lifted his hand and turned back to the prow of the flat-bottomed punt as it crunched slowly around the next bend in the icy river. He was the shorter of the two brothers and built like a halfback, with sprinter's legs, a narrow waist, and thickly muscled shoulders. His sandy blond hair, strong jaw, and clear blue eyes completed the picture of Norman Rockwell charm. While Mark watched warily, he slid down onto the cross slats of the punt, leaned back, cradled his head in his hands and shut his eyes.

Mark scanned the river ahead. The bare trees on both banks hung so heavily with icicles that some branches nearly touched the snow carpeting the meadows beneath them. "This is insane," he said, flicking a final salvo of drops onto David's face. But he didn't mean it. If his younger brother hadn't driven down from the 8th

13

Air Force base at Deenethorpe, this winter day would have been like any other at Oxford: a bleak fourteen-hour newsreel watched through foggy laboratory windows. Rain changing into sleet and then back into rain, falling in great gray sheets that spattered the cobbled quads of the colleges, shrouded the Bodelian Library, and swelled the lazy Cherwell and Thames into torrents.

"This is the life," David murmured. "This is exactly how we picture you eggheads when we're on the flight line. Living the life of Reilly, canoeing around a goddamn college campus. We risk our asses every day while you bums sit up here, supposedly winning the war with your little gray cells."

"You mean *punting* around a goddamn college campus."

David opened one eye, looked back and snorted. "Jeez, you sound more like a limey every year. If you called Mom on a telephone, she wouldn't even know you."

Mark studied his younger brother's face. It was good to see him again, and not merely because it provided an excuse to get out of the lab for an afternoon. Mark needed the human contact. In this place that offered so much comradeship, he had become a virtual outcast. Lately, he'd had to fight a wild impulse to simply turn to a sympathetic face on a bus and begin talking. Yet looking at his brother now—an Air Force captain who spent most days on white-knuckle bombing runs over Germany—he wondered if he had the right to add his own pressures to those already on David's shoulders.

"I think my hands are frostbitten," Mark grumbled, as the punt pushed on through the black water. "I'd give a hundred pounds for an outboard motor."

Once already he had resolved to talk to David about his problem—three weeks ago, on Christmas Day—but a last-minute bombing assignment had scotched their plans to get together. Now another month had almost slipped by. It had been that way for the last four years. Time rushing past like a river in flood. Now another Christmas was gone, and another New Year. 1944. Mark could scarcely believe it. Four years in this sandstone haven of cloisters and spires while the world outside tore itself to pieces with unrelenting fury.

"Hey," David called, his eyes still closed. "How are the girls down here?"

"What do you mean?"

David opened both eyes and craned his neck to stare back at his brother. "What do I *mean?* Has four years away from Susan pickled your pecker as well as your brain? I'm talking about English dames. We've got to live up to our billing, you know."

"Our billing?"

"Overpaid, over*sexed,* and over here, remember? Hell, I know you love Susan. I know plenty of guys who are crazy about their wives. But four years. You can't spend every waking moment holed up in that Frankenstein lab of yours."

Mark shrugged. "I have, though."

"Christ, I'd tell you about some of my adventures, only you wouldn't be able to sleep tonight."

Mark jabbed the pole into the river bottom. It had been a mistake to send Susan home, but any sane man would have done the same at the time, considering the danger of German invasion. He was getting tired of paying for that particular misjudgment, though. He'd been on the wrong side of the Atlantic longer than any American he knew.

"To hell with this," he said. As they rounded the bend at St. Hilda's College, he levered the punt into a sharp embankment near Christ Church Meadow. The impact of the bow against the shore practically catapulted David out of the boat, but he landed with an athlete's natural grace.

"Let's get a beer!" David said. "Don't you eggheads ever drink around here? Whose dumbass idea was this, anyway?"

Mark found himself laughing as he climbed out of the punt. "As a matter of fact, I know a few chaps who'd be glad to take you on in the drinking contest of your choice."

"Chaps?" David gaped at his brother. "Did I hear you say *chaps,* Mac? We gotta get you back to the States, *old sport.* Back to Georgia. You sound like the Great Gatsby."

"I'm only playing to your Tom Buchanan."

David groaned. "We'd better go straight to whiskey. A little Kentucky bourbon'll wash that limey accent right out of your throat."

"I'm afraid they don't stock Kentucky's finest here in Oxford, Slick."

David grinned. "That's why I brought a fifth in my muzette bag.

Cost me thirty bucks on the black market, but I wouldn't drink that high-toned limey swill if I was dying of thirst."

They crossed Christ Church Meadow mostly in silence. David took several long pulls from the bottle stowed in his flight bag. Mark declined repeated offers to share the whiskey. He wanted his mind clear when he spoke about his dilemma. He would have preferred to have David's mind clear as well, but there was nothing he could do about that.

Walking side by side, the differences between the brothers were more marked. Where David was compact and almost brawny, Mark was tall and lean, with the body of a distance runner. He moved with long, easy strides and a surefootedness acquired through years of running cross-country races. His hands were large, his fingers long and narrow. Surgeon's hands, his father had boasted when he was only a boy. David had inherited their mother's flashing blue eyes, but Mark's were deep brown, another legacy from his father. And where David was quick to smile or throw a punch, Mark wore the contemplative gaze of a man who carefully weighed all sides of any issue before acting.

He chose the Welsh Pony, in George Street. The pub did a brisk evening trade, but privacy could be had if desired. Mark went up to one of the two central bars and ordered a beer to justify the use of the table, then led David to the rear of the pub. By the time he was halfway to the bottom of his mug, he realized that David had drunk quite a lot of bourbon, with English stout to chase it down. Yet David remained surprisingly lucid. He was like their father in that way, if in no other. The analogy was not comforting.

"What the hell's eating you, Mac?" David asked sharply. "All day I've had the feeling you wanted to say something, but you keep backing off. You're like an old possum circling a garbage can. You're driving me nuts. Get it out in the open."

Mark leaned back against the oak chair and took his first long swallow of the night. "David, what does it feel like to bomb a German city?"

"What do you mean?" David straightened up, looking puzzled. "You mean am I scared?"

"No, I mean actually dropping the bombs. How does it feel to drop stick after stick of five-hundred-pound bombs on a city you know is full of women and children?"

"Hell, I don't drop 'em. The bombardier does that. I just fly the plane."

"So that's how you do it. You distance yourself from the act. Mentally, I mean."

David squinted at his brother. "Jesus, let's don't start, okay? It's not enough I had to listen to all that crap from Dad when I enlisted? Now that he's gone, you're going to take over?" He swung a heavy forearm to take in the pub and the snowy alley visible through a frosted window. "You sit up here in your little land of Oz, playing paper games with the other eggheads. You lose touch real quick. You start forgetting why we got into this war in the first place."

Mark held up his hand. "I know we have to stop the Nazis, David. But we're destroying so much more than that."

"Wake up, Mac. It's 1944. We're talking Hitler here. The fucking Führer."

"I realize that. But do you notice how Hitler is used to justify any Allied act, any Allied sacrifice? Area bombing. Suicide missions. The politicians act as if Hitler sprang fully formed from the brow of Jupiter. Men of conscience could have stopped that madman ten years ago."

"Coulda, woulda, shoulda," David muttered. "Welcome to the real world. Hitler asked for it, and now he's gonna get it."

"Yes, he did, and he is. But must we destroy an entire culture to destroy one man? Do we wipe out a whole country to cure one epidemic?"

David suddenly looked very angry indeed. "The Germans, you mean? Let me tell you about those *people* of yours. I had a buddy, name of Chuckie Wilson, okay? His B-17 went down near Würzburg, after the second Schweinfurt raid. The pilot was killed in flight, but Chuckie and two other guys got out of the plane. One guy was captured, another was smuggled out of France by the Resistance. But Chuckie was captured by some German civilians." David downed a double shot of whiskey, then lapsed into a sullen silence.

"And?"

"And they lynched him."

Mark felt the hairs on his neck rise. "They what?"

"Strung him up to the nearest tree, goddamn it."

"I thought the Germans treated captured flyers well. At least on the Western Front."

"Regular Kraut soldiers do. But the SS ain't regular, and the German civilians hate our guts."

"How do you know about the lynching?"

"The guy who made it out saw the whole thing. You want to know the worst part? While these civilians were stringing Chuckie up, a company of Waffen SS drove up in a truck. They sat there laughing and smoking while the bastards killed him, then drove away. Made me think of that colored guy that got lynched on the Bascombe farm back home. The lynchers claimed he raped a white girl, remember? But there wasn't any evidence, and there damn sure wasn't any trial. Remember what Uncle Marty said? The sheriff and his deputies stood there and watched the whole thing."

David slowly opened and closed his left fist while he knocked back a swig of bourbon with his right. "The guy who saw Chuckie lynched said there were just as many women there as men. He said one woman jumped up and hung on his feet while he swung."

"I see your point." Mark leaned back and took a deep breath. "Down here we lose sight of how personal war can be. We don't see the hatred."

"Damn right you don't, buddy. You oughta fly a raid with us sometime. Just once. Freezing your balls off, trying to remember to breathe from your mask, knowing ten seconds of exposed flesh could mean frostbite surgery. The whole ride you're cursing yourself for every time you ever skipped Sunday school."

Mark was thinking of an offer he had recently made to a Scottish brigadier general. In a fit of anger he'd threatened to leave his laboratory and volunteer to carry a rifle at the front. "Maybe I should get closer to the real war," he said quietly. "What are my convictions worth if I don't know what war really is? I could request a transfer to a forward surgical unit in Italy—"

David slammed his whiskey glass down, reached across the table and pinned his brother's arm to the scarred wood. Several patrons looked in their direction, but one glare from David was enough to blunt their curiosity. "You try that, and I'll break your friggin' legs," he said. "And if you try to do it without me knowing, I'll find out."

Mark was stunned by his brother's vehemence.

"I'm dead serious, Mac. You don't want to go anywhere near a real battlefield. Even from five miles up, I can tell you those places are hell on earth. You read me?"

"Loud and clear, ace," Mark said. But he was troubled by a feeling that for the first time he was seeing his brother as he really was. The David he remembered as a brash, irrepressible young athlete had been transformed by the war into a haggard boy-man with the eyes of a neurosurgeon.

"David," Mark whispered with sudden urgency, feeling his face grow hot with the prospect of confession. "I've got to talk to you." He couldn't stop himself. The words that became illegal the moment he uttered them came tumbling out in a flood. "The British are after me to work on a special project for them. They want me to spearhead it. It's a type of weapon that hasn't been used before—well, that's not strictly true, it *has* been used before but not in this way and not with this much potential for wholesale slaughter—"

David caught hold of his arm. "Whoa! Slow down. What are you babbling about?"

Mark looked furtively around the pub. The background hum of voices seemed sufficient to cover quiet conversation. He leaned across the table. "A secret weapon, David. I'm not kidding. It's just like the movies. It's a goddamn nightmare."

"A secret weapon."

"That's what I said. It's something that would have little to guide it. It would kill indiscriminately. Men, women, children, animals—no distinction. They'd die by the thousands."

"And the British want you to spearhead this project?"

"Right."

David's mouth split into an amazed smile. "Boy, did they ever pick the wrong guy."

Mark nodded. "Well, they think I'm the right guy."

"What kind of weapon is this? I don't see how it could be much more destructive or less discriminating than a thousand-bomber air raid."

Mark looked slowly around the pub. "It is, though. It's not a bomb. It's not even one of the super-bombs you've probably heard rumors about. It's something . . . something like what wounded Dad."

David recoiled, the cynicism instantly gone from his face. "You mean *gas?* Poison gas?"

Mark nodded.

"Shit, neither side has used gas yet in this war. Even the Nazis still remember the trenches from the last one. There are treaties prohibiting it, right?"

"The Geneva Protocol. But nobody cares about that. The U.S. didn't even sign it."

"Jesus. What kind of gas is it? Mustard?"

Mark's laugh had an almost hysterical undertone. "David, nobody knows the horrific effects of mustard gas better than you or I. But this gas I'm talking about is a thousand times worse. A *thousand* times worse. You can't see it, you don't even have to breathe it. But brother it will kill you. It's the equivalent of a cobra strike to the brain."

David had gone still. "I assume you're not supposed to be telling me any of this?"

"Absolutely not."

"Well . . . I guess you'd better start at the beginning."

3

Mark let his eyes wander over the thinning crowd. Of those who remained, he knew half by sight. Two were professors working on weapons programs. He kept his voice very low.

"One month ago," he said, "a small sample of colorless liquid labeled *Sarin* was delivered to my lab for testing. I usually get my samples from anonymous civilians, but this was different. Sarin was delivered by a Scottish brigadier general named Duff Smith. He's a one-armed old warhorse who's been pressuring me on and off for years to work on offensive chemical weapons. Brigadier Smith said he wanted an immediate opinion on the lethality of Sarin. As soon as I had that, I was to start trying to develop an effective mask filter against it. Only in the case of Sarin, a mask won't do it. You need protection over your entire body."

David looked thoughtful. "Is this a German gas? Or Allied stuff?"

"Smith wouldn't tell me. But he did warn me to take extra precautions. Christ, was he ever right. Sarin was like nothing I'd ever seen. It kills by short-circuiting the central nervous system. According to my experiments, it exceeds the lethality of phosgene by a factor of thirty."

David seemed unimpressed.

"Do you understand what I'm saying, David? Phosgene was the most lethal gas used in World War One. But compared to Sarin it's like . . . *nothing.* One-tenth of one milligram of Sarin—one speck the size of a grain of sand—will kill you in less than a minute. It's invisible in lethal concentration, and it will pass through human skin. *Right through your skin.*"

David's mouth was working silently. "I've got the picture. Go on."

"Last week, Brigadier Smith paid me another visit. This time he asked how I would feel if he told me Sarin was a German gas, and had no counterpart in the Allied arsenal. He wanted to know what I would do to protect Allied cities. And my honest answer was nothing. To protect the inhabitants of a city from Sarin would be impossible. It's not like a heavy-bomber raid. As bad as those are, people can come out from the shelters when they're over. Depending on weather conditions, Sarin could lie in the streets for days, coating sidewalks, windows, grass, food, anything."

"Okay," David said. "What happened next?"

"Smith tells me Sarin *is* a German gas. Stolen from the heart of the Reich, he says. Then he tells me I'm wrong—there *is* something I can do to protect our cities."

"What's that?"

"Develop an equally lethal gas, so that Hitler won't dare use Sarin himself."

David nodded slowly. "If he's telling the truth about Sarin, that sounds like the only thing to do. I don't see the problem."

Mark's face fell. "You don't? Christ, you of all people should understand."

"Look . . . I don't want to get into this pacifist thing again. I thought you'd come to terms with that. Hell, you've been working for the British since 1940."

"But only in a defensive capacity, you know that."

David expelled air from his cheeks. "To tell you the truth, I never really saw the difference. You're either working in the war effort or you're not."

"There's a big difference, David, believe me. Even in liberal Oxford, I'm an official leper."

"Be glad you're in Oxford. They'd beat the crap out of you at my air base."

Mark rubbed his forehead with his palms. "Look, I understand the logic of deterrence. But there has never been a weapon like this before. *Never.*" He watched with relief as the two professors left the pub. "David, I'm going to tell you something that most people don't

BLACK CROSS ❖ 23

know, and we've never discussed. Until one month ago, poison gas was the most humane weapon in the world."

"*What?*"

"It's the truth. Despite the agony of burns and the horror of chemical weapons, ninety-four percent of the men gassed in World War One were fit for duty again in nine weeks. Nine weeks, David. The mortality figure for poison gas is somewhere around two percent. Mortality from guns and shells is twenty-five percent—ten times higher. The painful fact is that our father was an exception."

David's confusion was evident in his bunched eyebrows. "What are you telling me, Mark?"

"I'm trying to explain that, until Sarin was invented, my aversion to gas warfare was based primarily on the paralyzing terror it held for soldiers, and the psychological aftermath of being wounded by gas. Figures don't tell the whole truth, especially about human pain. But with Sarin, chemical warfare has entered an entirely new phase. We're talking about a weapon that has four times the mortality rate of shot and shell. Sarin is one hundred percent lethal. It will kill *every living thing* it touches. I would rather carry a rifle at the front than be responsible for developing something that destructive."

David's whole posture conveyed the reluctance he felt to stray onto this territory. "Listen, I swore I'd never argue with you about this again. It's the same argument I always had with Dad. The Sermon on the Mount versus machine guns. Gandhi versus Hitler. Passive resistance can't work against Germany, Mark. The Nazis just *don't give a damn.* You turn the other cheek, those bastards'll slice it off for you. Hell, it was the Germans who gassed Dad in the first place!"

"Keep your voice down."

"Yeah, yeah. Jeez, I don't like where this conversation's ended up." The young pilot scratched his stubbled chin, deep in thought. "Okay . . . okay, just listen to me for a minute. Everybody back home calls you Mac, right? They always have."

"What does that have to do with anything?"

"Just listen. Everybody calls me David, right? Or Dave, or Slick. Why do you think everybody calls you Mac?"

Mark shrugged. "I was the oldest."

"Wrong. It was because you acted just like Dad did when he was a kid."

Mark shifted in his seat. "Maybe."

"Maybe, hell. You know I'm right. But what you don't know, or don't want to know, is that you *still* act just like him."

Mark stiffened.

"Our father—the great physician—spent most of his life inside our house. *Hiding.*"

"He was blind, for God's sake!"

"No, he wasn't," David said forcefully. "His eyes were damaged, but he could see when he wanted to."

Mark looked away, but didn't argue.

"God knows his face looked bad, but he didn't have to hide it. When I was a kid I thought he did. But he *didn't*. People could've gotten used to him. To the scars."

Mark closed his eyes, but the image in his mind only grew clearer. He saw a broken man lying on a sofa, much of his face and neck mutilated by blistering poisons that had splashed over half his body and entered his lungs. As a young boy Mark had watched his mother press cotton pads against that man's eyes, to soak up the tears that ran uncontrollably from the damaged membranes. She would retreat to the kitchen to weep softly when she was sure his father slept.

"Mom never got used to them," he said quietly.

"You're right," said David. "But it wasn't his face. It was the scars inside she couldn't handle. Do you hear what I'm saying? Dad was a certified war hero. He could've walked tall anywhere in America. But he didn't. And do you know why, *Doctor* McConnell? Because he brooded too goddamn much. Just like you. He tried to carry the weight of the fucking world on his shoulders. When I enlisted in the air corps, he threatened to disown me. And that was from his deathbed. But long before that, he'd made you so scared and disgusted with the idea of war that he charted your whole life for you." David wiped his brow. "Look, I'm not telling you what to do. You're the genius in this family."

"Come on, David."

"Goddamn it, drop the phony bullshit! I was eight years behind you in school, and all the teachers still called me by your name, okay? I'm a flyer, not a philosopher. But I can tell you this. When Ike's invasion finally jumps off, and our guys hit those French beaches, it's gonna be bad. Real bad. Guys younger than me are gonna be charging fortified machine-gun nests. Concrete bunkers. They're gonna be dying like flies over there. Now you're telling me they might have to face this Sarin stuff. If you're the guy who can stop Hitler from using it, or invent a defense against it, or at least give us the ability to hit back just as hard. . . . Well, you'd have to do a lot of talking to convince those guys it's right to do nothing at all. They'd call you a traitor for that."

Mark winced. "I know that. But what you don't understand is that *there is no defense*. The clothing required to protect a man from Sarin is airtight, and it's heavy. A soldier could fight in it for maybe an hour, two at the most. GIs won't even wear their standard gas masks in combat now, just because of a little discomfort. They could never take a defended beach in full body suits.

"So what are you saying? We're whipped, let's lie down and wait until we're all eating Wiener Schnitzel?"

"No. Look, if Sarin *is* a German gas, Hitler has yet to use it. Maybe he won't. I'm saying I won't be the man that makes Armageddon possible. Someone else can have that job."

David blinked his eyes several times, trying to focus on his watch. "Look," he said, "I think I'm going to drive back up to Deenethorpe tonight."

Mark reached across the table and squeezed his brother's arm. "Don't do that, David. I should never have brought this up."

"It's not that. It's just . . . I'm so tired of the whole goddamn thing. All the guys I knew that never came back from raids. I stopped making friends two months ago, Mac. It isn't worth it."

Mark saw then that the bourbon had finally taken effect.

"I think about you a lot, you know," David said softly. "When I feel those bombs drop out of Shady Lady's belly, when the flak's hammering the walls, I think, at least my brother doesn't have to see this. At least he's gonna make it back home. He deserves it. Always trying to do the right thing, to be the good son, faithful to the wife. Now I find out you're dealing with this stuff . . ." David looked down, as if trying to perceive something very small at the center of the table. "I try not to think about Dad too much. But you really are just like him. In the good ways too, I mean. Maybe you're right. Maybe he was right, too. I just don't want to think about it anymore tonight. And if I'm here, there's no way not to think about it."

"I understand."

Mark tipped the bartender as they left the pub, an act that always brought a wry smile from a man unused to the custom. David carefully tucked his nearly-empty bourbon bottle inside his leather jacket, then paused on the corner of George Street. "You'll do the right thing in the end," he said. "You always do. But I don't want to hear another word about any forward surgical unit. You're a real asshole sometimes. You must be the only guy in this war trying to think of ways to get closer to the fighting instead of away from it."

"Except for officers," Mark said.

"Right." David looked up the blacked out street, then down at his captain's bars. "Hey, I'm an officer, you know."

Mark punched him on the shoulder. "I won't tell anybody."

"Good. Now where did I park that goddamn jeep?"

Mark grinned and took the lead. "Follow me, Captain."

Twenty miles from the dreaming spires of Oxford, Winston Spencer Churchill stood stiffly at a window, smoking a cigar and peeking through a crack in his blackout curtains. The three men seated behind him waited tensely, watching the cigar's blue smoke curl up toward the red cornice.

"Headlights," Churchill said, a note of triumph in his voice.

He turned from the window. His face wore its customary scowl of pugnacious concentration, but these men knew him well. They saw the excitement in his eyes. "Brendan," he said gruffly. "Meet the car outside. Show the general directly to me."

Brendan Bracken, Churchill's former private secretary, Man Friday, and now minister of information, hurried to the main entrance of Chequers, one of the country estates that the prime minister used as a wartime hideaway.

Churchill quietly regarded the two men left in the room. Sitting rigid by the low fire was Brigadier General Duff Smith. The fifty-year-old Scotsman's empty left coat sleeve was pinned to his shoulder; the arm that should have filled it was buried somewhere in Belgium. A personal friend of Churchill, Smith now directed Special Operations Executive, the paramilitary espionage organization whose primary directive, penned by Churchill in 1940, was to "SET EUROPE ABLAZE."

To Brigadier Smith's right stood F. W. Lindemann, now Lord Cherwell. An Oxford don and longtime confidante, Lindemann advised the prime minister on all scientific matters, and monitored the work of a gaggle of geniuses—gleaned mostly from Oxford and

Cambridge—who labored twenty hours a day to increase the Allies' technological advantages over the Germans.

"Are we quite ready, gentlemen?" Churchill asked pointedly.

Brigadier Smith nodded. "As far as I'm concerned, Winston, it's an open and shut case. Of course, there's no guarantee Eisenhower will see it our way."

Professor Lindemann started to speak, but Churchill had already straightened at the sound of boots in the hallway. Brendan Bracken opened the door to the study and General Dwight D. Eisenhower strode in, followed by Commander Harry C. Butcher, his naval aide and friend of long standing. Sergeant Mickey McKeogh, Eisenhower's driver and valet, took up a post outside the door. The last American to enter was a major of army intelligence. He was not introduced.

"Greetings, my dear General!" Churchill said. He moved forward and pumped Eisenhower's hand with all-American enthusiasm. His red, black, and gold dressing gown contrasted strangely with the American general's simple olive drab uniform.

"Mr. Prime Minister," Eisenhower replied. "It's good to see you again, though unexpected."

The two men's eyes met with unspoken communication. Last month's conferences at Cairo and Teheran had not gone off without tensions between the two men. With the invasion less than five months away, Churchill still had reservations about a cross-Channel thrust into France, preferring to attack Germany through what he called the "soft underbelly" of Europe. Eisenhower, though he had just been named supreme commander of the Allied Expeditionary Force, was still adjusting to the mantle of power and had yet to assert his primacy in matters of strategy.

"An uneventful trip up from London, I hope?" Churchill said.

Eisenhower smiled. "The fog was so thick on Chesterfield Hill that Butcher had to get out and walk ahead of the car with a flashlight. But we made it, as you can see." He crossed the room and respectfully shook hands with Brigadier Smith, whom he'd known since 1942. Everyone else was introduced, excepting the American major of intelligence, who remained silent and stiff as a suit of decorative armor beside the closed study door.

Churchill rescued his dying cigar from an ashtray and walked over to his desk. He did not sit. This was the atmosphere he liked—

his Parliamentary milieu—him on his feet, speaking to a captive audience sitting on its collective ass. He picked up something small off the desk and rolled it in his palm. It appeared to be a bit of ornamental glass.

"Gentlemen," he began, "time is short and the matter at hand grave. So I'll be brief. The Nazis"—he pronounced the word *Narzis,* with a slur that managed to simultaneously convey both contempt and menace—"are up to their old tricks again. And some new ones as well. At the very moment when the tide seems to be turning irrevocably in our favor—I daresay on the very cusp of invasion—the Hun has sunk to new depths of frightfulness. He has apparently decided that no scientific abomination is too ghastly to use in his quest to stave off disaster."

Though well-accustomed by now to Churchill's flamboyant rhetoric, Eisenhower listened intently. He had only just arrived from North Africa via Washington, and any hint of new information about the European theater tantalized him.

Churchill rolled the piece of glass in his hand. "Before I proceed, I feel I must restate that this meeting, for official purposes, never occurred. No entries should be made in private diaries to record it. I am even breaking my own inviolate rule. No one will be asked to sign the guest book when they leave."

Eisenhower could stand no more buildup. "What the devil are you talking about, Mr. Prime Minister?"

Churchill held up the piece of glass he'd been fidgeting with. It was a tiny ampule. "Gentlemen, if I were to shatter this vial, every man-jack of us would be dead within a minute."

This was vintage Churchill, the dramatic prop, the verbal bombshell. "What the hell is it?" Eisenhower asked.

The prime minister bit down on his cigar and lowered his round head in a posture of challenge. "*Gas,*" he said.

Eisenhower squinted his eyes. "Poison gas?"

The prime minister nodded slowly, deliberately, then pulled the cigar from his mouth. "And not the kitchen stuff we choked on during the last war, though God knows that was bad enough. This is something entirely new, something absolutely *monstrous.*"

Eisenhower noted that Churchill had used the word "we" in reference to suffering poison gas attacks. He wondered if this was a veiled allusion to the fact that he had not seen combat in the First

World War, having served those years training tank troops in Penn-
sylvania. If Churchill was probing for a sore spot, he had found it.
"Well," he said curtly, "what kind of gas is it?"

"They call it *Sarin*. And it's a bloody miracle we've even found
out about it. We can all thank Duff Smith for that." Churchill
looked at the one-armed SOE chief, willing him to his feet.
"Brigadier?"

Duff Smith, a seasoned veteran of the Cameron Highlanders
regiment, stood with quiet confidence. "Thirty days ago," he said
with a vestigial Highland lilt, "we learned that our worst suspicions
about the German chemical effort were accurate. Not only have
they been pursuing weapons research at breakneck speed since before the war, but they've also been *producing* new gases and stockpiling them all over the country."

"Just a minute," Eisenhower broke in. "We've been doing the
same thing, haven't we?"

"Yes and no, General. Our programs didn't really get cracking
until we realized how much Germany had accomplished between
the wars. And, quite frankly, we've never managed to catch up."

"Are we talking about nerve agents?" asked the American major
of intelligence, speaking for the first time. "We've known about
Tabun for some time."

"Something of quite another magnitude," Smith said a bit tes-
tily. "The clearest indication of danger is that the Nazis have resumed testing these gases on human victims, mostly at SS-run
concentration camps in Germany and Poland. These experiments
have resulted in death for the exposed inmates in one hundred percent of the cases. We believe the Germans are setting up to deploy
nerve gas against our invasion troops."

Eisenhower cut his eyes at Commander Butcher.

"Did you say a hundred percent fatalities?" asked the army major. "Due strictly to the gas?"

"One hundred percent," Smith confirmed. "Thirty days ago, the
Polish Resistance managed to smuggle a sample of Sarin out of a
camp in northern Germany. Two days later we delivered that sample
to one of Lindemann's chemical weapons specialists at Oxford."

This time it was Eisenhower who interrupted. "I thought the
British chemical warfare complex was at Porton Down, on Salisbury
Plain."

"In the main," Smith responded, "that is correct. But we also have scientists working independently in other locations. Helps to keep everyone honest."

Churchill broke in. "I think Professor Lindemann is better equipped to fill us in on the technical details. Prof?"

The famous British scientist had been fussing with a battered pipe which stubbornly refused to light. He made one last attempt and was surprised by success. He puffed seriously for a few moments, then looked at the Americans and began to speak.

"Yes . . . well. In the Great War, you'll remember, chemical agents were classified by the Germans under the "cross" system. That is, each gas cylinder or artillery shell was painted with a cross of a particular color, depending on what type of gas it contained. There were four colors. Green denoted the suffocating gases, mainly chlorine and phosgene. White for irritants, or tear gases. Yellow Cross indicated the blister gases, primarily mustard. Blue was for the gases that blocked molecular respiration—cyanide, arsine, carbon monoxide."

General Eisenhower lit a second cigarette off his first and inhaled with great concentration.

"Eleven months ago," Lindemann continued, "just after the German surrender at Stalingrad, we learned of the existence of Tabun. Tabun was interesting because it worked in an entirely different way than any previous gas, by crippling the central nervous system. Yet because it was not significantly more lethal than phosgene, we didn't overreact. But we did realize that our own chemical weapons weren't much further along than in 1918, and we moved to correct the imbalance. *Sarin*—while it shares some characteristics of Tabun—is a completely different animal."

"I'm a little fuzzy on my chemistry," Eisenhower said with disarming frankness. "What makes Sarin so different?"

Lindemann knitted his eyebrows. "Unlike most poison gases, General, Sarin is absolutely lethal. In 1939, the deadliest battlefield gas in the world was phosgene." He paused to give his next statement the necessary emphasis. "Sarin is *thirty times* as deadly as phosgene. In sufficient concentration it can kill within seconds, and it need not even enter the lungs. It can pass directly through human skin."

"Jesus Christ." Eisenhower had blanched. "How does this stuff work?"

Lindemann considered the American commander for some moments. "General, every function of the human body, both conscious and unconscious, is controlled by the brain. Much as a general controls his troops. The brain passes its orders down to the organs and the limbs by means of nerve branches. The nerves are the couriers of the brain, you might say. When the brain sends a message down a nerve, a compound called acetylcholine is produced. Now, at this point, the nerve has temporarily lost its conductivity. The courier, having delivered his message, can no longer run. The nerve can only be restored to its conductive state by an enzyme called cholinesterase. Without this enzyme, the nerves of the body are nothing but dead tissue. The couriers die where they lie."

"And this gas," said Eisenhower, "Sarin. It destroys this enzyme, this . . . ?"

"Cholinesterase," supplied the major of intelligence.

"Precisely," said Lindemann.

Eisenhower pursed his lips. "Exactly how much of this stuff would it take to kill a soldier?"

Lindemann answered with his pipe clenched between his teeth. "One thousandth of a raindrop. A droplet so small most of us couldn't see it with the naked eye."

Churchill noted the stricken look on Eisenhower's face. The meeting was going just as he'd planned.

"Our people at Porton have been working round the clock to copy Sarin," Lindemann went on, "but I'm afraid they haven't had much luck. It's devilish difficult to reproduce."

"I'm afraid the Germans are having all the luck just now," Churchill said dryly. "And there's worse to come. Prof?"

"Yes. General, Brigadier Smith brings word of a still deadlier gas than Sarin. It is called *Soman*. We don't have a sample, but I've seen a detailed report. Remember your lethality ratios. Phosgene was the deadliest gas in 1939. Sarin is thirty times as deadly as phosgene. And according to the reports, Soman is to Sarin as Sarin is to phosgene. Worse, it's persistent."

"Persistent?" Eisenhower echoed.

The American major chose this moment to reassert himself. "General, persistence was one of the primary gauges of gas effectiveness during World War One. How long the gas stayed at ground level after it was released."

Lindemann nodded. "We have reports that Soman can remain stable for many hours, even days, clinging to whatever it comes into contact with. A soldier exposed even several hours after a battle would still likely die. And it would be a horrible death, General, I can assure you."

"Do we have any idea how much of this stuff the Germans have stockpiled?"

Brigadier Smith cleared his throat. "General, our best estimate is upwards of five thousand tons, ready for use."

The intelligence major was stunned enough to preempt his general. "Did you say *tons?*"

Churchill nodded crisply. "Conventional cylinders, aircraft bombs, artillery shells, the lot."

Eisenhower held out his right hand to Churchill. "Let me see that damned thing."

Churchill tossed the sealed vial toward the sofa. Commander Butcher and Brendan Bracken jumped, but Eisenhower caught the vial and held it up to a lamp. "I can't see anything," he said. "Just some condensation at the bottom."

"That's because it's invisible," Churchill said. "Prof?"

"Eh?" Lindemann was fussing with his pipe again.

"The delivery system. *Aerosols vecteurs?*"

"Right. General, when the Nazis overran Belgium in 1940, they scoured the universities for technology that might further their weapons research. I'm sorry to say that they came across the work of a rather talented chemist named Dautrebande. Dautrebande had been experimenting with a new concept he called *aerosols vecteurs*. In plain language, he'd found a way to reduce almost any substance refined to its smallest stable state: charged particles in suspension, refined to ninety-seven percent purity. He intended to use this technology to disperse healing agents in sealed hospital rooms. Obviously, the Nazis have other uses in mind."

"Remember," said Churchill, "the paramount consideration in gas warfare is the element of surprise. With Dautrebande's system, the Nazis could saturate an entire battle area with Soman before anyone even knew they were under attack. And we have no idea how *aerosols* might affect current protective equipment. It could render it totally obsolete."

Eisenhower stood and began pacing the room. "All right, you

didn't invite me here to describe the problem. What do you want to do about this?"

Churchill didn't hesitate. "I want the Eighth Air Force and Bomber Command to begin hitting the German stockpiles immediately. All known nerve gas factories should be added to the master target lists and given top priority."

"Good God," murmured Commander Butcher, whose former job had been a vice presidency at the Columbia Broadcasting System. "A direct hit could send clouds of lethal gas rolling across Germany. Thousands of women and children might be killed. From a propaganda standpoint alone—"

"*If,*" Churchill interrupted, "our air forces, in the course of bombing Germany's industrial base, happen to set free something we had no way of knowing was there . . . I don't see how we could be blamed."

The ruthlessness of Churchill's suggestion silenced the Americans.

Eisenhower stopped pacing. "Correct me if I'm wrong, but up to this point the Germans have not deployed poison gas on the battlefield. Not even against the Russians. True?"

"That's true," Churchill admitted. "Though they are murdering captive Jews with cyanide gas."

Eisenhower ignored this. "Therefore, we must assume that Hitler is restraining himself, even in the face of terrible losses, for the same reason that he has not used biological weapons. Because our intentional intelligence leaks to the Germans let them know in no uncertain terms that we have the means to retaliate in kind."

Churchill gave a conciliatory nod. "General, in the case of biologic weapons our leaks were quite truthful. However, in the area of chemical weapons you'll find that we exaggerated a bit. All in a good cause, to be sure. To buy ourselves time. But with the invasion imminent, our time has run out."

Eisenhower turned to his intelligence major. "Just what *do* we have in our chemical arsenal?"

"Loads of phosgene," the major said defensively. "We're stockpiling sixty days' worth of retaliatory gas for D day. And new shipments of mustard are arriving all the time."

Eisenhower frowned. "But nothing like Sarin?"

"No, sir."

"Nor Soman."

The major shook his head. "Not even close, sir."

"Jesus H. *Christ.*" Eisenhower looked around the room. "Gentlemen, I think it might be better if the prime minister and I continue this conversation alone."

"Brendan," Churchill said, barely controlling the excitement in his voice, "you and Duff give our American friends some tea and biscuits. Clemmie will show you where everything is. And I believe the Prof has a late appointment."

Lindemann glanced suddenly at his watch. "Good Lord, Winston, you're right." The tall don gathered up his hat and coat and started for the door, only at the last moment remembering that he was leaving the presence of the supreme commander of the Allied Expeditionary Force. He turned and tipped his hat to Eisenhower.

"Godspeed, General," he said, and was gone.

D wight D. Eisenhower furiously smoked a cigarette at the very window where Churchill had awaited his arrival. During the past forty minutes, he had sat mostly in silence, chain-smoking Lucky Strikes while the prime minister painted nightmare scenarios of the eleventh-hour appearance of Sarin and Soman on the D-day beaches. Finally, Eisenhower turned from the window.

"Frankly, Mr. Prime Minister, I don't know why you came to me with this. You know I don't have direct control over the strategic bombing forces. I've been fighting for that control for weeks, and *you've* been resisting me. Are you changing your position?"

Seated in a wing chair several feet away, Churchill stuck out his lower lip as if pondering an unfamiliar question. "I'm sure we can come to some reasonable compromise, General."

"Well, until we do, I couldn't make the decision to bomb those stockpiles even if I wanted to. Besides, this is a political matter. It's a question for President Roosevelt."

Churchill sighed heavily. "General, I spoke to Franklin about this matter in Cairo. I had an early report about Sarin. But I don't believe he fully grasped the threat. He seems to think the tide has turned sufficiently in our favor that no single German secret weapon could stop it. The air marshals are making similar noises, and they resent my meddling. That's why I came to you. As the man in charge of OVERLORD, I thought you couldn't fail to see the danger."

"Oh, I see the danger, all right."

"Thank God." Churchill spoke quickly. "The mind recoils. Rommel could bury canisters of Soman weeks before our troops arrive, then detonate them from a safe distance. Half a dozen planes spraying aerosol-borne Soman could stop your entire force on the sand. D day would be a disaster."

Eisenhower raised his hand. "Why do you think Hitler will deploy nerve gas on the invasion beaches if he didn't use it at Stalingrad?"

Churchill answered with confidence. "Because Stalingrad, however terrible a defeat, was not the end. He could still take the long view. But Hitler now faces the lodgement of an Allied army on the Continent. If we breach his Atlantic Wall, it means the end for him, and he knows it. Also, there is some question as to whether the Germans had effective protective gear for their own troops at that time. Remember, Sarin and Soman can pass through human skin. One gust of wind blowing the wrong way could decimate a German battalion as easily as one of ours. It happened often enough in the Great War. But given the stakes of the invasion, will Hitler hesitate to sacrifice his own men? Not for a moment. I tell you, that devil will stop at nothing."

Eisenhower found Churchill's eyes in the gloom. "Mr. Prime Minister, at this stage of the game, we've got to see Hitler straight. We can't afford not to."

"Whatever do you mean?"

"I mean I know for a fact that in 1940 you planned to use poison gas on the Germans if they reached the beaches of England."

Churchill did not deny it.

"So," Eisenhower plowed on, "let's stop pretending we have some special moral obligation to stop Hitler from using gas under circumstances where we would probably do the same."

"But that is precisely my point! Hitler will soon be in the very circumstances in which we would resort to gas ourselves. Can we afford to hope he will not?"

Eisenhower violently stubbed out his cigarette. "How the hell did we get into this mess?"

"I hate to say it, General, but it goes back to the non-competition agreements signed by Standard Oil and I. G. Farben in the 1920s. The arrangement was that Standard would stay out of chemicals if Farben stayed out of the oil business. Both companies held to that deal up to and even after the outbreak of war. It's the Germans who've revolutionized commercial chemistry. We have nothing to compare with the Farben conglomerate."

"What about French scientists?"

Churchill shook his head sadly. "Hitler alone holds this card." He picked up a pen and began doodling on a notepad. "May I speak with absolute frankness, General?"

"I wish to God you would."

"Duff Smith and I have a theory. We think Hitler hasn't used Sarin yet for one simple reason. He is *afraid of gas*. He was temporarily blinded by mustard gas in the Great War, you know. Made quite a thing of it in *Mein Kampf*. He may well have an exaggerated fear of our chemical abilities. We believe the real danger isn't Hitler at all, but Heinrich Himmler. Sarin and Soman are being tested at camps run by Himmler's SS. The sample of Sarin came from a remote SS camp built *solely* for the purpose of manufacturing and testing nerve gases. Himmler also controls much of the Nazi intelligence apparatus. Therefore, he is the man most likely to know we possess no nerve gases of our own. Duff and I think Himmler's plan is to perfect his nerve gases and protective clothing, then present the whole show to Hitler at the moment he most needs it—to stave off our invasion. At a single stroke Himmler could save the Reich and raise himself to an unassailable position as successor to the Nazi throne."

Eisenhower pointed a fresh cigarette at Churchill. "Now *that*, Mr. Prime Minister, is a motive that makes sense. Do you have proof of this?"

"Duff's Polish friends have a contact very close to the commandant of one of these camps. This agent believes a tactical demonstration of Soman—a demonstration for the Führer—may be scheduled in a matter of weeks, possibly even days."

"I see. Mr. Prime Minister, let me digress a moment. Professor Lindemann said your people are working around the clock to copy Sarin. I assume that is strictly for retaliatory purposes?"

Churchill took a deep breath. "Not if you agree with me, General. I believe there is an option more desirable than bombing the German stockpiles. I'm speaking of a demonstration raid. If our scientists succeed in copying Sarin, I believe we should launch a limited attack with our gas as soon as possible. Only by doing this will we leave no doubt whatever in Himmler's mind that he is wrong in his estimation of our capabilities and our resolve."

Eisenhower looked at Churchill with unveiled amazement. The

cold-bloodedness of the British continually stunned him. He cleared his throat. "But so far your scientists' efforts to copy Sarin have been unsuccessful, correct?"

Churchill turned up his palms. "They're dabbling with something called fluorophosphates, but progress is slow."

Eisenhower turned to the window and stared out over the snowswept English landscape. In the dark it looked as quiet as a cemetery. "Mr. Prime Minister," he said at length, "I'm afraid I can't support you on this. Neither the bombing nor the . . . the demonstration raid." Hearing Churchill's soft groan, Eisenhower turned. "Wait—please hear me out. I deeply respect your judgment. You have been right many times when everyone else was wrong. But things aren't so clear cut as you're trying to make them seem. If we bomb the German stockpiles and nerve gas plants, we tip our hand to Hitler. We show him what we fear most. Also, by bombing the stockpiles we indirectly use nerve gas on the German people. That's practically the same as first use. What would then stop Hitler from using Soman against our troops?"

Churchill hung on every word, searching for a chink in the American's logic.

"No," Eisenhower said firmly, "it's absolutely out of the question. President Roosevelt would never authorize a gas attack, and the American people wouldn't stand for it. There are still thousands of veterans walking American streets who were terrorized by gas in the first war, some scarred horribly. We will retaliate if attacked ourselves. The president has made that clear. But first use? Never."

Eisenhower steeled himself for the familiar roar of the British lion. But rather than rise to his feet for a spirited argument, Churchill seemed to withdraw into himself.

"What I will do," Eisenhower said quickly, "is push for full American cooperation in developing our own version of Sarin. That way, if Hitler *does* cross the line we can show our people that we're giving as good as we get. I'll press Eaker and Harris for aerial surveys of the gas plants and stockpiles. If Hitler uses Sarin, we'll be ready to start bombing immediately. How does that sound?"

"Like we're planning to shut the stable door after the horse has run away," Churchill mumbled.

Eisenhower felt his notorious temper reaching the flashpoint, but he managed to check it. He would have to endure countless hours of negotiations very much like this one in the coming months, and he had to keep relations civil. "Mr. Prime Minister, I've heard tales of doomsday weapons on both sides since 1942. In the end, this war will be won or lost with planes, tanks, and men."

Sitting there in the great wing chair in his dragon dressing gown, hands folded across his round belly, Winston Churchill resembled nothing so much as a pale Buddha resting on a velvet pillow. His watery eyes peered out from beneath heavy lids. "General," he said gravely, "you and I hold the fate of Christendom in our hands. I beg you to reconsider."

In that moment Eisenhower felt the full weight of Churchill's indomitable will projected against him. But his resolve held firm. "I'll keep all this in mind," he said. "But for now I must stand by what I said tonight."

The Supreme Commander rose and moved toward the study door. As he reached for the knob, something stopped him. A brief intimation that perhaps he had won too easily? He turned and fixed Churchill in his gaze. "As I'm sure you will, Mr. Prime Minister."

Churchill smiled in resignation. "Of course, General. Of course."

When Eisenhower's party had gone, Brigadier Duff Smith joined Churchill in his private study. A single lamp burned at the prime minister's desk. The one-armed SOE chief leaned forward.

"The air seemed a bit chilly when Ike collected his men," he observed.

Churchill laid both pudgy hands on his desk and sighed. "He refused, Duff. No bombing of the stockpiles, no demonstration raid if we develop our own gas."

"Bloody *hell*. Doesn't he realize what Soman would do to his sodding invasion?"

"I don't think he does. It's the same old American song, the same schoolboy naivete."

"That naivete could still cost us the war!"

"Eisenhower has never seen combat, Duff, remember that. I don't hold it against him, but a man who's never been shot at— much less gassed—lacks a certain perspective."

"Bloody Yanks," Smith fumed. "They either want to fight this war from six miles up in the air or by the Marquess of Queensbury rules."

"Steady, old man. They've acquitted themselves quite handily in Italy."

"Aye," Smith conceded. "But you've said it yourself a hundred times, Winston, 'Action This Day!' "

Churchill stuck out his lower lip and fixed the brigadier with a penetrating stare. "You never thought Eisenhower would agree to the bombing, did you?"

The SOE chief's poker face slipped ever so slightly. "That's a fact, Winston. I never did."

"And of course you have a plan."

"I've had thoughts."

"No matter how desperate a pass we've come to, I've never gone against the wishes of the Americans. The risks are enormous."

"The threat is greater, Winston."

"I believe that." Churchill paused. "You couldn't use any British personnel."

"Give me some credit, old man."

Churchill tapped his thick fingers on the desk. "What if it failed? Could you cover your tracks?"

Smith smiled. "Bombers go off course all the time. Drop their loads in the strangest of places."

"What would you need?"

"To start, a submarine that can hold station in the Baltic for four days."

"That's easily enough done. The Admiralty is the one place where my word is law."

"A squadron of Mosquito Bombers made available for one night."

"That's quite another matter, Duff. Bomber Command is the sharpest thorn in my side."

"It's an absolute necessity. Only way to cover up if we fail."

Churchill raised both hands in a gesture of futility. "I hate going to Harris hat in hand, but I suppose I can suffer through it once."

Smith drew in a breath. He was about to ask for the near-impossible. "I'd also need access to an airfield on the southern Swedish coast. For at least four days, preferably longer."

Churchill drew back in his chair, his face impassive. Dealing with putatively neutral countries was a tricky business. For Sweden, the price of aiding the Allies could be fifty thousand uninvited guests from Germany, all wearing parachutes. He aimed a stubby forefinger at Smith. "Can you pull this off, Duffy?"

"Someone had better, old man."

Churchill studied his old friend for several moments, weighing his past successes against his failures. "All right, you'll get your airfield. In fact, let's just save some time." He took a fountain pen from his desk, scrawled on a sheet of notepaper, then handed the page across to Smith. The brigadier's eyes widened as he read:

To All Soldiers of the Allied Expeditionary Force:
Brigadier Duff Smith, Chief of Special Operations Executive, is hereby authorized to requisition any and all aid he deems necessary to prosecute military operations inside Occupied Europe from 15 January to 15 February 1944. This applies to both regular and irregular forces. All inquiries to No. 10 Annexe.
Winston S. Churchill

"Good God," Smith exclaimed.

"That won't buy as much as you think," Churchill said with a trace of irony. "See how far it gets you with Sir Arthur bloody Harris of the Air Force."

Smith deftly folded the note with his one hand and slipped it into his tunic. "You underestimate your influence, Winston. Give me one of these good for three months and I'll bring you Hitler's head in a basket."

Churchill laughed heartily. "Godspeed, then. You've got thirty days. Don't put your foot in it." He extended his hand across the desk.

Smith squeezed the plump hand, then saluted smartly. "God save the King."

"God bless America," Churchill said. "And keep her ignorant."

6

Two days after Dwight Eisenhower politely warned Churchill to leave the German gas stockpiles alone, Brigadier Duff Smith sat alone in the back row of a meeting room in one of the sandbagged defense buildings in Whitehall. At a long raised table in the front of the room waited two majors and a general of the British army. Smith cared nothing about them. For the past forty-eight hours he had been trolling through the SOE files at Baker Street, searching for the man he needed to lead his mission into Germany. His luck had not been good.

The exclusion of British agents was the most frustrating restraint, but he knew it was justified. If British agents were captured on a strategic mission expressly forbidden by Eisenhower, the fragile Anglo-American alliance could be shattered overnight. SOE had hundreds of foreign agents on file, but few had the skills necessary to lead this mission. The typical SOE job—inserting agents into Occupied France—had become so routine that some officers called it the French shuttle. But sending men into Germany itself was another matter. The leader of this mission would have to be physically fit, fluent in German, unknown to the Abwehr and the Gestapo, yet experienced enough to move undetected inside the tightly controlled Reich on false papers. Most of all, he needed to be cold-blooded enough to kill innocent people in the accomplishment of his mission. This last requirement had disqualified several likely candidates.

Brigadier Smith had stumbled upon today's lead quite by accident. While lunching at his club, he'd overheard a discussion at a nearby table that tweaked his mental radar. A staff officer was telling a story about a young German Jew who'd fled to Palestine before the war and become a Zionist guerrilla fighter. Apparently, this young fellow had just blackmailed his way into a passage from Haifa to London, by promising to reveal guerilla techniques used by the *Haganah* to terrorize the British occupation forces in Palestine. Due to arrive today, his solitary demand had been that he be granted an audience with the C-in-C of Bomber Command. He supposedly had a plan for singlehandedly saving the Jews of Europe. The terrorist would get an audience, the officer joked, but not quite the one he expected. Smith had listened long enough to learn the young Jew's name and the address of the meeting, then driven to Baker Street and wired an old friend in Jerusalem to see if there was a file on a Mr. Jonas Stern.

There was. And the more Smith learned, the more intrigued he'd become. At twenty-five, Jonas Stern had been twice decorated by the British Army for his exploits guiding their forces in North Africa. Yet he was wanted by the British military police for crimes against His Majesty's forces in Palestine, as a terrorist of the feared Haganah. He had less than five pounds to his name, but carried a bounty of one thousand Arab dinars on his head. The responding officer added a postscript, informing Smith that Jonas Stern was the prime suspect in three separate murders, though as yet no one had gathered sufficient evidence to try him.

Smith turned at the sound of voices in the corridor behind him. An armed guard entered first, followed by a tall suntanned young man wearing shackles on his hands. Smith registered a lean, angular face and piercing black eyes, then Jonas Stern was past him and moving toward the officers who waited at the front of the room. Stern carried what appeared to be an oilcloth-wrapped package under one arm. Last through the door was a shorter man wearing the light khaki uniform and crimson sunburn of a British officer serving in the Middle East. Smith followed the group up the aisle and took a seat at the side of the room, where he could see more clearly.

The senior officer, General John Little, addressed the sunburned Englishman. "Captain Owen?"

"Yes, sir. I'm terribly sorry we're late. We'd have been here yesterday if it weren't for the U-boats."

General Little looked down his nose at Owen. "Well, you're here now. Let's begin. Is this the notorious Mr. Stern?"

"Yes, sir. Er . . . I wonder if it might be possible for me to remove his handcuffs now?"

A florid-faced major seated to the general's right said, "Not just yet, Captain. He is a wanted fugitive, after all."

Duff Smith focused on the man who had spoken, a staff intelligence major of rather modest achievements.

"I am Major Dickson," the man went on. "You've got a lot of cheek coming into this building. In case you don't know, you're the leading suspect in a rash of Arab house-bombings around Jerusalem, thefts of British lend-lease arms, not to mention the murder of a British military policeman in Jerusalem in 1942. The only reason we agreed to see you is that you saved Captain Owen's life at Tobruk. You probably don't know, but Captain Owen's father had quite a distinguished career in the Welsh Guards."

Jonas Stern said nothing.

"Captain Owen tells us you've got some daring plan for single-handedly winning the war in Europe. Is that right?"

"No."

"It's a bloody good thing," Dickson snapped. "I should think Monty can handle the invasion without any help from the likes of you!"

"Hear, hear," chimed the other major, who was seated on General Little's left.

Stern took a deep breath. "I'd like to state for the record that the officers that I requested be here are not present."

Major Dickson's face went completely scarlet. "If you think Air Chief Marshal Sir Arthur Harris has nothing better to do than listen to the ranting of a bloody Zionist terrorist—"

"Clive," General Little interrupted. "Mr. Stern, we have gathered here at some considerable inconvenience to hear what you have to say. You would do well to get on with it."

Brigadier Smith watched the young Jew try awkwardly to slide the package that was under his arm into his cuffed hands.

"Bloody waste of time," muttered Major Dickson.

"Mr. Stern," General Little said with seemingly paternal concern, "do you mind my asking if Moshe Shertok or Chaim Weizmann know you are in London?"

"They don't."

"I thought not. You see, Mr. Stern, there are proper channels for pursuing matters relating to European Jews. His Majesty's Government generously maintains excellent relations with the Jewish Agency here in London. Messrs. Weizmann and Shertok are the men you should be seeing about this matter. And I think you will find, having done so, that they are doing all in their power to help the European Jewry."

General Little waited what he considered to be a suitable time for his wisdom to be assimilated, then said, "Have I put your mind at rest, Mr. Stern?"

"You've done nothing of the kind," Stern replied. He took a step closer to the table. "I'm well aware of the efforts of Shertok, Weizmann, and the Jewish Agency. They have the best of intentions, I'm sure. But I have not come here to plead for Palestinian entry certificates for trapped Jews, or to ask you to declare them protected British persons, or to beg you to buy their freedom with war materiel. I don't believe any of that will be done. General, I have come here to speak to you, to military men, about a purely military solution."

Duff Smith pricked up his ears. As the tall young man gathered himself to deliver his appeal, Smith noted a certain self-possession, a *centeredness* that was remarkable in one so young. It was the mark of the natural soldier—or agent.

Stern gestured with the package in his shackled hands. "The depositions in this file contain eyewitness accounts of a program of mass extermination being carried out by the Nazis at four concentration camps in Germany and occupied Poland. I have precise tallies of the dead and detailed descriptions of the killing methods employed by the Nazis, from mass shootings and electrocutions to the most widely practiced method: death by poison gas and subsequent cremation of the corpses."

General Little glanced uncomfortably at Major Dickson. "May I see those reports, Mr. Stern?"

Stern took a step forward, but Little raised his hand. "Please do not approach the table," he said coolly. "Sergeant Gilchrist?"

A military policeman took the folder and carried it to the general. Little opened it and briefly scanned the papers inside. "Mr. Stern," he said, "do you have any evidence that this information is accurate? Other than the testimony of other Jews, I mean."

"General, reports of Jewish deaths in the hundreds of thousands have appeared in the *London Times* and *Manchester Guardian*, sometimes quoting the exact names and locations of death camps. I believe one such story even appeared in the *New York Times*. What I do not understand is why the Allies still refuse to do anything about them."

General Little brushed the edge of his neat gray mustache with his left forefinger. "*I believe*," he said with cold precision, "that you have accomplished what you set out to do here. I can assure you that these reports will be given all the attention they deserve."

Jonas Stern snorted in contempt. "General, I have not begun to accomplish what I came here to do. I've given you those reports merely to justify the desperate action I am about ask you to undertake on behalf of the Jewish people."

"I've had about all I can stand from this whelp," Major Dickson said. "Let's stop this charade."

"Just a moment, Clive," said the officer on General Little's left, a Guards major. "Let's hear him out. I suspect he's a member of the 'bomb the railways' school. That's it, isn't it, Mr. Stern? You want the RAF to bomb the railways leading to the concentration camps?"

"No, Major."

"Ah. Then you must be one of the advocates for forming a Jewish Brigade to take part in the invasion. I should have known. You saw some action in North Africa, didn't you?"

"That is not why I've come."

General Little slapped his palm down on Stern's file. "Then why the devil *have* you come? Put an end to the bloody suspense, will you?"

"General Little," Stern said, "I understand politics. I know that a Jewish Brigade would contain the seeds of a Jewish army, which could return to Palestine after the war and fight the British and the Arabs. I do not ask for that. I know it's been suggested that the Polish Resistance try to destroy the Nazi gas chambers. But the Poles are too weak to do this, and even if they weren't, they would not risk their lives to save Jews."

"Too bloody right," Major Dickson muttered.

Stern ignored him. "I do have a certain amount of military experience, and I realize that bombing the railways leading to the camps is impractical. Rail tracks are relatively easy to repair, and the Nazis could always substitute trucks for rolling stock."

Brigadier Smith could see that the young man's realistic assessments had gotten the attention of General Little and the Guards officer, if not Major Dickson.

"General," Stern concluded, "my request is simple. I am asking you for four heavy-bomber sorties over Germany and Poland. I have the names and exact locations of four concentration camps at which Jews are being gassed and shot to death at a conservatively estimated rate of over five thousand per day. That's five thousand per day in *each camp*. In the name of humanity—in the name of *God*—I ask that those four charnel houses be wiped from the face of the earth."

The silence in the room was total. Major Dickson sat up and stared wide-eyed at Stern. After the initial shock dissipated, General Little cleared his throat. "Do you mean, Mr. Stern, that you want these camps bombed *with the Jewish prisoners inside them?*"

"That is exactly what I mean, General."

Duff Smith felt a thrill of satisfaction.

"He's mad," said Major Dickson. "Absolutely barking."

"I'm quite sane, Major," Stern said. "And quite serious."

"And *I* am quite sure," General Little said, "that Messrs. Shertok and Weizmann, in all their desperate pleadings, have suggested nothing so drastic as this. You claim to speak for the Jewish people in asking for this madness?"

Stern spoke calmly and clearly. "General, Weizmann and Shertok are political men—distant from the truth of what is happening in Europe. The idea of bombing the camps was first suggested by members of the Jewish Underground in Poland and Germany. I have talked to some who escaped. General, I have looked into the eyes of women who had their infants snatched away by the heels and crushed against walls by SS officers. I have listened to fathers who watched their sons bayoneted as they stood weeping not a meter away—"

"That's enough," Little said sharply. "I don't need a lecture on the horrors of war from you."

"But these people are not at war, General! They are civilian noncombatants. Innocent women and children."

General Little gazed down at the papers Stern had brought, then looked up and began speaking in a soft voice. "Lad, I can't help but admire the courage it takes to make a request like that. But your request simply cannot be considered seriously. Not even from a purely military standpoint. Our bombers don't have the range to reach these camps. Their fighter escorts can't fly that far—"

"That's no longer true, General," Stern interrupted. "The new American P-51 Mustangs have a range of 850 miles. That puts the camps within striking distance from Italy."

"You're surprisingly well informed," Little rejoined. "But even so, there's the question of diverting military resources for nonmilitary missions—"

"But those Jews are being used as slave labor for the war industries!"

Little raised his hand. "The sole objective of the Allied air forces is to wipe out the war-making capacity of the Reich. That means oil production, ball-bearing plants, synthetic rubber—not civilian detention camps. If we were to bomb these camps, our raids would give Hitler the perfect opportunity to claim that *we* killed all the Jews who have died in captivity. And there remains the issue of our acting specifically for Jewish civilians. If we redress the grievances of the Jews by reprisal bombings, every other wronged group will line up for the same service."

"And don't forget," Major Dickson added, "these Jews are legally German citizens. Hitler has said from the beginning that the Jewish question is an internal German problem, and he is technically right."

General Little frowned at Dickson. "What we cannot ignore is the fact that the Nazis have close to a million Allied prisoners in their hands. Forty thousand British taken at Dunkirk alone. We have relatively few German prisoners. We can't afford to start playing the reprisal game, especially with prison camps. Hitler could resort to even more unpleasantness than he has already."

"Unpleasantness?"

"Look here, Stern," Little went on, "Captain Owen wrote to me about your father being trapped in Germany. That's a hard thing, I know. We've all lost loved ones in this war. But that's the nature of the game. I lost a brother in France in 1940. Bloody senseless. A British girls' school could have put up more of a fight than the Frogs did. But in times like these . . ."

Duff Smith nearly groaned aloud. Here was the fatuous, patronizing Englishman at his worst. *I lost a relative, so why should you*

*raise a wind about yours? Much less a million of them, eh? So hard
to get one's mind round numbers of that size, what?*

"It seems to me," Little said, examining a page from Stern's file,
"that these numbers are exaggerated. In all honesty, I've found that
to be a Jewish trait. Don't blame you at all, really. Best way to get
attention in a crowd. Two million Jews murdered? Why, in the
bloodiest battle of the Great War only six hundred thousand lives
were lost. Let's be rational, Stern. Let's face facts. It's my guess
someone's fiddled these figures. With the best of intentions, perhaps,
but fiddled them just the same. Someone with political motives, as
you said before."

Brigadier Smith saw the young man's shoulders sag as he began
to absorb the futility of his mission. "I don't know why I expected
you to believe what is happening," he said. "Most Jews in Palestine
don't even believe it."

General Little motioned for a sergeant to escort Stern out.

"But let me say this!" Stern cried as the British soldier took his
arm. "My father *is* somewhere inside Germany at this very moment.
Alive or dead, I don't know. But if he is alive, he would beg you to
do exactly as I have asked. General, to refuse to bomb these death
camps on the grounds that it would kill innocent prisoners is merely
misplaced sentiment. Destroying the gas chambers and crematoria is
the only way to slow down Hitler's extermination program. By killing a few thousand innocents, you could save millions! Isn't that the
most fundamental idea of warfare? Sacrificing the few for the
many?"

Duff Smith clenched his hands; Stern's words had electrified
him.

General Little looked hard at the young Zionist. "You've made
an eloquent case, Mr. Stern. This board will take your comments
under advisement. Sergeant Gilchrist?"

Stern stared at the general with alarm. "Could I have one more
moment, General?"

Major Dickson groaned in exasperation.

"Be quick," Little said.

"If you won't bomb the camps, will you allow me to take a
small commando force into Poland and attempt to liberate one concentration camp? I know the British Army is training a few Jews to
parachute into Hungary to try to warn the Jews there to resist. Gen-

eral, I'm not asking you to risk a single British life. If I fail, what would you have lost? A dozen Jews. I'm an experienced guerrilla fighter—"

"I'll bloody bet you are!" Major Dickson bellowed with sudden savagery. "Experienced at murdering British soldiers!"

The red-faced major was on his feet. Stern made no move toward or away from him. Instead, he raised his cuffed hands to the zipper of his jacket and pulled it down. From the left breast of his khaki shirt flashed the glint of silver and blue. It was the George Medal, the second-highest British decoration that could be awarded to a civilian.

"Major Dickson," said Stern, "this medal was pinned on me by General Bernard Law Montgomery for reconnaissance actions at El Alamein. The second award I received for aiding the British Army at Tobruk. Auchinleck pinned that one on. Both those officers are better men than you, and if you had any brains or heart whatever you might have understood at least part of what I've said here today. I've stood here as a soldier asking only for the chance to fight. To show Hitler something he has never seen—something he *needs* to see—a Jew who can fight, who *will* fight. Myself and twenty Haganah guerrillas, properly equipped, could destroy a concentration camp, I am sure of it."

"Now we've got to it!" Dickson roared. "The bloody Haganah!"

Duff Smith felt like boxing Dickson's ears for him. Thankfully, General Little waved the major down. "Such a raid is out of the question, Mr. Stern, for more reasons than I can name. Take a bit of advice. The best thing you can do is go back to Palestine and help your own people."

"My people are dying in Germany," Stern said.

"Yes . . . well. There are a lot of people dying all over the world just now."

Duff Smith watched the shackled hands rise up and point accusingly at Little. "General!" Stern said in a voice booming with prophetic power. "One day soon the world is going to ask England a very embarrassing question. Why did you refuse to grant sanctuary to the Jews who were being slaughtered by the millions in Europe? Why did you throw the lucky handful who managed to reach Palestine into British concentration camps? And most of all—"

"*Enough!*" shouted Little. His cultivated British reserve had finally cracked. "You *dare* march in here and preach to us? You insubordinate upstart! You're not a soldier. You're a bloody terrorist! It takes a lot more than a gun to make a soldier, Stern. Why, if it weren't for us standing alone against Hitler in 1940, your people would have been wiped out years ago!"

Major Dickson pointed at Stern. "The only reason you were allowed to come to England was to answer our questions about terrorism in Palestine." Dickson's eyes glowed with a cruel light. "And I'm happy to say that, as a major of intelligence, your interrogation will fall to me!"

Stern flexed his fists in rage and frustration. Duff Smith saw Captain Owen edging closer in case his friend's self-restraint snapped. General Little gathered up the papers from Stern's file and dropped them into a satchel at his feet.

"Place him under arrest, Sergeant Gilchrist," he said calmly.

Captain Owen shouted, "Wait!" but he was too late. As the sergeant approached, Stern swung his cuffed hands straight up from his waist with animal quickness. Gilchrist was grabbing for his truncheon when the steel cuffs caught him on the point of the chin. He hit the floor with the deadened thud of an unconscious boxer.

Major Dickson groped for his sidearm, then remembered he had left it with an aide for cleaning.

"Stop this nonsense!" cried General Little.

"Jonas!" Peter Owen yelled. "For God's sake!"

But it was all for naught. As the second guard charged, Stern swept up Gilchrist's truncheon from the floor and jabbed him in the belly, then spun to the wall beside the door as the man went down. Almost on cue, a sentry burst into the room with his revolver drawn. Stern's stolen truncheon crashed down, snapping the man's wrist and sending the pistol clattering to the floor. Stern lunged for the door, but the sentry caught him by the collar with his good hand and jerked backward.

There was a sound of ripping cloth. Stern's jacket came off, and his khaki shirt fell around his waist. He whirled.

"Bloody hell!" gasped the guard. "Look at that!"

The sight of Stern's exposed torso stunned even Brigadier Smith. The young Zionist's back, shoulders, and abdomen were transected by a netting of livid purple scars, some made by blades, others obviously by fire. The scars on the abdomen ran straight down past the waistband of his trousers. The moment of stillness lasted several seconds. Then Stern knocked down the sentry, snatched up his shirt and bolted through the door.

"After him!" Major Dickson screamed as footsteps pounded down the stairwell.

Captain Owen threw himself in front of the door. "General Little! Please let me talk to him!"

"Out of the way," Major Dickson growled, "or I'll order my men to shoot you down."

"For God's sake, General!"

"*Attention!*" General Little roared.

The guards froze where they stood. Duff Smith had remained motionless throughout the confusion, as if watching a staged musical.

"Steady, Dickson," General Little said. "I'm going to let Captain Owen bring him back. There's no sense in unnecessary bloodshed. You can question Stern at your leisure after you've calmed down."

"Sounds like a good plan, Johnny," Duff Smith said, speaking for the first time.

Major Dickson stood white-faced and shaking. "I'm going to throw that bastard in irons and sweat him until he diagrams the Haganah's whole batting order! He's one of the ringleaders. You can just *tell.*"

"He's only twenty-three, sir," Owen said. "But you're probably right about him being a leader."

"I'd hate to see that chap chained to a wall," said General Little. "He's got guts, even if he is a Yid."

"Interrogating him would be useless anyway," Owen said in a monotone.

"Why's that?" asked Dickson.

"Major, Jonas Stern could probably tell you every key man in the Haganah's ranks. Probably in the Irgun, too. But he *wouldn't* tell you. He'd die first."

"A lot of men say that," Dickson said. "In the beginning. That attitude doesn't last long."

Owen shook his head. "Stern's different."

Dickson smirked. "How's that?"

"Didn't you see the scars? He's been there before. Tortured, I mean. And nothing like our methods, believe me. He was running from a raid near Al Sabah one night when his horse broke its leg.

He was only seventeen. The Arabs were hot behind the raiding party. They ran him down almost immediately."

"What the hell did they do to him?" asked General Little.

"I'm not sure, sir. He doesn't talk about it. They only had him for a night and a day, but they were real tribesmen, the ones that got him. Murderous brutes. Stern somehow managed to escape on the second night. He never told them a thing. I heard some of his mates whispering about it during the North African campaign. He's a legend to the Zionists. I never saw him with his shirt off before today."

"Good God," Little muttered. "I saw the results of some Arab interrogations in the Great War, near Gallipoli. It's a miracle the fellow survived."

"Like I said, sir. Not much use in questioning him, to my mind. He won't talk unless he wants to."

"I see what you mean," Little agreed. "We'll sort out this mess tomorrow. You've got four hours to bring him in of his own volition, Owen. After that, Major Dickson's men will have a free hand."

"I'll find him, sir."

Little nodded. "That's all, Captain."

"Thank you, sir." The Welshman darted through the door.

Brigadier Duff Smith rose slowly, nodded to Little, and followed Owen outside.

Jonas Stern stood alone in a coal-dark doorway, his shivering body pressed against cold stone, and watched the broad avenue of Whitehall. He had nowhere to run. He had come so far to get here. All the way from Germany at age fourteen, with his mother in tow and his father left behind. Thousands of miles overland in a refugee caravan where smugglers robbed them of all they had before taking them farther down the illegal route to Palestine. Weeks in a battered freighter that bled salt water through its rusting hull while people belowdecks died of thirst. Years of struggle in Palestine, fighting the Arabs and the British, then in North Africa fighting the Nazis. Then finally from Palestine to London, to the room with the British staff officers with their trimmed mustaches and haughty blue eyes. Major Dickson had at least told the truth: the only reason they'd let him come at all was to interrogate him about the Haganah.

Stern tensed at the sound of running feet. Peering around the brickwork, he breathed a sigh of relief. The feet belonged to Peter Owen, and the Welshman was alone. Stern reached out and caught him by the jacket.

"Jonas!" cried Owen.

Stern let go of the jacket.

The young Welshman rolled his shoulders angrily. "What the hell was that back there?"

"You tell me, Peter. Are Major Dickson's men after me?"

"They will be if you don't turn yourself in within four hours." Owen struggled to light a cigarette in the frigid wind. Stern finally did it for him. "Thanks, old man," he said. "Christ, I'll take the desert over this any time."

"Those smug bastards," Stern muttered.

"I told you you were being unrealistic. It's a matter of scale as much as anything. Compared to the amphibious landing of a million men in Occupied Europe, a few thousand civilians—particularly Jews—don't garner much attention in military circles."

Stern held up his cuffed hands. "Get these off, Peter."

A pained look crossed Owen's face. "Dickson will have me up on charges."

"*Peter*—"

"Oh, hell." Owen fumbled in his pocket and brought out a key.

Stern snatched it away and began walking toward Trafalgar Square. The opened handcuffs tinkled on the cement like change thrown to a street urchin. He put the key in his pocket and kept walking. With blackout regulations still in force, the stars over London shone like distant spotlights, illuminating a sign advertising bomb-shelter space in the Charing Cross tube station.

"You've got to turn yourself in, Jonas," Owen said, struggling to stay abreast of him. "You've no alternative."

Stern noticed that he had begun leaning into the wind with his head turned slightly away as he walked. He hadn't walked with that gait since his childhood in northern Germany. Some habits never died.

Owen grabbed his sleeve and stopped him in the road. "Jonas, I won't blame you for anything you do at this point. But I can't be responsible for you, either. No matter what happens now, I consider the Tobruk debt paid."

Stern stared at the young Welshman with eyes that said many things, but he did not speak.

"I said Tobruk is wiped clean," Owen repeated, but the tone of his voice was uncertain.

"Sure, Peter." Stern started to add something, but his words were drowned by the sudden growl of an engine. A long silver Bentley floated over to the curb and stopped beside the two men, engine running.

Stern shoved Owen against the passenger door and began to run. He heard the Welshman's voice calling him back. He turned. Owen had snapped to attention beside the Bentley. Focusing on the car's interior, Stern saw only a driver and a single passenger. He walked cautiously back. Someone had rolled down the rear window. Framed in its dark square Stern saw a weathered face lit by bright eyes, and the shoulder boards of a brigadier general.

"Recognize me?" asked a deep voice with a Scottish accent.

Stern stared at the face. "You were at the meeting."

"I'm Brigadier Duff Smith, Mr. Stern. I'd like to have a word with you."

Stern looked at Peter Owen, silently asking if this could be a trap. The Welshman shrugged.

Brigadier Smith held up a silver flask. "Have a dram? Beastly cold out."

Stern did not accept the flask. As he stared at Brigadier Duff Smith, he felt a sudden certainty that he should run like hell. Get clear of this man and all his works. Almost before he knew what he was doing, he was walking away from the Bentley.

The car kept pace, coasting along beside him. "Come on, lad," Smith called. "Where's the harm in a little chat?"

"What kind of chat?"

"A chat about killing Germans."

"I'm German," Stern said, still marching into the wind. He glanced up at the dark face of Admiralty House. "According to Major Dickson, anyway."

"Nazis, I should have said."

"I killed plenty of Nazis in North Africa. That's not what I'm after."

Smith's reply was barely audible above the rumble of the Bentley's motor, but it stopped Stern in his tracks. "I'm talking about killing Nazis *inside Germany.*"

The Bentley rolled to a standstill beside Stern. The brigadier's eyes glinted with black humor. "That sound like your line of country, lad?"

The Bentley's driver got out and opened the rear door opposite Smith, but Stern still hesitated.

"You speak good English," Smith said, to fill the silence.

"Don't take it as flattery. Know your enemy, that's my motto." Stern pointed at the brigadier. "Can you get Major Dickson off my back?"

"My dear fellow," Smith said expansively, "I can make you disappear off the face of the earth, if I so choose."

Stern was vaguely aware of Peter Owen shouting something as he climbed into the Bentley, but all he remembered was Brigadier Smith's final exchange with the Welshman before he rolled up the rear window. Owen was protesting that General Little wanted Stern in custody, and that Major Dickson would be hunting him with a vengeance if he was not. Smith did not seem at all perturbed. He said something to Owen in a language Stern would later learn was Welsh. The gist of the translation was, *"You don't have a problem, laddie. You never found him, you never saw me, and that's the end of the story. Find yourself a pub and stop worrying. Nobody ever found anything Duff Smith hid, and nobody ever will."*

During the next two hours, as the Bentley rolled through the bleak winter streets of the blacked-out city, Stern learned more about the reality of the coming European war than he had dreamed in his most cynical fits of depression. In the beginning he pressed the brigadier about the mission he'd hinted at, but the Scotsman had his own way of coming to the meat of things. The first thing he did was deflate any hopes Stern had of the Allies saving the Jews still trapped in Europe. Several phrases would come back to Stern much later, and he would marvel at how frankly Smith had laid it all out.

"Don't you see, man?" Smith had said. "If we offer sanctuary to the Jews still alive in Europe, Hitler might say *yes*. And the truth is, we don't want them. Neither do the Americans. You Jews are a highly educated race. Consequently, you take away jobs faster than any other immigrant group. There are military reasons, as well. Little wasn't joking in there. The Nazis already laid down the law to the Red Cross. 'Touch the concentration camps, and we will no longer keep the Geneva Convention regarding military POWs.' That's no empty threat."

The Bentley rolled past the Royal Hospital. "You're ahead of your time, Stern. Though not by much, I'll wager. It won't be long before Chaim Weizmann goes to Churchill with the same request you made this afternoon. Bomb the camps. But it won't make any difference. Bomber Command is practically a law unto itself. There are a hundred ways to bury a request like that in committees and feasibility studies. You'd lost the battle before you even went in there today. To men like Little you're nothing but a meddling civilian. That's enough reason to deny your request, no matter how much sense it might make." Smith chuckled. "I don't know what you thought you were playing at. The bloody Archbishop of Canterbury lobbied for sanctuary in England for European Jews, and he failed. And you a wanted terrorist!"

"I had to try," Stern said. "If you knew the sheer numbers of innocent people dying, you would—"

"Numbers aren't the half of it." Duff Smith shook his head.

"I've seen eyewitness transcripts myself. Polish girls raped and tortured and thrown into the street with blood streaming from their bodies. Entire families stripped naked and made to stand on metal plates to be electrocuted. Jewish women being sterilized and sent to military brothels. Children wrenched from their mothers' teats. The whole hellish circus. What you don't understand is that *none of that matters.* War is supposed to be hell, Stern. That kind of thing has lost its shock value, especially to soldiers like Little, who watched their friends slaughtered by the thousands in the Great War. To men like that, civilian deaths are regrettable but irrelevant. They have no direct relation to the prosecution or outcome of the war."

"You can't all be like Little," Stern said. "I can't conceive of that."

"You're right. There are a lot more like Major Dickson."

The brigadier paused to pack and light a hand-carved pipe.

"There must be some decent men in England."

"Of course there are, lad," said Smith, puffing gently. "Churchill is one of your strongest advocates. He's all for establishing a Jewish National Home in Palestine after the war. Not that that means anything. Those bastards in Parliament will drop Winston like a hot brick just as soon as he's won the war for them."

After convincing Stern of the utter futility of his journey to England, Duff Smith finally got around to his proposition. "What I said back there," he drawled, "about killing Germans inside Germany. I wasn't joking."

"What do you have in mind?" Stern asked suspiciously.

Smith's face grew very hard, very quickly. "I'm not going to lie to you, lad. I'm not trying to save the pathetic remnants of European Jewry. Frankly, it's not my bailiwick."

"What *are* you trying to do?"

Smith's eyes flickered. "Not much, except alter the course of the war."

Stern sat back against the plush seat. "Brigadier . . . who are you? Who do you work for?"

"Ah. Officially, we're known as SOE—Special Operations Executive. We raise mischief in the occupied countries, France mostly. Sabotage and the like. But with the invasion round the corner, that's rather tapered off. We're mostly dropping supplies now."

"How can you alter the course of the war?"

Smith gave him an enigmatic grin. "Know anything about chemical warfare?"

"Hold your breath and put on your gas mask. That's all."

"Well, your former countrymen know quite a bit. The Nazis, I mean."

"I know they're using poison gas to murder Jews."

Brigadier Smith waved his pipe in scorn. "Zyklon B is a common insecticide. Oh, it's deadly enough in a closed room, but it's nothing compared to what I'm talking about."

In two minutes, Smith gave Stern a thumbnail sketch of the Nazi nerve gas program, including Heinrich Himmler's private patronage. He leaned heavily on two points: Allied helplessness in the face of Sarin, and the Nazis' predilection for testing their war gases on Jewish prisoners.

"We've pinpointed parts of their testing program to three prison camps," Smith concluded. "Natzweiler in Alsace, Sachsenhausen near Berlin, and Totenhausen near Rostock."

"Rostock?" Stern exclaimed. "I was born in Rostock!"

Smith raised his eyebrows. "Were you now?"

"What is it you want to do? Disable one of these plants? A commando raid?"

"No, I've something a little more complex in mind. Something with a little *flair.*" The brigadier cracked his knuckles, beginning with his left little finger. "What I want to do is frighten the Nazis so badly that they won't dare to use their nerve gas, not even when the Reich is falling down around their ears."

"How can you do that?"

"I neglected to tell you one fact about the Allied gas program,

Stern. After intensive analysis of the stolen sample of Sarin, a team of British chemists has managed to produce a facsimile nerve agent."

Stern breathed faster. "How much do you have?"

"One-point-six metric tons."

"Is that a lot?"

Smith sighed. "Frankly, no."

"How much do the Nazis have?"

"Our best estimate is five thousand tons."

Stern went pale. "Five *thousand*—? My God. How much would it take to seriously damage a city?"

"Two hundred fifty tons of Sarin could wipe out the city of Paris."

Stern turned away from Brigadier Smith and pressed his cheek to the cold car window. His head was starting to throb. "And you have one metric ton?"

"One-point-six."

"How wonderful for you. What do you plan to do with it?"

Brigadier Smith's voice cut the air like a rusty saber. "I plan to kill every man, woman, child, and dog inside one of those three camps. SS men, prisoners, the lot. And I'm going to let Heinrich Himmler know exactly who did it."

Stern wasn't sure he had heard correctly. He took a moment to try and digest the enormity of what he thought the brigadier had suggested. "Why in God's name are you going to do that?"

"It's a bluff. A gamble. Perhaps the biggest gamble of the war. I'm going to use our thimbleful of gas to try to convince Heinrich Himmler that we not only have our own nerve gas, but the will to use it. When he finds one of his precious camps wiped out to the last man, yet with every piece of German equipment in pristine condition, he will have no choice but to reach the conclusion I want him to reach. That if the Nazis were to deploy nerve gas against our invasion force, their cities would be *annihilated* by the same weapon."

"But how do you know Hitler won't retaliate with his superior stockpiles?"

"I don't. But if I'm right about Himmler running the nerve gas program on his own, Hitler will never even find out about our raid. Himmler will sweep the whole thing under the rug. Even if Hitler were to find out, he wouldn't have any evidence to hold up to the world as an excuse for a retaliatory strike. Not the way I've planned this show."

"You're mad," said Stern. "Hitler doesn't need to justify his actions to anyone."

"You're wrong," Smith said confidently. "Hitler doesn't hesitate to massacre Jews, but he *does* try his best to cover up the fact that he's doing it. He cares about public opinion. Always has."

Stern felt a sudden apprehension. "Brigadier this is a *strategic* mission. Why have you come to me?"

"Because my hands are tied by some regrettable political considerations."

"Such as?"

"The Yanks are against it." Smith grunted. "Bloody schoolboys. They're content to fight with sticks and pebbles and hope no one gets angry enough to go home for his father's shotgun. American opposition rules out my using British or American commandos for the operation."

"What about your SOE operatives?"

"The Americans have elbowed their way in there as well. They've demanded that we set up two-man parachute teams—one Yank, one of ours—to go into France and prepare the Resistance for D day. It's pathetic. I haven't met one Yank who can speak enough French to order Boeuf Bourguignonne, much less fool a German."

"So you're scraping the bottom of the barrel. Refugees."

Smith grinned. "Bloody terrorists, at that."

"Do you have the authority to undertake this operation? Brigadier general isn't exactly Supreme Commander."

Duff Smith reached into the pocket of his beribboned tunic and pulled out an envelope. From it he withdrew Churchill's note, which he handed to Stern. Stern didn't blink once while he read it.

"Satisfied?" Smith asked.

"*Mein Gott,*" Stern whispered.

"I want you to lead this mission. Are you my man or not?"

Stern nodded in the darkness. "Yes."

Smith reached into his jacket and pulled out a map of Europe. Swastikas covered the paper from Poland to the French Coast. Stern felt his pulse speeding at the prospect of action.

"Doesn't look like we've accomplished much in five years, does it?" Smith said. "Look here. There is one thing you can help me with tonight. You may already have done it."

"What?"

"Picked the target. I mentioned three camps. To be honest, I've already narrowed my list to two. Sachsenhausen is simply too large for the type of operation I have in mind. It's Natzweiler or Totenhausen."

Stern looked greedily at the map. He knew which camp he wanted to attack. Still, he didn't want to seem too eager.

"Natzweiler is the larger by far," Smith said. "The SS are almost certainly killing more Jews there."

"A larger camp would be easier for me to slip into unnoticed," Stern pointed out.

"You won't be infiltrating the camp. Not the way I've designed this show."

"Well," Stern said in a neutral tone, "since you have only a limited amount of gas, you could increase your chances of success by targeting the smallest camp."

"Quite," Smith agreed.

"How far is Totenhausen from Rostock?"

"Twenty miles, due east. It's on the Recknitz River."

Stern could not keep the excitement out of his voice. "Brigadier, I know that area. My father and I used to hike the wilderness all around Rostock. I used to follow the *Wandervögel* around when I was a boy."

Smith studied the map. "Totenhausen is practically on the Baltic Coast. Much closer to Sweden than Natzweiler is. That would simplify both infiltration and escape."

"Brigadier, it's got to be Totenhausen!"

"I'm afraid I can't make the final decision tonight." The Scotsman rolled up the map. "But I can tell you this. Totenhausen was designed solely to test and manufacture Sarin and Soman. From a political standpoint, it's the perfect target."

Stern tried to control his impatience. "What do I do now? Where do I go?"

"Some of my people will look after you." Smith leaned forward and opened a window in the partition separating them from the Bentley's driver. "Norgeby House," he said, then closed the window and turned to Stern. "There is more to this mission than killing people. There are other objectives which are extremely important. After the SS garrison is destroyed—"

"Just a minute," Stern interrupted. "You said we had to kill the prisoners?"

"Yes. I'm afraid there's no way around it. We can't jeopardize the mission by trying to warn them. Even if we did warn them, there's no way to get them out of the camp, much less out of Germany."

Stern nodded slowly. "Are they all Jews?"

"God, man, it's an odd time to get squeamish. Didn't you just propose bombing four concentration camps with no warning at all?"

Stern felt a strange hesitancy. He *had* just proposed that. But somehow this was different. Bombing the death camps would have been an unmistakable assertion of Allied support for Jews, and a potentially crippling blow to the Nazi extermination system. Brigadier Smith's plan also meant sacrificing Jews, but without any direct benefit to the Jewish people. Or was there? If Eisenhower's invasion stalled on the beaches of France, Hitler would almost certainly have time to complete the genocide he had begun eleven years ago. Stern cleared his throat.

"You mentioned other objectives, Brigadier?"

Smith was watching him carefully. "Right. After the garrison is neutralized, you'll move into the gas factory. First and foremost, we need a sample of Soman, their newest and most toxic gas. Second, we need photographs of the production apparatus. Nerve agents are extremely difficult to mass produce. A lot could be learned by studying photos of the German equipment."

"Brigadier, I'm no scientist," Stern objected. "I can operate a camera, but I wouldn't know a poison gas factory from a herring cannery."

"Don't worry about that. Your job is neutralizing the camp. Someone else will give you technical directions regarding the gas."

"Who?"

"An American. He's the foremost expert on poison gases outside Nazi Germany. Not only that, he speaks fluent German."

"I thought you said the Americans were against this mission."

"They are. But this man's a civilian. Perfect for the job."

Stern's eyes narrowed. "You sound like you're trying to sell him to me."

"I'm afraid *he's* the one we'll have to sell on this operation. He happens to be a pacifist."

"A pacifist! I don't want him."

"You'll take him, though," Smith said harshly. "You'll do whatever I bloody tell you to do. And the first thing you're going to do is help me sell him on this mission. Lay on the sob stuff about the plight of the Jews. Moral duty, all that rot."

Stern's voice communicated his disgust. "You want me to help you convince a pacifist to murder defenseless prisoners?"

A wicked smile touched the corners of Brigadier Smith's mouth. "Nobody needs to say anything about killing anybody. This is a sales job. And the first rule of sales is, know your mark. In this case, that advice can be taken quite literally."

"What do you mean? Who *is* this person?"

Brigadier Smith leaned back against the seat and closed his eyes. "Mark McConnell, M.D. And I can tell you right now, Stern, you're going to hate him."

Two hours later, in a forest deep in northern Germany, a black Volkswagen skidded to a stop beneath a thick stand of fir trees. Two figures—one male, one female—climbed out and hurried into the wood. The woman wore a heavy wool coat over a white nurse's uniform, and a fur hat over her blond hair. The man wore a ragged buttonless jacket to cover his gray shirt, which was lined with prison stripes.

The man stopped at the edge of a clearing and stood guard. The woman moved forward and called out a few words in Polish. Two men materialized out of the trees and stepped into the moonlight. One was huge, almost a giant, with a thick black beard. He carried a Sten submachine gun in one hand and wore a meat cleaver on his belt. The young man beside him weighed only half what his comrade did, and carried only a suitcase. With his long thin arms and delicate fingers, he looked like a refugee from a paupers' symphony.

"You're late, Anna," said the giant. "We already took down the antenna."

"Then put it back up," she said. "We almost didn't get here at all."

The giant grinned, then said something to his comrade in Polish. The thin man opened up the suitcase and pulled out a coil of wire. The giant tied one end to his belt and scrambled up the nearest fir tree.

The woman called Anna took a small notebook from her coat and knelt on the ground beside the suitcase. The simplicity of the concept fascinated her. Transmitter, receiver, battery, antenna—all in one battered leather suitcase. This wireless set had been hand-built by Polish partisans, but it worked almost as well as the factory-made German set where she worked. She patted the young man on the arm while he dialed in a frequency.

"Do you think we're too late, Miklos?" she asked.

He looked up at her with hollow eyes and smiled. "My brother likes to tease you, Anna. London is always waiting." He took a codebook from his pocket, opened it, then looked up toward the dark branches. "Ready, Stan?"

"Fire away!" called the giant. "Just keep it short."

Miklos rubbed his hands together for warmth, then did a musical dexterity exercise to limber his fingers. The blond woman opened her notebook to a marked page and handed it to him.

"This is it?" Miklos asked, scanning the nearly blank sheet. "Can it be worth all this trouble?"

Anna shrugged. "That's what they asked for."

Sixty miles from London, on the site of a former Roman encampment, stood a horrid Victorian pile known as Bletchley Park. Since the beginning of the war the mansion had served as the nerve center of Britain's covert battle against the Nazis. Radio aerials sheltered in the trees gathered hurried transmissions from across Occupied Europe, then routed them to former ships' radio operators on duty inside the mansion, who finally passed the decoded signals to the synod of dons and scholars responsible for piecing together a picture of what was happening in the darkness that lay across the Continent.

Tonight Brigadier Duff Smith had driven his Bentley at alarming speeds to reach Bletchley. He could have phoned, but he wanted to be there when—or if—the message he awaited came in. Smith had stood at the shoulder of a young rating from Newcastle for an hour, watching a silent radio receiver until nervous tension got the better of him. He was about to give up and drive back to London when a staccato of Morse dots and dashes filled the tiny room.

"That's him, sir," said the rating with controlled excitement. "PLATO. I don't even need to hear his identifying group. I know his fist like Ellington's piano."

Brigadier Smith watched the young man copy down the groups as they came through. They came in three short sets. When the radio fell silent, the rating looked up with a puzzled expression.

"That's it, sir?"

"I won't know until you decode it. How long were they on the air, Clapham?"

"I'd say about fifty-five seconds, sir. Plays that Morse key like a musician, PLATO does. A bloody artist."

Smith looked at his watch. "I make it fifty-eight seconds. Good show. The Poles are the best at this game, bar none. Decode that lot right now."

"Right, sir."

One minute later, the rating tore off a sheet of notepaper and handed it to the SOE chief. Smith read what he had written:

Wrapped steel winch cable, due to copper shortage.
Diameter 1.7 cm. Ten pylons. 609 meters.
Slope 29 degrees. 6 wires. 3 live, 3 dead.

Brigadier Smith laid the notepaper on a table and pulled a different sheet from his pocket. He consulted some figures that had been scrawled there earlier in the week by a brilliant British engineer. The rating saw the brigadier's hand stiffen, then crumple the sheet of paper in his hand.

"By God, it could work," Smith said softly. "That woman is gold in the bank. It could *work.*" He carefully placed both pieces of paper in the inside pocket of his jacket, then took his cap from the table. "Good work, Clapham."

Smith laid a hand on the rating's shoulder and said, "From now on, all transmissions from source PLATO will be passed under the name SCARLETT. SCARLETT with two 'T's."

"As in *Gone With the Wind,* sir?"

"Right."

"Noted." The young rating grinned. "Nice to know the Jerries are short of a few things too, eh?"

Duff Smith paused at the door and looked back thoughtfully. "They'll never know what that missing copper cost them, Clapham."

It was late afternoon in London when Brigadier Smith's silver Bentley rolled onto the A-40 and headed for Oxford. Smith was driving himself today, making use of an ingenious shift mechanism designed for him by SOE engineers. Jonas Stern sat beside him, studying a topographic map of Mecklenburg, the northernmost province of Germany.

"I remember it all," he said excitedly. "Every road, every brook. Brigadier, the target has to be Totenhausen."

"Be patient, lad."

"I don't see the concentration camp marked here."

"I told you, Totenhausen isn't like any camp you've ever heard of. It's strictly a laboratory and testing facility. Compared to a place like Buchenwald, it's minuscule. The SS let the trees grow right up to the electric fence. You need a larger scale map. Himmler is serious about hiding that camp."

Brigadier Smith had not worn his uniform today. He looked professorial in a tweed jacket and stalker's cap. "Listen," he said, "I've changed my mind about this meeting."

"What do you mean?"

"I mean I don't want you to say anything unless I ask you to."

"Why not?"

Smith looked away from the road long enough to let Stern know he meant what he was about to say. "Dr. McConnell is not like most men. He's too smart to be manipulated—by you, anyway—and he's too principled to be shamed or bribed into doing anything he doesn't believe in. He's also too bloody pigheaded to listen to reason."

Stern gazed out of the car window. "What kind of man calls himself a pacifist in 1944? Is he a religious fanatic?"

"Not at all."

"A philosopher? Head in the clouds?"

"In the sand, more like. He's a different sort of chap. Brilliant, but down to earth. Probably a genius. The pacifism comes from his father. He was a doctor too. Gassed in the Great War, one of the worst cases. Badly scarred, blinded. That's why the son chose the field he did. Wanted to prevent that kind of thing from ever happening again. Didn't muck about, either. His uncle owned a dye factory in Atlanta, Georgia. When McConnell was sixteen, he used the chemicals in that plant to brew his own mustard gas. Phosgene too. Tested it on rats he trapped in the basement. Building bloody gas masks at sixteen."

"He sounds like a dangerous sort of pacifist."

"Oh, he could be, if he chose. He's a riddle. He was a Rhodes scholar in 1930. Took a First at University College. Went back to America for medical school. Graduated top of his class there, then decided to go into general practice. Master's degree in chemical engineering. Holds five or six patents in the U.S. for various industrial compounds."

"He's rich?"

"He didn't grow up rich, if that's what you mean. I'm sure he's comfortable enough now. My point is this. He may say things that seem truly outlandish to you, or to anyone who really understands war. But don't lose your temper, no matter what. And don't mention his father. In fact, don't say anything at all."

Stern tossed the map of northern Germany onto the floor of the Bentley. "Why did you bring me along, then?"

"I want you to get a look at him. If he agrees to go on the mission, he'll be your only partner."

"*What?* You're saying this is a two-man job?"

"As far as you're concerned, yes." Brigadier Smith revved the Bentley past a U.S. Army truck.

Stern shook his head slowly. "This sounds more like a suicide mission every day."

"It may well be. But keep one thing clear in your mind. The mission you hear me propose to McConnell will be somewhat different than the mission I discussed with you. For obvious reasons, certain aspects of the offensive side of things will be . . . minimized. No matter what I say, you will show no surprise. Clear?"

"No matter what anybody says, I keep my mouth shut."

Brigadier Smith glanced at the young Zionist one last time. "So far, you haven't shown much of a talent for that."

Stern showed his right palm to the brigadier and wiggled his middle finger up and down, the most obscene Arab gesture he knew.

9

In Oxford it was raining. McConnell stood inside a bewildering maze of metal pipes, pressurized storage tanks, rubber hosing and racks of gas masks—a maze of his own construction. There were enough skull-and-crossbones POISON signs tacked around the lab to scare off a German regiment. Two elderly white-coated assistants worked quietly at the far end of the lab, preparing for the afternoon's experiment.

McConnell leaned against a window and looked down into the sandstone courtyard three floors below. Cold rain pooled in the cracks between the stones, running through channels carved over the past six centuries. He wondered if his brother was flying today. Did weather like this ground B-17s? Or was David navigating the sunny ether above the clouds, humming a swing tune while he pressed on towards Germany with death stowed under him?

Hardly a day had passed since their last meeting that Mark had not gone over his brother's words again. His determination not to participate in the race for a doomsday gas remained as strong as it had been that night, yet something within him would not let the issue rest. How many scientists had faced similar dilemmas during the war? Certainly those on the Tube Alloys project, men who labored in the shadowy, Faustian field of atomic physics. They had much in common with the men working in the sealed chemical laboratories at Porton Down. Good men living in bad times. Good men making compromises, or being compromised. How could he explain why he couldn't help them?

He watched the raindrops spatter on the window glass, wiggle like bacteria on a slide, then coalesce and run down, seemingly without direction, to join the water collecting in the gutter pipe, a liquid momentum with force enough to wear away the stone below. He thought of what David had said in the Welsh Pony, about the American boys gathering for the invasion. A rain of young men falling on England, out of airplanes, spilling out of the holds of ships, coalescing into groups that formed the cells of a colossal human wave. An incipient wave that grew each day, leaning eastward, that would soon be poised for a great leap across the Channel. It would leap as a whole, but it would break on the opposite shore and shatter into its component parts, individuals, young men who would water the ground with their blood.

That cataclysmic event, though still in the future, was already as unstoppable as the setting of the sun. The men behind it had come together in England, and around themselves were drawing young lives by the millions. They breathed the scent of history, and across the Channel perceived nothing less than the Armies of Darkness, *Festung Europa,* the fortress of the Antichrist, waiting to receive their mighty thrust.

But something else awaited them there. McConnell had seen it for himself, and heard it. He had traveled across the Channel to Belgium, and to France, and walked the fields that had once been crisscrossed with trenches and mud. He had stood awhile above the intermingled regiments of bones resting fitfully in shallow graves beneath the soil. And there, in whispers just beneath the wind that howled across the stark terrain, he had heard the puzzled voices of boys who had never known the inside of a woman, who never had children, who had never grown old. Seven million voices asking in unison the unanswered question that was an answer in itself:

Why?

Very soon those boys would have company.

"You okay, Doctor Mac?"

Startled, Mark turned from the window and saw his assistants holding four small white rats beside the hermetically sealed glass chamber he called the Bubble.

"Fine, Bill," he said. "Let's get to it."

The Bubble stood nearly five feet high, not tall enough for a man to stand in, but plenty of room for a small primate. Rubber hoses of various gauges snaked across the floor from storage cylinders to fittings in the Bubble's base. Inside the chamber lay four round, variously colored objects about the size of English footballs. One by one, the assistants picked up the containers, opened small hatches in their sides, and stuffed the rats inside. One rat per football. When the containers were sealed, the assistants rolled them back into the Bubble and secured its main hatch. McConnell was reaching for the valve on a gas cylinder when someone knocked on the lab door.

"Come," he said.

Brigadier Duff Smith strode into the lab, an enthusiastic smile on his face. He carried a few extra pounds around his middle, the inevitable toll of middle-age, but the muscle beneath was fit and hard. The second man through the door stood over six feet tall, and his skin had the burnished tan of a desert dweller. His dark eyes focused on McConnell and stayed there.

The brigadier surveyed the array of equipment. "How goes it, Doctor? What are we up to today? Bringing the dead back to life?"

"Quite probably the reverse," McConnell said sourly. He reached down and opened the valve. The muffled hiss of gas released under pressure sounded in the room.

Smith glanced at the glass chamber. "What's in the Bubble today? Rhesus monkeys?" He craned his neck. "I don't see anything."

"Look closer."

"Those four footballs?"

"That's exactly what we call them. Inside each of those footballs is a rat. The surfaces are made of mask filter material."

"For what class of gases?"

"Blue Cross. That's hydrocyanic acid going in now. If you feel the slightest irritation in your nasal passages, hold your breath and run like hell. The gas is odorless and nonirritant, so I've added a small amount of cyanogen chloride to let us know we're about to die."

"How long do we have to get clear after we smell it?"

"About six seconds."

Brigadier Smith's dark companion stiffened. Smith grinned and said, "Plenty of time, eh, Stern?"

McConnell shut off the valve. "That should be enough to tell. Go ahead and clear it."

An assistant started a noisy vacuum pump.

"Your friends at Porton Down think the Germans have given up on this gas, Brigadier," McConnell said over the rattle. "I don't. It's difficult to build up a lethal concentration on the battlefield, but that's just the kind of challenge the Germans love. Hydrocyanic acid can kill you in fifteen seconds if it saturates your mask filter. We call that 'breaking' the filter. Our current filters are easily broken by hydrocyanic acid, and I think the Germans know that. I'm trying to develop virtually unbreakable filter inserts for the M-2 through M-5 series canisters."

"Any success so far?"

"Let's take a look." McConnell signaled an assistant to shut off the pump, then donned a heavy black gas mask and motioned for Smith and his companion to move back against the wall. The Bubble gave off a sucking sound as he opened its door. He lifted one of the footballs, held it at arm's length, opened its hatch and stuck two fingers through the aperture. Brigadier Smith watched, fascinated, as McConnell drew the white rat from the football by its pink tail.

The rodent hung motionless in space.

"Damn!" McConnell said, pulling off his mask. He turned and watched his assistants pull dead rats from the other three footballs. He shook his head in frustration. "Dead rats. That's my life for the last three months."

"I don't see any obvious signs of suffocation," Brigadier Smith observed.

McConnell took a scalpel from a soapstone table and neatly sliced the rat's throat. Then he squeezed its body to express arterial blood. "See that? The blood is cherry red, as if it were fully oxygenated. Cyanide attaches to the hemoglobin molecule in place of oxygen. A soldier will look like he's in the bloom of health while he's suffocating."

While the assistants disposed of the rodents, Smith leaned closer. "I'd like to speak to you in private, Doctor. How about the Mitre Inn? We could take a room."

"I'd prefer to talk here." McConnell glanced over Smith's shoulder at the silent stranger, then called to his assistants, "We'll start back up after dinner."

When the assistants had gone, Smith pulled up a chair and straddled it, resting his right arm on its back. The gesture emphasized his missing limb. "We've had some more disturbing news," he said. "Out of Germany."

"I'm all ears."

"First, if you don't mind, I'd like you to bring Mr. Stern here up to speed on the chemical warfare situation. He's a Jew, originally from Germany. Fresh in from Palestine, if you can believe it. Gas isn't his line. Just a brief overview. German nomenclature, if you please."

"You've read the classification manual."

"But you helped write it," Smith said patiently. "I like my information from the horse's mouth."

McConnell directed his answer to Stern. "Four classes, designated by colored crosses. You just saw Blue Cross in action. White Cross is tear gas. Green Cross denotes chlorine, phosgene, diphosgene, et cetera. They're the oldest chemical weapons, but still first-rank battlefield choices. They kill by causing pulmonary edema—internal drowning. The last is Yellow Cross, which also dates back to World War One." McConnell wiped his brow and spoke in a mechanical voice. "Yellow Cross denotes the 'blister' gases, or vesicants. Mustard . . . Lewisite. Highly persistent gases. Wherever they touch the body, they produce burns, blisters, and deep ulcers of the most painful kind. The body's ability to heal is impaired, making the effects of Yellow Cross especially long lasting."

"Thank you," Smith said. "But you left out a class, I believe."

McConnell's eyes narrowed. "The last class has no cross classification," he said carefully.

"As of yesterday it does. Black Cross."

"*Schwarzes Kreuz,*" McConnell said softly. "A fitting name for a tool of the devil."

"Come now, Doctor. If I didn't know you were a scientist, I'd swear you were superstitious."

"Get to the point, Brigadier. You didn't drive up here from London to chat about gas classifications."

Smith smiled gamely. "Quite right, Doctor. I drove up here to enlist you body and soul in the war effort."

"What are you talking about?"

"As of last week, Sarin took second place in the Nazi arsenal. An even deadlier nerve agent is now being tested on human subjects inside Germany. It is called *Soman.* According to reports,

Soman is exponentially more toxic than Sarin, and far more persistent."

"I can hardly imagine anything more lethal than Sarin."

"Oh, it exists. The Porton lads are going over the report now. To be frank, the threat posed by Soman has been deemed so dire that I've been authorized to send a team into Germany to disable the production plant and bring back a large sample."

Stern cut his eyes at the brigadier.

"Into *Germany?*" said McConnell. "But . . . why tell me?"

The Scotsman wove his lie into the cloth of the truth. "Because I want you to go in with them, Doctor. I've finally found the ideal job for you: a mission that is entirely defensive in nature. It's the equivalent of preventive medicine."

"There's nothing defensive about sabotaging a nerve gas factory. You could send a cloud of death rolling right through the heart of Germany. You might as well call your mission a nerve gas attack."

"That's all the more reason for you to take part in the mission, Doctor. Having your expertise on the ground might prevent just such a disaster."

"Frankly, Brigadier, I don't believe you would perceive such an event as a disaster."

Smith started to reply, but McConnell held up his hand. "This discussion is pointless," he said. "I'll do everything in my power to develop a defense against this new gas, but that's all. I'm sorry, Mr. Stern. The brigadier could have saved you the drive from London. He knows my position on this."

"And a damned infuriating one it is, too!" Smith said with surprising force. "You call yourself a bloody pacifist, yet you've been in this war longer than practically any other American!"

"I refuse to have this argument again," McConnell said evenly. "There must be other scientists who could take this on."

"None who is fluent in German."

McConnell's eyes widened. "You consider me a fluent German speaker?"

"Three years of German in high school, three more in college."

"That hardly qualifies me as a spy."

"I've seen men with half your linguistic skills go into situations twice as dangerous as the one I'm asking you to take on."

"Did they come back?"

"Some did."

McConnell shook his head in amazement.

"Ten words of German could get you past a border post, Doctor, and you're better than that. There's no degree in espionage, you know. Every moment in the field is part of your final examination. Besides, Stern here is a native German. He can polish your delivery while the preparatory work is being done."

McConnell took a step toward Smith. "I'm not going, Brigadier. And you can't order me to. I'm an American civilian and a registered conscientious objector."

"You think I don't know that? Have you forgotten who ensured that you were granted that classification? It's bloody odd when you think about it. You call yourself a conscientious objector, but you're not hiding back in the States with the Quakers and Mennonites. You're nothing like the other pacifists I've seen. No, Doctor, to me"—Smith hesitated—"to me you look more like a man who's afraid of getting killed."

McConnell laughed outright. "I *am* afraid of getting killed. I assume every soldier is, if he's not mad. You won't shame me into helping you, Brigadier. This isn't a grammar school playground."

"You're damn right it isn't, laddie! If Jerry hits us with Soman, we've got to be ready to hit back twice as hard!"

McConnell smiled icily. "Why don't you spray the countryside with anthrax? That would render the whole of Germany uninhabitable for fifty years. Maybe even a hundred."

"We can't risk that, and you know it. They could do the same to us. It's tit-for-tat, and the enemy always has the prerogative to strike first. That's the hell of being a democracy."

"Our unwillingness to use such weapons is what separates us from the Nazis, Brigadier."

"Bring out the bloody violins," Smith growled.

Jonas Stern was the first to hear the footsteps in the corridor. He touched Smith, who moved quickly to the door and opened it a crack. McConnell watched him step outside, heard the hum of low voices. Then Smith walked slowly back into the room, followed by a young captain wearing the dark blouse and pinks of an 8th Air Force officer. The captain had an envelope in his hand.

"Doctor," the brigadier said in a soft voice, "this chap needs a word with you."

Mark felt a strange tingling in his fingertips. "What is it? Has something happened to David?"

The captain glanced at Brigadier Smith. "I'm not supposed to say anything until you've opened the letter. But . . . Doctor, your brother was shot down last night. I'm sorry, sir."

The captain extended the envelope. McConnell took it and tore open the seal. Inside was a sheet of paper, the words on it typewritten in the manner of a telegram.

REGRET TO INFORM CAPTAIN DAVID MCCONNELL KILLED IN ACTION
19 JANUARY STOP CAPTAIN MCCONNELL'S ACTIONS ALWAYS REFLECTED
THE HIGHEST HONOR UPON HIMSELF THE USAAF AND THE UNITED STATES
OF AMERICA STOP I EXTEND MY PERSONAL CONDOLENCES STOP

COLONEL WILLIAM T. HARRIGILL
401ST BOMB GROUP, 94TH COMBAT WING
U.S. 8TH AIR FORCE. DEENETHORPE, ENGLAND

"Doctor?" Brigadier Smith said softly. "Mac?"

McConnell held up his hand. "Please don't say anything, Brigadier." He had imagined this moment many times. Daylight bomber crews suffered horrifying rates of attrition. And yet something about this seemed wrong. It was the timing, he realized. Two minutes after refusing Brigadier Smith's biggest sales pitch ever, a messenger shows up to tell him his brother has been killed by the Germans? McConnell looked up from the paper and into the Scotsman's pale blue eyes.

"Brigadier?" His voice was barely a whisper. "Is this your doing?"

Smith looked at McConnell in astonishment. "I beg your pardon, Doctor?"

McConnell took a step toward him. "It *is*, isn't it? This is some damned SOE trick. You're trying to push me into your mission, aren't you? The end justifies the means in your business, right? If the pacifist won't go, we'll make him go." McConnell's face was white. *"Right,* Brigadier?"

The Scotsman straightened his back and raised his chin. It was the British equivalent of a cobra puffing out its hood. "Doctor, as much as I resent your insinuation, I am going to ignore it. I realize that in moments like this the mind grasps for any straw, however thin. But you are absolutely wrong."

McConnell felt his face growing hot. The captain was staring at him as if he were a dangerous mental patient. He looked down at the telegram. *Killed in action.* So goddamn *vague.* He cleared his throat.

"Can you tell me any more than this, Captain?"

The young officer pulled at the tails of his dress jacket. "The colonel said you had a top secret clearance, and that I could tell you what we knew. David's plane sustained catastrophic damage returning from a raid over Regensburg. It was hit by flak, probably fighter cannon as well. Nobody saw the aircraft hit the ground, but no chutes were sighted."

McConnell's eyes and throat were stinging. "Did—did you know my brother, Captain?"

"Yes, sir. Hell of a pilot. Always a joke for the ground crew. He even made the colonel crack a smile a few times. The colonel would have come himself, but we had—well, he was busy."

Mark blinked away tears. "Does our mother know yet?"

"No, sir. That's a draft of her telegram there."

"Jesus. Ask the colonel not to send this, please. I'd like to be the one to tell her."

"No problem, sir. It'll eventually have to be sent, but I think the colonel can hold off a few days."

McConnell looked from the brigadier's ruddy face to Jonas Stern's dark one, then at the captain. The messenger shifted uncertainly. "Sorry again, Doc," he said. He saluted Brigadier Smith and backed out of the lab.

Mark put his hand over his mouth and tried to swallow. All he could see was David, not as he had seen him four days ago, but as a little boy in a muddy Georgia pond, trying to learn to hold his breath.

"I'm sorry, Brigadier," he said softly. "I apologize."

The Scotsman held up his hand. "There's no need, man. I know this is difficult. I lost a brother myself. At Lofoten, in forty-one. But by God, Doctor, if this isn't the final reason to come on board with us, nothing is. The bastards killed your brother!"

McConnell shook his head hopelessly. "You've never understood me at all, have you? You have no idea why I am the way I am."

Smith bristled. "I understand you, all right. I know about your father. But what would he say now, eh? I'm asking you to go on a mission of mercy. Christ, Doctor, the Nazis are testing the nerve agents on *human beings*. Why do you think Stern here is going? Most of those human guinea pigs are Jews. The Germans are slaughtering his people while the world stands by and does nothing!"

McConnell studied Stern's face. He saw no sadness or pleading in the young man's features. All he saw—or thought he saw—was disgust. "I'm truly sorry," he said, "but I'm afraid I must ask you to leave. I need to be alone."

To McConnell's surprise, Brigadier Smith turned on his heel and walked out of the room without further argument. The young Jew, however, remained behind. He had stood silent throughout the meeting, but now he walked slowly forward until he stood only inches from McConnell. Mark had six or seven years on the stranger, but he sensed a fearsome intensity in the young man.

"Smith doesn't understand you, Doctor," Stern said softly. "But I do. You're not a coward. You are a fool. You're like my father was. You're like a million Jews across Europe. You believe in reason, in the essential goodness of man. You believe that if you refuse to commit evil yourself, someday you will conquer it." His voice dripped contempt. "All the fools who believed that are dead now. Fed into poison gas and flames by men who know the true nature of humanity. The only difference between you and those fools is that you're American." Stern switched suddenly from English to German, but McConnell caught most of it. "You have yet to taste even a sip of the pain so many have drunk to the bitter dregs in the last ten years."

McConnell opened his mouth to reply, but no sound came. The weight of Stern's words seemed incongruous when paired with the young face speaking them. But not with the eyes. The young Jew's eyes were like David's had been when he spoke of losing his friends. Ageless, emotionless—

"Stern!" Brigadier Smith stood in the open doorway. "Leave him be."

The dark young man nodded slowly at McConnell. "I'm sorry about your brother. But he was only a drop in an ocean beyond counting. You should think about that." He turned and followed the brigadier into the corridor.

Alone at last, McConnell reread the telegram in a daze. *Regret to inform ... killed in action ... McConnell's actions always reflected the highest honor ... my personal condolences ... condolences. ...* Mark put his left hand behind him and found the edge of a desk. He couldn't breathe. He stumbled to the nearest window and tried to open it, but the latch was stuck. He raised his right foot and kicked furiously at the ironwork.

In his anger at McConnell's refusal, Smith was pushing the Bentley beyond the limit of sanity, much less legality. The fact that he was doing it in the dark with only one arm would have terrified Jonas Stern at any other time. But just now his fury burned as hot as the brigadier's.

"Just find another damned chemist!" he shouted above the roar of the Bentley's engine.

"It's not as easy as it sounds," Smith snapped back. "I can't use enlisted personnel, American or British. Besides, McConnell's the best man for the job. Under the age of sixty, anyway."

Stern slammed his hand against the door. "Then what the hell are we going to do? You can't let one idealistic fool stop us."

Brigadier Smith glanced over at the young Zionist. "I haven't given up on the good doctor yet."

"No? You're mad, then. He'll never do it. You might as well ask Albert Schweitzer to start carrying a bazooka."

"I think he will," Smith insisted. "I think he almost agreed today. That telegram nearly pushed him over the edge."

Stern laughed harshly. "You're crazy."

"Mark my words," Brigadier Smith said, his eyes focused on the dark road. "He'll come around. Tragedy has a way of changing people's minds."

Stern turned suddenly to the Scotsman and stared. "Brigadier, you didn't set up that scene, did you? I mean ... his brother *was* really killed?"

Smith glanced at Stern, a look of genuine shock on his face.

"Christ, how devious do you think I am? I'd better hire more Jews while I can get them. You're born conspirators."

Stern searched the brigadier's face for a sign of deceit, but the Scotsman gave away nothing. Stern saw no point in questioning him further. But as he withdrew into his own thoughts, he could not help but wonder. How far *would* Brigadier Smith go to get what he wanted? The answer to that question would be of great importance after the war, in Palestine.

If he lived that long, of course.

McConnell was kicking at the ironwork of the window when the first doubt struck him. Why had he taken Brigadier Smith at his word? If the SOE chief had faked David's death, would he admit it when confronted?

"That bastard is cold enough to do it," he said aloud.

Mark knew how improbable the idea was, but a fierce hope overrode every rational objection his mind could conjure. With shaking hands he called the university operator and asked to be connected to the 8th Air Force base at Deenethorpe. He drummed his feet on the floor at the operator's infuriatingly polite: *I'm trying to connect you*—then at last he was through.

"I'd like to speak to someone about casualties, please."

"One moment, sir," said a young male voice.

McConnell heard several clicks, then a male voice with a Southern drawl came on the line. "Colonel Harrigill here."

Harrigill. McConnell remembered the name from the telegram. *Doesn't mean anything,* he thought. *Brigadier Smith could easily get the right names.* "Colonel," he said, surprised by the quaver in his voice, "this is Dr. Mark McConnell. I'm calling from Oxford University. Was there a raid over Regensburg last night?"

"I'm afraid I can't give out information like that over the phone, Doctor."

Part of McConnell's brain placed Harrigill's accent—the Mississippi Delta—while another made his face flush. The timbre of Colonel Harrigill's voice held more than official courtesy. The undertone sounded almost like sympathy.

"What information *can* you give me, Colonel?"

"Well . . . have you received a telegram today, Doctor?"

McConnell shut his eyes. "Yes."

"I can confirm that your brother's aircraft was lost in the line of duty over France. Visual reports from other aircrew led us to classify the entire crew as Killed In Action."

Mark found himself unable to say anything further.

"Is there anything I can do for you, son? I was about to send a telegram to your family Stateside."

"Don't! I mean not yet, at least. There's only our mother, and she's seen enough—just—I'll tell her, Colonel."

"That's fine with the Army Air Corps, Doctor. I'll try to slow down Western Union a little bit. And again, let me express my sorrow. Captain McConnell was a fine officer. A credit to his squadron, his country, and to the South."

Mark felt a strange chill at this archaic expression of respect from a fellow Southerner. Yet somehow it touched him. It seemed to fit David. "Thank you, Colonel."

"Good night, Doctor. God bless."

McConnell hung up the phone. Colonel Harrigill had dashed his last hope. David was gone. And to think Brigadier Smith had believed his death would finally wipe away Mark's hatred for war.

This time the grief washed over him without warning. His brother was dead. His father was dead. In his entire family, he was the last male McConnell left alive. For the first time since returning to England he felt an almost irresistible urge to go home. Back to Georgia. To his mother. His wife. The thought of his mother brought a wave of heat to his scalp. How was he going to tell her? What could he possibly say?

When he kicked the window latch this time, the iron-bound panes crashed open and a cutting wind stung his face. Slowly, his throat began to relax. He could breathe. He gazed out over a snowy scene that appeared much as it had four hundred years before. Oxford University. His island of tranquility in a world gone mad. What a pathetic joke. He felt the telegram slip from his hand, watched it brush the window casement and then flutter down to the cobblestones three stories below.

The first sound that escaped his throat was a great racking wail that burst from the depths of his soul. Several windows opened across the quad, revealing white faces alive with curiosity. Somewhere a gramophone was playing Bing Crosby's "I'll Be Seeing You." By the time the second verse wafted across the quad, the tears were freezing on McConnell's cheeks.

He was alone.

Y our tape machine stopped," said Rabbi Leibovitz.
"What?"
The old man pointed a long finger at the Sony microcas-
sette recorder lying on the end table beside his chair. I blinked twice,
unable to break the vision of my grandfather at that Oxford window, or my thoughts of my great uncle, whom I had never known.

"You need another tape," Leibovitz said. "And I need another
brandy. Pass the bottle, please."

I did. The rabbi glanced up at me while carefully pouring the
amber liquid into the glass. "So, Doctor, what do you think?"

I shrugged. "I don't know what to think."

"Does that sound like your grandfather to you? Does it ring
true?"

I pondered the question while I changed cassettes in the Sony. "I
guess it does," I said finally. "I can't see him compromising his principles simply for revenge."

"Are you so sure, Mark?"

I studied the rabbi's wizened face. "I guess I'll have to wait until you tell me, won't I? It's some story, all right. But the detail. . . .
How could you know all this?"

Leibovitz smiled fleetingly. "Some very long afternoons with
Mac in my office. Letters from other persons involved. Once I
learned about this story, it . . . possessed me for a while."

"What about the girl?" I asked, reaching down to the floor.
"The woman in this photograph? Who is she in the story? Is she the
woman who sent that coded message to Brigadier Smith? What the
hell was that about, anyway?"

Rabbi Leibovitz took a sip of his brandy. "Be patient. I'm getting to the girl. You want everything wrapped up in an hour, like a nice television movie." The old man cocked his head and listened to the relentless *cheeeep* of the crickets in the humid darkness outside the house. "It's time to shift focus for a little while. All this wasn't happening in a vacuum, you know. Other people were pursuing their own ends, quite oblivious to Brigadier Smith in London. Some very evil people. Monsters, I would say, if you don't object to the word."

I watched the old rabbi's eyes flick restlessly around my grandfather's study. It seemed to me that we had come to a part of the story he did not like. "Where are we shifting our focus to?" I asked, trying to prompt him.

"What?" he asked, his eyes fixing on mine.

"Where," I said again. "I guess you mean Germany, right?"

Leibovitz sat up straighter in the chair. "I do, yes," he said in a hoarse but resolute voice. "Nazi Germany."

Every prisoner in Totenhausen Camp had been standing on the hard-packed snow in roll-call formation for forty minutes in a freezing Arctic wind. Wearing only wooden shoes and gray-striped burlap prison clothes, they stood in a line seven deep and forty persons long. Nearly three hundred souls, all told—withered old men, mothers and fathers in their prime, strong-limbed youths, small children. One colicky infant screamed ceaselessly in the wretched ranks.

This *Appell* had been a surprise. The two scheduled roll calls—seven in the morning and seven at night—had already taken place. The camp veterans knew no good could come of the change in routine. In camp, all change was change for the worse. After only five minutes standing in the *Appellplatz*, they had caught the faint sound of the Polish prisoners whispering the feared word *seleckja*—selection. Somehow the Poles were always the first to know.

The newest prisoners in the line were Jews. Yesterday they had been clubbed out of an unheated rail car that carried them here from the concentration camp at Auschwitz, where they had been pulled from lines leaving trains newly arrived from the far corners of Western Europe—France and Holland mostly. They were the last of the lucky who had avoided the early deportations.

Their luck had run out.

One of the Jews standing in the first rank was no newcomer. He had been in Totenhausen so long that the SS called him not by his number or name, but by his occupation—*Schuhmacher*. Shoemaker. A lean and wiry man of fifty-five, with a hawklike nose and gray mustache, the shoemaker did not shiver like the other prisoners, nor did he try to whisper to those on either side of him. He simply stood motionless, burning as few calories as he could, and watched.

He watched SS Sergeant Major Gunther Sturm strut before the ragged assembly, his face clean-shaven for once, his lank blond hair combed across his bullet-shaped head. The shoemaker saw that the screeching of the infant annoyed the sergeant to no end. He had studied Gunther Sturm for two years, and could easily imagine the thoughts churning behind the slate eyes: *How did that brat's whore of a mother slip it through the selection net? Under her skirts, no doubt. The Auschwitz SS stay drunk and the prisoner Kommandos are lazy. How the hell do those laggards expect to win a war when they can't outsmart one crafty Jewess?* Sturm's growing frustration was of great interest to the shoemaker. On any other night the sergeant would have walked over and strangled the infant on the spot. But tonight he did not. This fact told the shoemaker something.

Tonight was special.

He studied the impressive display of force assembled to insure that tonight's activities—whatever they might be—proceeded in an orderly fashion. Eighty storm troopers of the SS *Totenkopfverbände*—Death's Head Battalions—stood stiffly at attention in their earth-brown uniforms, rifles at the ready in case some witless newcomer should make a dash for the wire. They were backed up by Sturm's beloved German shepherds—canines carefully bred with wolves to enhance their killing instinct—and also by the two machine gun towers at the forward corners of the camp.

A slamming door heralded the arrival of Sturm's immediate superior, Major Wolfgang Schörner. The senior security officer of Totenhausen marched smartly across the snow and stopped two meters from the shoemaker. Unlike the Death's Head guards, he wore the field gray uniform of the Waffen SS. He also wore a black patch over his left eye socket—a souvenir from his participation in the bloody retreat from Kursk, the turning point of the war in Russia—and a Knight's Cross at his throat.

Though only thirty years old, Schörner understood instinctively the dynamics of intimidation. Prisoners were forbidden to move during Appell, but the entire mass of bodies had drawn back slightly at his approach. With his good eye Major Schörner inspected the front line from end to end, looking for something or someone the prisoners could only guess at. Few had the courage to return his probing stare.

One who did was the shoemaker.

Another was a young woman of about twenty-five, a Dutch Jewess by the name of Jansen. Unlike the shoemaker, she had her entire family with her: husband, two small children, her father-in-law. The shoemaker had seen them arrive on yesterday's train. The woman's head had been shaved, but her large brown eyes flickered with a quick intelligence that had long since faded from the eyes of most of the other camp women. The shoemaker admired her bravery in returning Schörner's gaze, but he knew that it was hollow. She had no idea what lay in store for her family.

The shoemaker did. He didn't need to hear the whispers of the Poles. During the afternoon he had seen SS men taking great pains to avoid the area of the gas storage tanks behind their barracks. Obviously some new and potent poison had been pumped into the tanks from the laboratory. Yes, tonight there would be a selection. And selections were the exclusive province of the Herr Doktor.

"Excuse me, sir," the young Dutchwoman whispered in Yiddish. "I am Rachel Jansen. How long must we stand here in the cold?"

"Don't talk," said the shoemaker, keeping his face forward. "And keep your children quiet, for their sakes."

"No talking!" Sergeant Sturm shouted. At the sound of his voice the German shepherds burst out barking.

The shoemaker looked up at the sound of another slamming door. SS Lieutenant-General Herr Doktor Klaus Brandt, Commandant of Totenhausen Camp, stood before the rear door of his quarters wearing his elegant pale gray dress uniform. The tunic was immaculate. With a slow, purposeful tread he walked toward the Appellplatz and his assembled prisoners. It always intrigued the shoemaker to watch this man. Not only was Klaus Brandt exactly his own age—fifty-five—but to his knowledge was the only concentration camp commandant who was also a medical doctor. This had been tried once before, at a different camp, but the chosen physician had made a muddle of the administration. Not Brandt, though. The balding, slightly podgy Prussian was an obsessive perfectionist. Some believed he was a genius.

The shoemaker knew he was insane.

The commandant's SS uniform also signaled that tonight was a special occasion. Klaus Brandt considered himself a doctor first and a soldier second, and on most days wore his white lab coat over a business suit. He also insisted that he be addressed by his subordinates as *Herr Doktor* rather than *Herr Kommandant*. Of course he might be wearing the uniform simply to keep out the cold. The shoemaker could not remember a wind like this for many weeks. Earlier he had seen SS men building fires beneath their vehicles to keep the motor oil from freezing in the crankcases.

When Brandt came within ten paces of the line, Sergeant Sturm snapped to attention and yelled: "All prisoners present, Herr Doktor!"

Brandt acknowledged this report with a curt nod. He examined his watch, then leaned over and spoke quietly to Major Schörner. Schörner checked his own watch, then looked toward the main camp gate forty meters away. One of the gate guards shook his head in reply. Schörner looked questioningly at Brandt.

"Let us begin, Sturmbannführer," Brandt said.

Major Schörner signaled Sergeant Sturm with a flick of his head. Sturm marched toward the far end of the line and began pulling men from the ranks. The shoemaker saw immediately that this selection was different from all others he had seen. The criteria for selections were usually self-evident—sometimes certain adult men were selected (those of a certain approximate weight, for example) other times women having their menstrual cycle. Never had the shoemaker seen more than ten adults selected at one time, and for a simple reason: Brandt's testing chamber had not been designed to handle more.

Also, the usual procedure was for Brandt to walk along just behind the sergeant, approving the selections or, in rare cases, granting an on-the-spot dispensation. The Lord of Life and Death at Totenhausen savored his divine authority. But tonight Sturm was snatching men from the ranks with hardly a glance. Already thirteen stood under guard apart from the main group. With a chill of foreboding the shoemaker realized that all thirteen were Jews. Had his turn finally arrived?

His hands trembled. None of the Jews looked over fifty, but who knew? He saw the Jansen woman lean out of the line to try and see what was happening. An SS private stepped forward and shoved her back. Five storm troopers converged as Sergeant Sturm waded into the ranks to collar a reluctant prisoner. A hysterical wail echoed up the line, forcing the dog handlers to restrain the German shepherds.

The shoemaker began to pray. Nothing else would do any good. He had made his mistake years before, when he refused to flee from Germany with his wife and son. At least they were safe now, he thought—he *hoped*—safe in the Promised Land. Palestine. He was certainly luckier than the Jansen family on his right. Tonight the old grandfather would lose his son, the young wife her husband, and the children their father. He saw panic in the woman's eyes as she sought some means of protecting her husband. There was nothing. This was Nazi Germany, and Sergeant Sturm was getting closer.

"You!" Sturm snapped, pointing his finger. "Out of the line!"

The shoemaker watched a forty-year-old clerk from Warsaw shuffle out of the line and join the doomed men huddling in the center of the frozen camp yard. Rosen was his name, but no stone would ever mark his remains—

"*You!*" Sturm bellowed. "Out of the line!"

From the corner of his eye the shoemaker saw the young Dutch father turn and look into his wife's face. His eyes showed no fear for himself, only a withering guilt at leaving his family to suffer without his protection, however meager it might be. Their two children, a tiny boy and girl, clung to the hem of their mother's gray shift and stared up in mute terror.

"*Austreten!*" Sergeant Sturm barked, reaching for the Dutchman.

The young man raised one hand and tenderly touched his wife's cheek. "*Ik heb er geen woorden meer voor,* Rachel," he said. "Take care of Jan and Hannah."

The shoemaker was German, but he knew enough Dutch to translate: *I have no more words, Rachel.*

As Sergeant Sturm's hand closed on the young Dutchman's sleeve, a white-haired man bolted from the ranks and threw himself at Sturm's feet. The shoemaker cut his eyes up the line. Forty meters away Major Schörner was engaged in conversation with Dr. Brandt. Neither had seen the movement.

"*Spare my son!*" the old man begged in a whisper. "Spare my son! Benjamin Jansen begs you on his knees for mercy!"

Sergeant Sturm waved away a storm trooper who was hurrying

over with a dog. He drew his pistol, a well-oiled Luger. "Get back in line," he growled. "Or we'll take you instead."

"Yes!" said the old man. "That is what I want!" He rose to his feet and capered like a madman. "I will serve just as well!"

Sturm shoved him back a step. "You're not what we need." He pointed his pistol at the son. "Move!"

The elder Jansen's right hand burrowed inside his coat pocket. Sergeant Sturm pressed his Luger to the Dutchman's forehead, but the wrinkled hand emerged from the pocket holding something that flashed like stars under the arclights. The shoemaker heard Sturm catch his breath.

The Dutchman's palm was full of diamonds.

"*Take them,*" Ben Jansen whispered. "*For my son's life.*"

The shoemaker watched Sergeant Sturm's face go through several changes of expression. He could hear the thoughts turning in the sergeant's brain. Who else had seen the diamonds? What were they worth? A small fortune, by the look of them. How long would he have to carry them before he could hide them in his quarters?

"*They're yours,*" the old man whispered, pressing the gems toward Sturm's pocket.

The sergeant's left hand closed over the diamonds.

The shoemaker cringed. He knew what would happen now. He saw Sturm's finger tighten on the Luger's trigger—

"What is the delay here?" asked a sharp voice.

Sergeant Sturm froze as Major Schörner leaned over his shoulder.

"Yes," said Doctor Brandt, who had walked up beside Schörner. "What is the problem, Hauptscharführer?"

Sturm cleared his throat. "This old Jew wants to take his son's place."

"Impossible," Brandt said in a bored voice. He turned and stared impatiently at the front gate.

"I beg you, Herr Doktor!" Jansen implored. The old man had been astute enough to pick up on Brandt's preferred title. "My son has young children who need him. Herr Doktor, Marcus is a lawyer! I am but a tired old tailor. Useless! Take me instead!"

Klaus Brandt pivoted on his heel and regarded the old man with a sardonic smile. "But a good tailor is infinitely more valuable here than a lawyer," he said. He pointed to a nearby prisoner's tattered shift. The skin beneath it looked blue. "What need has he of a lawyer?"

With that, Brandt turned and moved a few steps up the line.

Benjamin Jansen stared after him with wild eyes. "But Herr Doktor—"

"*Quiet!*" Sturm roared, reaching for Marcus Jansen, who had knelt beside his children.

The old man shook as if from palsy. He reached out and caught the back of Major Schörner's gray tunic. "Sturmbannführer, take half the diamonds! Take all of them!"

Schörner turned back with narrowed eyes. "Diamonds?"

"I'm ready," said Marcus Jansen. The young Dutchman stepped resolutely from the line. His wife crouched and hugged her children, hiding their eyes.

Sergeant Sturm grabbed the lawyer and jerked him away.

With a wild shriek Ben Jansen clenched both hands into fists, took an uncertain step toward Major Schörner, then lunged to his right in the direction of Dr. Brandt.

The shoemaker felt something inside him snap. Despite the risk to himself, he threw his right fist and caught Ben Jansen on the side of the jaw. The old Dutchman dropped flat on his back in the snow in the same moment that the shoemaker whipped back into line and stood rigidly at attention.

It happened so fast that no one knew quite what to do. Sergeant Sturm had been a fraction of a second from shooting the old man. Now he looked uncertainly from the shoemaker to Schörner, then to Brandt, who had turned to see what was happening. Marcus Jansen stared in horror as Sturm's pistol hovered above his father's head.

The sudden blast of a car horn saved Benjamin Jansen's life. Its blaring echo reverberated over the snow like a royal clarion.

"It's the Reichsführer!" shouted Sergeant Sturm, hoping to turn all attention toward the front gate.

For the most part he succeeded. But while Klaus Brandt hurried toward the gate with an honor guard of SS troops, and the shoemaker wondered if he had actually heard the word *Reichsführer*, Major Wolfgang Schörner said in a soft voice: "Open your left hand, Hauptscharführer."

"But the selection!" Sturm protested. "I must finish!"

Schörner's hand closed around Sturm's thick wrist. "Haupt-scharführer, I order you to open your hand."

"*Zu befehl*, Sturmbannführer!" Sturm's voice was tight with fear and anger. As the roar of engines drew nearer, he opened his hand.

It was empty.

Major Schörner stared into the hand for a moment, then said, "Remain at attention, Hauptscharführer."

Without hesitation Schörner reached into Sturm's trouser pocket. A pained expression came over his face. He dug in the pocket, then removed his hand and opened it inches from the ser-geant's face.

The diamonds glittered like blue fire.

"I thought we had settled this issue," Schörner said quietly.

Sturm lowered his eyes. "We did, Sturmbannführer."

"Then would you like to explain these diamonds to the Reichsführer?"

Sturm paled. Himmler's edict against looting Jews for personal gain was quite explicit: the penalty was death. "Nein, Sturmbann-führer," he said.

Schörner grabbed Sturm's left hand and forced the diamonds into it. "Then get rid of them."

"Get rid of them? How?"

"*Schnell!*"

The shoemaker watched in amazement as Sergeant Sturm flung the diamonds across the snow like a man feeding chickens.

"Now," Schörner said in an even voice. "Finish the selection."

He turned and marched off toward the front gate, his knee boots gleaming under the lights.

Sturm stared down at Ben Jansen in silent rage. Then he hol-stered his Luger and kicked Marcus Jansen toward the condemned men. "*All male Jews aged sixteen to fifty step out of the ranks!*" he shouted. "*If anyone in that category is left in line one minute from now, every second woman in line will be shot!*"

The shoemaker felt the terrible, wonderful flood of relief he ex-perienced every time he survived a selection. Out of a total of thirty-nine adult male Jews, twenty-eight had fallen into the condemned category. As the remainder of these stepped from the line, a convoy of gray field cars and one heavy troop transport truck roared across the Appellplatz toward the rear of the camp. A square flag showing two triangles and a Nazi eagle flew from the left mudwing of the longest car.

So it's true, thought the shoemaker. *Heinrich Himmler has finally come to observe his handiwork.*

S ergeant Sturm's troops clubbed the condemned men toward the
rear of the camp with rifle butts and truncheons, while the balance of the prisoners remained standing in the snow. Rachel
Jansen remained on her knees, hugging her children. Her father-in-
law had not yet regained his senses. The shoemaker swept his eyes
over the decimated Jewish section, looking for his few remaining
friends. Nothing but gray heads now.

"All prisoners return to blocks!"

The shoemaker drifted to the edge of the pack as the dazed
crowd broke into small groups and moved toward the six inmate
barracks. He knew he should follow, but something held him back.
The emotions surging through him were so powerful that he hesitated to face them. Not for a year had he visited the rearmost area
of the camp, and for good reason. Behind the hospital, half-buried
in the earth, stood a small airtight chamber designated the Experimental Block, but called simply the "E-Block" by the camp population—when it was mentioned at all.

Only once had the shoemaker observed one of the "special
actions" that occurred at the E-Block—and he had observed it from
the inside. He had been wearing a heavy rubber body suit at the
time, with a sealed gas mask connected to a cylinder of oxygen. The
other man in the chamber—a Russian POW chained to the steel
wall and designated a "control" by Klaus Brandt—had been stark
naked. What the shoemaker saw happen to the Russian when the invisible gas hissed into the chamber had driven him nearly to suicide.
And tonight, Heinrich Himmler had come to see a similar spectacle
for himself.

Without further reflection the shoemaker broke away from the crowd of survivors and walked purposefully toward the rear of the camp. The risk was great, but less for him than for other inmates. His leatherworking skills were legendary in Totenhausen, and all SS knew him by sight. He had done at least one repair job for every soldier in camp. A boot here, a shoulder strap there. A pair of slippers for a mistress somewhere. Such was the currency of his survival. If someone stopped him, he would claim he had been called to examine a pair of shoes in the hospital.

Ignoring the searchlights, he entered the shadow of the hospital, hurried forward and peered around the corner of the three-story structure. The troop transport truck had been parked in the mouth of the alley, so that it blocked his vision. He squeezed between the truck and the hospital wall and edged forward until he could see.

Sergeant Sturm had halted the prisoners halfway up the alley. At the other end stood the gray field cars of the convoy, motors running. Two dozen SS soldiers of the *Leibstandarte Adolf Hitler* had already surrounded the autos. Several doors opened as one. Men wearing pale gray uniforms stepped into the icy night. The shoemaker's eyes settled on a smallish officer who had just removed a pair of pince-nez glasses. The glasses must have fogged as he stepped from the heated car, for he passed them to an adjutant, who wiped them clear with a handkerchief and then returned them. When the man put the pince-nez glasses back on, the shoemaker felt his hands begin to shake. He was standing less then forty meters away from SS Reichsführer Heinrich Himmler.

Himmler listened patiently while Doctor Brandt explained some arcane detail of the presentation he was about to witness. As they moved toward the E-Block, the shoemaker saw that one side of the alley was lined with thirty or so technicians and chemists from Totenhausen's poison gas plant. In their white lab coats they had been almost invisible in the snow. Himmler nodded affably as he passed them. Brandt motioned toward the E-Block, then turned to speak and saw that the Reichsführer was no longer beside him.

Himmler had stopped to address one of Totenhausen's six civilian nurses. Four of the women were old battlewagons, but two— Greta Müller and Anna Kaas—were blond and single and barely thirty. The shoemaker had mistaken them for lab technicians. Himmler seemed quite taken with Fraulein Kaas, and no wonder: he was middle-aged, pudgy, and chinless, while she could have posed for one of Goebbels' posters celebrating the Aryan female ideal. Brandt stood by impatiently; he'd intended for the nurses to be scenery, not full-scale diversions. At last Himmler gave a little bow and moved away from Anna Kaas. Brandt led him quickly to the hospital's rear steps, from whence he could observe the entrance to the E-Block, just across the alley.

Two camp spotlights had been pressed into service to focus on the chamber's sunken entrance. Himmler's guards craned their necks in curiosity. A muffled bang startled several of them, causing a ripple of suppressed laughter among the Totenhausen SS. It was only a corpse, they knew, swelling and bursting as it settled into the shallow grave pit beyond the electrified rear fence.

The condemned men crowded together like a herd of antelope sensing predators drawing around. The shoemaker could clearly see the young Dutch lawyer who had so stoically accepted his fate. Sergeant Sturm barked an order for the men to strip. Sharp blows from rifle butts convinced those who responded too slowly. The shoemaker put a hand over his mouth. Was there a more pathetic sight than a group of adult men stripped naked by force? In the biting cold their genitals shrank beyond any sexual recognition. One of Himmler's men brayed something about circumcised Jews and their lack of manhood. The shoemaker had to admit that from where he stood, only the lack of breasts marked the prisoners as men.

When the clothes and wooden-soled shoes lay piled in the snow, the first of their owners were herded down the four concrete steps that led to the entrance of the sunken chamber. The steel door had a great wheel set in its face, like a watertight hatch inside a U-boat. The shoemaker shivered when he heard the hermetic *pfft* that signaled the opening of the door. What went on in this alley day after day was horrible, but what he was seeing now was completely beyond his experience. The E-Block had been designed to accommodate ten men in standing positions. Tonight nearly thirty were being forced into the steel chamber. He could imagine the nightmarish scene that must be taking place as Sturm's troops forced the naked men in on top of one another.

When the last prisoner had been beaten through the door, it was levered shut and the wheel cranked into its closed position. Major Schörner signaled to a man who stood by the corner of the E-Block.

This man—who wore a striped prison shirt—flipped a switch, causing the double-paned porthole observation windows set in the low walls to come alight.

Acid flooded the shoemaker's stomach. The man who had thrown the light switch was named Ariel Weitz, and he was a Jew. The wiry little homosexual had worked as a male nurse in Hamburg before the war, and after being sent to Totenhausen, had wheedled his way into the job of Brandt's assistant. His behavior in this job quickly made him the most hated man in camp. Were it not for the terror of reprisals, Weitz would have had his throat cut long ago. The shoemaker watched him hover at the corner of the E-Block, eagerly awaiting his next order.

Brandt led Himmler to the side of the E-Block, with Major Schörner following at a discreet distance. They stopped beside an odd machine that stood man-high on a pallet in the snow. The shoemaker had never seen this machine before, but it looked like a sophisticated pump of some kind. Brandt removed something from his pocket and held it up for Himmler's scrutiny. No bigger than a rifle cartridge, it flashed in the light. *Glass,* the shoemaker thought. Himmler nodded and smiled at Brandt, seeming to express good-natured skepticism. Then Brandt turned to the machine and inserted the piece of glass into a compartment in its face. At that moment the shoemaker noticed a small-gauge rubber hose connecting the machine to a fitting on the side of the E-Block.

Major Schörner assisted the Reichsführer onto a stool beside one of the E-Block's observation portholes. He turned back to Brandt, who moved his left hand to a switch on his machine, then raised his right and said:

"I begin the action . . . now."

There was a quick, low-pitched hum from the machine, then silence. Faint screams emanated from the soundproofed E-Block. The shoemaker saw Himmler jerk backward and nearly fall off the stool, then right himself.

Ten seconds later the screaming stopped.

Himmler got up from the stool and backed away from the window. He wobbled on his feet, but when Major Schörner rushed to steady him he jerked away as if he had been burned. Very slowly, he seemed to come back to himself.

"*Danke,* Sturmbannführer," he said. "Herr Doktor?"

As Brandt scampered across the snow to Himmler's side, the shoemaker edged as far as he dared along the side of the truck.

"Yes, Reichsführer?" said Brandt.

"You have surpassed yourself. Are you positive those men were killed by the gas in that phial you showed me? Nothing else?"

"Absolutely, Reichsführer. Soman Four. The aerosol form is particularly fast-acting."

"Remarkable. I saw nothing in that room but dying men."

"That is what you ordered, Reichsführer."

"Brandt, you are a genius. You will be lionized for a thousand years. You and von Braun."

Klaus Brandt snapped his arm skyward. *"Heil Hitler!"*

"Will this gas kill as efficiently in the open air?"

"It will work exactly as you have seen tonight."

"Astounding. Will any further testing be required?"

"Not on the gas. However, beyond *aerosols vecteurs,* we are working on hand-held gas grenades and several other delivery systems. Our problem is protective equipment, Reichsführer. Weeks ago I was promised new lightweight impermeable suits from Raubhammer Proving Ground, but they have yet to arrive. Before we can deploy Soman on the battlefield, we must be sure that our own troops are safe."

"You shall have your suits, Herr Doktor. After what I have seen tonight, I intend to schedule a full-scale demonstration of Soman for the Führer. Let us say in . . . a fortnight." Himmler gave Brandt a reptilian smile. "The test will take place at Raubhammer Proving Ground. If those swine do not have their suits ready, I shall place them naked in the area to be saturated by Soman!"

Brandt laughed obligingly. "Reichsführer, if you can assure me a steady flow of test subjects, the perfection of ancillary delivery systems would be hastened. I've recently had trouble replenishing my stocks. I need healthy males now, and Speer is taking them all for the munitions factories."

"You will have your specimens, Herr Doktor. I'm afraid that even in 1944, Jews are something we still have a surplus of."

Himmler raised an arm and took in Sergeant Sturm's assembled SS troops. *"Kameraden!"* he shouted, his breath steaming in the cold. "I know that your work here is difficult. Yes! It takes a strong constitution to witness what I have just seen and yet remain good and decent men. You men are our finest flower, the seeds of the Reich's future. You alone have the strength to do what must be done. That is why we will win this war. The Englishman—and, yes, the American too—merely does his best in all contests. The German does what is *necessary! Kameraden, Sieg heil! Heil Hitler!"*

During the answering salvo of *Sieg heil*s, the shoemaker lay prone in the narrow space between the truck and the hospital wall with the snow soaking through his burlap clothes. He saw Brandt escort Himmler back to the waiting vehicles and join him in his field car. As they sped away, joined soon after by the troop truck, Major Schörner signaled to two SS men standing behind the E-Block. Within seconds, scalding jets of high-pressure steam and detergent chemicals blasted into the chamber to flush the corpses, walls, ceiling, and floor clean of nerve gas. The remaining mixture of air and toxic liquid was sucked out by powerful vacuum pumps. Finally, two small steel vents were opened in the roof, and scorching dry air treated with decontaminants removed all traces of Soman from the chamber.

Major Schörner looked around expectantly. Ariel Weitz scurried up to him like an obedient terrier.

"The usual, Weitz."

"*Jawohl,* Sturmbannführer!"

Schörner seemed entranced by the sight of the little Jew hurrying down the steps that no other man would tread without a stutter in his heartbeat. When Weitz disappeared, the major hastened back toward the front of the camp.

The alley was empty.

The shoemaker listened to the fading engines. Impelled by morbid curiosity, he darted across the alley to the far side of the E-Block, crouched in the snow, and pressed his face to an observation porthole.

The sterility of the scene stunned him. There was no blood or feces, not even a speck of dirt. The steam had taken care of that. But the position of the dead revealed the madness of what had gone before. The twenty-eight Jewish men who died tonight had been packed inside the E-Block like tinned herrings. Most had died standing up. Their corpses were tangled in a general riot of limbs, their dead skin blistered pink by the high-pressure steam, their open eyes glazed and protruding horribly. One man's head was jammed against the window from which Himmler had watched.

The shoemaker almost screamed when the corpses near the door began to move. Then he saw Ariel Weitz pushing his way in among the dead like a grave robber. The man was not even wearing a gas mask! Perhaps his guilty conscience had spawned a death wish. Weitz turned up his nose and sniffed the air like a *Hausfrau* checking her bathroom. Apparently satisfied, he reached into his pocket and withdrew a pair of precision pliers. Then he leaned over one of the fallen corpses. The shoemaker saw the face clearly, its pink mouth frozen in a rictus of pain and horror. It was the young Dutch lawyer, Jansen.

Weitz pulled a small torch from his back pocket and shined it into the oral cavity. His grisly effort was rewarded by the glint of gold. Carefully, he inserted the pliers into the corpse's mouth, fitted the tongs around the tooth and yanked it free of the bone. Weitz brushed away skin that had sloughed onto his hand, then pocketed his prize and put the pliers back into the lawyer's mouth.

The shoemaker felt his hands shaking. What kind of monster could plunder the corpses of his own tribe for its exterminators? He stared with murder in his eyes as Weitz fitted his pliers around yet another gold-crowned tooth. Then, as if suddenly aware that he was being watched, Ariel Weitz looked up—straight at the window from which the shoemaker watched.

The shoemaker froze. He met Weitz's startled gaze for a few seconds, peered into the twin abysses of his eyes. Then he ran across the empty alley and along the wall of the hospital.

He forced himself to slow down as he neared the inmate showers. Running could draw gunfire from the watchtowers at any time. As he passed the Appellplatz, an image of the old Dutchman's diamonds flashed into his brain. Was it worth the risk? The value of gems had been low throughout the war, in the camps at least. A treasured brooch might fetch four potatoes in a black market trade. But times were changing. As the Red Army offensive gained momentum, some SS had shown an interest in goods that would help them buy their way westward in the event of a Russian breakthrough.

He made five quick passes over the well-trodden snow where he and the Jansens had stood during the selection. Just as he decided that Sturm had defied Major Schörner and returned for the diamonds, he saw a flash on the ground to his right. He bent down, scooped up a handful of snow, then moved quickly toward the inmate blocks, sifting the snow as he walked. He counted four loose diamonds in his palm. Slipping the stones into his pocket, he silently scaled the wire fence and dropped to the other side.

"*Bitte!* Please do not shoot!"

The shoemaker clutched his chest in shock. Only when he recognized Rachel Jansen, the wife of the Dutch lawyer, did he begin to calm down. She was standing in the shadow of the Christian Women's Block with her tiny boy and girl clinging to her legs. "What are you doing out here?" he asked furiously.

The Dutchwoman hesitated too long. "My children needed the toilet. They have loose bowels."

"Don't lie to me! You came to look for the diamonds, didn't you?" He saw by her expression that he was right. Rachel Jansen either had courage or she was a fool. "The SS took the stones already," he said in a gentler tone. "You must go back."

She nodded hesitantly. "Can you tell me anything of my husband? The truth."

The shoemaker felt a sudden and surprising rush of emotion. Against his better instincts, he took the young woman's soft face between his hands. Very quietly, so that the children would not hear, he said, "You must be strong, Rachel. Your husband was a fine man, but he is dead. They are all dead."

He expected a hysterical response, but after an initial shudder, a quick blinking of the eyelids, Rachel Jansen pulled away from him. Her right hand went to her forehead, then covered her eyes. "Oh dear God," she whispered. "We are alone."

The shoemaker caught up a child in each arm and began walking to the Jewish Women's Block. Rachel followed. At the door he set the children down.

"Thank you," she said. "You are *de schoenmaker,* yes? I've only just arrived, but . . . already I've heard of you. Some people . . . they say bad things."

The shoemaker shrugged. He was thinking about Ariel Weitz.

"They say you collaborate with the Germans."

He glanced anxiously toward the Jewish Men's Block. He had no time for questions, but something about this young woman had struck him. Perhaps it was her children, or the brave husband she had lost, or her ability to sustain the blow of losing him and not shatter, as so many had. He reached into his pocket and closed his hand over the four diamonds. He started to pull out a single stone, then brought out two. He placed them carefully in her hand.

"That's all I could find," he told her. "Use them well."

Before she could respond, he turned and hurried toward the Jewish Men's Block.

As he passed under the faded yellow star over the door, the musty stew of caked sweat and mold and naphtha hit him, the smell of home. He lay on his hard bunk, stunned to find himself not sharing a blanket for the first time in many months. No shortage of bunks tonight. None of the eleven survivors of his block asked where he had been.

He wanted to sleep, but he could not get Ariel Weitz out of his mind. In the darkness above him hovered the image of the Jewish traitor, the *golem,* startled in the midst of his ghoulish work. What had shocked the shoemaker—what made him run—was not the fear of getting caught. It was the tears. As the little ferret looked up from the corpse, huge wet tears had been streaming down his face. That sight had shaken him to his core. Because if Ariel Weitz still possessed some secret well of compassion, some vestige of identity from the world of light, then could not the shoemaker as well?

He let his mind reel back through time, to his life before Hitler. The pungent stench of the block gave way to the warm colors and smells of his home. Bread cooking in the oven, good matzo, his wife working over the kitchen stove. And in the back of the apartment, his shop. There, shaping leather at the last, his son, only fourteen yet nearly as tall as his father. So quickly becoming a man. He heard his wife calling, "Avram? Avram! Come! There are men in the street! Brown Shirts!"

The shoemaker hugged himself and shivered in his bunk. That Nazi rally had marked the beginning of the end for him, the end of the time when he would be known by his given name. Soon after his wife and son fled Germany, Hilter's thugs began rounding up Jewish combat veterans along with all the rest, just as his son had predicted. Avram was arrested with a truckload of other Jews from Rostock and taken to a distant camp. There he had become prisoner 6065, a number of prestige now in the hellish universe of the camps, where a low number indicated either survival skills or luck—both treasured commodities.

When all his comrades died, he was transferred north to help build another prison in the land of numbers—Totenhausen Camp, not fifty kilometers from Rostock, his home city. There—*here*—he had carved out a small place for himself, existing in darkness, moving through life in single steps, with each step hoping to avoid the god of the camps, which was Death. So far he had been lucky, if survival was luck. Some believed the dead were the lucky ones. Sometimes he believed that too. But tonight, in some nameless slice of time between seeing the tears staining Weitz's ratlike face and giving the two diamonds to Rachel Jansen, the shoemaker had become Avram Stern again. And that terrified him.

Because once again he had something to lose.

One hour after the shoemaker found sleep, Anna Kaas was standing beneath a tree in a dark clearing five miles northeast of Totenhausen. A giant of a black-bearded Pole stood beside her, ravenously chewing the salted ham she had stolen from the camp stores. Kneeling on the ground at her feet was the gaunt young man with wild hair and violinist's fingers. He bent over an opened suitcase and began tapping out coded number groups on a Morse key. The numbers had been encoded to conceal the words on the sheet of paper in Anna's hand. While the young Pole tapped and his older brother wolfed down the ham, Anna reread her message.

Himmler personally observed Special Action tonight.
Field test of Soman Four to be held at Raubhammer Proving
Ground in fourteen days. The Führer will be present.

She took a match from her purse and set fire to the paper. It burned quickly. With her eyes she followed the dark antenna wire from the suitcase to the tree branch high above them.

She wondered exactly where the dots and dashes were going.

Six hundred miles away, in Bletchley Park, England, young Clapham received the message, transcribed and decoded it. Then he lifted the telephone and placed a call to SOE Headquarters in Baker Street.

Brigadier Duff Smith was awakened from sound sleep on an office cot to take the call. When he heard the word SCARLETT, followed by the contents of the message, he thanked Clapham, hung up, reached into a nearby tumbler and splashed water on his face. Then he calmly walked to the next office up the hall and said: "Barry, where's Winston tonight?"

13

Rachel Jansen spent her first morning as a widow trying desperately not to fall asleep. She had not rested for many hours, but until she was certain that her children were relatively safe, she would not sleep. She sat stiffly on the floor, her back pressed against the narrow bunk she had been assigned, one of three stacked like bookshelves against the front wall of the Jewish Women's Block. Her father-in-law stood unsteadily beside her. Her two children—Jan, three, and Hannah, two—sat on either side of her, their heads pillowed upon her shrinking breasts.

With stinging eyes Rachel looked warily around the barracks. For the last hour, women of every size and condition had been staring at her. She could not understand it. During her short time here, she had taken great care to offend no one. The women she had mentally christened the "new widows"—those who had arrived with her and also lost their husbands last night—were not staring. They seemed to be suffering various degrees of shock. But the others were. The only characteristic the staring women shared was their hair. Most of them had several inches of it.

It's the old-timers, she thought uneasily. *The camp veterans are staring at us.* Rachel pressed her thighs tightly together and thought of the two diamonds the shoemaker had given her. It was a bit of an indignity to hide them in so intimate a place, but she had seen female veterans of the camp hiding coins, rolled photographs, and other small treasures there in the showers, and she had quickly followed their example. It proved a wise decision. Since then she had witnessed two surprise searches.

Why do they stare so? she thought anxiously.

"My son," Benjamin Jansen whimpered for the hundredth time. "My home and my business weren't enough? They had to take my only son?"

"Quiet," Rachel whispered, pointing to the snoring children. "Sleep is their only refuge."

The old man shook his head hopelessly. "There is no refuge from this place. Except through the back gate."

Rachel's young face hardened. "Stop whining. If it hadn't been for that shoemaker knocking you down, you'd already be out the back gate."

The old man closed his eyes.

Though exhausted, Rachel stared defiantly back at the toughest looking of the women—a thickset Slav with ash-colored hair—and blocked out the old man's fatalism. It was not easy. The thought of the "back gate" was enough to paralyze anyone. Already she had learned that the irregular tattoo of muffled bangs echoing in the trees behind the camp—which she had thought were gunshots—were actually explosions of gas through the swollen skins of decomposing bodies, buried in shallow pits behind the camp. Her husband's resting place. . . .

"Hey!" barked a gravelly voice. "Don't you know why everyone is staring at you?"

Rachel lashed out blindly with her right hand and blinked her eyelids. She had fallen asleep just long enough for the big Slav to cross to her bunk. "Leave us alone!" she snarled.

The coarse-featured woman towering above her did not back away. She squatted down and jabbed a stubby finger at Benjamin Jansen. She wore leather-soled shoes, Rachel noticed, the only pair in the barracks.

"They're staring because of *him*," the woman said in a thick Polish accent. "This is the Jewish Women's Block. He can't stay here. The SS tolerate a certain amount of movement between the women's and the children's blocks. Helps to keep mischief down. But no men are allowed in the women's block. The old goat can listen to what I have to say, then he has to go."

Rachel looked at her father-in-law to make sure he understood.

"You've never been in a camp before, have you?" the woman asked. "None of you."

"We passed through Auschwitz," Rachel answered, "but only for an hour. I'm afraid this is all quite new to us."

"It shows."

"How, exactly?"

The woman wrinkled her wide, flat-boned face in scorn. "A hundred ways. But that doesn't matter. Now that your rich husband has gone through the back gate, maybe you're not too good to socialize with us, eh? Or maybe you want to be transferred to the Prominents' Block?"

"No, no. We want no special treatment."

"Good. Because there is no Prominents' Block here. That's Buchenwald. In Totenhausen everyone is equal."

The woman seemed to take great satisfaction from this statement. Rachel extended her hand. "I am Rachel Jansen. I am honored to meet you."

Rachel's formal manners brought a sneer to the woman's face. "I'm Frau Hagan," she announced. "I am Block Leader. I am also a Pole and a Communist." Frau Hagan said this as if it were a challenge to the devil. "I am *kapo* of Jewish women prisoners. Because I understand Yiddish, of course. Not everyone in this camp is Jewish, you know. There are Christian Poles, Russians, Latvians, Estonians, Gypsies, Ukrainians . . . even Germans. More Communists, too. A whole world behind an electric fence."

Frau Hagan frowned again at Benjamin Jansen. "I came over to tell you the facts of life—*camp* life—before your ignorance gets you and others killed."

Rachel nodded quickly. "We appreciate your kindness."

Frau Hagan snorted. "The first thing I tell you is this: whatever you were outside, forget it. The sooner the better. The higher up the ladder you were, the harder it will be for you to get used to the camp. What were you? What did your husband do?"

"He was a lawyer. A very good one."

Frau Hagan turned up her heavy hands in mock despair. "You see? That's terrible. Another spoiled princess."

"My father was a carpenter," Rachel added quickly.

"That's a little better. I was a washerwoman on the outside. A maid to a German businessman's family. Yet here I am Block Leader."

"That's very impressive," Rachel said carefully.

Frau Hagan stared at Rachel, trying to see if she was being made fun of. She decided she wasn't. "Now, the badges. Your children are wearing the plain yellow star. *Jood.* That means Jew in Dutch, eh? Some language. Well, a Jew is a Jew, no matter what the letters. Yellow triangles mark them all. But there are other colors, you'll see. People here have been brought from many camps, but in general the badges are based on the Auschwitz system. Knowing the badge colors can mean life or death for you here."

Rachel looked down at the cloth badge sewn onto the left breast of her tunic. It was made of two triangles, one superimposed upon the other to form the Star of David. The top triangle, which was red and pointed up, bore a large "N" on its center. Beneath this was a bright yellow triangle pointing down.

"The red triangle," Frau Hagan explained, "means Political Prisoner. It's nothing to do with anything you've done, it's just a convenient tag for the Germans. They think they have to label everything in sight or it doesn't exist. The big capital letter marks your country of origin. Same with all foreigners. Yours is 'N' for Netherlands, see? Mine is 'P'."

"I see."

"You'll see a lot of green triangles, too. Green marks the criminals, people who were actually convicted of crimes before they got here. Not all the greens are bad, but don't cross any of them. They stick together." Frau Hagan scowled suddenly. "Keep your boy away from the pink triangles. Pink marks the homosexuals. Keep him away from any man who gets too close. There are pederasts here, Dutch girl, and they aren't required to wear badges."

As Rachel absorbed the import of Frau Hagan's words, Hannah began to stir. Her movements woke Jan, her three-year-old, who reached into his pocket and took out a small wooden *dreidl.* Rachel had managed to smuggle the top all the way from Holland. Neither child could really spin it yet, but the *dreidl* was a reminder of a safer place and time. She started a game where the children slid it back and forth between them. Frau Hagan glanced at them.

"You haven't told them what last night meant?"

"No," Rachel whispered. "Their father told them he was going on a long trip. To work. There is nothing to be gained by telling them otherwise."

Frau Hagan seemed to agree with this judgment. "I'm surprised

they let you keep your son," she mused. "Young as he is, and blond.
It's a miracle he wasn't taken away to be Aryanized."

Rachel shivered in horror. "Marcus's grandfather was blond,"
she said. "A Gentile."

Frau Hagan had already forgotten the children. She silently
counted off badge classifications on her fingertips. "Black," she
said. "Black marks the asocials. Don't trust them. You'll also see an
armband with the word *Blöd*. It's worn by the feeble-minded. Re-
tards. They're generally harmless. Jehovah's Witnesses wear purple
triangles. They're kind, but don't make friends with them. They
don't last long in here. They're too hardheaded." Frau Hagan
sighed. "There are other badges and colors, but you can't learn them
all in a day."

The big Polish woman fell silent at a sudden rapping on the barracks wall. The other women scrambled for their bunks. Frau
Hagan pointed at Benjamin Jansen. "Under the bunk!"

The old man rolled under Rachel's bed and tried to conceal himself as best he could. An inmate at the window whispered, "It's all
right! It's only Anna!"

Rachel heard a collective sigh of relief. A half dozen voices murmured, *Nurse Kaas!* like a speaking round. Rachel watched in fascination as a small group of prisoners—almost like a delegation, with
Frau Hagan at their head—lined up to receive the revered visitor.
There was no knock. The door was simply thrust open and left that
way despite the winter wind. A tall, shapely blond woman wearing
a white uniform with blue trim stepped inside and pulled a small
parcel from beneath her skirt.

"We thank you most humbly, Fraulein Kaas," Frau Hagan said,
taking the package and passing it to another inmate.

Rachel was shocked by this formal speech from the woman who
had only moments ago ridiculed her own courtesy.

The blond nurse looked slightly embarrassed. "How is Frau
Buhle today?"

Frau Hagan shook her head. "No better, I'm afraid. But she
holds on. If you could possibly take time to examine her—"

"Not today. We're quite busy in the hospital."

"Of course."

Rachel stared at the two women. The physical differences between them were startling. Next to the blond nurse, Frau Hagan's

skin looked gray and dry as a dust rag. It suddenly dawned on her that Nurse Kaas was *German.* She was part of the camp staff!

The nurse glanced anxiously at the open door behind her. "Perhaps just a quick look," she said.

Frau Hagan led her to a bunk at the far end of the barracks. Camp veterans melted away before them, as if yielding a path for an earthly saint, then closed in behind. When the nurse knelt down, Rachel lost sight of her.

Rachel was curious about the nurse, but she remained beside her own bunk. Better not to interfere. She took advantage of this break to rest her eyes a bit. The last seven days had been a blur of withering terror and unspeakable indignity. The cattle car had been the worst. Endless hours sitting without heat or food on frozen railroad sidings, Marcus fighting like a dog for a handful of water for the children. Both of them sleeping standing up in the press of filthy bodies as the train crossed into Poland, each with a child in their arms. Holding Hannah naked and feverish over an overflowing bucket while she emptied her roiling bowels, then squatting herself in the filth. And finally, choosing a space among the dead for her family, not bothering with the bucket or anything else anymore, but only with breathing and keeping away those who had lost their reason.

The stop at Auschwitz had been a merciful deliverance. A silent man in a business suit pulled them out of a glassy-eyed throng queuing before a doctor and loaded them into an open truck which carried them to another train. That train hauled them northwest for three days, back into Germany, and finally disgorged them in a bomb-shattered marshaling yard in Rostock. And from there by truck to this place—Totenhausen—the place where Marcus died.

So I am a widow, she thought with a strange detachment. The idea did not seem difficult to grasp, considering the totality of transformation she had been forced to endure in the last thirty hours. She could still feel the bite of the shears as they scissored her hair to the skull. She remembered the last feeble protest of her dignity as she was forced to strip naked in the snow beside a barbed-wire fence and parade before snickering SS troops who called the dehumanizing procedure a "medical inspection." Then in rapid succession came delousing, the tattooing of her inner forearm, the distribution of striped uniforms and wooden shoes, the application of badges to the uniforms, and the taking of a detailed medical history. And now—with seeming inevitability—widowhood. The tears had stopped a little while ago, and Rachel had vowed not to let them return. She had to force herself to think, to concentrate on one thing only. Survival.

It was a skill she had learned while very young. As a German Jewish child orphaned during the Great War, she had been sent to Amsterdam to live for a while with a childless Jewish couple. She had grown to love them, but more importantly, she had made sure they grew to love her. Even at four, she knew she never wanted to be hungry again. She quickly mastered the Dutch language and manners, and when the time came for her to return to Germany, the couple had adopted her. Her marriage to Marcus Jansen—a native Dutch Jew—had completed her transformation from German orphan into Dutch wife.

When the Nazis invaded Holland in 1940, and her family was forced to go into hiding, she adapted to the attic room above the Christian family's shop with such grace that her whole family was able to follow her example. She had actually given birth to Hannah in that attic. But the events of the last week—beginning with the bloodcurdling sound of the Gestapo beating down the door of their hiding place—had stretched her adaptive capacity near to breaking.

"She won't last much longer," said a voice in German.

Rachel opened her eyes to see the German nurse moving toward her, instructing Frau Hagan as she walked. The nurse carried a stethoscope in her right hand. "Her ration will not help her now," the nurse was saying. "Share it amongst yourselves. Just keep her warm and—"

The blond nurse froze in midstep. "What's *he* doing in here?"

Rachel followed the nurse's gaze. She was staring at Benjamin Jansen, who was trying unsuccessfully to hide under Rachel's bunk.

"He only got here yesterday," Frau Hagan explained. "He sneaked in here to visit his grandchildren. We'll boot him out as soon as you're gone."

"You'd better. If Sergeant Sturm catches him here, he'll be on the Tree by nightfall."

"I'll take care of it," Frau Hagan promised. "What about the selections? Last night was the worst yet."

Nurse Kaas seemed suddenly in a rush. "We can only pray the worst is past."

Frau Hagan nodded. "You'd better go."

Before stepping outside, the nurse straightened her luxuriant hair with both hands. To Rachel, she looked like a knight adjusting armor.

"We pray you will come again soon," Frau Hagan said hopefully.

"Don't expect too much."

"Only what you can do. *Auf Wiedersehen.*"

Anna Kaas was gone. Frau Hagan turned and marched like a sergeant major back to Rachel's bunk. "Get up from there, old man!"

Benjamin Jansen rolled out from beneath the bunk and stood beside Rachel.

"Listen to the rest, then get your ass out of my barracks for good. You heard the nurse mention the Tree?"

"Yes. But I have seen no trees inside this camp."

"It's not a real tree, *glupi*. It's a tall post driven deep into the ground. There are two crossbars nailed to it. One down low, another up high. You've seen that?"

"To the side of the hospital?"

Frau Hagan nodded. "The Germans call it the Punishment Tree. We just call it the Tree." She motioned for a woman to move Rachel's children out of earshot. "There are three official punishments in this camp. All are administered at the Tree, and all can be fatal. There's the whip, the rope, and the dogs. The whip is for a first infraction of the rules. They take you to the Tree, tie your hands, and make you let down your pants or lift your skirt in front of the assembled prisoners. Then they bend you over the lower crossbar and lash you with a horsewhip. They lash you until you're bloody, with the whole camp staring up your backside. The tough ones survive it, others don't. Some die from exposure, some from shock.

"The rope is worse. They tie your hands behind your back, then loop a heavy rope around the first one and hoist you up to the top crossbar by your hands. Your shoulders pop out of joint immediately. If you lose consciousness—and most people do, after fifteen minutes of agony—the SS throw buckets of water on you to revive you. The rope can drive you mad or it can kill you. In winter it can kill you very quickly."

Rachel glanced fearfully at her children, who sat silently against the far wall with wide eyes.

"And the dogs?" Benjamin Jansen asked.

Frau Hagan chuckled bitterly. "I think you can figure that out. There's a set of manacles on a chain attached to the lower crossbar of the Tree. They strip you, manacle one ankle, then Sergeant Sturm sets his dogs on you." The Pole made a sudden snapping gesture with her hand, like canine jaws. Ben Jansen jumped. "No one survives the dogs, old man. Sergeant Sturm feeds and trains them, and he's honed them to a fine pitch of killing. It's a gruesome sight. Sturm was a dog master with an *Einsatzgruppe* in the East. One of the SS 'hunters.' His duty was tracking stubborn Jews into cellars and sewers, then killing them. He brags that he has even trained one of his shepherds to rape women who have been tied down."

Rachel felt her stomach flip over.

Frau Hagan's bland face hardened. "If you hear screaming during the night, don't get up. And when morning comes, don't let your children look toward the Tree. What they'd see there would be worse than your most terrible nightmare of what Hell could be."

Rachel buried her face in her hands. "Where in God's name have they brought us?"

"Forget about God," Frau Hagan advised. "He's forgotten about you. There is some good news, though. This camp is better than some. We're guinea pigs here, not work slaves. You were brought here for Herr Doktor Brandt to experiment upon, and Brandt likes his guinea pigs in reasonably good health. That means the food is edible and we don't have to sleep in our own shit. Of course, this paradise lasts only until the day you're selected. Or until you break a rule. Sturm and his men are always watching for infractions. The rule-breakers are their source of entertainment."

"But what *are* the rules? Where are they posted?"

"In the Germans' heads!" Frau laughed harshly. "That's why it's so hard to stay within them! You've got one mark against you already, little Dutch girl."

"What do you mean?"

"You're too pretty. You haven't been starved yet, so you've still got your breasts." The big Pole reached out and ran her hand over

Rachel's skull. Already a fine coat of black stubble had sprung up. Rachel instinctively jerked away. Frau Hagan laughed again. "Yes, someone might get very creative to get you into a bed. Schörner is drunk most of the time, but sometimes he perks up. His drinking is the best and worst thing about him. Sergeant Sturm is the one to watch out for. He's a pig. I advise you to start looking as ugly as you can as soon as you can, although I'm sure they already noticed you during the medical inspection."

Rachel shuddered at the memory.

"The SS may be animals, but remember one thing." Frau Hagan glared at Benjamin Jansen. "You too, old man. It's the unwritten law of every camp: The prisoner's worst enemy is the prisoner!"

The Block Leader squinted at Rachel, as if trying to gauge whether any of her hard-earned wisdom had taken root. "You know, I survived Auschwitz for three years," she said. "I have no tattoo number. You know what that means? I am less than zero. I helped build that stinking place. I was a *kapo* there, a good one. I saw a lot of Dutch, and they never lasted long. Especially the women. They couldn't accept the change. They never bathed, never ate. I hope you're different, Dutch girl. At Auschwitz the Dutch women became *musselmen* after only two weeks."

"What is a *musselman?*"

"A bag of bones, princess. A bag of bones that doesn't care if it eats anymore. A walking corpse."

"But I have seen no one like that here!"

"I told you, this camp is different. They didn't bring you here to work you to death. They brought you here to work *on* you."

"But what can you mean?"

Frau Hagan glanced at the children. "You'll find out soon enough." The big Pole placed both hands on her wide hips. "Do you understand these things I've told you?"

Rachel nodded uncertainly.

"Rations in two hours. Guard your shoes, spoon, and cup with your life. Keep your children's things yourself. Eat your bread as soon as you get it. Your stomach is the best safe against thieves." She grabbed Ben Jansen by the collar. "Out you go!"

Rachel watched in amazement as the Block Leader hauled the old man to the barracks door and shoved him out into the snow. She darted to the doorway. As her father-in-law plodded toward the

Jewish Men's Block, she heard a rapid shuffling behind her. When she turned, she saw Frau Hagan passing out small sausages from the parcel Nurse Kaas had brought. The Pole met her starved gaze, but did not offer her a sausage.

Rachel turned away. She felt sure that a diamond would buy a few sausages for Jan and Hannah. But they were not starving yet. She would have to use the stones more wisely than that. With luck, they might last through the war. She wondered what the shoemaker would say if he knew that when he found her hiding in the shadows by the fence, she had not been sneaking out to the Appellplatz to search for the lost diamonds, but sneaking *back*. It had been a frightful risk to leave Jan and Hannah while she searched, but the three diamonds she had found—plus the two the shoemaker had given her—made five, and she had no regrets. Clearly, life inside the camp functioned on the same principle as life outside: economics.

She had told her father-in-law nothing about the diamonds, and she never would. He had proved last night that he was no judge of when to expend his treasure. He had been desperate, of course, but Rachel was sure that the diamonds could not have saved Marcus from the selection. Bribery was not a public business. She would need allies to survive, and she would choose them very carefully. Someone like the shoemaker, perhaps, or even Frau Hagan. The Block Leader would soon learn how far a Dutchwoman would go to survive.

As she walked across the floor toward her children, Rachel kept her genital muscles flexed. It was probably not necessary, but she had no experience in such things. She would walk that way until she knew the diamonds were as secure as if locked inside a vault. She might not yet know how best to spend them, but she would have them to spend when the time came.

J onas Stern lay on a threadbare mattress and stared sullenly at
the stained ceiling of his jail cell. It had been five days since he
and Brigadier Duff Smith drove to Oxford to speak with the
American doctor, and Stern had spent four of those in a cell. Where
the hell was Smith? After McConnell refused the brigadier's request,
Smith had driven Stern back to London and dropped him at a
rooming house run by "some good friends of mine." Stern soon realized that Smith's "good friends" were off-duty London policemen.
But evading British police had become second nature to him in Palestine, and the London variety proved no more adept at surveillance
than their Middle Eastern cousins.

Stern had passed most of that first day in various London pubs,
where he ran into more than his share of American soldiers. With
Allied troops massing for the invasion, GIs were thick on the
ground. It wasn't long before Stern began trying to take out his anger at McConnell on the nearest Americans to hand. He survived
one brawl in Shoreditch without serious damage. Then he ran into
a squad of marines outside the entrance to the Strand Palace Hotel
bar. The liquored-up gyrenes did not take kindly to being called pac-
ifistic dilettantes, especially by a suntanned civilian with a German
accent. The military police found Stern lying flat on his back with
two glowing shiners and the fragments of a chair scattered around
him.

He had awakened in jail with ribs so bruised he could barely
breathe, and a new American slang term added to his growing list.
Shitbird. He railed at his jailers to call Brigadier Smith—and they
claimed they had—but the Scotsman never showed up. Either the

police were lying, Stern decided, or else he was precisely where the brigadier wanted him. Yesterday he had used Peter Owen's handcuff key to unlock his manacles and attempt an escape, but the coppers had been ready. That escapade had caused his transfer to his current accommodations.

His body jerked at the harsh clang of metal against metal.

"Shove yer bucket through the bars and make it quick!" barked a jailer. "If you spill any, you'll clean it up wiv your shirt!"

Stern rolled over and faced the stone wall. He couldn't decide whom he hated more, Brigadier Smith or Doctor Mark McConnell.

At that moment McConnell was going over some notes in his laboratory in Oxford. When the telephone rang, he tried to ignore it, but the caller was persistent. McConnell glanced at his watch. Ten P.M. Perhaps it was Mrs. Craig, the woman of the house he billeted in, offering him a late supper. He picked up the phone.

"Yes?"

"Yeah, hey," said a male voice with a Brooklyn accent. "Is this Dr. McConnell?"

"Yes."

"I need to see you, Doc. I got a problem."

"Excuse me, I think you have the wrong number. I'm a medical doctor, but I don't see patients. I'm associated with the university."

"Right," said the caller. "You're the one I want. I been patched up pretty good already. It's something else. I really need to see you."

McConnell wondered who in God's name had recommended him to a man with mental problems. "I'm afraid I'm not a psychiatrist either. I can recommend a good man in London, though."

The voice on the phone grew agitated. "You got it all wrong, Doc. It's *you* I need to see. Not a sawbones or a head-shrinker."

"Who is this?" McConnell asked, bewildered. "Do I know you?"

"Nah. But I knew your brother."

"You knew David?" McConnell felt his heart thump. "What's your name?"

"Captain Pascal Randazzo. Dave just called me Wop, though. I was his copilot on *Shady Lady*."

McConnell's heart rate was still rising. A member of David's crew had *survived*? "Where are you, Captain?" he asked excitedly.

"Right here. Oxford."

"My God. How did you get out of Germany? Do you have word of David?"

A long pause. "That's what I need to talk to you about, Doc. Do you think we could meet tonight?"

"Hell yes, Captain. You can come to my lab, or I could buy you supper somewhere. Have you eaten yet?"

"Yeah. I'll come to you, if you don't mind. Sooner the better."

"My lab's sort of tucked away in the university. Do you think you can find it?"

"I'm from New York, Doc. Long as it's streets and buildings, I can find it. It's trees and woods that screw me up."

McConnell couldn't help but smile. What a strange pair Randazzo the Wop and David the Georgia redneck must have made. "Where are you now, Captain?"

"The Mitre Inn."

He gave Randazzo detailed directions, then hung up. What the hell was going on? If there was word of David's crew, why hadn't the Air Force called him? Five days ago he had made the most difficult telephone call of his life, to tell his mother that her youngest son was presumed dead. Had that status changed? He paced the floor while he waited for Randazzo to arrive. What could the copilot's survival mean? No chutes had been sighted by the other bomber crews on the raid, but that didn't necessarily mean there weren't any. In the last four years he had heard stories of miraculous survival that defied all explanation. Perhaps David had managed to crash-*land* his bomber, instead of just crashing. He was a fantastic pilot. He had the medals to prove it.

McConnell jumped the first time he heard the sound: *thump-thump-bump*. It was irregular in tempo but continued to grow louder. He decided it must be a janitor pushing something heavy up the three flights of stairs. Probably a mop and a bucket of water. Then he heard a knock on his lab door.

"Doc?" said a muffled voice. "Hey, Doc!"

He hurried over and opened the door. Before him stood a short young man with dark eyes, curly black hair and a thick five-o'clock shadow. He leaned heavily on crutches, and his left leg was encased from ankle to hip in heavy plaster. The air force uniform was soaked with sweat.

"Captain Randazzo?"

"The Wop in person."

"I had no idea you were wounded. I'm sorry."

"No problem, Doc."

Randazzo *thump-bumped* his way across the floor and collapsed into a chair beside the very window Mark had dropped the telegram from just a week before. "Still ain't used to these fuckin' things," he said.

"What happened to your leg?"

"Broke it in two places."

"In the crash?"

"Bad parachute landing. Never had much practice."

Mark could hardly contain his excitement. "You mean you got out of the plane? Did David get out?"

"Sure did."

"But the air force said no chutes were sighted!"

Randazzo snorted. "I ain't surprised. We're flying in coffin corner to start with. And we were so goddamn low by the time we jumped that the squadron had already left us behind." The Italian thumped his plaster cast with the tip of a crutch. "That's how I got this fuckin' thing. We jumped too late. Still, it's better than dying, I guess."

McConnell studied the olive-skinned face and bleary eyes. Randazzo had been drinking. Probably for several days. "Maybe you should just tell me what happened, Captain."

The young officer looked out of the window at the dark skyline of Oxford. Only black spires broke the indigo screen of sky and stars. "Yeah," he said. "That's what I came for."

McConnell waited.

"The raid went okay. Made the Initial Point with only two losses in the squadron. We dropped all ten bombs within a thousand feet of the Mean Dropping Point. We creamed 'em. Won't be no fighters rolling out of Regensburg for a while."

"The problem came after?" McConnell prompted.

"Fuckin 'ay right. After we left the Rally Point. The return leg. A *real* problem."

"What happened?"

"About five flak shells, that's what. They happened to blow about ten holes in *Shady Lady*. The Germans had us conned before we ever passed over. Add in about twenty ME-109s attacking wingtip to wingtip."

Randazzo licked his lips and stared out of the window. "Looks like some kind of castle out there, huh? Like an Errol Flynn movie or something."

McConnell waited, but the captain said nothing further. "What do you remember about David, Captain, after the flak hit the plane?"

"Those fuckin' bastards!" Randazzo screamed suddenly. *"Goddamn murderers!"*

McConnell rocked back on his feet. Spittle flew from Randazzo's mouth as he tried to get to his feet using one crutch. Mark hurried over and gently pushed him back down onto the chair. "Take it easy, Captain. You said you were hit by flak. What happened then?"

"Flak," Randazzo said in a remote voice. "Yeah. After five or six hits, *Shady Lady* was buckin' like a Jersey hooker. Guys were screamin' in back. Joey, our ball turret gunner, was dead already. I told Dave it was time to bail out, but he wanted to try to nurse her back to England. We were somewhere near Lille. That's in France. After the Messerschmitts made their pass, I knew the *Lady* wasn't ever gonna see England again. The engines were on fire and she was dropping like a brick off the Empire State Building."

McConnell felt his mouth going dry. He actually heard the scrape as Randazzo drew a hand across his heavy black cheek stubble.

"I screamed at Dave to hit the silk, but he says we gotta wait 'til the crew gets out. I tell him I think the crew's dead. He tells me go check. Pilots sit way up high in a Fortress, you know. So I go back. Radio man, waist gunners—dead. I hump down the chute. Bombardier and navigator cut to shreds. Nobody on the interphone. It was time to bug out. *Shady Lady* was shaking herself to pieces. Dave held her steady while I jumped. He jumped a few seconds later."

Randazzo cleared his throat and took a deep, shuddering breath. "Dave had got us away from the flak batteries, thank God, or they'd have shot us while we fell. We landed about a quarter mile apart. I stayed put. My leg was broken. I didn't know that then, but I knew it hurt like a son of a bitch. Dave got unharnessed and started working his way toward me."

"Were you in a forest? Fields? What?"

"I was at the edge of a tree line, in a big bunch of bushes." Randazzo looked at the floor. "But Dave was exposed for the whole walk. Open field."

McConnell looked at the floor.

Randazzo's voice was barely a whisper. "We didn't know it, but we'd landed fairly close to a village. An SS unit saw us coming down. They sent out a patrol to follow the chutes. A *Kubelwagen*—that's a German jeep—came over the top of a little rise while Dave was still walking. He dropped to the ground when he heard the motor, but they'd seen him. Drove straight to him."

Randazzo scratched violently in his hair. "They started interrogating him on the spot. There was a lieutenant there, and four other guys. All SS. One sergeant, I think. They were asking Dave where I was. He wouldn't tell 'em. Name, rank, and serial number, just like in the movies. John fucking Wayne." Randazzo buried his face in his hands, sobbed once, then fell silent.

Mark struggled to find his own voice. "Then what happened, Captain?"

"Well . . . three of the SS guys stood Dave up in front of the lieutenant. Lieutenant pulls out his SS dagger. Ever seen one? Like some kind of miniature sword. This Kraut holds the dagger up to Dave's chest and starts asking questions."

"In German or English?" McConnell asked, not knowing why except that David understood no German.

Randazzo looked temporarily at a loss. "German," he said finally. "Yeah. Didn't matter, though, 'cause Dave wasn't having any. After about the third question, the lieutenant slaps him. Hard. Right then, Dave spits in the guy's face."

Mark closed his eyes.

"The Kraut lieutenant stabbed him. The guy just exploded, went crazy."

"No."

Randazzo's face worked strangely as he spoke. "The other guys let go of Dave. He fell. He laid there on the ground a minute, then rolled over onto his back. Then they . . . uh—"

Mark held up his hand. "Don't tell me the rest, Captain. I don't think I want to know."

"I gotta tell you," said Randazzo. "It was *my fucking fault!*"

McConnell realized then that the young copilot was wounded far more extensively than in the leg. "All right," he said softly. "What happened?"

"I never seen nothin' like it. Dave was still alive, but they started puttin' dirt in his mouth. *Dirt.* Then the sergeant finds a stick and starts shoving the dirt down Dave's throat." Randazzo was crying now. Mark couldn't stop himself either. "He died like that, Doc. Those Kraut lowlifes choked him with dirt, and . . . and I just laid there and watched it happen!"

McConnell could scarcely move. He forced himself to reach out and squeeze Randazzo's shoulder. "There was nothing you could have done, Captain. Not without sacrificing your own life."

The Italian looked up with tear-filled eyes. "Dave would have done something."

McConnell wanted to deny this, but he knew it was true.

"That redneck son of a bitch would have come screamin' out of those bushes like a whole goddamn division, armed or not." Randazzo was sobbing and laughing at the same time. "Not the Wop though." He shook his head pathetically. "I just laid there like a goddamn yellow coward and pissed my pants."

McConnell waited until the man had regained his composure. "Captain?"

"Goddamn it—"

"Captain, I'd like to know the rest. How did you get out?"

"Well . . . the SS kind of seemed to lose interest after Dave was dead. They poked around the field awhile, but by the time they got to the woods it was getting dark and I'd been crawling for all I was worth. I was damn lucky. The next morning some Resistance guys from the village walked right over me. They were half crazy, arguing all the time like a bunch of senators, but they got me to some people who'd taken flyers out before." Randazzo shook his head. "So here I am. And Dave is still back there in France. I don't know, Doc. HQ doesn't like these kinds of stories to get out, but . . . I just had to make sure you knew the truth. Your brother was the bravest son of a bitch I ever met. He was a goddamn hero."

"You're probably right, Captain," McConnell said, absurdly trying to maintain some semblance of professional distance. "But you're no coward." He let his gaze wander to the window. "What will you do now?"

Randazzo leaned over and picked up his crutches, then struggled to his feet. "If this leg heals up right, I'm goin' straight back to the flight line."

McConnell looked back at him. "You must be joking."

Randazzo's face was set in stone. "I ain't joking, Doc. I'm gonna drop bombs on those bastards until Germany ain't nothing but a crappy footnote in some dusty old book in a broken down college like this one."

McConnell felt suddenly lightheaded, as if he might simply float up to the ceiling. *I'm in shock,* he thought.

"Thank you for coming tonight, Captain. It means a lot to me to . . . to know the truth. I wish you well."

Randazzo worked his way over to the door. He saluted Mark, then turned without a word and hobbled from the room. McConnell heard him *thump-bumping* his way slowly down the stairs. The three flights took him nearly three minutes.

After the echoes faded, McConnell went to the window, pushed it open, and sucked in great gulps of cold air. His skin was tingling. Just as he had finally begun to accept the idea that his brother had perished bravely in an air battle, Pascal Randazzo had appeared like a specter to shatter even this grim comfort. David had not died in battle. He had been brutally murdered in cold blood. Murdered by Hitler's infamous Black Corps. The *Schutzstaffeln.* The SS.

One of McConnell's clearest childhood memories was of the day his younger brother was born. Their father had delivered David himself. His medical practice had long been moribund, but he insisted upon bringing his own son into the world. Mark remembered the look of pride on his father's scarred face, one of the only times the pride was in himself and not his sons.

He braced his hands on the stone window casement and leaned out. The air here was so different from the sweltering nights of his youth. The dark parapets and spires rising from the icy English cobbles *did* look like something out of *Robin Hood.* A great castle. A fortress. And wasn't that what he had used it for? A place of refuge from the war? For five years he had worked here in safety while braver men had given their lives to fight the Nazis. They had watched friends die, just as Randazzo had, yet they fought on in spite of their fear.

I know you, Doctor, the young Jew with Brigadier Smith had told him. *You're no coward. You're a fool. You believe in reason, in the essential goodness of man. You believe that if you refuse to commit evil yourself, someday you will conquer evil. You have yet to taste even a sip of the pain so many have drunk to the dregs in the last ten years . . .*

"I've had my sip of pain," McConnell said softly.

The feeling churning in his belly was like nothing he had ever known. Bitter, burning, volatile. It was fury, he realized, an inchoate anger so profound he could not give shape to it.

He tried to fight it, to remember the words thoughtful men had spoken about the futility of violence as a means to a better world. But compared to the images flashing behind his eyes, those words meant nothing. They were merely aggregates of letters, symbols of the futility of language in the face of deeds.

He turned away from the window and went to his small, cluttered desk. He rummaged in the top drawer for a few moments, then pulled out a small white card. He lifted the telephone and placed a call to London, to the number on the card. Despite the late hour, the phone was answered on the third ring.

"Smith here," said a gruff voice.

"Brigadier, this is Doctor Mark McConnell."

There was a pause. "What can I do for you, Doctor?"

"That trip you mentioned. Germany."

Smith grunted. "What about it?"

"Whatever it is, I'll do it."

The brigadier said nothing for some time. "Get some sleep," he said finally. "Don't say any goodbyes. We'll take care of all that. I'll send a driver to your house at 0600 sharp."

McConnell set the phone in its cradle and walked out of the laboratory without looking back.

At ten before midnight, the telephone rang in a London police station. The duty officer listened to the gruff voice on the line for a few moments, then hung up and grumbled, "Thinks he's the bloody First Sea Lord, that one."

"Who the 'ell was it, Bill?" asked the night jailer.

The duty officer squared his shoulders with exaggerated crispness. "Brig*adier* Duff bloody Smith, that's who."

"Who's he when he's at home?"

"I'm not sure. Curses like a Regimental Sergeant-Major, though."

"What did he want?"

"The Jewboy. Told me to have him washed and ready by six in the morning or he'd have my balls for breakfast."

"You going to oblige?"

The duty officer scowled. "Aye, I reckon. Smith's got connections with the Commissioner. That's how the Jewboy's been here all week without being charged."

The night jailer raised a bushy eyebrow. "I'd hop to it, Bill. It'll take a while to clean him up."

The duty officer hiked his belt over a bulging belly. "I'm glad to be rid of that bastard, to be honest. Makes me nervous. Hardly said a word since his first day in. It's his eyes. I think he'd cut both our throats for a shilling."

"That's a flippin' Jew for you, Bill."

McConnell rolled over and read the clock hanging on his bedroom wall. It was after three A.M., but he could not find sleep. He had gone to bed at midnight, dozed for an hour, then sat bolt upright in a fit of compulsion. One facet of the proposed mission had not been discussed—anti-nerve agent protection—and he did not intend to rely on any gear Duff Smith might supply. He dressed quietly and bicycled back to the university, let himself into his lab, and quietly removed two prototype anti-gas suits he had been secretly experimenting with for the last month. The ride home with the heavy gear strapped to the bike had nearly exhausted him, but the suits and tanks now lay packed in two suitcases at the foot of his bed.

Yet something else had kept him twisting in the bedclothes long after that. Brigadier Smith had ordered him not to say any goodbyes, and he had tried to obey. But the sense of something important left undone, of words left unsaid, was too powerful to ignore. With a soft curse he climbed out of bed, lit a candle at the small desk in his room, and picked up his fountain pen.

The letter to Susan came fairly easily. It was probably not much different than the millions of letters written by other husbands during the war. He apologized for sending her home during the Battle of Britain, and told her he had been faithful during the years since, which was true. There had been no children yet, and he regretted that, but in the end it would make it easier for her build a new life, should the worst happen.

The second letter took more time. When he thought of his mother, he felt a terrible guilt, a sense that he had no right to risk his own life no matter what the cause, no right to risk taking away her only surviving son. Yet it was his life, and in the end she would understand that. He lifted the pen and wrote:

Dear Mother,

If you have received this letter, I am no longer in this world. You have taken hard blows in your life, and do not deserve this one, but what I went to do, I had to do. Dad would say that I threw my life away in a useless attempt to revenge David's death, but you know me better than that. I have learned that there is truly an infinite capacity for evil in the human heart, and because of my abilities I have an opportunity, and probably an obligation, to do what I can to stop it. There just comes a time when a man says, Enough.

There are some practical matters to be attended to. Back during the Blitz, I wrote a will and mailed it to old Mr. Ward in town. As you know, the monthly payments he disburses to you and Susan come from my six industrial patents. It is a strange irony, but with the war expansion, the proceeds from those patents have grown to a substantial amount of money. In the will, I assigned three of those patents to Susan and three to you. It gives me great comfort to know that you will never have to worry about getting by again, or work so hard as you did during the Depression.

In my letter to Susan, I wrote that she should remarry and try to make a new life with the children she deserves. I hope you will encourage her in that, but she is not the only one who needs encouragement. It may not be a son's place to speak of these things to his mother, but I am. After Dad passed, I think you sealed away a part of yourself in the belief that David and I would never understand if you ever loved another man. That is a noble sentiment, but it is wrong. David and I, and yes, Dad too, wanted nothing so much in life as your happiness. You always said you were a tough old girl, but you are not so old, and no one should have to spend their life with only memories.

Not one day of my life passed without you in my thoughts. I know the same was true for David. God bless you and keep you.

Your son,
Mark

He sealed each letter in a separate envelope, then wrote a short covering letter asking the don he billeted with to forward the letters to Georgia if he had not heard from Mark in ninety days. He laid both envelopes on top of the letter, blew out the candle and went back to bed. This time sleep did not elude him. It came without warning and without dreams—a sleep so deep it was almost like death.

At one-twenty A.M. Brigadier Duff Smith's telephone rang for the last time that night.

"Smith here," he answered.

"I gave it my best shot, Brigadier."

The Scotsman leaned back in his chair. "You earned your money, Corporal."

"It worked?" asked the voice.

"I wrote the bloody script, didn't I?"

"Christ, sir, you did that all right. I felt so sorry for the poor bastard I could barely tell the story. It was the details that clinched it. And the plaster cast. Wow. It was like it really happened. It was *easy*."

"That story was not fiction, Corporal. It *has* really happened."

"Jeez, it really got to me, hurting the guy that bad."

"You don't want the money, then?"

"Hey, I want every fucking cent. I earned it. Five hundred simoleans."

Brigadier Smith chuckled cynically. "I foresee a stellar career for you in the American cinema, Corporal."

He hung up the telephone, consulted a calendar, scrawled a few notes on a pad, then made his last call of the night. It was answered by a male secretary, but after eight minutes the brigadier was rewarded with the unmistakable voice of Winston Churchill.

"I hope this is bloody important, Duff," the prime minister growled. "You pulled me away from the Marx Brothers."

"The doctor is in, Winston."

There was a pause. "How soon can you get here?"

"By the end of the film, probably."

"Don't let any Yanks see you, Duff. They're creeping around London like phantoms at the bloody opera."

"Pour me a Glenfiddich, if you have it."

"Done."

15

A woman was speaking Yiddish in the darkness. She spoke with the guttural inflections of Eastern Europe, but Rachel Jansen had no trouble understanding her. She would have understood even if she had not known Yiddish. Despair needs no translation.

Every woman in the block had gathered in a tight circle around a guttering candle hooded by a tin can. They sat on the floor with their knees under them, listening like mourners in a dark temple. The candlelight did little to smooth their stark, prematurely old faces, and it absolutely died in the hollows of their eyes. All but Frau Hagan wore the yellow triangle on their shifts.

Rachel had never seen or imagined anything like this ritual. The women called it *der Ring*—the Circle. Each night they gathered in this way and spoke by turns, emptying their memories. Children were banished from the block during the Circle, and Rachel soon learned why. The stories told here would have plunged children's minds into black depression and nightmares, scarring them forever. They were difficult enough for adults to endure. But every woman in the room already bore indelible scars. What could it hurt to hear others reveal their own? At least they could share their misery.

But sharing misery was not the purpose of the Circle. Its purpose was to record. A woman called the Scribe wrote down in shorthand everything that was said, paying particular attention to names, dates, and places. Each night the Scribe's annotated record was hidden in a space behind the wall where insulation would be, had insulation had been provided for the barracks, which it had not. After hearing a single night's entries into that record, Rachel had known she would never have the courage to read the full text. It was no less than a testament of the unwillingness—or perhaps worse, the inability—of God to protect his servants.

With great effort she managed to block out the speaker's voice. She admired the purpose of the Circle, but for the past four nights she had used this time to digest whatever she had learned during the day, and to try to apply that knowledge to her family's survival. Unlike the other new widows, who walked through the camp in various states of lethargy, Rachel strained to catch every conversation, sifting each for some scrap of information that might help protect her children.

Already she had experienced extremes of hope and despair. First she had learned that if she and her family had been captured a few months earlier, her children would never have been picked out of the line at Auschwitz, but sent directly to its gas chambers. But with international pressure building against the rumors of Nazi death camps, the SS had decided to create special "family sections" inside certain camps. Red Cross inspectors would be allowed admittance at the front gate, then steered down prepared routes to areas where they would witness scenes of family life not so different from that outside the camp fence, albeit with fewer material comforts. They would leave confident that the grisly rumors were the exaggerations of frightened Jews.

Frau Hagan told Rachel that when Reichsführer Himmler mentioned this program to Herr Doktor Brandt, Brandt had jumped at the chance. And the system had brought certain benefits. A few families were spared the agony of forced separation, which Frau Hagan claimed was worse than death for some, as she had seen such separations drive mothers to suicide. But the odd thing was, since the adoption of the family camp system, not one Red Cross inspector had ever been granted admittance to Totenhausen.

It was not until yesterday that Rachel learned why, and the answer had left her in a permanent state of terror. It seemed that, until recently, Klaus Brandt's talents were not sufficiently taxed by his poison gas experiments on behalf of Reichsführer Himmler. As a hobby he had taken up private researches into the etiology of spinal meningitis. Some said he had done this with an eye toward developing patentable medicines with which he could make a fortune after the war. In any case, Brandt's research used up children at a staggering rate, as his normal method was to inject meningococcus bacteria into healthy spines, then chart the effectiveness or failure of various compounds against the infection. Brandt's adoption of the family camp system insured a constant flow of children for his experiments.

Frau Hagan claimed the meningitis research had slowed considerably in recent weeks, but Rachel was not comforted. The thought that Jan or Hannah could be plucked from the Appellplatz at any moment and taken to the "hospital" to have deadly bacteria injected into their bodies was simply too horrifying to shut out. The thought that *any* children were at risk of this—that some in fact were dying in agony in the hospital on this very night—kept her in a constant state of near panic. She now devoted every waking moment to discovering some way to have her children exempted from these experiments.

A sudden sob from the Circle broke her train of thought. A listener had been moved to tears by the speaker's words. Rachel found herself drawn into the narrative by morbid fascination. The speaker's story was so much more harrowing than her own. It made her nervous to think what she would say when her turn came.

"The trucks were in the square," the woman said, determinedly focusing her eyes on the bare floorboards, as if her old village were standing there in miniature. "The SS beat everyone out of their homes. Those who were too slow about it, who stayed behind to pack some valuables or necessities, they died first. I had believed the worst rumors on the day before. I'd already packed a bag. There were rifle shots from every direction. They caused panic at first, but most of us hurried toward the trucks. We were like cattle. No one wanted to know what the shots meant. Mothers shouting to their children, children alone screaming. The men calling to each other, asking what they should do. What could they do? The SS had already shot the mayor and the police chief.

"From the bed of the truck we saw the worst of it. The children . . . the poor babies. On Praga Street the Germans were killing the babies outright. Smashing their heads with rifle butts, swinging them by the heels against walls. I myself saw an SS grab an infant from Hannah Karpik and dash its head against the street cobbles. Hannah went mad, tearing out her hair and beating her fists against the SS. After a few seconds he took out his pistol and shot her in the stomach, then left her for dead." The woman shrugged. "That was the Germans in Damosc."

"In Lodz, too," echoed a woman from the outer edge of the Circle. "The same, but worse. While we stood in lines in the square, the SS backed a flat truck up to the hospital wall. We could not understand what they were doing. Someone opened a third floor window. Then small packages began flying out of the window. When the second package landed in the bed of the truck, we realized what it was. They were throwing the newborn babies down from the nursery. Three floors. They laughed while they did it."

"Like barbarians from the Dark Ages," said the first woman. "Our rabbi was crying out to God to deliver us, while a young man cursed God in a voice twice as loud. On that night I felt the boy was right. How could God watch that slaughter and not be moved to act?"

"It's always the same," said another woman, a voice much older and cracked with phlegm. "Why write them down? The same story told a hundred times. A thousand times. No one cares."

"That is why we must write them all," Frau Hagan said forcefully. "To show what the Hun is really doing. Good men sometimes do bad things in war. But with the SS it is the rule. It is *policy*. Our stories, piled on other stories, each one documented, can prove this madness. Only then will it be impossible for them to deny it later."

"Later," scoffed a disembodied voice. "What is later? Who will be left to dig up our papers? Our stories. Who will be left to listen? Soon the Germans will own the world."

"Cover your stupid mouth," said Frau Hagan. "There is always a reckoning. The Red Army is coming to set us free. Stalin will crush Hitler into the ice of Russia, drown his tanks in the Pripet Marshes. We must be ready when the soldiers arrive. We must point out the butchers to them."

"Stalin won't come. Hitler almost took Moscow in 'forty-one. Anyway, Stalin hates Jews as much as Hitler. It doesn't matter. The streets of Moscow will soon have German names."

"Liar!" Frau Hagan snapped. "Empty-headed fool! Ask the Dutch girl. She came from Amsterdam. She had a radio. Ask her about Stalin. Ask her about the Red Army."

All eyes turned to Rachel. "Tell them," urged Frau Hagan.

"It's true," Rachel confirmed. "The Russians began a winter offensive in December. Only days before I was captured, I heard that they had advanced into Poland."

"As I told you!" Frau Hagan said triumphantly.

"I heard also on the BBC that they were driving the Germans back across the Ukraine."

Nearly fifty faces turned to Rachel and fired questions at her in a jumble of languages. What was happening in Estonia? In Warsaw? Italy? What about the Americans? The English?

"I'm afraid I don't know much," she apologized. "There are rumors of an invasion this year."

"They say that every year," said a disparaging voice. "They will not come. They don't care about us."

A long shriek suddenly pierced the night. The women in the Circle fell silent. Rachel had heard screaming earlier, like several women shouting for help, but it had come from farther away, from the direction of the SS barracks, and she had been unable to make Frau Hagan take notice of it. But when the second shriek sounded—this one obviously from close by—Frau Hagan's face told Rachel she sensed real danger.

"I may have to speak to Frau Komorowski," the Block Leader said.

"Don't risk it," said a woman. "Let them solve their own problems."

Frau Hagan ruminated. "I'll wait a few minutes. Finish the story, Brana."

"Should I hide the papers?" asked the Scribe. "What if the screams make them search?"

"Finish the story."

The woman called Brana resumed her narrative, telling of the open trucks driving through the winter blast to meet a prison train at an empty stretch of track. Of families loaded into unheated cattle cars, as Rachel's had been, without food, water, or toilets. Rachel found herself unwillingly reliving her own nightmare journey from Westerbork when something raised the hairs on her upper arms.

"*Quiet!*" she warned in a sharp voice.

Frau Hagan glared at her. "What is it, Dutch girl?"

"There is someone outside. Hide your papers."

Frau Hagan looked skeptical. "Heinke is listening at the door. She has heard nothing."

"Hide the papers, I tell you!"

Frau Hagan snatched the papers from the Scribe and stuffed them under her shift. Her eyes went to the woman called Heinke at the door. "Anything?"

The guard shook her head. Frau Hagan curled her upper lip at Rachel.

"SS!" Heinke hissed suddenly. "Into the bunks!"

The hooded candle was instantly extinguished. A wild scramble ensued as the women found their allotted places in the tiered bunks. Rachel realized then that they had practiced this maneuver a thousand times. The only sounds she heard were the grunts and curses of the new women as they stubbed toes and barked shins in their inexperienced haste. She admired the old-timers. Walking quickly without sound was a skill she had mastered long ago, in Amsterdam, and not an easy one.

Holding her breath in her own bunk, she waited for the slamming door and pounding boots of an SS search team. Instead she heard a furtive knock. Then the door cracked open and a shadow slipped through.

"Hagan?" whispered the shadow.

"Irina? Is that you?"

"Da."

"Everyone stay in your bunks," ordered Frau Hagan.

Rachel heard the muted thud of the heavy Pole's feet hitting the floor. Frau Hagan crossed the room in total darkness and held a whispered conversation with the kapo of the Christian Women's Block. In less than a minute the door opened and closed again.

"Another child has gone missing," Frau Hagan announced to the room. "A gypsy child."

There was a heavy silence.

"A boy child?" asked a quiet voice.

"Yes. Eight years old."

Rachel heard a whimper in the darkness.

"That was his mother we heard screaming. Frau Komorowski ordered her gagged and tied to her bunk. For her own protection. The gypsy had told them she was going to Doktor Brandt's quarters to get her son back."

"She named the right place," said a voice.

"God help the boy," said another. "It is unspeakable."

"Was it the same as before?"

Frau Hagan answered wearily. "A Latvian political saw Ariel Weitz talking to this gypsy boy earlier today."

Rachel heard spitting and cursing in the darkness, then voices that changed almost too rapidly to follow.

"Devil!" hissed one woman.

"One of the men should squash that worm."

"We should kill him ourselves."

"Don't talk madness," said Frau Hagan. "Kill Weitz and we all die. He serves Brandt, so Brandt protects him. Sturm protects him. Even Schörner protects Weitz, and Schörner despises him."

"Schörner uses him too," said a knowing voice. "Weitz informs for Schörner."

"To think he was born a Jew," mused another. "Weitz is worse than the SS. A thousand times worse."

"The shoemaker is also a Jew," observed Frau Hagan.

"The shoemaker makes shoes. Weitz summons children to be violated, then killed."

"What about the last boy?"

"Probably gassed with the men," someone speculated.

"No," said Frau Hagan. "He was shot last week. At the pit."

"Why didn't you tell us?" asked a dismayed voice.

"What could you have done, Yascha?"

Rachel realized then that Frau Hagan could recognize people by the timbre of their whispers.

"Enough talk," the Pole said conclusively. After a brief silence, she said, "You have good ears, Dutch girl. Irina flattened herself against the outside wall to avoid the searchlight. Is that what you heard?"

Rachel swallowed. "I heard something. I lived in hiding for three years in Amsterdam. Above a shop. There were customers in and out all day. The slightest noise meant danger."

"You learned well. From now on, you will guard the door."

Rachel closed her eyes. Was that a good thing, to be guard? If it kept her in Frau Hagan's good graces, it probably was. But would the woman called Heinke become her enemy now?

"Did you hear me, Dutch girl?" Frau Hagan asked.

"Tomorrow I guard the door."

"Yes. Now sleep. Everyone."

Rachel heard the creak of brittle wood as the Block Leader climbed into her bunk. Since her second day in camp, Rachel had watched the men with pink badges—and every other man—like a mother hen, but so far had detected no sign of impropriety toward Jan. Could the commandant of Totenhausen be the danger Frau Hagan had warned her about? Could there be two kinds of selection that had to be avoided to survive? If so, how could she protect her son? The Herr Doktor held absolute power of life and death over every inmate. He had already ordered the death of her husband. If Klaus Brandt wanted to abuse her Jan, she was helpless to stop him.

With a shiver of loathing, Rachel remembered Ariel Weitz. If Weitz was Brandt's procurer, perhaps he could be bribed to leave Jan alone. She had the five diamonds. Yet even if Weitz could be bought, would it help? Brandt probably chose his victims while walking through the camp in his white coat, pretending to be a healer. It *was* unspeakable. Yet it was reality. She could not fly back to Holland with her children beneath her wings. She would have to think of something.

Where could help lie? The shoemaker had proved he had compassion, but Rachel had hardly seen the man in the past four days. And what of Anna Kaas? The young nurse obviously felt some sympathy for the prisoners. Could she suggest some way to keep Jan out of harm's way? Rachel thought of Jan and Hannah lying in the Jewish Children's Block just meters away. A Sephardic Jewess from Salonica had the job of sleeping in the children's block to keep order. At supper Rachel had given her half of her own bread ration in exchange for a promise that Jan and Hannah would be allowed to sleep side by side. She'd considered offering the woman a full week's ration in exchange for her job, but finally decided against it. A week without bread would set her on the road to starvation, and while she would be closer to her children, she would be farther from the adult women who knew the rules of survival, particularly Frau Hagan. As a German shepherd howled on the camp perimeter, Rachel decided that the Block Leader was her tether to life, her bridge to survival. Whatever Frau Hagan needed, she would get from Rachel Jansen.

Guarding the door would be only the beginning.

16

McConnell's driver arrived in Oxford at six A.M. as Brigadier Smith had promised. One hour later he deposited his passenger and two extremely heavy suitcases at the entrance to King's Cross Station in London, with instructions to board Train 56, which departed at 7:07 A.M. for Edinburgh, Scotland.

The station echoed with the voices of servicemen from ten different countries wearing dozens of different uniforms, and all apparently more lost than McConnell. He did not see how he could possibly find Smith—or how Smith could find him—in the throng. Yet as he sidestepped a Canadian in the midst of bidding a tearful farewell to an English girl six inches taller than himself, he felt someone tug at his arm. He turned and looked into the twinkling blue eyes of Duff Smith. The SOE chief wore a natty tweed jacket with the left sleeve pinned to the shoulder.

"No uniform today, Brigadier?"

Duff Smith smiled but said nothing. He led McConnell to a private compartment, a luxury beyond price on the crowded train. Jonas Stern sat sullenly beside the window. After closing the door, Smith shook McConnell's hand and said in a jovial voice, "Glad to have you aboard, Doctor."

McConnell nodded at Stern, but the young man offered no greeting. McConnell's trained eye instantly noted the faded hematomas beneath his skin. Obviously Stern had not spent a peaceful week since their last meeting.

"What's all that rubbish?" sputtered Brigadier Smith, pointing at McConnell's bags. "You're not going to Brighton for the month, you know."

"I know. It's equipment, and it's necessary."

"We'll be supplying your gear for this trip, Doctor. You'll have to leave these behind."

"You can't supply this equipment, Brigadier."

Smith looked intrigued. "Let's have a look, then."

McConnell turned the heavy suitcases on their sides and opened them. One contained what appeared to be a pile of folded rubber, topped by some type of transparent rain gear for the head. The other case held two yellow cylinders about twenty inches long, and some corrugated rubber tubing.

"Is that *German* printed on those tanks?" Smith asked.

"Yes. These are portable oxygen cylinders taken from crashed Luftwaffe bombers. I figured if we're trying to pass ourselves off as German, we should be carrying German equipment."

"Good thinking, Doctor. Really. But I don't think I've ever seen a gas suit quite like that."

"It's the latest American impermeable suit."

"How in God's name did you get hold of it?"

"I still have a few friends Stateside, Brigadier. Edgewood Arsenal in Alabama. I've been experimenting with this suit for a month now. The clear vinyl gas mask was developed for soldiers with severe head wounds. I modified it to accept a hose from these oxygen cylinders, using some new equipment from the underwater diving field. I also developed and installed a specially trained acetate diaphragm to enhance speech capability. You're looking at the only airtight suit in the world that allows soldiers to see each other's faces and speak while fighting."

Brigadier Smith looked at Stern. "I told you he was the right man for this job, eh?"

For once Jonas Stern had no glib remark ready. "Do you have two of those suits?" he asked.

McConnell closed the cases and sat down opposite him. "Yes. And you're damn lucky we're about the same size."

Brigadier Smith picked up a straw basket from the floor. "Rations in here, lads. I won't be making the trip with you, but I'll see you sometime tomorrow."

"So where are we going?" Stern asked. "Can't you tell me, now that he's finally here?"

Smith stuck out his lower lip. "If you must know, you're going to Achnacarry Castle."

"Where in God's name is that?"

Duff Smith smiled. He'd heard that question repeated a hundred times before. *Achnacarry.* The name alone was enough to send some men into a cold sweat. "Some say it's the end of the world," he said. "But there's others who claim Achnacarry's the next thing to heaven. Mostly Scotsmen. Camerons, at that."

McConnell looked up sharply at the name Cameron.

"Why the hell are we going there?" Stern pressed.

Smith stopped smiling. "First, secrecy. Second, training. Third, time. Gentlemen, I cannot tell you why, but the time factor has suddenly become critical. In eleven days, the target of our mission will cease to have any strategic value."

"But if time is a problem," Stern argued, "why go all the way to Scotland? For God's sake, just tell me what you want done and put us into Germany. I'll make sure it gets done."

The brigadier shook his head. "You may have harried the Germans in North Africa, laddie, but you don't beard the lion in his den without some specialized training. We have eleven days. You are about to spend seven of those with the toughest men in the British Army. The C.O. at Achnacarry—which is now called the Commando Depot, by the way—is a friend of mine, and he has generously agreed to have his instructors pound their hard-earned knowledge into your thick skull. In seven days you will be a different man, Mr. Stern, a better man, and just possibly ready to accomplish the mission I'm sending you to do."

Smith ended the argument by stepping out of the compartment. "Change trains in Edinburgh," he told them. "You want Spean Bridge station. There'll be someone waiting for you. I'd conserve those rations. Charlie Vaughan runs a tight ship. If you reach the castle late, there may not be supper."

The brigadier looked at his two recruits for several moments. "Cheer up," he said. "By the time you reach Spean, you should be fast friends."

He laughed softly as he marched off down the corridor.

McConnell leaned back into the corner of the compartment. He wasn't sure exactly where Spean Bridge was, but he thought it was well up into the Scottish Highlands, possibly near Loch Ness. It was going to be a long trip.

The train lurched forward exactly on time and gathered speed rapidly as it moved north out of London. The day was clear and cold, the sky gray. After several minutes, Stern said, "What changed your mind, Doctor? What made you decide to come on this mission?"

McConnell kept looking out of the window. "None of your business," he said in a neutral tone.

"Are you sure you've got the nerve for it? This mission could get bloody, you know. I wouldn't want your pacifist sensibilities to be offended."

McConnell slowly turned from the window. "You obviously like fighting," he said. "But I'm not your problem. Whoever you're mad at, take it out on them. This is going to be a long ride."

He settled back into his seat and closed his eyes. Stern stared furiously at him for a while, then turned to the window and watched the winter countryside as the swaying train rumbled past Alexandra Palace.

The two men did not speak again for the next eight hours.

"Spean Bridge!" shouted a high-pitched voice, stretching out the syllables until the words were barely recognizable.

When McConnell blinked himself awake, Stern, the picnic basket, and one of the suitcases were gone.

"Spean Bridge!" shouted the conductor for the third and last time.

McConnell snatched up the other case and scrambled out of the compartment. He found Stern on the station platform, huddled beneath a green awning, eating a soggy sandwich from which the bread crust had been cut away. Cold rain poured relentlessly from a slate sky. Dark, forbidding hills rose on all sides of the village of Spean. They looked to be made of solid rock, cloaked with frost and crowned with snow.

It was still early in the afternoon, but McConnell had the feeling night was coming on. Then he realized that it was. Darkness fell early in the Highlands in winter, and dawn came very late. As the train chugged out of the station, he looked around the platform. It was as deserted as the green-and-white station building, which was locked tight.

"Smith said there would be someone to meet us," McConnell said. "I don't see anybody."

Sour-faced and puffy from sleep, Stern said nothing. McConnell reached into the picnic basket and took out a sandwich. Just then he saw a tall figure wearing a kilt and a green beret standing motionless at the end of the platform. The tartan was predominantly red, with highlights of yellow and forest green.

"Doctor McConnell?" the man called, rolling the *r* with a Highland burr.

"That's me."

The kilted man marched toward them. McConnell had never dreamed he would be intimidated by a man wearing a dress, but he was. Well over six feet tall, the newcomer stopped and stood in the freezing rain outside the awning as casually as if he were basking in May sunshine. There was an unsettling, animal strength about him. His chest was high and broad, and the calves that stretched his stockings looked sculpted from bronze. Short-cropped hair framed a chiseled, handsome face illuminated by sea blue eyes.

"Sergeant Ian McShane," the giant said mildly. "You're Stern, I ken?"

Stern nodded.

McConnell held out his hand, but the sergeant just looked at it.

"I dinna ken much about you," McShane said, "and I dinna need to know more. Our business has nothing to do with who you really are. From now on, McConnell, you're Mr. Wilkes." He looked at Stern. "You're Mr. Butler."

The Highlander eyed both men from head to toe. "Either of you ever in the military, then?"

Stern straightened. "I've had some experience."

"Have you now? Well. We'll find out tomorrow what we have to work with. It's fallen to me to shepherd you two through a wee bit o' training. Quite irregular, actually. Still, the MacVaughan ordered it. That's the way it'll be."

With a last appraising look at his charges, Sergeant McShane turned and walked back the way he had come.

Stern and McConnell looked at each other, then snatched up

their bags and hurried after him. At the end of the platform, they saw the Scotsman climb into a covered jeep and start the engine.

"Hey!" McConnell yelled. "Sergeant! Wait!"

McShane leaned out and said, "Follow this road west across the Caledonian Canal, turn north at Gairlochy, march along the loch till you sight Bunarkaig, then up the switchback road to the castle. It's about seven miles, all told. You can't get lost."

"But there's plenty of room in the jeep!" Stern objected.

McShane's blue eyes seemed to grow tired. "That's no' the point at all, Mr. Butler. Nobody rides to Achnacarry their first time up. All transport is by foot." He glanced at Stern's worn leather shoes. "We'll get you some proper gear at the castle. I will take those bags for you, though."

McConnell loaded the heavy suitcases into the jeep, then tossed Stern's leather bag after them.

"But it's pouring rain!" Stern shouted.

Sergeant McShane looked skyward and smiled. "Aye. It's pissin' it down, all right. I suggest you get used to it, Mr. Butler. It always rains at Achnacarry."

Stern whirled toward McConnell, perhaps to suggest that they try to board the jeep by force, but the American was no longer standing behind him. He was walking toward the main road, leaning grimly into the rain.

"See you at the castle, Mr. Butler," Sergeant McShane said. The jeep spun its tires and fishtailed onto the road, headed west, leaving Stern standing alone in the mud.

Stern slung the picnic basket over his shoulder and trotted after McConnell, catching him on the stone bridge for which the village had been named. "Where are you going?" he yelled. "Let's wait for the rain to stop!"

"It may not stop," McConnell said, walking faster on the rising grade.

Stern quickened his pace and punched McConnell on the right shoulder. "Do you really want to walk seven miles through freezing rain?"

"No, I don't. So I think I'll run it. Even with these hills, it probably shouldn't take more than an hour and a half. Two hours at the most."

"*What?*"

McConnell broke into a trot, leaving Stern fuming in the road, his dark hair plastered to his head. Stern took the last sandwich from the basket and wolfed it down. He watched the American top a ridge, disappear, then reappear a quarter mile farther on, a dim shadow against the gray wall of rain, growing steadily smaller.

"*Arschloch,*" he muttered. In Africa he had walked over endless miles of desert without water when forced to, but *schlepping* up these mountains in a driving rain when there were surely options available was insane. He kicked the empty picnic basket and began jogging up the road.

He kept up his pace for about a mile and a half, then slowed to a lopsided walk so that he could massage the knifelike stitch in his right side. All he could see ahead was more hills, a long black lake, and a few tiny stone houses. No traffic on the road. No sign of McConnell. No castle.

Then he saw the bicycle.

McConnell reached the top of the switchback road that led to Achnacarry Castle exactly sixty minutes after he started running. The steep hills combined with the thrashing wind and rain had nearly beaten him. But he'd made it. The outlines of a great baronial house emerged from the darkness. Warm yellow light glowed in one upper window. He slowed to a walk and made for the building. Down the shallow slope below the castle, the gleaming tin roofs of prefabricated Nissen huts made a strange contrast to the medieval landscape he had seen so far.

As he neared the castle, something else caught his eye. It was a row of graves. The graves followed the line of the drive. Each was marked by a white cross and a board which bore a name, rank, and brief epitaph. The first one McConnell stooped over read: *He showed himself on a ridge line.* The second read: *Failed to take appropriate cover under mortar barrage.*

As he stood puzzling over the inscriptions, he heard a slow creak. Then a familiar voice called out of the darkness: "The dead dinna mind the rain, Mr. Wilkes!"

Sergeant McShane.

"But I'd advise the livin' to get indoors!"

McConnell jogged up to the great wooden door, wiped his muddy shoes, and squeezed past McShane's broad body. He found himself in a spacious entrance hall which had been stripped of all furniture.

"Where's your friend, then?" McShane asked. "Mr. Butler."

McConnell shrugged. "Back out there somewhere, I guess."

The Highlander eyed him with new interest. "I'm not surprised. You must have set a cracking pace to make it that quickly."

"I've done a little running."

"Have you now? Well. That's a handy thing to have done if you're required to spend any time at Achnacarry, Mr. Wilkes. There's many a man who wished he'd done more of it. I've seen university distance runners fall flat in these hills." The Scot's lips cracked into a tight smile. " 'Course, eighty pounds of gear on their backs doesna help much."

Suddenly the front door was shoved open from outside. McConnell turned and saw Jonas Stern standing in the doorway with a satisfied smile on his face. He was wet to the skin, but didn't look at all winded.

Before McConnell or Sergeant McShane could speak, he said, "Butler reporting for duty, Sergeant."

McConnell looked at the sergeant with bewilderment, but the dour Scot was an old hand at appearing unflappable. "You made good time, Mr. Butler," he said. "I was about to lock the door."

"Go ahead."

McShane did, then led them through a hall dark with wainscoting and turned up a wide staircase. "You'll stay in the castle until further notice," he said. "You'll see hundreds of men coming and going in all manner of kit, speaking several languages. They're commando trainees. You leave them be, they'll do the same. Some will be instructors. They're not marked as such, but you won't have any trouble tellin' who they are."

Not if they all look like you, McConnell thought. Sergeant McShane looked like a Highland clan chief who'd stepped straight out of the eighteenth century.

"Remember," the Scotsman said, "you're Mr. Wilkes and Mr. Butler. Dinna be givin' those names unless you're asked. The C.O. of the depot is Colonel Vaughan. You two may not be military, but you'd better snap to if he comes near. The MacVaughan doesna suffer fools gladly."

They stopped in a dim passage with heavy wooden doors on either side. McShane pointed to the second door on the right. Stern pushed it open. Inside the small, square room were two cots, a paraffin lamp which had been burning for some time, and a bare clothes rack.

"Bath's up the passage," McShane said. "No hot water in this part of the castle." He put his forefinger between Stern's shoulder blades and shoved him into the room.

McConnell quickly followed, so as to stop any overreaction on Stern's part.

"You two must be important," the sergeant mused. "You're the first civilians I know of to pass through Achnacarry."

McConnell bent over one of the cots and picked up a horsehair rope about four feet long, with a permanent loop at one end and a straight wooden handle about six inches long attached to the other. An identical rope lay on the other cot.

"What's this?" he asked.

"Toggle rope," McShane said. "Every commando carries one at all times. You'll soon see why. I dinna want to see you without it. That's it then. I'll see you at breakfast. Six A.M."

He turned and started back toward the staircase.

McConnell went after him and called, "Is a Brigadier Duff Smith staying in the castle tonight, Sergeant?"

McShane didn't break stride. "I canna charge my memory about that just now, Mr. Wilkes."

Realizing he would learn nothing else until morning, McConnell went back to the room and began taking off his wet clothes. He stripped to the skin, as his shorts were soaked through, then climbed into bed. Stern paced the hall for a few moments, then did the same. McConnell thought it odd that Stern turned off the lamp before removing his clothes. It was almost as if he were trying to hide his body.

McConnell lay silent in the dark for some time. But he could not go to sleep without asking one question. "How'd you make it up here so fast?" he said finally. "You found someone to give you a ride?"

Stern answered in English, giving a fair rendition of McConnell's Georgia drawl. "None of your business, is it, Mr. Wilkes?"

McConnell took the barb in silence. He wondered if Stern realized that their code names had been taken from Margaret Mitchell's

Gone With the Wind. It had been the biggest picture of 1939, but God only knew what corner of the desert Jonas Stern had been living in then. Duff Smith had obviously selected the code names, knowing that McConnell would realize the significance of being named after the milquetoast Ashley Wilkes.

He was nearly asleep when Stern's disembodied voice said: "Did you see those grave markers?"

McConnell blinked in the chilly darkness. "I saw them."

"Nothing but dirt under those crosses."

"What do you mean? The graves are empty?"

"Right."

"How do you know?"

"I know the British Army. Fought with them in Africa. On their side, if you can believe it. Those graves are typical of their crap. They put those crosses there to scare recruits. 'Showed himself on a ridge line.' What rot. The British Army's just like those graves."

McConnell saw nothing to be gained by arguing with Stern about the British. "I guess we'll find out tomorrow," he said.

Stern grunted contemptuously in the darkness. "Sweet dreams, Mr. Wilkes," he said in German. "Come morning, I'll show those limey bastards commando training."

17

McConnell kicked Stern out of bed at nine A.M. After a quick trip to the toilet at the end of the hall, he dressed in the clothes McShane had provided: army denims, gaiters, and a heavy green cotton smock. Last, he put on the "toggle" rope, with its loop at one end and short handle at the other. He coiled it around his hand, then clipped the coil to the web belt he found in the clothes bag.

Stern was already dressed and standing by the door.

"You don't have your toggle rope," McConnell reminded him.

"I don't need it."

McConnell shrugged and led the way to the first floor of the castle. They met Sergeant McShane in the entrance hall. The Highlander wore his green beret, but he had forgone his kilt in favor of denims, a khaki shirt, and camouflaged rain smock.

"I was about to come lookin' for you," he said. "You missed breakfast."

"We're ready," said Stern.

"Ready?" McShane stared at him in amazement. "I dinna see your toggle rope."

"I don't need the damned thing."

"Oh, you'll be needin' it, Mr. Butler. Now, go back and get it. *Move.*"

When Stern returned with the rope, McShane led them outside into a gray Highland dawn. The smell of wood and peat smoke mingled with the scent of coffee and pine, bringing McConnell fully awake. At last he could see the place to which Brigadier Smith had sent them. Achnacarry itself was built of gray stone, with crenelated parapets and mock turrets at the corners. The gurgle of water from behind it announced a river he could not see, but beyond the castle roof rose wooded hills shrouded in mist like that in the foothills of the Appalachian Mountains in northern Georgia.

A majestic tree-lined drive led down from the castle to the glen below, where a great loch with a surface like burnished silver lay in the growing light. But the pastoral scene ended there. Achnacarry's expansive lawns were dotted with corrugated steel Nissen huts and canvas bell tents, a metropolis of instant housing. In the center of a field McConnell saw a tent as big as an aircraft hangar, and just across the drive the long row of graves Stern claimed were empty.

Not far from the graves, a powerfully built soldier of about fifty was speaking to a tall, bearded farmer twenty years his senior. The soldier's voice modulated quickly between apology and indignation, his accent the furthest thing imaginable from Highland Scots.

"That's the colonel," Sergeant McShane said.

McConnell was perplexed. "That's Colonel Vaughan?"

"Aye."

"But that's a London accent. I thought he was a Highlander, like yourself. I thought he was lord of the castle."

McShane laughed. "The *laird,* you mean? No, no. The real laird, Cameron of Lochiel, moved two miles up the loch to Clunes for the duration. But he keeps an eye on his place, make no mistake. It's his duty to all Camerons around the world."

McConnell regarded the heavy-jowled colonel. Vaughan seemed a bit on the bulky side for a commando, though he certainly looked as tough as an old army boot. "Vaughan's a commando himself?"

McShane shook his head. "Ex-Regimental Sergeant Major in the Guards."

"I don't see any commandos," Stern observed.

"They're on their thirty-six-hour scheme. Should be in any time, though."

"What's a thirty-six-hour scheme?" McConnell asked.

"Exactly what it sounds like. Thirty-six hours of running up and down the Lochaber hills in full kit under live fire. Be glad you missed it."

"They were out in that storm last night?"

"Aye. And it's a good thing they didna run across you two—"

A cacophony of wild, primitive screams rose out of the trees from behind the castle. "What the hell's that?" McConnell asked.

"Mock assault on the Arkaig bridge. Climax of the scheme."

McConnell watched in amazement as over a hundred commandos wearing strange cloth caps charged out from behind the castle with bayonets fixed. "What's that they're yelling, Sergeant?"

"Who knows? They're Free French blokes."

By the time the French commandos reached the Nissen huts, their enthusiasm had vanished. As they collapsed around their tents, Colonel Vaughan marched up the drive, cursing under his breath.

"What is it, sir?" Sergeant McShane asked.

Vaughan's face glowed red with anger. "Some fool pinched a bicycle from a crofter's hut down the hill. Bloody beggar's accusing one of our lads."

"One of ours, sir?"

"Right. Claims no one local would have pinched it. Says everyone knows it's his only transport other than his cart-horse."

McConnell looked Stern in the eye but saw no reaction.

"If he turns out to be right," Vaughan bellowed, "I'll flay the man who did it. We can't afford to offend the locals. And God forbid Lochiel should hear of it!" He glanced suspiciously down the hill at the exhausted Frenchmen. "Suppose one of the Frogs could have pinched it," he mused. "Seems unlikely, though."

At last Vaughan's eyes focused on Stern and McConnell. "What's this lot, then? Dummies for the bayonet course?"

"They're our special guests, sir."

Vaughan stuck out his lower lip and gave them a measuring look. "Duff's boys, eh? Very well. Carry on as we discussed, Sergeant."

"Yes, sir."

"And you look into that bicycle."

"Aye."

Colonel Vaughan started to go, then paused, tucked his chin into his chest and squinted at Stern. McConnell wondered what had caught his interest. The desert tan? Stern's languid posture? The insolent curve of his mouth? The colonel leaned his massive head in toward Stern's chest and spoke with paternal familiarity.

"You'd best get that chip off your shoulder, lad. Before somebody knocks it off." Vaughan cut his eyes at McShane. "Happens quite often round here, eh, Sergeant?"

"Seems to," McShane confirmed. "Now that you mention it."

Colonel Vaughan nodded once at McConnell, then disappeared into his castle.

Sergeant McShane stared pointedly at Stern. "Know anything about a missing bicycle?"

Stern silently returned the stare.

"Right," McShane said. "Let's get to business. Not much daylight in winter."

As the sergeant led them across the grounds, McConnell leaned toward Stern and whispered, "Where'd you hide the bicycle?"

"Don't know what you're talking about," said Stern.

Sergeant McShane eventually stopped on top of a small hillock. On the other side, a stocky man of about forty sat on a camp stool, smoking a cigarette with obvious enjoyment. A clipboard and a pen lay on the ground beside him.

"My orders," said McShane, "are to see where you two stand as far as taking care of yourselves. We're going to check your God-given ability first. Weapons come later. Let's see how you'd do if you were caught without one."

The instructor on the stool grinned up at McShane. "Funny how often that very thing tends to happen, isn't it, Ian?"

"True enough, John. Are you busy? These two will only be with us for a few days."

"Not at all. Just put a few Poles through their paces."

"You're the unarmed combat instructor?" Stern asked.

The man on the stool frowned at the sound of Stern's voice. German accents were seldom heard in the Lochaber hills.

McShane said, "All of us are qualified to teach any part of the course. But Sergeant Lewis does specialize a bit. This part of the course is actually called Silent Killing."

Sergeant Lewis stood up and grinned again, though this time his eyes stayed sober. "Step into my parlor, lad."

"I'll let my friend warm you up," Stern said.

McConnell turned to McShane. "Is this really necessary?"

"Get on with it, Mr. Wilkes."

McConnell eased cautiously down the bank. His felt his pulse quickening. His entire pugilistic experience consisted of one round of boxing in a makeshift ring in the Fairplay High School gymnasium. It was the week after Tunney hammered Jack Dempsey for the title in Philadelphia. The high school boys had caught a seven-day boxing fever. His opponent had been a head shorter and fifteen pounds lighter than himself. He remembered because in less than three minutes the smaller boy had hit him harder, faster, and more times than he had ever been hit in his life. Those three minutes had been an education. He suspected he was in for a similar experience now.

"Don't be shy," Sergeant Lewis said. "Come right in."

McConnell held up his fists in a classic boxing stance, right arm bent slightly at the elbow, left fist brushing his tucked chin. Sensing his hesitation, Lewis stepped forward and smiled, offering his head as a target.

McConnell tried the only ruse he knew. He let his eyes drop to his opponent's belly, feinted at the body with a left jab, then drove his right fist straight at Sergeant Lewis's chin.

When he ceased his forward motion he was sitting on his butt four feet beyond the spot where Lewis had been standing. The instructor had apparently converted the momentum of his punch into some kind of judo throw.

"You're no' a fighter, Mr. Wilkes," Lewis said. "That's plain enough. I won't even try to explain what I did then, because we don't have time for you to learn." He turned to McShane. "I'll do what I can, Ian. But I say fit him up with a pistol and pray he doesn't get caught without it."

McShane nodded in agreement, then motioned to McConnell, who climbed gratefully back up the bank.

"Your turn, Mr. Butler," Sergeant Lewis said. His voice had a rather unpleasant edge to it.

Stern walked easily down the bank, his long arms swinging lightly.

Sergeant Lewis took a step toward him. "Are you ready?"

"Ready enough."

The instructor shook his head. "Do you hear his accent, Ian? I pegged him for a Jew when I saw him, but he's a bloody German to boot." He turned back to Stern. "Say something else."

Stern straightened up to his full height. "All right, Sergeant. Shut your fucking mouth."

Lewis's face lit up with pleasure. "Blow me, he curses like an English sergeant!"

"He saw some action in North Africa," said McShane.

"Did he now?" Lewis began to slowly circle Stern.

Stern stood with his knees slightly bent, hands hanging loose at his sides. McConnell thought he looked birdlike, a thin statue of brown sinew and bone, with only his eyes tracking the British sergeant. Lewis kept his hands high, open, and in front as he moved. His body gave off a frightening intensity, like a ball of knotted muscle and adrenaline, but Stern gave no indication that he planned to move for the remainder of the morning. Finally Sergeant Lewis took a step forward, daring him to strike.

Stern did nothing.

Tired of this game, Lewis feinted with a curled right hand, then fired his left foot at Stern's head. Stern's response baffled both his opponent and his audience. He stepped back in a motion that appeared almost leisurely, at the same time driving his left hand sharply upward at a speed barely visible. The sergeant's whole body followed his kick skyward. He turned a half somersault and crashed onto his back at Stern's feet.

Lewis scrambled up, his face nearly purple with embarrassment and anger. "You're the clever-dick, aren't you!"

"John," Sergeant McShane cut in. "I think that's enough."

"Bloody hell it is! Ask Mr. Butler if it's enough. Or is it Mr. Birnbaum? Or Rubenstein?" He shook his finger in Stern's expressionless face. "You *are* a bloody four-by-two, aren't you?"

Stern replied in a perfect British accent. "Got something against Jews, have you, mate?"

"I knew it, Ian! Knew it the second I saw his desert tan." Lewis's face quivered. "This is one of the bastards that crippled my brother Wally in Palestine!"

"Could have been," Stern said quietly.

"You *bloody* bastard."

McShane shouted "John!" but it was too late. Lewis was already moving toward Stern, his hands a blur. McConnell watched in disbelief as Stern allowed himself to be struck twice, three times.

"Defend yourself!" he yelled.

Stern absorbed another blow that snapped his head back and left his cheek scarlet. Taking his reluctance to fight back as an opportunity to move in for the kill, Lewis abandoned the Oriental chops and threw a curled fist straight at Stern's throat.

Before the punch could land, Stern dropped to the ground, caught his weight on the fingers of his left hand and flung his right foot around in a great sweeping kick that snapped Sergeant Lewis's knee like a scythe-blade. McConnell heard a crack, then a high-pitched yell as Lewis went down, both hands gripping his leg. He moved instinctively toward the injured sergeant, but McShane's powerful hand restrained him.

"Mr. Butler! Move back up here. *Right now.*"

Stern looked up at the Highlander, then leaned over Sergeant Lewis and said, "An Australian taught me that. I guess you never met him." Then he walked slowly up to where McShane and McConnell waited.

"That wasna smart, Mr. Butler," McShane said. "Not smart at all."

"He asked for it."

"Maybe. But you're not here to advertise yourself." McShane looked down the bank. Lewis was massaging his rapidly swelling knee. "Better have the M.O. check that for you, John. I'll stop by his quarters tonight for a report."

"This is nothing!" Lewis yelled, and struggled to his feet. "I'm still going, Ian!"

McShane turned to Stern and McConnell and said, "Let's go."

"Where?" Stern asked.

"Firing range."

"Suits me."

McShane gave him a look of annoyance. "I thought it might."

At first, the firing range seemed merely another venue for Stern to demonstrate his martial prowess. They arrived to find two Frenchmen wrestling with a small, roughly finished machine gun. The weapons instructor, a Glaswegian named Colin Munro, watched the spectacle sadly. The gun would spit out a burst of bullets, jam, then clear just in time to startle the wits out of its operator.

"That, gentlemen," Sergeant McShane said, "is a British Sten Mark-Two-S. In trained hands it's prone to jamming. In untrained hands it's all but useless."

"Is that what we're taking in?" Stern asked.

"No." McShane reached into a crate on the ground and brought out a well-oiled submachine pistol of blue-black steel with a folding metal stock. McConnell saw Stern grin with anticipation.

"This is the German Schmeisser MP.40," McShane said. "Operates on roughly the same principle as the Sten. Much in the same way a Mercedes-Benz operates on the same principle as a Bedford truck."

Colin Munro laughed appreciatively.

"Fires a pistol cartridge, but it's reliable." McShane loaded a clip and handed the weapon to Stern. "I presume you're a dab hand with this, Mr. Butler?"

"I've held one." Stern took the Schmeisser and, holding it waist-high with both hands, aimed at a man-sized pile of sandbags thirty meters away.

"Hold on!" said Munro. "That's a close-in weapon, lad. Step out to the marker there. Give yourself a chance, man."

Stern smiled back at McShane, then pulled the trigger. He fired four three-round bursts—all of which struck the target in the chest area—then sprayed two nearby targets with the remaining shells in the clip.

"*That's* what I'm talking about!" Munro shouted at the Frenchmen. "Fire discipline!"

McShane gave Stern a sidelong glance. "This is my ringer, Colin. Calls himself Mr. Butler."

"Is he as good with a pistol?"

"Better," Stern said.

McShane loaded another clip into the Schmeisser and handed it to McConnell. "Mr. Wilkes?"

The submachine gun didn't feel entirely foreign in McConnell's hands, but when he fired—missing the sandbags completely—he realized he did not have even a semblance of control over the weapon.

"What do you say, Colin?" McShane asked.

"What can I say? Give me two weeks and I'll turn him around."

"We dinna have one week."

"Give him a ladies' gun, then. Small revolver. Best results without training."

McConnell flushed at this, though he knew he shouldn't give a damn. While Stern laughed, he stepped back and selected a worn bolt-action Lee-Enfield .303 from the rifle rack. "Anybody down in that target pit?" he asked, pointing two hundred meters downrange.

"Don't know," answered Munro. "But I don't see as it matters much." He grinned at McShane. "If you think you've hit it, you can run down there and fetch the target."

McConnell chambered a round, then raised the Enfield to his shoulder. He looked down the open sights and drew a bead on the black bullseye. It was odd, he thought, the way the body seemed to remember things the mind let slip away. He rolled his shoulders once, feeling the faintest breeze at his back, and adjusted his aim slightly for the drop of the bullet.

He squeezed the trigger.

Munro barked a short laugh. "Five quid says that was Maggie's drawers, Ian." Then he said more kindly, "Have another go, son."

McConnell worked the bolt three times in quick succession, feeling better with each shot. Then the chamber clicked empty.

"Dinna worry," McShane said, "we'll get you a revolver."

"Damn me, would you look at that!" exclaimed Munro.

Downrange, someone in the pit had raised the red pointer used to indicate hits. The red circle hovered over the bullseye. The weapons instructor picked up a walkie-talkie from the table.

"That you, Bill?" he asked.

"Righto, Colin," crackled the reply.

"Fun's fun. Now give us the real score."

"What do you mean? I was stowing some targets down here when you opened up. You shot the bleedin' eye out of it, as usual."

"Wasn't me, Bill. I think we've got ourselves another Alvin York up here."

McShane looked curiously at McConnell. "Mr. Wilkes?"

"Deer hunted when I was a kid," McConnell said. "Everybody did, where I'm from."

"Your family obviously didna go hungry."

McConnell enjoyed the look of puzzlement on Stern's face. "They tell me my grandfather was a sharpshooter for Benning's Brigade. Maybe that had something to do with it."

"U.S. Army?" Munro asked.

"Confederate States of America." McConnell laughed.

Sergeant McShane put the Lee-Enfield back into the rack. "Two bloody mystery men," he mumbled. "That's what I've got here."

Stern was still staring at McConnell.

"Right," McShane said. "One more stop this morning. The Death Ride. Get your toggle ropes ready."

The Highlander set off across the meadow, moving almost silently through the brown bracken like the expert hillman he was. As McConnell and Stern followed, Mark saw a huge vertical rock face in the distance. Something was moving across it like small insects. Then he realized that the insects were men. He breathed a sigh of relief when McShane turned away from the cliff.

The sergeant marched until they reached the river Arkaig, which was in flood from the recent rains, then worked his way along its bank. The cold gray water tumbled over rocks and tore through thickets with a high-pitched rushing sound. McConnell saw a huge limb slide past like a boat broken free of its moorings.

"Here we are," McShane said.

"Where?" Stern asked.

McShane pointed skyward. "The Death Ride, gentlemen."

Fifty feet above their heads, McConnell could just make out a black cable stretched taut from a treetop to the base of another tree across the river. The angle looked to be about fifty degrees. There was no safety net. Sergeant McShane laid his hand on a plank step nailed to the tree beside them. It was one of several dozen that led up to a tiny platform in the topmost branches, like the crow's nest of a ship.

"Death Ride," Stern said mockingly. "I don't see how this child's game can possibly help our mission."

McShane sighed with forbearance. "When you get where you're going, Mr. Butler, I think you'll find this exercise was a great help."

"You know where we're going?" Stern asked.

"I know you'd better be gettin' your backside up this tree."

McShane took Stern's toggle rope and threaded the wooden handle through the loop at the other end, creating a flexible hoop. "Throw the loop over the cable," he said. "Then twist your wrists into each end and jump. Gravity does the rest."

With a last scornful look, Stern scaled the ladder like a fireman. McConnell followed more slowly. Once on the platform, Stern tossed the looped toggle rope over the wire as McShane had instructed. Then, without any hesitation, he seized an end in each hand and threw himself out into space.

McConnell watched him sliding across the river like a runaway cable car. Stern's face remained confident until he reached a point halfway down the rope. At that moment someone on the opposite bank began firing a semiautomatic rifle. When McConnell saw Stern jerk his knees close up into his body, he knew something was wrong. A few blank gunshots added for show shouldn't worry a combat veteran like Stern. Then McConnell realized what was happening.

Stern was dodging real bullets.

Sergeant McShane was signaling for McConnell to go. His conscious mind screamed that he should climb back down to the ground, but something pushed him on. He tossed his toggle rope over the cable, twisted his wrists into loops on either side of it, and leaped off the platform. He felt the wind in his face, saw the river flashing up to meet him, heard the shriek of rifle bullets passing within inches of his body. Then the river bank knocked his knees up into his chin.

Stern pulled him to his feet. "Come on! I'm going to get that bastard!"

Two bullets slammed into a tree less then a meter away. Stern dove to the ground and screamed, *"Arschloch!"*

"All right, gents!" McShane shouted across the river. "You've seen one use for the toggle rope. Plenty more to come. Back on this side, now."

Stern beat the bushes for five minutes, but the sniper had vanished. He was still seething when they finally managed to ford the river and rejoin Sergeant McShane.

After lunch—a brief affair of beans and cabbage soup—Sergeant McShane led Stern off to receive some special instruction that apparently he alone needed. McConnell was handed a sealed box which he soon discovered held a textbook and a notebook. The textbook was a volume on colloquial German, prepared by some branch or other of British intelligence. Into it someone had inserted a loose sheet headed "Common SS Commands and Responses." The notebook contained some very interesting handwritten information on organic phosphates—the building blocks of nerve gases—and also some schematic drawings of apparatus that would likely be involved in the production of such gases. He wondered if this information had originated in Britain or Germany.

At the bottom of the box, he found a note from Brigadier Smith. It read: *This should keep you busy while Stern capers about in the forest, Doctor. Don't let a misplaced "du" trip you up, eh? I'll see you soon. Duff.*

McConnell spent the afternoon studying in the shadow of an old stone Episcopal church. He was grateful for the books. They allowed him to focus his mind on facts, rather than giving free rein to the guilt and grief that had troubled him for the past few days. By the time Sergeant McShane rounded him up for dinner, darkness had fallen and he was starving.

Near the center of the Nissen hut village, several long mess tables had been set up. They were long wooden affairs, scarred by years of use. He was reminded of "dinner on the ground" at some Baptist churches he'd visited as a boy, but the impression did not last long.

Sergeant McShane had made the mistake of seating him and Stern with the French commandos. Stern had not spoken more than three sentences before an ex-legionnaire noticed his German accent. McConnell tried to explain in high school French that Stern was a German Jewish refugee, but the situation deteriorated much too quickly for reason to play a part. True to form, Stern did nothing to defuse the situation. When the ex-legionnaire emptied a glass of ale in his face, Stern launched himself across the table like a man diving from a cliff.

Before the astonished Frenchman could react, Stern's thumbs were attempting to punch a hole in his windpipe. Within seconds a half-dozen French commandos had come to their comrade's rescue, but Stern refused to let go. McConnell saw elbows thrashing as the Frenchmen mercilessly pummeled him.

Then, almost as suddenly as it began, the brawl was over. The conclusive force was Sergeant Ian McShane. The huge Highlander waded into the mob and snatched out bodies like a man yanking roots from the earth. One well-placed blow dislodged the last of the Frenchmen, and a mighty heave brought Stern to his feet, dazed and bloody. The ex-legionnaire was lying on the floor, his face white, his neck red and swollen.

"What the bloody 'ell happened here?" roared a voice

McConnell recognized as Colonel Vaughan's. "The milling isn't for a week yet!"

The red-faced C.O. of Achnacarry sorted out the melee in a matter of seconds, his last order banishing Stern from the mess area. Without speaking, Sergeant McShane hustled both Stern and McConnell between the trainees' huts and across the drive, then onto a dark path behind the castle. As they approached the river, the silhouette of a small Nissen hut appeared directly in the path. McShane shoved Stern up against its steel wall.

"Listen, you," he said in a controlled voice. "That's never happened at our mess before, and it never will again. If it does, I'll wring your bloody neck myself." He poked a thick finger into Stern's chest. "And I can do it, laddie, fancy fighting or no."

McConnell had no doubt of it.

"You've got a problem, Mr. Butler," McShane said, still holding Stern to the wall. "And like the colonel said, you've come to the right place if you want it cured. From now on, this is where you'll eat and sleep. I'll have your gear sent out tonight."

The Scot shook his head and glared at them. "I dinna ken who decided to send you two here for training, but he must be short of a full shilling. You're about the least likely candidates for an important mission I can possibly imagine."

Just as Stern seemed about to reply (and McConnell was praying he wouldn't) they heard the muted thump of feet running up the path. A uniformed orderly appeared and saluted Sergeant McShane.

"What is it, Jennings?"

"Mr. Butler's wanted at the castle, Sergeant! At the double. Colonel Vaughan's office."

McShane sighed. "I tried to warn you," he told Stern. "I'll have your bags waitin' by the door."

"It's not the colonel, sir," the orderly said. "It's an officer from London. A Brigadier Smith."

"About bloody time," Stern muttered. He shouldered past McShane and headed back toward the castle.

McConnell shrugged at the Highlander and the astonished orderly, then walked into the Nissen hut and closed the door. There were two cots inside, but no blankets. A small paraffin lamp sat in one corner, but he saw no matches. He lay down on the bare cot and tucked his face into his forearms. On balance, the day's events had disturbed him. Brigadier Smith might believe Stern's propensity for violence was an asset, but McConnell did not. The calculated use of force to achieve an objective was one thing, explosive reflex aggression another. For whatever reason—past trauma or simply a bellicose temperament—Jonas Stern was unstable. And an unstable man was a poor leader. Wherever they were really going, McConnell decided, he would follow no orders but his own.

18

Stern found Brigadier Smith seated behind Colonel Vaughan's desk, wearing a tweed coat and stalker's cap. Smith waved Stern to a chair against the opposite wall.

"You started quite a stramash out there, I'm told," he said. "This morning, too."

"A what?"

"*Stramash*. Brawl. Fisticuffs."

Stern shrugged.

"I told you before, lad, I'm a flexible sort of fellow. But Charlie Vaughan isn't. In case you don't know, former Guards RSMs get extremely annoyed by a lack of discipline. And they go absolutely purple over the flouting of authority or tradition. Do you see what I'm getting at, Stern?"

"His instructors are anti-Semitic! One of them tried to kill me. And that French bastard was begging for it."

Smith sighed wearily. "You're not getting my point at all. No one knows you're up here but myself, the good doctor and these commandos. If you happened to disappear while visiting these lovely Scottish hills, well, there wouldn't be much that I or anyone else could do about it. You see? In fact, I doubt anyone would ever find you. So let's just concentrate on the business at hand." The brigadier gave Stern his most engaging smile.

Stern drummed his fingers soundlessly on his knees. "So?"

Smith opened a map case and spread it across Colonel Vaughan's desk. "Totenhausen Experimental Concentration Camp," he said. "In Mecklenburg. Your old stamping grounds."

Stern sat up, his anger forgotten.

"The camp is fairly isolated. The nearest large city is Rostock, twenty miles to the west. What used to be Poland is sixty miles to the east. Berlin is a hundred miles south."

Stern nodded impatiently. He'd known all this since he was a child.

"The camp's support village is Dornow, three miles north," Smith went on, pointing at a spot on the map. "There are German troops in the area, but no elite formations. Except at Totenhausen, of course."

"What's at Totenhausen?"

"A hundred and fifty Death's Head SS troops."

"*Totenkopfverbände,*" Stern murmured.

"Right. And a particularly nasty bunch, according to the reports. The commandant is a physician named Brandt, an SS Lieutenant-General and chemical genius. You don't find many scholars in the ranks of the SS, but Brandt is one. The senior security officer is Sturmbannführer Wolfgang Schörner. Interestingly enough, he's not a Nazi." Noticing Stern's puzzled expression, Smith said, "That's not as uncommon as you might think. At one time the SS was considered by some to be a potential enemy of the Party in internal Nazi power struggles. Schörner is what's known as *nur Soldaten* among the old SS fighters. Only a soldier. It means he's not a superloyal party fanatic. He fought in Russia under Paul Hausser, one of the few SS officers with a real military background. Lost an eye at Kursk."

Surprised by the depth of Smith's knowledge, Stern gave him an inquisitive look.

"The curious thing is why Schörner's there at all," Smith continued. "The rest of the troops are former Einsatzgruppen butchers or career concentration camp guards. I rather think Schörner was stationed there as a spy for the Wehrmacht. The Army High Command doesn't like Himmler having a monopoly on weapons as powerful as Sarin and Soman. I think they wanted an SS officer at Totenhausen who would keep them informed. Schörner's older brother is a big cheese on Kesselring's staff in Italy. Wolfgang had just been invalided out of the Russian theater because of his eye, and he needed a job. Getting the picture?"

"Simple enough." Stern said. "Schörner spies on the SS for the Wehrmacht. What's the inmate population of Totenhausen?"

"Very low. Fluctuates between two and three hundred, depending on the pace of the gas tests."

"So we're going to sacrifice three hundred innocent people to kill half as many SS men?"

"No, we're going to sacrifice three hundred doomed prisoners to save tens of thousands of Allied invasion troops."

"A matter of perspective?"

"Everything is in war, Stern. To Major Dickson you're a bloodthirsty terrorist. To your own people you're a hero."

"And what am I to you, Brigadier?"

Smith smiled thinly. "Useful. Let's get back to business. Totenhausen is separated from Dornow by a small group of forested hills. The only hills anywhere thereabouts, actually. The camp is nestled against the east side of them, on the north bank of the Recknitz River. The trees grow right up to the electrical fence. They're meant to conceal the camp from aerial surveillance."

Smith pulled another map from his case. It showed a close-up view of the hills, the village of Dornow to the north of them, and a detailed diagram of Totenhausen Camp itself, abutting the southernmost hill.

"What's that on the central hill?" Stern asked.

"Electrical transformer station. It's the key to the whole mission."

"Do we have to blow it up? I've had experience with that."

"No, we want the lights burning right up until the last second. Look here." Smith used his pipe stem to indicate six parallel lines that connected the power station to Totenhausen. "These are the overhead electrical transmission lines that power the camp and factory. They run straight down the hills from the power station into the camp. The total line distance is two thousand feet on a twenty-nine degree slope. One night before you go in, a British commando team will suspend eight cylinders of British nerve gas from a wire on the pylon nearest the power station. The cylinders will be hanging from roller mechanisms rather like those used on cable cars."

Stern frowned. "The cylinders roll down the hill, into the camp, and detonate?"

"Basically, yes. Our technical people have rigged pressure triggers on the bottoms and sides of the cylinders, rather like those on conventional mines. Once a trigger is tripped, a small bullet charge blows out a cap on the cylinder head. The cylinder releases its contents under high pressure, diffusing a lethal gas cloud at ground level. It's World War One technology, but damned efficient."

Stern took a moment to visualize the plan. "But if the cylinders are hanging from a power line," he said, "what keeps them from slamming into the crossarms that hold up the line on the way down?"

"That's exactly what I asked," said Smith, taking a pen from his pocket to illustrate his explanation. "It's a rather neat trick, actually. Don't think of the cylinders as *hanging down* from the line—even though they are. The roller wheel mechanism is like a man riding a bicycle on a circus wire. The wheel sits *on top of* the outermost wire on the pylon. Now, imagine the bicycle rider holding his arm straight out from his body. In his hand is a four-foot metal bar hanging straight down. And attached to that bar—well beneath the wire—is the gas cylinder, which is positioned so that its center of gravity is *directly below* the wire. You see? As long as the roller rides atop the outermost wire, the bar holding the cylinder—which curves up and outward before going down—will strike nothing. It's a bloody miracle of engineering."

"I believe it. What do these cylinders weigh?"

"One hundred thirty pounds apiece. Sixty kilograms. That's full."

"Can the power line hold that weight?"

Smith smiled like a gambler confident of his cards. "Do you have any idea what a two-inch thick coating of ice weighs along a hundred meters of wire? Quite a lot. But in northern Germany the lines are designed to hold it. And that's in *normal* times. The war has caused copper shortages all over the world. Everyone has had to fall back on steel wire for conductor material, including the Germans. Our intelligence reports indicate that the wires at Totenhausen are actually made of wrapped steel winch cable, some of the highest tensile-strength wire in the world."

Stern nodded in admiration. "What about the electrical current?"

"It's fairly high-voltage, but that's one of the reasons we chose this method. Because electrical transformers tend to blow out quite frequently, many key power stations maintain a backup set of transformers, ready to go on-line the moment the primary set is blown. Totenhausen not only has backup transformers—they've got a set of backup *lines*.

"Now, listen closely, you can't afford to muck this up. Totenhausen uses a three-phase electrical system. That means three live wires are required to run the camp's plant and equipment. The pylons that support these wires consist of two tall support legs joined at the top by wooden crossarms. There is a live wire running across each end of each crossarm, and one running right over the middle. For a normal three-phase system, that would be enough. But Brandt doesn't want his lab without power even for an hour. At Totenhausen, there is a backup line for each of those live wires, running right alongside it. These backups carry no current, but become live whenever the primary lines are short-circuited. This could be caused by lightning, falling limbs, or—"

"Sabotage," Stern finished.

"Right. Leave it to the Germans to be so efficient. But in this case, I'm afraid their efficiency has doomed them."

"How so?"

"Because we're going to hang our cylinders from one of those auxiliary lines. And there they'll wait, until you arrive to send them down the hill."

Stern nodded slowly. "What if the auxiliary lines become active?"

"Not to worry. The gas cylinders are metal, as are the suspension bars, but the rollers are fully insulated. It's exactly like a squirrel running along a power line, Stern. As long as he doesn't ground himself to a pole or a branch, he can run for miles. The whole scheme is brilliant. Barnes Wallis himself sketched out the roller wheel/cylinder combination. He designed the Dam-buster and Tallboy bombs, you know. Bloody genius."

Stern waved his hand impatiently. "How do I release the cylinders from their positions on the line?"

"Child's play. When you arrive, each roller will be held in place by a lubricated cotter pin. You'll find a heavy gauge rope of pure rubber connected to all eight cotter pins. All you need do is yank the rope to pull out the pins. Gravity will do the rest.

"It sounds simple enough. But tell me this. Why don't you have whoever hangs the cylinders go ahead and carry out the attack? It would be a lot simpler."

Smith looked down his nose at Stern. "Because they're British, old boy. I thought you understood that. Our American cousins have not given their seal of approval for this mission, and I cannot risk having British commandos caught *flagrante delicto*. Also, the men who are doing that job know a lot about soldiering, but damned little about chemistry. We need McConnell on the ground."

"But McConnell is American. What if he's captured?"

Smith hesitated. "We'll discuss that later."

After staring silently at the brigadier for several moments, Stern laid his index finger on the diagram of the camp. On it were marked electrical fence voltages, barracks and who occupied them, dog pens, gas storage tanks, a small cinema, and various other facilities. "You can't get this kind of detail from the air," he said. "Especially that information on the SS major, Schörner. You've got someone inside, haven't you?"

When Smith did not respond, Stern said, "An agent inside a concentration camp! How do you get their information out?"

"Tricks of the trade, lad. You Haganah chaps aren't the only ones who know how to play shadow games."

"My God, is it Schörner himself?"

Smith chuckled. "If only it were, eh?"

Stern looked back at the map. "When McConnell and I go into the camp, how can we be sure all the SS troops are dead?"

"You can't. Not until you're close enough to be shot, probably. That's why you'll be wearing German uniforms."

Stern went still. "What?"

"You don't fancy the idea? Standartenführer Stern?"

"I won't wear one."

"Suit yourself. No pun intended. But give ear: Hitler's Commando Order of 1942 specifies that any troops captured on a commando raid—in uniform or out, armed or unarmed—will be slaughtered to the last man. An SS or SD uniform is about the only hope you'll have of bluffing your way out if things go wrong. Besides, you're a native German. You could actually pull it off."

Stern glowered at the Scotsman. "I'll think about it. How long will it take the gas to dissipate?"

"I can't be sure of that. But since McConnell brought along his special suits, it really won't matter. You'll be able to go in immediately. That should greatly reduce any chance of SS reinforcements arriving from elsewhere before you finish."

"What do we do once we're inside?"

"Go straight to the factory. First, get a sample of Soman.

McConnell will know how to use the mini-canisters and universal couplers. After that, let him take you on a tour through the plant. Anything he points at, you shoot a picture of. Laboratory logs, notes, things like that, take them. Then steal a German vehicle and run for the Baltic coast. You'll find an inflatable boat cached there, and a Royal Navy submarine waiting to pick you up."

Stern laid his elbows on the desk and looked into Smith's eyes. "An inflatable boat? You do know the Baltic coast is often frozen this time of year?"

"Quite. That's why they won't be expecting you to leave in a boat. You'll find the raft cached by a shipping channel maintained by icebreaker. I'll give you all the details later."

Stern felt far from reassured. "How are we getting *into* Germany?" he asked.

"From here we stage to Sweden by air, then—"

"We? You mean McConnell and me."

Smith leaned forward. "I mean myself as well. I'll be bivouacked on the Swedish coast, waiting for confirmation of success." The brigadier could not conceal his excitement. "This is no hop into the French countryside to keep the Resistance in biscuits, man. It's a thrust to Jerry's vitals! If we pull off this bluff, we'll have changed the course of the war."

Stern studied Smith's craggy face. "Do your masters know you're flying over occupied territory? If you were captured—"

"No chance of that. I've arranged special transport for this trip. You won't believe it until you see it. From Sweden, you and McConnell will go into Germany by Moon plane. That's a single-engine wooden kite, painted matte black."

"A Lysander?"

"Right. You'll be landed just west of the hills, hopefully out of sight and sound of both Dornow village and the camp."

"We'll be met?"

"Yes, but you won't know by whom until you get there."

Stern's eyes flickered with apprehension. "Password?"

"Your password for the reception party is Black Cross. That's what I've named the mission as well. Black Cross is the Allied code name for nerve agents—it's meaningless to the Jerries. You'll get a more detailed set of codes before you leave."

"When will that be, exactly?"

Brigadier Smith leaned back in the chair and folded his hands together. "In exactly ten days, Stern, Heinrich Himmler is going to stage a demonstration of Soman at Raubhammer Proving Ground on the Lüneburger Heath. Among those present will be Adolf Hitler. Himmler intends to convince the Führer that nerve gas is the only weapon that can stop the coming Allied invasion. And, my boy, Himmler is *right.*"

Smith held up his hand and splayed his fingers. "Five days before that test—six nights from now—you and McConnell are going in. That gives you a four-day window in which to make your attack. Four days to wait for the proper wind and weather conditions. Four days to convince Heinrich Himmler that the Führer's fears of Allied gas capabilities are extremely well founded."

Stern stood up and flexed his fists with nervous energy. "I want to know about this contact of yours, Brigadier. Our lives will be in his hands from the moment we're inside Germany. Is it someone in the village? A soldier in the camp? Who?"

Smith's face gave away nothing. "If I told you that, his life would be in *your* hands. And right now, he is a lot more valuable than you are."

"I see." Stern leaned over the maps in silence for nearly a minute. "One question. It seems to me that a place like this would have a lot of safety equipment. Gas masks, suits, safety drills, that kind of thing."

"I think the reality will surprise you. Remember, Sarin and Soman can kill simply by contact with the skin. I'm sure Brandt and his staff have special protection, but to really protect the SS troops, everyone would have to wear a full body suit and mask at all times. It's just not practical. There are gas alarms in the factory itself, but the SS troops don't even carry masks with them. If you ask me, Himmler considers the Totenhausen detachment expendable. Satisfied?"

"This sounds like it could actually work."

"It's *going* to work."

Brigadier Smith fired his pipe and leaned back in Colonel Vaughan's chair. "Tell me," he said, "how are you and the good doctor getting along?"

Stern shrugged. "He'll do his job, I suppose. As long as he doesn't figure out that the real objective is to kill people, not disable the lab and factory."

"He won't. As long as you don't help him."

"Don't worry about that. Are we finished?"

"Finished?" Smith slapped the desk with a bang. "Not nearly. You've still got some training to do before bed."

"Training?"

"Climbing that pylon is going to be ticklish, especially in the dark. We've rigged a dummy here for you to practice on. We've got climbing spikes, harness, the lot."

"I've climbed a hundred telegraph poles," Stern objected. "I can do it without spikes and without practice."

Smith chuckled. "The pylons at Totenhausen are sixty feet tall, laddie, and may well be covered with ice."

"More games," Stern grumbled.

"Look, I know you've no use for us," Smith said equably. "We're not too fond of you either, to be frank. But you've got to set that aside. It's Jerry you want to kill, remember."

He stood up and walked to the closed door and rapped sharply on it. Someone pushed open the door. It was Sergeant McShane, dressed for foul weather. From the Highlander's hands dangled leather belts and straps fitted with medieval-looking spikes of iron.

Brigadier Smith folded his maps with amazing dexterity for a one-armed man, then tucked his case under his arm.

"Take him up the hill, Sergeant," he ordered.

When Stern finally trudged into the Nissen hut behind the castle, all his muscles were shaking with fatigue. By then someone had sent an orderly to the hut with blankets, pillows, and matches, but McConnell was not yet asleep. He was reading his German textbook by the light of the paraffin lamp.

Stern collapsed onto his cot and lay staring at the ceiling.

McConnell closed the book. "What were you doing to get so wet?"

"Studying electricity. What about you?"

McConnell dropped the textbook on the floor. "Colloquial German. SS protocols and orders. Plus a little organic chemistry.

"Say something in German."

"*Wie geht es Ihnen?*"

"*Ach,* your accent is terrible!"

"Tell me something I don't know."

"Don't worry," Stern said in an exhausted voice. "I'll do any talking that needs to be done. I doubt we'll have to do much."

"I suppose we're going in dressed as Germans?"

Stern turned his head and looked across the narrow space that divided them. "Why do you say that?"

"Christ, they're fitting us up with German weapons, they've got me studying SS orders. . . . What else could it be?"

Stern said nothing.

"I've been doing a lot of thinking lying here," McConnell said. "And I've got to tell you, this mission doesn't make sense."

Stern's voice was suddenly wary. "What do you mean?"

"I mean how the hell are two men going to disable a nerve gas plant? One man, really. As far as I can tell, I've got nothing to do with the sabotage. There must be other men going on this mission. Men we have yet to meet."

"Is that all you're worried about?"

"No, frankly. It's the whole concept. Look, Stern, whether you believe it or not, I am committed to this mission. But I don't like problems that don't add up. It's the logic—or rather the absence of it—that bothers me. I just don't see how Brigadier Smith can be telling us the truth. At least he isn't telling *me* the truth."

Stern tried to sound unconcerned. "Why do you say that?"

"Think about it. If the Allies possess no nerve gases, as Smith claims, this mission of ours isn't going to solve the problem. So we disable one plant. Big deal. I know for a fact that the Germans already possess massive stockpiles of Tabun, and probably Sarin as well. My seeing the inside of the plant that produces Soman would help Allied research, granted, as would photographs. But is that worth letting Hitler know how much we fear his nerve gases? That's what this raid is going to do.

"Also, Smith claims he's sending us in there to steal a sample of Soman. He doesn't need us for that. SOE already managed to smuggle out a sample of Sarin without our help. I analyzed the damned thing myself."

Stern watched McConnell closely.

"But if the Allies *do* possess nerve agents, this mission is completely unnecessary. We could simply send a sample of our gas to the Reich Chancellery. 'Sorry, Adolf, we've got it too.' "

"The British wouldn't do that," Stern said.

"Why not? We know the Germans already have the stuff. And by doing that we would avoid any chance of a massive retaliatory gas strike. If we cause a large release of Soman in the process of disabling this plant, Hitler might well hit London with every ounce of nerve gas he's got."

Stern forced himself to keep silent. The American's questions were disturbing—unless you possessed the missing pieces of the puzzle. Unless you knew that the British did possess their own nerve gas, but only a minuscule amount. And that in ten days, Heinrich Himmler was going to convince an uneasy Adolf Hitler that the super-weapon best suited to destroying the Allied invasion on French sand was nerve gas. And that the only chance of stopping Himmler was to convince him that Hitler's fears were true: that the Allies not only had nerve gas of their own, but would not hesitate to use it.

Stern knew McConnell would instantly grasp the logic of that. But he also knew the American would never willingly take part in the ruthless attack required to do the convincing. Yet one question McConnell had raised stuck in Stern's mind. If the British possessed a limited amount of their own nerve gas—as Brigadier Smith claimed—why didn't they simply send a sample to the Reich Chancellery as McConnell had suggested? Or at least leak evidence of their capability to Himmler? Why risk massive chemical retaliation by wiping out everyone in Totenhausen?

As he tried to fall asleep, Stern could not suppress a suspicion that even he was not being told the whole truth about the mission. And only then did he realize that the first worm of doubt had entered his mind long ago, probably the moment he realized Brigadier Smith intended to lie to McConnell. Because if the SOE chief was willing to lie to an American to manipulate him, he would not hesitate to lie to a Jew he considered a terrorist.

The question was, what could he be lying about?

Deep inside the Porton Down chemical research complex, a frustrated chemist stared through a heavy glass window at the hairy face of a Rhesus monkey. The monkey was strapped to a metal chair inside a chamber not very different from the E-Block at Totenhausen Camp, though much smaller. The chemist knew it must be his imagination, but he had the distinct feeling that the monkey was grinning at him in mockery.

"Increase the dose," he said.

The hiss of gas released under pressure sounded in the lab.

The monkey bobbed its head several times, but continued to breathe. And yes, it was very definitely grinning now.

The chemist slammed a hand down on his knee, then went to his desk, picked up the telephone and asked to be connected to a telephone number he had been given early that morning. There was a bit of a muddle at the other end, but soon an authoritative voice said, "Brigadier Smith here."

"This is Lifton, sir. Porton Down. We've established a new limit, but I'm afraid the news isn't quite what we'd expected."

"Well?"

"Nonlethal after forty-two hours."

"Bugger all!" Smith bellowed. "What's the problem?"

"It's stability, sir. We've got lethality, and if I may say so, we're lucky to have that. The Germans have had their best people on this for years. Given time, I'm sure—"

"Doctor, you have exactly five days to give me a gas that will remain lethal for one hundred hours. Keep me posted."

The chemist jumped at the sound of the disconnecting line.

"Oh, Richards?" he said to his assistant.

"Yes?"

"Do we have a pistol near to hand?"

"Not that I know of, Doctor Lifton. One of the guards outside might lend us one, I suppose. Why?"

The chemist stared furiously into the gas chamber. "Because I'd like to *shoot* that damned monkey."

19

Rachel's plan to gain Frau Hagan's confidence had worked. She wasn't sure why. Perhaps it was the fanatical vigilance with which she guarded the door each night during the Circle. Or perhaps the detailed answers she gave when Frau Hagan asked about war news she'd heard on the BBC in Amsterdam before being captured. Once she had even sensed a vague sexual interest on the Block Leader's part. In the end she did not care why Frau Hagan had taken her under her wing—only that she had.

For the last two days, the big Pole had invited Rachel to come on what she called her "morning patrol" of the camp. Rachel felt terribly nervous without Jan and Hannah beside her, but Frau Hagan assured her that the children were safe. The "patrol" was really more of a morning constitutional, though the Block Leader did notice many things Rachel missed. She noted which sentries were posted where, which of the three SS doctors under Brandt had slept late, the volume of black market traffic in clothing and utensils and sexual favors exchanged behind the showers, and a dozen other things.

Rachel noticed the prisoners more than the guards. They traveled in small groups, most often with those who shared the same badge color. Asocial with asocial, political with political, criminal with criminal, Jew with Jew. Above all she watched the children. Many clung to their mothers' shifts, as Jan and Hannah did whenever possible, but others seemed to have free run of the camp. Like a grimy-faced army of midget partisans, they darted in and out of alleys, crouched under steps, squabbled in the barracks, spied on everyone and stole anything that wasn't guarded or nailed down, including food from those too old or weak to protect themselves.

Rachel found it all bewildering. For four years she had heard
that the camps in the East were labor camps. Totenhausen was more
like a sanitarium, except that its staff was homicidally insane and
armed to the teeth. There was little to do but idly pass the time and
hope to avoid random death—unless of course you counted Frau
Hagan as your friend.

This morning the Block Leader had ordered Rachel to memorize
the layout of the camp, pointing out which buildings were to be
avoided and which areas were safe from the view of the tower gunners. The task did not take long. Totenhausen was surprisingly
small, and laid out with the usual German precision. In a perfect
square of electrified barbed wire, the inmate blocks occupied the
west side and the SS barracks the east, these alternate universes separated by the Appellplatz, where roll was taken twice each day, once
in the morning and once at night. The administration building and
officers' quarters stood at the front of the camp and faced south, towards the river, which flowed less than forty meters from the main
gate. And backed against the wooded hills at the rear of the camp
was Brandt's "hospital," with the half-buried E-Block squatting in
its shadow like a vicious dog in uneasy sleep. The only building
which compared to the hospital in size was a large wooden barn
which occupied the entire northeast corner of the camp, and was
surrounded by a ten-foot wire fence.

"That is where they make the gas?" Rachel asked, pointing to
the tops of two brick smokestacks that jutted from openings in the
high barn roof.

Frau Hagan quickly crossed herself. "The furnace of the devil,"
she said softly. "Don't point."

"I thought you were a Communist," said Rachel. "Communists
don't believe in God, do they?"

Frau Hagan pulled her gray coat around her. "God may be
dead, Dutch girl, but the devil is alive and well. I'm getting cold.
Let's walk."

They skirted the factory fence until they reached the SS barracks, then cut between the barracks and the dog kennels. Rachel
felt a prickle on her skin as she passed the watchful shepherds.

A sudden wild shouting from the direction of the Appellplatz
made her cringe.

"Football," Frau Hagan said without breaking stride.

Rachel squeezed her nails into her palms and walked on. "What happened early this morning?" she asked. "I heard screaming and shouting in the yard."

Frau Hagan sighed wearily and kicked a mound of snow. "The Gypsy woman tried to run to the wire. Someone stopped her. They should have let her go."

Rachel was horrified. "To the electric fence?"

"Of course. It happened all the time at Auschwitz. It's the most popular method of suicide there. The wire could have ended it for the Gypsy. Now something worse will happen. Maybe for all of us."

"What do you mean?"

Hagan turned her flat face to Rachel as she walked. "If they took your child from you, Dutch girl, what would you do?"

"I would go mad."

"Just so. And a madwoman is capable of anything. Very dangerous for the rest of us."

Hagan stopped, stretched her thick arms, then methodically bent and touched her toes several times. "Exercise," she puffed. "I know how shocking it is. You heard the talk. Yes, the distinguished Doctor Brandt is the pederast. There are some among the prisoners too, but Brandt is the worst. That mongrel Weitz brings them to him. One, sometimes two little boys in a month since the family camp ruse started. So, you see? The world is turned upside down. It would have been better for the Gypsy and her son to have been gassed at Chelmno than to have been saved and brought here."

"Can't we do anything to help the boy?" Rachel asked, thinking of her hidden diamonds. "Couldn't we bribe someone?"

Frau Hagan looked puzzled. "Bribe them to do what? Kill the boy? That is his only escape from here. And if something happens to that boy, Brandt will merely send Weitz for another. Perhaps your Jan."

Rachel shuddered. "What about that nurse? Anna Kaas. Can't she do something?"

Frau Hagan grabbed Rachel by the shoulders and shook her violently. "Are you a fool after all? Never again mention that name in the yard! Never! Do you understand?"

"I—yes. I mean, I won't."

"Since this whole insanity began, she is the only German I have seen do anything to help prisoners. The *only one*." The Pole shook

Rachel again. "Her life cannot be risked in a useless attempt to save a doomed child. Put that out of your stupid head!"

Rachel jerked away, but before she had gone five steps Frau Hagan caught her by the arm. "Not so fast, Dutch girl. You talk of bribes. What have you got to bribe *with?*"

"Nothing." Rachel's face grew hot. "Only my food, like everyone else."

"Sergeant Sturm has been questioning people, you know. He's asking about some diamonds he says were lost in the yard the night of the last selection."

"I don't know anything about that." Rachel immediately regretted her lie. Frau Hagan could order her searched anytime, and she knew every trick of concealment. She would search Rachel's inner body *first.*

"Someone said it was your idiot father-in-law who had the diamonds. You still don't know about it?"

"No. I mean I didn't know he had the diamonds, not until that night. Major Schörner made Sturm throw them into the yard."

Frau Hagan considered this. "That night, after the selection . . . you went to the toilet. You stayed a long time."

"My children were sick."

Frau Hagan's gaze didn't waver.

"The diamonds were in the Appellplatz!" Rachel blurted. "On the other side of the fence!"

"You could have climbed the fence."

"And left my children behind?" Rachel recalled the wild moment of madness it had taken to let go of Jan and Hannah's little hands and climb the cold wire. "If I were caught doing that I would never have seen them again!"

Frau Hagan nodded. "That is true, Dutch girl. I wonder if you have that much courage?"

"I assure you I don't."

"So if I searched you now I would find no diamonds?"

"No."

The Block Leader cocked her square head to one side. "Did you see anyone else that night, when you went to the toilet?"

Rachel felt cornered. She hesitated, but then, feeling like a traitor, she said, "The shoemaker. I saw him outside the block fence that night."

Frau Hagan's eyes flashed with satisfaction. "I should have known."

"You won't tell Sturm?"

More yells sounded from the direction of the main gate.

"Come on, Dutch girl." Frau Hagan pulled her along.

Emerging from behind the headquarters building, Rachel saw a dozen SS men stripped to their brown undershirts charging wildly around the parade ground in their knee boots. Sergeant Sturm was leading one team in a game of soccer in which a couple of large ammunition crates served as goals. A fairly large audience of both prisoners and SS men had gathered to watch the game, as there was no physical barrier separating the SS parade ground from the Appellplatz.

Rachel saw immediately that Sturm and his men approached sport with all the brutality they brought to their normal duties. Two players on the opposing team were already limping from injuries received at their hands.

"That's Willi Gauss leading the team against Sturm," Frau Hagan said as they moved into a press of ragged spectators. "He's a technical sergeant—inferior to Sturm in rank. Gave me a piece of cardboard once to mend my shoe."

Frau Hagan's comment made Rachel think of the shoemaker. Scanning the crowd, she spied him by the block fence, a wiry dark-skinned man standing a head taller than the other prisoners. "Who runs the Jewish Men's Block?" she asked in an offhand tone.

Frau Hagan's gave her a guarded look. "After the last selection, the shoemaker has the lowest number. The survivors will probably elect him. There are only a handful left. He has been at this camp even longer than me."

"You don't like him."

"He helps the SS."

"By making shoes for them?"

"And boots. And slippers for them to send home to their slutty wives. Why are you so curious, Dutch girl?"

Rachel was spared having to answer by the unmistakable crack of bone echoing across the yard. On the field, one of Sturm's men stood laughing and pointing over a prostrate figure. As the fallen man was carried off the field, Sergeant Gauss called out to a lone figure leaning against the headquarters building.

"Please, Sturmbannführer! My goalie's out of action. Give us a hand!"

Rachel had not noticed Schörner beneath the overhang of the roof. The major waved away the sergeant's entreaty, but more players joined in, pleading that they would have to stop the game unless someone made up the deficiency in numbers. Schörner finally stripped off his gray tunic and the bright Knight's Cross that hung around his neck, then folded both and laid them carefully on an electrical junction box.

"Well," Frau Hagan mused. "This might be interesting."

"Why?"

"Schörner against Sturm. Ever since he got here last September, Schörner has been riding Sturm and his men about security. When he's not drunk, that is. He can't get them to care. We're in the middle of Germany. They can't see any danger."

"*Is* there any danger?"

Frau Hagan shrugged. "Schörner's afraid of old ghosts. Russian ghosts, I expect." She chuckled. "For him the danger might be out on that field."

After conferring with Schörner, Sergeant Gauss took over as goalie and allowed the major to take a forward position. Within two minutes it became apparent that Schörner was no amateur. He stole the ball twice and moved it upfield alone, only to be brought to a sudden stop by the rough tactics of Sturm's men, who were expert at "accidentally" overshooting the ball and smashing head-on into their opponents. To the delight of both teams, however, Schörner did not call a penalty, which he could have used his superior rank to enforce. Instead, he played all the harder.

"Kick it down their throats, Sturmbannführer!" Sergeant Gauss shouted gleefully from the goal.

Schörner succeeded in stealing the ball a third time. He moved across the parade ground with deceptive ease, sidestepping Sturm's brown-uniformed men and keeping the ball dancing on the toe of his boot. He passed off once, only to find the ball coming right back at him. Obviously his team believed he represented their best chance of scoring.

He picked up speed as he neared the goal. Only one man—a brawny corporal—blocked his path, but several were racing up from behind. With only one eye, Schörner's peripheral vision was seriously impaired. He counted himself lucky that the two men pursuing him—one of whom was Sergeant Sturm—were closing from his left side. The right side would just have to take care of itself.

He neatly bypassed the corporal, leaving him befuddled in the center of the field and drawing some laughter from the sidelines, but Sergeant Sturm and a thickset private angled in from his left. The goalie crouched and spread his arms wide in anticipation. Schörner drew back his foot and let fly, but at the last minute pulled the force behind his kick.

The ball rolled forward two meters and stopped.

He planted both feet, ducked, and threw his left shoulder backward, catching Sturm full force just above the groin. The explosion of air from the sergeant's lungs silenced the field, so that when he flipped over the major's back and hit the ground the thud was audible to all. The other pursuer stood dumbfounded while Schörner darted back to the ball, drove it past the goalie and into the ammunition crate with a bang.

A shout went up from Gauss's team, though even they were stunned by the major's willingness to give Sturm a dose of his own medicine. Grinning as though he had never felt better, Schörner walked over to Sturm, who lay gasping on the ground, and offered him a hand. Sturm did not so much bat the hand away as refuse it, but his rage was plain. Schörner turned, waved to Sergeant Gauss, then walked back over to the headquarters building and collected his clothes.

Frau Hagan was shaking her head. "Schörner will pay for that one day," she said.

"But he's a major," Rachel pointed out. "Sturm is only a sergeant."

"That doesn't matter. Nearly every man here is loyal to Sturm. You see the brown uniforms. They're all Death's Head troops. Schörner's from a different division, the *Das Reich*. They fought everybody from the French to the Russians. Sturm and his men never shot anything but unarmed prisoners in rear areas. Schörner despises them, and they hate his guts."

"Maybe they'll kill each other," Rachel said, "and we can go home."

When the bell rang for the midday ration, Rachel took Jan and Hannah with her to the soup pot, where a Russian "green" dispensed watery soup and a little bread. She also took Frau Hagan's bowl, to save the Block Leader the trouble of the queue. She had already learned to position herself in line so that her family's ration was dipped from the bottom of the pot, where the cabbage leaves had settled. Still, the food was not enough to keep Jan and Hannah healthy. Frau Hagan chastised her for it, but Rachel divided half her ration between the children.

When Jan and Hannah were asleep, Rachel followed the Block Leader back outside. She had just caught up with her when a shadow darted out from behind the Punishment Tree and blocked their way. Before Rachel even recognized the man, Frau Hagan spat at him.

"Back, worm!"

Ariel Weitz flinched before the Block Leader's anger. "You'd better listen," he warned. "Or you'll be on the Tree."

"State your business," Frau Hagan growled, "then piss off."

Weitz pointed at Rachel. "The major wants to see her."

"Schörner?" Frau Hagan's brows drew together. "What does Schörner want with this girl?"

"Why don't you ask him, my fat *Blockführer?*"

"She'll be at his office in a moment." Frau Hagan glowered at the informer. "Leave us, worm."

The informer scowled, then hurried off.

Frau Hagan spat again. "Weitz is a tick growing fat on the Nazi wolf. One day I will squeeze him until he bursts with hot blood."

"What can Major Schörner want with me?" Rachel asked. "Not Jan? Not my little boy!"

"No, no," Frau Hagan said reassuringly. "Weitz would simply snatch the boy and take him to Brandt's quarters. With Schörner it could be anything. He may want you to clean his quarters. He may want to ask you something about Holland. Then again . . . it could be you he wants."

"Me?"

Frau Hagan gave her a knowing gaze. "The night after Himmler was here, women were brought into the camp. As a reward to Sturm and his men. That was the screaming you heard the night you became door guard. The screaming I refused to hear. Don't look that way. There was nothing I could do for them. Anyway, the women were from Ravensbrück. The main women's camp. I don't know exactly what happened, but Schörner didn't take part in it. He doesn't mix with Sturm and his thugs. Considers himself a German gentleman. Still, Sturm's little party may have excited him. He is a man, after all. Usually he buries his anger in a bottle. But who knows? Be careful, Dutch girl."

Rachel tried to control her rapid breathing. She felt lightheaded. "Should I resist?"

"This isn't Amsterdam. Choice doesn't exist here. Remember your children. I'll make sure they're watched until you return."

"Please . . . thank you." Rachel squeezed her arm. "Oh, what am I to do?"

The older woman looked uncomfortable. "Go now. If you're late, he will be harder on you."

20

Rachel stood terrified before Major Wolfgang Schörner. After her experiences with the SS and Frau Hagan's warnings, he seemed more apparition than man. He sat calmly behind his desk, wearing a clean gray uniform. He had changed clothes since the soccer game. Rachel could hear Ariel Weitz behind her, shuffling his feet. Schörner inclined his head toward the door, which then opened and closed quietly behind her.

Schörner frowned. "A crude man," he said. "But useful."

Rachel said nothing. She found herself trying to guess Schörner's age. Thirty seemed about right, though the eyepatch made him look older. Unlike Sergeant Sturm and the other SS men, Schörner was not scrupulously clean shaven. A day's shadow of dark beard grew evenly from his cheeks to his jawline. The two top buttons of his tunic were undone. He drummed his fingers on the desktop.

"You are Frau Rachel Jansen?"

Rachel nodded. *"Ja, Herr Major."*

Schörner's face brightened instantly. "But I thought you were from Holland!"

"Ich bin Holländerin, Herr Major."

"But your German is perfect! *Perfektes Hochdeutsch!"*

"I spent the first seven years of my life in Magdeburg, Herr Major. I was moved to Holland as an orphan, after the Great War."

Schörner leaned back in his chair and regarded Rachel. "I'm sorry they cut your hair. In this camp that is done before the medical inspection, so I had no opportunity to intervene. The barber told me it was quite beautiful."

Rachel tried not to appear in a hurry to leave the office.

"I noticed you at that inspection," Schörner said softly. He sounded almost embarrassed by this confidence. After what seemed an age, he said, "You remind me of someone."

Rachel swallowed. "Who is that, Herr Major?"

"It doesn't matter."

The longer Rachel stood there, the more uncomfortable she felt. "Herr Major," she said hoarsely, "what is it that I have done?"

"You have done nothing yet, Frau Jansen. But that will soon change, I hope."

Schörner stood and stepped from behind the desk. He was a tall man, lean but strongly built. Only now did Rachel notice the bottle of brandy standing open on the bookshelf against the wall, three quarters empty. Schörner poured himself a glass and drank it in one swallow. Then he tipped the glass toward Rachel.

"No, thank you, Herr Major."

Schörner turned his palms upward as if to say, "What can I do, then?" He took a step toward her, hesitated, then took another. Rachel felt a shiver run across her shoulders. She suddenly realized that Major Schörner was very drunk.

"Did you come here straight from Amsterdam?" he asked.

"Yes, Herr Major."

"This place must be a shock to you."

She didn't know how to respond. "I try to make the best of adverse circumstances."

Schörner's eyes opened wider. "Just so! That is exactly what I am doing myself!"

Rachel's puzzlement showed on her face.

Schörner sighed deeply. "The SS, Frau Jansen—the true SS—was established as an elite order. Like knights. At least that was the idea in the beginning. Lately, all manner of men wear the Sig Runes. Estonians, Ukrainians, even Arabs. My God, when I joined the SS a single dental filling was enough to disqualify a man." He closed his eyes briefly. "Nothing is as it used to be."

Rachel tried not to move a muscle. The change from the enthusiastic athlete of the soccer game to the drunken officer before her was disorienting.

"You've seen the guards here," said Schörner, moving closer. "Scum, most of them. Some were press-ganged from the Bremen jails. Not one of them has seen real combat." He lifted her chin with his right hand. "Does this talk surprise you?"

Schörner's touch had paralyzed her. "I—I'm sure I don't know what you're talking about, Herr Major."

Schörner let his hand drop. "Of course you don't. How could you? While I was fighting in Russia, you were hiding in a cellar in Holland, yes?"

"As you say, Herr Major."

Schörner seemed to find humor in this. "I don't blame you for hiding, you know, not a bit. The world is a difficult place for your people just now." He looked into his bookcase. "Have you ever been to England?"

"No, Herr Major."

"I was at Oxford, you know."

It's remarkable, thought Rachel. I am standing here having a *conversation* with an SS officer. A member of the murderous legion that never speaks except to command, and those commands given almost exclusively to order preparation for death. "I didn't know that," she said awkwardly. "You were one of the German Rhodes scholars?"

Schörner shook his head. "A regular student. A *paying* student. Anyway, Oxford terminated the German Rhodes scholarships in 1939. I was at King's College. My father's ideal of a gentleman was the English public school man. Absurd, isn't it?"

He walked slowly around Rachel. With great effort she remained perfectly still. When Schörner next spoke, his mouth was practically in her right ear.

"Miles from the battle," he murmured.

Without any preamble he slipped his right hand into Rachel's shift and cupped her left breast. She felt a jolt like an electric shock, then a sudden weakening of her bladder. Just as quickly she remembered the diamonds and forced her legs together. Schörner squeezed her breast gently, like a woman at market appraising a melon. She shivered.

"Be still."

Rachel obeyed. Schörner stroked her breast for several moments, then removed his hand. She felt tears welling in her eyes. His hand fell to her right hip. His breathing grew shallow. She could endure no more. Only a moment ago he had been speaking to her like a human being. Now. . . . She took one step forward and turned sharply to face him.

"Herr Major!" she said in the most indignant and aristocratic German she could muster. "Does a gentleman force himself upon a lady?"

Schörner stared at her with a mixture of anger and fascination. Rachel searched frantically for some frame of reference the SS officer might relate to. "Would you have me against my will?" she asked. "I should think that would be like stealing a war medal."

Schörner seemed intrigued by her reaction.

Rachel pushed ahead. What had she to lose now? "You say you are a man of honor. Would you falsely wear a medal for gallantry? It is the same with the act of love."

Schörner smiled sadly, then scratched at the edge of his eyepatch. "There is an important difference, Frau Jansen." He pulled his Knight's Cross from beneath his collar. "Medals cannot keep a man warm at night," he said, fingering the fine ribbon of red, white, and black. "They cannot erase the loneliness of this place for even a moment. But you could, I think. One hour in your arms could do it. At least for a while."

Rachel was speechless. Here was one of the men who had murdered her husband and God knew how many others in cold blood, now asking her to go to his bed. "Herr—Herr Major," she stammered, "I appeal to you as a gentleman. I am a new widow. I am not ready for this."

Schörner's face locked itself into a mask of formality. "I see," he said stiffly. "You are still grieving. You require time to purge the memory of your husband from your mind." He walked to the window and looked out at a squad of Sturm's soldiers drilling in the yard. "How long do you think you will need?"

Rachel was dumbfounded. "I don't. . . . Six months?"

Major Schörner took a deep breath and paused, as if mentally consulting a list of social mores. "Impossible," he said finally. "Outside, the normal mourning period is quite long, of course. Up to a year." He turned from the window. "Here things are different. We are at war, after all. Thousands of women are made widows every day. You cannot let your youth pass by simply because of a little sentimentality."

Rachel tried to think of some further argument, but came up with nothing.

"I shall give you one week," Schörner said. Then he moved back behind his desk and sat down.

"Is that all, Herr Major?"

"Yes. Oh, just a moment. From now on you will receive a special diet. When the evening meal is finished, go to the alley between the hospital and the Experimental Block. Inmate Weitz will meet you there with food."

Schörner picked up a pen and began scratching on a form that lay on his desk. Rachel felt a sudden wild courage, like the implacable instinct that had driven her over the block fence to search for the diamonds. "May I bring my children, Herr Major?"

"What?" Schörner looked up and blinked.

"May I bring my children to eat this special food?"

"Oh." A knowing gleam came into his eye. "Yes, I suppose so."

Rachel turned and stepped toward the door. She stopped at the sound of Schörner's voice.

"If you change your mind before the week is out, you can find me in my quarters. I am there every night. Do not take too long." He returned to the file on his desk. *"Auf wiedersehen."*

Rachel nodded to the door. *"Auf wiedersehen,* Herr Major."

Frau Hagan was waiting behind the cinema annex of the administration building. Rachel did not walk directly toward her, but toward the barracks area. Frau Hagan contrived to walk in such a way that their paths seemed naturally to intersect in the Appellplatz.

"What did he want?" she asked.

"Me."

"For sex?"

"Yes."

"I told you. You came here too healthy. I'm surprised it was Schörner, though." They walked for a few moments in silence. "At least it isn't Sturm. You might not survive a night with him. He's an animal. He would throw you to his pack when he was finished."

"God, what am I to do?"

"You must go to him tonight?"

"No. He gave me a week."

"What?"

"He said I could have one week to finish mourning. As if even a year would be enough!"

Frau Hagan stopped walking. "I think the major is taken with you, Dutch girl. As far as I can recall, Schörner has never had a woman in this camp. And why else would he let you wait a week? He could have you right this minute. There is nothing to stop him."

Rachel drew a quick breath. "He told me I remind him of someone. I think perhaps . . . perhaps he has some remnants of decency left."

The Pole seized Rachel's wrist in a clawlike grip. "Don't ever think that! If you walked within a meter of the wire he would shoot you himself. If you disobeyed an order he would have you on the Tree without a second thought."

Rachel felt herself losing control. As they neared the block, she threw her arms around Frau Hagan like a terrified child. "Why me?" she wailed. "I am a Jew. I thought I was like a disease to the SS."

Frau Hagan stroked Rachel's nearly bald scalp. "That is what Goebbels and Himmler say. But people are people. I know of a case where an SS man actually fell in love with a Jewess. They were both shot."

"What am I to do, then?"

Frau Hagan gently disengaged Rachel and held her at arms' length. "At the end of the week you will have to give in," she said firmly. "This is not Amsterdam. You have no choice."

But as they entered the block, Rachel decided that maybe she did have a choice. If she had to yield to Schörner in seven days regardless, why shouldn't she try to get something out of it?

Something for her children.

It is a curious fact that men who share extreme hardship—even those who previously dislike or even hate each other—form unspoken bonds that last forever. Not because of insensitivity or stupidity do armies train their recruits by driving them up to and beyond the point of maximum endurance. For thousands of years this system has forged the callow young men of numberless nations into soldiers ready to die for their comrades—even if these comrades are bound only by common hatred of their tormentor: the army.

Of course the process that bonds people need not be so extreme. Strangers standing at a bus stop will studiously ignore each other for quite some time. But let the bus be late, let a hard rain begin lashing the street, and the fragmented crowd quickly becomes a group united by resentment against the bus company and its lazy drivers.

It was a range of experiences between these two extremes that began to bridge the chasm between Mark McConnell and Jonas Stern. Though McConnell spent much time alone studying German and organic chemistry, and Stern climbed ice-slickened poles until he could do it wearing a blindfold, the two men found themselves thrown together on night marches, obstacle courses, at meals, and, most importantly, in the dark hut behind the castle in the exhausted minutes before sleep took them. A thaw was inevitable, and Smith should have seen it. There was simply no escaping the fact that the two men had no supporters at the castle other than themselves. No grumbling cadre of brothers-in-arms, as the commando recruits had, no friendly colleagues, as the instructors had. They were two civilians alone, training in a program wholly outside the normal routine of the Commando Depot.

For the staff they were an inconvenience, a disruption to be tolerated only at the request of the commanding officer, who was merely doing a favor for a friend. And excepting Sergeant Ian McShane, that tolerance was markedly thin. Some of Stern's early remarks about McConnell's pacifism had gotten around, and the instructors quickly came to view the American with the jaundiced eye that many in Oxford had. In Stern's case the prejudice was more open. Anti-Semitism was widespread in the British army, but Stern's German accent put him right over the top. He could hardly pass anyone at the castle without drawing a dark look or muttered imprecation.

And so by the fourth day, the two men, so different in philosophy, had been forced by prejudice onto common ground. Stern had maintained his fierce mask of cynicism, but McConnell soon sensed the somber, reflective intelligence behind it. Stern's reappraisal of McConnell occurred more slowly—until something quite unexpected taught him that first impressions can be far from accurate.

At the toggle bridge—a long net of intertwined toggle ropes that spanned a wide stretch of the river Arkaig—Sergeant McShane was taking great pleasure in pointing out to Stern this ingenious use for his favorite tool. Stern retorted that the bridge suspended above the rushing waters had required at least fifty toggle ropes to construct, whereas he and McConnell would have only two.

While they traded barbs on the castle bank, a group of French commandos were being instructed on how to properly negotiate the flexible bridge under fire. The Arkaig was still in flood, concealing rocks that could snap bones like twigs if a man fell the twenty feet from the bridge to the river. A concealed sniper fired near-miss shots with a rifle, and to further enhance the realism of the exercise, explosive charges had been laid in the riverbed. Consequently, several furious commandos found themselves bunched at the middle of the sagging bridge while an instructor with a clipboard shouted cockney epithets from the bank, maligning their ancestors back to William the Conqueror. Every time a bomb exploded in the river, the Frenchmen screamed at each other with redoubled fury.

Between bouts of laughter, Sergeant McShane explained to Stern and McConnell what the Frenchmen were doing wrong. His laughter died when, after a particularly violent explosion, one of the young commandos lost his footing and slipped down through the spiderweb of toggle ropes, somehow catching his throat in the tangle. His body jerked taut like that of a man being hanged—then his head snapped up and he plunged into the river.

Only the observers on the bank realized what had happened, and of them only McShane and the other instructor knew that two men had recently lost their lives under identical circumstances. In that case an explosion had shaken two men off the bridge. The flooded stream quickly swept them past all chance of aid, and their drowned bodies were later recovered at the mouth of Loch Lochy. A grappling net had since been suspended from the iron footbridge downstream, but Sergeant McShane was taking no chances. By the time the Frenchman's absence had been noticed by his comrades, the Highlander had already dived into the flooded river and begun swimming after the floating body.

McShane swam strongly and, urged on by the shouts of the men on the bridge, managed to overtake the Frenchman in time. The commandos on the bridge fought their way over the toggle ropes while McShane dragged their fallen comrade up the far bank.

Even from where McConnell and Stern stood, it was plain that the young commando was badly hurt. Sergeant McShane had all he could do to keep the man's friends far enough back to let him breathe. It was the Highlander's cry for a medical officer that broke the spell on the near bank. McConnell splashed into the shallows, then dived into the rushing water and fought his way across. Stern raced up the bank and scampered across the toggle bridge.

When McConnell broke through the circle of men on the far bank, he saw a young man gasping like a landed fish, but getting no air into his lungs. The commando's lips were already turning a deathly gray.

Cyanosis, he thought. *Not much time.*

The French commandos shouted wildly in their own language that someone should pump the water from their comrade's lungs. The young man's eyes bulged with terror as he tried vainly to suck air into his chest. McConnell elbowed two commandos aside, saying sharply, *"Je suis un medecin! Le Docteur!"* This parted the clamoring mass of Frenchmen. He knelt beside Sergeant McShane and palpated the Frenchman's throat. The larynx had been fractured.

"I need a penknife," he said. *"J'ai besoin d'un couteau!"*

"What are you doing?" McShane asked. "The man's got water in his lungs!"

"No, he doesn't. He just can't breathe. *Un Couteau!*"

"We've got to lay him on his stomach!" McShane insisted. "Push the water out. Help me turn him."

McConnell knocked the sergeant's arm aside, then grabbed the young Frenchman's hand and held it to McShane's face. "Look at his nails, Sergeant! He's suffocating!"

While McShane stared transfixed at the blue skin beneath the nails, someone thrust a small Swiss-made pocketknife into McConnell's hand. He flicked open its two blades and chose the smaller for its sharpness. The young Frenchman's face was turning bluer by the second. Using his left index finger, McConnell probed carefully for his primary landmark—the cricothyroid membrane at the center of the Adam's apple—then brought the point of the knife blade in contact with the skin.

"Dinna try that!" Sergeant McShane said. "He'll choke on his own blood! I've seen it happen in the field. If his throat's crushed, we've got to get him to a hospital!"

"He's dying!" McConnell snapped. "Hold him down!" He raised the knife, blade turned horizontally so as to pass cleanly between the cricoid and thyroid cartilages. *"Hold him, Sergeant!"*

Stunned by the American's sudden assumption of authority, McShane restrained the Frenchman with his left forearm, but grabbed McConnell's arm with his right. "Wait, damn you!"

"I'm a doctor!" McConnell shouted, turning on the big Scotsman. Then he shouted in French, *"Mets-le deahors! Get this man away!"*

A dozen hands jerked the astonished Highlander clear. Three French commandos took his place and pinned their young friend's head and body to the cold ground. With one clean stroke McConnell punched the knifepoint through skin and membrane.

The Frenchman's chest heaved.

"Mon Dieu!" gasped a dozen commandos in unison.

"I need something hollow!" McConnell told them. *"J'ai . . .* shit! *J'ai besoin de quelque chose de creux.* A reed, a straw, a pen . . . *un stilo?* Anything, quickly!"

As blood trickled from the small incision, he rotated the knife blade caudally to widen it. Then he slid his right index finger down the side of the blade and into the hole, drew out the blade, and left his finger in place to preserve the integrity of his incision. He was about to shout again when Jonas Stern knelt beside him and slapped a dismantled pen into his hand.

"The toggle-bridge instructor was using it to mark his charts!"

Stern had already snapped off the end of the pen's barrel, creating a hollow tube. McConnell took the fat end and slowly fed it down the inside of his finger and into the incision, exactly as he had slid his finger down the knife blade. The moment the barrel entered the trachea, the young Frenchman's chest heaved again, then slowly began to fill with air.

"Regardez!" shouted a soldier.

McConnell ordered two commandos to hold their man's legs higher than his head while he squatted beside the man's neck and held the tube in place. In less than a minute the Frenchman's face lightened a shade. In three minutes he had regained some pink and his pulse was strong.

"How is he, then?"

Sergeant McShane had squatted just behind McConnell.

"His larynx is in bad shape, but he's stable. He needs a good surgeon now."

"There's an ambulance on the way from Fort William. Should be here in a few minutes."

"Good."

A French medic appeared and knelt beside the patient. He nodded in silent admiration of McConnell's work, then began taping the pen barrel to the skin so that it would remain in place during transport. Mark stood up and shook out his hands. Only now did he realize they were quivering.

"Been a while since I've done anything like that," he said. "Nothing but lab work for the last five years."

Sergeant McShane's voice carried open respect. "That wasna a bad show, Mr. Wilkes. Bloody good."

McConnell extended his right hand. "It's McConnell, Sergeant. Doctor Mark McConnell."

"I'm pleased to know you, Doctor," McShane said, firmly shaking it. "I thought you were some kind of chemist, man."

McConnell smiled. "You were right about not trying a tracheotomy. It's a dangerous procedure, even for a surgeon in a hospital. I performed a cricothyroidotomy. Almost no danger of nicking an artery that way."

"Whatever you did, it was the right thing." The sergeant's blue eyes held McConnell's. "Doing the right thing at the right time . . . that's a talent."

McConnell shrugged off the compliment. "Where did Stern get off to?"

"You mean Butler?"

"Uh . . . right."

"Right here," said Stern, rising from the crowd of Frenchmen. "Thanks for that pen."

To McConnell's surprise, the young Jew leaned forward and offered his hand.

As McConnell shook it, Stern turned to McShane and said, "I think he might do after all, eh, Sergeant?"

McShane nodded once. "Aye. He might at that."

Walking back to the castle, McConnell realized that he had not enjoyed praise so much in quite some time.

That night, lying on the cots in the cold Nissen hut, Stern and McConnell spoke for the first time about something other than their impending mission.

"I've often wished I was a doctor," Stern said quietly. "Not really for the day to day life, you know, but since I got to Palestine. In North Africa, as well. I've seen a lot of men die."

He was silent for a while. Then he said, "The funny thing is, I remember them all. Not their names especially, but their faces. Their last seconds. It's struck me a dozen times how alike we all are at the end. They never get it right in the pictures. Most men want their mothers. If they can talk at all. Isn't that something? I'll bet they haven't written their mothers in a year, but at the end it's the only thing that could ease their fear. Some call out to their wives or children. I've stood and watched them die like that, miles from any kind of hospital. No first aid kit. Nothing."

McConnell lay in the dark and said nothing. Stern was only twenty-five years old, yet he had seen more death than most men would in their entire lives. He slid up onto one elbow.

"Have you ever helped anybody in that position, Stern?"

"What do you mean?"

McConnell could just make out Stern's silhouette in the darkness, a prone body with arms crossed over its chest. "You know what I mean. Stopped their pain. When I was an intern, I saw a few patients I thought would have been better off dead. But my hands were tied, of course. I just wondered what a man would do if there were no constraints."

Stern waited a long time to answer. McConnell had closed his eyes and turned on his side when he heard a soft voice say, "Once."

"What?"

"I did that once. In the desert. Some friends and I had raided an Arab settlement. Horseback. One man—a boy, really—got hit in the back as we rode away. Half his insides were blown out through his stomach. He couldn't ride any farther. The Arabs were behind us. If we'd doubled up, we never would have got away. Not with him dripping blood all over. Arabs are madmen for tracking you over sand. There wasn't much choice, it was death or torture for him. Still, nobody wanted to do it. We kept hoping he would die on his own. But he didn't. We waited as long as we could, but he just lay there, gurgling and crying and begging for water." Stern paused. "He didn't tell us to leave him, either."

"So?"

"So I did it. Nobody ordered me to. But if we'd waited any longer we would all have been taken."

"You did it while he wasn't looking?"

Stern chuckled bitterly in the darkness. "You watch too many films, Doctor. He knew what was coming. He put his hand over his eyes and whimpered. Bang. We rode away."

"Jesus."

"Not a good thing for a Jew to do."

"Somebody had to, I guess."

"I just wish I could have helped him. Really helped him, like you did today."

McConnell pulled the blankets up against the chill. What could he say? As the minutes passed, he wondered whether Stern was sleeping. If he was, what was he dreaming of? What peace had he ever known? His childhood was back in Germany, in the decade of despair and dementia that spawned Adolf Hitler. Could his brain still conjure images of a Rhineland lost forever?

McConnell closed his eyes. Without setting foot on a battlefield, the fear, the shame, the raw intensity of human beings purposefully killing each other had already entered into him. What lay behind all this? What had brought a Georgia-bred pacifist to a drafty Nissen hut behind a castle in the remote Scottish Highlands? His brother's murder? It was absurd. The entire Western world stood poised to invade Hitler's Fortress Europe.

What could he and Stern possibly accomplish there?

The next afternoon, McConnell was summoned to the castle by Sergeant McShane. When he arrived, he found Brigadier Smith waiting by the main entrance in his tweed jacket and stalker's cap, obviously in a state. Smith tossed his head sideways, indicating that McConnell should follow him, and led the way to a spot behind the castle where the rush of the Arkaig over the rocks would cover his voice. He faced the river as he spoke.

"What the hell do you think you're playing at, Doctor?"

McConnell stared at the brigadier's back without comprehension. "What are you talking about?"

Smith whirled. "I'm talking about you wagging your bloody tongue around that empty skull of yours!"

"Are you drunk, Brigadier?"

"Listen, Doctor. Whatever your opinion of this mission, you have no business infecting Stern with your bloody pessimism, do you hear?"

Suddenly McConnell understood. For the last few days, while he had tried to reason his way through the logic of their mission, Stern had confidently deflected all questions by claiming that his objections could be explained away by simple facts that were being witheld from him for reasons of security. But perhaps the truth was different. Perhaps Stern had become worried enough to voice his own concerns to Brigadier Smith.

"Did he speak to you?" he asked.

Smith reddened. "*Speak* to me? After that Lazarus act of yours by the river yesterday, he sneaked into Charlie Vaughan's office and used the telephone to track me down in London. Had a bloody grocer's list of questions."

McConnell couldn't help but smile. "Did you answer them?"

"I did nothing of the kind. And I'll answer none for you, either. What I will tell you is this: You're not half as smart as you think you are. There's more to this mission than you will ever know, and you had better leave it to the professionals."

"Like you?"

"Right. Unless you plan to back out now. Is that it?"

McConnell squatted beside the river and said nothing for some time. The great manipulator deserved to sweat a little.

"I'm tempted," he said finally. "I know you're lying to me about the mission, Brigadier. And I think you're lying to Stern as well. You never planned on the two of us becoming friends, did you?"

Smith laughed harshly. "If you think Jonas Stern is your friend, you're more naive than I thought. Believe it or not, Doctor, I'm the only friend you have in this business."

McConnell stood up and faced him. "If we're such asshole buddies, like you say, maybe you should be going into Germany with me. Since this is going to be such a bloodless mission and all."

"Don't be ridiculous," Smith said. "But I will be only a hundred miles away. On the Swedish coast."

"That's interesting."

Smith clicked his tongue against the roof of his mouth. "Well? Are you pulling out or staying in?"

McConnell skipped a flat stone across the river. "I'm in. I just want you to know I know you're lying. I don't know exactly how or why, but I know." He wiped his hands on his pants and smiled at the SOE chief. "I wouldn't miss this insanity for the world."

He left Smith standing beside the river with his mouth open.

Four days had passed since Schörner spoke to Rachel. Three days left before she had to go to him. Of course she did not *have* to go to him. She could run into the wire like the suicides at Auschwitz. But then Jan and Hannah would be left alone. In a particularly black mood Rachel had considered running to the wire with both children in her arms, thinking it better that they die with her than have Brandt take them for his ghastly experiments.

But she was not ready to do this. The instinct to live was strong inside her. She could feel it like a separate will, motivating her actions without hindrance of thought. In some prisoners, she saw, this instinct was not so strong. Several of the new widows had been steadily descending into terminal melancholia since the night of the big selection. Soon they would be *musselmen*. The new voice inside Rachel told her to ignore those women. It was an echo of Frau Hagan: *Despair is contagious.* This new voice also suggested a plan to save Jan and Hannah, and Rachel heeded it.

The plan centered around food.

Her nightly trips to the alley for Major Schörner's special rations did not escape the notice of the other inmates, but she endured the glares and epithets in silence. Because what she was doing in the alley was not what the other prisoners thought she was doing. When Ariel Weitz met her with the food each night—good vegetables and real sausage—Rachel let Jan and Hannah eat their fill, but did not touch her own portion. While Weitz stood watching from the end of the alley, she would sit hunched over with her face in her hands, seemingly despondent while her children ate. *Sooner or later,* the new voice told her, *he will tell Schörner you are not eating. And the*

*major wants you fat and soft for his bed, not bony and dry like the
other women. In order to get what he wants from you, perhaps he
will grant you what you want from him.*

It was really a small thing Schörner wanted, she told herself. It
was what every man had wanted from her since she was thirteen.
On the day he first spoke to her, his proposition had horrified her.
But now—though Rachel would admit this to no one—the prospect
no longer seemed so repugnant, especially in light of the other fates
possible in Totenhausen.

She thought also of her marriage: of how she had believed it
would be, and then how it actually was. As a child she had been
taught that marriage was a partnership, and to a large extent this
had proved true. But in the area of sexual relations, sometimes it
had not. As gentle as Marcus had been, there were times when he'd
wanted her and she had not wanted to give herself. And on some of
those occasions, he had not accepted her refusal. He had never actually raped her, but he had insisted until he'd got what he wanted.
And that, essentially, was what Major Schörner was trying to do
now. Or would do in three days' time.

Schörner was a straightforward sort of man, and far from ugly.
And whatever inhuman crimes he might commit in the name of Germany, he seemed to possess a personal code of honor. How difficult
a thing would it be for him to help her? By lifting his little finger at
the right moment he could save her children's lives.

This thought strengthened Rachel for a while. But on the afternoon of the fourth day, she realized how deranged her thinking had
become. Marcus might have occasionally demanded his way with
her, but hadn't she vowed to be his wife forever? Hadn't she sworn
her love to him a thousand times? A few nights of confusion and anger weighed against years of kindness and support were as nothing.
She was a prisoner here. Wolfgang Schörner was her jailer. One of
the legion that had murdered her husband and thousands, perhaps
millions of her people.

Schörner was a killer.

Rachel was reflecting on this when the gypsy woman finally
snapped. For the past few days—ever since her suicide attempt—the
women in the gypsy's block had kept her tied to her bunk except
during *Appell*. But today, since she had lain absolutely still for seven
hours, the gypsy was allowed to leave her block.

One glimpse of Klaus Brandt pushed her over the edge.

Rachel was standing alone near the headquarters building when she saw Brandt step out of the hospital, his white medical coat shining like a bright flag over a gray sea. Almost immediately a bundle of rags began running toward him from the block fence. It was the gypsy woman. She ran without sound, arms windmilling wildly, her eyes locked onto the oblivious doctor.

A tower-gunner saw her first. To run in camp was to invite execution. The gunner shouted a warning toward the ground, then laid both hands to his machine gun. Rachel waited for the rattle that would end the gypsy's life, but another German shouted to the gunner not to fire. It was one of Sturm's dog handlers, patrolling the factory fence. She watched in horror as the guard unhooked the leash of his German shepherd, then shouted "*Jüde!*" and clapped his hands together.

It was the most horrifying thing Rachel had ever seen. The dog bounded over the snow at three times the speed of the gypsy woman. The barking startled Brandt from his reverie. The corpulent doctor blinked at the fast-approaching woman, who began shouting words no one in camp could identify.

The shepherd leaped when the gypsy was still ten meters from Brandt, knocking her facedown onto the snow. Within seconds another dog joined the attack. Like everyone else in the yard, Rachel stood rooted to the earth. Watching the dogs savage the woman, she understood for the first time the urge some men had to hunt down and kill wild animals. Somehow, it was an affirmation that this terrible thing could never happen to them, this thing that must have happened countless times to their primeval ancestors.

When the third dog joined the melee, Rachel turned away and hurried toward her block, where Frau Hagan was watching the children. She did not want Jan or Hannah coming outside to see what the noise was about. She heard someone—possibly Brandt himself—shout an order in German to restrain the dogs, but it really didn't matter.

No one could survive the butchery she had just seen.

Anna Kaas stood over the gypsy woman, working quickly against great odds. The canine teeth had torn much of the woman's skin to shreds, but that was incidental. The real damage had been done to the blood vessels. And of course there was the shock.

Anna risked the ire of Doctor Brandt by clamping a major artery before any physician arrived. Then she set about treating the shock. She raised the woman's legs and covered her with a blanket. In less than a minute large patches of the blanket were soaked with blood. She was on the verge of taking further steps when Greta Müller rushed into the surgery.

"Be careful!" said the young nurse.

"Why?"

"I just heard the Herr Doktor say he would be attending to this woman personally."

Both nurses knew what this meant. It would have been better to let the gypsy bleed to death. Anna watched Greta busy herself with trays and disinfectant, anything to take her mind off the matter at hand, and also to look busy when the Herr Doktor arrived.

Thirty seconds later, Klaus Brandt strode through the swinging doors of the surgery. With his fringe of gray hair, white coat, and Prussian bearing, he was a perfect cinema picture of the concerned and able physician rushing to an emergency.

Nothing could have been further from the truth. He moved to an autoclave against the far wall and removed a 20cc syringe.

"Will you be assisting me, Nurse Kaas?" he asked.

"That is my honor, Herr Doktor," Greta said quickly.

Anna looked at the diminutive nurse, silently thanking her. Greta cut her eyes toward the door, meaning that she should get out while she could. From the main hallway, Anna heard Brandt's cold voice requesting something. She wrung her hands furiously and walked outside.

The Appellplatz was empty. Sergeant Sturm's troops had herded everyone into the blocks. Sixty meters across the snow, she knew, eyeballs would be pressed to cracks in the block doors, watching for the slightest indication of an SS reprisal. She looked up at the guard towers. Every machine gun was trained on those doors. Four of Sturm's dog-handlers appeared from the direction of the kennels, each holding a straining shepherd on a chain leash. None of the dogs wore muzzles.

Anna heard the hospital door open. She felt a brush of clothing against her shoulder, saw the back of a white coat as Brandt passed her and negotiated the icy concrete steps down to the ground. She knew she should keep silent. It would be madness to speak. But she could not stop herself.

"Herr Doktor?"

Brandt paused, then turned and looked up, his face expressionless.

"The patient?" Anna said.

Brandt's face suddenly came alive, like a still picture shocked into motion. "The patient expired, Nurse Kaas. Cardiac arrest, I'm afraid. The shock was too much for her."

He took a step toward her. "It was you who clamped the femoral artery?"

Anna nodded hesitantly.

"You know that is not within your professional competency." Brandt gave her a mechanical smile. "Still, it was a good job. Initiative is to be encouraged. You might have saved her."

If you hadn't killed her! Anna screamed silently. But she said nothing. She simply watched him turn and walk across the Appellplatz toward his quarters.

She went back into the hospital. Greta was cleaning the surgery. The blood-soaked blanket now covered the gypsy woman's face. On the tray beside her corpse lay the syringe and a half-empty vial.

Anna picked it up and read the label: PHENOL.

Brandt had injected carbolic acid directly into the woman's heart muscle, causing an agonizing death that had probably lasted one or two minutes. It was his favorite method of "elimination," as he called it.

"He murdered her," Anna said in a monotone.

Greta looked up and stared as if Anna were mad.

"We're nurses, Greta. Aren't we?"

Greta Müller looked away. She seemed caught between anger and compassion. Finally she said, "Politics. I don't understand it. I'm just a country girl. The Führer says the Jews and the gypsies are an infection. You have to kill an infection to save the host. The host body is the nation. I understand that principle. Many of our greatest physicians have endorsed it. Even Sauerbruch."

Anna shook her head hopelessly.

"But I don't understand one thing," Greta said.

"What?"

The little nurse pulled back the blanket and pointed at the mutilated throat. "This one. She would have died anyway."

"What are you saying, Greta?"

The nurse shrugged and pulled the blanket back over the corpse's face. "Sometimes in life it is necessary to do difficult things. But it is not necessary to like it."

Rachel sat rigidly in a back corner of the Jewish Women's Block, hugging Jan and Hannah to her chest. Frau Hagan stood across the block, watching the Appellplatz through the crack in the door. Every block veteran believed a reprisal was imminent.

Rachel knew nothing about reprisals. She had not been in camp long enough to experience one. Some women had been hissing that the SS should kill every gypsy in the camp, since it was a gypsy who had gone after Brandt. What madness. Madness when fear could pit good people against a woman whose only crime was trying to exact justice from her son's murderer. If Brandt had violated Jan, Rachel knew, she would have done the same, and probably suffered the same fate.

She prayed that the gypsy woman was dead. To be torn to pieces by dogs! She shuddered. She could not keep waiting for Schörner to ask why she was not eating the food he was sending her. She had hoped by her fasting to convince him that fear for her children's safety was driving her toward starvation, and that by offering protection he could bring her willingly and in good health to his bed.

But she could wait no longer. Brandt might decide in the next five minutes that he wanted Jan to replace the gypsy boy in his quarters. He could order a selection and take *both* of her children to the meningitis ward. No, she would simply have to go to Schörner's office today and try to baldly bargain with him. He could have what he wanted. Frau Hagan could call it collaboration—*she* had no children to protect. To Rachel, only one thing mattered. On the day the Allied armies finally arrived—Russians, Americans, she didn't care who—they would find Rachel Jansen at the gate of Totenhausen with her two children in her arms.

Alive.

As it happened, Rachel did not have to steel herself to walk into Major Schörner's office and ask to speak to him. Fifteen minutes after the gypsy woman died, Schörner sent Weitz to the block with orders to bring Rachel to him.

Her first response was panic. Had Schörner grown tired of waiting and decided to punish her?

"The Pole will take care of your brats," Weitz muttered as he pulled Rachel across the Appellplatz. "I think that bitch is in love with you."

At Schörner's office, they walked right past the clerk and into the major's presence. Schörner sat behind his desk, his face clean-shaven today, his tunic buttoned to the throat. He dismissed Weitz and opened his mouth to speak, but Rachel started first.

"A moment please, Sturmbannführer! May I ask you a question?"

Schörner looked discomfited by her directness. "Go ahead, then."

"It is a difficult question, Herr Sturmbannführer."

"I'm not squeamish."

Rachel concentrated on speaking perfect German. "Are you a man of your word, Sturmbannführer? A man of honor?"

Rather than explode with indignation as Rachel had feared, Schörner leaned back in his chair and regarded her with interest. He chose to answer her question with a question of his own.

"Do you know what honor is, Frau Jansen? I will tell you. When our armies marched into Athens, a German officer ordered a Greek soldier to strike the Greek flag from the Acropolis. The Greek

206

took down the flag, wrapped himself in it and stepped off the parapet. He plunged to his death. That is honor."

Schörner sniffed and looked toward his office window. "Do you think Sturm and his men know anything of honor?"

Always Sergeant Sturm, Rachel thought. *Why do they hate each other so much? Why does a major trouble himself about a sergeant?*

"If the Russians overran this camp tomorrow," Schörner said, "Sturm would kiss the ass of the first private through the gate and offer to sell him a watch."

"And you, Sturmbannführer?"

Schörner steepled his fingers and gazed into Rachel's eyes. "Only the day of action can answer that question. But I can tell you this. My word is my life."

"I am glad to know that, Sturmbannführer. Because I have a favor to ask of you."

Schörner's eyelids lowered a little. "A favor?"

"You have asked something of me. I wonder if I might ask something from you?"

"I see. What is it?"

Rachel felt her words slipping away. She had rehearsed them all the way across the Appellplatz, but to stand here like a beggar and offer to trade herself . . . it was too difficult.

"Speak!" Schörner demanded, coming to his feet. "What is the matter with you? Weitz tells me you refuse to eat any of your food. I go to great trouble to send that to you! The other prisoners endure the same hardships as you, yet they have no trouble eating. In fact they gobble their food like swine."

Rachel felt the floodgates burst. "It is my children, Sturmbannführer! My son! I'm worried that—" Her throat closed involuntarily. If Schörner perceived Jan as an obstacle to sexual congress with her, might not he simply order the boy taken to the E-Block and—

"Out with it, woman!" Schörner shouted.

Rachel could think of nothing but the truth. "Sometimes . . . sometimes children disappear here, Sturmbannführer."

This statement took Schörner completely aback. He stood motionless for a few seconds. Then he walked to the door and made sure it was completely closed. "You're speaking of Herr Doktor Brandt, of course," he said in a low voice.

Rachel nodded quickly.

Schörner sighed. "The commandant has . . . a problem, it is true," he said softly. "A weakness. As a man and a German officer, I despise him. However, I tolerate him. Not because he is my superior, but for one very simple reason. He is competent. In fact, he is probably a genius. Can you understand? Brandt is not like Mengele and the other quacks they call doctors at Auschwitz. Brandt was educated at Heidelberg, and then at Kiel as a medical doctor. He was a senior chemist with Farben for a while, after which he moved into pure research. He worked with Gebhardt Schräder himself." Schörner rubbed his chin, as if mulling over how much to reveal. "Research is what he is doing here. Farben provides him with equipment and materials. And what he is working on, Frau Jansen, well . . . never mind. I have forgotten myself in the presence of a beautiful woman." He looked Rachel from head to toe. "You have some sort of accommodation in mind, I take it."

"Yes, Sturmbannführer."

"That would be fair, of course. But I must be honest. The simple fact is that I cannot protect your son. As commandant, Brandt has absolute authority over everyone here, including me."

"But you are second only to him! And I have heard some people say that—well, that Brandt is afraid of you."

Schörner laughed. "I can assure you that rumor is false."

"Sturmbannführer, I think that a small gesture from you at the right moment might save my son, even my daughter."

Schörner made a sound indicating great weariness. "Frau Jansen, I can only give you advice. Keep the boy out of the Appellplatz except during roll call. Make him look sick. Rub his skin with something to give him a rash. Give him lice. It won't kill him, and it might save him. Make his skin look yellow, jaundiced."

"But what about medical inspections? I've heard that they periodically remove the sick and . . ." She faltered.

"Eliminate them," Schörner finished. "Sometimes they do, yes. SS doctors are bloodthirsty, even when working on their own brothers-in-arms. They would rather hack off a leg than try to save it for you." Schörner's right hand went to his eyepatch. "You would come to me tonight?"

"Sturmbannführer, please. Promise me you will try. For that . . . for that I could come."

As Schörner's eyes bore into hers, Rachel felt wretched and ridiculous. What was she offering? To have her body, the major had only to lock the door and bend her over his desk. She could not afford to scream, much less fight him. Yet that did not seem to be how he wanted things to happen.

"Perhaps," Schörner said carefully, "I could help about the medical inspections. I could send word to you just beforehand. You could clean your boy up a bit, so that he wouldn't be eliminated for sickness."

Rachel put her hand over her mouth. "But then Dr. Brandt would see him up close and clean. He might decide he wants him for the medical experiments. Or for—you know what."

Schörner threw up his hands. "There is only so much I can do! That is the system. I didn't devise it. I am merely trapped inside it, as you are."

Rachel let this remarkable statement pass unchallenged. But in a way, Schörner was right. He could only do so much to thwart the desires of his superior officer. It was a miracle he had offered even this much. Of course, he didn't have to live up to his word. And he would probably grow tired of her after a few nights. Then what would she do?

"Frau Jansen!"

"I'm sorry, Sturmbannführer?"

"Come to your senses, please. We are agreed? You will come to my quarters tonight?"

Rachel felt the coldness of a crypt seeping out from her heart. "Tonight," she said.

Naturally it was Weitz who escorted Rachel to Schörner's quarters. The camp was dark, blacked-out to conceal it from Allied bombers. Once she was inside, the physical act happened quickly. The major had obviously been waiting at the door. She did not fully undress. She merely became bodiless for a few minutes, a mind that absorbed the inanimate environment around her. Cherry furniture, of which Schörner had a few nice pieces, scrounged from God knows where. A phonograph, an old gramophone that clicked steadily, insisting that the end of the record had been reached. A framed picture on the wall, the obligatory stern-faced father and mother, with Schörner in front in civilian clothes and a tall, smiling young man beside him in a Wehrmacht captain's uniform. His older brother, of course. Also a little blond girl, smiling at the level of Schörner's belt. There were other photos stuffed between a bureau mirror and its frame. A group of gray-uniformed men standing in deep snow, and beyond the snow a white haze of sky split by bare black trees. A pile of burning scrap metal behind the men materialized into a tank that would never move under its own power again. The men's faces were grim, but every man was touching a comrade in some way, as if to reassure himself he was not alone on the great white plain.

Rachel had assumed that when Schörner finished she would be told to go back to the women's block. Or at least *allowed* to go. But after she pulled on her underpants and rose from the couch, Schörner asked if she would stay a bit. She hesitated, wondering what he could want. Had he not satisfied himself? He looked quite at ease.

Schörner led her into his front room and bade her sit down in a wing chair. He poured some brandy, which Rachel left standing on the low table before her. Then Schörner simply looked at her. To Rachel the room seemed filled by a brittle silence. She did not feel particularly uncomfortable, or particularly comfortable either. She simply noticed that the major's quarters, unlike the Jewish women's block, did not stink of sweat and disinfectant and worse things. It smelled of leather and gun oil and faintly of cigars. While he sat there watching her, she wondered if she was a different person for what she had allowed him to do. She didn't feel different. At least not any different from when she had walked in the door fifteen minutes earlier. But perhaps she was not thinking clearly, like a person who has had a limb torn off by a shell.

While Rachel sat thinking these things, Major Schörner began to talk. It struck her as quite odd, the things he said. He began by talking about the city of Cologne, how he missed it. And then about his older brother. He talked about hunting trips they had taken together as boys. He required no response from Rachel, only that she listen. She was glad he had not done all this talking before. Somehow she knew it would have been more difficult to block him out. To erase him as a person. After some time talking like this, he fell silent again. He studied Rachel with a wistful intensity so great that she suddenly realized she knew what he was thinking. This strange certainty gave her the courage to ask a question.

"Who is it that I remind you of, Sturmbannführer?"

Schörner answered effusively, as if during all his silence he had been waiting for her to ask this very thing. "A young Fräulein from my hometown. Cologne, as I told you. Her name was Erika. Erika Möser. We were sweethearts from a very young age, but no one knew it. She was the daughter of a rival banking family. You've read Shakespeare, I'm sure. It was the Montagues and the Capulets all over again. The coming of Hitler made things even worse for us. Unlike my father, Herr Möser openly condemned the Führer and anyone who supported him. He was an arrogant man—too powerful to eliminate—but Goebbels forced him out of the country in 1939. Erika stayed behind to wait for me." Schörner swallowed and looked at the floor. "It was a mistake. She was killed in the British thousand-bomber raid of 1942."

Rachel listened in amazement. It was all so unbelievable. One imagined SS officers to be monsters, sterile machines that obeyed orders to rape and massacre—not human beings who quaintly compared their childhood romances to *Romeo and Juliet*. Yet Schörner had killed many times, she was sure of it. At Totenhausen alone he had presided over the executions of hundreds, perhaps thousands of prisoners. And tonight he had pressured her into submitting to his will.

"You went to university?" Schörner asked suddenly.

"Yes. At Vrije. For two years only, though. I married before graduating."

"But that is excellent! Now perhaps I can converse for a while in words not prescribed in the manual of orders. I told you I was at Oxford, didn't I?"

Rachel could hardly believe he remembered, he had been so drunk. "Yes, Sturmbannführer. You said you were a paying student. Not a Rhodes scholar."

Schörner laughed. "That's right. My father wanted me to be the German Asquith. Strange, isn't it?"

"Strange that a man like that would let his son join the SS."

"*Let* me?" Schörner slapped his knee. "The old hypocrite *made* me join! It's true! Let me tell you a funny story. Secretly, my father despised Hitler. The Führer was a bounder, an upstart, a nobody. But after 1935 or so, my father began to see which way the wind was blowing. So did a lot of aristocrats, as well. He decided Hitler might take Germany where it needed to go after all. Given that, he decided he should cover his bases. My brother Joseph was already in the Wehrmacht, as per family tradition. He's on Kesselring's staff now, in Italy. And so young Wolfgang was 'encouraged' into the SS. The National Socialist aristocracy. The Nazi elite."

"You swore the personal oath to Hitler?" Rachel asked quietly.

"Yes. It didn't seem such a difficult thing to do in 1936. Now . . . well, let us say that the SS is not the ideal organization for an educated man. Not even for a half-educated man like me. Educated men tend to ask questions, and questions are *verboten* in the SS."

Rachel's curiosity struggled with her fear of provoking retaliation. "But even if the SS began as an elite unit, how can a man of your education ignore the things they have done over these years? What I have seen myself—the stories I've heard. . . ."

Schörner's face seemed suddenly to grow heavy. "There are excesses, certainly. There are things I do not agree with. War brings opportunities to men who in normal times suppress darker appetites. You should see what the Russians did to some of my friends." He curled his lip in disgust. "But frankly, if we win the war, none of that will ever be brought up in polite conversation, much less in a court of law. The butchers will be heroes."

Rachel was too stunned to consider her words. "If you win? Surely you don't—I mean, *can* you win, once the Americans and the English invade?"

Schörner smiled with surprising confidence. "That is exactly the problem we are working on here at Totenhausen. I almost told you the other day." He leaned back on the sofa, a man in a good humor, munificent in his superiority. "What is this power you have over me?" he asked. "You make me want to pour out my soul. What a fool I am, telling all to a woman."

Yet he did not stop. He seemed to enjoy the absurdity of the situation. "Frau Jansen, what I told you about Doktor Brandt's abilities is true. He is a pioneering chemist, a man of genius. His war gases are Germany's only hope of throwing the Allied invasion army back into the sea. Believe me when I tell you that Soman can stop literally an infinite number of troops. It is what we call a 'denial' weapon. No one can occupy the same area it does. And if we deny the Allies a foothold in France this year, we can stop the Russians in the East."

BLACK CROSS ❖ 213

Schörner bristled. "We might. If not, we can negotiate an end to the war with respectable territorial gains. That would be satisfactory. The alternative is the destruction of Germany." Schörner leaned forward. "*That* is why I tolerate Herr Doktor Brandt's eccentricities, Frau Jansen. It is an interesting intellectual problem, yes? Brandt's weakness is one for which I might kill him during normal times. But we are at war. Thus his value to Germany is determined by a different equation. Perhaps by a different mathematics altogether."

Rachel wondered where she fit in Schörner's "different" mathematics. There he sat, a scion of the "master race," having a parlor chat with a member of the tribe he was pledged to eradicate from the face of the earth.

"Sturmbannführer," she said quietly, "are you not in danger, sitting here with a Jew in this fashion? Doing what we have done?"

Schörner cocked his head slightly to the side. Then he chuckled softly. "I suppose so. But in this crazy camp, I would say that what I did tonight hardly qualifies as a misdemeanor."

Rachel would not be put off. "I am a Jew," she said again. "What does that mean to you?"

Schörner turned up his palms. "To me you are a woman," he said. "I don't really care about religion. I never did. Brandt doesn't care either, to tell you the truth. To him we are all guinea pigs."

"If I was old and ugly," Rachel said, "would you still not care about my religion?"

Schörner laughed. "You are not old and ugly. Even nearly bald you are quite beautiful. But please, do not push me on this. There are paradoxes in all societies, Frau Jansen. You did not grow up as I did, so you cannot possibly understand what led me to the position in which I now find myself. Nor can I really understand yours."

"No," Rachel said under her breath.

Schörner stood, not hurriedly, but with enough emphasis to indicate that the conversation was over. "I have absolutely no doubt that these things I've said tonight will not leave this room. You understand, of course."

Rachel felt as if an electrical switch had been thrown in her chest. What she had taken as a strange intimacy was merely Schörner speaking freely in the certainty that she would eventually die like all the other prisoners. She could scarcely believe she had dared speak to him, much less pressed him about personal matters.

"I understand completely, Sturmbannführer," she said submissively. "Should I go now?"

"You may go. I look forward to your next visit."

Rachel turned to the door.

"Just a moment. Take the brandy with you."

Schörner was holding out the glass she had left untouched on the table. Rachel considered taking the brandy to Frau Hagan. The old Pole would have no scruples about drinking Nazi booty. But Rachel could not touch the glass. Somehow, she felt, if she accepted anything material from Schörner, she would be lost. That she might never find herself again, even if she did someday manage to escape this place.

It was only a small victory, but she clung to it.

Outside Schörner's quarters, Rachel saw a man standing in the shadow of the administrative building, smoking a cigarette. She cringed, thinking it might be Sergeant Sturm.

As she drew closer she realized it was only one of Sturm's dog handlers. He did not challenge her, but he smiled in a way that made her rush past as quickly as she could.

T he money's as good as in my pocket!" Sergeant McShane
     shouted.
           Jonas Stern stood at the foot of one support leg of a
sixty-foot power pylon, his eyes glued to those of Ian McShane, who
stood twenty feet away beneath the pole's twin. The huge supports
were joined at the top by a twenty-foot crossarm, forming an approximate mockup of the pylon Stern would have to scale in Germany. Three electrical wires stretched from the crossarm to a second
pylon one hundred yards down the hill, then on again to a third on
the banks of Loch Lochy. McShane had bet Stern five pounds that
he could beat the younger man to the top of the pylon and release
one of the cylinders hanging from the wires.

"Ready?" he prodded.

Stern glanced down at his boots. The iron climbing spikes were
strapped securely to his calves, leaving two razor points jutting inward from the arches of his feet. He would have discarded the safety
belt that held his waist loosely to the pole, but McShane had insisted
he wear it as part of the wager. Stern raised his left foot three feet
above the wet ground and dug a spike into the pole. Then he slid
the belt up high enough so as not to restrict him when he leaped.

"Ready," he said.

"See you at the top!" cried McShane.

Stern began climbing with a herky-jerky motion, moving quickly
up the pole but fighting the safety belt all the way. With every step
he vowed that he would abandon it as soon as he got to Germany.
He glanced to his left and marveled at how smoothly Sergeant
McShane climbed. The man outweighed him by twenty kilograms,

yet he scampered up the pylon with the natural grace of a jungle ape. Stern focused on the crossarm high above his head and redoubled his efforts, scraping both cheeks and inner forearms as he struggled upward.

His right hand had just caught hold of the rough-edged crossbeam when McShane shouted: "That's five pounds you owe me, mate!"

Stern looked up. The huge Highlander was already sitting above him on the crossarm, his bare legs hanging beneath his old kilt, his face laughing beneath his green beret. Stern heard a soft whirring sound and looked down the hill. Thirty meters along the wire that began beneath McShane's kilt, a dark green gas cylinder trundled smoothly downhill toward the second pylon.

Stern reached out and jerked the rubber rope hanging from the pulley roller nearest him, yanking out the cotter pin that held the cylinder beneath it in place. Powered only by gravity, the green cylinder began to move away from the pylon and gather speed. The whole contraption looked something like a large oxygen bottle tied by its neck to a runaway ski-lift chair, but this did not stop it from working with absolute precision.

"I don't have five pounds," Stern grumbled, settling into an uncomfortable perch on his end of the crossarm.

McShane waved his hand. "You can stand me a pint in Fort William. Beats money anytime."

Stern nodded, still trying to catch his breath.

"There's Ben Nevis," McShane said. "See it? I call her the crouching lion. Tallest mountain in Scotland."

Stern raised his eyes and looked out over the glen. Far to the south he saw the wooded hump of the mountain shrouded in mist. Loch Lochy shimmered like polished slate in the pale sun.

"I think you've about got the knack of it," McShane said above the rising wind. " 'Course it'd take you another month to get up to my level."

Stern nodded with resignation. "You're damned good," he admitted. "But why in God's name do you work so hard at it? You're not the one who's going into—"

Stern stared hard into the Highlander's blue eyes.

McShane winked. "Finally figured it out, have you? Christ, it only took you a week."

"You close-mouthed bastard. You're going in to hang the cylinders!"

McShane made an indignant face. *"Goin'*, you say? I'm leading the bloody mission!"

"Who else is going with you?"

McShane looked around cautiously, which appeared ridiculous sixty feet off the ground. "Three other instructors," he said. "We get a little tired of wet-nursing pups like you. This is probably going to be the last real commando raid of the war, you know. In the classic sense, I mean. Hit and run. Shoot 'n scoot, as we used to say."

"It's all a game to you, isn't it?" Stern said in an accusatory tone. "The war, I mean."

McShane's lips maintained their smile, but his eyes narrowed. "It's one way of looking at it. That way, no matter how bad things get, you keep some perspective. But I'll tell you this, man. When the Luftwaffe was pounding London into dust and the RAF lads were dying like flies over the Channel, it wasna any game. Churchill sent us across just to show Britain wasna lyin' down for Hitler. We got chewed into little pieces. I lost many a mate those first two years. I dinna mind tellin' you, the day of reckoning is at hand."

McShane reached out with his boot and rocked a third gas cylinder, which hung from the wire beneath him. "I reckon most are content to wait for the invasion. But we Highlanders are a vindictive lot. To our own detriment sometimes. Smith offered me a chance to hit the bastards where it hurts, so I took it."

Stern had never thought he would feel empathy for a British soldier, but in that moment he did. "How much do you know about the mission, Sergeant?"

McShane gazed past him to the gray hills. "I know all I need to know. Same as you. Dinna look to know more." He glanced down to check his spikes for the descent. "You ought to be glad it's me going. You need all the help ye can get."

"What do you mean? I can take care of myself."

"Can you?" McShane chuckled softly. "I hope you can hide yourself better than you hid that bicycle. I found the bloody thing four days ago."

Stern's mouth fell open.

"Dinna be worryin' about that. The colonel doesn't know. I slipped it back to that crofter's hut for you." The Highlander reached down and took hold of the cotter pin holding the third cylinder in place. "You'll do fine," he said. "Smith knew what he was doing. You're the perfect man for your job."

He yanked the pin from the roller wheel. "And I'm the perfect man for mine. If anyone can hang those cylinders, stow your gear and get out without the Hun any the wiser, it's the boys from Achnacarry."

Stern watched the cylinder glide smoothly down the wire. He *was* glad to know McShane would be preparing the way for him. He didn't like any of the other instructors much, but after five days of training under them, he had to admit that he'd never met better or tougher soldiers in his life.

The rolling cylinder jumped the crossarm on the second pylon, then settled into a steady run down toward the loch.

"When are you jumping off?" Stern asked. "By my count, it's time to go."

"The cylinders from Porton Down are scheduled to arrive in one hour," McShane said calmly. "My lot shoves off then."

Stern felt a rush of excitement. "Tonight?"

McShane unclipped his safety belt, slid off the crossarm and dug his spikes into the thick pole beneath it. He looked over at Stern and grinned. "I just wish I was going to be there to see those cylinders land in that camp. It'll be some show, that. One night only, and no one leaves alive."

"No one but me and McConnell," said Stern.

"Right," McShane added quickly. "That's what I meant."

Beyond the Arkaig River where it bent north of the castle, McConnell wearily stuffed his chemistry and German books into a leather bag and started back toward the commando camp. He'd had enough studying, and his stomach was audibly begging for nourishment. To shorten his trip, he turned into a section of forest known as the *Mile Dorcha,* or Dark Mile. The origin of the name was plain enough. What had once been a forest lane was now a tunnel of overarching trees, with the road itself sunk between high banks covered with deep moss and lichens. It was the kind of place where one half-expected to hear the thunder of hoofbeats as a headless horseman galloped out of the trees.

But it was no horseman that stepped out of the forest to

McConnell's right, causing his heart to momentarily stop. It was a tall man of about sixty, wearing a beautiful kilt, a green beret and scuffed brogues. The gray-eyed stranger stood motionless beside the lane. When McConnell drew near, he lifted his walking staff and raised two fingers in greeting.

"Hello," said McConnell.

"Fine day for a walk," the man replied, then fell in beside him.

"Yes, it is," Mark agreed.

The stranger said nothing else. Strangely, McConnell felt no urge or obligation to speak. The kilted walker seemed in absolute harmony with his surroundings, as if he were as much a part of the landscape as the moss and the crooked trees. In the easy silence, McConnell found himself reflecting on the past week. His time at Achnacarry had been a revelation. The emergency surgery on the riverbank had left him exhilarated, reminding him of what he had given up to work in the labs at Oxford. It had also marked the genesis of a careful friendship between himself and Stern. The taciturn Jew still refused to reveal what kind of training he was doing alone, but whenever McConnell heard the *ka-whoom* of explosions echoing through the hills, he pictured Stern with his hand on the detonator.

Twice more since the episode at the river, he had managed to surprise Stern. Yesterday, Sergeants McShane and Lewis had trotted up to them carrying a massive ten-foot log on their shoulders. Lewis's knee was heavily taped, but he was making a great point of showing everyone that Stern had not crippled him. When the two sergeants pretended to pass the log to McConnell, Mark stunned everyone by taking it on his shoulder and marching off across the hill with little apparent strain. He didn't tell them that during high school he had worked summers at a creosote plant, where with twelve tireless Negroes he had hauled sizzling black poles nine hours a day under the Georgia sun.

And last night, when he and Stern stumbled upon a sergeant giving an outdoor lecture on survival cooking, McConnell had entered Achnacarry folklore. The cook had challenged his audience to guess which animal's flesh they were eating from his fire. When the stumped French commandos—and Jonas Stern—heard that the roasted delicacy in their mouths was Achnacarry Rat, there was a race to the river to vomit. Only McConnell finished his full portion, explaining that during the Depression he had eaten alligator, possum, nutria, snake, and racoon. He earned the cook's eternal friendship by pronouncing Achnacarry Rat superior to nutria, which was a large water rodent of the American Southeast.

Such moments had been rare, though. The uncertainty of their impending mission, and their impatience to get on with it, set them apart from the soldiers at the castle, who knew that their own battles with the Germans would not begin until spring arrived.

"You're the American, aren't you?"

McConnell jumped at the sound of the voice. So smooth and silent were the movements of the kilted man beside him that he had almost forgotten his presence.

"The pacifist I've been hearing about?"

McConnell glanced over at the weathered face of the stranger in the beret, then looked ahead. At the end of the tunnel of trees, an arch of light glimmered like a great cathedral window. "Yes," he said. "But I'm afraid you have me at a disadvantage."

"Sorry. I thought you'd know me by the tartan. I'm Donald Cameron."

McConnell tried to recover gracefully from the hitch in his stride. "*Sir* Donald Cameron? Laird of Achnacarry Castle?"

The Highlander smiled. "Aye. A mouthful, isn't it?" He gazed high into the shadowy treetops as they moved toward the forest's edge. "Beautiful in the gloaming, eh?"

"Yes, sir. The hills here remind me of some mountains back in my home state."

"Where would that be?"

"Georgia. Your hills have the same mist, the same wooded slopes as the Appalachian Mountains."

"I've heard of these mountains. A great many Americans come over here, you know. Searching for roots, they say. Quite a few Camerons were pushed off the land during the Clearances, and many went to America. Some to those very mountains of yours."

The arch of light had grown closer, but it seemed to dim as they approached. "Is that right?" said McConnell. "When I first heard your name, it was a bit of a surprise."

"Why's that, lad? Camerons have owned this land for seven hundred years."

McConnell heard the sound of rushing water. "That's what I mean. You see, my middle name is Cameron."

The laird didn't stop walking, but he turned to face McConnell. "Is that a fact, now? And your last name?"

"McConnell."

"Hm. Mostly Irish, that."

"My grandmother was a Cameron."

"Well, there's two sets of Camerons hereabouts. The Camerons of Lochiel, and the Camerons of Erracht." Sir Donald winked at McConnell. "Let's hope she was a Lochiel, eh?"

The two men emerged from the Dark Mile into lambent winter light. The cool spray of falling water misted the air. The laird led McConnell onto an arched stone footbridge and gestured up toward two waterfalls that cascaded into a peaty brown pool below the bridge. He took a deep, satisfied breath.

"I suppose the men have been giving you a lot of trouble about this pacifist business?"

McConnell hesitated. "A bit."

"Don't think you're cut out for battle, eh?"

"I just think there must be a better way to solve problems."

The laird smiled wistfully. "Aye, you'd think so, after all this time. Men are bloody-minded creatures though."

The light was changing fast on the falls, the frothing white turning silver in the twilight.

"When Bonnie Prince Charlie started to raise the rebellion," Cameron said, "my ancestor—the Gentle Lochiel, they called him—rode straight on to talk the prince out of it. An ill-timed enterprise, he called it."

"Did he succeed?"

"Oh, no. The rebellion was born, and Lochiel fought like the rest. But he knew it was doomed from the start, ye see. Ended in blood and death at Culloden." Sir Donald nodded slowly at McConnell. "My point, lad, is that a man isn't measured by how regularly he struts around beating his chest. A wise man loves peace better than war." He raised his forefinger. "And a wise man picks his battles. When he can, leastways."

McConnell was surprised to hear such a philosophy from a Highland Chief, a warrior breed if ever there was one.

"It's a strange world," the laird mused. "In 1746 the redcoats

burned our old castle. Now Charlie Vaughan and his English commandos have occupied the new one. I don't like it, but it's in a good
cause. Hitler, I mean. I've no use for the man. No use for a German
at all, to be honest. Going to Germany yourself, are ye?"

McConnell felt a shock of disbelief. Brigadier Smith had certainly not confided the target of the mission to a civilian, even if he
was the landlord.

"Don't look so surprised, lad. Not much gets by me. Why else
would you be paired with that German Jew? And dinna be worryin'.
I'm no' a talker."

"It's true," McConnell said, feeling an almost confessional relief.

"Must be important, then." The laird's blue eyes bore into
McConnell's. "Going into the enemy camp means bloodshed. I
guess you know that."

"I'm figuring it out."

"Well . . . if they picked you for this job, you must be the right
man."

Mark set his elbows on the stone rail of the bridge. "I didn't
think so at first. But now I have a queer feeling. Almost like . . .
well, destiny or something. Take the name Cameron. Right now I
may be standing on land my ancestors walked, and only because of
this mission."

Sir Donald nodded. "You listen, lad. When the time comes—
when you get to the sharp end of things—you'll know what to do.
I heard how you saved that Frog down by the river."

"That was my medical training. I'm not trained for this."

Cameron's bright eyes flashed. "Bugger all that! If you've got
Cameron blood in your veins, ye've got the fight in ye. You'll bear
up when the time comes."

He leaned his staff against the bridge rail and pulled a deer-
skinning knife from the stocking of his right leg, then looked
McConnell in the eye. "I wish I were going with you, that's God's
truth. But I'm too old now. My son is about your age. He's with the
Lovat Scouts. In any case, you're a Cameron by one branch or the
other, and you're entitled to wear the tartan."

McConnell watched in amazement as the laird sliced off a six-
inch swatch of his heavy woolen kilt.

"You take this, Doctor," he said. "Might bring ye luck in the
hard places." He slipped the knife back into his stocking. "There's

not a Hun in the world could stand before a Cameron with his blood up. Mark my words."

McConnell stood straight and carefully folded the green, red, and yellow cloth into the pocket of his army denims. "Thank you, sir," he said. "I'll keep it close by."

"You do that, lad."

The light was nearly gone. In the distance McConnell heard a muffled explosion, yet another prelude to the great cataclysm that would soon smash to rubble what was left of Europe.

He leaned on the bridge rail and watched the water sluice over the falls. You could lose yourself in that sound, he thought. In the sound, and the smell of wet stone and woodsmoke and mist. As he stared, a great salmon leaped from the shadowy pool below the falls. Its sides gleamed like pewter dipped in oil, and its tail flashed darkly in the dusk.

"Did you see that!" he cried, looking to his right.

No one was there. Only the empty stone bridge, and the lane leading back into the mossy tunnel of the Dark Mile. The Laird of Achnacarry had vanished. As crazy as he felt doing it, McConnell reached into his pocket to make sure the swatch of tartan was still there, to make sure he hadn't hallucinated the whole damned thing.

He hadn't. The cloth felt reassuringly coarse against his fingers. He started back toward the castle, thinking of what Lochiel had told him. *Pick your battles.* He hadn't picked this one. Duff Smith had picked it for him. It was odd. In war you ended up taking orders from men like Smith, pragmatic generals who assessed casualty projections with all the detachment of actuaries at Lloyd's. Why couldn't it be a man like Sir Donald Cameron who sent you in harm's way? A man of flesh and blood and compassion. A leader who didn't manipulate, but inspired?

McConnell slung his book bag over his shoulder and broke into a run, feeling his temples throb with frustration. He'd had it up to the neck with training. It was time to get on with it.

While McConnell ate alone in the solitary hut behind the castle, Jonas Stern sat in Colonel Vaughan's office, still half expecting to be raked over the coals by the colonel for stealing the bicycle. It was not Charles Vaughan who appeared at the door, however, but Brigadier Smith. The SOE chief wore a heavy raincoat and his stalker's cap, but tonight he carried no map case. He sat down heavily in Vaughan's chair, pulled a bottle of single-malt whiskey and two glasses from a file cabinet, and poured two fingers into each glass.

"Drink that," he ordered Stern.

Stern sat motionless. "What's wrong? You haven't scrubbed the mission?"

"Scrubbed it? I should say not. McShane and his men are flying toward Germany as I speak."

"What is it then?"

Smith's voice carried a note Stern had never heard from him before. Almost . . . compassion. "I drove over from the takeoff point just to see you." he said. "We've had some news out of Germany. It may concern you."

"How?"

The brigadier pulled a folded sheet of paper out of his inside coat pocket. "Three days ago, SOE scraped a Pole off a Baltic ice floe. He'd worked wonders for us, but he was blown. He managed to bring out one last haul. Among his papers were several lists of names. People who'd died at certain camps. One of those camps was Totenhausen."

Stern nodded slowly. "And?"

Smith handed the sheet across the desk. Scanning it quickly, Stern saw about fifty names, some obviously Jewish, others not. There were numbers beside each name. He found it near the bottom of the page, a name that stood out like letters of fire among the others: *Avram Stern (87052).*

Stern cleared his throat. "How old is this list?" he asked in a shaky voice.

"We don't know. Could be months, could be as recent as a week. Is it your father, lad?"

"How the hell do I know?" Stern exploded. "There could be a hundred Avram Sterns inside concentration camps!"

"In the Rostock area?" Smith asked softly.

Stern raised his right hand, pleading for silence. "I told him," he said, staring at the floor. "I begged him. But he wouldn't leave. I was fourteen and I could see it. But he'd fought for the Kaiser in the Great War. Said Hitler would never betray the veterans. What shit. What *shit!*" He stood up and moved to leave.

"Hold on a minute," Smith said. "I know this is a hard blow. I debated whether or not to show you that list. But it's a man's right to know. You may not come back from Germany yourself."

Stern nodded dully.

"You're going in tomorrow night. Almost the dark of the moon." Smith seemed hesitant to proceed. "I've got to say this. You know you can't bring anyone out with you?"

"What do you mean?"

"I mean Jews," Smith said firmly. "No one is coming out of Germany but you and McConnell. If you do bring anyone out, the sub won't take them aboard. Clear? No one can ever know about this mission, Stern. *Ever*. Especially the Americans."

"To hell with the Americans. How can I bring anyone out if I'm not going inside the camp until after the attack?"

"That's exactly my point. See that you don't."

Smith examined his fingernails. "Is the good doctor still trying to talk you out of going?"

"What? Oh. No. He talks. Doesn't mean anything. Talking never adds up to anything."

"So you're ready, then? Even if McConnell loses his nerve, balks, whatever. You'll carry it through?"

Stern looked up in exasperation, his burning black eyes answer enough.

"And the prisoners?"

"I know what has to be done."

"There's a good lad." Smith gave a satisfied grunt, then poured himself another whiskey and took a measured sip. "There's one last bit of business we have to discuss. It's rough, but necessary. And you're the man for it, I can see."

"I'm listening."

"You've been in hostile territory before. You know how it works. There can be no question of either of you being captured alive. Especially McConnell, with all he knows. It simply wouldn't do."

Stern reached into his shirt and brought out a small round medal with the Star of David engraved on it. Smith had never noticed the chain before. Stern worked the dull silver between his fingers, then opened his hand. In his palm lay an oblong black pill.

"I've carried it ever since North Africa," he said.

The brigadier raised his eyebrows in surprise. "Good show. Usually best for everyone, yourself included. However, I doubt whether

Dr. McConnell shares your philosophy of preparedness. In fact . . .
I doubt the man would take cyanide even if he had it."

"He wouldn't," agreed Stern.

Duff Smith sat without speaking for nearly a minute. Finally, he
said, "You understand?"

Stern's black eyes never blinked. "If that's the way it has to be,"
he said in a toneless voice. "*Zol zayn azoy.* So be it."

When Stern had gone, Brigadier Smith folded his list of names
and put it back into his pocket. Then he drank the whiskey Stern
had left on the desk. He hadn't really wanted to lie, but he had no
alternative. In all his experience, he had never ordered a mission
quite like this one. War always required blood to achieve victory,
but never had he seen the equation so starkly laid out. BLACK
CROSS did not require the sacrifice of trained soldiers at the hands
of the enemy, but the murder of innocent prisoners by one of their
own people. Under the cold light of a planning table, it was a simple
calculus of casualties versus potential gain—*enormous* gain. But
Smith had enough experience in the field to know that for the man
on the ground, who would himself have to take those innocent lives,
cold reason might not be enough. In that situation a man needed
conviction that burned like lye in his belly.

He had just given Jonas Stern that conviction. SOE really had
scraped a Pole off the Baltic coast three days ago. And the Pole *had*
been carrying a list of dead Jews. But there was no Avram Stern
among the names. Smith had no idea whether Avram Stern was alive
or dead, and he didn't much care. He'd gotten the name from Major
Dickson in London, who had a file on Jonas Stern an inch thick,
requisitioned from the military police in Palestine. The funny thing,
Smith reflected, was that his lie about Stern's father dying in Totenhausen was probably as close as anyone would ever come to knowing his true fate. And if that lie gave the son the fire he needed to
carry out BLACK CROSS, then the old Jew would not have died
in vain.

"Cheeky sod!" thundered a familiar voice. "Drinking my whiskey! I'll pin your ruddy ears back, Duff!"

Smith blinked up at the massive bulk and florid face of Colonel
Charles Vaughan. "Sorry," he said, rising to his feet. "I was breaking a bit of bad news. A dram softens the blow, what?"

Vaughan's expression changed instantly to paternal concern. " 'Ere now, Duff, I was only 'aving you on. Let's drain the bottle, eh? Absent friends."

"Thanks just the same, Charles." Smith stepped out from behind the desk and patted the colonel's upper arm. "I need to get back to Baker Street."

Vaughan frowned in disappointment. "All right, then. Cloaks and daggers. Did your special cargo come through all right?"

"Fine. I appreciate your lending me McShane and the others. A tough job wants tough men."

"They're my best, no mistake. And no one will ever know they were gone, Duff. Rest assured of that."

"Thanks, old man."

Smith stepped through the door, then turned back, his lips pursed thoughtfully. "You know, Charles, it's frightening how committed some of these Jews are. Cold-blooded as Gurkhas when it comes to the killing. We'd better look to our guns in Palestine after the war's over."

Vaughan rubbed his square chin. "I wouldn't lose sleep over that, Duff. I don't think Adolf's going to leave enough of them alive to start a riot, much less a war."

SS Oberscharführer Willi Gauss peered through the trees into darkness. Then he turned back and looked deeper into the forest, at the house he had left behind. Through the pouring rain he could see that Frau Kleist had already switched off the lamps. With a satisfied sigh he stepped out of the trees and began following the narrow footpath that led around the wooded hills and back to Totenhausen.

It would take him forty minutes of trudging through wind and rain to reach the camp, but he didn't really care. His trips to Frau Kleist's engendered an entirely different sort of fatigue than that produced by close-order drill. Frau Kleist's husband was captain of U-238, stationed in the Gulf of Mexico. But the "old man" hadn't been home for eighteen months, and his wife was not the type to martyr her sexuality for the German Navy. Willi thought the situation funny. Sybille Kleist hated the sea, but she'd married a submarine captain because she loved his dashing uniform. So typically German! Claiming that her husband didn't get home frequently enough to warrant living in a seaport, she had chosen to live alone in a very comfortable house outside her home village of Dornow.

The captain's misfortune was Willi Gauss's salvation. Sybille Kleist was insatiable in bed. Willi was twenty-three years old, she forty. Yet Sybille drained him to exhaustion twice a week, sometimes three times. Some nights she would not even let him step outside the house to have a pee. She waited for this need to make him hard, then used him again. And Willi wasn't complaining. Only lately had she begun to talk nonsense. She claimed she loved him. Even at twenty-three Willi knew that was dangerous. When the war was over, Captain Johann Kleist would return. U-boat captains were notoriously proud and tough men. Willi planned to have broken off the affair long before that day. Still, one or two more trips to Sybille's bed wouldn't make the ending any more difficult.

As he approached a dogleg on the dark path, he heard a muted thump somewhere ahead. It sounded vaguely familiar, but in the rain he couldn't place the sound. As he rounded the turn, he heard a swish in the trees to his left. Then another thump. Had Sergeant Sturm finally decided to follow him and see what he was up to in the forest at night?

Seconds later Willi stopped dead in the slushy path. Ten meters away stood a giant of a man wearing a dark uniform. Only the whites of two eyes flickered in the space where the face should have been. When Willi saw the parachute and shroud lines flap in the wind, a small voice in his brain said *Kommando*. He discounted it. After all, he was standing on German soil, far from any battlefront. Perhaps Major Schörner had laid on some type of exercise to test the Totenhausen guards. This thought stayed Willi's hand for a moment. Then he grabbed for the holster on his belt.

A bright flash bloomed in front of the parachutist.

Willi felt a tremendous blow in the stomach. Then he was looking up into the stormy sky over Mecklenburg. The parachutist bent over him. Willi felt more puzzled than afraid. And tired. Unbelievably tired. As he stared upward, the blacked-out face above him swirled, disappeared, then coalesced into the soft features of Sybille Kleist. She looked different somehow. She looked . . . beautiful. As he lost consciousness, Willi realized that perhaps he loved her after all.

"He's dead, Ian," said a voice in English.

Sergeant McShane kicked the body. It didn't move. "Make sure," he ordered.

A dark figure dropped to the ground and drove a dagger into the fallen German's heart.

"Papers," McShane said.

The kneeling figure rifled the dead man's pockets and came up with a brown leather wallet. "He's a sergeant. SS Oberscharführer Willi Gauss. Here's a ration card with the word Totenhausen."

McShane nodded. "I dinna think a lone sergeant with a pistol constitutes a patrol, Colin. Still, someone might be expecting him back at camp."

The Achnacarry weapons instructor looked up from Willi Gauss's corpse. "I smell liquor on him, Ian."

McShane watched the path while he freed himself from his parachute harness. Within seconds two more shadows raced up and stopped beside him. Both men instructors from Achnacarry. One was Alick Cochrane—another Highlander built on the McShane model—the other John Lewis, the judo instructor Stern had embarrassed on the first day of training. By taping his knee, exercising it furiously each day and packing it in ice each night, Lewis had made good his promise to be fit enough for the mission.

"Do you know where we are, Ian?" Alick Cochrane asked.

"Between the two main groups of hills. West of the village and the camp, as planned, but we're too far south. Bloody storm. Still, it could have been worse, jumping blind like that."

"Aye," Cochrane agreed. "I dinna think I could have done it if you hadn't jumped first."

"Where are the cylinders and the other gear?" asked Lewis.

McShane looked up at the dark hills and shielded his eyes from the driving rain. "Should be north of us, on the plain. Where we're supposed to be. The electrical station should be at the top of these hills to our left. Due east."

Colin Munro wiped his dagger clean and rose to his feet. "How do you want to play it, Ian?"

McShane looked down at the dead man in the path and forced himself to think clearly. From the moment they entered German airspace things had begun going wrong. They'd flown out of Wick airbase in Scotland, in the most secret aircraft of the Special Duties Squadron, a Luftwaffe JU-88A6 that had forced-landed in Cornwall and then been refitted by SOE for high-priority missions into Europe. The Junkers and a German-speaking RAF pilot had carried the team unchallenged over the occupied Low Countries, but the weather soon intervened. A Baltic storm had unexpectedly veered south and settled like a wall over the old German border. The pilot wanted to turn back, but McShane had forced him to fly straight into the storm. Using the Recknitz River as a landmark, he was able to bring the commandos almost directly over their target.

They had jumped blind, without flares or radio to guide them, and miraculously landed without injury. However, their cargo chutes and gas cylinders had been dropped too long after them. McShane knew he could eventually locate the cargo chutes; he'd watched them falling as long as he could. The dead man at his feet was the problem. Oberscharführer Willi Gauss could wreck the entire mission before McConnell and Stern even reached Germany, simply by having been in the wrong place at the wrong time. McShane glanced around the dark forest. Someone could easily have heard the fatal shots fired. The silencers on the Stens were far from silent.

"Ian?" Alick Cochrane asked gently.

"We bury him in the woods," McShane barked. "Right here. Bury our chutes in the same hole. No time for anything else. Then we'll retrieve the cylinders, bury the cargo chutes and move up the hill."

"Those cylinders," said Colin Munro. "I'll bet if we ditched the carrying poles, and each of us took a cylinder on his shoulder, we could cut the transport time in half. Especially through these woods."

"Those bloody tanks are heavy," Lewis reminded them.

"No tougher than the logs at Achnacarry," said McShane. "Will your knee take the weight then, John?"

"I'll manage."

"Right. This is where we live up to all that blarney we give the recruits about—"

"Everybody down!"

McShane hit the wet snow beside Willi Gauss's corpse. "What is it, Alick?"

Cochrane grabbed his arm and pointed toward the woods.

Forty yards to the north, a yellow light had appeared in the trees. After thirty seconds of absolute concentration, McShane decided the light was stationary.

"What do we do?" Lewis asked.

"Keep your bloody mouth shut and pray it goes away."

Sybille Kleist stood at the front window of her cottage and peered into the darkness. She knew the sounds of her forest, and the brief *Brrat!* that had punctuated the night after her lovely Willi left was not part of the normal Mecklenburg nocturne. She wondered if her paramour might be returning for one more round of lovemaking—she hoped so—but Willi did not reappear.

She took a drag on her cigarette and wished again for a telephone. Not that she could call anyone about her fears. They might stumble onto Willi, and that would be that. Life was becoming far too complicated. What would she do when her husband returned? Divorcing a heroic U-boat captain would brand her as a faithless, unpatriotic slut, no matter how boring the man was.

Nothing ever worked out as it should.

After another anxious minute of watching and listening, Sybille reluctantly went back to bed and lit a second cigarette. The sheets were still damp from Willi's enthusiastic attentions. Thinking of him, she remembered the sharp sound from the path. It was probably only a stag, she told herself, scraping his antlers on a tree. But she would be glad when she saw Willi again, all the same.

"Everybody up," McShane ordered softly. "We've only got seven hours till dawn. After we've hung the cylinders and stowed the radio, we've still got to make it to the beach."

Colin Munro pulled a folding spade out of his pack. "Let's haul this bastard into the trees and get him buried."

It took ninety-six minutes to bury Willi Gauss, find all eight cylinders, attach the roller mechanisms and suspension arms to the cylinder heads and bury the cotton cargo chutes that had brought them all down. It required a further two hours to lug the eight cylinders—plus one box that was to be cached for Stern and McConnell—to the top of the highest hill.

They set up their base at the foot of the first pylon beyond the transformer station fence. The station itself was blacked out to keep it from the eyes of Allied bomber formations. A deep humming in the forest told the commandos that it was functioning, but a quick recon by Cochrane confirmed that it was deserted.

Lewis grumbled that to climb the pylon and work around the high-voltage wires in the rain was suicide. Ignoring him completely, McShane donned spikes and harness, tied a long coiled rope to his belt, and quickly climbed one of the sixty-foot support poles. Colin Munro was right on his heels. At the top, buffeted by wind and icy rain, McShane tied his toggle rope around the crossarm as a safety measure, then uncoiled the long rope and used it to haul up the block and tackle necessary to hoist the gas cylinders to the top of the pylon.

The commandos worked mostly in silence, albeit at a frantic pace. They had rehearsed the operation a dozen times at Achnacarry. Cochrane and Lewis attached the cylinder/roller wheel combinations at ground level, then used the block and tackle to haul the apparatus to the top of the pylon. McShane and Colin Munro handled the transfer to the auxiliary conductor wires.

At Achnacarry, Munro had likened the transfer process to hanging a 130-pound Christmas ornament on a tightrope. The cylinder was the ornament, and the roller wheel and suspension bar formed the hook. The analogy was apt, and it stuck. Hanging the ornament required perfect balance and enormous strength, as it had to be lifted off of the tackle hook that had brought it up to the crossarm, then raised still higher and set down on the outermost auxiliary wire—all without man or metal touching the live wire that ran just inches away.

McShane provided the strength, Munro the balance. Once the roller wheel had been fitted onto the wire, Munro would climb from the crossarm onto the cylinder itself, while McShane held both man and machine in place with a rubber rope attached to a hook on the cylinder's bottom. Then McShane would let the cylinder—with Munro astride it—roll down a predetermined distance from the crossarm. When it stopped, Munro would remove a lubricated cotter pin from a pouch on his belt and fit it through a hole in the roller wheel. Then he would simultaneously arm the six pressure triggers that protruded from the hard wire netting covering each cylinder. The final step was to attach clips on a heavy gauge rubber rope to the oversized ring at the end of the cotter pin. It was this rope—attached in reverse sequence, so that the cylinder farthest from the pylon would be freed first—that Jonas Stern would use to initiate the gas attack.

Everything went according to plan until the last cylinder. McShane and Munro had decided to rest for sixty seconds before fitting the last tank into place. It hung just beneath them, still suspended from the block and tackle controlled by Cochrane and Lewis below. The two men were resting side by side on the crossbeam—McShane sitting, and Munro squatting with uncanny balance—when they heard a loud boom from the power station behind them.

Whether it was a lightning strike or a limb that had fallen across a live wire, neither man knew, but Ian McShane grunted explosively as the auxiliary wire energized and the rubber rope came alive in his hands. The Highlander did not know he had made a sound; he knew only that his arm had been yanked by a gorilla, so he tried to yank back. Then suddenly the current was gone and he toppled off the crossarm.

His toggle rope saved him. Tied from his belt to the crossarm, it held him suspended fifty-seven feet above the ground, in a perfect position to watch his mission end in catastrophe. He stared helplessly as the farthest cylinder from the crossarm began to roll down the wire toward Totenhausen.

Then he saw the most remarkable feat of bravery or madness he had ever witnessed. A black shadow flew through the air above him and caught itself on the four-foot suspension bar between the moving roller wheel and the cylinder head. At first he thought the shadow was an owl or a nighthawk.

Then he realized it was Colin Munro.

The weapons instructor had heard McShane's grunt and seen him try to jerk free, in the process yanking the pin from the cylinder farthest from the crossarm. Without an instant's reflection Munro had leaped off the crossarm.

McShane stretched out his hand in a futile attempt to snatch Munro back, but the moment was past. Man and machine trundled away down the wire, quickly gathering speed. Seconds later he lost sight of both in the darkness.

Forty yards down the auxiliary line, rolling rapidly toward the second pylon, Colin Munro felt electricity crackle in his hair. The knowledge that the wire above him was live—that he *himself* was "live"—nearly made him lose his stomach. It was a miracle he was not dead already, in that he had landed atop the cylinder without tripping one of the armed triggers. Yet he knew that for the next few seconds, at least, he was safe. Just as a bird can perch on a live conductor wire, so can a man if he is not grounded and if the voltage is not too high. This knowledge calmed him long enough to make some very quick calculations.

He had perhaps thirty seconds before the roller wheel reached the next pylon, smashed the porcelain insulator there and shorted out the entire system. Then his "Christmas ornament" would roll the remaining distance down to Totenhausen, crash to the ground and detonate with him aboard, filling his lungs with deadly nerve gas—if he had not already been killed by the fall. The mission would be blown, his friends hunted down and killed. All he could hear was his own voice saying something he had told the Achnacarry recruits a thousand times: *No matter how well we train you, lads, there will always arise a situation for which you cannot be prepared. It is then that the men separate themselves from the boys. . . .*

Steeling himself against pain, Munro clutched the suspension bar in his hands and swung both legs up and over the conductor wire to try to slow his descent. The friction of the wrapped steel wire burned right through his woolen trouser legs and his skin. The cylinder slowed, but not enough. When the wire sliced though his calf muscles to the bone, Munro screamed, and he knew then that he did not have the courage to mutilate his hands the same way.

He was less then forty feet from the second pylon when he remembered his toggle rope. With his left hand he reached behind him and snatched it off his belt. Then he swung the wooden handle over the wire, just ahead of the roller wheel.

The wheel snapped the handle like a twig, but the toggle rope itself tangled in the aluminum forks and began to foul the roller mechanism. The cylinder skidded for two yards, then began rolling again. This final motion jerked the remainder of the toggle rope up into the mechanism.

The rope took Colin Munro's arm with it. His hand went under the wheel and snapped with a louder crack than the wooden handle had made. Roller and cylinder skidded down the last ten feet, dragging the flailing commando behind it.

Just before it struck the crossarm, the wheel jerked to a stop. Colin Munro did not. His body was flung up over the pulley and onto the crossarm, closing a circuit between the live wire and the earth.

From two hundred feet up the hill, Ian McShane saw a bright yellow flash with a sizzling blue core. Then he saw the distant lights of Totenhausen dim once, twice . . . and come back on.

McShane "burned" the pole in his haste to get to the ground.

Creosote and splinters raked his arms and face as he slid earthward. When his boots hit the snow, he raced down the hill, leaving Cochrane and Lewis to tie off the rope holding the final cylinder in place.

At the foot of the next pylon, McShane found his friend's body. Munro was lying on his stomach. His right hand was mangled, the arm torn and broken, and his tattered trouser legs were soaked in blood. The air smelled of ozone, as if a bolt of lightning had struck here. Munro himself smelled of burnt hair and cooked flesh. McShane dropped to his knees and felt for a carotid pulse, knowing it was useless.

He crouched there thinking until Cochrane and Lewis appeared.

"What the hell happened, Ian?" Alick asked breathlessly.

"Damn damn *damn!*" McShane cursed. "The auxiliaries energized. Shocked me blind. I accidentally jerked out one of the pins. My rubber gloves must have been dirty, and let the current bleed up to my arm. The cylinder got away, but Colin jumped out onto it. By God, he stopped the bloody thing."

McShane stood and peered into the darkness high above them. "That looks like what's left of a toggle rope up there. Colin managed to foul the wheel with it."

"Damn me," muttered Cochrane, looking closer at Munro's body.

"He grounded himself on the pole," said McShane. "He was dead before he hit the ground."

"What the hell happened to his foot?" asked Lewis.

Munro's right foot was bare and split open at the ankle, as if it had burst from within.

"The current must have come out there," McShane said. "Blew his damn boot off. Either I didna catch the full current, or it must have traveled down an arm and a leg on the same side. Missed my vitals. Colin wasn't so lucky."

"No," Cochrane murmured. "But he saved the mission, Ian. He saved *us.*"

"That he did, Alick." McShane waited until he knew his voice was steady. "But we've still got two cylinders to hang. The one back there and the one over our heads."

"What about the Germans?" asked Lewis. "I saw the lights flicker down below."

McShane walked over to the nearest support pole and jammed one of his spikes into the wood. "Either they noticed or they didn't. If they come, it's a fight we'll be givin' them. If not, we'll finish the job. Give me your rope."

Lewis handed over a long coil.

"I'm going to cut Colin's toggle rope free. Then we'll use this rope to tow the cylinder back up and pin it beside the others."

Alick Cochrane stared. It was something to witness the kind of determination that could block out a dead comrade and push on with an impossible mission. But he knew his friend wasn't thinking clearly. "Ian," he said gently, "if we try to tow the thing, we'll be electrocuted ourselves."

"I dinna think the auxiliary wires are live anymore," McShane said. "Whatever shorted the main lines was temporary, because Colin shorted the auxiliaries and the lights are back on below."

Cochrane considered this. "Colin's body may only have faulted the backups for a second, Ian. They could still be live."

"Well then . . . I'll just jump clear out onto the cylinder, like Colin did, and pin the bastard right where it is. I'll use something easily breakable, like a heavy twig. The momentum of the other cylinders will knock it free when the time comes."

Cochrane began scouring the snow for a suitable stick.

"What about Colin?" Lewis asked. "You want me to bury him while you're up there?"

McShane had already driven both spikes into the pole and started climbing, but he stopped and looked down, finding Lewis's eye. "By God, if we can break our backs to haul gas cylinders, John, we can haul Colin to the beach. He'll be buried in Scotland or I'll die gettin' him there."

Cochrane handed two twigs up to McShane. "It's sixteen miles to the beach, Ian."

The big Highlander's eyes narrowed. "Then we've no time to waste, have we?"

26

Sergeant Gunther Sturm strode with great satisfaction through Totenhausen Camp. It was a fine morning with fine prospects. The arrogant bastard who had been riding him since September had finally made a mistake. He had taken a fancy to the bald Jewess who strutted around the camp like a princess. And that made him vulnerable.

Schörner had been tolerable up until the night Himmler came, allowing Sturm to run the camp as he had before the major's arrival from Russia. There had been some misunderstandings in the beginning, but once Sturm realized it was a matter of principle with Schörner not to profit from the prisoners' bad luck—and not simply a matter of greasing his palm—Sturm had kept a low profile and limited his looting to easily concealable and highly profitable items. Like diamonds. The two men had never gotten along personally, but who ever said officers and noncoms had to be friends?

It was all the old Dutch Jew's fault. He had shoved the diamonds into Sturm's hand just as Schörner blundered up to see it. And of course the major had reminded him of their previous misunderstanding, holding his past mistakes over his head just like every officer loved to do. The bastard wanted Sturm to know he could be cashiered for looting anytime Schörner chose.

But the major had made his own mistake now. Sleeping with a Jewess! Raping one in the heat of action was one thing, but this was something different. Three times already Sturm's men had reported seeing the Jansen woman leaving Schörner's quarters late at night. The only question had been how best to respond.

The normal procedure would be to report Schörner to the Herr

Doktor. But denouncing an officer for violations of the Nuremberg racial laws was a tricky business when the man you had to denounce him to was guilty of the same crime, and to an even more disgusting degree. Sturm had considered going outside the chain of command and reporting Schörner to a higher SS authority—perhaps Colonel Beck at Peenemünde—but breaking the chain of command was practically a crime in itself. On top of that, Schörner came from a wealthy family. There was no telling how much influence his father might be able to bring to bear in Berlin—not to mention his stinking Knight's Cross.

No, there was only one way. Private satisfaction. And Sturm had come up with the perfect answer. He would provoke the Jansen woman into some desperate act. Then he would be fully within his rights when he shot her. Brandt would have no complaint, and Schörner could do nothing without admitting he'd become romantically entangled with a Jewess. It rankled Sturm to no end that he had to plan this way. At any other camp he could simply walk up to Rachel Jansen and shoot her. Here, he had to have a good reason to damage one of Brandt's guinea pigs. And that was where the diamonds came in. It would cost him the stones to get the bitch, but it would be worth it.

The spot Sturm had chosen for his ambush was a narrow alley between the SS barracks and the dog kennels. He had picked his day and his hour well too. Brandt was gone to Ravensbrück to witness some experiment or other, and Schörner was in Dornow, questioning the locals about the missing sergeant, Willi Gauss. Finally, it was the time of morning when the Jansen woman usually walked a circuit of the camp with the Block Leader, Hagan. Sturm's plan for luring the Jewess to the alley was simple. All he needed was one of her children.

He chose the son.

"You're digging your own grave," Frau Hagan said. "Nothing good can come of it."

Rachel kept her eyes fixed on the snow as she walked. "My children eat well. They are gaining weight."

"But for how long? How long will Schörner stay interested? You don't know how their minds work. Schörner was lonely enough to come to you, but soon he'll hate himself for it. You'll be the one to pay for his disgust with himself."

"I have no choice. He can protect Jan and Hannah."

"You believe that? If Brandt selected Jan tomorrow, what could Schörner do? If he disobeyed an order, Brandt would put him in front of a firing squad. He just tells you what will keep him between your legs. Like all men."

"He chose me, remember? Let's don't talk about it."

Frau Hagan raised her hands in a gesture of futility. "Always you listen to my advice. But not about this. You think I've never seen this before? How do you think I've survived so long?"

Rachel looked up at her. "I would like to know that."

"Not by doing what you are doing. Or what the shoemaker does. Listen, in 1940 I and seven hundred other Poles from Tarnow were transported to Oscweicim—what the Germans call Au- schwitz—in Upper Silesia. We built that camp. Digging all the time, no food or water. Only the strong survived.

"It was there that I became a Communist. We built a synthetic rubber plant at Buna. They called it Auschwitz Three, but that place was Hell on earth. There was a man there named Spivack, a Pole from Warsaw. Small, but wiry like a monkey. I worked with him, hauling bricks and cement. After a week, I knew he was the tough- est man I had ever seen. At the end of the day when the big oxes had fallen down, he was still working. It was his *mind* that was tough, you see? He was a Communist. Nothing but death could beat him."

Frau Hagan waggled a finger at Rachel. "It was the German Communists who tried to stop Hitler in the beginning. But the Ger- man people were afraid of Marxism. Even the German Jews. Cow- ards. Afraid to let go of their bourgeois comforts." The big Pole laughed bitterly. "Where did all their comforts get them, eh? Up the chimney, that's where."

"What happened to Spivack?"

Frau Hagan shrugged. "I was transferred here. But I'll tell you this. He didn't let the SS treat him like a dog. Even some of those bastards respected him, all the punishment he could take. That's what I've done, and I'm still here. Still alive. But you, Dutch girl, you're riding on the back of a tiger."

"Not everyone is as strong as you," Rachel said. "I judge no one here."

. *"Rachel! Hagan! Hurry!"*

An older woman raced into the alley between the hospital and the E-Block. Frau Hagan shouted for her to slow down, but she ran right up to them and grabbed Rachel's shift.

"They took Jan! Hurry!"

A sudden heat suffused Rachel's skin. "What?"

"One of Sturm's dog handlers came for your boy! There was nothing I could do!"

Rachel grabbed the woman's arm. "Hannah?"

"She's safe."

"Where is the boy now?" Frau Hagan asked.

"They took him to the kennels."

Rachel started to run, but Frau Hagan grabbed her upper arm. "Walk," she commanded. "Running will get you a bullet in the back."

"I must go to him!"

"You must also be careful. Sturm has planned this well, I think."

"What do you mean?"

"Brandt is out of town, and Schörner left for Dornow this morning. Too much coincidence."

"Schörner is away?" Rachel felt suddenly faint. "My God, what can I do?"

"I don't know." Frau Hagan set her jaw in a grim line. "But I will come with you."

When Rachel rounded the corner of the SS barracks, she saw Jan standing with his back to the dog kennels. Sergeant Sturm was squatting in front of him, his broad face pressed close to the little boy's. Jan was crying. An SS private stood to the side, his subma-chine gun pointed leisurely at the three-year-old.

Rachel screamed and raced toward her son, but Sturm stood up and caught her in a bear hug.

"Please!" Rachel shrieked, kicking wildly. "Let him go!"

"Moeder! Moeder!" Jan whimpered.

Frau Hagan scooped up the boy and started to run, but the SS private backed her against the barracks with his submachine gun. Sturm lifted Rachel off her feet dropped her beside the kennels.

"Against the wall!" he ordered. "Face the wall!"

Rachel craned her neck to catch of glimpse of Jan. Frau Hagan was holding the boy tightly against her bosom.

Sturm slapped Rachel's face. "Bend over and grab your ankles, whore!"

"I will! Please don't hurt my son!"

"I'll do whatever I like. Now, bend over! Let's have those diamonds."

"Jan! Shut your eyes!"

Frau Hagan covered the boy's eyes as Rachel bent over.

The Kubelwagen carrying Major Wolfgang Schörner barreled through the front gate of Totenhausen without slowing and screeched to a stop in front of the administration building. Schörner had learned nothing about Technical Sergeant Gauss in Dornow, but a little extra effort had paid off. He'd decided to question the occupants of some of the outlying houses between Dornow and Totenhausen, and the fourth house he came to belonged to Sybille Kleist. Schörner had scarcely gotten Sergeant Gauss's name out of his mouth when Frau Kleist broke down completely.

"Something's happened to Willi!" she sobbed. "I knew it! I wanted to come forward, Sturmbannführer, but . . . I swear to you, twice this morning I started to come to the camp to report, but I couldn't."

"Why not, madam?" Schörner had asked.

Frau Kleist attempted some semblance of haughty dignity. "I am a married woman, Sturmbannführer. Willi—Sergeant Gauss—assists me with certain heavy work around the house. There is nothing improper, of course, but if my husband ever misconstrued—"

"My inquiries will be conducted with the utmost discretion," Schörner said with forced patience.

"Sergeant Gauss was here last night. Just after he left, I thought I heard something. I *know* I did. I looked outside but saw nothing. God help me, Sturmbannführer, but the more I've thought about it, the more I think the noise sounded like gunshots. Soft but very fast."

At that point Schörner had read Sybille Kleist the riot act. Ten minutes later he ordered all search parties to concentrate in the area of the Kleist residence, then left for Totenhausen to summon Sergeant Sturm with his best dogs.

As he climbed out of the Kubelwagen, Schörner saw a wireless operator emerge from the HQ building. "Rottenführer!" he shouted. "Where is Hauptscharführer Sturm?"

"I'm not sure, Sturmbannführer. I heard the dogs barking a moment ago. Perhaps he is exercising them."

Schörner entered the alley between the dog kennels and the SS barracks just as Sergeant Sturm hiked up Rachel's shift and bunched it around her waist. Marching stiffly up the alley, he saw Sturm pull down her underpants, brace his left hand in the small of her back and reach between her thighs with his right.

"Achtung, Hauptscharführer!"

Sergeant Sturm snapped straight and gaped at the advancing major. Clean-shaven and dressed in his field gray Waffen-SS uniform, the eyepatch tied across his face like a wound badge, Schörner personified the nightmare of every SS noncom.

"ACHTUNG!"

Sturm squared his shoulders and thumbed the seams of his trousers. Rachel pulled up her underwear and ran to Frau Hagan.

"Exactly what is going on here?" Schörner asked.

Sturm regrouped rapidly. "I am conducting a search, Sturmbannführer."

"It looked to me like you were conducting a rape."

"Sturmbannführer, this woman is concealing contraband on her person."

Schörner's eyes flicked to Rachel. "What kind of contraband? Food? Explosives?"

"No, Sturmbannführer. Diamonds. The very gems you instructed me to get rid of some nights ago."

Schörner pursed his lips, surprised by this response. "I see. And how do you know she has these diamonds?"

"I have reliable information, Sturmbannführer. A report from another prisoner."

Rachel felt her stomach twist. What fellow prisoner would inform on her to the SS?

"And where is she hiding these gems?"

Sturm felt a surge of confidence; for once the facts were in his favor. "She hides them in her private parts, Sturmbannführer, like all these shameless Jewish cows."

Schörner was silent for a moment. "If that is the information you received, Hauptscharführer, you should have informed me. I would have instructed a civilian nurse to search the prisoner. Your conduct was highly irregular, and quite unbecoming a German soldier."

Sturm reddened. He would not be humiliated in front of a Jew. "I know my duty, Sturmbannführer! If this prisoner is breaking the rules, I will search her wherever I find her."

"Your duty, Hauptscharführer?" said Schörner, raising his eyebrows. "While you were molesting women in alleyways, I was out doing *your* duty for you. Not only have I discovered that our missing sergeant was carrying on an illicit affair with the wife of a hero of the Kriegsmarine, but also that he was dallying in bed with this woman just last night. The woman reported hearing gunshots soon after he left. I hurried back here to enlist the help of you and your dogs to search the area. And what do I find? You, acting in an even more disgusting manner than Gauss!"

The news about Gauss surprised Sturm, but he did not intend to let Rachel escape. "Sturmbannführer, I will personally take the dogs and search the area. But first we must relieve this prisoner of the contraband."

Schörner glanced around the alley. The SS private was making a point of looking the other way. Sturm's strategy of isolation had backfired on him. "I suggest, Hauptscharführer," Schörner said icily, "that you gather your dogs and stop wasting my time. This prisoner is known to me. I doubt seriously whether she possesses any diamonds, or that she would hide them in the disgusting manner you describe. Apparently your mind works in the same direction as Sergeant Gauss's."

Sturm knew he should have dropped it there. But he couldn't. "How do you know what is or isn't hidden between her legs?" he asked.

Schörner's head snapped back as if Sturm had slapped him.

"That's right," Sturm said, this time more confidently. "I know your game. You're no better than Gauss or anyone else. By my standards, you're a damn sight worse."

Schörner's hand was around Sturm's throat in less than a second. He slammed the stunned sergeant up against the wall of the kennel and squeezed his neck with enough force to kill. The German shepherds went wild.

Sturm was trying to speak, but no air could escape his throat.

Schörner's voice grated like broken glass. "You wish to say something, Hauptscharführer?" He loosened his grip just enough for Sturm to whisper.

The sergeant sucked in as much air as he could, then rasped, "You're not fit to wear that uniform, you Jew-fucking bastard."

Schörner's face went completely white. To hear such words from a man who had never fought in a single battle, who had never even come under hostile fire, made him temporarily lose his reason. He drove his right knee into Gunther Sturm's groin. When Sturm doubled over in agony, he smashed his fist down on the back of his neck. Before the sergeant could react, Schörner's boot was across the back of his neck, crushing his face into the gravel.

Rachel watched from the hospital wall in horror and fascination. She could tell that Frau Hagan was even more stunned than she was. Sturm's red face was being ground into the gravel like a willful dog's. Major Schörner seemed to be considering whether or not to go ahead and snap Sturm's neck with his finely polished hobnailed boot. He regarded the back of the sergeant's bare head for several moments, as if carefully weighing the pros and cons of the choice.

Rachel heard a sudden roar of engines from the other side of the barracks. A motorcycle with an empty sidecar swept into the alley and skidded to a stop beside Schörner. Its rider removed his goggles and stared at the prone figure on the ground.

"What is it, Rottenführer?" Schörner asked.

The rider's eyes stayed on Sergeant Sturm. "Sturmbannführer, it's . . ."

"Speak up, man!"

"Sergeant Gauss, Sturmbannführer! We found his body. He's been murdered! Shot by an automatic weapon!"

"*What?* Where?"

"Near the Kleist woman's house, just as you said. Buried in the snow. We had to dig up half the yard, but we found him. And Sturmbannführer, that's not the worst of it. We found four parachutes buried with him. *British* parachutes."

Schörner lifted his boot off of Sturm's neck. "Get up, Haupt-scharführer! Get every dog and man you have and meet at the Kleist house immediately." He leaped into the sidecar of the motorcycle. "Take me to the spot, Rottenführer!"

"*Zu befehl*, Sturmbannführer!"

Sturm got slowly to his feet as the corporal kicked the bike into gear.

"What are you staring at?" Schörner asked him, as if nothing had passed between them. "There may be British commandos in the area. Everything else can wait!"

Sturm nodded dully. Too much had happened too quickly for him to take it all in. "*Jawohl*," he mumbled. Then he hurried into the kennel and lifted six chain leashes off a hook inside the door.

Schörner looked at Rachel, his eyes full of intense but unreadable emotion. Then the motorcycle roared out of the alley.

Rachel hugged Jan to her breast and looked at Frau Hagan. The Polish woman shook her head. "He's mad," she said. "He has lost his mind."

"Jan, Jan," Rachel crooned in a low voice. "Everything is all right now."

"No, it isn't," Frau Hagan said. "This is just beginning."

"What do you mean? Will Sturm report him?"

"I don't think so. I think those two will settle this privately. Schörner must have something on Sturm, something bad enough that Sturm is afraid to bring charges against him for consorting with you. That's why he tried to get you this way. Whatever it is will probably keep him from reporting this."

The Pole rubbed her grayish-brown hair with both hands. "It won't keep him from killing Schörner, though. It may take a little time, but he'll find a way. You're the one who has to worry now. You're the pawn between them."

Rachel shuddered. "Let's go back to the block. I want to find Hannah."

They moved out of the alley, Rachel carrying Jan. "You know the worst thing Sturm said? That he had reliable information that I had the diamonds."

"Do you?" Frau Hagan asked bluntly.

Rachel hesitated, then finally gave up her pretense. "Yes. I'm sorry I lied to you."

Frau Hagan waved her hand. "You keep them where he said?"

"Yes."

"Where do you hide them when you go to Schörner?"

"Don't ask." Rachel quickened her pace. "I can't believe anyone would inform on me. Someone in the same position we are! Someone must have watched me in the toilet or the showers."

"If I find out who," Frau Hagan said matter-of-factly, "I'll strangle them with a bootlace."

"But how could they do it?"

The Block Leader grunted with a sound that summed up a lifetime of disillusionment. "I told you your first day here, Dutch girl. The prisoner's worst enemy is the prisoner."

W hat? What?"

McConnell came awake in the dark the way he once had as an intern in Atlanta, eyes wide open but full of sleep, shaking his head to jar his brain into action.

Someone was shaking him by the arm.

"Get up, Mr. Wilkes! Wake up, sir!"

McConnell's eyes focused. Where he expected the face of a nurse, he saw the young face of one of Colonel Vaughan's orderlies. The orderly pulled him to his feet.

"Is that your only bag, sir?"

"What the hell's going on?" McConnell demanded.

"Is this all your gear, sir?"

"No, damn it, I have suitcases at the castle. Just wait a minute. Jesus . . . is this it? Tonight?"

"Leave everything in the hut behind, sir. You won't be needing it. Follow me."

The orderly marched out. McConnell groped in the dark for his shoes, pulled them on and went after him. It was raining outside, no surprise at Achnacarry. The orderly waited on the path to the castle, bouncing on the balls of his feet.

McConnell walked rapidly but did not run, another habit he had developed as an intern. It gave him time to get his thoughts together. Where the hell was Stern? Just after supper they had both lain down in the hut. Now Stern was gone. The day had been a washout, the first time Sergeant McShane had not shown up at dawn to work them to death. He had not appeared during the re-

248

mainder of the day either, and Stern—quite out of character—had shown no curiosity about the matter.

McConnell sidestepped the rear corner of the castle and moved quickly along the wall. When he rounded the front, he saw only the dim yellow bulb over the castle door, burning through the rain. A stiff hand bumped him in the chest.

"Hold here, Mr. Wilkes," said the orderly.

"What the hell—?"

"Shut up, Doctor," snapped a familiar voice.

McConnell's eyes focused slowly on the figure crouched against the castle wall. There was a leather bag beside him.

Stern.

McConnell squatted down. "Is this it?"

"I heard Smith's plane land a little while ago," Stern said.

McConnell felt his heartbeat quicken. He realized he was clutching the swatch of Cameron tartan in his hand. As the cold rain ran down into his collar, he noticed that the hut village in the meadow across the drive looked empty. No campfires, no singing.

"Where is everybody?"

"Night Assault," Stern replied.

"What's that?"

"The colonel's graduation exercise," said the orderly. "Closest thing in the world to real combat. The Frenchies are rowing across the loch now."

McConnell heard a low rumble in the dark. An engine. A canvas-backed army truck slowly ground its way up the drive and stopped by the main entrance of the castle. Over its tailgate climbed three men who looked as if they could barely walk. McConnell caught his breath when they stepped into the glow of the bulb over the door.

One of the men was Sergeant Ian McShane.

Stern jumped up and ran toward the truck. McConnell followed, but before they reached it the castle door opened and Brigadier Smith stepped out into the rain. No tweed coat and stalker's cap tonight—he was wearing his army uniform. Two orderlies behind him carried McConnell's heavy suitcases and two large duffel bags.

"Load them into the lorry," Smith barked. He caught sight of

Stern and McConnell. "Into the truck, you two. You'll find new clothes in those bags. Put them on."

In the shuffle at the tailgate, McConnell looked into the eyes of Sergeant McShane. What he saw stunned him: fatigue, anger, the remnants of shock. When he touched the sergeant's arm, McShane jerked suddenly, as if in pain. McConnell saw then that his inner arms had been scraped raw and scabbed over, as if he had skidded fifty yards on cement.

"Where the hell have you been, Sergeant?" he asked.

"Where you're going, Doctor."

Suddenly Brigadier Smith was between them. "Into the castle, Sergeant. Whisky and fire. You've earned it."

McShane, flanked by John Lewis and Alick Cochrane, said nothing. Glancing over Smith's shoulder, McConnell saw that Lewis and Cochrane looked worse than McShane. McShane started to say something, but before he could Brigadier Smith said:

"Carry on, Sergeant."

Cochrane and Lewis moved toward the door, but McShane stepped around the brigadier and laid a finger on Stern's chest.

"You mind how you go, over there," he said. "Look after the doctor here, right? You might be findin' a warmer welcome than you've been led to expect."

The Highlander looked Brigadier Smith dead in the eye, then turned and trudged into the castle.

"What's he talking about?" Stern asked.

"They lost a man," the brigadier said. "That's all. You've lost a few yourself, haven't you? It was Colin Munro, the weapons instructor. They hauled his body fifteen miles overland to the pickup point. Now, get on with it, eh? We've got to be in Sweden by three A.M. Germany by dawn."

Stern pulled McConnell toward the truck. "Nothing we can do," he said.

Inside his duffel bag McConnell found not only dry civilian clothes—with proper German tags inside them—but also a neatly pressed and folded military uniform of field gray winter wool. He saw the silver SS runes and the Death's Head badge on his captain's cap and felt a chill. Stern's uniform was gray-green, with the feared green piping and sleeve patch of the SD. On the breast was an Iron

Cross First Class and a Wound Badge. The left collar patch indicated that its wearer was a colonel—*Standartenführer*.

"The civvies or the uniforms?" McConnell asked.

"The uniforms," said Stern.

McConnell was still dressing when the truck began to roll. Stern bent over the suitcase that contained McConnell's anti-gas suits and began rummaging beneath them.

"What are you doing?" McConnell asked.

"That bicycle's not the only thing I stole at the castle," Stern said over the rumble of the truck. "Smith is crazy if he thinks I'm going into Nazi Germany with nothing but a Schmeisser and a pistol."

McConnell knelt down and looked into the case. He saw several hand grenades, a small box, and a package wrapped in brown paper.

"What is all that stuff?"

"Plastic explosive. Time pencil detonators. Grenades."

"Where did you get it?"

"Vaughan's private arsenal. Thank God those orderlies didn't search your suitcases."

"They still might."

"No. From now on, you and I carry these bags every step of the way."

Three minutes later the truck stopped. Brigadier Smith appeared at the tailgate.

"At the double," he said. "No time to lose."

McConnell dropped to the ground. They had stopped beside an airplane, but no ordinary airplane. It was a high-wing monoplane painted matte black. From fifty yards away it would be totally invisible. Smith's pilot had put the ominous-looking craft down in a wet field that didn't look long enough for a flock of geese to land in. Stern bumped past McConnell with the suitcases. Then suddenly the night was shattered by a thunder of guns like a summer storm sweeping across Georgia.

"Christ!" McConnell yelled. "What the hell is that?"

"Into the plane!" the brigadier shouted. "If we hurry we'll see the best of it!"

McConnell squeezed the duffel bags into the plane, and before he could even catch his breath the grumbling Lysander was climbing the crest of a hill with scant yards to spare. On Smith's order, the pilot banked over Loch Lochy for a sightseeing run. McConnell had never seen anything like the spectacle below him. Tracer fire arced through the night like something from an H. G. Wells novel. Flares exploded around the plane, illuminating a dozen or so dinghies on the loch below like ducks in a shooting gallery.

"Those Frogs are scared out of their wits right now!" Smith shouted. "Charles's lads are firing real bullets inches from their arses!"

Smith told the pilot to swing around and head for 'checkers,' whatever that meant. As the Lysander swept along the beach, just a hundred feet above exploding mortar shells, McConnell saw an ambulance parked with its headlights on high. Standing in the wet glow of the twin beams was a barrel-chested figure with his hands clasped behind his back. He raised his right arm in farewell as the Lysander buzzed past him, waggling its wings.

"Look at him!" Brigadier Smith shouted. "Standing there like C. B. DeMille himself. What a show! The War Office says Charlie Vaughan uses more ordnance for his Night Assault than Monty used at Alamein!"

The pilot banked into the worst of the storm. It was all McConnell could manage to hold down the contents of his stomach. He tried to take his mind off the nausea by questioning Smith, but the brigadier ignored him. Rain slapped steadily against the perspex windows. The pilot was only the back of a leather cap, Stern a silhouette in the darkness close beside him.

For the first time since David's death, he realized how irrevocable it all was. He was adrift in a black airplane under a starless sky, droning over an island that had shown no lights to heaven since 1939. The idea that there was a worldwide war going on, perhaps for the soul of mankind, had never seemed more real than it did now.

Were these the smells David had known? The duck-blind smell of rainsoaked wool and leather? The bite of aviation fuel and oil? The scent of anticipation emanating from Stern, a sweaty tang of the hunter at first light? And of course the metallic odor McConnell fancied he smelled on himself—

The smell of fear.

For the first time, the reality of his destination entered into him. Nazi Germany. There was a square yard of the glorious Reich waiting for his two feet to touch down on, maybe waiting for his corpse. He tried to banish this thought while the Lysander plowed doggedly southward against the storm, and by the time the plane began to descend, he had been asleep for over an hour.

The impact of the wheels on earth knocked him awake. "Is this Sweden?" he asked woozily.

"Not quite, lad."

Brigadier Smith's voice. The plane turned and taxied back the way it had come. Outside, McConnell saw only darkness. Then a pair of auto headlights blinked three times.

The pilot rolled up to the car and stopped.

"Out," Smith ordered.

They trundled out of the plane and into the car, a polished Humber. The pilot stayed in the Lysander. The driver of the Humber wore a chauffer's black uniform and drove like a man late for his daughter's wedding. The German uniforms drew several glances in the rearview mirror, but very shortly the car drew up beside a large, trimmed hedge. Smith got out and led them through a formal English garden. McConnell saw a faint reflection of moonlight on mullioned windows, then he was standing with Smith and Stern beside an oak door.

"Where the hell are we?" asked Stern.

"Clean up your language," the brigadier said tersely.

Smith opened the door and led them into a dim corridor. McConnell smelled leather bookbindings and old chintz, oiled wood and tea. As they moved through the dark house, he saw the gleam of brass and crystal. For a moment he thought they'd entered the rooms of his tutor at Oxford. But that was impossible.

Brigadier Smith turned suddenly into another corridor lit by an electric wall lamp. He stopped before a door. The paneling beside it looked four hundred years old. Smith put his hand on the doorknob, then looked back at Stern.

"Look sharp," he said. "Speak only when spoken to, and keep a civil tongue in your head."

McConnell noticed with some uneasiness that the brigadier's usual informality was nowhere in evidence. Every word and gesture was distinctly military. When Smith opened the door, he realized why.

The first thing he saw was the bald top of a round head. The head was leaning over a huge map that, even upside down, McConnell recognized as the Pas de Calais. The portly body was encased in a navy pea jacket, which seemed odd until McConnell noticed that the interior of the house was barely warmer than the frigid air outside. He smelled the long cigar in the ashtray before he saw it, then the aromatic brandy in the crystal glass.

Winston Churchill looked up from the map and blinked.

"By thunder!" he cried, standing straight. "Himmler's hooligans have come for me at last!"

McConnell laughed, a little hysterically perhaps, but the prime minister had found exactly the right gambit to put them at ease. It couldn't be too often that Winston Churchill found himself face to face with jackbooted SS officers. His grin as he looked them up and down seemed to indicate that he was enjoying it. McConnell marveled at the vitality radiating from the man. Churchill was seventy years old, but his watery blue eyes shone with humor and almost unnerving intelligence. When he stuck the cigar between his lips and spoke directly to McConnell, Mark felt a sudden magnifying of his own importance, like a subtle shift in the earth's gravitational field.

"So, how did you like Scotland, Doctor?" he asked, his voice far richer than his radio broadcasts. "Quite a tough little course, eh?"

The forward thrust of Churchill's prodigious head seemed an implicit challenge. "Pretty tough," McConnell agreed.

"Duff tells me you passed with flying colors."

McConnell was aware that the prime minister exploited every facet of his daunting charisma to sway others to his cause, yet despite this awareness he could not but be affected by it. He felt almost defensive when he heard Stern mutter behind him:

"Games."

"What's that?" Churchill asked, cocking his chin and puffing on the cigar. "Stern, isn't it?"

"I said *games*. That's what they play up there."

McConnell had no doubt Brigadier Smith was on the verge of knifing Stern in the kidneys.

"Mr. Stern," said Churchill, "they play games at Achnacarry because war *is* a game. It is a game you play with a smile. If you can't smile, you grin. And if you can't grin, you get out of the way until you can!"

He set his cigar in the ashtray and leaned across the desk, his hands splayed on its polished surface. "I asked to see you men for two reasons. Because you are civilians, and because you are not British subjects. You are undertaking a mission of the most hazardous nature. I want to impress upon you the supreme importance of this mission. This mission, gentlemen, *must not fail.*"

He hiked both trouser legs and sat behind the desk. "I wanted to speak especially to you, Doctor McConnell. I understand you're a follower of Mr. Gandhi?"

McConnell found himself surprisingly willing to answer. "To a degree, yes."

"I hope not to the degree that some of your scientific colleagues are. Do you know Professor Bohr?"

"Niels Bohr? The Danish physicist?"

"That's the man."

"I know of him."

"That utopist has the most muddleheaded perspective on war I've ever heard. He's like a bloody child. He sat in front of me and rambled for three quarters of an hour and I still had no idea what he was talking about. I think it all boiled down to resisting violence with humility. At least Gandhi says it in one tenth the time."

Churchill's eyes narrowed with incisive curiosity. "What about you, Doctor? Do *you* believe humility is the best weapon to use against Herr Hitler's armies?"

McConnell did not answer immediately. The mention of Niels Bohr had distracted him. The renowned physicist was supposed to be in Sweden. How had he "sat in front of" Winston Churchill? This strange revelation dovetailed with the whispered rumors he had heard at Oxford about accelerated research into atomic physics.

"Doctor?" Churchill prompted.

"I think events have gone beyond that now, Mr. Prime Minister. But I also think Hitler could have been stopped with little or no violence years ago."

"I quite agree. But we live in the present." His voice rose a semitone. "Duff tells me your father won the Distinguished Service Cross in the Great War. At the St. Mihiel salient."

"That's right," said McConnell, wondering why Churchill's knowledge of his past should take him by surprise. "Also the Silver Star. Of course, he threw them both into the Potomac River in 1932."

Churchill tucked his chin into his chest and gave McConnell a froglike stare. "Why the devil did he do that?"

McConnell wasn't sure the prime minister would like the answer, but he told him. "Remember the Bonus Army Riot in Washington? During the Depression?"

"Veteran's pensions or something?" rumbled Churchill.

"Exactly. Some men from my father's old unit had gone up with the vets who were trying to get relief from the government. There were about twenty-five thousand of them, with their families. They called and asked my dad if he would go up and try to give them some medical help. He went. The D.C. police were feeding the vets and their families, but President Hoover had no sympathy. After three months of peaceful demonstration, he called in the army. The army attacked the unarmed crowds with tear gas, bayonets, cavalry, and tanks. Several vets were shot, some infants gassed to death." McConnell paused. "My father was in that crowd."

Churchill watched with unblinking eyes. "Do I sense some deeper moral to this story?"

"A footnote. I have since learned the names of some of the officers who attacked that crowd. The troops were led by a man named Douglas MacArthur. MacArthur disobeyed Hoover and went far beyond his original orders. MacArthur's aide was a Major Dwight Eisenhower. The saber-wielding cavalry were led by Captain George Patton. So, Mr. Prime Minister, perhaps you understand why my devotion to the military is less than blind."

"I do indeed. Politics can be a difficult business, Doctor. I must sadly admit that I have made similar mistakes. But none of that affects the current situation. I don't have to explain to a man of your gifts the threat facing Christian civilization."

McConnell had no doubt that Stern had noted the omission of Jews from that formulation.

"For your own reasons, whatever they are, you have agreed to go on this mission. For that I thank you. I am not exaggerating when I say that the liberation of Europe may hang upon it."

Churchill's eyes played over McConnell's face for some moments. Then he took a sheet of notepaper from his desk and lifted a pen from its well. "There is bound to be loss of life during this mission," he said, writing quickly. "I want you to know that final responsibility rests with me."

Churchill tore off the sheet of paper and handed it to McConnell, who read it with astonishment.

On my head be these deaths.
W

"I'm half-American myself, you know," said Churchill. "And I reckon you're at least half-English, Doctor."

"What?" McConnell mumbled, still looking at the remarkable note. "What do you mean?"

Churchill clamped his teeth down on his cigar and grinned. "Any man who has survived both Oxford University and Achnacarry Castle has earned his citizenship!"

McConnell heard Brigadier Smith's feet shifting impatiently on the floor behind him. Then Stern's German-accented voice cut the air of the study.

"What about my people?" he asked in an accusatory tone. "Is there a place for Jews in your Anglo-American paradise?"

"Hold your tongue!" bellowed Brigadier Smith.

"Let him speak, Duff," Churchill said. "He has a right to be angry."

Stern took a step forward. The SD uniform and German accent gave his words a chilling intensity. "I want to know if you will really support the establishment of a Jewish homeland in Palestine after the war."

Churchill punctuated his words with his cigar, using it like a pointer. "I most certainly will, Mr. Stern. But the key phrase in your question was '*after* the war.' There's a damned great lot of fighting to be done yet."

"And I'm ready to do it," Stern said.

"Are you? Well then. When you get back from this mission, I shall personally see to it that you get a commission in the Jewish Brigade." He smiled. "You'll need a different uniform, of course. They wouldn't like that swastika."

"There *is* no Jewish Brigade! It's been buried in paperwork for years."

"Not any longer," said Churchill. "I've unburied it. The Jewish Brigade will fight in the liberation. So, are you interested?"

Stern actually snapped to attention.

Churchill beamed. "This is my sort of fellow, Duff. You've chosen well, I think."

"He'll do," Smith said grudgingly. "But I'm afraid we really must go. The schedule, you know."

"H-Hour," Churchill said with relish. "And right into Germany! What I wouldn't give to go with you." He stood up and vigorously shook both McConnell's and Stern's hands.

McConnell thought of something else he wanted to ask, but by then the brigadier had whisked them out of the room and along the dim corridor.

The driver of the Humber met them at the outside door.

"Follow him," Smith said. "I'll join you in a moment."

As they passed outside, McConnell looked back. They were exiting from a different door, and above it he saw the words: *Pro Patria Omnia.* Now he realized what Duff Smith had said to his pilot over Loch Lochy. He had not said to head for "checkers" but *Chequers,* which was the country residence of the British prime minister. As he followed Stern back to the Lysander, McConnell wondered if Adolf Hitler knew what words were engraved above the door of that house, and what they meant.

All for the Fatherland.

Churchill was studiously smoking his cigar when Brigadier Smith returned. Smith took a chair opposite the desk and waited for the inevitable grilling the PM always gave before important operations. Churchill exhaled a great cloud of blue smoke, sniffed, then rested his cigar on the rim of the ashtray.

"This is the only operation I have ever sanctioned that goes directly against the wishes of the Americans," he said soberly. "I'm still not sure I fancy using an American to do it. Even if he is the right man from a technical standpoint. It could cause problems later."

"There won't be any problems, Winston. If this mission succeeds, it succeeds in producing a negative: the *nonuse* of nerve gas by the Nazis. And if it fails, both Stern and McConnell will in all likelihood be dead."

"What if it succeeds, but the good doctor decides to unburden himself afterwards? For reasons of conscience."

Smith peered into the blue eyes, trying to read the subtext of the conversation. At length he said, "This is a dangerous mission. Even if it succeeds, it's quite possible that McConnell and Stern might not get back alive."

Churchill steepled his fingers and focused his eyes somewhere in the shadows beyond Smith. "Does anyone know McConnell is going on this mission? Anyone at all?"

"He left two letters with an Oxford don. For his wife and mother. The usual stuff. I confiscated them."

Churchill sighed heavily. "If Eisenhower or Marshall learn I've bypassed them to make a strike of this magnitude—"

"They've left you no alternative, Winston! If Eisenhower's armies fall dead after thirty seconds on the French beaches, Roosevelt and Marshall will scream to high heaven about what should have been done, and Ike will resign, but by then it will be *too late.*"

Churchill was nodding. "I agree, Duff. The question is, will the mission succeed? Is there a real chance?"

"Absolutely."

"What about our gas? How long will it remain stable now?"

"It varies from lot to lot. The last two batches from Porton remained stable for ninety-seven hours."

"What's that? Four days?"

"Just over that."

"And it was lethal?"

"Oh, quite, yes. Dispatched two large primates rather handily."

Churchill winced. "Don't tell me where you got your test subjects. I don't want the Royal Society beating down my door. How old is the gas your Achnacarry men took in?"

Smith looked at his watch. "Twenty-six hours and counting."

"Cutting it a bit fine, aren't you?"

"The Raubhammer demonstration is in four days," said Smith. "If we don't pull it off by then, we're probably too late anyway. If the wind is under seven miles per hour when they arrive, Stern will release the gas tonight. If not tonight, then tomorrow."

Churchill picked up his pen and began doodling on a notepad. "That's why you want the submarine to stand by for four days. The weather must be right for the attack?"

"That, and the exhibition for Hitler. I want to give them every possible chance to make the attack. As for weather, four miles an hour is optimal wind speed for a gas attack of this type, preferably without rain."

"Does Stern or McConnell know the gas may not work?"

"Of course not."

Churchill pulled the heavy pea jacket around his neck. "Duff, if you had to give me a percentage chance of success, what would you say?"

Smith ruminated. "Fifty-fifty for the attack itself. But if the attack is successful, I think there's a ninety percent chance the bluff will work. Winston, I'm absolutely positive that this nerve gas initiative is an all-Himmler show. Everything points to it. When we hit him discreetly with his own personal 'miracle weapon,' we'll knock his legs right out from under him. As far as he'll know, we've got ten thousand tons of British Sarin ready to drop on Berlin. He'll *have* to call off his show."

"Will he be able to prove we were behind the attack?"

"No. We're using German cylinders, World War One vintage. But he'll know who was responsible. I'll see to that."

"And if our Sarin doesn't work?"

Smith shrugged. "Then the bombers go in."

Churchill made a growling noise in the back of his throat. "What will happen if we have to bomb that camp?"

"That depends on several factors. Again, the weather. How much gas is stored on-site. Our planes will be carrying incendiary bombs, to try to incinerate as much of the gas as possible before it leaves the area. Still, there's a chance that the nearby villages could be wiped out. We just don't know enough to predict. If they *are* wiped out, I'm sure Himmler will simply announce a regrettable industrial accident. Whatever happens, all traces of our mission will be destroyed."

"What if you don't hear anything from Stern and McConnell?"

"If I don't have positive confirmation of success three nights from now, the bombers will go in, no matter what."

"Do Stern and McConnell know about the bombers?"

"Good God, no."

Churchill rubbed his forehead with both hands. He had looked vital to McConnell, but Duff Smith knew the prime minister had only just recovered from pneumonia in December, and that after surviving two heart attacks in the same month. The pressures on him were enormous. Yet he insisted on shouldering moral responsibility for every mission.

"They're civilians, Duff," Churchill pointed out.

"They'll sign releases before they leave."

"That's not what I meant. You don't think that with his brother murdered by the SS, you could entrust McConnell with the real purpose of the mission?"

Smith shook his head. "I don't think Doctor McConnell would kill a human being even to save his own life."

The telephone on Churchill's desk rang, but he ignored it. "There is one flaw that could bring disaster, Duff. What if they're captured and tortured before they can carry out the attack? You gave them L-pills?"

"Stern carries one at all times, if you can believe it. But I wouldn't trust McConnell to take cyanide even if he had it." The brigadier felt in his pocket for his pipe. "No need to worry on that score, though. If capture appears imminent, Stern is under orders to shoot the good doctor where he stands."

Churchill's phone finally stopped ringing.

"That's a hard order, Duff. It wouldn't sit well with a lot of people, on both sides of the Atlantic."

Smith had anticipated this last spasm of conscience. "There is a precedent, Winston. At Dieppe, when we sent our radar experts to reconnoiter the German radar station, we sent gunmen in behind them—disguised as bodyguards—just in case the Jerries closed in."

"I don't see how that makes this situation any better."

Smith smiled. "One of those bodyguards was an American FBI agent. If the Yanks had no qualms about an FBI man shooting our scientists, I don't see how they could object to us doing the same."

Brendan Bracken opened the study door and said, "Hayes Lodge. General Eisenhower is standing by for you."

Churchill nodded and waved his aide out of the room. "It's a moot point, Duff, but if *any* of this ever gets out, who shot whom will be irrelevant. All that matters is secrecy and results. But tell me . . . do you think Stern would really shoot McConnell down in cold blood?"

Duff Smith stood up and patted his khakis flat. "Winston, there is absolutely no doubt in my mind."

T he Moon plane dropped out of the dark sky like a night-hawk, swooping through ghostly clouds in a dive McConnell thought would tear off its wings.

"Hold on to your seats!" advised the pilot.

McConnell closed his eyes as the rattling Lysander hurtled toward the earth. The plane was packed full. They had crammed the suitcase containing the anti-gas suits and stolen explosives in the small space behind the seats. He held the case with the air cylinders on his lap. He also had his personal bag, which contained food, his Schmeisser, a change of civilian clothes, and some medical supplies.

"Are you going to be sick?" Stern shouted over the roar of the engine.

McConnell opened his eyes. He felt like a man plunging to his death, but Stern's face was impassive. He wondered if he looked as authentically Nazi as Stern did. He wore a captain's uniform and carried papers identifying him as an SS physician, but he felt about as German as a Hormel frankfurter. In the dark gray-green SD uniform and cap, with the Iron Cross First Class on his tunic, Stern radiated a sinister authority.

"*Damn* this plane!" Stern cursed, adjusting the scuffed leather bag and Schmeisser on his lap.

"Bad luck!" yelled the pilot. "Couldn't be helped!"

McConnell said nothing. The line of pale blue light silhouetting the eastern horizon was comment enough. Dawn was coming, and they had yet to reach the ground. The entire night had been a race against time. After the meeting with Churchill, they'd made a brief hop to a restricted airfield. There Brigadier Smith and an aide had led them aboard a captured Junkers bomber Smith claimed was so secret that they could not be allowed to see its pilot. The Junkers bore all its original Luftwaffe markings, which had made for a dangerous run out of British airspace, but allowed an uneventful trip to neutral Sweden. During the flight, Smith actually ordered the pilot to open the bomb bay so that he could point out German battleships on blockade duty below them.

Their problem began in Sweden. The Lysander detailed to carry them from Sweden to Germany—the plane they were in now—had developed engine trouble on its way back from a mission into Occupied France. And because the tiny black plane had but one engine, they had been forced to wait hours in a freezing shack while its pilot and the mysterious Junkers pilot repaired the problem. By the time they finished, dawn was scarcely an hour away. McConnell had suggested they wait until the next night, but Smith wouldn't hear of it. He practically shoved them into the Lysander and ordered their pilot not to turn back for any reason.

McConnell had expected to fly just over the wave tops to avoid German radar, but the pilot told them there was more chance of being shot down by a Kriegsmarine vessel than by a Luftwaffe night fighter. They'd crossed the Baltic at nine thousand feet. Ten minutes ago they'd flown over the coast of northern Germany.

And then the dive.

"Thank God," McConnell said, feeling the plane start to level out over the lightless plain.

"We're going to touch down in a farmer's field!" yelled the pilot. "The Met people say there's been a hard freeze, so I'm not expecting problems with mud." He looked back over his shoulder, revealing the face of a jaded twenty-year-old daredevil. "I won't be turning off the engine. Himmler himself could be waiting down there, for all we know. I expect you to get yourselves and your gear out of the plane in less than thirty seconds."

"Nice to know we can count on you!" Stern shouted back.

The pilot shook his head. "I take SOE people into France all the time. But Germany . . . you two must be daft."

Great, thought McConnell. *Even the help knows we're idiots.* Far out on the western horizon he saw a faint orange glow. "What's that?" he asked.

"Rostock," answered the pilot. "We bombed it practically into

rubble in forty-three, but the Heinkel aircraft factory is still opera-
tional. They must have used incendiaries tonight. The fires are still
burning."

McConnell noticed that Stern had pressed his face to the perspex. "What are you looking for?" he asked.

"I grew up in Rostock," Stern said. "I was just wondering if our
apartment block was still standing."

"Doubtful," the pilot said needlessly. "The center of town is
pretty well smashed. Looks like a bloody Roman ruin."

"So *that's* why Smith chose you for this," McConnell said, forgetting his airsickness for a moment. "You know the area."

"That's one reason."

"There's the signal!" cried the pilot. "Get ready!"

He pulled back on the controls and climbed, then circled around
for a high-angle approach. All McConnell could see in the blackness
below were three dim yellow lights in a line, with a red one off to
the side, forming an inverted "L." The red light appeared to be
blinking a Morse code letter again and again.

The Lysander fell like a hailstone on the wind. McConnell
gripped his seat and watched the "L" race upward. The wheels hit
hard, bounced, then settled onto the bumpy ground and quickly
rolled to a stop near the red light.

"Get out!" bellowed the pilot. "Go!"

Stern already had the hatch open. The roar of the engine filled
the cabin. McConnell saw him drop his bag out, then jump down.
McConnell hefted his suitcase across the seat and handed it out,
then climbed down himself.

"You've left a bloody case!" the pilot yelled.

McConnell hopped back into the plane and with a groan lifted
out the suitcase containing the anti-gas suits and stolen explosives.

"Good luck!" the pilot called. Then the black plane was off,
turning quickly on the frozen earth and accelerating back in the direction it had come. Only the fading grumble of the engine told
them anything was there at all.

"You're the athlete," Stern said in the darkness. "You carry the
air cylinders."

When McConnell reached down for the case, it was gone. A
huge man with a black beard, heavy fur coat, and an old bolt-action
rifle strapped over his shoulder stood less than a yard from him. The

heavy suitcase hung from one hand as if it held only a weekend's clothes. While McConnell stared, the flare path that had guided in the plane winked out, and two more figures quickly materialized out of the blackness. One was a tall thin man with a fisherman's cap pulled low over his eyes, the other smaller and bundled to the eyeballs in a thick scarf and oilskin coat. The smaller man carried no weapon, but was obviously the leader.

"Password?" he asked in muffled German.

"*Schwarzes Kreuz,*" Stern replied. "Black Cross."

"You are . . . ?"

"Butler and Wilkes. He's Wilkes. You?"

"Melanie. Follow us. *Schnell!* We've been here all night. If we're caught in the open at dawn, we're dead."

The shadowy escorts moved so quickly across the flat ground that even McConnell had trouble keeping up. Once, the leader dropped flat and motioned for everyone to do the same. McConnell thought he heard the faint rumble of an engine, but wasn't sure. After three minutes, the leader got up and continued on.

Hurrying across the frozen fields, McConnell realized that the cold here was of an entirely different magnitude than that in Scotland. He should have prepared himself. Did it take a genius to figure out that in northern Germany, wind blowing from the north was coming from the Arctic? They were only twenty miles from the Baltic coast. The wind blasted across this plain like the fulfillment of a Norse curse, the uniforms he and Stern wore useless against its power.

He saw a few dim lights out to his left. A road? A rail line? To his right he saw nothing at first. Then the faintest corona of blue began to highlight the crest of a range of hills. He shivered. Beyond those hills the sun was rising.

As they rounded the foot of one of the hills, he saw dim yellow lights close ahead. The leader stopped and spoke quietly to the two escorts, who melted away into the shadows without a word. Stern and McConnell picked up their suitcases.

They were approaching a small village. Already they had passed two outlying farmhouses. A dog barked but apparently awakened no one. McConnell found himself recalling the advice Stern had given him about moving in hostile territory. First: never smoke in the field. Stern claimed the smell of cigarette smoke on the wind had saved his life many times. McConnell had made a joke then, but it didn't seem funny now. As they neared the next cottage, the leader made no effort to circle around it. Instead he walked right up to the front door, unlocked it with a key and motioned them inside.

There was hardly any light, but McConnell could see that the walls of the narrow entrance hall were adorned only by a coat rack. Stern dropped his bags and sat down on them, breathing hard.

"Pick up those cases," the leader ordered. "You're going to the cellar."

"Give us a moment, eh?" Stern pleaded in German. "That was some hike."

The leader grunted in disgust and stalked out of the foyer. Mc-Connell set down his bags and felt his way into a room that had to be a kitchen. He smelled coffee warming on the stove. It took great restraint to keep from feeling his way to it and drinking straight from the pot.

The leader lighted two candles and placed them on a wooden table at the center of the room. McConnell took in the sparsely stocked shelves and yellow-painted walls, then said, *"Mein Name ist Mark McConnell. Thank you for meeting us."*

The leader shrugged and took off his hat. A mane of blond hair fell around his shoulders. He unwrapped the scarf from his face.

"My God," McConnell said in English.

"I am Anna Kaas," said the young woman, pulling off her heavy coat and revealing anything but a man's figure. "Tell your lazy friend to take those suitcases down to the cellar. You're in Germany now."

"Ach du lieber Hergott!" Stern said from the doorway.

"You were expecting a man?" Anna said. "Sorry to disappoint you."

McConnell watched in amazement as the young woman poured the coffee. She appeared to be close to his own age, and she had deep brown eyes—unusual in a woman who otherwise fit the Aryan stereotype of the flaxen-haired, blue-eyed Brunhild.

"You're hours late," she said. "You are trying to kill us?"

"Mechanical trouble," said Stern, stepping into the kitchen. "You work in the camp?"

"Yes. I'm a nurse. There are six of us."

"You enjoy your work?"

Even by candlelight, McConnell saw the woman color at this remark. "If I did, would I be putting up two rude Englishmen for the
night?" she rejoined.

"I'm American," McConnell told her.

"And I'm German," said Stern. "I was raised thirty kilometers
from here, in Rostock."

"How wonderful for you," Anna said. "Perhaps you can stay
alive long enough to complete your mission."

Stern walked to the kitchen window and peered through a crack
in the curtains. McConnell could see the glow of daylight even from
where he stood.

"If the wind lets up," said Stern, "I'll only have to survive half
an hour or so to do that."

"What do you mean?" Anna asked.

"I mean we're executing the mission as soon as the wind falls
off."

"Not if you want to succeed."

Stern turned from the window. "Why not? The daylight is a
problem, but we've got the German uniforms. We'll make it to
the hill. Getting away alive afterward won't be easy, but. . . ." He
waved his hand dismissively.

"London didn't tell you?" Anna Kaas shook her head in astonishment. "Major Schörner discovered the body of an SS sergeant today, buried in the hills. He'd been shot by a submachine gun. The
SS found four parachutes buried with him. *British* parachutes."

"*Verdammt!*" said Stern. "That's what McShane meant by a
'warm welcome.' They killed someone during the preparatory mission. Smith must have ordered him not to tell us about it."

"Terrific," McConnell said.

"It's a miracle we reached the cottage," Anna told them. "Major
Schörner has half the garrison out on patrol. A motorcycle unit
stopped here five minutes before I left for the pickup point. If they'd
returned while I was gone, we would be running for our lives now."

"How far are we from the power station?" Stern asked.

"About three kilometers, uphill all the way."

"Heavy tree growth? Plenty of cover?"

"Yes, but a switchback road crosses your path a dozen times between here and there."

Stern winced. "What about the wind? Has it been blowing this hard all night?"

"What is so important about the wind?"

When Stern did not reply, she said, "It gusts, but it hasn't dropped below a hard breeze all night."

"Just a minute," McConnell cut in. "What's all this about a power station? Now that we're finally in Germany, maybe you can tell me exactly what the plan is? How are the two of us supposed to disable this plant so that I can get a look at the machinery? Are some of Vaughan's commandos parachuting in behind us or what?"

"No," said Stern.

"I am also confused," Anna said. "Since only two of you landed, I assumed your team must already be here, hiding in the woods. What can two men do against the garrison at Totenhausen?"

"More than you think," said Stern.

"*You* don't know what the mission is?" McConnell asked her. "No."

"Come on, Stern," he pressed. "Out with it."

"Thank you for telling her my real name, Doctor."

"Code names are childish at this point," Anna said. She looked at McConnell. "Your German is terrible."

"*Danke.*"

"I mean your grammar is perfect, but your accent. . . ."

"I already tried to avoid this mission on those grounds. It didn't work."

"He's not here for his language skills," Stern said. "He's a chemist."

Anna looked at McConnell with sudden understanding. "Ah. Perhaps you weren't such a bad choice, then."

Stern opened a door that led onto a small bedroom, looked inside, then closed it. "You want to know how the two of us are going to disable the plant, Doctor? We're not. We're going to leave it exactly like we find it, except for one thing. Everybody in it will be dead."

"What?" McConnell felt suddenly lightheaded. "What did you say?"

"You didn't hear me? We're going to gas the camp, Doctor. That's why I asked about the wind. The ideal windspeed for the attack is zero to six miles per hour."

"Gas the camp? With what?"

"With nerve gas from the Totenhausen storage tanks?" Anna guessed.

Stern shook his head. "With our own nerve gas."

"We didn't bring any," said McConnell. "We don't even *have* any. Do we?"

Stern smiled with the satisfaction of secret knowledge.

"But . . ." Anna trailed off, pondering Stern's words.

"I see," McConnell said. But he didn't see. He had known Smith was holding back facts about the mission. Yet of all the possibilities he had imagined, this was not one. "Is the target really a gas factory and testing facility, as I was led to believe?"

"Yes."

"But . . . how are you going to gas the SS without killing the prisoners?"

"I'm not."

McConnell sat down at the kitchen table and tried to digest this.

"There's no way to warn the prisoners without risking the success of the mission," explained Stern. "Even if we could separate them, there's nowhere for them to go."

"*Mein Gott,*" Anna whispered.

"Why didn't you tell me this back at Achnacarry?" asked McConnell. "I asked you enough times."

"I didn't tell you because you wouldn't have come. Smith was not lying about one thing, Doctor, time is critical. There was no time to find someone else."

"Couldn't you at least have given me the choice?"

"You *have* a choice. Are you going to help me?"

McConnell was tempted to refuse merely out of anger at being tricked so completely. But even underneath his anger, he knew that what Smith wanted them to do was wrong.

"No," he said. "I'm not going to help you kill innocent prisoners."

Stern turned up his palms. "You see? We were right not to tell you."

"Christ, what did you gain by lying?"

"You're here, aren't you? Look, all you have to do is assist me in the final phase. Go into the factory and tell me what to take pictures of. Help me get the samples. Smith thought you'd see the necessity after thinking it through."

"Well, I don't see it! I knew something like this couldn't be done without loss of life. I prepared myself for that. But this . . . Jesus, Stern, you're talking about murdering hundreds of innocent people! I thought we understood each other. Don't you think you owed me a little honesty?"

"*Owed* you?" Stern's face reddened. "I only met you two weeks ago! I'll tell you who I owe, Doctor. The Jews waiting to be murdered in fifty death camps across Germany and Poland. I owe the soldiers who are going to risk their lives to liberate Europe and free those Jews. It may not be their top priority, but they'll get to it sooner or later. As for you, you can sit here and wait for the Second Coming or whatever you believe will finally stop Hitler. I'm going up that hill."

"Is that where the gas is?"

"Yes."

"How are you going to get it into the camp?"

"Easily. There are ten electrical pylons connecting the power station on top of a nearby hill to the prison camp at the bottom. Last night, Sergeant McShane and his men hung eight cylinders of British nerve gas from a power line at the top pylon. My mission is to climb that pylon, release the cylinders, and send them down into Totenhausen."

"So that's it," Anna said, staring into one of the candle flames. "London had me out at all hours of the night sketching poles and wires and transformer boxes. All the electrical junctions at the camp. I had no idea why until now. I assumed they were planning to defeat the electrical fence before a general assault."

She sat down opposite McConnell and looked up at Stern. "Is that really the only way? To kill *everyone?*"

"What are a few hundred lives sacrificed if it saves tens of thousands later?" Stern said.

Anna's eyes didn't waver. "You say that very easily, Herr Stern. There are women and children in that camp."

"Jews?"

"There are many Jews there, yes. Others too. You don't like Jews?"

"I am a Jew."

She blinked in disbelief. "My God. You are a Jew and you have the nerve to come here? You must be mad."

"No. But I am ready to die for my people. If other Jews must die also, so be it."

"Is that your choice to make?" McConnell asked.

"Those prisoners were doomed long before we got here, Doctor. This way at least they'll die for a reason."

"Count me out," McConnell said.

"I never counted you in." Stern went back to the window and watched through a crack in the curtains. "I told Smith he was a fool to think you would help me. It doesn't matter, though. I can make the attack without you."

McConnell wasn't listening. He was thinking. "You say those cylinders on the hill have British nerve gas in them?"

"That's right."

"What kind of nerve gas?"

Stern shrugged. "I don't know. Nerve gas."

"Have you seen it work?"

"Seen it? Of course not. It's invisible, isn't it?"

"Sometimes. Do you know where it came from?"

"What is your point, Doctor?"

McConnell didn't answer. His silence obviously infuriated Stern, who glared angrily from the window. Anna looked from one man to the other, stunned by the hostility displayed between them.

Stern suddenly turned back to the window curtains, as if he had heard something. "I see a bus!" he said, picking up his Schmeisser. "A gray bus full of men. They're driving from the village toward us. Who are they?"

"The factory technicians," Anna said. "They're quartered in Dornow. The bus takes them back and forth to work every day."

When McConnell began to laugh, Anna and Stern stared at each other like funeral goers who have stumbled into the wrong parade. The laugh began as a few short barks, then settled into the dry chuckle of a man who realizes that he is the butt of a joke of cosmic proportions.

"What the hell is wrong with you?" Stern asked. "What are you laughing at?"

"You," said McConnell. "Us."

"What do you mean?"

"Stern, we're both so goddamn stupid it's pathetic. What did I tell you back at Achnacarry? That this mission as explained to me didn't make sense. But since you knew Smith was lying to me, it didn't bother you too much that I couldn't make sense of it. But don't you see? The mission as told to *you* doesn't make any sense either."

"Explain, damn you!"

"Are you blind? If the British really have developed their own nerve gas, where is the logic in wiping out the people in this camp?"

Stern tried to recall his first conversation with Brigadier Smith, that night in the Bentley. "The British only have a limited amount of gas," he said slowly. "One-point six tons, something like that. The Nazis have thousands of tons stockpiled around Germany. Smith said the Allies could never catch up before the invasion, that their only chance was to bluff the Nazis into believing they not only have their own nerve gas, but also the will to use it. Plus the sample, re-member? The Soman sample."

McConnell watched him like a teacher willing a student toward an answer. *"Think,* Stern. They got a sample of Sarin out without our help, remember? They don't need us for that. They've got Anna here. No, the point of this mission is *killing the people.* To kill ev-eryone inside that camp and leave the machinery intact. That is the plan, right?"

"Yes."

"I couldn't see it because I had accepted the idea that we were coming to disable the plant. But assuming Smith told you truth—at least about the objective—what does that tell us? If you wipe out this camp with nerve gas, you will have committed the first offensive chemical weapons strike of the Second World War. The risks are in-calculable. And if I know one thing about Duff Smith, he's a prag-matic bastard. The same for Churchill. Neither would take such a risk unless they had no choice."

"They *don't* have a choice," Stern told him. In four days Hein-rich Himmler is going to demonstrate Soman to the Führer, in the hope of convincing him to use nerve gas against the Allied invasion troops. Hitler believes the Allies have their own nerve gases. Himmler doesn't, and for once he is close to being right. Churchill and Smith believe this attack—this bluff—is the only chance to convince Himmler he's wrong, and embarrass him into calling off his demonstration."

McConnell remained unconvinced. "Even if all that is true," he said, "you're missing the point. If the British possess even one liter of their own nerve gas, all Churchill would have to do is get one vial of it into the right hands in Germany. Even leaking the written formula would be enough. By doing that, they would show Hitler they have strategic parity, but without risking massive retaliation. Because the Nazis would have no way of knowing whether the British had only one vial or ten thousand tons!"

McConnell drummed his fingers on the table. "No, Stern, only one possible scenario justifies a risk like this. The British *have* developed some form of nerve gas, but there's a problem with it. Maybe multiple problems."

"What do you mean? What kind of problems?"

McConnell shrugged. "Could be anything. It usually takes three to six months to copy a war gas, and that's with *conventional* variants. Sarin is a revolutionary toxin, and as far as I know, the British have had it for less than sixty days. With Churchill breathing down their necks, the scientists at Porton might just have been able to crack it. But even then their problems would only have begun. War gases are extremely difficult to mass produce for battlefield use. They must be heavier than air, resistant to moisture, non-corrosive to standard steel. They must be stable enough to retain toxicity during long periods of storage and transport, also to survive the detonation of the artillery shells that carry them. A nerve gas should ideally be odorless and colorless, insofar as is possible. If you see a gas cloud coming—or smell it in low concentration—its effectiveness as a weapon is greatly inhibited—"

"Get to the point!" Stern shouted.

"Sorry. My point is that the British team at Porton has probably developed a facsimile of Sarin that has one or more of those flaws. They can't send a sample to the Germans, because they know their gas can't withstand close analysis, i.e. it's not in the same league with Sarin."

Stern moved away from the window and planted a boot on one of the kitchen chairs. "Why couldn't they send Hitler a vial from the stolen sample? Send the Nazis their own gas and claim it's British?"

McConnell considered this. "That's not a bad idea, actually. I'll bet Smith thought of that. But German chemists are very good. An *exact* chemical copy of German Sarin would be greeted with extreme suspicion. They'd probably figure out that bluff."

He drank some of his coffee, which had grown cold. "No, I think Smith and Churchill looked at the situation and decided they had only one option. To gamble that whatever problems exist with the British Sarin, the stuff *will kill*. That's why there are only the two of us, Stern. If the copycat Sarin kills effectively, it may well convince the Nazis that they would be foolish to risk attacking the Allies with nerve gas. But if it *doesn't* work, what have the British lost? You and me. Two expendable civilians. Whether the British Sarin works or not, it will be gone on the wind in a few hours. And I'll bet you fifty bucks that the cylinders hanging from your pylon are of German manufacture."

"They are."

McConnell shook his head, awed by the boldness of Smith's plan. "We're sacrificial lambs, Stern. You may fancy that role. I don't."

Stern had gone very still. Anna was watching McConnell with a strange mixture of respect and fear.

"It stings, doesn't it?" McConnell laughed softly. "The great Haganah terrorist, fooled by a British general."

Stern slung his Schmeisser over his shoulder. "The gas might work," he said. "You admitted that yourself. If it does, the mission will succeed regardless of all this. I guess I'll just have to find out the hard way, as you Americans say."

He turned and started for the foyer.

"Wait!" Anna pleaded. "It's daylight. You'll never reach that pylon without being caught. Major Schörner has doubled the guard on the transformer station."

Stern lifted his hand from the door handle. "What?"

"I told you, there are patrols everywhere because of the dead sergeant. Even if you managed to attack the camp, half the SS men wouldn't be there. I've made a place for you in the cellar. You can hide there today and decide what to do. It will be dark by six tonight. Where is the harm in waiting until then?"

Stern came back into the kitchen. "I want to speak to someone higher up in your group."

"There is no one higher," Anna said.

"*You* are the senior person?"

"There's no one else."

"I don't believe you. Who were those men who helped us at the plane?"

"Friends. They know nothing about the situation in camp."

"You're Brigadier Smith's only contact?"

"Who is Brigadier Smith?"

McConnell couldn't keep from grinning. "What's wrong with her? I like her just fine. Our own Mata Hari."

"Shut up, damn you!"

McConnell stood up. "Kiss my ass, Stern. You know that idiom yet? Add it to your collection."

Stern gave both of them withering stares, nodding like a man who has just discovered he is surrounded by enemies. Then he turned, walked through the foyer and out the front door.

Anna looked at McConnell with wild eyes, then jumped up, ran to the door, and shouted for Stern. He apparently did not stop, for she came back into the kitchen wearing the blank gaze of a witness to a terrible accident.

"He is walking toward the hills," she said. "He will kill us all."

"I don't know," said McConnell, standing up from the table. "He's got that SD uniform. He speaks perfect German. He might make it."

Anna looked around her kitchen as if it had suddenly become an alien environment. "They should have told me," she said, her soft voice full of resentment. "It is too much to ask." She focused on McConnell, her face now illuminated by sunlight. "Would he really do it?" she asked. "Would he really kill all those prisoners? All those children?"

McConnell realized then that Stern's revelation had shocked the nurse as deeply as it had him. He felt an urge to touch her, to try and comfort her, but he didn't want her to misinterpret his action. "I'm afraid he's perfectly capable of doing that," he said. "If he really wants to, you could only stop him by killing him. Unless you're ready to do that, I don't think you'd better go in to work today."

"But I must!" Anna looked at him with new fear in her eyes. "If I don't, Major Schörner will send a patrol here."

"Can you call in sick?"

"I have no telephone."

"How do you get to work?"

"Bicycle."

"Well . . . you'd better ride damn slowly."

29

Only twenty-four hours had passed since Major Schörner humiliated Sergeant Sturm in the alley, but in those hours Gunther Sturm had boiled with a rage unlike any he had ever known. It consumed him. Ultimately, he would kill Schörner. But the discovery of the British parachutes had caused enough of an uproar to draw the attention of Colonel Beck at Peenemünde. Sturm knew he would be crazy to try to get rid of Schörner under the nose of that devil.

He'd flirted with the idea of challenging Schörner to a duel. SS law entitled a man to demand satisfaction in a dispute where honor was involved. But in practice, actual duels were discouraged. Besides, even with one eye missing, Schörner was an expert fencer and a crack shot. No, the only revenge he could get immediately would be through Schörner's Jewish whore.

The man he had chosen to carry out his vendetta was a certain Corporal Ludwig Grot. Not only was Grot the most violent man in his unit, but he also owed the sergeant major nearly four hundred marks in gambling debts. Sturm had put the matter to him over a bottle of excellent schnapps, a treat he had been saving for a special occasion. Grot had been more than happy for the chance to erase his debts with a single favor. And so simple! One beating. A couple of well-placed blows. Where was the difficulty? If a Jew insulted the honor of the Reich as he passed, it was his duty to teach her a lesson. If she died, so what? One less Jew fouling the good German air.

Sturm had made sure Grot had a clear field for his attack. Schörner was meeting with Colonel Beck at Peenemünde about the parachutes, and Brandt had driven down to Berlin again to meet

with Reichsführer Himmler. As Sturm walked his favorite shepherd—an enormous male called Rudi—down to the vantage point
he had chosen from which to observe the ambush, he saw Grot
lounging in front of the SS enlisted barracks. He gave the corporal
a smug grin and reflected on how good a choice he had made.

During their time in Einsatzkommando 8, clearing Jews from
Latvia, Ludwig Grot had frequently complained of boredom. He
also lamented the great waste of ammunition expended in the dis-
posal of Jews. One day he discovered a way to simultaneously as-
suage his two pet peeves. He ordered several Jewish prisoners to
stand in a line, each man pressing his chest to the back of the man
in front of him. He then took bets on how many Jews he could kill
with a single bullet. In eastern Poland he had won thirty marks by
killing three fully grown males with a single shot from his Luger.
Near Poznan he had killed five women this way, but the last in line
had taken several hours to die, so she didn't really count.

Sturm affectionately scratched Rudi's coat behind the powerful
neck. He almost wished Schörner could be around to see the show.

Rachel was crossing the Appellplatz with Hannah and Jan when
a guttural German voice brought her up short.

"What was that you said, Jew?"

She stopped and looked up into the perpetually angry face of
Corporal Ludwig Grot.

"What did you call me, *Judenlaus?*" he barked.

Rachel noticed that the corporal was speaking very loudly, as if
for the benefit of an audience. She clenched Jan and Hannah's
hands. "I said nothing, Herr Rottenführer. But if I offended, I
apologize."

"You did offend, you stinking slut."

Rachel crumpled to the ground under the force of the first blow.
She wasn't sure what had happened. It felt like she had walked
blindly into an iron lamppost. When Grot kicked her in the stomach
she nearly blacked out, but she forced one string of words from her
throat. "Run! Children, run to Frau Hagan!"

Jan caught little Hannah's hand and began pulling her toward
the inmate blocks.

Grot dragged Rachel to her feet and slapped her twice—very
hard and very quickly—like a man for whom violence is an old

habit. The right side of her face stung as if it had been scalded. The left side felt numb. An image of a silver Death's Head ring hung before her eyes. For an instant she thought of Wolfgang Schörner, then in the next remembered he was eighty kilometers away in Peenemünde. There would be no rescue today. She closed her eyes and prayed that Frau Hagan would look after her children.

Grot balled his right fist and punched the side of the head, dropping her onto the snow, then kicked her savagely in the ribs with his hobnailed boot. Rachel heard something crack as her left side collapsed inward. Grot's boot stopped in its path toward her head as a woman's voice shouted at him in a foreign language.

He looked up.

Frau Hagan was striding across the yard with all the confidence she had displayed digging peat at Auschwitz or hauling bricks at Buna. When she was ten meters from the corporal she began berating him in German, waving her hands and shouting that Major Schörner had unexpectedly returned to the camp and wanted Grot in his office immediately.

Confronted by this disconcerting spectacle, Grot stood up straight. The *kapo* of the Jewish Women's Block, though a prisoner, had an official position and she was screaming about Major Schörner. He turned and sought out Sergeant Sturm, who stood beneath a watchtower forty meters across the yard.

While Corporal Grot looked to Sturm for guidance, Frau Hagan covered the last few meters to him. Rachel gasped when she saw the gardening spade appear from beneath her gray shift.

Grot whirled just in time to see the flash of metal as Frau Hagan buried the spade up to the hilt in his neck. She jerked the spade back out, allowing a fountain of blood to spurt from Grot's carotid artery. Both hands flew to his throat.

"*Dosyç!*" Frau Hagan bellowed. "Enough! To hell with you, SS!" The big Pole nodded at Grot, defiance in her eyes.

The SS man, his eyes bulging in dumb incomprehension, fell to the ground in a spreading puddle of blood.

Frau Hagan knelt over Rachel. "Are you all right, Dutch girl?"

Rachel could barely breathe, much less speak. Tears of gratitude stung her cheeks. She heard cries of rage and confusion reverberating through the camp. No one could quite believe what had happened.

"Run," she croaked. "Get away . . . while you can."

A savage barking chilled Rachel's blood. But instead of cowering before the fearsome noise, Frau Hagan rose into a crouch, turned, and braced herself for an attack. Rachel saw her face contort into a mask of fury—an anger that had been building for years, perhaps for a lifetime.

Rudi, Sturm's favorite shepherd, was charging across the yard with his teeth bared. He tore over the frozen ground faster than a racing hound and leaped at Frau Hagan while he was still four meters away.

The Block Leader shouted something in Polish and held up her left forearm. Rudi's jaws snapped shut on unprotected flesh as he landed, flailing his head from side to side and fighting to push the woman off her feet.

With all the power in her thick body Frau Hagan slashed upward and plunged the spade into the animal's throat. An explosive squeal echoed across the snow. The dog kept thrashing its head, teeth ripping flesh, but its motions seemed mechanical, confused. Frau Hagan yanked out the spade and struck lower, ripping open its belly from groin to breastbone.

Rudi let go. Frau Hagan threw herself upon the beast like a madwoman, mauling it with maniacal strength. Steam rose from the dog's open belly.

Rachel tensed when heard the first shot, but she saw no immediate effect. The second bullet thudded into flesh, but Frau Hagan continued to slash away. Rachel realized then that an excited guard had shot the dog—either by mistake or to put it out of its misery.

Frau Hagan looked back over her shoulder. *"Get up!"* she shouted. *"Run! You'll be shot!"*

Rachel struggled to move but her limbs would not obey. "No!" she yelled back. "Come with me!"

Another rifle bullet slammed into the dog. One of the tower-gunners fired a short burst to take his range. Frau Hagan looked at Rachel one last time, her eyes shining with a strange elation, then gathered up her shift and dashed toward the base of the guard tower where Sergeant Sturm stood watching in disbelief.

The enraged Pole was running at full speed with the spade held high when the tower gunner cut her down. The bullets blew her over onto her back, where she lay without moving.

Totenhausen lay perfectly silent. From the ground Rachel searched the faces of the women prisoners that had formed a loose perimeter around her. For the first time since her arrival, she sensed a real potential for violence among them. Frau Hagan was known to them all. Dozens in the crowd owed her favors, some owed her their lives. She was a symbol of survival in the face of the worst the Nazis could do. For some seconds Rachel was seized by the feeling that the women might actually follow Frau Hagan's example and charge the guards.

She heard an SS man shout an order to return to barracks. No one moved. Across the yard, in the shadow of the hospital, Rachel spied Anna Kaas. The blond nurse was standing beside the concrete steps, looking directly at her. In her white uniform she looked strangely like an angel. When she had caught Rachel's eye, Anna raised both hands sharply toward the sky. Rachel stared back. The nurse signaled again, more violently.

Get up? Rachel thought. *Is that what you are telling me? Yes. Get up and walk or you will die where you lie.*

She scrabbled up onto her forearms, then her knees. Frau Hagan lay motionless twenty meters away. Sergeant Sturm was bellowing orders one after another. Some of the women prisoners were moving *en masse* toward the main gate, where a small group of SS stood with their weapons leveled. Rachel got unsteadily to her feet.

Someone fired a shot into the air.

The mob pushed on toward the gate. At any other camp they would have been shot down without a thought, but these were Brandt's guinea pigs. The guards hesitated. Rachel stepped over the mutilated dog and moved toward her fallen friend. She could not stop herself. She felt a remarkable sense of calm. For the first time, she realized, her children were not uppermost in her mind. Death was beckoning, yet she felt no fear.

She had almost reached Frau Hagan when someone seized her arm. She looked up into the face of Anna Kaas. The nurse pulled her away from Frau Hagan, toward the hospital.

Rachel looked back at the dead Pole. "Where are you taking me?"

"Shut up and follow me!"

There was a sudden hail of gunfire. Rachel turned toward the main gate. The SS were shooting into the ground at the mob's feet. The line of advancing women wavered, but several shouted defiantly. Then Sergeant Sturm pointed his revolver at the crowd and fired three times in quick succession.

"He's shooting people," Rachel said.

The mob broke and ran, leaving its wounded behind.

Anna dragged her up the hospital steps and into the main corridor. Instead of taking her to an examining room, she pushed Rachel into a dark alcove that smelled of dirty linens.

"Before the yard is cleared you must return to your block," she said quickly. "You don't want to see a doctor. The doctors here will use your injuries as an excuse to kill you. Do you understand?"

Rachel stared.

Anna took hold of her shoulders and shook her. "Hagan is dead! You are alive! Without you, your children will die! Do you hear?"

Rachel nodded dully.

"It is madness!" Anna said, a hysterical tone underlying her voice. "I thought we would all be dead by now. And now this! God knows what Sturm will do after what Hagan did!"

She pulled Rachel out of the alcove and marched her to the back door of the hospital. "You know where you are. Go left, toward the latrines. Get into your block any way you can." She opened the door and looked out. The alley was empty. "Go now!" She shoved Rachel down the steps and closed the door.

Rachel went.

30

McConnell had been waiting alone in the cellar of Anna's cottage for eight hours when he heard someone knock at the front door. He turned off the gas lamp and sat completely still in the darkness. He knew the knocking might be Stern, but Stern had taken off without a word and he could find his own goddamn way back in.

Besides, it might not be Stern. Stern could have been caught by a German patrol ten minutes after he left the cottage and been tortured ever since. He could have given up its location only minutes ago. The sound of the knocking was faint, probably because there was a staircase and a heavy door between McConnell and the kitchen, and then the foyer beyond that.

The knocking stopped.

McConnell didn't try to relight the gas lamp. He took several deep breaths and tried to slow the pounding of his heart. He wasn't sure if it was light or dark outside, but he figured dark.

Where the hell *was* Stern?

After his dramatic dawn exit, Anna had shown McConnell through a narrow door in the corner of the kitchen that led to the cellar. Down a steep flight of wooden steps was a low-ceilinged room stacked with bellied boxes and rusted farm machinery. There was a sofa at the back, and a couple of old duvets. He'd collected the bags from the foyer and hauled them down the steps one piece at a time while Anna watched him with a hopeless look in her eyes. She'd spoken a few puzzled words, then left for Totenhausen.

During the first two hours McConnell had jumped at every sound, expecting to hear sirens or gunfire or whatever alarms might result from Stern gassing the prison camp. After that, he'd begun having visions of Stern in the hands of the SS, trying to hold out against God only knew what kind of tortures. But when no storm troopers arrived to break down the cottage door and arrest him, he calmed down enough to eat some cheese from his bag and consider his situation.

Brigadier Smith had proved to be even more devious than McConnell had given him credit for. The moment McConnell climbed out of that Lysander onto German soil, he had become an accessory to the mission, helpless to stop Stern except by killing him or turning him in to the SS—both moral impossibilities.

Smith had counted on that.

So here he was, cowering in the cellar of a frightened German nurse, unable to escape Germany without Stern's help. The nurse intrigued him. She was the furthest thing imaginable from his idea of a spy. Had it been she who smuggled out the sample of Sarin that he'd tested in his Oxford lab? It was certainly possible. But if so, what had motivated her to take such a risk? In the absence of facts, he found himself certain that Anna Kaas had endured some great tragedy at the hands of the Nazis. Why else would she risk her life to fight them? Very few Germans had.

Her reluctance to embrace Brigadier Smith's plan had surprised and pleased him. She must have been excited at the prospect of action, especially after months or even years of living a double life, always under threat of discovery yet never seeing any benefit from the risks she took. But now that the day had arrived, she seemed appalled by what "London" had decreed must be done. Before leaving the cottage, she'd looked back at him and said, "It's odd, isn't it? The Nazis say we must kill Jews to save the German people. Your Brigadier Smith says you must kill Jews to save the Jewish people. I wonder . . . do any of these men care about saving individual human beings?" A simplification, perhaps, but she had gotten to the heart of the matter. Maybe together they could convince Stern to abandon the idea of killing the prisoners.

Perhaps they could work out a compromise.

McConnell gripped the arm of the sofa. Something had made a crashing sound upstairs. He heard a quick scream, then voices. He felt along the sofa cushion until his left hand closed over the folding stock of his Schmeisser. He'd never thought he would really use the weapon, but if SS men were coming for him—

A shaft of light sliced down through the darkness.

He pointed the submachine gun at the top of the stairs.

"Are you down there?"

A woman's voice. Anna. But she was not alone.

"Come on, Doctor!"

Stern.

McConnell exhaled in relief. Keeping the Schmeisser in his hands, he climbed the steps to the kitchen. He arrived in time to see Anna pour a glass of vodka and drink it in a single swallow. With trembling hands she poured another.

"What's the matter?" McConnell asked. "What happened?"

"I frightened her," said Stern, leaning in the foyer doorway. "I tried to get in earlier, but you wouldn't answer the door. I didn't want to break in, because I thought you might shoot me. I waited for her, then shoved in behind her when she opened the door."

"Where the hell have you been all day?"

Stern walked over to Anna and drank a shot of vodka from her bottle. "Rostock," he said, and wiped his mouth.

Anna's glass clinked on the countertop. "You are insane! Why did you go there?"

Stern took another swallow of vodka. "It was too windy to make the attack. Besides, I knew we'd never reach the coast without being caught if an alarm was raised. Not in daylight."

"But how did you get to Rostock?"

"I stole a car from the village."

Anna shook her head. "You are mad."

"I returned it to its owner," Stern said casually. "But never mind that. When you got here, you dropped your bicycle and ran to your door. Something had frightened you long before you saw me. What was it?"

Anna looked away from him and drank from the glass. "You were right last night," she said. "Totenhausen must be destroyed, whatever the cost. It is an abomination."

McConnell stared at her in confusion.

"Tell me what happened," Stern demanded.

She took a step back, retreating from Stern's sudden intensity. "There was a killing today."

"Is that unusual?"

"Only because it was a prisoner who killed an SS man."

"What?"

"It was a woman. The Blockführer of the Jewish Women's Barracks. She stabbed a corporal in the neck with a gardening spade. The biggest brute in the camp."

"Why did she do that?"

"The guard was beating another prisoner to death. A Jewess from Amsterdam."

Stern shook his head angrily. "This Blockführer was also a Jew?"

"No. But she and the Jewess were friends."

"Did the Jewish woman die?"

"No. I got her away and sent her back to her block." Anna half-turned away and looked at the floor as she spoke, as if she were being forced to reveal some terrible family secret. "Hauptscharführer Sturm went berserk after seeing that his man was really dead. With Brandt and Schörner gone, he was the senior officer in camp. He ordered immediate reprisals. Two women were hanged from the Punishment Tree, and eight more shot by firing squad. Ten people murdered."

Stern grabbed her shoulder and spun her around. "Jews?"

"No," she said, her voice barely audible. "Polish Christians."

Anna pushed past him and sat down at the table, the glass still clenched in her hand. "If Schörner hadn't returned from Peenemünde, I think Sturm and his men would have murdered every prisoner in the camp."

"Major Schörner imposed order?" Stern asked, standing right over her.

"More than that. He ordered Sturm confined to quarters. That man has the nerve of the devil."

"But why would he do that?"

"I think it's something personal between him and Sturm. Something to do with the woman."

"The woman who killed the SS man?"

"No, the Jewess who was beaten. I think Schörner has pressured her into some sort of sexual arrangement."

Stern looked pointedly at McConnell, as if to say, *You see what these Nazi pigs are capable of?* "And this sergeant disapproves of the major's sexual arrangement?"

"I don't think he cares about that," Anna said. "There is something else between him and Schörner. Sturm really hates him."

"What kind of crazy camp is this? Is there no discipline?"

She shook her head slowly, unshed tears pooling in her eyes. "It's worse than anything you can imagine. Herr Doktor Brandt is in charge. Technically he is a lieutenant-general in the SS, but he has no military training. It is said he's a personal friend of Himmler. There are three other SS doctors—two captains and a major—to fill out the officer complement. Major Schörner is head of security. After that it drops to Hauptscharführer Sturm and his men."

"No midlevel officers?"

Anna shook her head. "That's the way Brandt likes it. He wants doctors around him, not soldiers."

At last Stern moved away from her and began pacing around the table. McConnell sat down so he wouldn't have to keep stepping out of his way.

"What would happen if I attacked the camp now?" Stern asked.

"The same as last night," Anna said in an exhausted voice. "You'd miss half of the SS garrison because Schörner has them out searching for parachutists, but you'd kill all of the prisoners. Not only that, since you told me about the wind I've been thinking about it. The wind at the camp blows faster than on this side of the hills. It blows down the river."

Stern made a frustrated sound in his throat.

"Also, Brandt had not returned from Berlin when I left."

"*Verdammt!* Will he be back tonight?"

"Probably, but it could be quite late." Anna stood up and went to the sink, where she ran some water over a cloth and held it against her face. "The whole camp has gone mad," she said through the rag. "Himmler's visit set all this off. The very next night, Sturm and his men raped and murdered six women brought from Ravensbrück. Schörner used to be drunk all the time. Now he's like a hawk, watching everything. It's like something woke him from a deep sleep. Brandt abusing the children . . . it's madness, I tell you. Like the end of the world."

"What was that about children?" McConnell asked.

Anna hung the cloth on the basin and turned to him. "Brandt

performs experiments on children. He calls it medical research, but it's unspeakable. Three times in the past ten weeks he's had boys brought to his quarters. Little boys. He keeps them there for a while, a week or so, then . . . then the gas, I suppose. Oh, God forgive me, I don't know." She wiped more tears out of her eyes. "I don't know and I don't want to."

Stern stopped pacing and stared at McConnell, his face contorted with rage. "And still you won't help me destroy this place?"

McConnell found himself eyeing the vodka bottle with more than passing interest. "Listen, you want to kill this man Brandt. I understand that. I do. A man who tortures children doesn't deserve to live. But you're asking me to kill every innocent prisoner under his power as well. Does that make sense to you?"

"We're talking about the outcome of the entire war!"

"If you believe Brigadier Smith." McConnell tried to summon his most persuasive voice. "Look, Stern, we need to hash this thing out. We're in a pretty tough spot here. Maybe we can find some kind of middle ground if we just calm down—"

Stern kicked over one of the chairs and took a step toward him. "You should have come with me to Rostock today, Doctor. Perhaps you wouldn't be so calm yourself. Are you interested in what I saw there?"

McConnell suppressed an urge to pick up his Schmeisser in self-defense. "Sure," he said softly.

"Our pilot was wrong."

"What do you mean?"

"My family's apartment building was still standing. In fact, I went inside and asked a few questions."

Anna closed her eyes and moved her lips silently, a gesture McConnell read as the equivalent of a Catholic crossing herself.

"Oh, I wasn't in any danger," Stern said in a sarcastic voice. "A policeman stopped me in the city, but when he saw the SD uniform he nearly pissed his trousers. He couldn't wait to get away from me. Being an SD colonel in this country must be rather like being God."

More like the devil, thought McConnell, but he didn't say it.

"Yes, our building is still there," Stern went on, "but things aren't *quite* the same. No bloodstains or anything unpleasant like that. Only when I lived there it was a Jewish building. Now it's full of little blond girls and boys, miniature versions of Fräulein Kaas here."

McConnell saw Anna flinch.

"No one seemed to remember my family," Stern said. "And why should they? It was mostly children. Little Aryan princes and princesses, all living happily in flats haunted by the ghosts of little dark-haired children. I do not think they are troubled by ghosts, though. Do you, Doctor?"

"Stern—"

"Are *you* troubled by them, Doctor?" Stern banged his Schmeisser against a cabinet, startling Anna. "Of all the men in the world, I had to be stuck with you! This woman has more courage than you!"

He stalked down the cellar stairs, but quickly returned with his personal bag, which held the supplies he'd stolen from Achnacarry.

"Where are you going now?" Anna asked anxiously.

Stern slung the bag over his shoulder. "I'm going up that hill to end this madness. The wind is blowing again, but as soon as it dies I'm sending down those cylinders."

"Jesus," said McConnell, coming to his feet. "Just give me a minute to think, for God's sake."

"You've been thinking for your whole life, Doctor. Would another minute make any difference?"

McConnell knew there was no stopping him. "Are you going for the sub afterwards?"

"Since you're not going to help me, there's really nothing I can do in the factory after the attack. I wouldn't know what I was looking at, much less what to take pictures of. I'll steal the nearest vehicle I can find and make a run for the coast."

"What about us?"

"You mean you?"

"We can't leave Anna to face the Gestapo."

Stern barked a short laugh. "We can't take her back with us. Smith was plain about that. The sub wouldn't take her on board. You know the British."

"Every man for himself, eh, Stern?" McConnell shook his head in disgust. "That's been your style from the beginning, hasn't it?"

Stern pulled open the door. "Don't worry, Doctor. I'll get you back to your warm little laboratory, even if it kills me. I want you to explain to Smith why you couldn't compromise your sacred principles to save the Allied invasion army." He hefted the leather bag over his shoulder. "I wish you had to explain it to your dead brother."

McConnell went for him then, but Stern simply slipped out and pulled the door shut after him. By the time McConnell got it open again, he had vanished into the darkness.

Wolfgang Schörner clicked his boot heels together with the report of a parade ground inspection. Before him, seated at an obsessively tidy desk, was Doctor Klaus Brandt. The commandant of Totenhausen had returned from Berlin an hour earlier. He looked up from a piece of notepaper he'd been studying when Schörner entered and regarded him over a pair of rimless reading glasses.

"You asked to see me, Herr Doktor?" Schörner said.

Brandt pursed his lips as if mulling over a complex diagnosis. Schörner felt the familiar discomfort he always experienced in Brandt's presence. It wasn't only the man's perversions. After four years at the sharp end of the war, Schörner found it irksome to be around men who worried more about their careers than the survival of the Reich. He was depressingly certain that whether Germany won or lost, Klaus Brandt would be a millionaire after the war, while the barbed wire on the Fatherland's borders would be tangled with the corpses of men like himself. Yet, ironically, Klaus Brandt was one of the few who held in his hands the means for German victory.

After what seemed an age to Schörner, Brandt said, "You heard Reichsführer Himmler say that he intends to give the Führer a demonstration of Soman Four?"

Schörner nodded. "In three days' time, yes?"

"Correct. I have just learned that Erwin Rommel will be there as well."

Schörner felt a thrill of surprise. Of course it made perfect sense: Hitler had just put Rommel in charge of his Atlantic Wall. It would be the Desert Fox's responsibility to destroy the Allies on the beaches of France.

"Is the demonstration still to take place at Raubhammer Proving Ground, Herr Doktor?"

Brandt sniffed peevishly. "Yes. The test will take place in three days. The Raubhammer engineers claim they've finally perfected a lightweight suit that can insulate a man from both Sarin and Soman."

Schörner raised his eyebrows. "I would like to see that suit, Herr Doktor."

"So would I, Schörner. And we will. They're sending over three for our inspection." Brandt took a very thin cigarette from a gold case on his desk and lit it with almost feminine delicacy. "This demonstration will be quite a show, it seems," he said, leaning back and blowing smoke to the side. "Concentration camp prisoners from Sachsenhausen will be dressed in captured British uniforms and made to charge across a mock beach where Soman has been deployed. SS volunteers defending the 'beach' will be wearing the new protective suits. It should really be something to see. A fitting reward after all our hard work."

"And well-deserved, Herr Doktor."

"Quite so, Sturmbannführer. The Reichsführer believes this demonstration will at last overcome the Führer's irrational—but quite understandable—aversion to chemical weapons."

Brandt held the cigarette between his lips while he examined the manicured fingernails of his left hand. "This will be quite a feather in Himmler's cap, Schörner. And he knows how to reward loyalty."

"I know it well, Herr Doktor." Schörner waited for further information, but Brandt had lapsed into silence.

"Will that be all, Herr Doktor?"

"Not quite, Schörner. This matter of the British parachutes. You have the situation under control? I would hate to think anything might interrupt our production schedule, with the test so near."

"Herr Doktor, Standartenführer Beck and myself believe the parachutists had their sights set on the Peenemünde complex. Most of the sensitive rocketry equipment has been moved into Poland or the Harz Mountains to keep it out of reach of the Allied bombers, but the Allies may not know this. Beck has deployed a great deal of his strength between here and Peenemünde. If by some remote chance these commandos *are* attempting to penetrate our facility, my patrols will catch them long before they get close."

"See that they do, Sturmbannführer."

Schörner clicked his boot heels again.

Setting the cigarette aside, Brandt adjusted his reading glasses and looked down at the paper he had been studying when Schörner entered. "One more thing, Sturmbannführer. I understand that you have placed Hauptscharführer Sturm under house arrest?"

Schörner stiffened. "That is correct, Herr Doktor."

"Why?"

"The Hauptscharführer instigated the incident that resulted in the death of Corporal Grot, as well as that of the *kapo* of the Jewish Women's Block, Hagan."

"And his motive?"

"I believe his motive involved some diamonds, Herr Doktor. Sturm has a habit of trying to loot prisoners as they are brought in from the Occupied Territories. I warned him once, but he apparently did not take the warning to heart."

"Looting is a serious charge, Sturmbannführer." Brandt looked up over his glasses. "The Reichsführer himself has mandated the death penalty for profiteers."

"The basis of my action, Herr Doktor."

"However," said Brandt, tapping his fingers on the desk, "when I returned from Berlin, I found a note on my desk giving a somewhat different version of events."

Schörner felt blood rising into his cheeks. "Was this note signed, Herr Doktor?"

Brandt smiled, but the effect was more like a grimace. "Yes, it was. By four noncommissioned officers. This note contained some serious charges of its own. Charges leveled at you, Sturmbannführer. Charges relating to infractions of the Nuremberg racial laws."

Schörner did not flinch. He knew Brandt was on thin ice himself here. "I am prepared to stand in an SS court on any charges you see fit to authorize, Herr Doktor."

Klaus Brandt instantly raised his hands in a placating gesture. "At ease, Sturmbannführer. I don't think it will come to that. Still, it might be better if you released Sturm under his own recognizance. For the good of the corps. You understand. The last thing any of us want is a pack of SD officers down here turning over every stone and bed."

A hot wave of revulsion washed over Schörner. He wouldn't be surprised if Sturm's comrades had made some oblique reference to Brandt's perversions in their letter. He pressed down his disgust. "As you say, Herr Doktor."

"I'm sure Hauptscharführer Sturm has seen the error of his

ways." Brandt patted the desk with both hands. "Let us concentrate our energies upon the upcoming test, Sturmbannführer. Destiny is at hand."

Schörner fired his boot heels together and marched out.

Jonas Stern moved swiftly through the trees, his steps almost soundless in the newly fallen snow. He'd moved uphill after leaving the cottage, away from the village of Dornow, toward the power station. Toward the cylinders. Twice he had heard patrols pass within thirty meters of him, but he found it easy to avoid them. Usually the orange light or smell of cigarettes betrayed the SS men. Thirty minutes after leaving Anna Kaas's cottage, he was standing beneath the tall wooden pylon where the gas cylinders hung.

He stood in the darkness beside the two great support poles and stared up through the foliage. It took some time for his eyes to adjust, but eventually he made out the silhouettes of the steel cylinders hanging in a neat row from one of the outermost electrical wires. He felt a sudden dizziness when he realized that the heavy tanks were swaying in the treetops. Even without the portable anemometer, he was certain that wind sufficient to move those cylinders was moving faster than the ideal speed for the attack.

He stomped on the snow around the base of the support leg nearest him. Buried beneath his feet, in a box with the anemometer and the emergency radio and the submarine signal lamp, were the climbing spikes and harness that would carry him to the top of the pylon. Within five minutes he could initiate the nerve gas attack on Totenhausen. The brisk wind might dilute the gas's effects, but if the British nerve agent worked at all, it should certainly kill some SS men. On the other hand, if he waited for a while, the wind might drop off to nothing.

As he stood there in the snow, the hum of the nearby transformer station buzzing in his ears, he felt something even stronger than his hatred for the Nazis turning inside him. Something he would never admit to McConnell or the nurse or anyone else. Something he could hardly admit to himself. The visit to Rostock had dredged it up, and the longer he stood there, the more powerful it became until, to his surprise, he found himself moving again. Down the hill, away from the power station. Away from the cylinders.

He was moving toward Totenhausen Camp.

D o you think he will do it this time?" Anna asked.
McConnell sat opposite her at the kitchen table, two
mugs of ersatz coffee made from barley between them. The
brew tasted terrible, but it was hot.

"If he makes it up the hill alive, he probably will. Do you think
he *should* do it?"

"Someone must do something," Anna said. "I don't know if it's
right to kill the prisoners. But he is right about one thing."

"What?"

"Everybody in that camp is doomed no matter what we do.
They'll never survive the war."

"Do you think what he said is true? Do you think I'm a coward
for not helping him?"

Anna looked into her coffee. "People are different. What he
calls courage you call stupidity. What you call courage he calls
weakness. Some men are not made for war, I think. And that must
be a good thing." She looked up at him. "Why *did* they select you
for this mission? It doesn't seem to make sense."

"They said they picked me because I'm not British and because
I'm an expert on poison gases. I guess the idea was that together
Stern and I would make one perfect soldier. A killer with the brain
of a scientist. What about you? You're a civilian nurse?"

"Yes. They said there was a shortage in the medical corps, but
I think Brandt just prefers civilians."

"I'm a civilian myself."

She nodded. "A chemist, yes?"

He laughed. "By avocation only. I'm actually a medical doctor."

Anna's face underwent a subtle yet profound change. She seemed to be looking at McConnell through different eyes. "You are a physician?"

"Yes. Before the war, anyway."

"You had a practice?"

"Briefly."

She sat in silence, reflecting on this new information. Finally she said, "Is that the reason you are so hesitant to kill?"

McConnell hedged. "Part of it, I suppose."

"It's part of the reason I do what I do, too."

"How do you mean?"

Anna glanced at the kitchen window. "It's dangerous for you to be up here. Schörner might order a house-to-house search."

"You want me to go down to the basement?"

She stood up and refilled their mugs, then took the half-empty vodka bottle from a sideboard. "I'll come with you," she said. "I guess we're both waiting for the same thing."

"What is that, exactly?"

"The alarms at Totenhausen. If Stern carries out the attack, we will hear sirens, even in the basement."

McConnell went down the steps first and lit the gas lamp. They sat on the sofa he'd slept on the night before, half-hidden behind the boxes and old farm-machinery parts.

"Can I ask you something?" he said. "You don't have to answer if you don't want to. But I'm curious."

She looked at the floor and smiled sadly. "Why do I work against the Nazis? Yes?"

"Yes. You have to admit, not many Germans have."

"Oh, I'll admit that. The few who had the courage to fight were hunted down early on. The rest fall into two categories: those who love the new order, and those who simply take the path of least resistance. The latter is a highly developed feature of the German political character."

"But not of yours."

Anna poured a stiff shot of the vodka into her coffee. "It could have been." She drank. "But it didn't turn out that way. The funny thing is what changed me. I thought about it a moment ago, when you talked about yourself and Stern. About the two of you making one complete soldier."

"What do you mean?"

"What made me different than other Germans. It was a man, of course."

"A man like myself and *Stern?* I can hardly imagine a man like that."

She laughed. "This man was more like you than Stern. He was a doctor, in fact."

"A physician?"

"Yes. But he was also a Jew."

Anna said this with a certain defiance, and it was the last thing he expected. He didn't know what to say. But he did want to hear the story. "This was in Dornow?"

"No, Berlin. I was raised in Bad Sülze, not far from here. My parents were rural people. Well-enough off, but very provincial. My sister and I had grander ideas. At seventeen I went off to Berlin to become a sophisticated city girl. When I completed my nurses' training, I went to work for a general practitioner in Charlottenburg. Franz Perlman. That was 1936. The Nuremberg Laws had been passed by then, but I was a foolish girl. I had no idea how ominous it all was. The restrictions on Jews were being enforced in different fields at different speeds, and many doctors were still practicing. Franz really seemed too busy to notice. He worked from morning till night, and on everyone—Jews, Christians, whomever."

Anna sipped from her coffee and stared into the soft light of the gas lamp. "There were three of us: Franz, the receptionist, and me. You can imagine how it happened. It's not so uncommon a situation, is it? A doctor and a nurse? I was twenty at the time. I'd fallen in love with him by the third week. It wasn't so hard to do. He was a kind and dedicated man. He tried to discourage me at first. He was a widower, and older. Forty-four. I didn't care how old he was. I never thought about him being a Jew, either. After about a year he stopped discouraging me. Poor man. I was shameless. I wanted to marry him, but he wouldn't hear of it. He wouldn't even let us be seen together outside the office. Only twice in all that time did he sneak into my flat, and he never allowed me in his.

"I grew angry at him after a while. About his refusal to marry me, even secretly. I was a fool. One day he pulled the scales from my eyes. He told me about all his friends who had been forced out of business, or who had simply disappeared. I didn't believe him at first. I lived in . . . *in einem Traum.* In a dream. Jewish professors had already been badgered out of the medical schools. Franz had received threatening letters. He showed me some. Only then did I understand. It was for my physical safety that he'd kept up the illusion that we had no relationship. He wanted to marry me more than anything."

McConnell detected a hitch in Anna's voice, but she got control of it again.

"The practice was almost as busy as ever. A few patients stopped coming, but not many. A caring doctor is not so easy to find. Too many worship the scalpel, yes? Or themselves."

McConnell smiled. "I've known a few of those."

"Franz was different. He felt a deep obligation to his patients. That's why he wouldn't stop. Finally the Nazis left him no room to squirm. They forbade Jewish doctors practicing at all. The line was drawn. Our receptionist refused to come to work. But not me. Every day for five weeks I did the work of two. And Franz was doing the work of ten. Visiting the old, delivering babies—he was one of the last. The funny thing is, many Aryans continued to see him. And he continued to treat them!" She drew a deep breath. "I apologize for dragging this out. It's just . . . I haven't told anyone about this since it happened. I couldn't, you understand? Not my parents. Not even my sister. Especially not my sister."

"I understand, Fräulein Kaas."

"Do you? Do you know what finally happened?"

"They dragged him off to a concentration camp."

"No. One fine morning a well-scrubbed SS boy—I mean it, he was younger than I—he walked into the waiting room and demanded to see the doctor. He had four friends with him, all dressed in black with their Death's Head badges. Franz came into the waiting room wearing his white coat and stethoscope. The SS man informed him that the clinic was closed. Franz said no one had the right to stop him from treating the sick, no matter what uniform they wore. Franz told the boy to go home, then turned around to go back to work."

A chill ran along McConnell's neck and arms. "They didn't kill him—"

"The boy pulled out a Walther and shot Franz in the back. The bullet shattered his spine." Anna wiped tears from her cheeks. "He died within a minute on his own waiting-room floor."

McConnell found nothing to say.

She raised her eyes. "You know what the worst of it was? There were German Christians in that waiting room when it happened. People Franz had treated for fifteen years. And not one of them— not *one*—uttered a sound of protest. Not even to the *boy* who had murdered their doctor before their very eyes!"

"Anna—"

"And Stern wonders why I hate the Nazis?" She balled her fists. "I tell you, if I weren't such a coward I would kill Brandt myself!"

An odd thought struck McConnell then. "How in God's name did you end up working in a concentration camp after that?"

She drank another slug of the vodka-laced coffee. "This really takes the prize. After I came back from the city, depressed and nearly destitute, my older sister took pity on me. And of course, she was in an excellent position to 'help' me. Her way of escaping the boredom of country life had been to marry the Gauleiter of Mecklenburg. Can you believe it? My sister Sabine is a rabid Nazi! She got me the job at Totenhausen, and I was in no position to turn it down. Honestly, the first time I toured Brandt's hospital, it seemed almost like a civilian institution. What a fool I was!"

It was insane, thought McConnell, but typical of what the war had done to people around the world. "You mentioned courage before," he said. "Your Franz Perlman had the kind of courage I admire. He had principles. Character. Conviction."

"Yes," Anna said to her coffee. "And now he is dead. In this world we have made, that's where principles get you."

"Maybe. But I'll take that over capitulation anytime."

"What about you, Doctor?" she said. "I gave you my confession. Give me yours. What keeps you from going up that hill and helping Stern?"

McConnell slid off the sofa and sat on the floor with his back against the leg rest. "It's simple, really. It was my father. He was a doctor too. He's dead now. He fought in World War One. Against the Germans, of course."

"My uncle, too. He died at the Marne."

"My father was gassed at St. Mihiel. Badly burned by mustard. He never really recovered."

Anna touched his shoulder. "I'm sorry."

"I'm sure Freud would have a lot to say about my career choice," McConnell said lightly. "I don't really give a damn. I saw very young what war did to people, and I didn't like it. I still don't. When this one started, I tried to use my talents to prevent suffering, not inflict it. As you can see, the British weren't satisfied with that."

She leaned forward and looked down into his eyes. "You remind me a lot of Franz, Doctor. I think you are a good and kind man. But I don't think you really understand what is happening in Germany."

Anna got up and walked over to a shelf lined with what appeared to be old account books. "I would like you to look at something."

She removed several books, then reached into the space behind and pulled out a small leather-bound volume, its cover worn to a dull shine. "This is my diary," she said. "I began it the day after Franz was killed. In some ways it has been my only friend. The first part contains nothing of consequence—merely personal things. But somewhere around page thirty, I began to record my experiences at Totenhausen. I recorded every experiment I witnessed myself, as well as things I overheard Dr. Brandt confide to other doctors, either in person or on the telephone. Some passages are things he said directly to me after visiting other Reich medical facilities. Concentration camps, euthanasia centers, various clinics." She carried the book part of the way to the stairs, then turned and tossed it to McConnell.

"You're a doctor," she said. "Read the *Curriculum Vitae* of one of your fellow physicians."

When she had gone, McConnell opened the diary and began to read.

Rachel Jansen sat motionless in the wing chair in the anteroom of Major Schörner's quarters. Schörner sat on the sofa opposite her, sipping from a glass of brandy.

"Why didn't he kill me in the reprisal?" Rachel asked in a monotone.

Schörner held his glass up to a lamp and watched the light play through the amber liquid. "Sturm is just the slightest bit afraid of me," he said. "And well he should be. I'd like to cut his throat with his own dagger. When I look at those bruises on your beautiful face . . . my blood burns. And I can tell by the way you sit and breathe that you are hurt in the side. Did that bastard Grot kick you?"

"This is madness," Rachel said softly, the act of speech sending stabbing pains along her damaged ribs. "What if I am discovered here? Now? Tonight?"

A reckless smile played at the corners of Schörner's handsome mouth. "That is the last thing that would happen tonight, *Liebling*. Brandt wants no conflict, nothing that might disturb his arrangements with Reichsführer Himmler. To Brandt, Sturm and I are merely a sideshow. Besides that"—his voice softened—"I had to see you. I had to know that the pig had not hurt you badly."

Schörner leaned forward on the sofa. "Did he? If you are unable tonight . . . I will understand."

Rachel shivered in the chair.

"You are cold?" Schörner asked, his voice full of concern. "Here, *Liebling*, come and sit beside me."

Rachel hesitated, then rose and walked to the couch like a woman going to the guillotine.

Jonas Stern stood in the shadow of a wooden barracks building and listened. At first he heard only the wind, blowing down the Recknitz River. Anna Kaas was right. It was stronger here than in the treetops on the hills.

It took time to separate the snoring from the wind. But that was the sound, he realized: snoring. He moved silently along the row of barracks buildings.

A combination of stealth and boldness had brought him this far. Just before reaching Totenhausen's back fence, he had crossed over three long, shallow pits dug under the trees. He remembered the smell of burnt flesh from North Africa, and recognized the pits for what they were.

It was the trees that gave him his plan. Tall evergreens grew right up to the electrical fence on three sides of the camp. Since he was outside the fence, he simply slung his Schmeisser over his shoulder, climbed a fir tree, shinnied out along a branch and dropped to the snow beside the barn that concealed the gas factory.

Before his nerves had time to stop him, he straightened his back and marched toward the gate that separated the factory from the camp proper. There was one sentry there, an SS private wearing the earth-brown uniform of a concentration camp guard. Stern made ready to get out his papers, but his gray-green SD uniform and Iron Cross were apparently all the identification he needed. He rapped out a "Heil Hitler!" as he passed the respectful guard.

It was easy enough to get his bearings. Walking with obvious purpose—for the benefit of the men in the watchtowers—he moved through the alley that separated the hospital from the E-Block, turned left, then walked up to the mesh fence that bordered the inmate blocks. He strolled along the fence until he found a spot out of sight of the tower guards. One sentry stood watch at the camp's rear gate, but he was facing the woods. Stern saw no insulators on the fence wires—no electricity here. He quickly scaled the fence and dropped to the other side.

He'd heard the snores at the first block. He heard the same thing at the next three. Only at the fifth barracks, when he bent low to listen at the crack beneath the door, did he see a faint yellow glow, as from a candle. Then he heard a voice. A whisper, really. The hairs on his neck rose like quills.

The voice was speaking Yiddish.

He took a quick breath and slipped his right forefinger into the trigger guard of his Schmeisser. Then he stood erect, walked up the three steps and into the block.

The candle went out instantly. He heard a frantic scuffling like rats in the walls—then silence. The air was warmer here, thick with the smell of soiled wool and disinfectant.

"Listen to me," he said softly in Yiddish. "Are you all Jews here?"

No one answered.

"Listen. I am not what I appear to be. Please, are you all Jews?"

Nothing.

He wished he had stripped off the SD uniform outside. "I myself am a Jew," he said. "I have come to Germany from Palestine. I am a spy. I have come to learn the truth of what the Nazis are doing to our people."

Stern realized that if he had claimed he was the Messiah sent from God, he could not have stunned the prisoners more. He saw a faint reflection from eyes peering at him in terror and astonishment, like a den of rabbits surprised in the dark.

"Who is leader here?" he asked.

"Our leader is dead, SS man," said a harsh voice from the darkness. A woman's voice. "You know that."

"Who spoke? Please, I have not come to harm you, but I haven't much time."

"You know who we are," hissed another voice. "What do you want, SS man?"

"This is an SD uniform," Stern said in measured tones. "But I am neither SS nor SD. I am a Jew from Rostock who fled to Palestine. I am ready to prove that to anyone who will speak to me."

"Say kaddish then," someone challenged him, "for all the people you have murdered."

Stern began: "*Yis-ga-dal v'yis-ka-dash sh'may ra-bo, B'ol-mo dee-v'ro hir u-say, v'yam-leeh mal-hu-say*—is that enough?"

"He knows it," said a hesitant voice.

"That means nothing," whispered another.

"What year is it?" someone asked.

"By the Hebrew calendar 5705." Stern felt the pressure of time, but he was proud of the women for testing him this way.

"What are the Four Questions?"

He smiled in the darkness, remembering the Passover seders of his youth. "Why do we eat matzo? Why do we eat bitter herbs? Why do we dip our vegetables? Why do we recline?"

"He knows."

"More lies," said the skeptic. "No Jew would come here by choice."

"There is only one way to tell," said a more confident voice. "The same way the SS pick our men from the crowds."

Stern was confused only a moment.

"Can you pass that test, SS man?" asked the skeptic.

With a flush of anger and embarrassment, Stern unfastened the trousers of the SD uniform and let them down a little.

"Light the candle," said the confident voice.

In the uncertain light of the candle flame Stern saw five women wearing striped gray shifts. Sallow faces, dull eyes, hair cropped almost to the skulls. Beyond them others waited, watchful in the darkness.

"Come closer," said one of the women. She was young, with a dark thatch of hair and onyx eyes.

He obeyed.

The dark-haired woman crept forward with the candle and crouched in front of him. "He speaks the truth," she said. "He is circumcised."

Several women gasped. Stern pulled up his pants. When the woman before him straightened up, he peered deep into her eyes. She seemed younger than the other women. Healthier, too. When he looked down, he saw not only skin over her bones, but also feminine contours.

"I am Rachel Jansen," she said. "You must be mad."

McConnell had been reading Anna's diary for an hour. He did not want to go on, but he could not stop. He felt numb. Even now, he could not quite accept it. The nurse's diary described nothing less than the systematic perversion of a renowned national medical community into the utter negation of everything medical science had sought to achieve since the time of Hippocrates.

He had expected some horror stories. For months rumor had been rife in England about the brutality of the Nazi detention camps. But Anna's diary had little to do with brutality. Brutality was a universal flaw in the human character, commonplace in every society. This diary described atrocities committed on another scale altogether. Even outright murder seemed banal in the face of what he had read in the last hour. One of the most alarming passages had had its effect because of who was involved, as much as what was done.

1-6-43 Dr. Brandt returned from a trip to Auschwitz Main Camp in Silesia. All afternoon he complained to Rauch and Schmidt how the Reich's money is being wasted there. He said Dr. Clauberg has allowed his professional standards to fall deplorably, that Clauberg's experiments with mass sterilization border on quackery.

McConnell knew well the name Clauberg. But could Anna's diary really implicate the physician who had developed the standard test for progesterone action? A test that still carried his name? If the diary could be believed, it could.

Clauberg has apparently taken to "castrating" both men and women by means of massive doses of X-rays. Brandt claims the inefficiency of this method is obvious to anyone with even rudimentary experience of gamma rays and their effects. To prove his point, Brandt requested a male prisoner, which Hauptscharführer Sturm promptly provided (17-year-old Russian POW). After the prisoner had been forcibly restrained by SS troops, Brandt proceeded to perform a vasectomy, to show his protégés how rapidly the procedure could be executed by a skilled surgeon. He accomplished the procedure in four minutes. A discussion of female sterilization followed, in which Brandt again claimed surgery as the most efficient method.

He said Clauberg will never regain his prewar eminence. Brandt plans to sterilize six women tomorrow morning to prove his point, before scheduled test of Sarin IV aerosol compound . . .

The shock of this entry had lasted only until McConnell reached the first detailed description of one of Klaus Brandt's "research projects." This passage alone was enough to damn the Nazi state for all eternity.

6-8-43 Eight days ago, Brandt purposely infected four boys and four girls with rapidly fulminating Group I meningococcus bacteria (by the droplet infection method, droplets being obtained from live carriers held prisoner in the isolation room.) Greta Müller and I were instructed to rotate 12-hour shifts in the experimental ward until the study had run its course. This is my first opportunity to record what happened.

Our functions were to (a) record the onset of symptoms (b) take blood samples and white counts when indicated (c) administer sulfadiazine (and also Dr. Brandt's own formulation) to the separate patient groups at the proper intervals (d) administer fluids to prevent dehydration (e) chart the progress of each patient until recovery or death. The youngest patient was six months old (female) the oldest five years (male). The average age was three and one half years.

On the fourth day after infection, meningococcus was recovered from the blood of all patients. Most had characteristic rashes at this time. Brandt ordered oral administration of sulfadiazine to two patients, simultaneously giving his secret preparation to two others. The remaining four patients (including the female infant) he designated as controls.

The control group quickly exhibited symptoms of the septicemic stage of the disease: irregular fever, hypersensitivity, rapid pulse and respiration. Most curled up in the characteristic position and cried out when disturbed. All four developed serious rashes, three of these hemorrhagic. White counts of all controls hovered between 16,500 and 17,500.

First fatality in the control group (four-year-old female) caused by overwhelming septicemic infection. 80% of body covered by hemorrhagic rash. Routine postmortem by Dr. Rauch.

Infant control quickly exhibited bulging of the fontanelles due to massive infection. Experienced convulsions, low pulse rate and respiration. Death occurred six days after initial infection.

*The two patients given sulfadiazine showed marked improve-
ment within 48 hours. Those given Brandt's preparation were
slower to improve. The controls quickly progressed into the next
stage of the disease. The bacteria disappeared from their blood-
streams and localized in the meninges. Patients experienced vomiting and the familiar bursting headache caused by increased pressure
of the cerebrospinal fluid. Also constipation, urine retention, and
stiffness of neck muscles due to nerve root involvement. Two of the
smaller children's spines and necks drew backward into the characteristic "bow." None could flex his chin.*

*Third fatality in control group (three-year-old male) died in ag-
ony on Greta's shift. I had managed to feed him some aspirin that
morning, nothing else. Brandt's postmortem revealed cause of death
to be internal hydrocephalus. Ventricles of the brain were dilated,
and the brain convolutions flattened by the pressure of a thick, purulent fluid. Also optic nerve involvement: patient was blind in one
eye at time of death. Purulent exudate extended all the way into the
spinal canal.*

*Throughout the course of the experiment, Brandt performed
several spinal punctures to examine cerebrospinal fluid. He was infuriated by the slowness of his own preparation compared to that of
sulfadiazine. The children were terrified of these spinal punctures,
and had to be restrained by Ariel Weitz and SS men. On day six
Brandt resorted to direct injection of his preparation into the spine
of one child. This leads me to believe that his secret preparation is
unrelated to the sulfonamides, as local therapy is not required when
using those. Brandt plans to duplicate this entire experiment in one
week, using a different preparation. Also, one box of polyvalent
antimeningococcus horse serum arrived yesterday. . . .*

McConnell looked up from the diary. He realized then that he
was in a kind of shock. There were at least a dozen separate entries
recording similar experiments on children, and references to nearly fifty more performed by Brandt and his assistant physicians—
all accurate down to the last medical detail. But what horrified
him most was that these experiments had no valid medical reason
behind them. It was known that meningitis could be cured by sulfadiazine. Was Klaus Brandt torturing children merely to try and find
some new pharmacological agent with which to enrich himself after
the war?

McConnell closed his eyes and pressed his fingertips to his temples. How could Anna Kaas record such things without apparent emotion? He had searched for some sense of guilt or revulsion in the record, but after the first few entries all references to her own perspective virtually ceased. Then he realized—or rather *hoped* he had realized—what she was up to. The German nurse was acting as a sort of verbal camera—recording what she saw in the manner that courts of law would demand evidence of a witness. Injecting emotion into her record would only cloud the issue after the war.

But still, he thought, to realize that she had stood by while these atrocities were committed—and in fact had *participated* in them— was difficult to grasp. He longed for some expression of anguish or plea for forgiveness, however insufficient or inarticulate, from the vulnerable soul that lies at the core of every human being. But as yet he had not found it.

He was certain of one thing: if he got out of Germany alive, the nurse's diary was going with him.

Jonas Stern sat in stunned silence in a corner of the Jewish Women's Block. More than forty women surrounded him. A single guttering candle flickered on the floor. He had never seen such eyes before, not even in the faces of soldiers unmanned in the midst of great carnage. Eyes like black mirrors, at once shallow and bottomless. He had the feeling that if he pressed his finger to one of those eyes, it would shatter and fall inward through a black cavern of grief and loss that could never be filled.

He had learned much in his short time here. He'd asked a few questions about the histories of the women, mostly to keep up the fiction of gathering intelligence for Zionist leaders in Palestine and London. But when he heard some of the answers, all else went out of his mind for a while. Each story was a variation on the same theme: We were doing all right; Hitler came to power; the rich fled; the Nazis came to our town, our village, our city, our house, our flat; they killed my father, my mother, my husband, my sons, my uncles, my sisters, my daughter, my grandparents. And almost every story ended with the same line: *I am the last of my family.*

As the women spoke, Stern learned that the Block Leader's death and the brutal reprisals that followed had thrown the block into disarray, and that the young Dutchwoman who questioned him had assumed the dead Pole's position by default. He had made up his mind to ask her the question he had risked his life to come here and ask, when she said:

"How do you plan to get out of the camp, Herr Stern?"

He knew what was coming. Some of the women had begun to dream of escape. He had to discourage them. They could not know that he had no intention of leaving the vicinity of the camp until— until what? Until he had killed them all, of course.

"Herr Stern?" Rachel said again.

"I'm walking out through the front gate. The same way I got in."

Rachel was silent for some moments. "But that doesn't make sense. An SS man without transportation?"

Stern shifted uncomfortably. "I told you before, this uniform is SD: Sicherheitsdienst. More feared even than the Gestapo. Not even the SS question the SD."

Stern saw a flash of hope in her dark eyes. "I have a favor to ask of you," Rachel said. "A great favor."

"I can't take you out," he said quickly.

"Not me. My child."

He stared at her. "You have a child here?"

"Two. A boy and a girl."

"And you want . . . you want me to take only *one* child?"

The young woman took hold of his hand and squeezed, her eyes blazing with urgency. "Better that one have a chance at life than both die," she said. "And they will surely die if they stay here!"

Stern saw desperation her eyes, but also a fierce determination. She meant what she said.

"They are very small," she said in a pleading voice that drove Stern into a rage of shame and impotence. "You could easily carry one—"

Stern jerked his hand away. The realization that this woman had so honestly confronted the impossibility of her own survival that she would give up her child to a stranger shook him to his core. He stared into the ring of faces surrounding him, searching for some sign of censure.

None of the other women seemed shocked by Rachel's request.

* * *

In Anna's cellar, McConnell had finally found the diary entry he was searching for. It was near the end, dated only two weeks ago.

2-1-44 More and more civilians are being killed by Allied bombs. In case I do not survive the war, I will here speak a little about things almost too painful to face. I know what the world will ask about me. How could this woman have stood by and watched these horrible things? She was a civilian. She was a <u>nurse</u>! She did not have to do these things. No one held a gun to her head. Well, that is both true and false. I am a civilian, but I live in Nazi Germany at war. And I knew enough about Klaus Brandt after one week here to know that a request to be transferred might mean death. Brandt has absolute power in Totenhausen. If he orders your death, you are dead. Only Sturmbannführer Schörner seems unafraid of him. I think Schörner saw too much death in Russia to be afraid of anything.

Some will call me a coward for not leaving this place, for not refusing to participate in these experiments, even at the cost of my life. Am I a coward? Yes. I have lain shivering in my bed with nightmares of Hauptscharführer Sturm beating down the door of my cottage to arrest me and take me to the Tree. I have been close to suicide. But the world's condemnation means little. Not all the torturers in the world could cause me the agony I have felt when the beseeching eyes of dying children looked to me for help, and I could not give it.

I have an answer for the world, but no excuse. When I first arrived at Totenhausen, I was already severely depressed, due to the fact that my lover had been murdered by the SS in Berlin. When I realized what actually went on here, I believe I entered a state of deep shock. After I regained some perspective, getting away from Totenhausen became my only thought. But then I considered my situation. If Brandt allowed me to leave the camp, I would succeed in distancing myself from the crimes. But the crimes would <u>still go on</u>. They would continue just as before, but unseen by anyone who was disturbed by them, as I was. I felt like a little fish swimming inside a tidal wave. I could try to swim in the other direction, but the wave would thunder on. For many days I hardly spoke. Then I decided I had been sent to this hell for one reason: to be a witness. To record what I saw. This I have done, and continue to do. I have become hardened to things that would shame a murderer. But I no longer think of suicide. Now I pray that I will survive this war. I pray that

my diary will be the noose that finally snaps Klaus Brandt's fat neck.
I worry sometimes that I am beyond saving, that I am damned in the
eyes of God. But more often I wonder if God even sees this place.
How could God exist in the same universe with Totenhausen Camp?

McConnell closed the diary. He had found the reassurance he
sought. Even in this crucible of human depravity, some measure
of hope—of human integrity—survived. Anna Kaas *had* rebelled
against the madness she described. But her rebellion was not the
empty whining of political dilettantes. She had not offered impotent,
moralizing words and then retired into the wings of rationalization
or self-delusion. Nor had she committed some brave but vain act of
self-sacrifice, as McConnell might have done. She had done something far more difficult. She had sacrificed her humanity in order to
attempt the only thing that might ever have some real effect on the
men who committed the horrors she witnessed each day—to tell the
world what they were doing.

When he realized this, McConnell also understood something
else. That Anna Kaas had accomplished something no one before
her ever had. She had changed his fundamental belief about the futility of violence. All his life he had stood with his father against
war. But tonight, simple written words had bred a cold light that revealed to him something worse than war—or perhaps a new kind of
war—a war of mankind upon itself. A self-consuming madness that
could only end in complete annihilation. His medical experience
gave him the perfect metaphor for his new understanding.

Cancer.

The system that had created Totenhausen—and the dozen other
camps he had read of in the diary—was a malignant melanoma fes-
tering within the human species. It moved maliciously, under cover
of a more conventional malady, but it would eventually destroy everything in its path. And like any melanoma, it could not be stopped
without destroying healthy tissue in the process.

As he sat with the closed book on his lap, McConnell came to
a conclusion inconceivable to him before tonight. If his father—a
physician and combat veteran who had preached nonviolence for
twenty years—could by some magic read Anna Kaas's diary, and
then come face to face with *Doctor* Klaus Brandt . . .

He would shoot him down like a mad dog.

* * *

"For the last time, I cannot do it!" Stern said. "It will be a miracle if I escape alive. With a child I would have no chance."

He forced himself to look away from Rachel Jansen's face. A light had gone out behind her eyes. Where there had been hope, he saw only ashes. "I want to ask you something," he said. "All of you. Come closer."

The gray faces drew nearer to him.

"What is it?" Rachel asked.

"I am interested in a particular man. A Jew from Rostock. We received reports that he died at this camp. I want to know if any of you can tell me anything about him. If you remember him. How he lived . . . perhaps how he died."

"What was his name? Between us we know everyone in the camp."

"Avram," Stern said quietly. "Avram Stern, from Rostock."

Rachel looked at the other women, then back at Stern. "You mean the shoemaker?"

Stern felt a flush of apprehension. "Shoemaker? He was a cobbler, yes."

Rachel slowly held out her hand and touched his chin. She lifted his face, turning both cheeks to the light. "My God," she murmured. "You are his son."

Stern's body tensed. "You knew him?"

Rachel looked puzzled. "Knew him? I know him. He's sleeping less than thirty meters from us right now."

W hen the door to the cottage banged open above him, McConnell threw down the diary and grabbed his Schmeisser. He heard Anna's voice, then a man's voice speaking German. He crept to the top of the cellar stairs and opened the door a crack. Stern was standing in the kitchen in his SD uniform, furiously rubbing his hands. His face was red and his eyes full of tears, as if he had run for miles in a cold wind.

"*Kaffee, bitte,*" he said to Anna. "Where is the doctor? Sleeping?"

Anna moved to the dented pot steaming on the stove.

"I'm starting to think you don't really mean to attack that camp at all," said McConnell, stepping into the kitchen.

Stern's eyes went to the Schmeisser. "You'd do better to hold that by the barrel and use it as a club."

"Go to hell." McConnell took a seat at the table.

"*Danke,*" said Stern, accepting a hot cup from Anna. "If your Christian Hell exists, my friend, I've just been there. And you know what? It's full of Jews."

"What do you mean? You went *into* the camp?"

Stern raised the cup to his windburned lips, watching McConnell over the rim. "Camps are made to keep people in, not out."

"So how did you get out?"

"Underneath a medical supply truck. A rather odd time to take deliveries, don't you think?"

Anna said from the stove, "There are as many Christians as Jews in Totenhausen, Herr Stern."

Stern surprised McConnell by not responding to this statement.

The young Zionist seemed preoccupied, his hair-trigger temper no-where in evidence.

"So why didn't you attack the camp?" McConnell asked.

"Too much wind," said Stern, his eyes fixed on the table.

"I see. Did you learn anything useful?"

"Useful how? You don't want this mission to succeed, remember?"

Anna looked over Stern's shoulder at McConnell. Her eyes seemed to be asking if this was still true.

"I have a proposition for you, Doctor," Stern said in a neutral tone.

"I'm listening."

"It's obvious that I can't carry out this mission as planned without your help. So, I propose a compromise."

Anna set a cup of barley coffee in front of McConnell. He nodded thanks. "What kind of compromise?"

"If you will help me to gas the SS garrison, I will do everything in my power to save the lives of the prisoners."

McConnell sat back hard in his chair. Had he heard correctly? Anna's eyes were riveted on him. Obviously she had heard the same thing. "Well hell," he said, "talk about Saul on the road to Damascus—"

Stern's chair crashed back against the stove as he came to his feet.

"Whoa!" said McConnell, raising both hands. "Take it easy! Four hours ago you were ready to kill everybody in the place. Now you want to save them?"

Stern felt his hands trembling. When he embraced his father for the first time in eleven years, it was if a jacket of ice had melted away from his heart. Everything he had planned to say if he ever got the chance—how stupid and stubborn Avram had been to remain in Germany, how cruel to make his wife and son strike out for Palestine without his protection—all went out of his mind the moment he saw the pathetic state his father was in.

Avram Stern had not even recognized his own son. When Jonas spoke his Hebrew name, and the name of his mother, the man known as the shoemaker had nearly fainted dead away. While Rachel Jansen kept the other women back, they spoke of many things, but Jonas had come quickly to the point. In an almost inaudible whisper he asked his father to come out of the camp with him.

Avram had refused. Jonas could not believe it. It was Rostock all over again! Only it was different. Ten years before, Avram had refused to believe that Hitler would betray the Jewish combat veterans. He no longer labored under such delusions, but he remained as stubborn as ever. Now he claimed it was impossible for him in good conscience to abandon his fellow Jews to the fate that awaited them in Totenhausen. Jonas had argued violently—and in fact came very close to revealing his true mission—but Avram had not been moved. The only concession he made was that if Jonas could somehow help the others to escape, he would go also. And so, brimming with anger and frustration, Jonas had told his father to sleep in the Jewish Women's Block until he came again.

Trekking back across the hills, Stern had calmed himself enough to settle on a plan. Because of his father's hardheadedness, he now had to try to accomplish something even the chief of SOE believed to be impossible: find a way to kill Totenhausen's SS guards with poison gas while sparing its prisoners. To do that, Stern knew, he would need McConnell's help. He hated this new dependence almost as much as he hated himself for being unable to follow through with the original plan. And he had no intention of revealing his weakness to the American.

"I am *willing* to try to save the prisoners," Stern said through tight lips. "*If* you will help me kill the SS men, get the photos the British need, and steal the sample of Soman. But I will still carry out the attack alone if you refuse to help me. Everyone will die then, perhaps even you and Fräulein Kaas."

"Calm down," McConnell told him. "Just sit down and be still for a minute. Please."

Anna righted Stern's chair and set it behind him, but he did not sit.

McConnell tried to penetrate the crystalline shine of Stern's eyes, but it was like trying to read through black quartz. Stern's reasons were his own, and for the time being at least, would remain that way.

"All right," McConnell said after a moment. "That sounds like a fair bargain to me. You've got a deal. I'll help you."

Stern was more shocked by this reversal of position than McConnell had been by his. He reached awkwardly for a chair and sat down opposite McConnell at the table.

"Easier sell than you thought, huh?" said McConnell. "Well, don't look so pleased with yourself. I want to know how you propose to kill a hundred and fifty SS soldiers without killing the prisoners as well."

"You're the one who wants to save them," Stern said, almost too quickly. "You find a way."

A fleeting intuition told McConnell that Stern's words had very little connection to what was in his heart. He had no evidence of this, but because Stern almost always said exactly what he thought, his words invariably had the ring of conviction. But his last remark had sounded forced, overdone. And yet, what could he possibly be hiding?

"You're supposed to be the genius," Stern went on, filling the silence McConnell had left. "Let's see you prove it."

"I will," said McConnell, his eyes and ears taking the measure of the new personality before him. "I'll find a way."

Half an hour and a second pot of coffee later, McConnell still had no answer. The three of them sat around the table like students trying to solve a complex calculus problem. Stern had suggested a couple of desperate commando-style plans to free the prisoners before gassing the camp, but each would have required at least a dozen men and split-second timing. His ideas brought McConnell no closer to a solution, but they did confirm his suspicion that Stern—for whatever reason—suddenly possessed a heartfelt desire to save the prisoners' lives.

It was Anna who put him on track. Stern was telling them about something his guerrilla band had tried against a British fort, when she broke in and said, *"Ach! The E-Block!"*

Stern stopped talking. "What?"

"The Experimental Block. It's the sealed chamber at the rear of the camp, where Brandt's gas experiments are carried out."

"What about it?" asked McConnell.

"The SS avoid it like a plague ward. I was thinking, what if we could slip the prisoners into it a few at a time, maybe half an hour before you attack? When the cylinders detonated, the prisoners would be safe inside the E-Block while the SS troops choked to death outside."

Stern gaped at her across the table. "That's brilliant."

"Just a minute," McConnell interrupted. "How big is this chamber?"

Anna's smile faded. "I've never been inside it, but you're right . . . it's small. From the outside it doesn't seem so small, but it's a double-walled chamber. A room inside a room. Let me think. I've seen the numbers on test reports. I think . . . nine square meters."

"That's only a hundred square feet," McConnell said. "How high is the ceiling?"

"Just enough room for a tall man to stand. Two meters?"

"Six and a half feet. How many prisoners in the camp?"

She shook her head. "After today's reprisals . . . two hundred and thirty-four."

"It's impossible."

"You're right," said Stern. "You couldn't squeeze even half of the prisoners inside. Damn! There's got to be a way."

McConnell spread his hands flat on the table and sat still for nearly a minute, his mind exploring every possible variant of Anna's idea. "Maybe there is," he said finally.

"What?" said Stern. "You have an idea?"

"Anna is right about the E-Block—in principle. The essential problem is exposing the SS to the gas while protecting the prisoners from it. But she's thinking backwards."

"What do you mean?" asked Anna. "Get the SS to go into the E-Block and kill them with the gas while the prisoners are safe outside?"

"In theory, yes."

"But the SS won't go near the E-Block! Besides, there are a hundred and fifty of them."

McConnell couldn't resist a smile. "I'm sure you're right. But I also feel sure that the architect who designed Totenhausen was thorough enough to include a bomb shelter in his plans."

Her eyes played over his face as she absorbed the full import of his words. "My God, you're right. It's a long tunnel, and it will hold *more* than every SS man in the camp."

"That's it," said Stern, his voice almost crackling with excitement. "We sneak two cylinders into the bomb shelter, trick the SS into it and *auf Wiedersehen*—mission accomplished. I'll bet that gas is twice as effective in an enclosed space."

"Probably ten times as effective," said McConnell. "Plus, the wind ceases to be a factor in the plan."

Stern shook his head. "Smith was right, Doctor. You are a bloody genius."

McConnell bowed in mock humility. "How many entrances does the shelter have, Anna?"

"Two. The main entrance is in one of the SS barracks. The other is in the basement of the hospital. The morgue."

"Do you think you could block the morgue entrance so that no one who entered from the SS barracks could get out that way?"

"I think so, yes."

"If it is more effective in a closed space," Stern reasoned, "one cylinder should be enough. But I'll use two to be sure. It's a simple matter of taking them down from the pylon and. . . ."

"What's the matter?" asked McConnell. "We can't get them down from the pylon?"

"No, we can do that. The problem is getting the cylinders into the camp. I dropped inside the wire from an overhanging tree limb. I can't do that with steel cylinders." Stern looked down at the table for a moment, then raised his eyes to Anna. "There's only one way to do it," he said.

"A car," she said quietly.

He nodded. "Can you get one?"

Anna bit her bottom lip as she considered this. "I have a friend, Greta Müller. Her father is a farmer who supplies food to the SS Oberabschnitt at Stettin. He not only has vehicles, but petrol to run them."

"With a car we could lay the cylinders flat on the backseat, or sling them beneath the undercarriage with chains. That would be better." Pure energy radiated from Stern as he visualized the plan. "You could drive in late tomorrow night and park by the hospital. I'd be waiting for you. After I unchained the cylinders, you could lead me to the morgue entrance of the bomb shelter. All I'd have to do is move them in and set them to detonate at the proper time." He leaned toward Anna, the full weight of his personality radiating from his dark eyes. "Can you get a car?"

"I'm almost certain I can," she said, looking back at him with a strange fascination. "Greta thinks I have a lover in Rostock. A married man. I've kept up that story so I can get the car sometimes without her asking questions. I've used it three times before. Though usually with more notice."

"Tell her it's a crisis. He's trying to end it with you."

"Just a minute," McConnell interjected.

"It's the only way," Anna said.

"I realize that. But you're both overlooking a serious problem."

"What is it?" Stern asked impatiently.

"To get the SS troops into that shelter, we need an air raid."

"Why? I can set off the siren myself. The SS won't know if the raid is real or not. They'll run straight into the gas."

McConnell glanced at Anna. She did not look confident.

"We've had only one air raid in the years I've been here," she said, "and that was a false alarm. All drills are scheduled. Also, there are officers for every phase of the raid. Soldiers who man the alarm, who fight fires, who make sure each building is evacuated— not including the prisoners, of course. They're left exposed."

"You're saying it wouldn't work?" asked Stern.

"I'm saying that if no bombs began to fall, many soldiers would probably never go into the shelter. I doubt very seriously whether the entrances would be closed unless bombs were actually falling. You couldn't rely on it."

"For God's sake," Stern muttered. "There's got to be a way."

"There is," said McConnell. "A real air raid." He tapped the tabletop with his fingers. "And I think we can get one. Brigadier Smith knows the exact coordinates of Totenhausen. He's the one who started this whole thing. The least that bastard can do is to send a handful of bombers over to help us finish the job. All we need is a radio."

"That's just what we don't have," said Stern. "McShane cached one for us, but it's useless. I dug up the parachute container on my way back from the camp, to take out the climbing spikes and harness. The container was cracked and half filled with water. The parachute obviously didn't open properly. Our signal lamp for the submarine was dry, but the radio was drowned and its vacuum tubes smashed."

Stern leaned back in his chair and stared at the ceiling. "Even if we get a radio," he said, "a real air raid gives us another problem. We can ask Smith to schedule the raid at a precise time, but there's no guarantee the bombers will arrive at that time. You see?"

"I do," said McConnell. "There's no way to time the cylinders in the bomb shelter so that they'll detonate just after the bombs have fallen and kill the SS men who've run for cover."

"Right." Stern relaxed his neck so that his head hung limp over the chair-back. "Unless. . . ."

"Unless what?"

Stern straightened up and gave him an odd smile. "Unless I'm waiting inside the shelter with the detonator in my hand."

"*What?*"

"It's the only way," said Stern. "I'll wear one of the gas suits you brought from Oxford."

"You're certifiably nuts."

"Are you saying the suit and mask you designed won't protect me?"

"In a sealed room full of nerve gas? I damn sure won't offer you any guarantee. Hell, that's like playing Russian roulette."

"I rather like the idea," Stern said, glancing at Anna. "The simplicity of it. And I'll be there to watch all those SS bastards claw each other's eyes out."

"Jesus," whispered McConnell. "You've got guts, I'll give you that."

"It's settled then."

"Which brings us back to the radio," Anna said softly.

Stern smoothed back his dark hair and gave her an appraising look. "You have a radio, don't you, Fräulein Kaas?"

She shook her head. "The nearest radio we can use belongs to the Polish Resistance."

"The Polish Resistance is operating nearby?"

"No, they're in Poland."

"But the border is two hundred kilometers away! You'd need a radio just to contact them."

"I can contact them, Herr Stern. But you will have to take my word for that."

"Why?"

"Because as reckless as you are, you might be captured. I cannot expose others to that risk."

"You think I would tell the SS anything?"

Anna regarded him with suspicion in her eyes. "There should be no question of your talking, Herr Stern. I'm sure the British provided you with a cyanide capsule. They went to great lengths to provide me with one. Are you telling me you would not take your capsule if you were about to be captured?"

"They didn't give me a cyanide capsule," said McConnell. "Not that I want one or anything."

Anna cut her eyes at Stern, but he avoided her glance.

"Do you have one?" McConnell asked him.

"Damn it," Stern snapped, "I want to know how you're getting word to these Poles. I must know if there's any real chance to get word to Smith."

"Word will get through," Anna said with serene confidence.

"I know Smith has someone else inside that camp," Stern insisted. "I know the codes for this mission. They were taken from that Clark Gable picture. We are Butler and Wilkes. You are Melanie. Smith's base in Sweden is Atlanta, and Totenhausen is Tara. So tell me please who is Scarlett?"

Anna said nothing.

"You don't have to give me a name," Stern said, "just tell me the method of contact."

She sighed. "Telephone. All right? Someone will call them for me."

"From the village?"

"I will say no more."

"I knew it!" Stern exulted. "Major Schörner is Scarlett. He is, isn't he? Tell me! I knew you didn't set up a link to London on your own."

Anna went into the foyer and put on her overcoat. "Think what you wish, Herr Stern. There is only a little darkness left. I must be on my way."

Anna arrived at Totenhausen winded and nearly frozen through from her bicycle ride over the hills. She had been rehearsing her excuse all the way: *I neglected to properly store some tissue samples in the lab.* . . . The words were on her tongue as the guard stepped up and peered at her through the electrified wire, but he just smiled and signaled for his comrade to open the gate.

She rode straight across the deserted Appellplatz to the hospital and entered through the back door. She made no attempt to move silently; stealth would draw more attention than noise. The hallway on the second floor was dark. She felt her way along the wide corridor until she came to the door she wanted.

She tapped softly, knowing it would be locked.

Almost instantly a threatening whisper said, *"Who's there? I have a gun pointed at you!"*

"It's Anna. Open the door."

She heard a click. The door was pulled back. Ariel Weitz stood there in his shorts, a pistol in his hand. She walked past him into the room. It was hardly more than a broom closet, but it had hot and cold running water—luxury compared to what the other inmates endured. The smell of cigarettes and cheap schnapps hung in the air.

"What are you doing here?" he demanded.

"I need a crash meeting."

"With who?"

"The Wojiks. And they must bring the radio."

"You are crazy! You want me to call them?"

"Yes. Tonight. Right now."

"I won't do it." Weitz shook his head with theatrical exaggeration.

"You must do it. Everything depends on it."

His feral eyes suddenly lit up. "The commandos are here?"

"Just make the call, Herr Weitz."

"How many? They are going to attack the camp?"

"Tell Stan to meet me at the same place as before."

"I can't," Weitz said stubbornly. "Schörner will catch me."

"I doubt that. He's probably in bed with the Jewish woman."

He gave her a sidelong glance. "You know about that?"

"I know many things. Why are you so anxious? I thought you were the nerveless one."

"It's Schörner. He's changed. He hardly drinks anymore, always watching everything."

"What do you expect, after one of his men is found murdered and wrapped inside a British parachute?"

"That was bad, you're right. But I think it's the Jansen woman as much as the parachutes. Schörner has come alive. He thinks he's in Russia again."

Anna summoned her most persuasive voice. "Herr Weitz, everything you have done up to this point has led to this one moment.

Everything is ready. But *nothing will happen* if you don't get the Wojiks to meet me tomorrow."

He hugged his hands to his chest like a mountaineer fighting hypothermia. "All right, all right," he said. "I'll try."

"You'll *do* it. As soon as I leave." Anna moved toward the door, then looked back. "And Herr Weitz . . . don't drink so much."

Weitz nodded, but his eyes were already far away. "I'm so tired," he said, his voice modulating into a feminine register. "Everyone thinks I'm a monster. Even Schörner. My own people hate me worse than they hate the SS."

"But that is what has allowed you to do what you have done."

"Yes, but . . . I just . . . it can't go on. I must explain. Make them see how it really is."

Anna walked back and laid a hand on his bony shoulder. She tried not to recoil from the feverish skin. "Herr Weitz," she said softly, "God sees how it really is."

The bloodshot eyes opened wider.

"The Wojiks will be there tomorrow?" she said again. "Midafternoon? With the radio?"

Weitz closed his clammy hands around hers and squeezed. "They'll be there."

34

Jonas Stern leaned out of the back window of Greta Müller's black Volkswagen and saluted a Wehrmacht private as they passed through Dettmannsdorf.

"Don't press your luck," McConnell snapped from behind the wheel.

Stern laughed and leaned back inside. He made a striking figure in the gray-green SD uniform and cap, and he seemed to be thoroughly enjoying himself. Anna had planned to meet the Polish partisans alone, after feigning illness near the end of the day's work shift. But when Stern heard that she intended to borrow Greta Müller's car for the journey, he had insisted on going along.

"I believe," he had said in an arrogant voice, "that a young woman escorted by Standartenführer of the SD will be much safer than a woman out driving alone."

Anna had been unimpressed. Ultimately he'd had to threaten to abandon the idea of saving the prisoners before she submitted.

While waiting in the cottage for her to get off from work, McConnell had decided to accompany them as well. He saw no point in waiting for the SS to arrive at the cottage and inform him that his fellow spies had been caught and he was under arrest. You're the big cheese, he'd told Stern. I can be your driver or something.

So that was how they played it. McConnell drove the car, while Anna and Stern sat in back like privileged passengers. The rendezvous was only ten miles from Anna's cottage, in a small wood northeast of Bad Sülze. As the VW rolled past the hamlet of Kneese Hof, she told them they were halfway there. They bypassed Bad

Sülze proper by swinging south and crossing a small bridge over the Recknitz River. Two kilometers of gravel road carried them onto a moor and to the edge of the wood.

"Pull into the trees," Anna instructed. "Off the road."

McConnell obeyed. Stern got out and looked around the car, his Schmeisser at the ready. McConnell followed, carrying a bag containing bread, cheese, and his own Schmeisser.

"I'll go ahead," said Anna. "Stan is very careful. I'll talk to him first, explain things before you come out. In those uniforms, he'd shoot you down without a second thought."

But when they arrived at the meeting place, no one was there. Stern and McConnell crouched in the snow while Anna walked into the middle of the clearing. A half hour later, a thin, nervous young man walked out of the trees and began speaking to her. He was unarmed, and looked strangely familiar to McConnell. They spoke a full five minutes before Anna motioned for Stern and McConnell to come out.

"Say something in English," she told McConnell. "Hurry."

"Well . . . fourscore and seven years ago, our fathers brought forth upon this continent a new nation, conceived in liberty—"

"Good enough?" she asked the thin Pole.

The young man mulled it over.

"Stan already saw both of you," she told Stern. "He could have killed you any time. I'm glad he's in a good mood today. Put your gun on the ground."

Stern reluctantly obeyed.

"They don't have their radio."

"*What?*"

"They share it among three resistance groups. But they can get to it by midnight tonight."

"That gives Brigadier Smith less than twenty-four hours to set up the bombing raid," Stern said. "It's going to be close."

McConnell started as a giant of a man stepped from the trees less than twenty meters away. He had a thick black beard and carried a World War One vintage bolt-action rifle—probably a Mauser—which he pointed right at Stern's chest. McConnell didn't blame him. Stern looked every inch an officer of the SD.

"*Co słychać?*" Stern said in a friendly voice.

The big man's face brightened. "*Pan mòwi po polsku?*"

Stern switched to German. "A little. I was born in Rostock. I knew some Polish seamen."

The bearded man held out a meaty hand. "Stanislaus Wojik," he said, vigorously shaking Stern's entire arm. "That's my brother, Miklos."

Stan Wojik looked like a man who had lived by his hands before becoming an amateur soldier, but his brother Miklos was almost a caricature of a starving artist—a second-chair violinist in an orchestra of modest reputation. Hollow cheeks, and large eyes as sincere as a child's. McConnell suddenly realized where he had seen the brothers before. They were the two other members of the "reception party" that had met the Moon plane on the night he and Stern landed in Germany. He reached into his sack and took out a block of English cheese. Stan nodded thanks and tossed it to his brother.

"Stan speaks fair German," Anna said.

"Good," said Stern, squarely facing the big Pole. "I think I should hold my gun on you while we talk. If someone comes up on us, I'll say you're both our prisoners. We stopped to eat."

Stan Wojik shrugged and laid down his rifle. Stern picked up his Schmeisser. McConnell noticed that Stan Wojik had a heavy meat cleaver hanging from a leather thong on his belt. The big man patted it and laughed.

"I used to be a butcher," he said. "I still cut meat occasionally." He grinned. "Nazi sausage, when I can get it."

Stern laughed appreciatively, then in a mixture of Polish and German began explaining what they wanted. Stan Wojik listened intently, nodding during each pause. McConnell only followed about half of the exchange. Stern and the elder Wojik ate cheese while they talked, but Miklos sat quietly beside Anna, his eyes hardly leaving her face.

When the conversation was finished, Stan turned to McConnell and said in German: "You are American?"

"Yes."

"Tell Roosevelt we need more guns. We need guns in Warsaw, but Stalin won't give us any. Tell Roosevelt with guns we can beat the Nazis ourselves. We aren't afraid to fight."

McConnell saw no point in trying to explain that the odds of him ever talking to FDR were slim to none. "I'll tell him," he said.

He was surprised when Stern took a sheet of notepaper from

an inside pocket and handed it to Stan Wojik. The Pole seemed surprised too. McConnell walked over to read it. Stern had hand-printed a message in English, followed by Polish and German translations:

CODE: ATLANTA Freq: 3140 Request diversionary air raid very near but not on TARA on 15/2/44 at precisely 2000 hours. Raid absolutely essential to success. BUTLER and WILKES.

"Is this smart?" McConnell asked. "What if he's caught?"

Stern shrugged. "If he's caught, that note will be the least of our problems. Without that air raid—in the right place and at the right time—our plan won't work. You said that yourself. It's worth the risk of him carrying the note to get the message right."

Stan Wojik nodded.

"Where do these men live?" McConnell asked, unable to curb his curiosity.

Miklos laughed. "We are from a place called Warsow, on the Polish border."

"Warsaw?"

"War*sow*," Stern corrected. "It's a small village near the island of Usedom. That's where the Peenemünde rocket complex was until the big bombing raid last August."

Stan Wojik understood enough of this to add, "Much experiments still go on. Rockets fly all across Poland. Airplanes without pilots. Very dangerous weapons."

"Is there still an SS garrison at Peenemünde?" Stern asked.

"Some SS, yes."

"They forced you out of Warsow?" McConnell inquired.

Stan shrugged. "Hard to fight the Germans in towns."

"You live in the forests now?"

"We live wherever London needs us. Move all the time."

The meeting was over. Anna gave the Poles the rest of the food from McConnell's bag. Miklos thanked her effusively, while Stan greedily eyed Stern's Schmeisser. On impulse, McConnell reached into his bag and took out his own Schmeisser, which he held out to Stan and indicated through hand motions that he was willing to trade for the bolt-action Mauser and a box of cartridges. Stern started to object, but then apparently thought better of it.

They made the trade.

As they were leaving, Stan Wojik gestured at Stern with his new submachine gun and said, "Can you fool the Germans in that uniform?"

In a transformation that stunned McConnell and Anna more than the Poles, Stern planted both feet wide apart on the ground, squared his shoulders, put his hands on his hips and barked several lightning commands at the Wojiks in harsh German.

The big Pole took a step back and laid his hand on the meat cleaver. Then he looked at McConnell and laughed nervously. "I think maybe he does that too well! Careful he doesn't get to liking it."

Stern relaxed and shook Stan Wojik's hand again. "Your radio set has adequate range?"

"Sweden is only a hundred and sixty kilometers across the water." The Pole grinned and thumped his broad chest. "If we don't get confirmation, I'll steal a boat and sail across myself! You'll get your bombs, my friend. Farewell."

"*Dowidzenia,*" said Stern.

As they drove back along the Dettmannsdorf road, Stern said, "That's the kind of brave son of a bitch who won't survive this war. He'll never win a medal, and he'll die blindfolded and alone against some dirty brick wall."

"Shut up," Anna said from the backseat. "Even if that's true, there's no point in talking about it."

McConnell had to agree.

They had no trouble getting back to Anna's cottage. The trouble started after nightfall, when McConnell and Stern tried to slip up into the hills to retrieve the two gas cylinders they needed to booby-trap the SS bomb shelter. Three times they had to drop to their bellies in the snow to avoid SS patrols with dogs. The soldiers were working in pairs, mostly on foot, though one motorcycle with a sidecar had roared past on the narrow switchback road, spewing a rooster tail of snow behind it.

Before leaving the cottage, Stern had told McConnell that their German uniforms would be enough to prevent anyone taking a close interest in them. So far, he had shown no inclination to test his theory.

When they finally reached the pylon where the cylinders hung, McConnell caught his breath in astonishment. The two wooden support poles were as thick as oak trees, and joined at the top by a heavy crossarm. He could faintly see the outline of something hanging from one of the power lines, but in the confusion of the treetops he couldn't be sure what. He did not see how they could climb to that crossarm in the dark, but Stern lost no time proving the boasts he had made at Achnacarry. He quickly donned his climbing spikes, then the gas mask McConnell had persuaded him to wear (though without the full body suit it was practically useless), tied a long coil of rope to his belt, and went up the pole like a chimpanzee. Forty seconds after he put metal to wood, he was straddling the crossarm sixty feet above the ground.

McConnell heard a few metallic clinks above him, but nothing else. After about fifteen minutes, the first gas cylinder materialized out of the darkness above his head. The camouflaged tank descended silently, swinging in a gentle arc as Stern lowered it with the heavy rope. When McConnell tried to stop the swinging, to keep the protruding pressure triggers from striking the snow, the cylinder knocked him to the ground.

Seeing this, Stern tied off the rope at the crossarm and descended. He had wisely disarmed the triggers before lowering the cylinder, and the two of them let the tank down without serious incident. By the time Stern climbed the pole and repeated the process, his muscles were cramping from overexertion.

"You've got a big stain on your uniform," McConnell told him when he reached the ground the second time.

"Tar," said Stern, pulling off his sweat-soaked gas mask. "The nurse will have to get it off. Are you ready?"

"I don't suppose we can drag these things?"

"Not if you want to live until morning. The tracks would lead the SS right to us. What is it, Doctor? What are you thinking?"

McConnell crouched beside one of the cylinders. "I was thinking . . . we might be able to test the gas before the raid, to see if it works or not. Then we'd know whether the attack was even worth trying."

"Can we do that?"

McConnell lightly touched one of the pressure triggers, then examined the cylinder head. "I don't think so. Not without losing the entire contents of a cylinder. We'd have to trip a trigger to get the cap off, and after the cap is blown, there's no stopping the gas."

"What the hell?" said Stern. "Let's try it. One cylinder should be enough to kill everybody in that bomb shelter."

"You're missing the point. If we empty one of these things, and the gas works, it could kill every living creature for a hundred yards around. How long do you think it would take Schörner's patrols to discover that? Also, the SS would hear the detonator go off. And even wearing a suit, I wouldn't want to be anywhere close when it blew. It's just too goddamn dangerous."

McConnell stood up. "No dress rehearsal. Let's move."

"McShane said something about using carrying poles to move the cylinders," Stern said. "We can tie our toggle ropes between two long branches and cradle the tank like a body on a litter."

"Sounds good. It'll take two trips, but it'll be worth it."

It took a few minutes to find dead branches strong enough to take the weight, but once they did, the rest went quickly. They moved with silent purpose through the trees, each knowing that poor concentration could mean death for them both. Their spirits rose when new snow began to fall, mercifully covering their tracks.

They buried the two cylinders in a copse near the winding hill road. It would be a simple matter for Anna to stop Greta's VW there tomorrow night, just long enough for Stern and McConnell to chain the tanks under the car.

On the way back to the cottage, they kept off the road as much as possible. They were moving down the Dornow side of the hills when Stern smelled the telltale odor that had given him early warning of danger so many times in his past: cigarette smoke. He reached out for McConnell's arm, but felt nothing.

He dropped onto his belly without a sound.

A match flared in the darkness three meters ahead.

In the first second Stern realized many things: that they had blundered unawares onto a road cut; that there were two SS men standing in the cut, holding machine pistols in one hand and cigarettes in the other; that their heads were at the level Stern's knees had been before he dropped; that McConnell was too far away to warn without giving himself away. He could only hope the American had smelled the smoke in time.

He hadn't. By the time the match flared McConnell was already at the edge of the road cut. When he tensed, his weight broke the ledge of packed snow and he half-tumbled, half-slid down into the road and crashed onto his stomach.

The SS men nearly pissed themselves with fright, but they managed to throw down their cigarettes and aim their machine pistols at the groaning figure on the ground. A German shepherd broke into furious barking.

Seeing the dog, Stern simply ceased to exist in his own mind. He possessed no mass, made no motion. He knew the slightest sound or faintest odor might draw the animal's attention.

One of the SS men dragged McConnell to his feet and shined a flashlight into his face. The second man covered him with a machine pistol. The SS uniform and captain's rank badge confused them. They didn't recognize McConnell, but they weren't yet confident enough to treat him like a criminal. The man with the flashlight began asking questions in rapid-fire German while the shepherd growled menacingly. McConnell said nothing, merely handed over his forged identity papers.

The man with the flashlight examined them closely.

Four feet above them, Stern silently slipped his Schmeisser off his shoulder and crept forward like a mink over the snow. A fallen log stopped him. He felt the heat of battle in his blood, like a drug pounding through his heart and brain. But for the snow, he might have been in the desert again, scouting against Rommel's troops. It took tremendous restraint to keep from dropping into the road and shooting both SS men with a wild shriek.

He forced himself to think rationally.

If he killed the soldiers, they would soon be missed. Major Schörner would probably launch a massive manhunt. Stern would have no choice but to go immediately back up the hill and release the cylinders. And then his father would die. That was unacceptable, but he had to do something. McConnell's university German wouldn't fool the SS men for twenty seconds. At least they had no radio, he thought gratefully. He considered stepping out of the woods, bold as brass, and playing the role of Standartenführer Ritter Stern for all it was worth. But even if he succeeded in fooling them, the very least they would do was report his presence to Major Schörner. More likely they would demand that he return to Totenhausen with them.

When McConnell's frightened eyes glanced up to his hiding place, Stern realized he had a third option. Brigadier Smith's option. *Under no circumstances can we allow the good doctor to fall into enemy hands. If it looks like he's going to be captured alive, you're going to have to eliminate him.* That was an order. But Smith had given that order on the same night he told Stern his father had been killed in Totenhausen. The lying bastard. And yet . . . the order was logically sound. There was only one problem. If he killed McConnell, who would then help him save his father? *The Poles,* whispered a voice in his brain. *Stan Wojik would like nothing better than to add an SS garrison to his scorecard. . . .*

With a silent curse Stern rose up above the log and sighted his Schmeisser down on McConnell's chest. He would wait until the soldiers forced the American to start marching down the road back to Totenhausen. Then he would fire. Fire and run like hell.

He pressed his finger to the trigger.

It took all of McConnell's courage and concentration not to look up to where he knew Stern must be. All he could think of was Randazzo the Wop describing how David had been murdered by SS troops in a situation exactly like this one. Where the hell *was* Stern? Why hadn't he marched out of the woods doing his SD impersonation? The man with the flashlight jabbered something in a guttural voice, then shoved McConnell backward. The only words he caught were "Who is . . . ?" "Doctor," and "Peenemünde."

He opened his mouth to answer, but no words came out.

The officer with the machine pistol stepped forward and jerked McConnell's Walther from its holster.

"*Los, marsch!*" the man shouted, pointing in the direction of Totenhausen.

McConnell stole a last look in Stern's direction, then turned and started up the road. He had walked about ten yards when the *Brrat!* of the silenced Schmeisser split the darkness.

He felt a hammerlike blow between his shoulder blades. Then he was lying facedown in the snow, unable to move. He felt the German shepherd's teeth tearing into the SS uniform, teeth raking his shoulder.

Brrrat! went the Schmeisser again.

He heard a thud, then footsteps crunching rapidly up the road. The dog's jaws snapped shut on his neck.

An explosive howl assaulted his eardrums.

He flipped over onto his back in time to see Stern pin the German shepherd to the ground with his boot and fire a single shot into its mouth.

"*Get up!*" Stern ordered. "*Now! Up!*"

In spite of the shock of it all, McConnell quickly worked out what had happened. Stern had shot one of the SS men first. The startled shepherd had immediately pounced on McConnell, as it must have been trained to do. Stern then shot the second SS man, ran up and kicked the dog off his back and killed it.

"*Where the fuck were you?*" McConnell asked.

"Shut up!" snapped Stern. He was already dragging one of the dead SS men into the trees below the road. "Spread snow over those bloodstains!"

McConnell obeyed. *So, this is it,* he thought, feeling his blood pounding in his ears. *This is action.* By the time he covered the stains, Stern had already piled both corpses and the dog out of sight in the trees.

"What do we do now?" McConnell asked, dizzy with adrenaline. "Someone must have heard something! Where do we hide the bodies?"

"Shut up and let me think," said Stern. "We can't bury them. Dogs would find them too easily. I'd like to throw them in the river, but we wouldn't make it that far."

Stern snapped his fingers. "Sewers! Dornow must have a waste line running to the river."

"You mean carry the bodies into the village? The dog too?"

"There's probably an access hole near the edge of the village. Probably not too far from Anna's cottage. I'll scout it out."

"You don't think bodies will be found in a sewer?"

Stern bent over to lift one of the corpses. "If they start to stink, so what? Sewers stink anyway."

McConnell grabbed his shoulder. "Stern, you saved my life. I . . . thanks. Just thanks, that's all."

Stern's eyes flashed in the darkness. "Don't thank me too quickly, Doctor. It was a near thing."

McConnell wanted to ask what he meant, but Stern had already hoisted one corpse onto his shoulder and moved off under the trees.

McConnell awoke from a dead sleep, his heart pounding. After their return from the Dornow sewer, Stern had told him to sleep fully dressed; now he knew why. Someone was pounding on a door above them. Stern had already scrambled to his feet and was checking the clip of his Schmeisser. The muted hammering reassured McConnell it was not the cellar door being assaulted, but that was small respite.

Stern kicked him. "Someone's trying to get into the cottage!"

McConnell drew his Walther and followed Stern up the steps. Through a crack in the door they saw Anna sweep into the kitchen wearing only a nightgown. She glanced in their direction, hesitated, then went into the foyer to answer the knocking.

"Who's there?" she called.

"Fräulein Kaas? Open the door!"

Stern moved into the kitchen and crouched behind the cabinets nearest the foyer. McConnell stayed on the cellar stairs, but aimed his Walther through the door.

"Nurse Kaas! Open the door!"

Anna braced her back against the door and closed her eyes. "It's quite late!" she shouted. "Identify yourself!"

McConnell glanced at his watch. Just after midnight.

"I am Sturmmann Heinz Weber! You're needed at the camp immediately! Major Schörner's orders!"

Anna glanced back into the kitchen, then turned and opened the front door. A tall lance corporal stood there, his breath steaming in the cold.

"What is the problem, Sturmmann?"

"I cannot say, Nurse."

"You have a car?"

"*Nein,* a motorcycle with sidecar. Please, you must hurry."

"Wait here. I must put on some clothes."

"Hurry! The Sturmbannführer will have my head if we're late."

"Late for what?"

"Just hurry!" The soldier disappeared from the doorway.

Anna hurried through the kitchen without any intention of stopping, but McConnell threw open the door and grabbed her arm. "Don't go!" he said, surprising himself as well as her.

She looked strangely at him. "I must go. I have no choice."

Stern pushed her toward her bedroom, then shoved McConnell back onto the cellar stairs and pulled the door shut after them. When they reached the bottom, he said, "What the hell was that about?"

When McConnell didn't answer, Stern poked him in the chest with the butt of his Schmeisser.

Like a striking snake McConnell drove his open hand into Stern's chest and slammed him up against the wall.

"Don't ever do that again," he said.

Stern was so stunned by this reaction that he merely watched the American climb back to the top of the stairs and sit down beside the door. "She'll be all right," he said. "She's managed this long without your help."

McConnell glared down at him. "You don't know anything. Schörner and Brandt could be planning to torture every nurse in that camp right now. You don't know what those bastards are capable of."

"And you do? What do you know about it, Doctor? You've spent the whole war hiding in England."

McConnell descended the stairs and walked to the broken bookshelf near the far wall. He pulled Anna's diary from behind the old account books and tossed it to Stern. "That's what I know. You ought to read it sometime. It might even turn *your* stomach, though you want everyone to believe that's impossible."

Stern looked down at the diary. "Oh, it's possible. And I know exactly what those bastards are capable of. They've been doing their worst to my people for ten years, remember?"

McConnell squatted on his haunches and stared at the floor. "Do you think they found the bodies? Or maybe the cylinders?"

"Not the bodies. Not that quickly."

"Maybe we should wait on top of the hill," McConnell said. "If it looks like the game's up, you could still send the cylinders down into the camp."

Stern opened his mouth, but did not speak. McConnell's suggestion hung in the air like a challenge.

"I mean, if Schörner is onto us," McConnell went on, "that would be our only chance to execute the mission."

"Are you telling me that you're willing to kill the prisoners now?" Stern asked.

"What else can we do?"

"Forget it, Doctor. We're going to wait here."

"And if they come for us?"

"If they come, I'll hold them off as long as I can. You try to get around them and up the hill. The climbing spikes and harness are in my bag. You can send the gas down yourself."

Stern looked as if he believed what he was saying, but McConnell knew better. If the SS came for them here, he would never reach the gas cylinders. He probably wouldn't even make it out of the cottage. Stern had to know that. So what was keeping him from going up the hill to be in position to release the gas if it became necessary?

Something in his eyes kept McConnell from voicing the question.

The front gate of Totenhausen was wide open and waiting when the motorcycle carrying Anna Kaas reached the camp. The lance corporal raced across the parade ground and the Appellplatz and skidded to a stop before the hospital.

"They're waiting in the basement," he said. "The morgue."

Anna climbed out of the sidecar and walked up the hospital steps. Inside and to the left was the stairwell. Two flights led up, one down. She walked through the door and went down.

In designing Totenhausen's hospital, Klaus Brandt had given special attention to the morgue. For it was in this room that he did much of his work, analyzing the pathologic effects of his gases, and also of the meningococcus bacteria. Four autopsy tables stood in the center of the room, which was dominated by a mirrorlike wall that housed a set of stainless steel drawers, each of which could accommodate two adult male corpses, or four children.

Anna had a strong stomach, but she nearly fainted when she reached the bottom of the stairs. The autopsy table nearest her was bare, but the second was occupied by a naked man that, even from a distance, she instantly recognized as Stan Wojik. The Pole's black beard was matted with blood, his battered head swollen, his massive body covered with cuts and bruises. Jonas Stern's prediction had already come true—Anna had seen enough corpses to know—Stan Wojik was dead.

"Come in, Nurse," called a voice from across the room.

Major Wolfgang Schörner stepped out from behind a rack of metal shelves. He was carrying a telephone in his left hand and speaking into the mouthpiece, which he held in his right. He waved Anna farther into the room.

"That is correct, Herr Doktor," he said. "Two of Sturm's men are missing. They never returned from patrol. Of course, they could be lying drunk in one of the local villages, but this time I don't think so."

Anna knew she should try to listen to the conversation, but it was difficult. Her eyes were drawn inexorably to the third autopsy table. *Don't look yet,* said a voice in her head. *You can't stand it yet.* She forced herself to watch Schörner. He was pacing now, carrying the phone with him on a long line.

"Beck still thinks the target is Peenemünde," he was saying, "but I am not so sure anymore. I'm beginning to think the Allies may know about our facility after all. The Poles were caught between here and Peenemünde, but that tells us nothing about their activities or their target. Only questioning will do that. Standartenführer Beck is on his way down from Peenemünde with a Gestapo interrogator."

Schörner listened for a while, his face intense. "Herr Doktor, I don't think you should bother yourself. You know the Gestapo. Yes, I absolutely agree. I'll see that I'm present when they interrogate him. I've brought in one of the nurses to make the man presentable. Yes, *Gute Nacht.*"

Schörner put down the phone and signaled Anna over. She kept her eyes locked on his face. She did not want to meet the eyes of the man lying on the third table.

"I want this man cleaned up," Schörner said. "He's bruised a bit, but do what you can."

There was no way to avoid it. Anna looked down.

Miklos Wojik stared up at her with the eyes of an animal caught in a steel trap. When he recognized her, he began to cry.

God forgive me, Anna thought desperately, *but don't let him say my name.*

"How bad is he?" Schörner asked.

Anna pulled back the sheet that covered the young Pole's body. It wasn't nearly so bad as his brother's. His emaciated chest was bruised, and one wrist looked like it might be fractured, but there were no cuts or burns. She cleared her throat.

"What happened to him, Sturmbannführer?"

Schörner looked down at Miklos Wojik with clinical detachment. "He is a Polish partisan. I would have preferred to question the other man myself, but Hauptscharführer Sturm and his men apprehended them both. Sturm decided to question them on the spot. As you can see, he allowed his zeal to override his professionalism."

Anna looked back at the body of Stan Wojik. From this angle, she noticed that his genital area was particularly bruised—probably the result of repeated kicking. It was easy to imagine Sturm taking great pleasure in that. She wondered how the Hauptscharführer would have fared against Stan Wojik without armed storm troopers to back him up.

"A Gestapo agent will arrive shortly to interrogate this man," Schörner told her. "He is very annoyed that we have allowed one prisoner to expire prematurely. I trust you will have this one looking decent by the time he arrives."

Anna nodded. "I'll do what I can, Sturmbannführer."

"*Bitte.*" Schörner was staring into her eyes with almost priest-like intensity when the unmistakable crack of rifle fire echoed down the stairwell.

"Sturmbannführer!" Anna cried. "What was that?"

Schörner had not moved a muscle. "Another reprisal," he said quietly. "Hauptscharführer Sturm believes there is more to the mystery of his lost patrol than whisky or easy women. He has convinced Brandt that shooting prisoners is the way to find out what. They're being shot against the hospital wall." Schörner made a disparaging sound. "As if a spy network could be run by the wretches in this camp."

"Whom did they kill this time?" Anna asked.

Schörner's eyes narrowed. "You have an interest in particular prisoners?"

"No, Sturmbannführer. I was merely curious."

"I see. I believe they shot five Jewish women and five Polish men. He means to shoot ten prisoners every twenty-four hours."

Anna knew by Schörner's calmness that Rachel Jansen had not been among the condemned. But then she wondered. Perhaps that would be the easiest way to extricate himself from any future difficulties—

"You are Fraulein Kaas?" Schörner asked.

Anna felt a sudden flush of panic. "Yes, Sturmbannführer."

"Your sister is the wife of Gauleiter Hoffman?"

"Yes, Sturmbannführer."

"Listen to me. Obviously any nurse could clean this prisoner. I specifically called you here because I needed to speak with someone reliable. Someone at the center of things here, but . . . still outside. You understand?"

"I'm not sure, Sturmbannführer."

"Let me be clear, then. If you had to pick someone from the camp staff who might be capable of treason, who would it be?"

Anna's voice was a whisper. "*Treason,* Sturmbannführer?"

"Yes. Someone in this camp is leaking information to either the Polish Resistance or the Allies, perhaps both. And it's certainly not a prisoner. I've known for some time that there is an illegal radio transmitter operating in the area."

Anna knew then that the whole thing was a wicked charade. Schörner was about to place her under arrest. The Gestapo man was on his way to interrogate *her,* not Miklos Wojik.

"Do you know any of the lab technicians well?" Schörner asked.

"Technicians? No, Sturmbannführer."

"See them in Dornow? In the tavern?"

"I do not socialize, Sturmbannführer."

"A pity. You are a beautiful woman. What about your fellow nurses? Do you feel confident of their political loyalties?"

Anna could make no sense of her frantic thoughts. What would be the clever thing to say? What would Jonas Stern say?

Schörner tapped the autopsy table. He seemed wholly oblivious to Miklos Wojik. "Are we the target?" he murmured. "The radio, Gauss, the stolen car . . . and now these Poles." He gave the table a final slap. "I must go to Brandt's office for a while, Nurse. While I'm gone, I want you to think about what I asked you."

I can't stand it anymore, she thought. *I've got to get out of here.* "Sturmbannführer, may I retrieve a medical bag from the surgery upstairs?"

"I'll send a man for it. Please attend to this man immediately."

He hurried up the stairs.

Anna went to the sink and wet a cloth, then returned to Miklos's side and laved his brow with warm water. The young Pole was crying again.

"I'm sorry, Miklos," she whispered. "What happened?"

He shook his head hopelessly. "They killed Stanislaus," he croaked. "They . . . hurt him first. Oh, God *damn* them!"

Anna shut out her pity. "Miklos, did you send the message to Sweden? Did you get to your radio?"

"No. I'm sorry. We didn't get more than ten miles. The woods were full of SS. They were everywhere, as if they were looking for us."

"They weren't. They were looking for someone else."

"Your friends. The sergeant who killed Stan kept asking about parachutes. Did they catch your friends?"

"Not yet. Miklos, what about the paper? The paper the Jew gave you."

"Stan got rid of it in time. They didn't find it."

Anna felt a flutter of hope. "Are you positive?"

"He burned it just before they closed in." Miklos was breathing too fast. "Stan fought them. He kept on fighting so they shot him in the legs so they could beat him without him fighting and—"

Anna pressed her hand over his mouth. "Don't think about it, Miklos. Breathe through your nose. You're hyperventilating."

The Pole caught her wrist in a desperate grip and pulled her hand away. "Help me, Anna," he begged. "You must help me."

She fought back tears. It seemed that her fate was to stand at the side of the doomed and be unable to help them. "There's nothing I can do for you," she said.

"There is, Anna. You must."

She heard heavy boots pounding down the stairs. An SS private rushed into the room carrying a black medical bag. He handed it to her, then took up station at the foot of the stairs.

She leaned over Miklos's face and began to wash his chest with the rag. "What can I do?" she whispered.

"Kill me," said the Pole, in a voice no louder than a breath.

The color drained from Anna's face.

"You must. Stan told them nothing, but he was strong." More tears rolled down Miklos's cheeks. "I am not strong, Anna. I am afraid. I always was. If they do to me what they did to Stan, I will talk. I know it."

"I cannot do what you ask."

"What's he saying there?" called the SS guard.

Anna straightened up. "He's out of his head. I think he may have a concussion."

She leaned down again, as if examining Miklos's eyes.

"The Gestapo is coming," said the Pole. "They're worse than the SS. They use electricity."

"I cannot do it."

Suddenly Miklos Wojik's eyes focused with an intensity of pleading Anna had never seen in her life, not even in the eyes of the victims of Brandt's experiments. "I am a dead man," he whispered. "Nothing can change that. But if you don't do what I ask, you and your friends will be dead too."

An electric tingle raced across Anna's scalp and shoulders. What Miklos said was true. If he talked, they would all die. She would be tortured. How long could she hold her silence if Sturm were allowed to do whatever he wished to her? And if she somehow survived the ordeal, there was always the Ravensbrück camp for women—

She opened the black medical bag and scanned the neat rows of ampules and glass syringes lying in their fitted slots beneath elastic bands. Antiseptics, local anesthetics, sulfa drugs, insulin— Was that the answer? No, it would take a massive overdose to kill, and as his blood sugar plummeted Miklos would experience cramps that would panic the guard. *There*—

She reached into the bottom of the bag and palmed a vial of

morphia, then leaned down and put her head on Miklos Wojik's chest as if listening carefully.

"Guard!" she cried. "This man is having heart palpitations!"

"I'll call a doctor!" the SS man volunteered, starting toward the telephone Schörner had been using.

"No, I need adrenaline immediately! Run to the pharmacy room and get some!"

The guard shifted on his feet. "I'm not supposed to leave my post."

"He'll die without it!"

The SS man nodded. "I'll be right back."

Anna selected a 10cc syringe and drew six cubic centimeters of morphia into the barrel. She could not afford the time to tie a tourniquet to make a vein stand up, nor could she use a superficial vein that might leave clear traces of a puncture. Her eyes searched Miklos's naked body. The Pole's groin area was badly bruised, just as his brother's had been. Beneath one of those bruises, inferior to the inguinal ligament, ran the femoral vein. It took experience to hit a deep vein blindly, but Anna had been forced to use the femoral dozens of times when unable to locate superficial veins on emaciated prisoners. She pressed two fingers of her left hand hard into the flesh between Miklos's penis and his right hip bone. He groaned as she compressed the bruise, but Anna instantly felt a powerful pulse beating beneath her fingertips.

She glanced at the stairs, then angled the needle just beyond her fingers and punctured the bruised skin and tissue. When she drew back the plunger, dark blood swirled in the barrel of the syringe. With a silent prayer she closed her eyes and injected the entire contents of the syringe into the vein.

Miklos lifted his head as she drew out the needle. "Did you . . . ?"

Anna had not met his eyes since making her decision. Now she did.

They were closed. *"Boze,"* he murmured. "God bless you, Anna. How long?"

"Soon. May God forgive me for this terrible thing."

Miklos opened his eyes again. They were brown and very large. *"I* forgive you," he said forcefully. "I forgive you now, myself! God sent you to me, Anna. You are his angel and you don't even know it. I suppose that's how it always is."

There was a clattering of boots as the private rushed back in and handed Anna the adrenaline. "Is he still alive?"

"Yes. *Danke*. I think perhaps it was merely a panic attack. His heart is weak, though."

"He has reason to panic," the guard muttered.

Miklos closed his eyes so he would not to have to look at the SS man. Anna stood rigidly beside him as his breathing slowed. After the guard returned to his post, she walked around the table and held the young Pole's hand. Miklos squeezed back weakly. After two minutes he lapsed into a coma. She held his hand for another minute to be sure, then let it go. She had reached her limit.

"He's sleeping," she said to the guard. "I've done all I can for him. He is presentable for interrogation." She summoned her last reserve of courage. "Tell Wolfgang I will come again if he needs me, but I need sleep now. I am on duty tomorrow."

She pocketed the original ampule of adrenaline from the medical kit so at least that part of her story would hold up, then moved toward the door. She knew she should wait for Schörner to return; it would be madness to leave. She should wait and calmly play the part of dumbfounded nurse while Schörner apologized for the prisoner's death to the Gestapo man from Peenemünde. But she simply could not do it.

The private stepped into Anna's path as she neared the stairs, but her professional manner—and her use of Schörner's Christian name—intimidated him enough not to challenge her. She marched past him, up the stairs, and out of the hospital. With every step she felt as if she were condemning herself, but she kept walking. She kept walking until she had walked right out of Totenhausen's main gate.

Seventeen minutes later, Miklos Wojik died.

36

While Anna was gone, McConnell and Stern had sat in the cellar for an hour, then had grown so anxious they came up to the kitchen and ate some moldy cheese in the darkness. Every minute or so Stern would go to the front window to check the road for approaching vehicles. They heard a motorcycle once, but it turned out to be only an SS man headed into Dornow. When Anna finally did arrive, they never heard her coming. She simply opened the door and stepped inside the dark foyer.

Stern switched on the kitchen light.

She stood in the kitchen door, her blond hair tangled and plastered to her cheeks, her overcoat soaked through as if she had fallen a dozen times in the snow. She shivered uncontrollably.

McConnell jumped up and steadied her. "Put on some coffee," he told Stern.

Stern didn't move. "What happened?" he asked. "What did they want you for?"

Anna's eyes seemed out of focus. "It's over," she mumbled.

"What do you mean?" Stern grabbed his Schmeisser off the counter. "They know we're here?"

"I don't know. But Schörner caught the Wojiks."

"Oh God," McConnell murmured. "Did you walk back here?"

"Yes."

"Jesus."

"Schörner?" said Stern. "Schörner isn't Scarlett?"

Anna shook her head.

"Well . . . did they get the message to Sweden?"

"No."

"*No?* No message? No air raid?"

"No."

"*Scheisse!* Have the Poles talked yet? How long has Schörner had them?"

"They haven't talked," Anna said, half-turning as McConnell pulled off her wet overcoat.

"How do you know?" Stern pressed.

"They can't."

"What do you mean? They're dead?"

"Yes."

"Both of them?"

"Yes."

"What about the note? My note to Smith."

"Stan got rid of it before they were taken."

"How do you know that?"

"Miklos told me."

"You *talked* to them?"

"Only Miklos. Stan was already dead. Tortured."

"Tortured? Then how do you know he didn't talk?"

Anna finally focused on Stern. "Because Miklos told me," she said, her nostrils flaring in anger. "And because I knew Stan Wojik. He was tough. Tougher than you will ever be, Herr Stern. He hated the Nazis. He hated them so much he lived in the forest like an animal to fight them. You think the Jews are the only ones who have suffered in this war?"

"What about the other one?" Stern asked, undeterred. "The thin one. He was tortured as well? He didn't look so tough."

"He was, though. Tough enough to ask me to kill him."

McConnell and Stern looked at each other.

Anna spoke without inflection, certain now that events were beyond her power to change. "Hauptscharführer Sturm killed Stan before they ever reached the camp. A Gestapo man from Peenemünde was on his way to Totenhausen to question Miklos. Schörner told me to clean him up for questioning. We were alone. Miklos told me he knew he would talk if they tortured him like they had Stan. He said . . . he said he knew he was weak."

"He asked you to kill him?" Stern said.

"Yes." Anna touched her cheek as if to reassure herself she was really alive. "I refused at first. But then I realized what it would mean if he talked."

"You did it?" said McConnell.

She nodded listlessly. "Six cc's of morphia in the femoral vein."

McConnell lifted his hand to comfort her, but she drew back.

"Did you see him die?" Stern asked.

"I saw him go into coma."

Stern turned to McConnell. "Would that kill him? Morphia?"

"A full grain in the femoral vein would almost certainly do it. Respiratory arrest, then death."

"How is it you are here, then?" Stern asked, his voice harsh and relentless. "You killed a prisoner and they just let you walk out?"

"Stop interrogating her," said McConnell.

"You realize they could be outside right now?" Stern moved quickly to the window. "You damn fool! She could have led Schörner right to us!"

"See anything?" McConnell asked sarcastically.

"It's too dark."

"I know I should have stayed," Anna said, finally pushing her hair out of her eyes. "But I couldn't do it. I might have gone mad right in front of Schörner. I told the guard that Miklos's heart was weak, that I'd done all I could do. I told him Schörner could send for me if he needed me again."

"Stupid," Stern muttered from the window. "*Blöd!* Schörner is bound to send someone after you."

"I don't care," Anna whispered. "I just don't care anymore."

"You'd better care. Or you'll be dead."

"But I *don't*. Don't you see? I just killed a friend. A boy, really. I murdered him! No one should be asked to do that. *No one!*"

"It's war," Stern said flatly.

"War?" Anna started around the table toward him. "What do you know about war?" she asked.

McConnell watched in amazement as the German nurse put both hands on Stern's chest and shoved him backward against the sink.

"What have you done?" she demanded. "Talk, that's what! Talk, talk, talk. I'm *sick* of your talking. If you think the SS are coming, get your ass up that hill. Go on! Gas the whole camp! Kill all the prisoners, I don't care. I *dare* you to do it!"

The blood drained out of Anna's face. When she wobbled on her feet, McConnell reached out and pulled her to him.

She allowed it.

"Jonas," he said softly, "I think we've reached the point where we may have to consider that."

"What are you talking about?"

"What do you think I'm talking about?"

Stern turned back to the window and made as if he were watching the road. "But we agreed to try to save the prisoners."

"You'd better hurry," Anna said into McConnell's chest. "They shot ten more while I was there."

"*What?*" Stern whirled from the window and stared at her like a man steeling himself to take a bullet. "Who did they shoot?"

Anna raised her head. "Five Jewish women and five Polish men."

Stern blinked several times, his relief obvious. "But why did they shoot these people?"

"Schörner knows something is going on at the camp. At first he thought the parachutes and the rest of it had to do with Peenemünde. But not anymore. On top of everything else, they seem to have lost an SS patrol."

McConnell raised his head and caught Stern's eye.

Anna laid her hand on his chest as if to thank him, then straightened up and went to the sideboard and lit three short candles. It was easy to forget that the electric light could draw unwanted attention. "Schörner really called me to the camp so he could question me," she said. "He thinks someone on the camp staff is a traitor, either a nurse or a lab technician. It's Sturm who is pressing for the execution of prisoners—his way of rooting out the leak."

When Anna went to the stove to brew a pot of the awful barley coffee, McConnell decided she was all right, at least for the moment. He turned one of the chairs around and sat with his forearms resting on its back, the way the old guys did on porches back home. "Listen, Stern," he said quietly, "God knows I didn't come here to kill innocent people. But the things I've learned since I've been here . . . I'm starting to understand why the British tried this crazy bluff. We tried to save the prisoners. We did everything we could. Hell, two good men died trying to help us. But we've got to face facts now. We failed. We failed, and there's nothing to do but go back to the original plan."

Stern looked furtively around the kitchen. "I don't want to do that anymore."

"What *do* you want to do? Run for the coast? Go for the sub and leave this Nazi death machine ticking along like a Swiss watch?"

Stern actually seemed to be considering this. "You want a sample of Soman, Doctor? I can get you one tonight. I'll walk right into that factory and draw off a canister myself. Get me one of the mini-cylinders out of your bag."

McConnell turned up his palms in confusion. "What the hell is going on here, Stern? You know that isn't the main objective of this mission. We're supposed to convince the Germans that we have our own nerve gas and the will to use it."

Stern dropped his Schmeisser on the counter and sat down at the table. "Do *you* have the will to use it, Doctor? Do you have the will to kill every man, woman, and child in that camp?"

"God help me, I think I do," McConnell said, thinking of Anna's diary. "Until last night, I don't think I really believed the Nazis would use Sarin or Soman. But now . . . there's no doubt in my mind. You think I like admitting Smith is right? He's a devious, manipulative son of a bitch. But given what I know now, I believe this mission—or one like it—is probably the only chance of stopping the Nazis from using Sarin and Soman."

"What's turned you so bloodthirsty all of a sudden? Yesterday you were a goddamn pacifist. What's in that diary, anyway?"

Anna turned from the stove, her eyes on McConnell.

"I showed it to him," he confessed. "Stern, that diary describes something I never thought possible."

"What? The systematic murder of thousands of Jews?"

"No. That's bad enough, but it's been done before. All through history, in fact. What's different about what the Nazis are doing is that *they've put the doctors in charge.* They've succeeded in inverting human values so completely that they've transformed the healers into the chief killers."

Stern made a wry face. "You think doctors killing people is somehow different than other men doing it?"

"Yes. A doctor is sworn to preserve life. *Do no harm*—that's the first rule. A doctor who murders is worse than a priest who murders. Popes and priests have presided over some of the worst carnage in history. But intentional mass murder in the name of medicine? I've never heard of it before. Hitler's propaganda machine has instilled a sort of bio-political mentality in the German people. He's convinced them that certain races—yours, for example—are deadly bacilli that must be eradicated. There is apparently a whole generation of German doctors that actually *believes* it is healing the body politic by killing millions of people. You once lectured me about evil, Stern. Well, I'm convinced, okay? If there is pure evil in the world, the Nazis have achieved it."

Stern's laugh held bitter irony. "Words," he said. "You're an intellectual, so you have to draw some grand meaning from everything. What did I tell you the first time I saw you? The Nazis understand the true nature of man. They deal with what *is*. They took the lust for power and turned it into a religion. And it works! It could work anywhere, Doctor, even in America. I'll bet some of your colleagues would line up for the chance to say who should live and who should die. It's fun playing God."

"No it isn't, Stern. You know that. But I'm afraid we've got to do it tonight."

When Stern did not respond, McConnell said, "Hitler hasn't unleashed man's true nature. He's taken such a huge leap into madness that even now no one has begun to grasp what's really going on. But *we* know, Stern. And that obligates us to try to do something about it."

"But you said the British nerve gas won't even work!"

"It *might* work. We have to try."

Stern threw up his hands. "Go ahead then! You try!"

"I will if I have to. Why don't you tell me what's really going on here? You came to Germany ready to sacrifice yourself and anyone else to accomplish this mission. Now you're balking. For the last two days you've been ready to believe the gas worked. Now you're not. Something changed last night, Jonas. What was it? What are you keeping from me?"

"You're crazy," snapped Stern. He got up and started pacing the kitchen, the muscles in his forearms taut as wires.

"Maybe I am," McConnell conceded. "But I'll be *less* crazy if you just tell me why you won't go through with the attack."

"Tell him," Anna said from the stove. "Or I will."

Stern stopped dead and stared at her. After a moment, his eyes glazed with hatred. "You tell him and I'll kill you."

"You go to hell!" she shouted, fearless in her anger. "Or act like a man! That would be better!"

Something seemed to go out of Stern then. Hope, maybe, or the will to keep lying. He closed his eyes and leaned back against the sideboard, blocking the light from one of the candles.

"How long have you known?" he asked.

Anna's voice softened. "The night you got here, you said you were from Rostock. When I heard your real name I thought of the shoemaker, just for an instant. But you were so different—"

"Different how? What do you know about him?"

"Well . . . he repairs boots for the SS. Makes leather goods for them."

"Are you saying he's a collaborator?"

"No. Just that you seemed so different from him. Different enough that I dismissed the idea for a while. But yesterday I saw him up close again. Then I knew."

"What the hell are you two talking about?" McConnell asked. "You know somebody in that camp?"

"My father," Stern said, his voice almost inaudible. "My father is a prisoner in the camp, okay? He's been there for three years."

McConnell looked at Anna and saw the confirmation in her eyes. "Jesus, why didn't you tell me before now? All you had to do—"

Stern held up a hand for silence. "I have discovered that I'm a coward, Doctor. Not a pleasant thing. You were right, I was ready to sacrifice them all. Then I found out my father was one of the prisoners and I couldn't do it. It's pathetic."

"It's human, Stern."

"You are also right," Stern said to Anna. "He and I are different. But it is my duty to try to save him. For my mother."

"For yourself, goddamn it!" said McConnell. "Why don't you

just slip in and take him out tonight? I have no doubt you could do it."

"He won't come. He's crazy. He won't leave the others behind."

No one spoke for a while. McConnell stared at one of the candles, going back over the situation yet again. He blanked the people from his mind and tried to see it as a purely scientific problem, from every possible angle no matter how unlikely. Three minutes later he felt the hair on his arms rise.

"Anna, get me a pencil and paper," he said. "Hurry, please."

"What is it?" Stern asked. "What's wrong?"

"Nothing. Just be quiet for a minute." McConnell took the things from Anna and began scratching numbers and letters on the paper. Stern walked around and peered over his shoulder.

"What the hell is that?"

"Dalton's Law of Partial Pressures. You want to make a contribution or you want to be quiet?"

Stern scowled and moved away. Two minutes later, McConnell set down the pencil. "All right, listen," he said. "If you're willing to go back into that camp tonight, we can save your father."

Stern came back and stood over him. "How?"

"By doing what Anna originally suggested. Moving the prisoners into the E-Block before the attack. It's an insane risk for you—for all of us, really—but . . . well, it's your decision."

Anna looked at him in confusion. "But all of the prisoners won't fit into the E-Block."

"That's right," said McConnell. "All of them won't."

"But half of them will," Stern said softly.

"It's the only option, Stern. That or run."

"Playing God," Anna said.

"My father would never agree to be among the saved," Stern said, almost to himself. "He would give up his place to a woman or child."

"I'm afraid that's what it's going to come down to," McConnell told him. "Depending on who makes the final decision, of course."

"What do you mean? How many people can fit in there?"

"Anna said the chamber was three meters by three, and two meters high." He looked at her. "Right?"

She nodded. "After we talked about it, I checked a test record to see if I was right. I was."

"That's eighteen cubic meters of total space." McConnell looked down at his sheet. "Six hundred and fifty cubic feet to me."

"You can squeeze a lot of bodies into that," Stern said. "Especially underfed bodies."

McConnell nodded patiently. "If it were merely a question of space. But it's not. It's a question of oxygen."

"Eighteen cubic meters of air won't support everyone we can fit in there?"

"Not for long. Those movies you've seen, where ten men get trapped in a sealed bank vault or a gold mine and spend two days trying to figure out a way to get out?"

"Yes?"

"They're so much *Scheisse,* okay? Think about it like this. I tie a paper bag over your head. That's all the air you have. How long can you survive on that?"

"Not very long."

"Right. And that's all the E-Block is—a big paper bag. Only it's made of steel. You've got one hundred square feet of floor space. That sounds big, but believe me, it's not. You could probably force a hundred malnourished women and children inside. However, every single body that goes in displaces a certain amount of air from the chamber, reducing the available oxygen."

"Damn it, how many people can survive in there?"

"That depends on who goes in." McConnell picked up his pencil. "How does the inmate population break down?"

"There are six barracks buildings," Anna said. "Two for men, two for women, two for children. There are two for each because the Jews are separated from the other prisoners."

"Privileged as usual," Stern muttered.

"Normally there would be fifty persons in each barracks," Anna went on, "totalling three hundred. But Brandt has had trouble replenishing the ranks. The Jewish Men's Block has less than fifteen men in it. Both children's barracks are nearly full, and the Jewish Women's Block just under that. The Christian Women's Block is under quota. After the reprisals, the total camp population is probably about two hundred and twenty."

"I counted forty-eight women in the Jewish Women's Block," Stern said. "But they've shot five since then."

McConnell picked up his pencil and began scratching again.

"Figure for forty-five women and fifty children," Stern said. "We could fit that many inside—physically I mean."

McConnell looked up, "I know what you're telling me. Just give me a minute, please. These are big numbers. Total milliliters of air . . . oxygen percentages total and consumed . . . that's per kilogram per minute . . . a pediatric figure . . . Christ . . . mmm . . . okay. I've got it."

"How many?"

McConnell set down his pencil. "Assuming forty-five women and fifty children, the available oxygen would last one hundred and two minutes. That's only a guess, but it's a solid guess."

"One hour and forty-two minutes," Anna said. "Is that long enough?"

"Frankly, I don't think so. Smith's scientists planned this attack with only eight cylinders. That suggests a gas on the order of Sarin, which I'm certain it was copied from. If the British gas works, lethal amounts could persist for as long as four hours, maybe even longer."

"Four hours is too long," said Stern. "SS reinforcements could arrive from somewhere else."

McConnell considered this factor. SS reinforcements could be as deadly as Sarin if they weren't killed by the gas. "We must pare the numbers down to allow for two hours of oxygen. No less."

"Numbers?" Stern echoed. "You're talking about people!"

"I know that," McConnell said evenly. "The one hundred and twenty-five I already excluded from the equation are people too. They're just not Jews."

For once, Stern did not lose his self-control when faced with an unpalatable truth. "What's wrong with the fucking Nazis all of a sudden?" he grumbled. "They usually build everything twice as big as anyone else."

"The gases Brandt tests in the E-Block are the most toxic in the world," Anna explained. "Sometimes they run several tests in a day. The E-Block was designed small enough to be cleaned thoroughly and quickly with steam and detergents. The whole process is automated."

"It's just a bigger version of the Bubble back in my lab," said McConnell.

"Bubble?"

"I remember," said Stern. "Except you use rats. They use people. So tell me, how many people can survive for two hours in Brandt's bubble?"

"You want to save all the children or all the women?"

"My God," Anna whispered. "You have no right to do this."

"You're right," McConnell agreed. "But I am doing it."

"*Kinder,*" said Stern. "Save the children."

"But the children must have someone to take care of them when they come out," Anna argued.

"Women use more air," said Stern. "There'll be enough women left to take care of the children. Take out women."

McConnell carefully recalculated his equation. "If you took out ten women," he said, "the oxygen would last one hundred and nineteen minutes. Almost exactly two hours. If you want my opinion, I'd take out twenty women. It's horrible, I know, but by trying to save too many we could kill them all."

"Wait!" Anna cut in. "What about an oxygen bottle?"

McConnell's eyebrows went up. "Oxygen bottle? Depending on the type, it could make a significant difference."

"There are several large tanks in the factory, in case of accidents. I can't get access to those, but in the hospital we have two portable bottles. I don't know the exact amount of oxygen in them, but I think I could steal one. The other is being used on a pneumonia case, an SS private. It would be missed immediately."

Stern was nodding excitedly. "At least that would let us save all the women, yes? Maybe even the few men—"

McConnell held up his hand. "There's another concern here. These time limits I'm giving you are for total oxygen depletion. That means *death*. Before that there would be episodes of hysteria, fainting, possibly some violence. You're talking about terrified women and children packed inside a sealed chamber, probably without lights. They could be tearing out each other's eyes after an hour, trampling the children, God knows what. You understand?"

"You're saying don't increase the numbers at all?"

"I'm saying we should count that oxygen bottle as a reserve. There's no guarantee we can even get it into the E-Block. On top of that, these people may *have* to stay inside the chamber three or four hours before it's safe to come out."

Stern nodded in resignation.

"Can we even get the E-Block open?" McConnell asked.

"It's always open," Anna said. "Who would want to go inside it?"

"Point taken. Okay, Jonas, I think you should go back in right now, tonight. You've got about three hours of darkness left. Talk to your father, explain the situation, tell him to start slipping people into the E-Block just before dawn. That's when we'll attack."

Stern laughed. "Doctor, you may know chemistry, but you know nothing about military tactics." He sat down at the table and picked up McConnell's pencil. "What do you think is going to happen after this attack of ours? Where are these women and children going to go?"

"Where were they going to go if we saved them all? This isn't Hollywood, Stern. We can give those people a fighting chance. That's more than what they have now. Maybe they can make a run for Poland, try to reach the Resistance."

"You obviously don't know that half the Polish resistance groups will kill a Jew as quickly as a Nazi will."

"Goddamn it, Stern—"

"No, you're right, Doctor. They'll have to try for Poland. But they can't do that in the daylight. Women and children in stolen SS trucks crossing fifty miles of Nazi Germany by day? You're crazy! I don't fancy trying to find our British submarine in the daylight myself. Also, if I sneak back into the camp tonight—which might not be so easy, considering what Fräulein Kaas just did there—I've got damn little time to convince my father or those women to condemn their friends to death, then sneak out of the camp, up the hill, and send down the gas." Stern tossed the pencil on the table. "No, it's got to be tomorrow night." He turned to Anna. "What time is the final roll call?"

"Seven P.M."

"Then we'll attack at eight. The confusion will be much greater for the SS at night, and we'll have hours of darkness to escape."

"You realize that tomorrow night will be the fourth night we've been here," McConnell reminded him. "If we don't make it to the submarine by dawn the next day, it won't be there."

"We'll make it."

"And what about the gas? It could be degrading into harmless chemicals right now. And the reprisals. What if they shoot ten more people tomorrow? What about your—"

Stern slapped the table. "Shut up, goddamn you! I've made my decision. If you'd ever seen unarmed people hunted down by troops in the daylight, you'd know why."

McConnell hesitated, but reluctantly nodded his assent. "We'll just have to pray Schörner doesn't close the net on us by tomorrow night," he said. "But what about Anna? She can't go back into Totenhausen after what she did tonight."

Anna closed her eyes. "If I don't, they'll know something's wrong."

"They already know! They must. You killed Miklos and kept them from interrogating him."

"Maybe they don't know that," said Stern. "The SS had already roughed him up. She told the guard Wojik's heart was weak. Maybe they think he just died."

"I've also got to get that oxygen bottle into the E-Block," Anna reminded them.

McConnell started to argue further, but she cut him off by asking Stern a question. "Do you think your father will consent to go into the E-Block?"

"With the way the numbers have worked out, I very much doubt it." Stern stood up and leaned against the stove for warmth.

"You must persuade him. Perhaps he would agree to lead the women and children to Poland?"

"He might. I've got all day tomorrow to think of something." Stern snapped his fingers. "There is one thing I can do tonight, though." He walked around the table and disappeared through the cellar door.

Anna took McConnell's hand under the table and squeezed it. "You are a strange man," she said.

Stern came back up the stairs carrying his leather bag.

"What's that for?" asked McConnell.

"The two cylinders we were going to put in the SS bomb shelter. If we're going back to the original plan, we need every ounce of gas we can get for the attack, yes? I'm going to drag those two cylinders as close as possible to the camp fence. With the plastic explosive and time pencil fuses from Achnacarry, I can set charges on the cylinder heads and time them to coincide with the attack. Eight o'clock."

"I completely forgot!" said McConnell, feeling like an idiot. "You're right. We're going to need the highest saturation we can get at ground level. I'll come with you."

Anna squeezed his hand painfully under the table.

"No point in both of us risking capture," said Stern, slinging the strap of the bag over his shoulder. "I can drag the cylinders myself."

McConnell thought about it, then acquiesced. "Just don't get caught," he said. "I couldn't climb that pylon in a week."

Stern grinned, surprising both Anna and McConnell. "You could if you had to, Doctor. But don't worry about it. We're due some good luck." He picked up his Schmeisser and moved toward the foyer. At the door, he looked back and caught McConnell's eye, beckoning him to follow.

"What is it?" McConnell asked, pulling the front door closed after them.

"The SS may come for her," Stern said. "Frankly, it worries me that they haven't come yet."

"What are you saying?"

"I'm saying you should wait for me in the cellar. She should stay upstairs. If they come, and she goes with them voluntarily, they might not search the house."

"I'm not an idiot, Stern."

"I know that. But you . . . her. I'm not blind. All I'm saying is that now is not the time."

It irritated McConnell that Stern had seen through him so easily. "There may not be any other time," he said.

Stern shrugged. "Do what you have to. But if they do come here—and they don't find you—take the spikes from the cellar, climb the hill, and go up that pylon. When you get to the top, tie yourself on with your toggle rope and wait for me as long as you can." He laughed. "McShane was right about those ropes after all, wasn't he? Anyway, you'll be in the treetops, but you'll be able to see the camp road. If it looks like Schörner's men are coming up the hill for you, send down the gas. It's set up so a child could do it. After you've done it, forget about me, forget about her, and try to reach the coast. You just might get out alive."

McConnell was shaking his head, but Stern said, "If it comes to that point, Doctor, she and I are dead already."

Stern held out his hand for the first time since McConnell had known him.

McConnell took it.

"It's less than twenty-four hours," Stern said, squeezing his hand. "What can happen in a day?"

H e's gone," McConnell said, shutting the door against the cold.

"What did he say?" Anna asked from the table.

Without Stern's manic energy there to distract him, McConnell noticed for the first time the tremendous toll all of it was taking on Anna. Her skin, especially around the eyes, had completely lost the pallor of that first night, and taken on the shiny darkness of overripe fruit.

"He's setting the two cylinders for eight tomorrow night. He'll send the rest down at the same time. He said I should wait for him in the cellar, and you should wait upstairs."

She looked surprised. "I assumed he would tell you to wait on the hill, in case he was caught and you had to carry out the attack tonight."

"He doesn't plan on getting caught."

"What do you think?"

McConnell sat down opposite her. "To tell you the truth, I don't even know if I could climb the pylon. They didn't train me for that."

"You have to climb it to release the gas?"

"According to Stern."

"I could go with you," Anna suggested. "Help you. There's no reason for me to stay here."

"There no reason for you to risk going with me. Besides, you . . . you look done in. You really should try to sleep."

Anna folded her arms together as if she were cold. "I cannot sleep. I am exhausted, but I don't want to drop off. Schörner could send someone for me at any moment."

McConnell weighed the dangers of remaining at the cottage against trying to reach the pylon on the hill. "Anna, has anyone suspected you before now?"

"I don't think so. But it won't take Schörner long to put it together." She brushed her hair back from her face. "If they come for me—if Sergeant Sturm comes for me—I think I would kill myself rather than be taken."

McConnell looked into her eyes. She was not only exhausted, she was absolutely terrified. He felt stupid for not seeing it earlier. And she meant what she said about suicide.

"Look, I'm not leaving you behind," he said. "I'm taking you out with us."

"Stern said the British wouldn't let you take anyone out."

McConnell tensed at the sound of an engine on the Dornow road, but the vehicle didn't turn into the lane that led to the cottage. "How long have you been helping SOE?" he asked.

"Six or seven months."

"To hell with what the British say. I'm taking you out. Smith owes you that."

She kept looking at him. In her eyes he sensed, or hoped he sensed, some flicker of hope for herself. He could tell that she had been forcing herself not to think about what would happen after the attack. But now he had offered her a chance, and he saw that she wanted it.

"What about the hill?" she asked.

"To hell with it. I'd rather wait here."

"In the cellar?"

He slid his hand across the table. "With you."

She lowered her eyes, but did not take his hand. "Stern told me you're married."

"I am."

"Why didn't you tell me last night?"

"I don't know. You didn't ask."

She looked up at him again. "What is it you want, Doctor?"

"You."

"I know you want me. *Why* do you want me?"

He searched for some reasonable answer, but could not find one.

"Is it because you might die tomorrow? Or even tonight?"

He considered this. "I don't think so."

"Why, then?"

"Because I love you."

"Love me?" Anna's lips curled with a trace of irony. "You don't even know me."

"I know you."

"You're mad."

"No argument."

"Don't say you love me, Doctor. Not to persuade me to give my body to you. You don't have to say that."

"I don't say it easily. You're the second woman I've said that to in my entire life."

Her eyes searched his face for deception.

"I know a lot of men say it," McConnell went on, "just for that reason. It's the easiest way to get a woman to let you have your way with her, I'm sure."

"And you say it now."

His eyes didn't waver. "Yes."

"You have a wife."

"Yes."

"You don't love her?"

"I do love her."

"But she isn't here to comfort you. And I am."

McConnell watched the way her eyes changed when she talked. They seemed as much a part of her communication as her words, amplifying each question or statement with fine yet uncertain shades of meaning. "She hasn't been in England to comfort me for the past four years, either," he said. "I made it fine without any . . . comfort."

"There were temptations there? In England?"

"Enough."

"But you ignored them? You were noble?"

"Trying to be, I guess."

"But you are not feeling noble now."

He sighed wearily. "Look, is this a test or what? I certainly don't feel noble about this. I feel like I've been dropped straight into hell or the closest thing to it. A week ago I was a pacifist and a loyal husband. Tonight I'm planning mass murder and contemplating adultery." He laughed then, rather strangely. "Maybe I'm working my way up in stages. First adultery, then a little assault and battery to get warmed up . . . then I'll go for the really big time. Poison gas."

"Stop it," she said.

"Look, let's just forget it." He stood up. "Maybe we should go up the hill."

"What is your wife's name, Doctor?"

"What?"

"What is your wife's name?"

"Susan."

"You have children with her?"

"No. None yet."

Anna stood up slowly. Her left hand went to the button at her throat. She unfastened it and moved to the next button. "Then," she said deliberately, "with all humility I ask Susan's forgiveness for what I am about to do."

He watched the white blouse open, revealing scalloped collarbones, then her breasts. "Why are you saying that?"

She dropped the blouse from her shoulders. "Because she is your wife. Because she is here with us now, and there's no use pretending she isn't." Anna unfastened her skirt. It brushed the floor with a soft rustle. She took a step forward.

He could see the pulse at the base of her throat.

"I won't be ashamed for this later," she said, her voice trembling. "In spite of what we are about to do. This is what it is, but I *refuse to be ashamed.*"

He held his hands in front of him, as if to stop her. "Are you sure you want this?"

"Yes."

"Because you might die tomorrow?"

"Partly."

He winced. In spite of the impossibility of it all, he had hoped for something more. "Is it because of Franz Perlman? The man you loved?"

A faint smile touched her lips. "No. That's past."

She reached out and laid a finger on McConnell's lips.

He pulled her to him and kissed her mouth. He felt a sudden heat across the back of his neck, and his heart beat in quick, irregular bursts. She molded her body against his, withholding nothing. "Hurry," she said. "Schörner could come at any moment."

He backed toward her bedroom, kissing her and pulling her with him while she worked at the buttons of his shirt. After four years of self-denial, the mere touch of her skin, the pressure of her breasts as she drew breath against him made him flush with heat. At the edge of the bed Anna reached down, still kissing him, and pulled back the heavy duvet.

"*Zeig's mir,*" she said. "Show me how you love me."

As she opened to him, he had a sense of collapsing into her, of leaving behind more than the terror and uncertainty of the past three days. *Show me how you love me,* she had said. But what he heard was, *Show me we are still alive. . . .*

So he did. Yet even deep within her, in the sweat and the groans and the moments of oblivion, he could not escape the feeling that they were making love in the shadow of a great darkness, pressing toward each other with the desperation of the condemned.

Jonas Stern lay facedown in the snow on the east side of Totenhausen, just ten meters from the electric fence. His leather bag lay beside him. The darkness and the trees gave him cover from the watchtowers, but the dog kennels stood just on the other side of the fence. He held his breath while an SS man led a muzzled shepherd along the inside of the wire.

He had already buried the two gas cylinders in the snow, in shallow trenches dug at an upward angle perpendicular to the fence, leaving only the cylinder heads exposed. He'd molded the plastic explosive around the seams where the cylinder heads joined the tanks. All that remained was to prime and arm the plastic with time pencil fuses. If he did it right, at the instant of detonation the steel heads would be blown away from the tanks, allowing the pressurized nerve gas to spurt through the fence and saturate the area of the dog kennels and the SS barracks.

The cylinders weren't the problem. The problem was the patrols. Crossing the hills from the cottage to the camp, Stern had felt as if an entire SS division had descended on the area. It had taken him over two hours to get from the cottage to the camp fence, and he had twice nearly stumbled into patrols. The two missing SS men had generated even more of a response than he'd expected. Lying in the snow beside the buried cylinders, he tried to decide what to do next.

In his experience, military patrols, no matter what army they served, reached their lowest effectiveness in the hour before dawn. Sometimes it was better to wait them out. He had done it before, and it looked like the best course of action tonight. He would not let Schörner catch him because of impatience. The case he'd stolen from Achnacarry held a selection of time pencil fuses, giving him great flexibility in delay times. Even if he waited here until dawn, he could still set the cylinders to blow at eight tomorrow night. Thinking of Colonel Vaughan discovering the missing ordnance at Achnacarry made him want to laugh. But he didn't.

He heard the crunch of boot heels and the panting of another dog.

Klaus Brandt sat alone in his office in the hospital, the dim bulb of his desk lamp providing the only light.

"Absolutely, Reichsführer," he said into the black telephone. "And the sooner the better. The Raubhammer gas suits were my only worry, and they have arrived. I shall test them tomorrow."

"I have a surprise for you, Brandt," Himmler replied. "You must have wondered why I have always demanded schematic plans of all your equipment, as well as detailed updates on your new processes."

Brandt rolled his eyes. "I must confess some curiosity, Reichsführer."

"You will be gratified to learn that for the past year, I have had teams of Russian laborers carving a massive factory out of the rock beneath the Harz Mountains. If the Raubhammer test goes as planned—as I have no doubt it will—you will begin directing mass production of Soman Four at that factory in five days' time."

Brandt drummed his fingers on his desk. If Himmler had offered anything less he would have been insulted. "Reichsführer, I do not know what to say."

"Say nothing. The only thanks I require will be the maximum possible output of Soman from that day until the day the Allies invade France. We'll show Speer what the SS can accomplish!"

"You have my word, Reichsführer. But what of my work here? My laboratory equipment and staff, my hospital?"

Himmler made a clucking sound over the phone. "Forget that little workshop, Brandt. At the Harz factory you will have everything you need, but with twenty times the capacity. You will of course bring your technicians with you. I have already arranged to have Totenhausen converted into a poultry processing plant."

"I see." Brandt was taken aback by this. "And my test subjects?"

"You mean your prisoners? If your work is done, liquidate them. We must have absolute secrecy."

Brandt lifted a pen and doodled on the notepad on his desk. "Perhaps I should wait until the Raubhammer demonstration is completed, just to be sure."

There was a chilly silence from Berlin. "You have doubts about the demonstration, Herr Doktor?"

Brandt cleared his throat, cursing himself mentally for his overcautiousness. "None whatever, Reichsführer. I shall begin dismantling the laboratory tomorrow."

"And your prisoners?"

"Nothing will remain."

Fifty meters away from Klaus Brandt, Major Wolfgang Schörner poured a glass of brandy and sat on his sofa. Ariel Weitz had only just delivered Rachel to his quarters, as tonight's work had kept him much longer than usual. It had been a messy business, but now he could relax. Rachel nodded once to him, then moved toward the sofa, her fingers automatically lifting her shift over her head.

Schörner rose quickly and pulled the garment back into place. "Wait a moment," he said. "I have something to tell you. Something you will very much want to hear." He led her gently to the wing chair.

She sat with her hands folded on her lap and waited.

"Have you ever heard of *Eindeutschung?*" Schörner asked.

Rachel shook her head.

"*Eindeutschung* is a program for the reclamation of Nordic-Germanic racial elements from the occupied eastern territories. In this program, children between two and six years of age who exhibit Nordic traits—as yours do, especially the boy—are taken into one of the *Lebensborn* homes. Today, I am happy to say, I was able to obtain a promise that space could be made available for your children at the home in Steinhöring."

Rachel's pulse quickened. "What is a *Lebensborn* home, Sturmbannführer?"

"Ah, I forget. You have been isolated. *Lebensborn* is the Fount of Life Society. It was established by Reichsführer Himmler to assist unwed mothers of pure racial stock in delivering and raising their children. The facilities are models of cleanliness."

"And these homes . . . they accept children of parents who are not of 'pure' racial stock?"

"They do, yes. It's a matter of biological selection. But I have already vouched for your children. The senior man at Steinhöring is a friend of my father."

"I see." Rachel thought for a moment. "What happens to these children after they reach the age of six?"

"Oh, they are adopted long before then. The demand far exceeds the supply."

"The *demand?* Who demands them?"

"Why, good German families of course. Frequently families of childless SS officers."

Rachel closed her eyes.

Schörner could not contain his excitement. "I don't know why I didn't think of it sooner. It's the perfect solution!"

"They would be raised as Nazis?"

Schörner looked put out. "As Germans, Rachel. Is that so terrible?"

"I would never see them again."

A strange smile played over Schörner's lips. "Children are not the only ones taken into the *Eindeutschung* program, *Liebling.*"

Rachel cringed at the intimate word. Her relationship with Schörner had been nothing like she'd expected. Rather than simply using her for sexual relief, he seemed intent on creating some grotesque parody of domesticity.

"What are you saying?" she asked, trying not to trust the glimmer of excitement she felt. "I could go with my children?"

Schörner's smile disappeared. "That would not be possible. However, all is not lost. I shall be reassigned very soon. My parents are still alive in Cologne. I believe it might be possible for me to take you there and have you employed by them as a servant, as part of *Eindeutschung*.

"But I am a Jew, Sturmbannführer."

"Stop saying that! Papers are easily enough had, especially in the current situation. Do you want to survive or don't you?"

Rachel stared at him in wonder. It was a measure of the gulf between them that Schörner could sit there and offer what he thought was salvation, while she saw only grief and pain. "Sturmbannführer, I do not consider life without my children worth living."

Exasperation flared in Schörner's voice. "They would be given the best of care in a *Lebensborn* home!"

"Until they were adopted by an SS family."

"Of course!" He forced himself to calm down. "Listen . . . who knows? Perhaps after the war we—you—could locate the adopting parents and convince them to. . . ." Even Schörner fell silent at this ridiculous fantasy. "Rachel," he said firmly, "my ability to protect your children at this point is negligible. You must decide soon. The alternative is—"

"What?"

"Must I say it? Brandt's work here is nearly done. After that . . . I cannot tell you more."

"I cannot decide this! I must have time to think."

"But your children would *survive*. Isn't that what you want?"

Yes! cried a voice in her mind. *The war will be over before long, and the Nazis will lose. You could find them! You could tell every woman in the Circle what you are doing, so that after the war people would know you were telling the truth. Perhaps you could even mark the children in some way, give them a small scar to help prove they were yours after the war. They would probably have forgotten you, of course, and they might have changed a bit under the influence of SS parents, but—*

Rachel leapt to her feet. She was too torn even to make sense of her own thoughts. "Do you require anything further of me, Sturmbannführer?"

Schörner moved toward her, then stopped himself. "No. You may go. But think about what I told you. These are desperate times, Rachel. We must not close our minds to radical solutions."

She stared at him for a long time. Then she turned, walked to the door, and knocked for Ariel Weitz.

* * *

Anna swept back her hair from the dampness at her neck. She was lying naked beneath the duvet she had brought to the cellar from upstairs. Two pale candles on the floor gave the only light. McConnell lay on his back, with her head in the crook of his arm.

"It will be dawn soon," she said. "Maybe we should go up the hill. If Schörner catches Stern, we won't get another chance to carry out the attack."

McConnell pulled her closer. "Don't worry about that."

"Why not?"

"Because even if those bastards caught Stern—which they won't—they couldn't make him talk. Not in a week. That nut would slash his own throat with a broken bottle before he'd talk, just to spite them."

She laughed softly in the darkness.

"Why don't you try to sleep?" he said. "I'll watch over you."

"I cannot sleep," she said. "The way this has all happened . . . you and me . . . the Wojiks being caught . . . what we must do tomorrow—I can't force it out of my mind long enough to sleep. And it will all be over soon enough, in any case."

McConnell turned and looked into her eyes. "Do you think Stern came here with orders to kill me?" he asked, giving voice to his suspicion for the first time. "If I was captured, I mean."

Anna's face grew somber. "I think he did, yes."

"The cyanide capsule, right?"

"Yes. They always give one. Especially to someone like you, who is valuable because of what they know. I guess they were afraid you wouldn't take the capsule if you were captured."

He rose up on one elbow. "But I *was* captured, Anna. Last night. Stern told me not to tell you. The point is, he didn't kill me. He could have—easily—but he didn't. He killed two SS men instead."

She stiffened. "The missing patrol? Stern killed them?"

"Yes."

"*Ach,* where are the bodies?"

"The sewer in Dornow."

"My God. Schörner is bound to find them before tomorrow night."

McConnell took a deep breath. "Maybe. But it's odd, isn't it? About Stern disobeying his orders, I mean."

"No. He likes you."

McConnell laughed. "He doesn't like me."

"Perhaps 'like' is the wrong word. He respects you. You are something he can never be."

"What's that?"

"Innocent. Naive. Full of hope." She pulled the duvet up to her chin. "American."

"I don't feel very naive. And I've got damn little hope, if you want to know the truth."

Anna turned under the covers and pulled him close. "It's mad anyway, you know. Why didn't the Allies just bomb Totenhausen to rubble?"

"Because bombing it flat wouldn't change anything in Himmler's head." Feeling the moist heat of her skin, he turned and rolled her on top of him. She shifted only slightly and he was inside again, looking up into her eyes.

"Who thought up this mission?" she asked, refusing to move.

"One of Churchill's men." McConnell put his hands on her thighs and tried to gently rock her.

She used her weight to stop him. "Churchill is behind this plan?"

"Ultimately, yes. I saw him. He gave me a note absolving me of guilt for the people who would die on this mission. Like he was the pope or something. Anna—"

She sat up and flattened her palms on his chest. He watched her abdominal muscles contract as she slid slowly forward and back, her eyes never leaving his face. "Do you know what I'm going to do if I get out?" she said.

"You *are* going to get out."

"Well . . . if I do, I'm going to become a doctor. A children's doctor. It's the only way I could ever live with the things I have seen Brandt do to them."

McConnell didn't want to think about any of it. He pressed harder and watched her eyes as she moved above him. She seemed about to speak, but instead she leaned down and pushed her arms beneath his back, crushing her breasts between them. She buried her face in the hollow of his neck. She was physically very strong, he realized, strong enough that her arms around his back almost stopped his breathing as she clung fiercely to him. And as badly as he'd wanted her, he sensed an intensity in her that dwarfed his own. How had she survived this long? Living on a knife-edge between the mundane and madness, pretending to be unmoved by things that would sicken a coroner, holding her silence, praying for the day when she could somehow strike back?

Anna caught her breath and rose above him again, her nails digging into his arms. She had held back a great deal of herself upstairs. She had opened just enough to allow him in, offering herself as a refuge. And he had taken her. But now she had forgotten him—or at least the surface of him. What did she feel? he wondered. What did she see with her eyes shut tight and her face suffused with hot blood? The shade of Franz Perlman, the Jewish doctor murdered in Berlin? Or was she like some desperate swimmer in a dark ocean, glimpsing a faint and distant light that promised hope and life if only she could reach it? McConnell made himself believe that. That *he* was that light. That he could get her out of Germany alive. That he could get them both out. But when she cried out, her fingers tangled in his hair, her hips thrashing against his own, he heard only the anguished sound of someone whose light has disappeared.

"Raus!" shouted a male voice. *"Raus! Get up!"*

McConnell jerked awake and grabbed for his pistol. Anna had beaten him to it. She was sitting up with her breasts uncovered and the gun pointed straight at Jonas Stern's chest.

"You think that's funny?" she said.

"Put that thing down," Stern snapped. "Get up and get dressed. It's light outside."

Her face went white. "Morning? What time is it?"

"Eight-thirty. The cylinders are armed and buried by the dog kennels. They will detonate automatically at eight tonight."

Anna threw off the covers and began pulling on her clothes. McConnell noticed that Stern didn't look away while she did it.

"Wait," he said.

She had her blouse on and was buttoning her skirt. "I can't. I'm late already."

"Anna . . . Christ, you can't go back there."

"She's got to," Stern said. "We settled this last night."

"Bullshit." McConnell stood up and pulled on his shorts, then took hold of Anna's arm. "Schörner might be sitting there waiting for you. What the hell did he tell that Gestapo man last night when he arrived to question Wojik?"

"I don't know," Anna said, fastening a belt around her waist. "But if I don't go, they'll come for me here and you'll both be killed. Besides, I've got to put the oxygen bottle in the E-Block."

"Anna, that bottle won't make enough difference to—"

"Please stop." She took his hand. "Unless the worst has already happened, I'll be back long before eight." She stood on tiptoe and kissed him on the mouth. "I'll be all right. Keep your head down today. You too, Herr Stern. I'm counting on you to get me out of this country."

Stern looked from her to McConnell. "What is she talking about?"

Anna smiled at him, then hurried up the cellar stairs. She didn't look back when she went through the door.

"What the hell was she talking about?" Stern asked again.

McConnell pulled on the gray trousers of his SS uniform. "I'm taking her out with me. You have a problem with that?"

Stern shrugged. "That's between you and the Royal Navy, Doctor. Your wife might have something to say about it, though."

"Go to hell."

38

Anna knew something was wrong as soon as her bicycle coasted out of the heavy trees and onto the drive leading to Totenhausen's main gate. Not only had the gate guard been doubled, but even with the pale winter sun lighting the hillside and the river, the men in the watchtowers were probing the shadows beneath the trees on the perimeter with their spotlights. When Anna stopped at the gate, the guards exchanged odd glances but did not detain her. Why should they? She was riding straight into the lion's jaws.

She'd decided that if Major Schörner confronted her, her first line of defense would be that she had merely followed orders. He had asked her to clean the patient, not sit by him all night, and she had done that. She'd left the patient sleeping and in reasonably good shape. If pressed further, she would allow some anger to come through. After all, she was a civilian nurse, not an SS auxiliary. Medical research was one thing, torture another. Was it a crime to possess a weak stomach?

She turned left to pedal around the cinema annex. Activity in the camp seemed normal enough, except for the extra guards and the lights. She saw no sign of SS vehicles from Peenemünde. Perhaps Colonel Beck and his Gestapo torturer had already come and gone. Perhaps all was well after all. She held that thought until she rounded the corner of the cinema.

A naked woman was hanging from the Punishment Tree. Hanging by her hands, which had been tied behind her back so that when she was hoisted up her shoulders would be dislocated. The woman's torso was bloody, her legs dark purple. For a moment Anna thought

Sergeant Sturm had finally managed to kill Rachel Jansen, but as she pedaled on toward the hospital she saw that it was not Rachel. This woman had blond hair. It only appeared dark because of the matted blood.

"Please God, no," Anna whispered, as she stopped at the hospital steps.

The dead woman was Greta Müller.

The young nurse's hands were tied behind her back, and she swayed gently from the rope that held her to the bar. Anna knew she should not look too closely, but she could not look away. Someone had hung a large paper circle around Greta's neck. A target. A target for a firing party. Most of the circle, and Greta's chest, had been shot away.

Every instinct told Anna to run, to turn around and pedal out of the camp as fast as she could. But where could she run to? Schörner might be watching her at this very moment. She knew she should enter the hospital, but her legs had stopped moving. Greta's body told a long and terrible story. The bruises showed where the questions had started. A series of burns traversed the length of her left arm. More serious queries. Ragged wounds on her thighs revealed that Sturm and his dogs had taken a turn before the end.

"Why Greta?" Anna asked, her voice almost a child's whimper.

She looked across the Appellplatz. She knew that if she saw Schörner or Sturm or Brandt then, she would scream, *Why her, you stupid animals? I am the traitor! I am the spy!* She was actually speaking aloud when someone opened the hospital door and snarled, "Get inside, you stupid cow!"

Ariel Weitz stood in the hospital doorway, his ratlike face white with fear. "Stop gaping at her! Get to work!"

When Anna did not obey, Weitz reached out and jerked her into the building. He pulled her down the right-hand corridor and into an empty examining room. "Get hold of yourself!" he said, shaking her by the shoulders. "You're signing your death warrant if you can't act normally. Mine too."

"I don't under*stand*," Anna wailed. "What happened?"

"What do you think? They tortured her all night, then shot her."

"But *why*? She didn't do anything."

Weitz's face twisted in savage anger. "What did you think would happen after you ran out of here last night? You left your post and that stupid Pole died! Schörner wanted blood. I thought Sturm was bad. My God, when Schörner loses control—"

"But why Greta?"

Weitz threw up his hands. "Why? Because Schörner was raving about security and treason and God knows what. He didn't believe Miklos died naturally."

"But why didn't he come for me?"

"It *would* have been you!" Weitz ground his teeth. "Schörner was ready to send Sturm after you. I knew if they interrogated you all would be lost. I didn't have any choice. I had to give them someone else."

Anna stared at him. "What do you mean?"

"I told Schörner I saw little Greta slip into the morgue before you got there. I suggested that she might have done something to kill him."

"You didn't!"

"I did!" Weitz's eyes danced with maniacal light. "I told him I'd seen her before in Dornow, too, talking to suspicious characters. Poles, probably. I told him a dozen lies—all to save you!"

"But Greta didn't know anything! Why did they kill her?"

"You're such a little *fool!* They thought she did know something. They tortured her until she was useless and then shot her as an example."

Anna felt her legs go out from under her. Weitz managed to shove her backward so that she collapsed onto a doctor's stool. "I can't do it anymore," she moaned. "Nothing is worth this."

"I'm just glad Miklos died," Weitz said. "He would have told them everything. I would have killed him myself if I'd had the chance. Tell me, what time are they attacking the camp?"

Anna raised her hands to her face. Tears of hysteria welled in her eyes and a scream gathered in her throat. Only hours ago she had glimpsed a chance at a life beyond this place, some light of sanity beyond madness. But it had been an illusion. By leaving last night she had doomed her friend to unspeakable torture—

"What *time?*" Weitz pressed.

Anna squeezed her shaking hands into fists. Only anger could bring her through now. She thought of the day Franz Perlman had been murdered by the SS in Berlin.

"Eight o'clock tonight," she whispered.

Weitz nodded. "Good, good. I want to be ready. How many men?"

"No men."

"What?"

"There won't be any men."

"No men? But how . . . ? My God, they're going to bomb us from the air?"

"No."

"No? What, then?"

"Gas."

"*Gas?* Poison gas? How can they do that?"

Anna looked up with bloodshot eyes. "It's better that you don't know." She stood up. "I've got to get away from here."

Weitz blocked the door. "You can't go anywhere! You'll ruin everything. Everything I did will have been for nothing."

"I didn't ask you to do anything!"

Weitz gave her a chilling smile. "I see. You wish it was you hanging up there on the Tree? You didn't see what they did to little Greta."

Anna shuddered. "Better me than an innocent girl."

"Ha! None of us are innocent here. Even though we worked against them, we stood silent while it went on. We have *participated*. There are no clean souls in this building. Except the children. Don't shed any tears for Fräulein Müller."

"You sicken me!" Anna hissed. "Get away from me! Get away, you—you *filthy Jew!*"

Weitz clapped his hands together like a monkey. "Ha ha! You see? We've worked together six months, you and I. Plotting and scheming, we made this raid possible. But in the end you are a German and I am a filthy Jew!"

Anna held up her hands. "I didn't mean that, Herr Weitz. I have nothing against Jews. I once loved a Jew."

Weitz cackled still louder. "Of course you did! Every German has his pet Jew. The one that really doesn't deserve the gas. But somehow we all end up there."

"All but you," she said cruelly.

"Oh, I'll get there soon enough. But I'll be taking a few Germans with me."

Anna had no desire to know what he meant. "I can't face Brandt today," she said. "Or Schörner, or Sturm. Not any of them!"

"You'll have to face Schörner eventually," he said. "Go sit in the children's ward for a while. That should stiffen your spine. Go sit with the little boy Brandt uses as a living culture medium. He's deaf and mute now, from the meningitis. That should remind you of why we're doing this. What was the life of Greta Müller worth compared to the children we have seen murdered here?"

"I can't think that way," Anna whispered.

"Then don't think at all. Play your part for a few hours and go home. You can miss the final act."

"What will you be doing?"

Weitz put his hand on the door handle. "Dying, probably. But before I do, I'm going to finish Klaus Brandt. Gas is too good for that slug. For years I've dreamed of how I would kill him if I had the chance." Weitz held up a dirty-nailed forefinger. "You wouldn't want to see it, I promise you."

Hans-Joachim Kleber, deputy chief of police in Dornow village, was thinking that seventy years old was too old to be climbing down an icy iron ladder into a sewer tunnel. But he had little choice. Kleber had assumed his rank in the police department in late 1943, after the last Dornow men under sixty disappeared into the army. And since nothing illegal ever happened in Dornow—not since the SS had built the camp over the hill, anyway—he was placed in charge of maintaining the electric lights and the sewer tunnel. He didn't complain much. The work paid enough to keep him in tobacco.

He groaned as his rubber boots plopped down into the cold muck at the bottom of the ladder. At least it didn't stink so bad in winter. The complaints had started coming in just after noon. Several Dornow families were dealing with backed up sewage, and they didn't like it. So of course old Kleber had been called away from his warm fire to root through the filthy tunnel with his Wehrmacht flashlight.

The old man shone the beam southward, where the tunnel ran for nearly a mile before emptying into the Recknitz River. The tunnel itself was five feet high, with iron rungs set in its sides to assist maintenance workers. Only a trickle of waste flowed in the narrow channel at its bottom. That meant the blockage must be to the north, closer to the village.

Seconds after Kleber turned in that direction, his torch illuminated the corpse of a dog—a shepherd by the look of him—lying with its fanged mouth open in the middle of the shallow sewage stream. He had no idea why a dog would have entered the sewer, unless it was starving, which didn't appear to be the case. The old man scratched his chin and moved cautiously forward.

"*Ach*," he grumbled, as the torch beam lit up a thick tangle of branches, mud, raw sewage, and rats. Kleber unclipped a heavy, short-handled rake from his belt and, after beating away the rats, began pulling away branches. It was heavy work for a man of his years. He laid the flashlight on an iron rung and went to work with both hands. He could hear the rats splashing around him.

"Dirty shit-eaters," he cursed.

Then his rake hooked into something that would not give. Kleber let go of the handle and picked up his flashlight.

"*Mein Gott,*" he whispered, stumbling backward.

The metal teeth of his rake were caught in the sodden brown trousers of an SS man. A *dead* SS man. As the light beam played over the waxy features of the corpse, Kleber realized with horror that the body was lying in the arms of another. *This* was what had caused the branches and other flotsam to collect here.

And the rats.

He stood there a few moments, thinking. For two days the SS had been combing the hills with dogs, and in ever-increasing numbers. What they might be looking for had been the subject of quiet but extensive speculation in the main tavern in Dornow. Kleber figured he knew now what they were looking for. He shook his head slowly, then turned and splashed back up the tunnel to raise the alarm.

Otto Buch, Bürgermeister of Dornow, sat silently at his desk and tried to look appropriately submissive as the senior SS security officer of Totenhausen Camp shouted at him about parachutes, Polish partisans, and traitors. He really had no idea why this one-eyed war hero thought a village mayor could do anything about his problem. Buch had exactly two police officers under his command, one of whom was the old grandfather who had discovered the bodies. If things weren't so damned serious, he would have laughed. He found it funny that it was an interruption in the orderly flow of fecal matter that had brought a flood of the same substance down upon his head.

"Sturmbannführer Schörner," Buch said soothingly, "you have viewed the bodies yourself?"

"You see my uniform covered with excrement, do you not?"

Buch wrinkled his nose. "It is difficult to ignore, Sturmbannführer. But allow me to inquire: have you formed an opinion as to how these men died?"

"They were shot in the back with an automatic weapon!"

Buch folded his hands over his substantial belly. "Sturmbannführer, we in Dornow make every effort to assist the SS at Totenhausen, despite the great secrecy that surrounds your facility. But this . . ."—he waved his hand—"this sounds to me like a military problem."

Schörner raised himself to his full height. "It is about to become a civilian problem, Bürgermeister. As soon as I can get enough troops here, I am going to conduct a house-to-house search of the village."

Otto Buch's face reddened. "Are you *saying*," he spluttered indignantly, "that you suspect someone in *this* village of harboring anti-fascist partisans?"

"I am."

"Well I don't believe it! I've known everyone here for years! The only people I might even *consider* as suspects would be the civilian support personnel who have moved here since your camp was built."

Schörner listened as a motorcycle skidded to a stop in the street below the mayor's office. He moved to the window and saw the SS rider charging into the first floor doorway below. Schörner had the office door open by the time the rider reached the top of the stairs.

The rider pulled off his goggles and saluted sharply. "You're wanted at the camp immediately, Sturmbannführer! Herr Doktor Brandt has ordered a selection!"

"A selection?"

"Yes, sir." The messenger glanced at the portly mayor.

"You may speak freely," Schörner said.

"The Herr Doktor said something about testing new suits from Raubhammer."

"I am not needed for that," Schörner said with annoyance. "I have pressing business here."

"Is that what I should tell the Herr Doktor?"

"Tell him I have an emergency here. Hauptscharführer Sturm can easily stand in for me during a sel—" Schörner froze in mid-sentence.

Otto Buch narrowed his eyes with curiosity. "Sturmbann-führer?" he said softly. "Are you all right?"

Schörner's good eye focused on the mayor for an instant. Then he snatched the goggles from the messenger, bolted down the stairs and into the street.

The SS man and the mayor reached the window just in time to see him roar off on the motorcycle in the direction of Totenhausen.

39

Klaus Brandt stood in the snow before the steps of his hospital, a look of impatience on his face. He glared at his watch, then motioned for Sergeant Sturm to join him.

"I'm tired of waiting, Hauptscharführer," he said. "We'll start without him."

Sturm nodded crisply. "Ready when you are, Herr Doktor. Will you be making the selection?"

"Not today. There are no specific medical criteria. I need three subjects. Choose whomever you wish."

Sturm suppressed a smile. *"Zu befehl,* Herr Doktor. Heil Hitler!"

Rachel Jansen backed out of the latrine shed holding Hannah on her left hip and gripping Jan's hand with her right. When she turned, she saw Sergeant Sturm and three SS men waiting for her.

The struggle was one-sided and brief. Two storm troopers jerked the children away while Sturm and the fourth man pinned Rachel's arms. She was screaming and crying at once as they dragged her away, her eyes on her children. Jan stared after her with wide eyes, then bent over Hannah, who lay motionless on the snow.

"Third time pays for all," Sturm growled in her ear, as they passed through the block gate and into the Appellplatz. "This time I've got *permission* to kill you."

Rachel smelled garlic and blood sausage on his breath.

"I want you to know something," he went on. "After you're dead, I'll be getting those diamonds back from you. You think about that while your breathing the gas, eh? Three Jews in an oven."

Rachel's feet hung just above the ground as they marched her across the yard. Near the hospital steps she saw a knot of men. All wore earth-brown uniforms except one, who stood a little apart.

The shoemaker.

Three Jews in an oven? Rachel heard someone shouting behind her. She recognized the voice before she turned—Benjamin Jansen, her father-in-law. Now she understood. Sturm had found some way to get rid of everyone who had witnessed the incident with the diamonds. They dropped her beside the shoemaker. Sturm moved off to speak with Brandt, leaving her under the guard of four storm troopers.

"Don't try to run," the shoemaker said.

"We're going to the gas," Rachel told him.

"Not the way you think. They're testing a new type of chemical suit. We may have a chance. I survived one gassing inside a suit."

"Sturm means to kill me," Rachel said softly. "To get at Schörner. Oh God, spare my children. Without me—"

Her words were drowned by the yells of Ben Jansen as he was beaten toward them. The shoemaker leaned close and whispered, "There will be a control. There always is. You must volunteer to wear a suit, do you hear? Volunteer to wear the suit!"

Rachel heard the high whine of a motorcycle on the hill road. "Herr Stern, promise me that if your son comes back you will make him take my children away."

"Frau Jansen, the suit—"

"Promise me!"

The shoemaker sighed in resignation. "I promise."

Ben Jansen was babbling at Rachel, but she wasn't listening. She tried to catch sight of Jan or Hannah near the children's block. Was there any chance now that Schörner would send them into a *Lebensborn* home? Of course not. She had been a fool not to accept his offer instantly.

"To the E-Block!" Brandt commanded from the steps.

Two storm troopers caught Rachel by the arms and carried her up the steps into the hospital, straight down the main hall to the rear door, which led onto the alley and the E-Block. They were halfway across the alley when a motorcycle roared into one end of it and raced up to the hospital steps. A man wearing the field gray of the Waffen SS leaped off the cycle and let it fall in the snow. Only when he tore off his goggles did Rachel see the eyepatch and realize who the rider was.

"Herr Doktor!" Schörner shouted. "We must put all troops on full alert immediately!"

Sergeant Sturm shouldered his way between Brandt and Schörner. "The Herr Doktor is conducting an experiment," he said. "Everything else must wait."

Schörner did not even glance at the captives; he knew Rachel would be among them. "Herr Doktor, I must insist!"

"*Ach,* you stink," Sturm said under his breath. "Where have you been, in a sewer?"

"Yes."

"Just a moment, Hauptscharführer," Brandt said in a calm voice. "Let us hear what our security chief has to say."

"I have located the missing patrol, Herr Doktor," Schörner said. "Both men were shot in the back with submachine guns and hidden in the Dornow sewer."

Even Sturm rocked back at this news. Schörner pushed on, maximizing the sense of imminent danger. "I recommend an immediate house-to-house search of Dornow. Sturm should recall his men from the hills. Also the dogs. We will need them to sniff walls and floors."

Sergeant Sturm turned his back on Brandt. "That's what you'd like, isn't it?" he whispered. "But you're too late this time."

Brandt walked halfway down the steps. Something very much like fear had crept into his bland face. "Who do you think is responsible for these deaths, Schörner?"

"It could be anyone, Herr Doktor. Partisans, British commandos, possibly both working in concert. But with the Raubhammer demonstration so close, I don't believe we should take any chances. Think of Rommel. Think of the Führer!"

Brandt's face went white. "Sturm! Round up every available man and dog to search the village. Immediately!"

"But the test—"

"Will continue without you!" Brandt finished. "Move! *Schnell!*"

Sturm glared at Schörner, then started up the alley.

"Start with the mayor's house!" Schörner called after him. "That pompous ass needs a lesson in authority!"

"Good work, Schörner," Brandt said. "Now, let us continue the experiment. I'm testing the integrity of the Raubhammer suits today. Ah, here they are now."

Rachel turned and saw Ariel Weitz and three SS men backing carefully down the steps. They carried between them two shiny black suits which had some type of rubber bag and hose apparatus attached to their backs. She sought out Schörner's eyes, but he refused to look in her direction.

Schörner cleared his throat. "I understood that they had sent us three suits, Herr Doktor."

"They did. But I will not soil my own suit with the sweat of a Jew. Would you, Schörner?"

Schörner studied the commandant's face several moments before answering. "*Nein,* Herr Doktor."

"Of course not. Now, Sturmbannführer, we have a decision to make. One of these prisoners must function as the control. Do you have a preference?"

Rachel saw then that Brandt was toying with Schörner. Somehow, the doctor knew exactly what his security chief had been up to. Giving Schörner this choice was merely one more perverse experiment designed for Brandt's enjoyment. Before Schörner could answer, Rachel heard the shoemaker whisper softly behind her:

"He cannot save you. You must volunteer. Think of your children—"

"I have no preference," Schörner said in an emotionless voice, his eye never leaving Brandt's face.

A faint smile touched Brandt's lips. "I am very glad to hear it, Sturmbannführer. In that case—"

"I volunteer to wear a suit!" Rachel cried, stepping forward.

Brandt studied her with interest. "As would I, were I in your place," he said. He let his eyes play over her body, then looked pointedly at Schörner. "Well, Sturmbannführer? Give the young lady what she wants. By all means, a suit."

Schörner snapped his fingers at Ariel Weitz, who immediately carried one of the suits to Rachel and began unzipping it.

"I too volunteer!"

Rachel turned. Her father-in-law had followed her example. She watched Brandt's eyes examine the old tailor with clinical detachment.

"I think not," Brandt said. "Give the other suit to the shoemaker. Let's see if his luck holds, eh, Schörner? He survived one of these tests already, you know. Although that was an early version of Sarin, as I recall. Not nearly so toxic as Soman Four."

As Benjamin Jansen absorbed these words, Brandt said, "Bind the control hand and foot. We can't risk him tearing the suits in his death throes."

The old tailor began to struggle, but Rachel remembered little else until she found herself sitting in a floodlit corner of the E-Block, her head and body encased in rubber, breathing parched air that tasted like metal. The shoemaker sat motionless beside her. Just beyond him, lying against the wall, she saw a small metal gas cylinder. Was that where the Soman would come from? She decided not. The small tank looked almost casually left behind, its pale green paint blending perfectly with the paint inside the E-Block.

She looked over at Ben Jansen, who lay writhing in the opposite corner just three meters away. The old man had been spared the indignity of being stripped naked, but only to better approximate the effect of Soman Four on uniformed Allied soldiers. As Rachel watched him fighting the ropes, she wondered at the wild impulse to survive that had made her step away from him and grasp at the only choice that offered a chance at life. Had concern for her children driven her to it? Of course. But was it only them? Was there *anything* she would not do to survive one more day? As the hissing of the opened gas valves penetrated the rubber mask, she knew that there was not. She closed her eyes, knowing that her father-in-law would be dead when she opened them again.

She prayed only that she would live to open them.

Anna Kaas watched the steel hatch of the E-Block from an open window on the second floor of the hospital. By her watch, eight minutes had passed since the three prisoners were sealed inside. The gassing had not lasted more than a minute, she knew. She had seen SS men turning off the valves behind the E-Block. The rest of the time would have been spent cleaning the Soman from the chamber with neutralizing chemicals and detergents. The usual cleaning method—scalding steam and corrosive bleach—could not be used in a suit test, because Brandt always interviewed the survivors afterwards. She thanked God that no one had discovered the portable oxygen cylinder.

Not yet, at least.

Two men wearing gas masks and rubber gloves moved cautiously down the concrete steps and opened the E-Block's hatch, then dashed back up to ground level.

No one emerged.

As Klaus Brandt knelt beside one of the porthole windows and rapped on it, Anna looked down at her left hand. In it were the keys to Greta Müller's Volkswagen. She turned her arm to read her watch: 3:30 P.M. Four and one-half hours until the attack. If there was an attack. With Sturm already organizing Schörner's house-to-house search, she had to get back to the cottage and warn Stern and McConnell. They could make the decision: stay and try to carry off the attack, or run. She felt a powerful urge to run right now. But she would not go until she knew whether Stern's father had survived. Every moment she stood there felt like a dare to fate, but if Rachel Jansen had the courage to walk into the E-Block under her own power, Anna could stand to watch for two more minutes.

She started at a shout from below. A black figure was moving slowly up the E-Block steps, a bubbly white substance flowing off of the suit as it moved. It was soap, Anna realized, the detergent solution Brandt used to spray away gas residue after suit tests. When the black-suited figure straightened, she knew it could only be Avram Stern. He stood nearly a head taller than Brandt, and in his arms he carried a limp figure which also wore a dripping suit.

Rachel Jansen.

Anna stayed long enough to see the tall figure lay down its burden and pull off its mask, revealing the prominent nose and gray moustache of the man called Shoemaker. Major Schörner was hurrying toward the prostrate figure at the shoemaker's feet when Anna turned from the window and ran toward the stairs.

"How are we supposed to move in these things?" Stern yelled, trying to be heard through his vinyl gas mask.

He was standing in the kitchen of the cottage, wearing one of the oilskin anti-gas suits McConnell had brought from Oxford. He had gone up and down the cellar stairs three times wearing the suit, mask, and air tank, and he was already pouring sweat.

"You don't have to shout," McConnell told him. "The diaphragm set into the vinyl transmits your voice. You sound like an insect version of yourself."

He pulled up the oilskin shoulders of the suit so that Stern could lift the clear vinyl mask off his head. "It will be a little tougher when we're both wearing our masks," said McConnell, "but we'll manage."

"It's like wearing five sets of clothes," Stern complained, wiping sweat from his face. "How do we fight in them?"

"I wouldn't suggest hand to hand combat. One small rip and the whole thing is useless. If active nerve gas gets inside, you're dead."

"Why isn't air escaping from your hose now?"

McConnell held up the corrugated rubber hose of his air tank, which sat on the kitchen table. There was a bulbous device at the point where the hose met the cylinder. "This is called a regulator," he said. "It's sensitive enough so that the force of your breath opens and closes it. There's going to be a revolution in underwater diving after the war because of this gadget. A man named Cousteau developed—"

McConnell gaped at Stern, who had dropped into a crouch on the kitchen floor.

"What is it?" he whispered.

"A car just pulled up outside."

McConnell knelt beside him. "SS?"

Stern picked up his Schmeisser from a chair. "If it is, we don't have a chance in these suits."

McConnell heard the angry clicking of a key in the front door. Someone jerked the door handle up and down, but the lock held fast.

"*Scheisse!*" cursed a muffled voice.

"A woman?" McConnell asked softly.

Stern tiptoed to the kitchen window and peeked through a small crack between the curtains. "It *is* a woman."

"Maybe it's one of the other nurses. She'll go away eventually."

Stern shook his head. "She's not going away. She's getting a suitcase out of the boot. It's a nice car, too. A Mercedes. Too expensive for a nurse. Wait . . . she's coming back to the door."

"Anna!" the woman shouted. She jerked the door handle up and down again. "Why have you changed your locks?"

"What's she doing now?"

"Sitting down on her suitcase. She's opening a book! She's not going anywhere."

"We'd better get down to the cellar."

Stern shook his head. "She might hear us moving in these suits."

"Jesus," McConnell murmured. "We should have hit the camp last night."

"Everything's fine," Stern said quietly. "If she doesn't leave soon, I'll drag her in here and kill her."

Anna was driving too fast when she came down out of the wooded hills south of Dornow. She forced herself to slow down as the car passed the first outbuildings of the village.

She knew it was insane to have taken Greta's Volkswagen, but she had to beat Sturm's men to the cottage. The gate guards had seen her driving the VW often enough to let her leave the camp unmolested. She'd nearly killed herself several times on the hairpin turns in the hills, but tempting death had calmed her a little. Then she turned down the lane that led to her cottage.

"Oh God," she whispered. "Not today."

She rolled to a stop behind the Mercedes. Her sister Sabine was standing beside the front door, looking just as she always did: the perfect Gauleiter's wife. Too much makeup and too many jewels. Even her casual dresses were shipped from Paris.

"I've been waiting here for two hours!" Sabine complained.

Anna smoothed her hair and tried to look composed. "And *Guten Abend* to you, Sabine. Have you been inside?"

Sabine Hoffman's mouth puckered into a shrewish scowl. "How could I go inside? You've changed your locks!"

"Oh . . . yes. Someone tried to break in while I was at work. I didn't feel safe."

"You should fly a Party flag outside. No one would have the nerve to break in. I'll have Walter's office send you one."

Anna noticed the leather suitcase by the door. She felt almost too disoriented to hold a conversation. "Sabine, what are you doing here? I had no idea you were coming."

"I've come to stay the night. Walter went to Berlin again, to kiss up to the Party hacks. Goebbels is having some kind of function for the Hitler Jügend. They never ask the wives anymore. Not that I'd want to go. Magda's such a bore." She looked past her Mercedes at

388 ❖ GREG ILES

Greta's car. "Is that yours, dear? It doesn't look bad at all, for a Volkswagen."

Anna tried to focus her thoughts. "No, it . . . belongs to one of the other nurses. A friend of mine. She lends it to me sometimes."

"Too bad." Sabine picked up her suitcase. "Let's get inside. It's freezing out here."

Anna prayed that McConnell and Stern were in the cellar. Her pulse raced as she unlocked the door.

Not a chair was out of place.

Sabine set her suitcase in Anna's bedroom and installed herself at the kitchen table. "I'm positively starving," she said. "What do you have?"

Anna realized she was wringing her hands. "Not much, I'm afraid. I often eat at the camp." She felt a sudden hope. "We should go into the village. There's—"

"Nonsense," Sabine said. "A little coffee would be fine. I live on coffee and cigarettes these days. Walter too. You can't imagine how busy he's become. I feel like I'm married to the Party. The few hours he *is* home he does nothing but write speeches. No time for the children. To them Gauleiter is a dirty word. Their father's the biggest man in town and they never see him."

Anna began boiling water for coffee.

Sabine lit a cigarette and drew deeply. She let the smoke escape in little puffs as she talked. "The social scene in Berlin is practically nonexistent now. The Führer spends all his time in Rastenburg, in East Prussia. What's the point of being Nazi royalty if the king is never in town? Tell me, Anna, have you met any delicious officers at the camp? That Major Schörner is quite the hero, I understand. They know him in Berlin."

Anna shook her head distractedly. "I really have no time for that. Dr. Brandt keeps us working."

"Brandt," Sabine spat. "That man gives me the chills. Locked away day and night operating on Jews and God knows what else. Still, Walter says he's a genius, whatever that means. I suspect it means he's impotent." She cast her jaded eye around the kitchen, then into the bedroom. Anna was reaching for a coffee mug when her sister said, "Do I smell a man, dear?"

Anna froze. "What?"

"A man. You know the smell. Sweat and old leather. Come,

Anna, are you hiding a sturdy little SS lover in your virginal bower?"

Anna forced a laugh. "You're mad, Sabine."

Sabine stood up and pointed to the counter. "Mad, am I? You little sneak. I suppose you wear that to scare the burglars away?"

Anna felt her heart stop. In the corner beneath a cabinet lay Jonas Stern's *Sicherheitsdienst* cap.

"The SD, no less," Sabine said, picking up the cap. She ran her finger along the green piping. "Secret police. That fits, since you've been keeping him secret from me. And an officer, dear. Who is he?"

At the moment Anna realized she had no idea what to say, the cellar door crashed open and Jonas Stern burst into the kitchen wearing his SD uniform. He pointed his Schmeisser at Sabine.

"*Ach du lieber Hergott!*" she cried. "There's no need to get so excited. I don't care if you're married. Anna deserves all the fun she wants."

"*Sit down!*" Stern yelled. "Now! In the chair!"

Sabine's expression changed from mild amusement to anger. "You'd better improve your manners, Standartenführer," she said tartly. "Or I'll have my husband speak to Reichsführer Himmler about you."

"I don't care who your husband speaks to," he snarled. "Put your fat ass in that chair!"

Sabine looked at Anna for an explanation, but Anna had covered her face with both hands. McConnell stepped into the room wearing his SS uniform.

"What's going on here?" Sabine demanded. "Someone had better explain."

In the silence that followed, Sabine Hoffman fully apprehended the wrongness of the situation. She had never been slow on the uptake, and she sensed lethal danger now. Like a startled cat she snatched the coffee pot off the stove and hurled the boiling water at Stern, in the same motion darting in front of McConnell to reach the foyer and freedom.

Stunned by the water, and afraid of hitting McConnell, Stern fired late and high. The slugs from his silenced Schmeisser shattered some cabinet doors, but Sabine was already in the foyer.

Before Stern could follow and finish her, McConnell dove through the door and leaped onto the woman's back as she tore at the door handle. Sabine whirled, clawing and screeching like a wildcat.

"*Stop it!*" Anna screamed. "*Sabine, be quiet!*"

McConnell threw himself backward and whirled, crushing Sabine against the foyer wall and stunning her enough that she fell to the floor.

Anna threw herself over her sister to keep Stern from shooting her. "Lie still, Sabine! Don't say anything!"

Stern was trying to push his way into the foyer, but McConnell shoved him back into the kitchen. "You don't have to shoot her!"

"You heard her!" Stern shouted. "She's planning to stay here tonight. We can't risk her ruining everything. She's got to be eliminated."

"She's my sister, for God's sake!" Anna screamed from the foyer.

"She's a Nazi!" Stern yelled back.

McConnell held up his hands to keep Stern from charging the foyer door. "You can't kill her sister, Jonas!"

"I can't?"

McConnell pushed him back. "Look, the attack is only three hours away. We can tie her in the basement. She won't get out."

Stern looked past him. "Too much depends on this, Doctor."

McConnell spoke very low. "If you kill her, there's no telling how Anna might react."

"We don't need Anna anymore either," Stern said, his eyes cold. "All we need is this cottage."

McConnell lowered his hands but leaned close to Stern. "If you hurt Anna," he said, "I will kill you. And if you manage to kill me first, and I don't see that gas factory, Brigadier Smith will have your balls for breakfast. You understand? There's no need for more bloodshed. Let's just tie her in the basement."

"You can't hide here anymore anyway, you bastard!" Anna shouted at Stern. "Brandt ordered a house-to-house search of Dornow!"

McConnell and Stern looked at each other, their mouths open.

"How long do we have?" Stern asked.

When Anna didn't respond, McConnell said, "Anna, please, how long?"

"Sturm's men could be in the village already."

A knock on the door silenced them all.

All but Sabine. She screamed at the pounding. *"Help me! Help!"*

McConnell jerked Anna off of her sister and dragged Sabine into the kitchen.

"A Kubelwagen!" Stern said from the window. "They must have coasted up the lane! Get your rifle, Doctor!"

Stern pushed Anna up to the front door and motioned for her to reply. He stood behind her with the Schmeisser, ready to spray the entire foyer with bullets if necessary.

"Who's there?" Anna called, her voice near to breaking.

"Weitz," came the muffled reply.

Anna sagged against the door in relief. She motioned Stern back into the kitchen, then opened the door.

Ariel Weitz pushed past her and closed the door behind him. "What the hell goes on here?" he asked. "Who screamed? Whose Mercedes is that?"

"My sister's. What are you doing here? Are you crazy? Sturm and his men could be here any minute."

"You're the one who's crazy," Weitz snapped. "Taking Greta's car? Now, take me to them."

"Who?"

"Them. The commandos, or whoever is going to make the attack. I've got to speak to them."

Anna looked anxiously over her shoulder.

Stern stepped up to the door of the small foyer with his Schmeisser leveled. "Who are you?"

Weitz looked at the SD uniform in shock. "I am Ariel Weitz, Standartenführer. I apologize, I've obviously come to the wrong house by mistake."

"He's no SD officer!" Sabine screamed. *"Help me!"*

Weitz forced himself not to look beyond the Nazi specter before him.

"You're Scarlett, aren't you?" Stern said. "Smith's other agent in Totenhausen. It's you who calls the Poles."

Weitz looked to Anna with petrified eyes, then back at Stern.

"You've come to the right house," Stern assured him. "What have you to tell me? Hurry!"

"It's all right," Anna said.

"Well . . . Brandt has postponed the house-to-house search. He pulled in all the patrols."

Stern's eyes narrowed. "Why would he do that?"

"Sturm's dogs dug up more British parachutes near the Dornow road. Cargo chutes this time. The rains uncovered them. Sturm came back with the parachutes right after Anna left. Schörner wanted to cordon off the whole village, but Brandt overruled him. Brandt thinks that by searching for commandos, Schörner would be leaving him and his lab open to attack. So they're sealing off the camp."

Stern closed his eyes for an instant, the only sign that this news had disturbed him. "How did you get out?"

"Brandt sent me to Dornow to get the only four technicians who are not on duty at the factory. I heard him and Schörner discussing plans to dismantle the lab tonight."

"Dismantle the lab? Tonight? Why would they do that?"

"I don't know, but. . . ."

"But what?"

Weitz scratched his chin. "Well, if taking apart the lab means they are moving tomorrow, and the Raubhammer test is tomorrow, what can they be planning to do with the prisoners?"

Stern nodded. "Anything else?"

"No, Standartenführer."

"Stop calling me that. You are Jewish?"

"Yes, sir."

"If you come out of the war alive, you should come to Palestine. We could use you there."

Weitz's hand went to his mouth. "*You* . . . you are a Jew?"

"Yes. And I want you to do something for me, if you can."

"Anything."

"When the attack comes, some of the SS will probably run for their bomb shelter. And that shelter might well protect them. Unless of course some enterprising soul found a way to booby-trap it."

A slow smile crept over Weitz's face. "It would be my pleasure, Standartenführer."

"Good man. Now go. Get back to your work. And think of a reason why you stopped here, in case anyone saw you."

Weitz bowed his head and hurried away from the door.

Stern turned back to the kitchen. McConnell was restraining Sabine from behind in a wrestling hold.

Before Stern could speak, Anna said, "Brandt gassed your father."

Stern's face went white. "What are you telling me?" he whispered. "My father is dead?"

Anna held up a forefinger. "Give me your word that you will not kill my sister, or I tell you nothing."

"You're lying."

"I saw him walk into the E-Block with my own eyes," Anna said.

McConnell heard the truth of it in her voice.

"All right," said Stern. "You can take her to the basement and tie her. Now—*tell me what you know.*"

"Your father survived. It was a chemical-suit test. Your father wore one. I saw him walk out alive."

Without even waiting for a response, Anna grabbed Sabine by the arm and pulled her to the cellar door. Sabine fought no more. It was plain even to her that Stern would shoot on the slightest provocation.

"You'd better gag her," Stern called after them. "If I have to listen to any more mewling about Nazi high society, I'll kill her just to shut her up."

McConnell collapsed into a kitchen chair. "You heard that guy. They've sealed the camp. Schörner's expecting something. You'll never get in there tonight. You won't be able to warn the prisoners to go into the E-Block."

"I'll get in," Stern said with absolute conviction.

"How?"

Stern's boot heels fired together with the crack of a small caliber pistol. His voice took on a saber edge. "It appears that Standartenführer Ritter Stern from Berlin is going to have to make a security inspection."

40

At 6:00 P.M. Greenwich Mean Time, twelve RAF Mosquito bombers lifted off from Skitten field, a division of Wick air base in Scotland, and headed across the North Sea toward Occupied Europe. Their code name was GENERAL SHERMAN. The Mosquitoes took off just behind an RAF Pathfinder force which was leading a wave of Lancasters to the oil plants at Magdeburg, Germany. Each specially modified Mosquito carried 4,000 pounds of bombs in its belly.

GENERAL SHERMAN would remain with the Pathfinder force across the Netherlands, but when the Pathfinders turned south near Cuxhaven, the Mosquitoes would continue east, past Rostock, to the mouth of the Recknitz River. Flying by dead reckoning, they would follow the river south, ticking off the villages as they went. When they passed Bad Sülze, they would follow the line of the river with their H₂S blind bombing radars until they sighted Dornow village. There, the leading aircraft would drop parachute flares to bathe the area in light. Then the second plane would mark the Aiming Point with brilliant-burning red Target Indicators.

The "Mossies" would be near the limit of their range, but with no known antiaircraft guns to worry about, they could afford to make a slow, accurate bomb run. Their primary target was a prison camp sheltered between the hills and the river, known to them only as TARA. In tandem formation, they would pound the southern face of those hills with high-explosive and incendiary bombs until nothing remained but a fire burning hot enough to boil the nearby Recknitz River.

* * *

Jonas Stern walked into Anna's bedroom and checked his SD uniform in the mirror. He had forgotten to remove the creosote stain he'd gotten while climbing the pylon, but that was a small thing now. He straightened his collar, checked the Iron Cross on his breast, felt the pocket that held his papers.

Staring at his reflection, Stern found it easy to believe that his father had not recognized him. Even though he had shaved in the afternoon, the face and eyes under the peaked SD cap seemed to belong to a man he did not know.

Perhaps they did. So much had happened in the past three days. The visit to Rostock had hit him hardest. Finding his father alive had been a miracle, and yet some part of him had not been surprised by it. Such miracles were not outside his experience of war. But the trip into Rostock, into the neighborhood where he had lived until age fourteen, had overwhelmed him. Even though he and his mother had fled Germany in fear, even though he knew as well as anyone the outrages perpetrated against the Jews who remained behind, some inaccessible part of him had clung to that small neighborhood, those few streets and buildings that had nurtured him. That part, that repository of memory, had remained German.

When he entered his street, expecting to find his old apartment building smashed to rubble, and then saw it standing as tall and proud as it ever had, hope welled in him. He climbed the stairs to the second floor with the unreasoning faith of a fool, shedding years with each step, his cynicism left at the curb with the stolen car. But when he knocked at the door he had once been unable to open because he could not reach the handle, it was answered not by his mother or father or his uncle or anyone else he remembered, but by a bespectacled man of sixty with white hair and soup stains on his shirt.

Stern stood mute, staring past the stranger. The furniture in the apartment was the furniture he had grown up with. His mother's sofa and end tables, his father's bookcase and wall clock. He swayed on his feet, his sense of time in free fall. The stranger asked if the Standartenführer was all right. Finally focusing on the face before him, Stern realized that the old man was trembling in fear. The SD uniform had worked its spell.

Even as he mumbled his apologies, Stern caught sight of the two blond children beyond the old man. The boy was only half-dressed, but the tunic hanging open on his shoulders, exposing his white chest, was the familiar black of the Hitler Youth. He wore it as naturally as a British boy would have worn a Boy Scout uniform.

Stern almost stumbled down the stairs in his haste to get back to the car. He would rather have found the whole street leveled by Allied bombs and his relatives dead under the wreckage. The sight of that apartment, filled by the furniture of his memory but empty of the people he had known, had punched like a stake into that hidden part of him that remained what he had been as a child, that remained German. As he turned the car out of the familiar street, he truly understood something for the first time. He was not German. He was a Jew. A man without a country, without even a home. A man who was only what he could make of himself, who could call home only that land he could take and hold by force of arms.

Anna's voice rising in the kitchen brought Stern back to the present. He cocked the SD cap on his head, picked up his Schmeisser and walked into the kitchen. McConnell and the nurse were sitting at the table. They had spoken little to him since his attempt to shoot Sabine—who now lay trussed like a turkey in the basement—but he had no regrets. Leaving the woman alive was a mistake. If they couldn't see that, so be it.

"How do I look?" he asked.

"Just like one of them," said Anna. "Except for the suntan. Maybe you are one of them."

Stern ignored her. He set his Schmeisser on the table and folded his arms as he stood over them. "The whole thing is timing now," he said. "It's seven oh-five. I'm taking Sabine's Mercedes to the camp, and I plan to be at the gate in ten minutes. I'm going to leave the climbing spikes at the foot of the pylon on my way. I don't plan to be inside the camp longer than fifteen minutes."

"What are you going to tell the prisoners?" asked McConnell. "You think you can explain the situation and get them to decide who will live or die in fifteen minutes?"

"The less time they have to think, the better. If all goes well, you will hear an explosion at seven-fifty. That will be me blowing out the transformers in the power station on the hill. You will be waiting here. When you hear the explosion, take the Volkswagen and meet me where the road comes closest to the pylon. Have the gas suits with you. We'll go to the camp together and finish the job. If you haven't heard the grenade by seven-fifty, I've failed. Then you must take the car up the hill, put on the climbing spikes as I showed you, climb the pylon and release the cylinders."

"All in ten minutes?" McConnell asked. "Why don't Anna and I just wait on the hill?"

"Because the only thing that can stop this attack now is someone discovering those cylinders before the attack. I don't want either of you anywhere near that pylon until it's absolutely necessary."

"But that's not enough time."

"It is. I've seen you run, Doctor. I've seen you carry logs on your back. Even if you only climbed six feet per minute, you could climb that pole in ten minutes. You'll climb it a lot faster than that, if it comes to it."

Stern picked up a piece of cloth from the table. It was the swatch of tartan Sir Donald Cameron had given McConnell on the bridge. "The two buried cylinders will detonate automatically at eight," he said, rubbing the tartan between his fingers. "If you've had to send down the cylinders yourself, consider the job done. I'll be beyond help and there will probably be SS reinforcements on the way." He dropped the tartan and tilted his head toward Anna. "She knows the area. The two of you might be able to reach the sub. She can take my place."

"It won't come to that," McConnell said.

"Sure." Stern shifted uncomfortably on his feet. "Listen, if I don't get out, and you do . . . well, my mother lives in Tel Aviv. Leah Stern."

"It won't come to that," McConnell said again.

"Just promise you'll do it. I don't trust Smith. That lying bastard told me my father was dead." He slung the Schmeisser over his shoulder. "Just tell my mother I was with Father at the end, okay? That I tried to get him out."

"Smith told you your father was dead?"

Stern nodded. "He wanted me angry enough to kill anybody who stood in the way of getting this job done."

McConnell shoved his chair back and stood up. "If the worst happens, I'll get word to your mother. But you're going to tell her about it yourself. It'll be the big family story. The night Jonas saved his old man from the Nazis."

Stern took McConnell's hand and shook it.

"*Shalom,*" McConnell said, and smiled. "What do you say?"

Stern's mouth split into a grin. He looked unbelievably young then, too young for what he was about to do. "Kiss my ass, Doctor. Is that right?"

"Close enough."

Anna raised her eyes to Stern. He nodded at her, then moved toward the door. As his fingers touched the handle, she said, "*Auf Wiedersehen,* Herr Stern."

He stepped out into the night.

Anna pulled a strand of hair out of her eyes. "He looked like a boy," she said. "At the end."

"He is a boy," McConnell replied. "A boy who probably won't live the night."

"He's also a killer. He's a match for Sturm or any of them, that one."

McConnell nodded. "He has to be."

Airman Peter Bottomley watched the small single-engine plane float down through the dark Swedish sky and onto the abandoned airstrip. It taxied right up to the Junkers bomber and stopped, engine running. The side door opened and a one-armed man climbed down to the tarmac wearing a severe black business suit. He waved to the pilot. The light plane taxied away. The passenger hurried over to where Bottomley stood waiting.

"How was Stockholm, Brigadier?"

"Same as ever," said Smith. "Thick with intrigue, damned little of which will ever amount to anything. Any word from Butler and Wilkes?"

"None, sir. But Bletchley got an unconfirmed report that the Wojiks have gone missing."

A shadow of concern crossed the brigadier's face. "Missing?"

"Apparently someone from the SHEPHERD network reported that Scarlett called the Wojiks for a crash meeting. The Wojiks left for the meeting, but never returned."

Smith tugged at one end of his gray mustache. "Schörner may have tumbled to Weitz and the Kaas woman, then used them to draw the Wojiks in. He might even have bagged Butler and Wilkes." Smith looked down at his dour suit. "Looks like I'm dressed for the occasion."

"Bad luck, sir."

Smith sniffed and looked southward across the frozen Baltic. A black channel had been smashed through the coastal ice, but it was rapidly filling with small floes. "We don't know for certain," he said. "Still no Ultra traffic indicating anything out of the ordinary at Totenhausen? No foiled commando attack or anything like that?"

"No, sir."

"Well, this is the fourth night. The wind must have been calm enough for the attack by now, yet Butler and Wilkes have not attacked. The gas is nearly one hundred hours old now. It looks like they've failed, whatever the reason." He patted his pockets for his pipe. "Well . . . with a little luck on the navigation, GENERAL SHERMAN will wipe out all trace of the mission. Butler and Wilkes might never have been there at all. Poor bastards."

Bottomley raised an eyebrow and said with black humor, "Gone with the wind, eh sir?"

"Have a little respect, Bottomley."

"Do you still want me to monitor Butler's emergency frequency tonight? Once the Mosquitoes leave the main force, they'll be observing strict radio silence. We couldn't stop them if we wanted to. If you think Butler and Wilkes are done for—"

"Of course you monitor the frequency, man! Right up to the minute the bombs fall." Duff Smith's voice was edged with anger. "No matter how bleak it looks, one never knows in this business. Anyway, we might learn something about why the mission failed."

"Yes, sir."

Smith worried at his mustache again. "I thought Stern had it in him to pull it off," he murmured. "Blast."

"I beg your pardon, sir?"

"Nothing, Bottomley. Let's take the radio down to that hut by the beach. You never know who might crawl up out of the surf."

"Very good, sir."

Jonas Stern wheeled Sabine Hoffman's Mercedes up to the front gate of Totenhausen like Lucifer arriving in a black chariot. He'd seen the spotlights when he was still a mile away, like white fingers exploring the forest, and he had known then that trying to sneak back in would have been impossible.

He had to brazen it out.

As one of the six SS men guarding the gate approached the Mercedes, Stern prayed that Anna Kaas had given him an accurate description of the command situation at the camp. He rolled down his window and waited for the guard to arrive.

When the brown-uniformed SS private saw the SD uniform and rank badge, he reacted exactly as Stern hoped he would. He snapped to attention with eyes as big as spent bullets.

"Step up to the window, Schütze," Stern said in an offhand voice.

"*Zu befehl,* Standartenführer!"

"I am Standartenführer Ritter Stern, from Berlin. I have come here to make an arrest. Possibly several arrests."

The private's face lost what little color it had possessed.

"I want no one but SD personnel to enter or leave through this gate for the next hour. That includes Sturmbannführer Wolfgang Schörner. Do you understand?"

"*Jawohl,* Sturmbannführer!"

"Stop shouting. You will tell the other guards nothing. You will tell Hauptscharführer Sturm nothing. I shall speak to Herr Doktor Brandt and no one else. Anyone who interferes with these arrests will find himself in the cellars of Prinz-Albrechtstrasse by morning. Have I made myself clear?"

The private was too stunned to muster enough voice to answer, but he clicked his boot heels and nodded.

"Get back to your post and open the gate."

The private fled back to his comrades and obeyed the order.

Stern put the Mercedes into gear and rolled slowly forward into Totenhausen. The headquarters building looked deserted. He drove around it and onto the Appellplatz. Directly ahead of him stood the hospital, to his left the inmate blocks. Two heavy trucks were parked near the fence surrounding the large barn to his right, the barn Brigadier Smith had told him housed Brandt's lab and gas factory. Men wearing white coats were loading boxes into the trucks.

Stern drove straight on to the hospital and parked on the side away from the factory. His watch read 7:16 P.M. On schedule. He unscrewed the SOE-machined silencer from the Schmeisser and slipped it into his right boot, then got out of the Mercedes and walked around the hospital.

The alley was empty.

Halfway up it, he turned left and moved quite deliberately down the four steps that led to the half-sunken E-Block. The door worked by means of a steel wheel set in its face, like the wheel on a submarine hatch. The wheel turned under his hand; as Anna had predicted, the door was open. Warmer air ruffled his hair as he stepped inside. A faint bluish light passed through the porthole windows set high in the walls of the steel room. Only now did he realize how desperate was their plan. The E-Block felt exactly like what it was: a chamber of death. It was a supreme irony that in just over forty minutes it would be the one place in Totenhausen where life could survive.

If the British gas worked, he reminded himself.

He closed the door, checked to make sure the alley was empty, then climbed the icy steps and walked toward the inmate blocks. He wondered how much the gate guard had told his comrades about the man in the Mercedes. Under normal circumstances, the presence of an SD colonel would move quickly up the SS grapevine. But these were not normal circumstances. How long would it take the news to reach Wolfgang Schörner?

There was a sentry standing before the wire gate of the fence surrounding the six inmate blocks. Approaching him, Stern realized that he was walking beneath the mutilated body of a naked woman. Greta Müller. He erased the Goyaesque image from his mind and pulled out the leather case containing his forged papers, flipping it open before he reached the sentry.

"I need to speak to a prisoner," he said with perfunctory courtesy. "A Jewess. It's a matter of Reich security. I'm not expecting trouble, so you may remain at your post. If you hear women screaming, ignore it. If you hear a man shout for help, that will be me. Come running."

The guard barely glanced at the papers; again the SD uniform and rank were enough. Stern was through the gate in less time than it would take to light a cigarette.

"Standartenführer?"

Stern laid one hand on his Schmeisser as he turned.

"You'll need this."

The sentry hurried over and handed him a battery torch.

Stern nodded a curt thank-you, then stepped up into the block.

The room was totally dark. He switched on the flashlight, held it at arm's length and shined it on his own face.

"I am the shoemaker's son," he whispered. "I have returned. Is my father here?"

"*My son!*" The answer was a joyous whisper.

"Light the candle," Jonas commanded. "Hurry!"

There was a rustling of clothes in the darkness. A hooded yellow glow illuminated a circle on the floor. A shadow passed in front of the light, and Stern felt arms go around him and squeeze tightly. Raw emotion surged through him, so strong that he almost couldn't bear it. All he could think of was his mother sitting alone in her tiny flat in Palestine.

"How do you do it?" Avram Stern asked. "How do you get past them?"

"Never mind. I must speak to you. Bring everyone close around me. Quickly."

"Rachel!" Avram said sharply. "Form the Circle."

Stern sensed a great many movements around him, like leaves in a night forest. As the women drew closer, he backed against the door. He tried to make the movement seem natural, but he did it to block the escape route of anyone who panicked.

His father and Rachel Jansen stood closest to him. The other faces were a mixture of young and old, a human map of Europe.

"Listen to me," he said in Yiddish. "I must speak to you, and we have very little time. What I told you before was not completely true. I came here from Palestine, but not to verify reports of Nazi atrocities. I came here to help prepare for a great strike against Hitler.

"You all know what the Nazis are making here at this camp. They have tested it on people you knew, perhaps even family members. You know how deadly this gas is. I don't need to tell any of you how devastating it would be to the troops who will soon land in France to liberate Europe. It is for that reason that the Allies intend to kill Herr Doktor Brandt and destroy his laboratory."

There was a sudden wind of whispers. Stern gazed into the shocked faces. As much as he wanted to, he could not tell these women the truth. "In approximately forty minutes," he said, "Totenhausen Camp is going be attacked from the air."

Several women gasped.

"The shells that fall will be chemical shells, filled with a gas much like the one made here." Stern took a step closer to the women. He realized that he had been silently counting them. There were forty-four, plus his father. "Anyone unprotected from this gas will probably be killed during the attack. I have come here to suggest a way that many of you might be able to survive it."

"Why have you really come here?" asked a woman from the back. "The Allies don't care if we live or die."

Stern turned up his palms. "I am a Jew, not an Allied soldier. I fight for Haganah in Palestine. I fight for Israel. I have risked my life to come here. Will you listen?"

"We will listen," Rachel said.

"The only protection from this gas is complete isolation. The bombs will fall at eight o'clock. Ten minutes before that, you must move from here to the E-Block and lock yourselves inside. It is imperative—"

"The E-Block?" someone said. "There are more than two hundred prisoners in this camp. The E-Block would not even hold all of us here."

"I realize that," Stern said carefully.

The women looked at each other in puzzlement.

"What are you saying, my son?" Avram asked.

"I am saying that not everyone can be saved."

There was a long silence.

"What about the bomb shelter?" someone asked. "All prisoners could fit in there."

Jonas shook his head. "The SS are trained to run for the shelter during an emergency. Prisoners trying to take shelter there would be shot out of hand." He did not say that if things were working out properly, the SS shelter was already booby-trapped.

A middle-aged woman stood up in the center of the group. "Who claims the right that is God's alone?" she asked. "Who would say who shall live and who shall die?"

Stern closed his hand around the Schmeisser. This would be the mad minute, as each woman grasped exactly what he was suggesting.

"I'm glad there are no rabbis here," said a very old woman from the floor. "What an endless argument we would have to listen to. Sometimes one must follow the heart. And common sense."

"And what does common sense say here?" asked the woman who had stood.

"It is simple," said the old woman, speaking with calm certainty. "This camp is like a sinking ship. The E-Block is the lifeboat. There is a law for that. Unwritten perhaps, but sacred. Everyone knows it. Women and children first. And the young women before the old. The ones still able to bear children."

These words silenced the block.

"You speak wisely," Avram said to the old woman. "It is not an easy thing to do. But necessary."

Another woman stood up suddenly. "What are you saying?" she asked in a French accent. "That we should save ourselves but ignore the Gentile women?"

"They've ignored us long enough," said a bitter voice.

"And the children? Do we let the Christian children die? And what of the men? They have no right to live?"

"Of course they do," said the old woman. "But they do not have the duty to *choose*. That has fallen on us. We cannot take the opinion of every prisoner in camp. The secret could not be kept. It was wise of this young man to wait until the last minute to tell us."

"You knew about this attack two nights ago?" asked the Frenchwoman.

"Of course he did," said another.

Avram raised his hands. "Let me speak, please. With only minutes, we would only cause a general riot by telling the other blocks. The fact is that the E-Block is the only shelter, and it will only hold a few."

One of the women Rachel called the new widows stood hesitantly. "My daughter is in the children's block," she said in an almost inaudible voice. If we are going to die, I want to be with her."

"We can save the children," Jonas said. "And some of you. But we must hurry and decide the issue."

"*Some* of us?" It was the Frenchwoman again. "You can't even save all the children! Now you're going to condemn some of us?"

"Keep your voice down," Jonas said sharply.

"How many?" asked a familiar voice. It was Rachel Jansen. "How many people can be saved in the E-Block? I have been inside it, and it is very small."

"The E-Block was designed to conduct tests on ten men," Jonas said. "The number that can be saved is determined by space and oxygen. They'll need at least two hours of air."

"How many?" Rachel asked again. "That's all we need to know."

Stern nodded, grateful for her pragmatism. "Fifty children," he said. "Every child in the Jewish Children's Block."

"And women?"

He hesitated. "Thirty-five."

In the tomblike silence that followed, he looked at his watch: 7:23. It was taking too long. He removed the British silencer from his boot and screwed it onto the Schmeisser's barrel. "Talk among yourselves," he said. "I must speak to my father alone. But I warn you: if anyone tries to go through that door, I will have no choice but to shoot."

He took his father's hand and led him into the darkness beyond the circle of women.

"Mother will not believe it," he said, sitting on one of the narrow bunks. "Everyone tried to convince her that you were dead. To carry on. I told her that myself."

"I *was* dead," Avram said, taking a seat beside him.

"It doesn't matter now. God has given us a second chance. No matter what the women decide, I am taking you out when I go. You will pretend to be my prisoner. In five minutes you will be outside that fence."

Avram Stern looked into his son's face. "Jonas, I told you before. I cannot go out with you. Please, listen. I cannot leave women and children here to die."

Jonas took his father's arm. "You're not responsible for their deaths! It's the Nazis! The British and the Americans!"

"I would be responsible for one death, Jonas."

"One? Whose?"

"The child you could take out in my place."

"What are you talking about?"

"How many people can you take out with you? Out of Germany?"

Stern heard sibilant voices rising and falling as the women argued in whispers. "I'm not supposed to bring anyone out. We're going out by British submarine. Then from Sweden to England by plane. The plane is small. In the worst case, I'd planned to send you on from Sweden in my place and find another way back myself. Or we could both try to reach Palestine by an illegal route. I know some people."

Avram was shaking his head. "Stop worrying. You're going out just as you were supposed to. I've lived a long life, Jonas. My old friends are dead. I am not destined to go with you. But someone else is. You can take one Jewish child."

Stern opened his mouth to argue, but his father clenched his arm with the iron grip of a man who has labored a lifetime with his hands. "Listen to your father! Even those who survive in the E-Block may die in reprisals. That's how things work here, Jonas. The person that goes with you has the best chance for life. It must be a child. Small enough for you to carry in your arms, to smuggle into your submarine, to hold on your lap in the airplane. One child to live for all the thousands who have died in this insane country." Avram held up his right hand and closed it slowly as if around some precious treasure. "One seed, Jonas. One little seed for Palestine."

"You expect me to leave you to die again?" Stern said, seething with frustration. "What could I say to Mother? She would hate me forever."

Avram shook his head. "No. Your mother is a practical woman. When I refused to leave Germany, did she stay behind to die? No. She carried you as far as she could from danger. My son, it is the fulfillment of my life to know both of you reached Palestine. I was wrong in 1935, but this time I am right. You must do as I tell you." He looked up and motioned to someone in the darkness. Rachel Jansen appeared and knelt beside the bunk, her eyes wide with fear and hope.

"You remember her?" Avram asked.

Jonas nodded. The bright black eyes were not easily forgotten.

Avram reached out and squeezed Rachel's hand. "Both nights since then she has smuggled her children here on the chance that you might come back. She knew you must have told me to wait here in case you returned. She is a brave girl, Jonas. She is like the daughter of Levi, who put Moses into the ark of bulrushes. And you are her ark, my son."

Rachel's lips quivered as she watched Avram's face. "Is it—?"

"As I suspected," Avram said firmly. "One child, Rachel. One can go. One must stay with you. You must decide."

Jonas saw the young woman sway slightly on her knees. When

she spoke again, her voice was barely a whisper. "How long do I have?"

Jonas looked at his watch. 7:26. "Father," he whispered. "I beg you—"

"My decision is made."

Jonas turned to Rachel. "Two minutes," he said.

Rachel hesitated, as if he might say something else, might somehow offer more hope. But he didn't. She stood up slowly and walked over to the corner bunk where her children slept.

Avram laid his hand on his son's knee. "Come," he said. "Let us see what the women have decided."

"Wait a moment," Jonas said. "We have a problem. The women can't move to the E-Block with that sentry at the block gate."

Avram squeezed his son's knee. "I know what must be done. Let us see what they have decided."

41

One hundred and fifty miles west of Rostock, the RAF Pathfinder force turned southeast toward Magdeburg. But as the last of the Lancasters of the 300-bomber Main Force moved into position behind them, the twelve Mosquitoes of the Special Duties Squadron continued eastward.

In the cockpit of the lead Mosquito, Squadron Leader Harry Sumner spoke to his navigator, who was crowded into the seat behind his right shoulder. "Going to max speed, Jacobs. Strict radio silence from here out. Make a visual check to be sure everyone's with us."

"Right."

Sumner put his hand affectionately on the throttles. The De Havilland Mosquito had turned out to be the miracle bomber of the war. Built wholly of plywood for peacetime air racing, the "Mossy" carried no defensive armament, relying on its tremendous speed to avoid confrontation. It could cruise to Germany at 265 miles per hour with a full bombload, then accelerate to 360 to evade even the best Luftwaffe night fighters. When Harry Sumner went to max speed, the Merlin engines roared like lions loosed from cages.

"Everyone still there, Jacobs?"

"Right with us, sir," said the navigator.

"H$_2$S radar working?"

"So far."

"Let's find that bloody river."

Rachel Jansen knelt beside the prison bunk and looked down at her two sleeping children. They lay side by side, impossibly small and vulnerable, their faces placid above the tatty prison blanket. For two days and nights she had prayed for and dreaded this moment. There was no way to make a just choice, or even a logical one. It was like being asked which eye one would prefer to have plucked out.

She tried in vain to block out the memories that tortured her: Marcus's face after seeing the babies for the first time, especially Hannah, who had been born in the attic in Amsterdam; the hours Rachel had simply stared at the tops of their little heads while they suckled at her breasts, weeping with a rapturous awareness of mortality that closed the throat and made the skin prickle with heat—

Stop! she told herself. *You must choose!*

Her first instinct was to send Jan with the shoemaker's son. It was him she had feared for most these last two weeks. But now it appeared that Klaus Brandt was going to die. The danger would be equal for both children after that. Rachel thought briefly of Marcus; if her husband were still alive, he would choose Jan. *Continuation of the family name,* he would say sternly. Yet Rachel felt little obligation to the Jansen name. Marcus was dead. A blade of guilt pierced her when she thought of his father dying beside her in the E-Block, but she drove the image from her mind.

Gazing down at the children's faces, Rachel simply stopped trying to decide. She laid a hand on Jan's forehead. Three years old. Three years old and already one of the last survivors of his generation. It was impossible to comprehend. Yet it was reality. Hannah's second birthday had passed while she rode in a stifling cattle car full of sick and dying Jews. Rachel remembered wrapping the little *dreidl* in straw and giving it to her like a present. Hannah instantly recognized the old toy, but everyone had pretended it was a new and priceless treasure.

Rachel felt gooseflesh rise under her burlap shift. She had always felt a preternatural sense of peace when she looked at her daughter. It was almost like looking at herself. Not a mirror image, but rather a reflection in water, as if an imaginative and flattering artist had rendered Rachel as a child, widening her eyes, making her mouth fuller, her forehead a little higher. And every word Hannah said, each question she asked, bespoke Rachel's own curiosity. Jan was like Marcus: reserved, a little gentleman.

Rachel started as the voice of Avram Stern cut through the dark. Her time was running out. For an instant she actually considered taking the *dreidl* from her pocket and spinning the top on the rough floorboards. She could assign two of its four Hebrew letters to Jan, two to Hannah, and let God decide. But she did not do this. Even God had no place in this decision.

With that thought, Rachel suddenly understood exactly who and where she was. She was not like the mother of Moses, who had set her infant son adrift in an ark of bulrushes to save him from the soldiers of Pharaoh. She was a woman trapped on an island inhabited by a doomed race, an island sinking rapidly into the sea. She had the chance to send one child out upon that sea —an unfinished message in a bottle—her only message to the world.

She pulled back the prison blanket and lifted her baby to her breast.

Ariel Weitz was very pleased with himself. He had made a great deal of mischief in the last forty minutes, and every second had given him a warm and wicked satisfaction. During his years at Totenhausen, Weitz had managed to acquire keys to nearly every door in the camp. Some had been given to him by the SS to facilitate his daily tasks. Others he had stolen.

One key opened a storeroom at the back of the headquarters building, which housed the overflow from the main camp arsenal. From this storeroom he had removed six potato-masher grenades, two land mines and a submachine gun, all of which he packed into a crate marked SULFADIAZINE. He carried this crate to the morgue in the hospital basement and with another key opened the SS bomb shelter. A long string of hanging light bulbs revealed a ramp descending at a shallow angle into a tunnel that ran fifty meters underground and then up to a second entrance in one of the SS barracks. The tunnel was lined with musty shelves and benches.

With a mine in one hand and two grenades in the other, Weitz had scampered along the tunnel until he reached the barracks entrance. Just inside the door, square in the middle of the tunnel, he set the land mine on the floor and armed it. Then he took the two grenades and, using some string from his pockets, stretched tripwires across the tunnel and anchored them to the shelves. When pulled taut by panicked legs, they would detonate the potato-mashers and fill the tunnel with a hurricane of shrapnel. On the way back to the morgue, Weitz unscrewed every light bulb in the tunnel, cackling softly while he did it.

He had booby-trapped the morgue entrance in exactly the same way as the barracks entrance, and as a final touch unscrewed every light bulb in the morgue. Any SS men who managed to find their way to the bomb shelter entrance would have little chance of seeing the explosives that were about to kill them.

Yes, he was quite pleased with himself.

"Your time is up!" Avram told the women. He stood with his back to the barracks door, his son beside him. "You cannot decide not to decide. To do that is to condemn everyone."

Once again the Frenchwoman stood up and gestured fiercely. "I say it again! *No one here can choose fairly.*"

Avram took a step toward her. "I can choose fairly," he said.

"You!" she cried. "Your own son is the one who has come to kill us. Of course you will be saved."

"Am I not a man? The E-Block will be full of women and children. I will be with the other men during the attack. Thus, I alone among you can choose fairly."

The Frenchwoman looked incredulous. "You will die with the others?"

"If that is our fate. Now, please listen to me."

The old woman who had likened the E-Block to a lifeboat got to her feet and pointed at the Frenchwoman. "You've sung your song long enough, little bird. The shoemaker knows what must be done. Sit down and hold your tongue."

The other women nodded in agreement. Jonas wondered if it was his father's promise of self-sacrifice that had silenced them, or merely the fact that he'd volunteered to lift from their shoulders the responsibility of choosing.

"Here is my decision," Avram said. "Places in the E-Block will be given to Jewish women and children. No one outside this block will be told anything."

There was a sudden buzz of conversation, but it died quickly.

"Any woman among you who has a child will be given a place. If you have a child, please raise your hand."

Fifteen women raised their hands from the floor.

"Keep your hands raised. How many of those left are thirty years old or younger?"

Eight more women raised their hands.

"That's twenty-five adults," said Avram, "including Rachel Jansen and the Sephardic woman who sleeps in the children's block. How many women left are between thirty-one years and forty?"

Fourteen women raised their hands.

Avram counted silently. "That's thirty-nine. There is room for only thirty-five adults. Please keep your hands raised."

"For God's sake," snapped a woman with her hand in the air. "Do four extra matter so much?"

"Four extra could kill everyone," Jonas said. "Depending on how long you must stay inside to survive. I was told to allow only twenty-five adults. I'm stretching it as it is."

Avram looked at the women who had not raised their hands. Some of them were staring at the floor, others weeping openly. The old woman who had spoken about the lifeboat tried to comfort them.

Jonas blinked as he saw a hand drop. A woman who looked to be in her late twenties stood up where the hand had been. "I will stay here," she said.

"But you are young," protested an older woman. "You will have children someday. You deserve a place."

The volunteer looked at the floor and shook her head. "I will never have children. I was sterilized at Auschwitz. The other girls died, and I was sent here. I don't know why. It doesn't matter. I will stay."

"God bless you," said the old woman.

"That's thirty-eight," Avram said stoically.

Two more hands dropped. "I lost my children long ago," said a voice. "And my husband in the last selection."

"The same," said the other woman. "I don't think it matters much where we are anyway. I've been under bombs before. If one bomb fell on the E-Block it would kill everyone inside. I will take my chances here."

Stern felt a stab of guilt because of his lie, but there was no help for it. He glanced toward the rear of the block. No sign of Rachel Jansen. He was about to call her name when a bald woman jumped up and pointed at someone seated on the floor.

"She's lying! She's forty-two. How can you do it, Shoshana?"

The woman being pointed at kept her hand rigidly in the air. "I'm thirty-nine," she said.

The accuser shook her head violently. "I know her from Lublin! She's forty-two!"

The accused woman stood up, her face working in terror. "Yes, I'm forty-two! Is that so old? Why shouldn't I have a chance to live? Look at my hips! I can still bear children!"

She turned around in place in an almost lewd exhibition of her surviving sexual charms. Jonas saw that some of the other women who had been excluded were becoming upset. He stepped forward, ready to restrain the overwrought woman.

"If you want to keep living so badly, go in my place."

Another woman had stood up. She was emaciated and nearly bald, with skin like parchment, but certainly not older than thirty. "I lived in Warsaw," she said. "There is no one left in my family. Take my place."

"No!" protested several women. "You deserve your place!"

The young woman raised her hands, palms up, in a haunting gesture of resignation. "Please," she said. "I am so tired."

Jonas stepped in front of his father. "Hands down," he said. "It is decided." He called to the back of the barracks: "Frau Jansen, it is time."

"How will we reach the E-Block without the Germans seeing us?" asked a young woman.

"I plan to short out the electricity just before the attack. You only have to cross fifteen meters of open ground to reach the alley. Each woman must take at least one child to the E-Block, some two. Once inside, do whatever you must to fit everyone in. The ceiling is low, but you can hold the small children on your shoulders."

"What about the sentry they posted at our gate? We can't get out that way, and many of the children can't climb the fence."

"I'm going to kill the sentry," Jonas said. "My father will put on his uniform and stand in his place until it is time for you to move. I suggest you begin moving them at ten minutes until eight. Use your own judgment. But no matter what happens, the E-Block door must be sealed shut before eight."

"How will we get out?" asked a worried voice from the floor. "There is no door handle inside the E-Block."

"I will leave my machine gun. One of you will have to shoot out a window. It's the only way."

"How long do we wait?"

"Two hours, if you can stand it. There should be two hours of air, plus a small oxygen bottle as a reserve. After that, you must get away from here quickly. Take a truck and try to reach the Polish border. There are partisans there in the forest."

Jonas's chest felt suddenly hollow. Rachel Jansen was walking toward him like a specter out of the darkness. She held a small bundle in her arms, wrapped in one of the prison blankets. When she reached him, she immediately handed it over. There were tears on her face.

"Take care of her, Herr Stern," she said. "She won't make any trouble for you."

Jonas pulled back the blanket. He saw the raven-haired head of Hannah Jansen. The little girl was fast asleep. He passed the child back to Rachel. "Just a little longer," he said. "I have something to do before I go."

He handed the silenced Schmeisser to his father and drew the SS dagger from the black sheath at his belt. Its gleaming nine-inch blade was engraved with the motto, *My Honor Is Loyalty*. He closed his hand around the Nazi eagle on the black haft of the dagger and held it up before his father's face.

"Let's go."

"I need your assistance, Rottenführer."

The sentry standing at the block gate turned and peered through the darkness at Jonas Stern, who stood just inside the wire fence.

"*Jawohl*, Standartenführer." The sentry opened the gate, stepped inside, and closed it behind him.

Jonas led him toward the Jewish Women's Block. "I need to remove one of the Jews for further questioning, Rottenführer. Some of her friends may try to stop me."

"Allow me, Standartenführer!" The sentry shouldered his way in front of Stern and marched up the steps.

Stern stayed close behind him. The moment the guard passed through the barracks door, Jonas clapped his left hand around the man's forehead, jerked back his neck and dragged the double-edged dagger across his throat with his right hand. There was no cry, only a rush of air and warm blood. Stern held onto the head long enough to guide the body down to the barracks floor, then sheathed his knife and darted out of the block to stand at the gate while his father put on the sentry's clothes.

Within seconds the women stripped the dead corporal of clothes, boots, and weapons and gave all to Avram, who immediately put them on and went out to change places with his son.

Jonas opened the gate for Avram to pass out, then slipped back inside and stood just behind his father.

"Father, I beg you," he whispered. "Please come out with me. Get away from this place."

Avram reached back through the gateposts and clenched his son's arm. "No more talk of that."

"Then at least go into the E-Block. You can lead the women into Poland."

"No more, Jonas!" Avram looked back over his son's shoulder and whispered, *"Rachel."*

Jonas turned and saw the young woman standing behind him, tears glittering in her dark eyes. Hannah was in her arms.

"Open your hand, my son," Avram commanded.

Puzzled, Jonas slipped his hand between the gateposts. He felt something small and hard like seeds pressed into it.

"Those are diamonds," said Avram, finding Rachel's eyes. "Yes, I kept two for myself. But I give them now to your daughter. Give yours to Jonas as well, Rachel. He will need them to buy passage to Palestine."

Rachel had all her diamonds ready, but when she saw the shoemaker give up his stones for Hannah, she pressed only two into Jonas's hand.

After pocketing the diamonds, Jonas drew the bloody SS dagger from the sheath at his belt and held it out to Rachel. "If anyone tries to stop you in the alley," he said, "use this. Move close to them and strike quickly. Aim for the upper stomach."

Rachel took the dagger and held it beneath the bundle that was Hannah.

Avram turned his back to the fence again. "Listen to me, Jonas," he whispered. "When you get to Palestine, take this child to your mother. Tell Leah to raise her as if she were your sister. You understand?"

Jonas struggled to gain control of his voice. "Yes."

He was about to take the little girl from Rachel when he saw three SS men standing at the back gate of the camp. They were in easy sight of the open ground the women would have to cross to reach the E-Block. "Look!" he whispered.

"My God," said Avram. "What are they doing?"

Jonas couldn't make out faces or rank badges, only two men standing inside the gate smoking cigarettes and talking to the sentry who stood outside. He checked his watch. 7:35. He should be driving out of the front gate now.

"Do you think they'll go away in time?" Avram asked.

"I don't know. Father, walk with me to my car. With you in that uniform we can drive right out of here."

Rachel grabbed Jonas's arm. "You can't do that! You can't leave Hannah behind!"

"We'll take her with us."

Awakened by her mother's panic, the child whimpered softly in the darkness. Avram touched Rachel's arm. "Have no fear," he said. "Jonas, forget the men at the gate. Take this child and go. The E-Block was a long chance anyway."

Jonas stared at the three SS men, his mind whirling.

Avram held up the dead corporal's machine gun. "If they don't move, I will try to kill them."

As Avram spoke these words, Jonas spied two more SS men. They were standing in the shadow of the hospital wall, examining the polished black Mercedes that had mysteriously appeared in camp. In that moment Jonas knew he would not reach the gas cylinders in time. It would be McConnell or no one.

He slipped through the gate and hugged his father as tightly as he could, as if to cling to the moment for the rest of his life. "I will never forget you," he said in a choked voice. Then he snatched away the dead sentry's gun and threw it onto the snow. "That weapon isn't silenced," he said. "Take this."

He handed Avram his Schmeisser.

Avram made as if to speak, but his voice failed him. A brief light flickered in his eyes, something very much like second thoughts, but he pushed his son away. "Go!" he said.

"Have the child ready," Jonas told him. "If I'm alive in five minutes, I'll be back for her."

42

Jonas Stern marched across the frozen Appellplatz like Erwin Rommel inspecting the Afrika Korps. His only weapon was his Walther PPK; he'd given his silenced Schmeisser to his father and his SS dagger to Rachel Jansen. Whenever one of the SS men smoking at the back gate inhaled, an orange glow lit the upper half of his face. By this light Stern saw that two of the guards were privates, the other a sergeant major. The men still had not noticed him.

"Hauptscharführer!" he snapped, singling out the senior man. "You are not in the habit of saluting superior officers?"

Sergeant Gunther Sturm looked up in amazement at the gray-green uniform and Iron Cross First Class. An angry SD colonel was the last thing he expected to encounter at Totenhausen's back gate.

"Standartenführer!" he cried. "Heil Hitler!"

The privates quickly followed his example.

Stern raised his chin and looked down his nose at the bull-necked sergeant. "You are Hauptscharführer Sturm?"

Sturm's eyes widened. *"Jawohl,* Standartenführer."

"Don't look so frightened. I have bigger fish to fry than you. I am here to arrest Major Wolfgang Schörner for conspiring to reveal state secrets. I shall require your assistance, Hauptscharführer, and that of these men as well. Obergruppenführer Kaltenbrunner in Berlin will appreciate your help."

Sturm's stubbled face went slack, then brightened with malicious glee. "Standartenführer," he said unctuously, "I'm not one to complain about a superior, but I have had suspicions of my own about the Sturmbannführer."

"Why did you not report these suspicions?"

Sturm was momentarily at a loss. "I've been searching for proof, Standartenführer. One does not accuse a holder of the Knight's Cross lightly."

"Herr Schörner will not wear the Knight's Cross much longer, Hauptscharführer."

Sturm looked at the two privates, astonished by his good luck. "What do you want us to do, Standartenführer?"

Stern glanced at his watch: 7:37. The women would begin moving in thirteen minutes. Now he regretted giving up the silenced Schmeisser. "Here is the situation, Hauptscharführer. We believe Allied commandos intend to attack this camp tonight to assassinate Herr Doktor Brandt and destroy his laboratory. We believe Schörner arranged this attack through contacts with the Polish Resistance."

Gunther Sturm could barely contain his excitement. "The Herr Doktor was right!"

"SD reinforcements will arrive from Berlin within thirty minutes," Stern went on. "But with your help I will immediately arrest Schörner and remove him from the camp, to prevent him from assisting these commandos in any way. Are you ready?"

Sturm jerked a Luger from his belt and shook it in the air. "I know how to deal with traitors, Standartenführer. If Schörner resists, I'll blow his head off!"

Stern nodded. "Bring these men as well. Schörner is a dangerous man."

Sturm looked suddenly uncertain. "I must leave one behind, Standartenführer. The commandant could have me shot if I left this gate unguarded."

Stern glared at the private who stood on the other side of the wire. "This is your last smoke break," he said. "Don't take your eyes off of those trees. The commandos will almost certainly attack from the hills. Is that clear?"

"*Jawohl,* Standartenführer!"

The gray-faced private whipped around instantly, his eyes on the dark trees that had seemed benign only a moment ago.

"To the headquarters, Hauptscharführer!"

Stern walked a step ahead of the two SS men as they crossed the Appellplatz.

"Perhaps I should have my dogs patrol the back fence?" Sturm suggested.

"No need for that yet," said Stern. The last thing he needed was attack dogs prowling the area of the E-Block. "We will deploy the dogs only at the last moment. We want them fresh."

"Very good, Standartenführer."

They passed the rear of the cinema annex, which was contiguous to the headquarters building. As they reached the front door of the headquarters, it opened and a tall officer wearing a Waffen SS uniform and a black eyepatch stepped through it.

Wolfgang Schörner froze in midstep when he saw the SD uniform.

Stern calmly drew his Walther and aimed it at the astonished major. "Sturmbannführer Wolfgang Schörner, by order of the Führer I place you under arrest."

Major Schörner stared in amazement at Sergeant Sturm, who had drawn his Luger, then looked back at Stern. "I beg your pardon, Standartenführer?"

"You heard me. Relieve him of his pistol, Hauptscharführer."

Schörner made no move to resist as Sturm yanked his Luger from its holster. "Who is this man, Hauptscharführer?"

Stern held up his hand. "I am Standartenführer Ritter Stern from the *Sicherheitsdienst* in Berlin, as you can plainly see."

"I received no communication about your arrival."

"Of course you didn't. All will become clear in Berlin."

"Berlin?" Schörner's eyes moved up and down Stern's uniform, taking in each button, patch, badge, crease, and stain. "Hauptscharführer," he said, "the Standartenführer seems to be missing his dagger. Don't you find that interesting?"

Stern waved his pistol toward the hospital, where the Mercedes waited. "To my car, Hauptscharführer," he said tersely.

But Gunther Sturm was looking at Schörner. Sturm knew the face of guilt, and as much as he hated the major, Schörner was not acting guilty of anything.

"I am perfectly willing to go to Berlin," Schörner said equably. "But shouldn't we at least ask to see this man's papers first? An SD officer who loses his dagger is subject to arrest himself."

Sturm looked uncertainly at Stern. "Standartenführer?"

Stern glanced impatiently at his watch, an officer in a hurry. "You will regret this," he said. He brought out his wallet and handed it to Sturm, who passed it straight to Schörner.

"These papers give you authority to inspect security arrangements at Totenhausen." Schörner looked up. "Not to place me under arrest."

"By statute, the SD has complete powers of examination and arrest over the SS," Stern said. "I do not need a written order to arrest a traitor." He lowered his voice to a menacing pitch. "Now, move to my car."

"These orders are dated four days ago," Schörner observed, not moving an inch. "Did it take you four days to drive up from Berlin?"

Before Stern could respond, Schörner said, "The suntan interests me as well. Has the sun begun shining in the Tiergarten in the dead of winter?"

Stern raised his pistol to Schörner's face.

The major showed no sign of fear.

Stern wanted to pull the trigger, but he knew it would be the worst possible mistake he could make.

"Where *is* your dagger, Standartenführer?" Schörner asked.

Stern forced himself not to look down at the empty sheath on his belt. This showed considerable nerve, considering that his mind had gone blank.

A bemused look crossed Schörner's face. "With all respect, Standartenführer, on what day did you receive your dagger?"

It was funny in a way, thought Stern. He was replaying the scene in the Jewish Women's Block, when he had been questioned to prove he was a Jew. Only Major Schörner had not asked him what year it was on the Hebrew calendar. "I have not come here to answer your questions," he snapped. "You will answer mine."

Schörner glanced at Sturm. "What do you think, Hauptscharführer? A simple enough question, don't you think? Even you could answer that one."

Gunther Sturm wore the expression of an attack dog being given commands by two masters. He hated Schörner viciously, but those very qualities he hated most made the idea of Schörner betraying Germany an impossibility. With agonizing slowness he turned until his Luger was aimed just to the right of Stern's belly.

"If the Standartenführer could answer the question?" he said in an apologetic tone. "When did you receive your dagger?"

Stern had always known this moment would come someday. A moment without options. A truly impossible situation. He had simply overestimated his abilities, while underestimating those of a combat veteran named Wolfgang Schörner. He thought of the cyanide capsule he had earlier transferred from his Star of David medallion into his pocket, but he felt no inclination to try to swallow it. No matter what the bastards did to him, they would not break him before the gas descended on the camp.

"I don't recall the exact day," he said. "It was 1940."

"That's interesting," said Schörner, "since all ceremonial daggers are awarded only on November ninth."

Stern looked at his watch. 7:40. His only thought was to give the women time to get the children to the E-Block. And he knew he could do that. "There is only one solution," he said. "Call Obergruppenführer Kaltenbrunner at SD headquarters in Berlin." Stern reversed the Walther in his hand and handed it butt first to Sergeant Sturm.

Bewildered, the SS man accepted the weapon.

A faint smile touched Schörner's mouth. "Where did you meet this man, Hauptscharführer?" he asked.

"At the back gate, Sturmbannführer."

"You have someone guarding the gate now?"

"*Ja.*"

"How many technicians are in the factory?"

"The full shift. Thirty-four men. They're taking the place apart."

Schörner nodded while he thought. "I want every one of the technicians moved into the cinema immediately and placed under guard. Then bolt every door on the factory. Clear?"

"*Zu befehl,* Sturmbannführer."

"One call to Berlin will tell me if the major here is fish or fowl. I want those technicians locked in the cinema by the time I'm off the phone. The civilian nurses as well. Every one of them. Get moving."

Sergeant Sturm hurried into the headquarters building. Schörner turned back to Stern. "This has been most entertaining. If you are who you say you are, I will soon be without a dagger myself. If not, well. . . ." Schörner looked over Stern's shoulder. "You'd better come with us, Schütze."

With the barrel of a private's rifle between his shoulder blades,

Stern followed Schörner into the headquarters building. He stole one last glance at his watch as he passed through the door.

7:41.

"I've heard no explosion yet."

"He's still got nine minutes," said McConnell from the kitchen table. He turned to the stove, where Anna stood warming herself. "Would we definitely hear a grenade on the hill?"

"Yes. I think we should go now. Something feels wrong to me."

"That's just nerves. It's not time yet."

McConnell was feeling butterflies himself, as if he were waiting to run the biggest race of his life. He had just gulped a large glass of water to make up for the fluid loss from a half hour inside his anti-gas suit. His air cylinder stood on the floor, the corrugated hose wrapped around it.

Anna turned from the stove. "I think they've caught him," she said.

McConnell angrily slapped the table. "Then why haven't we heard shooting? An alarm? Something? You think he would let them take him without a fight?"

"He might. His father is there, remember."

McConnell took a deep breath and tried to stay calm. Arranged in front of him were his toggle rope, his clear vinyl head mask, the Mauser rifle he'd traded from Stan Wojik, and the bright swatch of tartan that Sir Donald Cameron had given him on the bridge at Achnacarry. The note from Churchill was folded in Anna's diary, which he'd hidden in the leg of his oilskin suit. Stern's gas suit was folded in the backseat of Greta's Volkswagen.

But where was Stern?

Anna touched his arm. "He's relying on us to send down the gas," she said. "I think we should wait on the hill."

"I'm doing what he told me," McConnell said doggedly. He took another long drink of water. "Eight more minutes. We'll make it to the hill in time."

She reached out and took his hand. "All right. Whatever happens, I'm glad for last night. It will make everything easier."

McConnell started to ask what she meant, but he didn't. He had a feeling he knew.

*　*　*

When Avram Stern saw his son walking back across the Appellplatz ahead of Sergeant Sturm and an SS private, he almost panicked. Instead, he tried to think like his son. Jonas had come this far without getting caught; he must know what he was doing.

The three men walked around the cinema and disappeared. Could Jonas be trying to reach the main gate? It was fifty meters away, and difficult to see clearly in the darkness, but Avram would know if a man passed through it.

No one did.

Two minutes after Jonas disappeared, Avram saw Sergeant Sturm burst from the rear door of the headquarters and sprint toward the factory with five SS men behind him. Had Jonas made a break for freedom? Had he concocted some diversion to draw the SS away from the E-Block? Avram felt a flash of fear as white-coated lab technicians began streaming out of the factory gate with Sergeant Sturm's men prodding them along.

The soft crunch of footsteps on the snow behind him told him Rachel and the other chosen women were slipping into the Jewish Children's Block in preparation for the move to the E-Block. He looked down at his wristwatch—an illegal item he had accepted as payment for a repair job on a pair of SS knee boots—the wristwatch of a dead Jew.

7:41.

Jonas had planned to short out the electricity prior to the attack. That would not happen now. Without the cover of absolute darkness, the women and children would have to cross open ground in plain view of the sentry standing at the back gate.

They would never make it.

With quivering hands the shoemaker unslung the silenced Schmeisser and started for the back gate.

"Berlin never heard of you."

Major Schörner put down the telephone and smiled.

Stern stared impassively into the black barrel of his own Walther.

"I talked to Kaltenbrunner himself," Schörner said. "He wants me to send you to Berlin for questioning. But—I have a few questions of my own for you first."

A door banged open behind Stern. He did not turn, but the clatter of boots told him at least three men had entered the office.

"Sturmbannführer, the technicians are locked in the cinema!" said Sergeant Sturm. "The factory is sealed!"

"And the nurses?" Schörner asked.

"The three who were on duty are in the cinema with the technicians. Greta Müller is dead, of course. I sent a rider for Frau Jaspers."

"That's five. And the sixth?"

"Fraulein Kaas, Sturmbannführer. It seems she left the hospital early today."

Schörner sighed impatiently. "*And?*"

"I just found out she was driving Greta Müller's car! In the confusion after finding the bodies in the sewer—"

"In the confusion no one noticed," Schörner finished. "In fact I did notice that. But because Fraulein Kaas is the sister of a Gauleiter's wife, I did not consider her a likely candidate for treason. How foolish of me. Now that I think of it, she was quite a friend of the Müller girl."

Stern stole a glance at his watch: 7:43. He prayed McConnell would leave the cottage on schedule.

Schörner tapped his right hand on his desk. "Do you know what I think, Hauptscharführer? I think our ersatz Standartenführer looks much too clean to have been hiding in the forest for the past few days. He looks like he's been enjoying local hospitality. Eating well, by the look of him. Where does Fraulein Kaas live, Sturm?"

"A old farmer's cottage on the southern edge of Dornow."

Schörner nodded. "I know that cottage." He stood up suddenly and pocketed Stern's Walther. "I'm going to take a detachment of men and search it."

"But Herr Doktor Brandt ordered the camp sealed."

Schörner's jaw tightened. "I am in charge of security here, not Brandt. This man is no longer a threat. His comrades are. The Allies might well be planning to kidnap Brandt. I want you to place the Herr Doktor under guard."

Schörner took an extra clip of ammunition from his desk drawer and retrieved his Luger from Sergeant Sturm. "If there's any trouble while I'm gone, Hauptscharführer, do whatever you must to prevent the Herr Doktor from falling into enemy hands." He looked up pointedly. "Do you understand?"

Sturm cleared his throat. "Does the Sturmbannführer mean that I should kill him?"

"Precisely."

Sturm nodded soberly. Schörner's sudden transformation from altar boy to ruthless commander had stunned him. "What about this one?" he asked, pointing at Stern.

"I need to know everything he knows. Who sent him, how many men in his unit, what their plans are, everything. I believe you're up to the task, Hauptscharführer?"

Gunther Sturm knew he was up to the task, but after killing the Polish giant by mistake, he was a little hesitant to take on another important interrogation. "Exactly how far may I go, Sturmbann-führer?"

Schörner pulled on a greatcoat and marched to the door of the office. "Don't kill him. Is that clear enough?"

Sturm saluted. "*Zu befehl,* Sturmbannführer! Good hunting."

Schörner went out.

Sturm lifted the phone and said, "Karl? Tell Glaub and Becker to guard the Herr Doktor until they hear otherwise from me."

He hung up and motioned to two SS privates standing at the back of the office. "Hold him in the chair," he said.

Stern tensed as four hands took him by the upper arms and squeezed tight enough to close off his circulation.

Sergeant Sturm quickly searched the SD uniform, laughing at the cyanide capsule and pocketing the keys to Sabine's Mercedes. Then he smiled and drew his SS dagger from the black sheath at his belt. It was identical to the one Stern had used to slash the throat of the sentry, the one he had in his ignorance given to Rachel Jansen. Sergeant Sturm casually cut the buttons off of the SD tunic, then sliced the undershirt beneath it down the middle.

"*Ach!*" he cried, staring at Stern's naked torso. "Look at this!"

The two SS privates leaned down and gaped at the livid scars that covered Stern's chest and abdomen. It was Sturm who first no-ticed that the scars extended down into the trousers.

"Stand him up," he said.

When Stern was on his feet, Sturm cut his belt in half and jerked the SD trousers down to his knees.

"He's missing his last inch!" Sturm crowed. "I'll be damned! He's a Jew! A stinking Jew in an SD uniform!"

Stern stopped breathing when the sergeant lifted his scrotum with the cold dagger blade.

"Look at him," Sturm said, laughing. "Shrinking like a wilted radish! How long do you think it will take me to make this one sing, Felix?"

One of the privates looked appraisingly at Stern's scarred chest. "Twenty marks says he holds out for two hours."

"That's a good bet," Jonas said in a soft voice. He looked straight into Gunther Sturm's eyes. "I hope you're a patient man."

If the two privates had not been holding him up, Sturm's fist would have doubled him over on the floor. As it was, he could not draw breath for nearly ten seconds.

"Put him back in the chair," Sturm said. "In an hour he'll be begging us to kill him."

43

Ariel Weitz stood motionless at the window of Klaus Brandt's office door. Brandt's back was to the door. He was reading some medical charts, but Weitz knew he was actually waiting for a telephone call. An hour earlier, the commandant had placed a long-distance call to Reichsführer Himmler in Berlin. Even the mighty waited like servants on the whim of the former chicken farmer who ruled the SS.

Weitz's hands tingled as he stared at Brandt's white-jacketed back. Every gray hair sprouting from the thick Prussian neck made him want to scream with hatred and disgust. He saw the shining dome of Brandt's balding head as a perfect spot in which to drive a dozen roofing nails. A hundred times he had thought of slamming the famous hands in the steel door of the isolation ward. A thousand times of injecting the meningococcus bacillus into his spine, as Brandt had done so many times to "his children." But tonight. . . .

Tonight would pay for all.

At the sound of boots in the main corridor, Weitz moved away from the door. Two SS men hurried past him and took up station on either side of Brandt's door.

A complication.

Weitz walked up the hall to a small examining room off the main corridor. Here he had cached the remainder of his weapons, and also his prize. Hanging in a narrow closet was one of the Raubhammer gas suits tested in the afternoon, now thoroughly decontaminated. Weighing less than half of what previous models did, it utilized a filter canister and a breathing bag which contained a small cylinder of pure oxygen. One of the other Raubhammer suits was hanging in Brandt's office, but Weitz didn't care about that. He would only need the one.

He wondered what the two SS guards would think when they saw Brandt's pet Jew rounding the corner with a submachine gun in his hand. Whatever it was would be the last thoughts they ever had. But why had they so suddenly appeared? Had Schörner finally comprehended the danger facing the camp? A minute ago Weitz had noticed Sergeant Sturm rushing a long line of factory technicians across the Appellplatz toward the cinema, but he saw no real problem in that. No matter what Schörner might have learned, he was way behind the game at this point. Too far behind to catch up.

Weitz was reaching for the Raubhammer suit when he heard the roar of a troop truck.

Avram Stern had taken three steps toward Totenhausen's back gate when shouted orders and the rumble of motors stopped him in his tracks. He turned to see Major Schörner's gray field car speeding out of Totenhausen's front gate, followed closely by an open truck full of SS troops, all armed to the teeth.

Avram felt his last hope wither away.

He closed his hand around the Schmeisser and started back toward the sentry, only to be stopped again by the sound of a slamming door. Ariel Weitz was standing on the front steps of the hospital, staring after the disappearing vehicles with a puzzled look on his face. Weitz cocked his head back, almost as if he sensed a human gaze upon him. When he finally looked toward the inmate blocks, the shoemaker made the fastest and riskiest decision of his life. He would never know why he did it. If someone had asked him at the time, he might have said something about the tears he had seen on Weitz's face on the night of the big selection. He had thought about Weitz many times since that night. How the hated informer had free run of the camp. How he was so trusted by the SS that they occasionally let him go into Dornow alone to run errands for them. And how to mount an operation like the one Jonas was involved in, the British would need a good source of information inside Totenhausen. And the conclusion Avram had come to was that no Jew could be so thoroughly corrupted by the Nazis as Ariel Weitz seemed to be. And so, when Weitz looked from the hospital steps toward the blocks, Avram motioned for him to come over to the block gate.

*   *   *

Weitz hesitated when he saw the sentry beckoning from the inmate blocks. He did not want to cross the Appellplatz. But the man signaling to him was SS; even so close to his moment of triumph, he could not very well refuse. He hurried across the snow and stopped before the sentry, looking up with his usual obsequious mask.

"*You!*" he blurted. "What are you doing in that uniform?"

Avram reached out and closed his left hand around the back of Weitz's neck. With his right he drew the SS dagger from his belt and held its point under Weitz's chin. "If you cry out," he whispered, "I'll cut your throat like a piece of scrap leather."

Weitz shook his head violently. "No! You don't understand!" He stared at the SS uniform. "I don't understand either."

Avram pricked the knifepoint into Weitz's skin. "Tell me one thing. Are you involved in what is about to happen?"

The little man's eyes grew wide. "I know what is going to happen. But I have my own plans."

"I knew it! You little bootlicker! You've been pretending all the time. Listen to me. My son has been taken by the SS. Unless he is freed, the attack will not take place."

"Your son . . . ? Your *son* is the Jewish Standartenführer?"

"Yes."

"My God. Where is he now? In the cinema with the workers?"

"I don't know. They're probably interrogating him somewhere." Avram shook Weitz's neck. "You must free him! You know everything about this camp."

Weitz looked furious at this interruption of his plans, but he nodded. "I'll see what I can do. What are you going to do? Stand here and wait to die?"

Avram let go. "You just free my son."

The moment Weitz turned back toward the hospital, Rachel Jansen stepped out of the shadows behind Avram. "Why were you talking to him?" she whispered. "He works for the SS."

"Never mind. Are all the women in the children's block?"

"Yes." She held up the bundle in her arms. "And here is Hannah. Where is your son?"

Avram shook his head. "Taken. You'll have to carry Hannah to the E-Block with you."

Rachel moaned softly. Avram heard a tiny frightened voice in the bundled blanket. Rachel comforted the child in Dutch, then switched back to German. "What are we to do, Shoemaker? I cannot move the children with that sentry at the back gate. He will surely see us and raise the alarm."

"Go back inside."

"But the gas is coming!"

"Be ready to move quickly. I'll be back here in one minute to get you. If I'm not, you're on your own. Do what you think is best."

Rachel grabbed his arm through the gateposts. "If you see your son anywhere, tell him to come and get Hannah. I *beg* you, Herr Stern!"

"I'll tell him."

Avram jerked back the bolt on the Schmeisser and started toward the back gate.

Jonas Stern tried to keep himself conscious as Sergeant Sturm worked on him. The man showed an aptitude for his job. He had enthusiasm, which was important. Physical torture was tiring work. The blows to the side of the head were the worst. Stern's ears were ringing so loudly he could hardly think. He wanted to let go, to give in to unconsciousness. But he forced himself to keep awake. Because he had one advantage over his tormentor. He knew exactly what was about to happen to Totenhausen Camp. And perhaps—just perhaps—when the plastic explosive he had molded around the heads of the buried cylinders detonated, he would still be physically able to make a run for the main gate. But to do that he would have to be conscious. Not an easy thing when someone was trying to pound your brain into jelly. When Sergeant Sturm switched to the knife, he was almost grateful.

Avram Stern had not killed a human being since 1918, but he did not pause to debate the issue with himself. As he moved across the snow toward the sentry, he wondered how loud the report of the silenced Schmeisser would be. As a veteran of World War One, he found it difficult to believe anything could completely silence the report of a machine gun.

He decided to use the dagger.

He tried to walk confidently, arrogantly, swaggering the way the SS guards did. He concentrated on the sentry's back. The man was standing just inside the gate, facing the trees. Avram thought of calling out softly so as not to startle him, but the man seemed oblivious. Avram looked down at the silver dagger in his hand. It would take a powerful stroke to penetrate a greatcoat and winter tunic. Jonas had made a great point of cutting the other sentry's throat, but Avram had no training in such things. He fleetingly wished for a bayonet like the one he had carried in the Great War, or better yet a trusty sharpened spade, the weapon of choice for trench combat.

But this was a different war.

"*Kamerad?*" he called in a surprisingly natural voice. "Do you have a match?"

The sentry was startled, but when he saw the brown uniform he relaxed and reached into his greatcoat. "I could use a smoke myself," he said with a nervous laugh. "That SD bastard scared the life out of me."

As the match flared, the young sentry's eyes played over Avram's face. There was an instant of shared recognition. Avram Stern saw a boy for whom he had crafted a pair of soft slippers as a gift for a girlfriend; the sentry saw the middle-aged face of the shoemaker.

Avram's arm seemed alive with rage as he drove the dagger straight up into the soft skin beneath the sentry's chin. He felt a sudden shock in his wrist. The dagger point had driven cleanly through palate, sinuses, and brain and hit the roof of the sentry's skull, stopping his thrust with the dagger's hilt still three centimeters below the jaw. Looking straight into the wide blue eyes, Avram yanked the haft of the dagger once to the left, then let the body fall onto the snow.

He tried to dislodge the blade from the sentry's head, but it was beyond his power. He sat the boy up against the fence, as if he had fallen asleep on guard duty. The haft of the dagger kept the head in a semi-upright position. Avram wiped his bloody hands on the sentry's coat and started back toward the inmate blocks.

His watch read 7:48.

He almost fired his Schmeisser in panic when a group of silent shadows brushed past him in the darkness. Then he realized what was happening.

Rachel Jansen had started the migration to the E-Block.

44

The Cameron tartan flew like a bright flag from the strap of McConnell's air tank harness as he carried it through the cottage door, Anna close on his heels.

"Wait!" he said. "It's Stern!"

A half mile away a pair of headlights was moving across the flat stretch of road that led from the hills to Dornow. A second pair appeared out of the darkness at the foot of the hills, following the first.

"Are they chasing him?" McConnell asked anxiously.

"It's not Stern," Anna said in a flat voice. "It's ten till eight now. If he was free, he'd be on the pylon. Look at the difference in those lights. That's a field car out front with a troop truck behind. My God. They're coming. Schörner must have caught Stern and broken him."

She jerked the air cylinder off of McConnell's shoulder and pulled him towards Greta's Volkswagen. There, she dropped the cylinder in the rear seat and took four grenades from Stern's leather bag.

"Get into the car!" she cried. "Get down on the floor! Hurry!"

"What the hell are you going to do?" McConnell asked.

"There's only one road to the power station, and they're on it. We can't drive past them. I'm going to have to stand in the cottage door so that when they get here they'll come straight for me. When they do, you—"

He grabbed her arms and shook her. "I'm not leaving you here to be killed!"

"Then we'll both die for nothing."

He could feel the rumble of the approaching vehicles. "There's got to be another way!"

Anna glanced back at the oncoming headlights. "All right," she said. She dropped the grenades back into the front seat. "Follow me!"

She raced into the cottage and switched on every light, then pulled open the cellar door and shouted, "Keep quiet, Sabine! There's going to be shooting! You could be killed by mistake!"

While McConnell stared in bewilderment, she slammed the cellar door and pulled open a kitchen drawer, from which she took a revolver he had never seen.

"Stan Wojik gave it to me," she said, pulling him into the bedroom.

A small door led onto the empty field behind the cottage. Anna went first, racing around the side of the building and dropping to her knees at the corner. McConnell followed more slowly under the weight of his suit and the Mauser rifle. As he reached the corner, she made a dash for the Volkswagen. He went after her, and was surprised to see her go for the driver's seat.

Before she could open the door, he pushed her aside, smashed the window with his rifle butt and shattered the interior light. Then he opened the door and shoved her all the way across the front seat.

"Get down!" he said. "All the way on the floor!"

Anna obeyed. McConnell stretched flat on his back on the seat, his head just beneath the passenger window, inches from her face, his feet angled down beneath the steering wheel. He held the rifle tight along his body, right forefinger on the trigger.

"Why the lights?" he asked.

"They'll assume anyone breaking blackout regulations so flagrantly must be inside. But if they do check the cars first . . ." She held up her revolver.

The squeal of automobile brakes mingled with the groan of a heavy truck gearing down. McConnell tensed and tried to decipher the sounds. The truck stopped between the car and the cottage, but kept its engine idling. Four doors opened and closed. Heavy boots crunched on the snow. McConnell raised his head to peek out, but his and Anna's breath had already fogged the window glass. He heard a loud rapping on the cottage door.

"Fräulein Kaas!" shouted a male voice. "Fräulein Kaas, open the door!"

"*Schörner,*" Anna hissed.

The sound of the submachine gun hit McConnell like an electric shock. Schörner had shot the lock off the door.

A muffled female voice shouted: "Help me! In the name of the Führer help me!"

"Christ, Sabine got loose!" McConnell heard boots clattering on the floorboards of the cottage.

Anna gripped his arm. "What can you see?" she asked.

He sat up slowly and rubbed a small clear circle in the fogged window on the driver's side. "A half dozen soldiers by the cottage door. Maybe a dozen more in the troop truck."

"Get ready. When you hear me shout, start the car."

McConnell had barely got his feet on the pedals when he saw Anna pull the pins out of two grenades. She opened the Volkswagen's door and stepped out as casually as if she were getting out at a restaurant, then turned toward the troop truck and tossed the grenades. She was firing her pistol into the knot of soldiers by the door even before the grenades exploded.

"*For God's sake move!*" she screamed, with only one foot in the car.

The Volkswagen's engine roared to life. McConnell floored the accelerator, but the tires spun in vain on the ice.

Two grenades detonated a split second apart in blinding white flashes. Anna kept shooting. McConnell saw an SS man charge through the cottage door, then fly backward like a dog jerked on a leash. Anna dove back into the car and pulled the door shut, and he eased up on the gas and the tires caught.

The Volkswagen fishtailed onto the road. He thanked God for the winters he had spent in England; most Georgia natives couldn't drive a car half a mile on ice like this. Anna reloaded her pistol and aimed it back over the seat toward the cottage as they sped away.

"They're not following," she cried. "What are they doing?"

"Questioning your sister!" McConnell kept his eyes focused on the road. "Put on Stern's gas suit. *Put it on!*"

Wolfgang Schörner picked himself up off the cottage floor and walked calmly to the door. He watched the taillights of the Volkswagen racing back up the hill road. The SS corporal who had been driving the troop truck stumbled up to him, his face white with horror.

"Five men dead, Sturmbannführer! Eight wounded! What do we do?"

"First you calm down." Schörner took a deep, satisfied breath. "The war has finally come to Totenhausen, Rottenführer. People die in wars."

"Do we go after them?"

"Not yet. The fools are running straight toward the camp." He turned and looked back into the kitchen. Sabine Hoffman was being helped off of the floor by an SS private. "I apologize for the inter-ruption, Madam. As I was saying, I met you several months ago in Berlin. Your husband is Gauleiter Hoffman?"

"Yes, Sturmbannführer!"

"Can you tell me who left in that car?"

"My sister! She's gone mad! There were two men with her most of the day. One American, the other a Jew. He was dressed as an SD officer!"

"We have that man in custody," Schörner said in a reassuring voice. "Do you know what your sister and this American planned to do tonight?"

"I heard the Jew saying something about an electrical station."

Schörner felt a prick of anxiety. "Anything else?"

"Anna was asking the American something about poison gas. He seemed to know quite a lot about it."

The color drained from Schörner's face. "Is there a telephone here?"

Sabine shook her head.

"Rottenführer, I want four men in my car! The rest follow in the truck."

"What about the wounded, Sturmbannführer? Some of them can't walk."

"Leave them in the road!"

Twenty-two miles north of Totenhausen, the navigator in the lead bomber of GENERAL SHERMAN sighted the mouth of the Recknitz River below him.

"That's it, sir. Time to turn."

Squadron Leader Harry Sumner banked the Mosquito to the south. "Everyone with us, Jacobs?"

"Right on our tail."

Sumner checked his fuel gauge. A headwind had put them slightly behind schedule, but they would benefit by the same wind on the ride home. They had lost one plane already, forced to turn back due to mechanical failure. That was the way of it. But they still had more than enough bombload and Target Indicators to carry out the mission.

"Think you can find this place, Jacobs? It's supposed to be almost covered with trees."

The navigator was holding a pen-sized torch in his teeth and studying a map. "Just stay over the river," he said in a garbled voice. "The H_2S will show me the bends. If this map is accurate, we can use Dornow village and the river as brackets. Flares will give us a visual on the power station and the camp."

Sumner peered through the dark windscreen. The silver line of the river led them southward like a magic road. A rum mission, this, even by Special Duties Squadron standards. All the way into Germany to bomb a tiny prison camp for SOE? The Air Marshals constantly fought Duff Smith tooth and nail to keep their precious planes out of his clutches. How had he managed to divert a Mosquito squadron for this? Sumner had mentioned it to his superior at Wick, but all he'd got in reply was a sour look and a mumbled, "If we want to fight this one, we'll have to go all the way to Downing Street."

He hadn't known what to make of that. But he did know one thing. From one thousand feet without ack-ack, his squadron could hit an outdoor privy dead center and leave nothing but a crater for a square mile around.

"Eight minutes out," the navigator said.

"They're still not following!" McConnell said, keeping his eyes on the rearview mirror and pushing the Volkswagen as fast as he dared.

"They will." Anna thrust her arms into the sleeves of the oilskin jumpsuit and started to zip up its front.

He caught her hand. "You have to put on the mask first, then zip the suit over the part that drapes over your shoulders. It's the only way to get an airtight seal."

Anna reached back for both masks.

"Put yours on now," he said. "I'll be able to hear you if you need to talk."

The road climbed sharply. McConnell reduced speed. Just ahead he saw the first curve of the switchback road that wound across the hills. As he took the turn, he caught sight of lights in the distance behind them.

"There they are," he said. "You know anything about compressed air bottles?"

"I've administered oxygen a hundred times."

"Same principle. Open the valve, attach the air hose to your mask and breathe normally." He wrenched the wheel to avoid colliding with a bank of birch trees. "Jesus! This is like a logging road!"

Anna had her mask on now. It blurred her facial features and dulled her eyes. She looked like an extra in a Flash Gordon feature. "The boots are too big," she said, her voice buzzing through the speech transmission diaphragm near her mouthpiece.

"Put them on anyway. And zip the legs down around them." He braked for another curve. "How far to the power station?"

"Not far."

"I'll drive the car into the trees. Schörner and his men should drive right past us."

Anna nodded and pointed to the left. "Slow down."

He let the VW drift past the transformer station. He saw a wooden watchman's hut inside the dark jungle of metal struts, a faint light glowing in its window. Thirty meters past the station, he turned off the road and rolled forward until tree trunks forced him to stop.

He pulled on his mask and zipped his suit, then climbed out. The silence was eerie after the frantic skirmish at the cottage. Anna helped him strap on his air tank. He felt like a draft horse wearing blinders. Before he attached his air hose, he leaned forward and said, "I guess we'd better take the guns with us."

She shook her head and handed him the Mauser rifle.

"What are you doing?"

"I'm staying here," she said. "Schörner may stop at the power station. He might even turn in here. We can't take the chance."

"But you couldn't stop them if they did."

"I've got Stern's grenades," she said. "And my pistol. You keep your rifle as a last resort."

"Anna—"

"Go!"

He started to say something else, but she slung the Mauser over his shoulder and pushed him farther into the trees. He turned back and looked at her. She was standing motionless in the dark beside the car, a fine-figured woman wrapped in heavy black oilskin and wearing a clear vinyl bag over her head. Ludicrous. Tragic. He thought of the diary she had labored over so long, that was now wedged into the left leg of his gas suit. He hoped she would be alive to make a final entry when this night was over.

He raised his hand, then turned and trudged across the snow toward the pylon.

Major Schörner raced up the hills at nearly twice the speed McConnell had. The excitable corporal occupied the field car's passenger seat, while three more SS men were scrunched into the back, each armed with a submachine gun. Somehow the troop truck was managing to keep up, probably because its driver was as angry and bent on revenge as the storm troopers in back. Schörner issued a quick volley of orders to the corporal.

"We'll split at the transformer station. You take two men and go back to Totenhausen in the car. Tell Sturm to expect a commando attack. The electricity may go off at any time. That means the electric fences will be off. Thank God I ordered those mines laid. Tell Sturm to put half his men around the gas storage tanks and the other half around the factory. Tell him" —the field car nearly skated off the road as Schörner took a dogleg curve, but he held it under control— "tell him I'll be there as soon as I can. I'll use the men from the truck to surround the power station. The American must be trying to detonate explosives laid earlier in the week. The detonator will probably be somewhere in the trees outside the station. *Ach*, what I would give for Sturm's dogs."

The corporal's face lit up. "But we have a dog, Sturmbannführer! In the cab of the truck!"

"At last, a little luck." Schörner slung the car around another curve and jammed the gas pedal to the floor. The strange thing, he thought, gripping the wheel like a Grand Prix champion, was that as bad as the situation was, he felt better than he had in months.

McConnell stumbled the last few meters to the pylon, his throat stinging from the dry air in the cylinder on his back. The climbing spikes and harness lay at the foot of the nearest support pole, as Stern had promised. He'd never worn anything like them before, but the principle was simple enough: one sharp iron spike for the instep of each foot, affixed to fishhook-shaped pieces of iron that fit beneath the feet and rose along the inner calves, with leather straps to hold them on. The safety harness was basically a broad, heavy belt with a steel ring in front, which clipped to a second belt sized to fit around the pole. McConnell dropped his rifle, sat down and strapped on the spikes.

That done, he slung the Mauser over his shoulder, fastened his safety belt around the support pole and drove his right spike into the wood. He expected it to break loose when he put his weight on it, but the spike held. He bear-hugged the pole and raised himself on the spike, then he slid the belt up, leaned back to steady himself, and drove his left spike into the pole two feet up. In this manner he began to ascend the pole at a surprising speed, although he seemed to be circling it as he went up, like a snake climbing a tree.

He couldn't see much in the darkness, but he knew from Stern's quick briefing that the double pylons marched down a narrow swath that had been cleared through the forested hills, their crossarms taller than all but the largest trees. A straight run of two thousand feet descending at a thirty degree angle—or so Stern had told him.

He cried out as his right spike broke free. He slid four feet down the icy pole before managing to hug it tightly enough to stop. The safety belt had done almost nothing to retard his fall. He prayed that no splinters had torn holes in his gas suit.

Three quarters of the way to the top, he saw the lights of the pursuing vehicles racing up the winding hill road. They seemed to flicker on and off as he stared down through the trees. He dug his spikes into the wood and forced himself higher, thinking of Anna waiting in the trees below. He had almost reached the crossarm when he heard an engine roar to life.

At first he thought the watchman from the power station had started a vehicle. But the sound had come from almost directly beneath the pylon. When he realized what was actually happening, he almost started back down the pole.

But of course he would be too late. Anna had planned it that way. There was nothing he could do.

She had decided to die for the mission.

45

Ariel Weitz stepped out of the front door of the hospital and hurried down the steps wearing Herr Doktor Brandt's SS greatcoat, which he had pilfered from a closet. Brandt's bulky coat was the only garment that minimized the odd hump at the small of Weitz's back caused by the breathing bag of the Raub-hammer gas suit. In his left hand he carried the accompanying gas mask, in his right a machine pistol.

He moved across the Appellplatz at a fast walk, his eyes on the headquarters building. Personally, he didn't care much what happened to the shoemaker's son. But the shoemaker had said that without him the gas attack would not take place. And having met the young commando, Weitz believed this might be true. He brought out a key to the back door of the headquarters, unlocked it, and walked inside.

He heard muffled screaming from the front of the building. Mentally he ran through the possibilities. Quartermaster's office. Wireless officer's room. Brandt's administrative office. Schörner's office. Down the corridor to his right—from the direction of the cinema—he heard a low buzz of voices. The factory technicians and their guards. He pulled the greatcoat close around him and moved quickly up the hallway.

He saw the brown-jacketed back of the wireless operator at his console. The quartermaster's office was empty. He kept moving. Brandt's administrative office. Empty. The screams grew louder now. He heard the sound of a blow. Men laughing. He heard Gunther Sturm's voice braying something about losing a bet.

He laid the Raubhammer gas mask on the floor and held the machine pistol in both hands.

*　*　*

Jonas Stern strained against the ropes that held him to the chair, his eyes bulging from pain. His face and torso were covered with blood. Sergeant Sturm had opened several long, shallow cuts on his chest. One of Sturm's assistants had brought salt from the mess and the sergeant had rubbed it into the wounds. He had also broken one of the fingers on Stern's left hand, not by bending it backward, but by snapping it at a right angle like a dry twig. For a man of Sturm's strength, the effort expended was minimal compared to the expected return.

Yet he'd gotten no return. The Jew masquerading as an SD officer had done nothing but scream, and he'd done damn little of that, considering. Sturm was beginning to worry that he might indeed lose his twenty marks.

For Stern's part, the searing fire of the dagger blade and the caustic burning of the salt had finally merged into a general agony. His head and neck throbbed mightily from the blows, and his left eye was swollen almost shut.

But he was conscious.

It would all be over soon. They had taken away his watch, but he'd stolen a glance at the sergeant's only a moment ago. It read 7:59. He hoped he would survive the gas long enough to see Sturm shitting his pants as he danced across the floor like a spastic and choked on his own vomit. He thought he could hold his breath long enough to see that.

"What are you thinking, you smug bastard?" Sturm bellowed. "I'll tell you what *I'm* thinking." He glanced at his two comrades, who leaned against the wall smoking cigarettes. "I'm thinking it's time to boil some water. It's not a pretty sight, seeing a man scalded. A little splash from the soup pot is enough to make a man yell. I wonder how you'll sound when we dump a steaming kettlefull down the front of your pants?"

One of the SS men dropped his cigarette and stubbed it out with his boot. "I'll get it from the mess."

Stern craned his neck to see if the private was really going to get the water.

What he saw was the brown back of the man's tunic explode into scarlet and he was lifted off his feet to the accompaniment of gunfire. A smallish man wearing an SS greatcoat walked through the doorway. A second later Stern recognized the man from Anna's cottage. It was Brigadier Smith's agent: Scarlett.

Things seemed to happen very slowly after that. The other SS private fumbled for his gun. Sergeant Sturm shouted, *"Put down that gun, Weitz! Have you gone mad?"* But the little man just kept walking forward until the barrel of his machine pistol touched the private's belly and he pulled the trigger. The muffled burst eviscerated the private and chewed a hole in the wall behind him.

Sergeant Sturm reached for the latch on Schörner's office window, but Weitz fired a burst into the wall beside him. Sturm looked up, his face white with panic and confusion.

"Weitz!" he screamed. "What madness is this?"

The little man began to laugh. Switching the gun from hand to hand, he slipped off the greatcoat and let it fall to the floor. Stern saw then that he was wearing a rubber suit very much like the ones McConnell had brought from Oxford.

"What the hell is that?" Sturm asked. "Why are you wearing that?"

A brief flash lit the window, followed instantly by a muffled explosion that rattled the window in its frame.

"What?" Sturm grunted.

A second explosion followed the first.

Now Weitz looked puzzled as well.

"That's the gas!" Stern shouted from the chair. "British Sarin! I buried two cylinders by the dog kennels!"

Weitz smiled with sudden understanding. "You wanted to go outside, Hauptscharführer? Go ahead. Right through the window, where I can watch you."

Sergeant Sturm conjured a conspiratorial smile. "How about a deal, Weitz? We've done business before, eh? What do you want?"

"I want to see your eyes popping out of your head while you breathe Sarin."

Men were yelling in another part of the building. Sturm bent over and flipped the latch and jerked up the window. When he hesitated, Weitz shot out the panes over his head.

"Wait!" Stern shouted from the chair. "He has my keys!"

Sergeant Sturm cut his eyes at Jonas, then turned and jumped through the window.

"Stop him!" Stern shouted. "Hurry!"

Weitz went to the window. Sturm was running toward the hospital, and he didn't seem to be suffering the effects of any gas. Weitz knelt and fired at the retreating figure until the chamber of his gun clicked empty. He saw Sturm fall, but the sergeant picked himself up and continued on toward the hospital.

"There's no gas out there," Weitz said. "Not Sarin, anyway."

"Untie me!" Stern screamed. "Did you hit him?"

"Yes." Weitz picked up the SS dagger and slashed the ropes binding Stern to the chair. "Can you walk?"

Stern jumped to his feet. "We've got to get away from here! I have a car but no keys!"

Weitz picked up the Raubhammer gas mask from the hall floor and put it on. Just before he snapped the air hose into place, he shouted through the hole in his face mask: "There's another suit in the hospital! In Brandt's office. Follow me!"

Stern had tried to shape the plastic explosive so that it would blow the cylinder heads straight off of the buried tanks. When the first pencil fuse fired, the charge blasted the cylinder head outward like an artillery shell, straight through the wall of one of the SS barracks. The six-pound piece of metal decapitated Private Otto Huth, and before his stunned friends could even take in what had happened, the second cylinder head tore through the wall, shattered the hip of a lance corporal and lodged in the opposite wall.

Fifty SS men at once scrambled for their weapons and charged the barracks door. The bottleneck created there forced them to regain some semblance of discipline. Twenty seconds later, three dozen nervous storm troopers were crouching outside, trying to pinpoint a threat that seemed to have vanished.

"Look!" said one, pointing past the dog kennels toward the woods. "Smoke. They're bombing us from the air!"

"Don't be an idiot," said a strapping soldier named Heinrich Krebs. "The snow must have detonated some of the mines we laid around the perimeter today."

"I don't remember putting any mines on this side."

But Krebs was already walking around the kennels toward the fence.

"What's wrong with the dogs?" asked a puzzled voice.

"Maybe they were killed by shrapnel," someone suggested.

Several men stepped up to the kennel fence. "They're not all down," said one. "Look."

"*Mein Gott,* they're sick. What . . . ?"

The other SS barracks had also emptied at the sound of the explosions. Now more than seventy men were strung out along the narrow alley between the barracks and the dog kennels.

"See anything, Krebs?" called a sergeant.

There was no answer.

"Heini?"

"Shhh!" someone said. "Listen."

It was a soft sound, like the hissing of a venomous snake. But almost immediately the hissing was drowned out by the sound of men gibbering, defecating, striking each other, and choking on their own tongues. A dozen storm troopers fell to the ground, convulsing like epileptics in seizure.

Heinrich Krebs was already dead.

Six miles north of Totenhausen, ten Mosquitoes of the GENERAL SHERMAN flight assumed a tandem bombing formation. A half mile south of them, Squadron-Leader Harry Sumner reached for his microphone to break radio silence.

"Leader approaching target," he said in a mechanical voice. "I will mark with flares from one thousand feet, then go to fifteen hundred to act as Master Bomber. Number Two will drop red, repeat red, Target Indicators. I will verify Aiming Point, then give the go-ahead. High explosive followed by incendiaries. Let's put one down Göring's bunghole, eh?"

Sumner hung up the mike. "Well, Jacobs?" he said.

The navigator remained bent over the fuzzy image on the screen of his air-to-ground radar. "Eighty percent sure, sir. It would help if we slowed a bit."

Sumner keyed his mike. "Leader reducing speed. Holding at one thousand. Two, drop Target Indicators on my mark."

"*Out! Out!*" Schörner shouted as the troop truck wheeled into the driveway of the power station and stopped behind his car. "Ten men out now!"

He slammed his gloved hand down on the roof of his field car. "Tell Sturm everything I said!"

At that moment a grenade landed just behind the troop truck and exploded with an ear-splitting boom. Shrieks of agony filled the air. Schörner ran around the truck just in time to see the taillights of the Volkswagen flick on at the next curve. Snow kicked up into the air as the car raced away down the hill.

The driver of the troop truck revved his engine and shifted into gear, preparing to turn and pursue the fleeing car, but Schörner leaped up onto the running board and grabbed the wheel.

"Stop, you imbecile! You're staying here! Let that dog out!"

He jumped down and told the driver of his field car to chase the VW only if it headed toward Totenhausen. The corporal saluted and sped away.

"We're looking for an American and a bomb detonator!" Schörner yelled to the confused mass of SS troopers. "He's wearing a Waffen SS uniform! I want four men inside the station. Everyone else into the trees!"

Anna pumped the brakes of the Volkswagen, waiting to be sure Schörner was following. After a few moments, she saw a pair of headlights skid around the curve behind her. The lights were low to the ground. The field car.

She kept pumping the brakes, but no other lights appeared. Why wasn't the troop truck following? She didn't think one grenade could have put it out of commission. When the field car closed to within four car lengths, she jammed the accelerator to the floor.

The Volkswagen glanced off a hard snow bank, but she maintained control and fought the car around the next switchback curve. Below her lay Totenhausen. She wondered briefly what was happening inside the camp, but thoughts of McConnell quickly returned. Would he be able to climb the pylon? Would he have the will to release the gas cylinders if he did? How odd it would be never to see him again, the man who had awakened her sleeping heart after so many years. She pumped the brake, preparing to take the next curve, but the car lurched forward, shuddering under the impact of machine gun bullets.

Anna momentarily lost control of the car, then righted it and hit the gas. She looked down on the seat beside her. She had saved the last two grenades for a reason. Major Schörner had once told her a story about a wounded SS officer left behind by his unit during a retreat on the Eastern front. The man had sat calmly against a burning tank as the Russian infantry approached. When they came within five meters of him, he smiled, pulled the pins on the grenades and blew a half dozen Russians to pieces with him.

Anna had endured many nightmares in which she was tortured by Gunther Sturm. She had no intention of enduring the reality. If they managed to stop Greta's VW with gunfire, she would surrender like the man on the Russian front. With a smile on her face and live grenades in her hands.

"Dark as a bloody coal chute down there!" the navigator complained.

"What about your radar?"

"All I see is the river bend. It *looks* like the right one."

Squadron-Leader Harry Sumner expelled air from his cheeks with a sound that betrayed the tripwire tension beneath his calm voice. "How sure are you?"

"Well . . . eighty-five percent?"

"That's not good enough, Jacobs. If we bomb the wrong target, they'll just send us back." Sumner paused. "I'm going to drop a single flare. You'll have to verify our location visually."

The navigator looked up from his radar. "One flare, sir? Everyone down there will know we're here, and we'll still have to do a full marking run."

"They'll know soon enough anyway." Sumner reached for a lever. "There's no known ack-ack between here and Rostock, and we've got to be sure."

"Yes, sir."

"I can't risk wasting the lot on the wrong bend in the river."

"No, sir.

"Here we go."

McConnell perched on the crossarm of the pylon like a man in the crow's nest of a clipper ship. He blinked stinging sweat out of his eyes and looked around. Above him hung the inverted black bowl of sky and stars, a cold sliver of moon. Below him, to the north, shone the faint lights of Dornow village. To the south curved the silver line of the Recknitz River, sheltering Totenhausen Camp on its near bank. He recognized the spot by the bluish glow of spotlights.

His nerves thrummed. A staggering amount of effort had gone into putting one man on top of this pylon with the gas cylinders under his control. He was not that man, but he was the man who had made it here. And if the British nerve gas worked, he could doom every SS man in Totenhausen as surely as Jonas Stern could have. If the gas worked. If the cylinders stayed on track during their run down to the camp. If, if, if—

He could hear Schörner's men beating the bushes below him. Flashlight beams ricocheted off the snow in all directions. He heard a dog barking wildly, someone encouraging the dog. They were trying to track his scent over the snow. He didn't see how they could, as he'd been wearing a rubber suit while he walked, but the torches were getting closer. He didn't feel particularly nervous. They would capture him eventually, of course, but too late.

Right now he was untouchable.

The drama that caught his attention was closer. On the south face of the hills, two sets of headlights careened down the switchback road through the trees. Anna was in front, the SS car behind. The field car was slowly closing the gap, the outcome a foregone conclusion. Anna would be overtaken and killed within minutes. He tried to focus his mind on the task at hand, but he couldn't tear his eyes away from the swerving lights below.

And then it hit him. In thirty seconds both cars would break out onto the flat stretch that led from the base of the hill around to Totenhausen's front gate. By road, they might be a third of a mile away, but as the crow flew—or the bullet—the distance was probably more like three hundred meters. With the shouts of Schörner's men ringing up from the woods below, McConnell swung down off the crossarm and drove his spikes into the support pole beneath it. Clipping his safety belt around the pole, he jerked Stan Wojik's bolt-action Mauser off his shoulder and laid it over the crossarm, aiming south.

He chambered a round from the magazine and waited.

As he stared, he realized that the shot was damn near impossible. The problem was not the rifle, but the darkness. He was staring across open sights into a wall of night. Even when the cars appeared beneath him, he would have no way to accurately judge distance. It would be like aiming at stars.

Anna's car burst out of the trees at the foot of the hill, her red taillights accelerating away from him almost directly in line with the descending pylons. She had opened up a lead, but her flight was leading her headlong toward Totenhausen, straight into death. He stuck his gloved forefinger into the trigger guard of the Mauser and began tracking her lights. He almost threw the rifle down in frustration. He would be lucky if his bullet struck within fifty yards of the car.

He heard the dog barking in the trees below him, closer now. A voice in his brain told him to drop the rifle, to climb back onto the crossarm and release the cylinders. He was about to do just that when he heard the rumble of powerful engines.

Had Schörner brought more trucks into the forest?

The SS field car broke out of the trees. McConnell sighted in on the dim taillights and shook the sweat from his eyes, his heart pounding with the futility of his effort. But as his finger touched the trigger, he heard something pop in the sky high above him. The hillside came alive with light as surely as if God had thrown a switch in heaven. He had no idea who had fired the flare, but his eye instantly oriented him to distance by pylons, treetops, the stretch of road. . . .

He led the field car high and pulled the trigger.

"Rifle fire!" Major Schörner shouted, his eyes turned skyward in an attempt to locate the flare. "Rifle fire in the trees! Move south!"

Led by the dog, Schörner and his men crashed through the trees toward the sound of the gunfire.

McConnell's second bullet tore through the canvas roof of the field car and into the neck of an SS man in the backseat. The storm trooper squealed like a dying pig. Blood sprayed over his comrades, who immediately ducked below the windows, assuming they were being fired on from the sides. Four seconds later another slug knocked off the car's wing mirror. The driver had hardly registered the impact when McConnell's fifth bullet drilled down through the trunk panel and punctured the fuel tank. Gasoline funneled onto the road behind the car, and the sparks from the overheated exhaust quickly ignited the mixture.

The tank blew with a dull *crump* like a mortar shot, breaking the rear axle and dropping the back of the car onto the road with a metallic screech. The SS men who were still alive dove through the doors before it stopped, leaving their wounded comrades behind in the burning vehicle.

Anna shut her eyes and swerved, stunned by the flash behind her. She had no idea what could have destroyed the field car. Could it have hit a land mine? She skidded back onto the road and took her foot off the accelerator, realizing that her diversionary sacrifice was no longer required. What should she do? What *could* she do? Go back to the pylon? It was too late to help McConnell now. What about the camp? If all went as planned, it would soon be saturated with gas. She let the VW coast forward, her mind spinning with confusion.

And then she remembered the children.

She had the gas suit. She had the pistol.

And she had a debt to pay.

"What the bloody hell was that?" Harry Sumner asked.

"No idea, sir. Small explosion."

"Well, damn it? Is this the place?"

The navigator took his eyes off the swirl of flame and scanned the land below. As the lone parachute flare drifted away on the wind, he caught sight of something like a metal cage on a hilltop to the northwest.

"There it is, Harry! The power station! This is it! One hundred percent sure!"

Squadron Leader Sumner pressed his back into the seat and banked the Mosquito.

"Second pass," he said into his mike. "Leader marking with all flares."

McConnell pulled himself back up onto the crossarm and turned his attention to the business at hand. In the dying light of the flare, the top of the pylon looked just as Stern had described it. The twenty-foot crossarm spanned two thick support legs and jutted out a few feet on either side. Six wires passed over the crossarm in three pairs, one pair at each end of the arm and one pair in the middle. Three porcelain insulators shaped like upside-down dinner plates kept the wires from coming into direct contact with the crossarm.

According to Stern, one wire in each pair was live and one merely an auxiliary. The gas cylinders themselves had been suspended from the auxiliary wire at the end of the crossarm nearest McConnell, about five feet away. The question-mark-shaped suspension bars curved up and out from the roller-wheels, then back under the wire and down to the cylinders. McConnell saw that Stern had removed the two cylinders nearest the crossarm for use on the SS bomb shelter. But the rubber rope that would pull the cotter pins from the six remaining rollers was just within reach. Stern had wrapped it around the head of the cylinder nearest the pylon.

McConnell shinnied out to the end of the crossarm, trying not to tear the crotch of his gas suit. He stopped just short of the porcelain insulator. Following the rubber rope with his eyes, he realized that when he pulled it, the cotter pins that held the roller-wheels in position would be jerked out in reverse sequence, releasing the cylinder farthest from the pylon first, and so on until the cylinder nearest him had been freed.

The shouts below were getting closer. As darkness settled over the hillside again, McConnell fastened his safety belt around the crossarm, leaned out, took hold of the rubber rope and gave one sharp tug.

The rope stretched, but nothing came loose.

He yanked harder, and almost lost his balance when the cotter pin pulled free. The rubber rope sang like a plucked bass string as the cylinder farthest from him began to roll.

McConnell blinked in disbelief. There were *two* cylinders rolling down the wire, and they were quickly gathering speed. Keep some space between them, Stern had told him. He had pulled too hard! He began counting slowly—meaning to count to fifteen—but before he even reached five he noticed red taillights nearing the Recknitz River.

Anna.

She was still driving toward Totenhausen. What the hell was she doing? Hadn't she seen the SS car explode? She must have! What did she think she could do in the camp? Staring down the hill in a panic, McConnell realized that Stern might still be alive somewhere down there. Was that it? Was Anna trying to rescue Stern? If so, she wouldn't even get past the gate guards unless—

With the courage of despair McConnell dropped the rubber rope and shinnied back toward the support pole he had climbed. Passing it, he continued toward the center of the crossarm and stopped just short of the middle insulator. Five inches from his crotch ran the center auxiliary wire, just beyond that the live one.

He felt a strong vibration in the crossarm caused by the current in the live wire. He was too close. He scooted backward until he was two feet from the center pair of wires.

Unslinging the rifle from his shoulder, he took the muzzle of the barrel in his right hand, leaned forward, and extended the stock away from him until it hovered six inches above the pylon's far support pole. His right arm quivered from the weight of the old rifle. He let the stock down until the breech end of the barrel rested on the crossarm, just a few inches from the far support pole. Very carefully, he lowered the muzzle in his hand to within four inches of the live center wire.

Then he shut his eyes and dropped the metal barrel onto the wire.

"Mein Gott!" screamed one of Schörner's soldiers. "The bomb!"

Wolfgang Schörner stood motionless in the snow, stunned by the blue-white flash that had strobed in the forest ahead of him. He had heard many bombs in the past, but the explosion he'd just heard was like none he had ever known. The flash had burst high and in front of him, but the sound had come from behind, from the direction of the transformer station. Just after the flash, he had sensed more than seen a blazing white light pass high over his head, moving rapidly toward the transformer station. Then he'd heard a brassy *whooom,* and then—at least a full second later—the detonation.

Four distinct events.

Then he understood. There was no bomb. Somehow, someone had faulted one of the power lines above them. And they had done it in such a way that the main transformers had exploded. Totenhausen would be without electricity for a few seconds, but the backup transformers and lines would automatically kick on. Schörner waited to hear some telltale sound that this had happened.

What he heard was a sharp crack farther down the hill. Staring high into the darkness of the trees, he saw a blue-white fireball rolling up the hill like a man-made comet. He was marveling at the impossible vision of something rolling *uphill* when the fireball flashed over his head and hurled itself into the power station.

The second explosion dwarfed the first.

When McConnell dropped the rifle barrel onto the live wire, 8,700 volts of electricity instantly sought the shortest route to earth. The heat of the flash charred the surface of his oilskin suit and knocked him off the crossarm. A sound like a lion's roar split the night as the current discharged itself into the ground sixty feet below him. Hanging from his safety belt, McConnell thanked God that his basic knowledge of electricity had proved accurate: the shortest route from the live wire to earth had been through the rifle barrel and down through the far support pole, allowing him to remain outside the lethal circuit he had created.

Relays in the station instantly attempted to open the circuit breakers, but the poorly maintained batteries that controlled this function had expended their last energy correcting the mishap of Colin Munro four night earlier. The tremendous electrical load placed on the lines by contact with the earth drew a massive overcurrent from the 100,000-volt transmission lines that fed into the station, allowing thousands of amps to heat the faulted line to an extreme temperature. At the pylon where McConnell hung suspended like a fallen mountain-climber, the current flashed across all three live wires, ionizing the air between them and creating an arc like a welder's flame.

It was this arc that rolled up the wires and over Schörner's head toward the source of the current. It flashed onto the copper bus bars of the station, ionizing the available air and crackling across the metal struts like something from a Frankenstein picture. Heated far beyond the tolerance they had been built to withstand, the contacts inside the circuit breakers instantly boiled the insulating oil they were submerged in and blasted apart their steel-drum containers like giant shrapnel bombs, spraying oil across the snow.

The sensors in the station responsible for rerouting the voltage to the auxiliary system did function, but they too failed in the end. The first poison-gas cylinder had already smashed two insulators, putting the auxiliary wire into direct contact with two cross-arms. When the rerouted voltage reached the first damaged insulator, the previous event repeated itself almost exactly. As the second explosion reverberated through the hills, McConnell—still blinking his eyes from the passage of the second fireball—looked down toward Totenhausen.

Every light in the camp had gone out.

While Schörner's men stared dumbfounded at the transformer station, the major aimed his flashlight along the boot tracks they had been following, toward the blue-white flash he had seen. Standing squarely in the middle of the tracks was a smooth, thick tree trunk. Schörner had shone his flashlight ten feet up the tree before he realized it was one leg of a power pylon.

"Bring your torches!" he shouted, running toward the pole. "Hurry!"

By the time Schörner's shout echoed up from below, McConnell had righted himself on the crossarm and gotten his hand around the rubber rope. Three flashlights converged on one leg of the pylon. Stern had told him put space between the cylinders, but there was no more time. He yanked the third cotter pin loose, waited two beats, then jerked out the fourth and fifth simultaneously.

A flashlight flicked over the crossarm.

The last cylinder hung three feet down the wire from the crossarm, swaying gently in the darkness. As he tightened his grip on the rope to pull the final pin, McConnell realized something that sent spasms of fear along his spine.

He was going to die.

In a matter of seconds four torch beams would fix his position like London searchlights pinning a Luftwaffe bomber to the clouds, and machine gun bullets would follow. With this certainty came something unexpected—something quite different from what he had been feeling only moments ago—a flood of pure animal terror.

He wanted to live.

"There!" Schörner shouted, holding his beam steady on the top of the pylon. "Do you see something?"

"Nothing, Sturmbannführer."

"The tracks end *right here.*"

"Maybe he doubled back."

"Look at this!" cried an SS private, who had bent over something in the snow. He screamed suddenly and fell backward.

Schörner whirled and shone his flashlight onto the snow. A bolt-action Mauser rifle, scorched black and smoking, lay in a shallow well of melting snow. It took him only seconds to put together what had happened. He aimed his flashlight toward the top of the pylon.

"Lights!" he shouted.

"Sturmbannführer!" screamed one of the men. "The power station is burning!"

Schörner cursed as three torch beams disappeared. *"The pylon, you stupid swine! Put your lights on the pole!"*

McConnell stretched out his legs, hooked both feet around the four-foot suspension bar that held up the last cylinder and yanked out the cotter pin. The rubber rope fell sixty feet onto the snow. Only his butt and his hands on the crossarm resisted the downhill tug of the cylinder hanging beneath him.

Twice already a flashlight beam had played over his black oil-skin suit, but he forced himself to look down.

Wire netting covered the dark cylinder, and from the netting protruded six pressure-triggers, any one of which could blow the cap out of the cylinder head and release the gas within. There was no time for caution. If the triggers tripped and the British gas worked, he would have to rely on the gas suit and mask he had modified in Oxford. He would live or die by his own hands. Three torch beams stabbed the darkness around him.

With fire in his stomach he leaped off the crossarm.

"There!" Schörner shouted. "There's someone up there!"

"Where, Sturmbannführer?"

Schörner threw down his flashlight and snatched a submachine gun from the startled SS man, then turned it skyward and fired a long burst up along the length of the support pole.

McConnell's breath went out of his lungs when his crotch crashed onto the cylinder head. He felt as if he'd been kicked in the balls by a mule. It was all he could do to hang onto the suspension bar, but the cylinder was rolling.

It was rolling *fast*.

He was already twenty feet from the pylon when Schörner's fusillade of bullets ripped into the crossarm behind him. He looked down frantically to see if his legs had tripped any of the triggers. He couldn't tell. More shouts and gunfire sounded behind him, but suddenly it was all meaningless. No one below understood yet what had happened.

McConnell did. And he knew his problems had only just begun. Somewhere out ahead of him, five cylinders of nerve gas were shunting along a length of steel winch cable toward Totenhausen, and he was almost certainly overtaking them. He was trying to work out just how quickly when the roller-wheel above his head jumped the shattered insulator on the second pylon.

He closed his eyes in terror until the wheel settled back onto the wire on the other side. It was a lot like riding a cable car, he thought, a very fast cable car with no operator. He would almost certainly reach Totenhausen alive. The problem was how to get off of the cylinder before it dropped sixty feet to the ground. He was squinting down the wire trying to answer that question when the whole night sky burst into flame like the Fourth of July.

S tern was right behind Ariel Weitz as the rubber-suited figure
burst out of the back corridor of the headquarters building and
into the Appellplatz. Weitz ran straight toward the hospital,
but Stern swung out to his left. He had no intention of running unprotected through the invisible cloud of nerve gas that might be
drifting across the yard from the SS barracks and dog kennels on his
right. As he ran, he saw a white flash burst above the hills behind
the camp.

A flare.

Was Schörner signaling for assistance? Had he trapped McConnell on the road?

"Herr Stern! Please stop!"

Stern looked left. A woman was running toward him with a
child in her arms. Rachel Jansen. He could scarcely believe it, but
she was there, with a crowd of confused prisoners streaming out of
the inmate blocks behind her.

"It's after eight!" he shouted. "Get to the E-Block!"

"My son is already there! You promised to take Hannah!"

Stern heard a distant peal of thunder like artillery in the hills.
The entire camp seemed to freeze and listen. A second explosion followed. Then every light in the camp went out.

Transformers, thought Stern, remembering the sound from his
guerrilla days in Palestine. "My God, he's done it," he said. He
grabbed Rachel's shoulders. "The gas is coming! Come on!"

Rachel held out the bundled blanket. "For God's sake, take her
with you!"

Stern took the little girl like a sack under his right arm and

459

seized Rachel's hand with his left. Paralyzing pain shot up from his broken finger as he sprinted toward the hospital with Hannah screaming for her mother and Rachel following behind.

"Where is my father?" he asked.

"Taking children to the E-Block!"

He raced up the front steps of the hospital and crashed through the front door into the darkness of the main corridor.

"*Weitz!*" he screamed.

No answer.

Rachel slammed into his back. "Where is Hannah? Did you put her down?"

"I have her! Now, go to the E-Block! Go to your son! Straight through this corridor!"

While Stern pointed down the hall toward the back door, the window in the door lit up like a cinema screen. White light poured over his shoulders from the window in the door behind him.

"My God, what's happening?" Rachel asked. "What is that?"

Spotlights? Stern thought, though why anyone would be shining spotlights on the hospital doors made no sense to him.

"Weitz! Where are you?"

He heard a crash off to his right, then a bloodcurdling scream. He handed the child to Rachel and stumbled down the hall to his right, into darkness, feeling his way along, his finger burning at the slightest contact. He heard more crashes, another scream. Someone was begging in German, but the words were slurred, confused. A beam of light sliced across the corridor. In its brief flash he caught sight of at least two dead SS men outside the doorway. He moved cautiously forward. He heard a sound like a rotten melon dropped onto concrete, then the shuffle of feet on tile.

"Weitz?" he whispered.

A blast of gunfire poured out of a doorway.

"SCARLETT! I'm the man you just saved!"

A pause. "In here," said a muffled voice.

Stern smelled blood when he passed through the door. Weitz shined the flashlight into his eyes, then moved it away. Stern's eyes tracked the yellow beam until it came to rest on what once had been a human face. The skull was grossly misshapen now, a mass of gore and blood, the white coat beneath it a riot of scarlet and black. On the desk before this mess lay a short iron bar.

"*Guten Abend,* Standartenführer," Weitz said in a hushed tone. "This isn't what I wanted, you know."

"Who is that?"

Weitz clicked his heels together and gave the corpse a fascist salute. "The distinguished Herr *Doktor* Klaus Brandt. I wanted it to take *longer.*"

Stern took the torch from Weitz's hand. The little man made no effort to resist. One sweep of the walls revealed a nauseating mural of blood and tissue. Stern shined the light on the killer's face.

"Where is the other gas suit, Herr Weitz?"

Weitz pointed to the floor behind the desk. "He was trying to put it on. Trying to get away."

Stern picked up the suit, mask, and the boots that lay beside them. "Is there a vinyl sheet anywhere close?" he asked.

"This is a hospital."

"*Get* me one then. In the main corridor you'll find a little girl. I want you to wrap her in the sheet. Can you do that?"

"For the gas, you mean? She'll need oxygen."

"Then get me a fucking bottle!"

A powerful explosion rocked the foundations of the hospital, shattering some kind of glassware in the dark office. Weitz cocked his head to one side, as if listening to a particularly fine piece of music.

"What the hell was that?" asked Stern.

"Little rats trying to leave the ship. But they went the wrong way! You told me to booby trap the bomb shelter, remember?"

Stern turned away from the grisly scene and moved toward the door. The telephone on Brandt's desk rang. He heard Weitz pick it up and say, "Yes?"

After a short pause, Weitz began to laugh. The sound chilled Stern's blood. "Who is that?" he asked, aiming the torch at the desk.

"Berlin." Weitz smiled eerily. "Reichsführer Himmler is holding for the Herr Doktor."

Weitz held the phone against Klaus Brandt's shattered skull and looked up at Stern. The flashlight reflected the whites of his eyes and the teeth of his grin.

Stern leaped forward and snatched the phone away before Weitz could say anything more. He held the receiver to his ear and heard an irritated voice: "Brandt? Brandt! Confounded telephone lines . . . the Allies have knocked them out again."

A chill raced across Stern's arms and shoulders.

"Brandt!" Himmler said again. "What the devil is going on up there?"

Stern touched his lips to the bloody mouthpiece. Very slowly and clearly he said, "Listen to me, chicken farmer. You lost the war tonight. Keep your cyanide pill close. We are coming back for you in the spring."

He set the phone gently in its cradle, picked up the Raub-hammer suit and walked out of the office. Weitz followed with his machine pistol. Before they reached the main hall, the telephone was ringing again.

Rachel waited in the corridor with Hannah in her arms.

"For God's sake, woman!" yelled Stern.

Rachel shook her head and clung desperately to her daughter. Stern saw in her eyes that she was close to collapse. He had seen it happen to men in the desert, a kind of cumulative shock that could make a man lie down to sleep in the middle of a blazing battlefield. If he took the time to put on the Raubhammer suit, Rachel Jansen would not cross the alley to the E-Block alive. He dropped the suit and the flashlight on the floor, took Weitz's machine pistol and pulled her toward the back door.

As he crashed through it he saw the rear of the camp—trees, fence, the roof of the E-Block, the alley—illuminated as if by day-light.

What was happening?

Halfway across the alley, he heard a babble of voices to his left. A tall figure wearing a brown SS uniform was running toward him, pulling two children along behind, one by each hand.

"*Father?*" Jonas shouted.

The figure stopped dead. "Jonas? My son?"

Stern threw his left arm around his father.

"The blood!" cried Avram. "What have they done to you?"

A pistol shot cracked at the far end of the alley. Jonas turned to his right. Just beyond the alley stood the huge barn that held the laboratory and gas factory. When the second crack sounded, he re-alized what he was hearing—the detonation of the trigger mecha-nisms on the gas cylinders.

"Into the E-Block!" he yelled. *"Now! Everyone!"*

He pushed the two children down the concrete steps that led to the gas chamber. Rachel and Hannah already waited by the hatchway.

"They saw me!" Avram said as they shoved the children through the hatch.

"Who saw you?"

"The men. It's a mob! They know something is happening, Jonas. The E-Block won't hold another soul! Every Jewish child and some of the Gentile children are inside. The women are holding them on their shoulders, squeezing them into every corner . . . it's a nightmare!"

Stern pulled Hannah from her mother's arms. "You are the last, Rachel! Say farewell!"

Rachel took her daughter's face between her hands. "Remember what I told you, little one. Do whatever Herr Stern tells you. Never"—her voice cracked—*"never* forget me." She kissed the terrified child hard on the forehead and then backed away.

"I am going to live," she told Stern, her black eyes bright with tears. "One day I will come to Palestine. I will want her back. Don't ever leave her!"

As Jonas pushed her through the hatch, Rachel reached into her shift and pressed something into his hand. It was too large to be another diamond. He looked down. A *dreidl*. He stuffed the little top into the trouser pocket of the SD uniform.

"She won't remember!" Rachel cried, backing hard against the wall of bodies behind her. "So you must tell her! It is all she will have of her parents!"

With that she turned and hurled herself into the mass of bodies seeking refuge in the gas chamber.

Another crack sounded from behind the factory. Jonas wrapped the blanket around Hannah's head and set her on a step. Then he took his father by the shoulders and shook him.

"Get your ass through that door! Now!"

Avram looked confused. "Jonas . . ." His face was working through stages of incomprehension. Things had not turned out as they were supposed to. He should have been dead before now. "I can't be the only man left alive. Not after—"

For the first time in his life Jonas Stern struck his father. He hit him so hard that Avram doubled over and fell as surely as if he had taken a bullet in the belly. Jonas dragged him to his feet and stood him up beside the hatch. He saw only blackness inside. The heat in the chamber was already stifling. A cacophony of wailing women and children filled his ears. He called for Rachel, but she had already been swallowed by the tangle of limbs. He grabbed the nearest arm to the door and pulled.

"*Can you hear me?*" he asked in Yiddish.

"Yes, sir!" answered a shaky male voice.

"How old are you?"

"Thirteen, sir."

"Help me pull him in. He's not SS. You know the shoemaker?"

"Yes."

Stern heard the crack of another detonator. When they'd got his father inside, he shoved Weitz's machine pistol into the boy's clammy hands. "Hold tight to that! Don't let anyone take it from you. Stay in here until there's no more air to breathe. Then shoot out a window, crawl out, and open the hatch. That's the *only way out*. Do you understand?"

"I think so."

The voice sounded frightened but resolute. Stern squeezed the boy's arm, then backed up, took hold of the heavy steel door and forced it shut. As he cranked the great wheel into the closed position, he felt he was sealing people into a tomb, not a lifeboat.

Only time would tell which.

Coming up the steps with Hannah in his arms, he saw a group of men enter the alley from the factory end. They wore prison stripes, not SS uniforms. Panic seized him. Even if he'd still had the machine pistol, he could not keep them away from the E-Block for long. Several men began throwing their arms about like puppets controlled by a madman.

Two fell to their knees, retching in the snow.

"God forgive me," Jonas said. He raced across the alley and up the hospital steps without looking back.

McConnell clung desperately to the suspension bar as the roller-wheel jumped over the shattered transformer on the seventh pylon and raced down the wire. He was three quarters of the way down the hill with no sign of slowing and no idea how to get off of the cylinder alive. The parachute flares floated down through the blackness like white stars, illuminating the landscape from the hillside to the river with a hypnotic light.

What did they mean? Had some emergency signal been triggered? If so, it was a hell of a show. He tore his eyes away from the flares and forced himself to think. He was moving too fast to catch hold of a crossarm, and he was too high to hope to drop into the snow and survive. He did not realize he had the means to save his life until he caught sight of the cylinder ahead of him. The image of it hurtling down the power line tripped a memory in his mind. The Death-Ride at Achnacarry, when he and Stern had been ordered to leap from a tree and slide across the Arkaig River on a taut wire using only their toggle ropes. . . .

Toggle ropes . . .

Anna felt a sense of peace when she saw the lights of Totenhausen wink out. Alarmed tower-gunners began firing on the Volkswagen when they realized it was not going to stop, but they were too late. She steamrollered the gate at sixty miles per hour and roared across the parade ground. Bullets shredded her rear tires, but she drove on.

A lone SS man caught in her high-beams fired at her.

She ran him down.

She swerved around the headquarters and headed toward the inmate blocks. Had the Jewish women and children reached the E-Block? Had Stern even reached the block to warn them about the attack? And what of the Christian children? They had nowhere to go. Perhaps she could lead them to safety somewhere.

She gasped and hit the brakes as her headlights revealed the block area. A frantic mob of ghostly figures was milling around like patients set free from a lunatic asylum. Some clung to the fence wires, others writhed in the snow, their backs arched in spasm like human bows. Anna saw children among them. Unconsciously she touched her air hose to make sure it was secured to her mask.

As the VW slowed, a group of men noticed the car and charged with suicidal recklessness. She yanked the wheel to the right and gunned the motor. To get out of the car here would be like leaping into the sea to save a hundred drowning people. Better to go to the E-Block by running through the hospital corridor.

She skidded to a stop beside the hospital steps. There were corpses here too. Her gas suit had no pockets, so she left the keys in the car. With shredded tires the Volkswagen was useless anyway. She reloaded her pistol, then hoisted the heavy air tank onto her back and struggled up the hospital steps.

"Looks like someone already had a go at the power station, sir," said the navigator. "It's burning."

Squadron Leader Harry Sumner started the climb to fifteen hundred feet. From there he would act as Master Bomber, using his radio to guide and correct the delivery of bombs by the other aircraft.

"We're going to hit it anyway, Jacobs. Following orders, right down the line. They must want the whole hill flattened, to send the two cookies with us."

Jacobs nodded. His squadron leader was referring to the two 4,000 lb. high explosive bombs carried in the bays of two Mosquitos which had been specially modified to carry the huge concrete-busting bombs to Berlin. Dropping those on the tiny power station and camp below would be like squashing ants with a mace.

Nothing would remain but holes in the ground.

But just in case it did, the additional 14,000 pounds of incendiaries carried by the remaining Mosquitoes would burn off anything left above ground.

"Overdoing it a bit, wouldn't you say, sir?" commented the navigator.

"We'll never know," Sumner replied. "God only knows what's down there. Could be the devil's own furnace, buried where we can't see it."

"Could be, sir."

"Verify placement of Target Indicators. I only want to do this once. And pray Jerry doesn't have any decoys down there."

"Ready, sir."

The Squadron Leader keyed his mike twice, then began transmitting orders to one of the ten bombers wheeling in the sky below him.

McConnell watched in mute terror as the cylinder ahead of him rocketed off the tenth pylon like a skier from a cliff and smashed into the rear of a huge barnlike structure, then fell the remaining distance to the ground. Looking down, he saw that the power lines dropped almost perpendicularly from the tenth pylon to a distribution shed at the base of the factory. There would be no gradual descent.

He had to stop *now*.

He gripped the loop-end of his toggle rope in his left hand and focused on the roller-wheel above him. If he tangled the rope in that wheel, he would probably die. There was only one way to make the throw. He slipped his right wrist through the loop-end of the short rope, and with the same hand gripped the wooden handle at the other end—a throwing weight.

He leaned back as far as he could.

The roller-wheel above him whirred like a fishing reel spinning under a shark's pull. Cocking his right arm, he threw the handle-end of the rope up and over the power line, aiming just behind the pulley-roller, and grabbed for the falling handle with his left hand.

He caught it!

Glancing down, he saw the crossarm of the tenth pylon rushing up to meet him. Thirty yards, twenty—had the British Sarin killed even a single SS man?—fifteen yards . . .

He twisted one end of the rope around each wrist and heaved himself up off the cylinder. The heavy tank shot out from under him like a wild bronco that had finally thrown its rider.

The horsehair toggle rope sang as it raked against the power line, slowing his descent. Was the friction enough? With all his strength he clenched the rope in his vibrating hands.

The toggle rope hit the crossarm with enough speed to snap McConnell's whole body out ahead of the pylon, parallel to the wires. Momentum tore at his air tank, the harness on his back, his shoulders and wrists—but everything held. Rope, tank, harness, bones, and ligaments. Two seconds after the impact he was hanging suspended from the tenth pylon like a parachutist caught in a tree.

His arms felt as if they had been yanked from their sockets, so he swung his legs up over the crossarm and, in the upside-down position so common to twelve year old tree-climbers, worked his way along to the nearest support leg of the pylon.

Then he looked down.

Sixty feet below, six gas cylinders lay on the snow beside the factory wall. They looked harmless, used up, like scrap metal fallen off a junk truck. For all he knew, they might *be* harmless.

But they might not.

He looked to his right, down into the camp proper. Black stick figures of varying sizes sprawled on the snow at crazy angles, many concentrated in the area of the inmate blocks.

"God in Heaven," he said, his voice alien inside the vinyl mask. "It works."

He struggled to hold down the wave of nausea rising from his stomach. Vomiting in the mask might be fatal, since he could not risk removing it. Had any of the women and children reached the E-Block? Had he released the gas too early? Where was Anna? Stern? Stern had no gas suit. He looked down at his waist. Christ. He'd left his safety belt clipped to the top pylon.

The goddamn thing was useless anyway.

He took two massive breaths from his air tank, then jammed his spikes into wood, bear-hugged the pole and started down.

47

Did you get the oxygen bottle?" Stern shouted, running toward the flashlight beam at the opposite end of the hospital corridor.

The beam moved down and illuminated a green bottle lying on a dark, reflective sheet. Stern set the kicking bundle that was Hannah Jansen on the sheet.

"Took it from a pneumonia case," came Weitz's muffled reply. "You'd better put on that suit."

Stern lost no time doing that. But as he tried to work the recessed zipper, he realized something was wrong. Weitz could not be holding the flashlight to help him see and at the same time be taping the little girl into the vinyl sheet—which the sounds Stern had been hearing indicated he was doing.

"Who else is here?" Stern cried, throwing himself out of the beam of the flashlight.

"It's all right!" Weitz said, shining the torch onto another black-suited figure wearing an air tank on its back. The figure looked up from its work. In the glow of the flashlight Stern first saw only a reflection. Then, through the clear vinyl mask McConnell had brought from Oxford, he saw the blond hair and dark eyes of Anna Kaas. She stared back at him for a moment, obviously stunned by the blood and bruising on his face, then pointed at his gas suit and went back to her work.

Stern lost no time zipping up the Raubhammer suit. Suddenly, the hospital lights blinked on, faded, then stayed on.

The bright light paralyzed Stern.

"The emergency generator," said Weitz. "There's someone in the basement!" He jabbed Stern on the shoulder. "What did you do with my gun?"

"I gave it to someone."

Weitz cursed and raced around the corner toward Brandt's office. Anna held up her revolver and called out, but the buzz produced by the speech diaphragm of her mask died after a few feet. She put down her gun and with Stern's help sealed the vinyl sheet as completely as possible with the roll of tape Weitz had provided. Stern picked up the bundle—much heavier now with the oxygen bottle added to the child's weight—and turned toward the hospital door.

Sergeant Gunther Sturm stood beside the stairwell, unsteady on his feet but holding an infantry rifle in his hands. The left side of his tunic was soaked in blood.

As Stern bent to set down the child, Sturm fired.

He missed.

The SS man jerked back the bolt for a second shot.

Though years of conditioned reflexes told Stern to attack the man, something stronger surged through him. He threw himself over Hannah Jansen's body, shielding her from the bullets even as the inner voice told him he would die for it.

He heard gunshots, but too many too quickly to be the bolt-action rifle in Sturm's hands. He looked up to see Ariel Weitz barreling out of the side corridor firing Klaus Brandt's Luger.

Sergeant Sturm returned fire at point-blank range.

The boom of the rifle in the wide hallway had not even died when Weitz hit the tile floor. The sergeant staggered over to the fallen man, pulling back the rifle bolt as he walked. Weitz struggled on the floor, but could not rise or even crawl away. Sturm's bullet had broken his back.

Jonas started to lunge toward the SS man—then a heavy caliber revolver exploded beside his right ear. He threw up his hand to protect his eardrum, watching in astonishment as Anna Kaas fired three more bullets, spiking Sturm to the hospital wall. The sergeant hung there a moment, his arms flung wide, then dropped like a sack of sausage filling, leaving scarlet streaks behind him.

Anna knelt beside Weitz. The little man was fighting just to breathe. She gently pulled off his mask and airhose.

Weitz was unshaven as usual. A faint smile lit his eyes. "Remember what you said?" he whispered.

The lights in the corridor dimmed again, but stayed on.

Anna squeezed the rubber that covered his right hand. "I'm sorry, Herr Weitz?"

"You said . . . God . . . sees how it really is." He tried unsuccessfully to swallow. "I hope that's true," he gasped, and died.

Anna bowed her head.

Stern touched her shoulder. "Do you have a car, Fräulein Kaas?"

As Anna turned to answer, the hospital lights went out and stayed out. Stern pulled her to her feet in the darkness.

"Greta's car won't take us far," she said. "They shot the tires to pieces. What about Sabine's Mercedes?"

"No." Stern heard the muffled screaming of the child in the sealed sheet. "Wait!"

He dropped to his knees and felt his way across Gunther Sturm's bloody corpse, searching for pockets. He almost shouted with relief when he felt his right hand close over car keys. "We've got it!" he said, sliding his palms over the cold tiles in search of the SS man's rifle. "We'll pick up McConnell at the pylon."

He found the rifle, stood up, and slung it over his shoulder. At first he thought the frantic buzzing was some type of insect beside his ear. Then Anna punched him and he realized it was the nurse screaming inside her gas mask. He snapped straight and followed her pointing arm.

At the rear door of the hospital, backlit by the dying white light of a parachute flare, stood a tall, black-suited figure. When it lifted an arm toward them, Stern's mind shouted *Gun!* so loudly that he had Sturm's rifle off his shoulder and aimed in an instant.

Anna fired her pistol but missed. Twenty meters was well beyond her effective range.

Stern pulled the rifle's trigger.

Nothing happened. Sergeant Sturm had failed to fully chamber another round. As he worked the bolt, a brilliant red light bloomed in the window behind the silhouette.

It was the flash of multicolored cloth against the black suit that made Stern pull his aim. His bullet smashed the window of the door behind the figure. He knocked Anna's arm wide, then waved both arms wildly. He had no idea how McConnell had gotten down the hill so fast, but he knew no German would be wearing a piece of Scottish tartan in the heat of battle.

When McConnell reached them, he leaned in close and said, "We've got to get out of here! The gas works! The alley is full of dead!"

Stern's gas mask had no speech diaphragm, so he took the risk of unclipping his air hose. "How the hell did you get here?" he asked, immediately sealing the hole with his palm.

"Air mail!" McConnell shouted, his voice rendered cartoonish by the buzzing diaphragm.

"What?"

"Forget it!"

"What about the factory?" Stern asked. "Do we run? Or do we finish the job?"

"Do we have a car?"

"The Mercedes."

"What about the camera and the sample canisters?"

"In Greta's Volkswagen," Anna said.

McConnell saw something move on the floor. "What the hell is that?"

"A little girl," Stern told him. "There's an oxygen bottle in there with her, but we've got to get her away from here."

"What about the other children?" Anna asked.

"The E-Block is full," said Stern. "The rest. . . ." He shook his head. "This is the one we can still save."

"Put your air hose back on!" McConnell yelled. "Anna, take the girl in the Mercedes and wait for us by the river. The wind blowing off the water will make that the safest place. Jonas and I are going to do what we came here to do. We'll meet you at the river. We'll use the Mercedes to make a run for the coast." He turned to Stern. "Good enough?"

Stern nodded.

"Any sign of Schörner?" McConnell asked.

"No," said Anna.

Stern shook his head.

"Find a dark spot to wait," McConnell told her.

"There's a ferry down there," Anna said. "A one-truck ferry used for bringing supplies from the south. If we used that, we wouldn't have to risk meeting Schörner on the main road."

Stern nodded with an exaggerated motion, then bent down and hoisted Hannah Jansen onto his right shoulder.

Anna led the way through the front door with her revolver. McConnell suddenly slammed into the air tank on her back. He squeezed past her and stood gaping at the Appellplatz. Two blinding red fires lay burning in the snow like Roman candle flares. He could see two more burning in a straight line beyond the front gate, probably hear the river bank. Seeing the ruby flare burst behind him at the rear door of the hospital, he had imagined a flare fired by a dying SS man.

This was something different.

There was almost a pattern to the fires, as if they were comets cast down by an angry but methodical god. McConnell might have kept staring had Stern not shoved him forward and run down the steps like a man with the devil at his heels. Anna pulled McConnell down with her and grabbed a leather bag from the backseat of Greta's car. Together they followed Stern around the hospital to the Mercedes.

They met him coming back. McConnell called out to ask what the hell was going on, but Stern had already passed him, running across the Appellplatz toward the headquarters building.

They found Hannah on the passenger seat of the idling Mercedes. The oxygen bottle inside the vinyl sheet was slowly inflating it like a balloon. McConnell helped Anna into the driver's seat. The air tank on her back pressed her chest into the steering wheel, but she managed to shift the car into gear.

"See you at the river!" he shouted, slamming the door.

The Mercedes' wheels began spinning on the ice.

On impulse McConnell pulled open the back door, jumped across the seat and yelled, "Drop me at the front of the camp!"

It took Major Schörner five minutes to cover the same distance McConnell had covered in eighty seconds. Where McConnell had crossed it in a straight line, Schörner had had to wrestle the troop truck down the tortuous hill road and around the wreckage of his field car just to get within a quarter mile of the camp. Counting the time it had taken him to regroup his men at the power station, he was running very late. With every red fire he passed, the sense of urgency grew in him. He knew what those fires meant. He had seen them in Russia. As the troop truck roared toward the camp gate, he leaned out of the window to shout at the gate guards.

He saw none.

"Slow down!" he shouted at the driver. "Slower, you swine!"

He opened the door and stood on the truck's running board. As the driver coasted forward, Schörner felt a sudden and powerful sense of dread. He never knew the source of these intuitions, but in Russia he had learned not to question them.

"Stop the truck!" he ordered. *"Stop!"*

The truck skidded to a halt.

Schörner jumped down onto the snow and took a couple of steps toward the gate. Peering into the darkness, his eyes were drawn to three dark forms on the ground about five meters inside the twisted gate. He looked up at the nearest watchtower. The upper half of the tower-gunner's body was hanging over the gun parapet.

Schörner blinked in disbelief. He backed blindly toward the troop truck, then turned and scrambled up into the cab. "Back up!" he screamed, rolling up the window as fast as he could. "Get us out of here!"

The driver stared at him as if he were mad.

Schörner drew his pistol and put it against the driver's head. *"There's been a gas release! I want this truck two hundred meters back up the road!"*

The panicked driver jammed the transmission into reverse and spun the tires for ten seconds before they finally caught on the icy gravel.

"Target Indicators down, sir," the navigator said. "Aiming Point verified."

"This is the Master Bomber," Squadron Leader Sumner said into the radio mike. "If there was any ack-ack down there, they'd be coning us now. Take your time and do it properly. The power station first, then the camp. Bomb on red indicators. Bomb at will."

Sumner's Mosquito continued to circle at fifteen hundred feet while the lead bomber went in. The modified aircraft made its run south to north, aiming for the red markers at the power station. It dropped its load one half second too late, causing the single 4,000 pound high-explosive bomb it carried to drift just past the hilltop.

Moments later, the village of Dornow ceased to exist.

*   *   *

McConnell was halfway out of the Mercedes when a shuddering blast wave shook the earth beneath his feet. He looked back toward the hospital and saw a mushroom-shaped fireball boiling into the night sky beyond the hills. As he stared, the crown of the highest hill disappeared in a daisy chain of star-white explosions. The flash arced over Totenhausen, freeze-framing a field of corpses.

Now he understood the red fires.

Now he understood what Stern had figured out the moment he saw the Target Indicators laid out like a grid over the camp. But what the hell did Stern think he could do about it? He couldn't call 8th Air Force HQ in England and ask them to cancel a bombing raid.

The roar of the fleeing Mercedes brought him back to his senses. He kicked open the door to the building he had seen Stern disappear into and stopped dead. Yellow light was pouring into an empty corridor from a doorway up the hall. Where was the electricity coming from? He stared in wonder at the empty corridor. Why were there no dead Germans here? Had the gas not yet penetrated this building? He closed the door behind him and concentrated on sounds.

It was difficult to hear through the vinyl mask, but there was no mistaking the sound of the diesel generator. He moved quickly up the hall toward the source of the light, which turned out to be the wireless operator's room. Stern was already seated at the console, searching for a frequency on the dial.

Another chain of explosions rattled the floorboards.

Stern pounded the desk in fury. McConnell immediately saw his problem. Stern wanted to use the radio, but couldn't risk removing his air hose to speak. He had no idea who Stern wanted to talk to, but the scientist in him knew instantly that there was only one solution. He grabbed a pen by the radio console and scrawled three words on a codebook beside Stern's hand.

COAL MINE CANARY!

Stern looked up through the bulging eyepieces of his gas mask. Then he grabbed the infantry rifle he had taken from Sergeant Sturm and bolted from the room.

McConnell heard another drumfire of explosions, much nearer this time. The blast waves jolted the radio sets on the shelf. Shit! How bad could their luck be? To be on the verge of success and have it all blown to hell because of poor organization? Duff Smith should have known Bomber Command or the 8th Air Force might unilaterally decide to wipe out a power station like the one on the hill above Dornow. He should have taken steps.

McConnell jumped as Stern shoved a young SS man into the room and slammed the door. The brown-clad soldier was not wearing a gas mask, but he was alive. Stern handed his rifle to McConnell and shoved the SS man down until his mouth and nose were at the crack between door and floor.

"There's our canary," Stern said. "Stand on his back, and if he tries to run, shoot him."

He jumped into the radio-operator's chair and yelled into the mike. *"Atlanta! Atlanta! This is Butler and Wilkes, repeat, Butler and Wilkes, calling Atlanta!"*

McConnell planted a boot between the German's shoulder blades and rested the muzzle of the rifle on his kidneys. "What the hell are you doing, Stern?"

"Butler, repeat, Butler, calling Atlanta!" Stern said again, waving at McConnell to shut up. *"May Day, May Day!"*

McConnell expected at any moment to hear the deafening blast of bombs landing inside the camp perimeter. "Try to raise the planes themselves!" he shouted. "Brigadier Smith can't stop the damn things!"

Stern whirled around and screamed, "Smith *sent* those planes, you idiot! He's the only one who can stop them!"

McConnell felt suddenly dizzy. He was an idiot. Brigadier Smith *had* taken steps. And those steps demonstrated a degree of ruthless professionalism that left McConnell dazed. He could only watch speechless as Stern bent back over the console.

"This is Butler, repeat, Butler, calling Atlanta. . . ."

"Ach du lieber, Sturmbannführer! What was that?"

Wolfgang Schörner watched with businesslike appreciation as the first incendiaries obliterated the Dornow power station. He shook his head in wonder. "I believe that last stick was phosphorous bombs, Koerber. Perhaps some thermite as well. Be glad you're not under them."

"But what are they doing?"

Schörner rubbed his chin thoughtfully. "They are preparing to flatten Totenhausen with their own agents inside. The question is *why?*"

The incendiary bombs were what Anna Kaas had been waiting for. Not them specifically, but something like them. Something that would draw the attention of Major Schörner and his men long enough for her to drive the black Mercedes out of Totenhausen's front gate without being seen. She had watched the troop truck race up to the gate, even recognized Schörner's movements as he climbed down from the running board, turned, and jumped back into the truck. She thanked God she'd had the sense to keep her headlights off as she drove across the camp.

The troop truck had retreated two hundred meters up the access road that curved around the camp toward the hills, but Schörner was no fool. The truck still blocked the main route of escape and maintained an oblique view of the front gate. Anna needed to cross the forty meters of downward-sloping open ground between the gate and the river, where the single-truck ferry that led to Totenhausen's secondary access road waited in the icy water. Without a diversion, she would never reach it unnoticed.

GENERAL SHERMAN provided that diversion. When she saw the orange flash reflected in her windshield from the enormous blast of flame on the hills behind the camp, she lifted her foot from the brake and idled forward between the smashed gateposts and dead SS men. The rubber bundle in the backseat was still jerking and fighting. Muffled screams pierced the silence. Anna knew the little girl inside must be nearly mad with terror, but she would have to wait. The dead sentries meant the nerve gas had drifted south at least as far as the gate.

She fed the Mercedes a little gas, all the while watching the twin beams of Schörner's troop truck and praying his eyes were on the hills. Twenty meters to the river. Ten. She took her eyes off Schörner's truck long enough to aim the Mercedes at the little ramp that led up onto the ferry. As the car's nose drifted down, a bolt of terror hit her. Would the brake lights betray her position to Schörner? *Yes.* With a prayer on her lips she shut off the engine and let the Mercedes coast up the ramp. When she felt the wheels bump onto the wooden deck, she threw the car into low gear, slammed her foot down on the brake pedal and set the parking brake.

The Mercedes skated across the icy deck with a hiss. If the front bumper had not struck an iron post jutting up from the edge of the deck near the wheelhouse, the car would have slid right off and crashed into the river. When it jolted to a stop, Anna glanced back at the troop truck. It had not moved. She spoke comfortingly to the half-inflated vinyl bundle in the backseat and peered through the front windshield. The river was frozen along most of its length this time of year, but the ferry ran frequently enough to keep a narrow channel open during the day. The channel froze again each night, only to be broken open again in the morning. How quickly did it freeze?

She could not risk opening the door to find out. She squinted into the darkness. Directly ahead of the car's hood there was ice, but it looked black compared to the white sheet that spread east and west along the river. The black ice ran in a straight line to the opposite bank. That blackness was river water. There was ice there, but it was thin.

She hoped it was thin enough.

Brigadier Duff Smith was monitoring the frequency of GENERAL SHERMAN when Airman Bottomley burst through the door of the little hut beside the runway.

"Switch to three-one-four-zero, sir! Hurry!"

Duff Smith had been in too many tight places to stand on form when he heard the strain of action in a man's voice; he obeyed his subordinate without question. Static filled the hut as he spun through the frequencies.

"I was in the Junkers, sir," Bottomley panted. "I was switching through the bands when I heard it."

"Heard what?"

"*Them*, sir! Transmitting in the clear!"

Suddenly a muffled voice with a German accent very like Jonas Stern's crackled, "*. . . repeat, Butler calling Atlanta! May Day! May Day!*"

Smith blanched. He pressed the transmitter key and barked, "This is Atlanta! Come in, Butler! Come in, Butler! We'd written you off. What is your situation?"

The radio crackled again. "*Mission accomplished! Repeat, mission accomplished! Abort bombers, abort bombers!*"

"Damn me," Smith gasped, his Highland accent breaking through the English veneer, as it always did in stressful situations. "Say again, Butler? Did you say mission accomplished?"

"Mission accomplished! Stop those bombers, you one-armed bastard!"

With shaking fingers, Duff Smith dialed in the emergency frequency of GENERAL SHERMAN.

Squadron Leader Harry Sumner's hands jumped on the controls when he heard the Scottish accent blare out of the Mosquito's high frequency radio. *"General Sherman, General Sherman! Attention!"*

Navigator Jacobs's head popped up from his radar screen with confusion and suspicion clouding his face. "Who the hell is that, Harry?"

"I'd like to know myself," Sumner said in a deadpan voice.

"I order you to abort your mission. I say again, abort your mission."

Sumner blinked in puzzlement. "There's no abort code for this leg of the mission, is there, Jacobs?"

"Not after we left the Main Force, sir. Strict radio silence."

"How does this bleeder know our frequency then? And our code name?"

Jacobs shrugged and looked out of the cockpit. "It's too late anyway, sir. The power station is gone. They're forming up for the run on the camp now.

"Attention, General Sherman! You are at fifty-four-point-oh-four degrees north, twelve-point-three-one degrees east. Your target code is Tara. I wrote the order authorizing this raid, and I am now countermanding that order. I know you are observing radio silence. I also know you can hear me. Break off your raid immediately and verify same action by verbal response. Break off raid immediately or face the consequences when you return to Skitten."

Harry Sumner's hands tingled at the controls. "Sounds kosher, Peter. What do you think?"

"It's your call, Harry. You've got about ten seconds to stop the run."

"I never heard a Jerry who could mimic a Highlander like that." Sumner keyed the mike. "This is General Sherman," he said tersely. "What year was the Battle of Harlaw fought?"

There was silence. Then the radio crackled: "Fourteen-eleven. Bless you, laddie, it was fourteen-eleven."

Sumner snatched up the VHF mike. "This is the Master Bomber. Abort bomb run, abort bomb run. This is your squadron leader. Return to base. Abort, abort. Return to base."

Navigator Jacobs sank back in his seat and sighed heavily. "I hope you know what you're doing, Harry."

"So do I," Sumner said. "So do I."

48

Walking across the dark Appellplatz after the bombs stopped falling, McConnell sensed for the first time the magnitude of what he had done. Sealed from head to toe in black oilskin, breathing air that had been compressed in an Oxford laboratory, he moved through the corpses like a ghost on a battlefield.

The dead lay everywhere, SS and prisoners together, men and women and children with their arms and legs thrown out at haphazard angles, mouths and eyes open to a sky scorched red by the sizzling Target Indicators. As horrifying as it was, McConnell knew this was but a shadow of the devastation that lay in store if twentieth-century science were completely harnessed to the engine of warfare. He looked over at Stern. The eyeholes in the young Zionist's gas mask were pointed at the factory, not the ground. But even Stern could not ignore the obvious. They had saved some, but they had killed more.

Yet as they approached the factory gate, one thought filled McConnell's mind. If a mere British copy of Sarin could accomplish this silent, bloodless slaughter, then in Soman the Germans possessed a weapon of truly apocalyptic power. He had understood that intellectually in Oxford. But to see a nerve agent used against human beings brought home to him in a way nothing else could how impossible were the dilemmas men like Duff Smith and Churchill faced.

Their bluff *had* to work. The alternative was Armageddon.

Stern was molding a charge of plastic explosive around the lock on the factory door. McConnell thought of all that had been done to bring him to this spot, to put him inside this German gas plant for fifteen minutes. Stern backed quickly away from the door and pulled McConnell with him. A moment later the plastic explosive blasted the doorknob into twisted fragments and the door fell gaping to one side.

When McConnell raised the powerful flashlight Stern had found in the wireless operator's room, and shone it around the interior of the dark factory, he knew that Duff Smith had been right to send him. He was the best man for the job. The production area was smaller than he'd expected, but it contained industrial equipment without equal in the world. The closest thing he had seen to it was a classified DuPont research-and-development lab that one of his professors had walked him through. The production room was two stories high, packed with copper U-tubes and compressors and shallow closed vats. Every few feet along the wall, signs with letters three feet tall read RAUCHEN VERBOTEN!—NO SMOKING! The floor was covered with wooden crates, some open, some sealed. Without electricity for the factory lights, the camera was of little value, but Stern had it out anyway.

McConnell felt like a London tour guide leading Stern through the maze of apparatus, aiming the flashlight here and there while Stern tried long-exposure shots. He found the *aerosols vecteurs* device chained to a pallet in the center of the room. Using tools taken from a workbench, he tore at the heart of the machine until he found the secret it contained: filter discs. He marveled at the sequence of ten superfine droplet traps arranged in order of decreasing tolerance. By the time a war gas had passed from one end to the other, it would exist only as charged ions in suspension, rendering it not only invisible, but also unstoppable by conventional gas masks.

He slipped five of the filters into Stern's bag, then moved on. It was only when Stern used up the first roll of film that they realized they could not change the film cartridge without removing their gas suits. Their oilskin gloves provided enough mobility to fire a gun, but not to thread film onto the tiny spool inside a camera. McConnell motioned for Stern to put the camera away. He wanted only two things from the building: a sample of Soman, and Klaus Brandt's laboratory logs.

He found both in a one-story room in the rear of the factory. The equipment here was made of glass, not metal. This was where the real work was done. One wall of the lab was lined with rubber suits hanging from pegs on the wall. McConnell pointed at a heavy steel door. Stern shot off the lock with a pistol he had taken off a corpse on the way to the factory.

Behind the door they found a treasure trove that would keep the scientists at Porton Down busy for a year. There were small metal gas cylinders marked GA, GB, and with other letters McConnell did not recognize. The cylinders marked GB had strips of adhesive tape fixed to them, with handwritten letters on the tape: *Sarin II; Sarin III; Tabun VII; Soman I; Soman IV.* At the bottom of the storage closet was an empty wooden box like an ammunition crate, but with vertical slots sized to take the eight-inch-long cylinders. McConnell assumed Brandt had used the box to transport gas samples to other testing facilities.

While he filled the crate with samples, Stern explored a higher shelf, pulling down a variety of paraphernalia including a small metal sphere with a stem at the top. It too was marked with adhesive tape that read *Soman IV.* It took Stern a moment to realize what it was—an experimental grenade containing nerve gas.

He slipped three into his bag.

McConnell found Brandt's principal laboratory log lying open on a desk. Sergeant Sturm had apparently evacuated the chemists in the midst of dismantling their equipment for transport. Everything had been left as it was, like a table set for dinner in a burned-out house. McConnell thumbed quickly through the thick notebook. There were passages written in several different hands, many with detailed chemical formulas, most based on organic phosphates. Each entry had been carefully initialed after completion. Several bore the letters *K.B.* beneath them. McConnell stuffed the log into Stern's bag, then picked up the cylinder-transport crate and motioned for Stern to follow him. They had got what they came for.

It was time to run.

"Rottenführer!" Major Schörner shouted. "By the gate! What do you see?"

The young corporal stared through the windshield. He had idled the truck forward fifty meters in the last minute, but he still saw nothing. "I'm sorry, Sturmbannführer."

"By the *gate,* fool! Look now! Crossing the road!"

The corporal followed the beam of the truck's headlights. At last he saw—or thought he saw—a brighter blackness moving against the general darkness. "What is that, Sturmbannführer?"

Schörner slapped his knee in frustration. "Commandos," he said. "They're wearing chemical suits. Move the truck forward, Rottenführer. Very slowly."

As the truck edged forward, its headlight beams caught two figures for an instant. They ducked and ran, flashing as if made of black foil.

Schörner slammed his hand down on the dash. "They're running for the ferry!"

"What should I do, Sturmbannführer?"

Schörner thought furiously. When the answer came to him, he felt a moment of doubt. But then a second realization hit him like a spike through the heart. If Allied commandos had just released the Soman stocks inside Totenhausen, Rachel Jansen was dead. The men in the black suits had not only wiped out the installation he had been ordered to protect, but they had also murdered the only woman he had felt anything for since the love of his life was killed by British bombs. With the calm deliberation of a man under sentence of death, he opened the door and climbed down from the cab.

He took one deep breath, then another. "Everyone all right?" he called to the men in the back of the truck.

"Hofer died from a shrapnel wound, Sturmbannführer. But the rest of us are all right."

"Get down. All of you."

Ten SS men leaped to the ground and formed a line with their rifles and submachine guns at the ready.

Schörner adjusted the patch over his eye and stood erect. "There are at least two Allied commandos on the riverbank near the ferry, possibly more. The ferry is probably iced in, but there may be poison gas between us and them. Bock, Fischer, remain in the truck in case they try to flee this way in a vehicle. The rest of us will advance to the ferry on foot."

Schörner moved up the line as he spoke, finding the eye of every man at least once. "I want five men to form a line in front of me, spaced at ten-meter intervals. I want one man on each side of me— twenty meters away—and one man behind, fifteen meters back. Fire on anything that moves. If any of us fall to gas, the rest will move in the opposite direction, but continue firing. Clear?"

Schörner had seen a few faces whiten when he mentioned gas, and the rest when they realized he meant to use them as human gas alarms. But situations like this were what the SS had been created for. Would Sturm's concentration camp scum live up to the tradition of their corps? They might be scum, but they were German scum. He swept his eyes once more up the line.

"Remember your oath to the Führer, gentlemen. *'I vow to Thee and to the superiors Whom Thou shalt appoint Obedience unto Death, so help me God.'* Heil Hitler!"

As one, ten pairs of jackboots cracked and ten arms lifted to the cold night sky. *"Heil Hitler!"* came the answer.

Rifle bolts clicked in the darkness. The troops assumed the exact formation Schörner had ordered and moved quickly toward the ferry.

Anna nearly fired her pistol when the black-suited figure hammered on the window of the Mercedes. She had been watching the headlights of the troop truck and had not seen anyone cross the road. The swatch of tartan wedged into McConnell's tank harness registered in her brain before she pulled the trigger. She got out of the Mercedes, closed the door, and hugged him tightly.

There was a sudden deep rumbling, and the ferry began to shudder in the water. Anna looked over the roof of the Mercedes. Stern was in the wheelhouse, giving the twin screws all the power they would take. The ferry heaved itself away from the bank and smashed into the sheet of ice covering the ferry channel, throwing Anna and McConnell to the deck. Stern shifted the engines into reverse, backed up and rammed the sheet again.

Nothing.

The third time, he backed the stern of the ferry flush against the dock, shearing off part of the access ramp with a screech of tearing metal. Then he shifted gears, gunned the engine, closed his eyes, and prayed. He heard the deep, shivering crack of ice as the first bullets shattered the windows of the wheelhouse.

"Faster!" Schörner shouted. "They've started the ferry!"

The major's formation had been advancing steadily, parallel to the river, firing as they closed on the dock. While the men shot at the spot they thought the ferry should be, Schörner had kept his eye on the line in front of him, watching for signs of gas. But when the ferry motor roared to life, he knew the time had come to risk all. Eighty meters away, the flat craft nosed out into the river, a clear target now against the white ice sheet. Schörner opened his mouth to order his men to charge the dock at a full run. Then he realized that the man he had posted on his left side was no longer there.

"Gas!" he shouted. "Move right! *Schnell!*"

The line of men broke toward the water, still moving forward, still firing at the ferry. Schörner slammed into the back of the man in front of him, losing his balance. Furious, he got to his feet and shoved the halted trooper forward. The man would not budge. Then Schörner saw why. Two soldiers lay squirming on the ground thirty meters ahead. His five-man frontal screen had been reduced to three, plus the right wingman, who had been forced up to Schörner's side when the squad pressed against the river. He glanced behind him. The rear guard was still on his feet.

"Hold here and give them everything you've got!"

Stern crouched low in the wheelhouse, trying to guide the heavy ferry without standing up inside the glass cube that enclosed the upper wheelhouse. Three sides of the enclosure had already been shattered by bullets.

Anna and McConnell were hunkered down behind the Mercedes, at the edge of the deck. There was no railing, and with Stern pushing the engines to the maximum—plus the give-and-take jolting of the bow smashing the ice—there was a real danger of falling into the river. Anna motioned for McConnell to get the little girl out of the backseat, but he thought the child was safer where she was.

Anna didn't. Using the door handle to steady herself, she pulled herself into a half crouch and opened the door.

The Mercedes' interior light clicked on.

One second later a rifle bullet tore through the opposite window and drilled through Anna's right shoulder.

All McConnell saw was her body flying backward. Then she was gone. Screaming for Stern to stop, he closed the car door and jumped after her into the swirling black water.

"We've hit the pilot!" Schörner shouted, seeing the ferry slow three quarters of the way across the river. "Pour it in!"

As the volume of fire increased, he heard a choked cry behind him. He whirled. The man he had posted behind him seemed to be trying to grab his face with his left hand. Then he suddenly bent double, vomited, snapped back up and fired his submachine gun skyward in an uncontrolled burst. Schörner stared in horror as the man fell backward on the snow and ceased all movement. His nostrils filled with the nauseating odor of feces and urine.

The stench of death.

He held his breath and kept firing at the ferry.

McConnell fought his way toward the gas mask he saw bobbing in the black water. The current was pulling Anna toward the shelf of white ice that covered the rest of the river. If she passed under that, she would be lost. His arms seemed suddenly made of lead. Even in the oilskin suit the water chilled him to the bone, and his heavy rubber boots were pulling him down. He drove his gloved hands against the water and reached out . . .

Two fingers hooked under the leather harness of Anna's air tank. He looked back. The ferry was twenty yards away. He got a firmer grip on Anna's harness, then began swimming.

He knew he would never reach the ferry under his own power. At some point he had torn his gas suit. Its oilskin legs were filling with freezing water, dragging him toward the bottom. Only the buoyancy of their air tanks was keeping him and Anna from sinking like boulders. He had actually stopped swimming when he saw the ferry moving slowly back toward them.

Wolfgang Schörner had not felt real fear since the retreat from Kursk. But when he saw two of the three riflemen in front of him begin jerking spasmodically, a film of cold sweat broke out over his whole body. Was he breathing the gas now? Was it entering his skin even as he knelt on the ground? With a last roar of anger and courage he stood erect and charged down the riverbank toward the dock.

McConnell shoved his right arm through a half-submerged tire on the side of the ferry and pulled Anna close to him. "*Go! Go!*" he shouted, gasping for air. "I've got her! Go!"

Stern firewalled the throttles. The ferry's twin screws lifted the foredeck right out of the water as it closed the last few yards to the far bank, smashing ice as it went. Stern looked back at the dock they'd left behind. A barrel-melting burst of yellow muzzle flashes strobed in the darkness, throwing a hail of bullets across the water. Stern dove out of the wheelhouse as the slugs shattered the remaining glass and riddled the side of the Mercedes.

The ferry would have to land itself.

He prayed that none of the tires on the Mercedes had been punctured.

Wolfgang Schörner was dying on his feet. Even as the bullets poured out of his weapon, a deadly poison was shutting down his central nervous system. The invisible nerve gas had entered his body through every exposed surface, but quickest through the mucus membranes of his mouth and nose, and through the moist sclera of his eyes.

His machine gun clicked empty. He wanted to throw it down, but his hand would not open. He felt a strange embarrassment as his bladder involuntarily voided. Then his bowels let go. He saw the ferry collide with the opposite bank. Almost immediately the taillights of the car clicked on. Schörner was nodding his head violently up and down, but could not understand why. At the last moment he realized that the river itself might afford him protection from the gas. With tremendous concentration he forced his right leg to take a step. Then he lurched forward and fell flat on his face at the end of the pier.

The last thing he felt was the icy water of the river tugging at his right hand.

Racing southwest on the hard gravel road that followed the river, Stern had left Totenhausen far behind. But McConnell knew the Mercedes had sat inside the camp too long not to have been contaminated. He leaned back over the passenger seat and cranked down the rear window beside Anna's still-masked head. He wanted to apply pressure to her shoulder wound, but if there was gas residue on his glove, he might kill her by doing it. He reached across the inflated vinyl bundle that held Hannah Jansen and rolled down the other window.

Cold air blasted through the car.

After a full minute, he ripped the air hose out of his mask and breathed deeply. He had never tasted air so sweet. He waited thirty seconds more, then removed Stern's mask. Stern's face was badly bruised and covered with dried blood, and one of his eyes nearly swollen shut.

"How far to the coast?" McConnell asked, unzipping his suit and pulling his hands out of the oilskin sleeves.

"Forty kilometers in a plane. Probably an hour by road."

Something jabbed McConnell in the crotch. He reached into his suit for the offending object. It was Anna's diary, soaked by river water. Churchill's note hung out of the top like a soggy bookmark. He dropped the diary into Stern's leather bag, then climbed into the back seat to attend to Anna. After she managed to follow his orders and unzip her own suit, he tore out a section of her blouse and stuffed it into the hole in her shoulder. Being careful to touch only the inner surfaces, he gently lifted the transparent gas mask off her head and threw it out of the window.

"We're about to cross the river again," Stern said over the seat. "This is Tessin. Stay down."

McConnell leaned across Anna's lap as they rolled through the blacked out village.

"Is the little girl alive?" Stern asked.

"She's still moving."

Using a British commando knife from Stern's bag, McConnell carefully cut away the rapidly deflating vinyl sheet that held the little girl and the oxygen bottle. "I doubt this thing was completely airtight," he said, "but the pressure of the escaping oxygen should have kept the nerve gas from getting inside."

A high-pitched shriek announced the re-entry of two-year-old Hannah Jansen into the land of the living. McConnell dropped the sheet out of the window and hugged the dark-haired child close, trying to comfort her as best he could. It would be a long time, he knew, before she purged the horror of this night from her mind.

"You know where we're supposed to go?" he asked.

Stern nodded, his eyes on the dark road.

"You think anybody knows what happened? I mean, do you think they'll have troops out looking for us?"

Stern looked back across the seat, his swollen eye sockets crusted with dried blood.

"Just take care of the women, Doctor. Leave the rest to Standartenführer Stern."

McConnell kept pressure on Anna's wound as the Mercedes rolled through the night. Whenever they came to a village, Stern would slow down and coast through at moderate speed. McConnell remembered the names for a long time after: Tessin; Sanitz; Gresenhorst; Ribnitz. Not long after Ribnitz, he smelled sea air. Stern didn't slow down as he expected, but instead accelerated.

"What are you doing?" McConnell asked.

Stern leaned forward and stared through the windshield. "Our inflatable dinghy is supposed to be hidden in the rocks beneath a certain jetty near Dierhagen. A two-man job. But I'm not about to take an inflatable out into a shipping channel cut by an icebreaker. Not with a wounded woman and a child. It would probably take us two hours just to find the damned thing and inflate it."

McConnell saw they had entered another village. "What *are* you going to do then?"

Stern hunched over the wheel. "Be ready to move fast, Doctor. I'll carry the child, you take the woman. No matter what happens, *don't get separated.*"

McConnell had no intention of doing that. "I'm ready," he said.

Stern drove right down the main street of the village. It looked deserted, but at the end of the street McConnell saw the faint silhouette of masts against the night sky. A light burned in a shack at the entrance to the jetty. Stern stopped long enough to wriggle out of his oilskin suit, then pulled up beside the shack and gave a loud blast on the horn.

"Are you crazy?" McConnell asked.

Stern pulled his SD cap out of his bag, set it on his head at an angle and got out of the car, leaving the engine running.

A uniformed officer of the coastal police stumbled out of the shack with a flashlight in his hand. He was about to curse to high heaven whomever had disturbed his sleep when the beam of his torch fell upon the blood-soaked uniform, the Iron Cross First Class, and the rank badge of a colonel in the SD.

"Get that light out of my face, idiot!" Stern barked. "Stand at attention!"

The policeman—a fifty-year-old veteran of World War One—snapped instantly erect, his thumbs at the seams of his trousers. "What can I do for you, Standartenführer?"

"Who are you?"

"Feldwebel Kurt Voss."

"Well, Feldwebel, I need a boat."

The policeman's face was gray with fright, but he was not stupid enough to mention the blood and bruises on the face of the Nazi apparition before him. "There are many boats here, Standartenführer. What type of boat do you require?"

"A motor launch. A seaworthy vessel, the fastest on the dock."

The policeman swallowed. "Most of the boats here are for fishing, Standartenführer. And with the ice this time of year . . . well, few go out at all."

"There must be something."

"There is the Kriegsmarine patrol boat. Its crew put in earlier tonight for . . . well—"

"I understand perfectly, Feldwebel." Stern smiled coldly. "Lead the way to this craft. I will follow in my car."

"But you must speak to the captain first, Standartenführer. He will certainly . . ."

The policeman fell silent under Stern's withering glare.

Stern cocked his chin and enunciated each word separately in the Gestapo fashion, like whiplashes. "The captain will do *what*, Feldwebel? Report to Berlin that he was unavailable to assist an SD officer on Reich security business because he was lying drunk in a brothel?"

The policeman shook his head violently. "You are right, Standartenführer! Follow me. I'll have the boat running before you get aboard."

There was some confusion at the boat when Anna and little Hannah appeared. The wide-eyed policeman could not convince himself that a wounded woman and a child were involved in official SD business, but he was trying hard. Stern carried Hannah into the cabin and laid her in a berth. McConnell and Anna sat down opposite her.

"I'll be on the bridge," Stern told them. He squeezed Anna's good arm. "We're almost there."

He found the policeman standing at the wheel. "How much fuel do we have, Feldwebel?"

"The tanks are full, Standartenführer. There's also an extra can in the hold."

"Enough to get us to Sweden?

"Sweden!" The policeman's terror of the SD battled with his fear of being charged in some treasonous scheme. "Standartenführer, if your business is that important, I'm sure Captain Leber would be glad to ferry you across. Let me call him for you. I know exactly where he is."

"I'm sure you do." Stern revved the engines of the *Schnellboot* and was rewarded with a powerful rumble. He motioned the policeman closer. "Feldwebel," he said softly, "what I am about to say you will repeat on pain of death. The woman and child you just saw are the mistress and child of Reichsführer Himmler. I am their bodyguard. Two hours ago, they were nearly kidnapped by officers disloyal to the Führer. We barely escaped with our lives. The Reichsführer personally instructed me to get them to Sweden by dawn. Now—*do I have enough fuel?*"

The policeman nodded hopelessly.

"How far to open water?"

"Six kilometers."

"That is all I require, Feldwebel. Return to your post."

The policeman climbed onto the dock without a word. Running up the jetty, he heard the thunder of the patrol boat's twin inboard engines as Stern sped north through the black channel that led through the ice sheet to the open waters of the Baltic. Once inside his hut, the feldwebel reached for his telephone, then pulled his hand back into his lap. Stern's scandalous story was sufficient to stay his hand for several minutes. But in the end he snatched up the phone again and called a certain well-known house in Dierhagen to inform Kriegsmarine Captain Leber that a son of a whore from the SD had hijacked his patrol boat to go to Sweden.

After one hour and twenty minutes inside the E-Block, Avram Stern knew the women and children could stand no more. There was no light. Children perching on their mothers' shoulders blocked all four porthole windows. The heat was stifling, almost unbearable; several women had already fainted, and there was nowhere for them to fall. The noise was unbearable. The ceaseless shrieks and wails of hysterical women and children hammered at the shoemaker's eardrums, raising the specter of panic in his own mind. He'd shouted a dozen times for them to be silent, but to no avail.

He felt the dead weight of an unconscious woman sag against him. The child who had been sitting on her shoulders screamed and toppled the other way, into the clawing, shoving mass. Avram tried to take a deep, calming breath, but the air that entered his lungs tasted like acid. He took the machine pistol from the boy Jonas had given it to and began climbing over the heads of the women. Fingernails raked his face and neck, but he struck back, fighting toward the only window whose position he was sure of relative to the door: the window from which Heinrich Himmler had observed the last selection.

He saw a glimmer of moonlight.

When he finally reached the window, he had to fight the urge to immediately shoot it out. No matter how bad things were inside the gas chamber, death might wait without. He pressed his face to the double-paned glass. Bodies lay strewn across the alley as if they had fallen off a plague wagon. Bile rose into his chest. Avram knew he would recognize every dead face in the alley. What had Jonas done? And why? Where was the benefit? As he stared at the hellish scene, something moved slowly into his field of vision.

A dog.

It wasn't one of Sturm's German shepherds with powerful haunches and a glowing coat, but a mongrel from the hills. A scavenger that survived on the refuse of Dornow. The mongrel moved from one corpse to another with boldness driven by hunger. It lingered at the corpse of a woman, tugged at her shift, then licked her face and backed up to gauge the response. Avram counted to sixty, warding off angry blows from below.

The dog was still alive.

Avram pressed the barrel of the machine pistol to the window and pulled the trigger.

Opening the hatch of the E-Block wasn't half as difficult as climbing through the jagged porthole had been. The moment he pulled back the steel door, limp bodies cascaded through it like corpses he'd once seen at a rail siding in eastern Germany. He backed up the cement stairs and waited for the hysterical mass of women and children to empty from the gas chamber.

When the alley was full of milling prisoners, he climbed to the top of the hospital steps and fired the machine pistol into the air. "Listen to me!" he shouted. "We have survived, but we are not yet saved. SS reinforcements are bound to arrive soon." A ripple of fear passed through the crowd. "We must get away immediately. The best hope for all of you is the forests of Poland. I want the two largest German-speakers among you to go to the SS barracks and put on uniforms like mine. Do not try to strip the dead! Gas on their clothing could kill you. Look for spare uniforms in closets or chests. I want ten others to search the camp for the troop truck. The trucks by the factory will be badly contaminated. Touch *nothing* unless absolutely necessary. There could be lethal gas on any surface."

As the frightened women spoke among themselves, Avram turned and reached through the shattered window in the hospital's back door and pushed down the handle with the butt of the machine pistol. Walking through, he felt a tug on his belt. He turned and looked into the eyes of Rachel Jansen, who carried her three-year-old son on her left hip. The boy's eyes were glazed with shock.

"Where are you going, Shoemaker?" Rachel asked.

"To look for money."

"I want to come with you."

Avram nodded and led her into the dark building.

In an office on the second floor he found a hundred Reich-marks, but it was not even a quarter of what he would need.

"Will money help us in Poland?" Rachel asked.

Still ransacking drawers, Avram did not answer.

"Do you really believe we can cross the border and contact a friendly resistance group?"

"There's a fair chance." Avram slammed a door shut and turned to face her. "But I don't think it's the best chance. You don't have to go to Poland if you don't want to."

"What do you mean?"

"If you have the courage, you can come with me. I have a friend in Rostock. A Gentile. He worked ten years in my shop. He offered to help me many years ago, but I was too stupid to understand the danger. I am going to try to reach him now."

"You mean go into the city itself?" Rachel asked fearfully.

"It will be dangerous," he conceded. "If we had money it would be better. We could try to buy our way across to Sweden. I've found a little, but not enough. And we don't have time to search the whole camp."

Rachel was silent in the darkness. At length she said, "Do you really think Rostock is the best chance?"

"For me, yes. For you and the child, yes. But no more."

"I have money, Shoemaker."

"*What?* How much?"

"Three more diamonds. I found them the night you caught me outside. The night Marcus died."

Avram seized her arms with joy. "I thank God you are a devious woman! Hurry, you'll need an SS uniform. I saw one in the closet here. It belonged to one of the assistant doctors. Rauch, I think."

They heard the bellow of the troop truck before Rachel finished dressing. When she had, Avram carried Jan down the stairs and they joined the crowd outside.

"Into the truck!" Avram said. "Everyone, hurry!"

While mothers passed children up into the bed of the truck, Avram sought out the two women he'd sent to the SS barracks to find uniforms. He found them by the cab. They'd taken it upon themselves to procure rifles as well as uniforms. *Perhaps they have a chance after all,* Avram thought. With their short-cropped hair they could certainly pass for SS men at a distance.

"We found it idling on the road with its headlights burning," said the larger of the pair.

"You can drive a truck?" he asked.

She nodded curtly. "You are not coming?"

"No. Listen to me. Drive eastward by as straight a route as you can, but stick to the back roads. It shouldn't take more than three hours. Stop for nothing. If anyone does manage to stop you, tell them you're taking typhus-infected prisoners into the forest to shoot them, by order of SS Lieutenant-General Herr Doktor Klaus Brandt. Do you understand?"

The women nodded.

"When you get close to the border, drive the truck into the trees. Cross on foot through the forest. If you are being chased, don't make a fight of it and don't stop to try to save any wounded. Run for your lives. Your only hope is contacting a friendly resistance group in the forest." He turned up his palms. "That is all I know to tell you. You'd better get moving."

The two women climbed up into the cab and shifted the truck into gear. Avram helped lift the last of the children into the back, then signaled to the driver. As the truck trundled past the dead and out of the alley, he thought of the old woman who had compared the E-Block to a lifeboat. She was dead now, but she had been right. Now the truck was the lifeboat. He lifted Jan from Rachel's arms and began walking out of the alley.

"Where are we going?" Rachel asked.

"They keep a Kubelwagen parked behind the gas storage tanks. That's perfect for us. Small but official."

Rachel had to hurry to keep up with his long strides. "Are you sure about Rostock? You'll have to get us through checkpoints, speak to policemen."

"I'm sure."

"Can you fool them?"

Avram laughed softly. "Frau Jansen, I was once a German soldier. I had a medal from the Kaiser. I can convince those bastards we're on a mission for Hitler himself if it will get us a step closer to freedom."

Rachel took his free hand in hers and squeezed hard. "To Palestine," she said.

One mile north of Dierhagen, Jonas Stern extinguished the running lights of the patrol boat and let it idle in the open water. At least the dangerous run through the narrow ice channel was over. He assumed the Kriegsmarine had been alerted by now, but hoped that his emphasis on reaching Sweden would cause them to establish a blockade line farther out to sea. He blinked the running lights on and off three times in quick succession, waited thirty seconds, then repeated the signal.

He saw nothing. Three hundred and sixty degrees of darkness. He wondered if there had ever been a submarine at all. Had Smith ever believed he and McConnell would get this far?

"Why have we stopped?"

McConnell had poked his head up from the cabin.

"How's the nurse?" Stern asked.

"Okay for now. There was no morphine in the first aid kit. I gave her some schnapps I found in a bag. I need real medical supplies, Jonas."

Stern nodded. "This is where we're supposed to meet the submarine. But there's no sub here."

"But Smith knows we're coming, right? I mean, he knows we succeeded."

Stern rubbed the stubble on his chin. "Did you ever consider the possibility that Brigadier Smith never meant for us to get out alive, Doctor? That the attack was the only real point of all this?"

McConnell said nothing. Stern's suggestion was more than a possibility. A man who would send bombers to wipe out all trace of their mission would not hesitate to leave them stranded in a black ocean between the SS and the German Navy.

"My God," Stern murmured. "Look!"

Forty meters off the bow, the massive conning tower of a submarine rose out of the waves like the Biblical leviathan.

"They must have been watching us through their periscope!"

Stern cried. "They were looking for a raft, not a German patrol boat. Get Anna and the girl ready."

By the time Stern brought the patrol boat alongside the submarine, its captain, first officer, two ratings, and a man not in uniform but wearing a black turtleneck sweater were waiting for them. The first officer carried a submachine gun. Stern saw "HMS *Sword*" painted on the submarine's hull. The ratings caught hold of the patrol boat with long hooks.

"Code names?" called the man in the black sweater.

"Butler and Wilkes!" Stern replied.

"Come aboard."

Stern went below and brought Hannah Jansen out of the cabin. McConnell followed, supporting Anna. As they approached the rail, the man in the black sweater pointed at them and said something to the captain.

"Hold!" the captain shouted. "We can only take the two of you aboard! No refugees!"

McConnell saw that this order had not surprised Stern at all. "Captain, I'm a medical doctor!" he shouted. "This woman has a gunshot wound. The other is a child. They need immediate medical attention!"

The captain's resolve seemed to waver. The man in the black turtleneck spoke angrily in his ear. The captain brushed him away and said, "I'm sorry, Doctor, but the normal rules do not apply. I have specific orders—only the two of you. You've got ten seconds to get aboard this ship."

Anna pulled McConnell's face close to hers. "Go," she said. "I can drive the boat. I'll point it north and try to reach Sweden. Thank you for everything you've done."

"Not a chance in hell," he said. "It's a hundred miles to Sweden, straight through the German Navy."

"We'll scuttle her!" Stern threatened. He reached into his bag and brought out a British grenade. "Then you'll *have* to rescue them. It's the law of the sea!"

"I won't have that!" the captain shouted. "I will not have it!" He looked from Stern to the man in the black sweater.

McConnell sensed the honor of a sea captain struggling with his sense of duty to an authority he wasn't sure he trusted. The captain leaned over and said something to his first officer. McConnell could scarcely believe it when the first officer turned and pointed the sub-machine gun at the man in the sweater.

"Come aboard!" the captain called. "Quickly."

McConnell went below to retrieve the crate containing the sample gas cylinders. He stared at the lid, thinking. He did not like what he had seen of their rescue party so far. He opened the crate quickly, then sealed it again and carried it topside.

The ratings were holding the patrol boat steady for the transfer. McConnell handed the crate up to the first officer, but the man in the sweater thrust himself forward and took it. The first officer took aboard Stern's leather bag—and his explosives—even before he took Hannah Jansen. As Stern climbed past McConnell, he whispered, *"The black sweater is Intelligence. Probably SOE."*

As they stood freezing in the darkness beside the conning tower, the captain said, "We'll use the radio to call Sweden. I can't disobey a direct order. Brigadier Smith must give me approval."

McConnell felt fury rising in his chest.

"I'm sorry, Doctor, but I've no choice. There's nowhere else I can put them off."

"We'd better hurry, sir," said the first officer. "The Kriegsmarine has been alerted. It won't take them long to find us."

The first officer escorted the SOE man up the ladder and into the sub, not exactly at gunpoint, but with a clear understanding of who was in charge. Stern carried Hannah up with ease, but both ratings had to help McConnell get Anna up the ladder and through the hatch. Her arm was stiffening, the pain and blood loss taking their toll.

The captain ordered that Anna and Hannah be held at the foot of the ladder while he used the radio. McConnell didn't want to leave them, but Stern shoved him along a claustrophobic passage toward the radio room. A half-dozen young faces gaped at the German uniforms as they passed.

While the wireless operator raised "Atlanta" and verified the codes, the captain, a rather short man with tired eyes, said, "Don't like irregular operations. Dirty business. Our job is sinking ships, not ferrying Joes all over the seven seas. Still—"

"Got him, sir," said the wireless operator. "Better make it quick. We're transmitting *en clair,* and the Kriegsmarine has DF gear all over the place."

"Right." The captain took the mike. "Tickell here. I've got a sticky situation. A wounded woman and a child in dire circumstances. I've brought them aboard for medical attention. Request permission to ferry them to you. Will you take them off there?"

The only answer was a high-pitched electronic whine and intermittent static. The captain was standing half in and half out of the wireless station. Pressed against his back, McConnell had to turn his head only two inches to look into Stern's eyes. Stern did not look confident. At last the voice of Brigadier Smith cut through the static.

"Tickell, there's more at stake here than you will ever know. I will only say this once. Put those refugees back into whatever craft they arrived on and make for your destination straightaway. Confirm."

The captain leaned farther into the wireless room and said in a strained voice, "You're condemning them to death, Smith. I won't have that on my conscience."

McConnell felt Stern jab him in the side. Looking back over his shoulder, he saw the intelligence man standing about two yards behind Stern, with the first officer behind him. There would be no getting past them to help Anna and the child.

"Nothing's on your precious conscience!" crackled Smith's voice. "You saw my authority. If you won't put them off, my man will. Confirm."

McConnell heard a long sigh, then the voice of the captain saying, "Message received and understood. Proceeding with all speed."

Captain Tickell looked back over his shoulder. "Put them back in the patrol boat, Deevers!" he called to his first officer. "Show the woman how to work the throttle and compass, then point her towards Sweden." He turned and shouted toward the other end of the corridor. "Prepare to dive!"

McConnell couldn't believe the man would really put off a wounded woman and a child. He laid a hand on Tickell's shoulder. "Captain—"

The captain shoved roughly past him, then stopped and looked back, his face full of disgust. "I'm sorry, Doctor," he said. "But there's nothing I can do. It's out of my hands." He turned and made his way along the passage toward the control room.

McConnell slipped a hand into his pocket. Duff Smith had left him no choice, and this would be his only chance. Just as Captain

Tickell reached the control room, McConnell stepped away from the door to the radio room and brought out the eight-inch metal cylinder marked *Soman IV.*

"Captain!" he shouted. "Your ship is in grave danger!"

Tickell turned slowly and peered back up the passage.

McConnell held up the cylinder in his left hand and clenched the valve key between his right thumb and forefinger. "This canister contains the deadliest war gas known to man. This is what we were sent into Germany to get. No one knows better than you that this submarine is nothing but a sealed tin can with a motor—"

McConnell heard the sound of running feet behind him. He glanced over his shoulder in time to see Stern shatter the nose of the SOE man with his right hand and flatten the first officer with his left elbow. The first officer tried to use his machine pistol, but he was no match for Stern in close quarters. A burst of gunfire ricocheted though the passage, ringing the steel hull like a mammoth bell. Then Stern was holding the weapon over two dazed and bleeding men.

"Did you shoot them?" McConnell asked in a shaky voice.

"No. *Watch the captain!*"

McConnell whirled, brandishing the cylinder. Tickell had already covered half the distance to him. "Don't let this go any further, Captain!" he shouted. He felt his control over the situation disintegrating fast. "If I release this gas in this submarine, every man on board will be dead within five minutes. Either close the hatch and dive, or preside over the death of your ship." His eyes bore into the British officer's. "So help me God, Captain, I will do it."

"He's bluffing," groaned the SOE man from the floor.

The captain stared wide-eyed at the cylinder.

"How long will it take us to get to Sweden, Stern?"

"Submerged . . . about six hours."

McConnell shook the cylinder again. "Six hours, Captain! I could keep my hand on this valve for twice that long if I had to. You have two choices. You know which is right. Which will it be?"

Captain Tickell gazed into McConnell's eyes with the cold-blooded assessment of a man accustomed to balancing lethal risks. As he did, McConnell felt a strange calm settle in his soul. He was *not bluffing.* That realization gave him a sense of power he had never known in his life.

Tickell's eyes narrowed slightly, then widened like those of a hunter who has followed a wounded lion too far into the bush. "Let my first officer up," he said. "Deevers, close the bloody hatch. Duff Smith can sort out his own mess."

A dizzying wave of relief washed over McConnell.

"Prepare to dive!" Tickell shouted to the control room. "We'll torpedo the patrol boat before we go."

"Thank you, Captain," McConnell said. "You did the right thing."

Tickell's jaw muscles clenched with cold fury. "I'll see you both hanged for this," he said.

"You'll probably have to watch them pin medals on us first," Stern said over McConnell's shoulder. "Let's get this stinking tub to Sweden."

Six hours later, HMS *Sword* surfaced one mile off the southern Swedish coast. The voyage had been a test of nerves, with McConnell treating Anna's wound while Stern stood guard with the revolver and the canister of Soman. They'd shut the door long enough for McConnell to set and splint Stern's broken finger, but the lacerations on his chest had had to wait. Hannah Jansen had drunk some powdered milk and vomited it up immediately. By the time they crawled out of the submarine's conning tower to be taken ashore, they were near to exhaustion.

Airman Bottomley had rented a motor launch to meet the sub. The sleek wooden craft rose and fell gently on the swell beside the sub's sail. When Bottomley refused to take Anna and the child aboard, Captain Tickell told him he would take them or be blown out of the water.

Bottomley took them.

The SOE man remained on the *Sword;* apparently there was other "dirty business" still to be done in the Baltic. The launch reached the Swedish coast after a ten-minute run, homing on a blinking green signal lantern.

When Bottomley cut the engine and drifted into the small dock, McConnell spied the two silhouettes waiting for them. One was Duff Smith. The other was a little taller, but bundled in a heavy coat and muffler. For a wild moment he thought Winston Churchill himself might reach down out of the gloom to pull them onto the dock.

In the event, he was even more stunned. The face at the other end of the assisting arm belonged to his brother.

McConnell froze for a moment, watched Stern hand the child up to David. Before he had time to think, Stern had helped Anna out of the launch. Like a sleepwalker he climbed out of the boat and faced them all on the jetty.

David broke into a huge grin and said, "Goddamn it, boy, you made it!"

McConnell could not speak. Despite the evidence before him, his mind tried to deny the reality. Then David passed Hannah Jansen to Stern, reached into his flight jacket and brought out a pewter flask.

"How about a shot of Kentucky's finest, Mac?" he asked. "It's cold as a welldigger's ass up here."

McConnell turned to Brigadier Smith. "Does he know . . . what I thought?"

Duff Smith shook his head very slightly, then pointed at the wooden crate. "Is that the gas sample, Doctor?"

McConnell nodded dully. "Soman Four. Fluoromethylpinacolyl-oxyphosphine oxide." He gestured at Stern's bag. "Brandt's lab log is in there." He brought out the cylinder he had used to blackmail the sub captain. "But I'm going to hang onto this one until we reach England, if you don't mind. Maybe even longer. Think of it as insurance."

"Dear boy," Smith said, "there's no need for histrionics. You're the hero of the hour."

"When are we going back to England?"

"Right now. Your brother will fly us in the Junkers. He flew you over from England four nights ago, though neither of you knew it."

"I did?" David said. "I'll be damned."

"It was David who fixed the Lysander engine. Made the whole jaunt possible, I daresay." Smith allowed himself a smile. "A credit to the Eighth Air Force, this lad. I hate to give him back. And he loves my JU-88A6."

"That's a fact," David chimed in, but by now he had sensed the tension between his brother and the brigadier.

All McConnell could think of was the transatlantic call he had made to his mother three weeks before.

"I wasn't counting on any refugees, Doctor," Smith said tetchily. "I'm afraid you've caused a spot of bother there."

McConnell looked at David again. Then he handed the cylinder to Stern and, before anyone could stop him, punched the brigadier in the belly with all his strength.

Smith doubled over, gasping for air.

Airman Bottomley leaped for McConnell, but he didn't get past David. Seconds later he was hanging by his throat from the crook of the pilot's elbow.

"Take it easy now, pardner," David drawled.

Duff Smith straightened up with some difficulty. "It's all right, Bottomley," he croaked. "I suppose I deserved that one."

"Damn right you did," said McConnell. "Now, let's get the hell out of here. All of us."

Brigadier Smith waved his agreement.

McConnell saw Stern staring at him in astonishment. He slipped under Anna's good arm and braced her for a walk. "Can you make it?" he asked quietly.

Her eyes were only half open, but she nodded.

As they moved along the jetty, David leaned over and said, "What did you punch that old coot for? He's okay, once you get to know him."

Mark hugged Anna to his side and shook his head. "Ask me in twenty years," he said. "It's a hell of a war story."

EPILOGUE

A hell of a story?" I said. "That's not the end of it!"

Rabbi Leibovitz looked at me a little strangely. Dawn was creeping around the edges of the drapes. We'd moved into the kitchen sometime during the night, where he told his tale over a pot of coffee. Later we'd come back to the study.

"What do you want to know?" he asked.

"Well . . . everything. But first my Uncle David. I thought he was killed in the war, but according to you . . ."

"He was killed, Mark. Five months after Mac's mission he was shot down over Germany. It happened to a lot of good boys. Too many, I'm afraid. They had a little time together, though. Brigadier Smith managed to keep David four extra days before returning him to the Eighth Air Force. He'd used Churchill's note and some valuable SOE intelligence to get David's superiors to go along with the deception. Anyway, Mac and David spent the four days following the mission in London. Mac remembered them as some of the best days of his life."

I shook my head. "What about the others? Who got out alive? You left me hanging at the camp. Did the shoemaker and Rachel get to Rostock with Jan? Did they reach Sweden?"

"Miraculously enough, they did. They hid in the house of Avram's old employee for three weeks. It took that long to arrange passage on a smuggler's boat. It cost them all three diamonds, but they reached Sweden alive. They were interned there for the duration of the war."

"What did Rachel do after the war?"

"She went to Palestine to find her daughter."

"Palestine? I figured Hannah wound up in some British orphanage."

"You underestimate Jonas Stern," said Leibovitz. "With the diamonds Rachel and his father had given him, Stern arranged to have Hannah cared for by a Jewish family in London. He fought with the British in France, then with the Jewish Brigade later. He won a hatful of medals, then went back to Palestine to drive out the British and the Arabs. He took Hannah with him."

"I'll be damned. And Rachel found them?"

"With Avram's help. The two of them traveled from Sweden to Palestine in the winter of 1945. Hannah was living with Jonas and his mother in Tel Aviv."

"My God. Were Rachel and Stern lovers, then?"

Leibovitz smiled. "I don't know. The two of them raised Hannah under the same roof for some years. They never married, though. From what I gathered, Stern's work kept him traveling around the world for longer and longer periods. He was a born fighter. He spent his whole life in one branch or another of Israeli intelligence. Eventually Rachel married another man. Hannah is a grown woman now. Well into middle age. Jan is a lawyer, like his father was. In Tel Aviv."

I shook my head. "And Avram?"

"Avram died twenty years ago. He was eighty-six."

I felt a disturbing dislocation of time. In my mind, Avram Stern was a man of fifty-five, Hannah Jansen a child of two. "How do you know all this?" I asked. "My grandfather kept up with everyone?"

"A little. Not so often, but enough to know the big things. Every two or three years he got a letter from Stern. Postmarked from the ends of the earth, usually."

I sat quietly, trying to take it all in. The man who raised me—the grandfather I thought I had known all my life—was really someone entirely different. Leibovitz was right. I felt different for hearing the story. How many gray heads had I passed in the street or spoken to in the emergency room, never imagining they had once hunched over the controls of a shattered bomber in the darkness over Germany or lain in an icy ditch while SS troops combed a forest for them.

"The rest of the story is not so happy," Leibovitz said. "Fewer

than half of the women and children who got away on the truck survived the war. I've spent several years trying to track them down.
Life in the forests of occupied Poland was hard. Some ran into the
wrong kind of resistance groups. Others died of sickness, even hunger. That's the way it was. The most dramatic escape from a death
camp in World War Two was from Sobibor. Three hundred escaped
through the fence, yet only a handful survived the mines and the
machine guns of the SS."

"Christ." I could see now why my grandfather felt confused
about what he had done. "Was it worth it, Rabbi? How much of
what my grandfather guessed was true? How much of what Brigadier Smith told them was the truth?"

Leibovitz straightened in the chair. "As costly as that mission
was, I believe it was worth every life lost. Heinrich Himmler *had*
been trying to persuade Hitler to utilize nerve gas to stave off the invasion. But after the raid on Totenhausen, he had little choice but to
buy Brigadier Smith's bluff. The evidence was before his eyes. The
Allies possessed nerve gas and they had used it. They had used it to
destroy Himmler's pet project one day before his demonstration for
the Führer. That left him two choices. Tell Hitler about the devastating raid and accept the shame of being proved wrong—not to mention admitting that Allied saboteurs had penetrated a top-secret SS
facility—or—"

"Cover it up."

"Yes."

"How did he do it?"

"He simply exaggerated the effects of the bombs delivered
by the Mosquito flight. Who would argue with him? What had been
the village of Dornow was hardly more than a crater in the snow.
The power station was obliterated. The day after your grandfather
left Totenhausen, Himmler ordered the camp demolished and the
debris plowed under the ground."

"Jesus."

"I went there, Mark. Four years ago. I was on a trip with some
other rabbis, to see the concentration camps. I took a side trip to
Dornow. I went down to the spot between the hills and the river."

"And?"

"There was nothing there. Just a rough, uneven field with the
river flowing past it. I said kaddish and drove away."

Leibovitz touched a finger to his chin. "Some justice did come out of it. Anna's diary was used as evidence in the infamous Nazi medical trials. One of Brandt's assistant physicians had been away from Totenhausen at the time of the attack. He was hanged, largely on the evidence of the diary."

"What about the record kept by the Jewish women? Did Rachel take that out?"

Leibovitz smiled sadly. "How symmetrical it would be to think she did. But when that last night of horror came, no one thought of it. They thought only of survival."

"Perhaps if Frau Hagan had still been alive. . . ."

"Perhaps. But in any case, they were not the only prisoners who kept records. After the war, similar journals were found buried in jars, cans, under barrack floorboards. Some of them . . ."

For the first time I saw moisture in the rabbi's eyes. He leaned his head back and blinked, then fell silent. I picked up the Victoria Cross from the floor. "I think I'm beginning to understand," I said. "What happened at Totenhausen had nothing to do with glory."

"Not in any conventional sense. Winston Churchill thought so, though. He awarded Mac the medal in a private meeting near the end of the war." The old man squeezed his hands together, then reached out and took a sip of brandy. "I've sometimes wondered whether or not that VC is real. As I told you, the only other American ever to receive it was the Unknown Soldier. Technically, it's not supposed to be awarded to civilians. The highest British medal that can be is the George Cross, and Jonas Stern received that for the Totenhausen mission. I believe the VC is real, though. I believe Churchill liked your grandfather, Mark. I think he deeply respected him, and his ideals. I think Churchill saw in Mac the best part of America. And Mac had given a great deal to England. He'd been working for them since 1940, remember, long before Pearl Harbor."

Leibovitz set down his glass. "Mac respected Churchill as well. Churchill asked him as a favor to preserve the secret of BLACK CROSS, and as you know too well, Mac did so until his dying day. He once told me Churchill's note meant far more to him than the VC."

The rabbi got up from the chair and walked over to my grandfather's bookshelves. "We had a bit of a shock in 1991," he said, moving slowly along the row of books. "Mac and I were in my home, watching CNN. The Desert Storm deadline was near to expiring. We saw a clip of American soldiers being briefed on how to inject themselves with atropine in response to poison gas attacks. The announcer specifically mentioned Sarin as the most feared weapon in the Iraqi arsenal."

"My God."

Leibovitz turned from the shelves. "It's true. To this day, Sarin and Soman remain the deadliest poison gases in the world."

The rabbi's revelations were shocking, but the truth was that my mind was no longer on weapons and military medals. I picked up the old wooden box and took out the black-and-white photograph, the one showing the blond woman's face against dark wood. She really was beautiful.

"This woman is Anna Kaas, isn't she?"

Leibovitz nodded. "That was the real secret of your grandfather's life, Mark."

"What happened to her?"

"She lived in Britain until the end of the war. I don't know whether she and Mac lived together there or not. But when the war ended, he came back to America alone."

"She stayed behind?"

"Yes."

"And he never told my grandmother about her?"

"Never. Two years after the war, Anna Kaas emigrated to New York. She graduated from the Cornell Medical School in 1952."

"Wow. Did my grandfather ever see her after that?"

The rabbi seemed hesitant to answer. "Two or three times," he said finally. "Over all those years. Medical meetings in New York, Boston. What does it matter now? He shared something with Anna that no one but Jonas Stern could understand, and probably not even him. Stern was made of different stuff, I think."

I stood up, tired from lack of sleep, yet alive with a strange energy. "It's difficult to take in," I said. "I don't really know what to say, or do. I guess there's nothing I *can* do."

Rabbi Leibovitz gave me a meaningful glance.

"What is it?" I asked. "Wait a minute. Do these people know my grandfather is dead?"

He smiled wistfully. "Jonas Stern is dead himself, Mark."

"What?"

"He died in 1987. One day a telegram came to Mac's office. It was from Hannah Jansen—under her married name, of course. It said that Stern's will had instructed her to notify Mac of his death. Nothing else, though. We never found out how he died. I contacted some friends in Israel, but Israel is obsessive about security."

"What about Rachel? Does she know?"

"She knows. I called her the day of the crash."

I was pacing the room, growing inexplicably more nervous with each passing minute.

"*Anna* doesn't know, however," said Leibovitz. "And I think you should be the one to tell her."

I stopped. "Me? Why me?"

He cocked his head to one side. "I think it would be fitting."

"Where did you say she was? New York?"

"Yes. Westchester. Her name is Anna Hastings now."

"She got married?"

"Of course. She wasn't one to pine away the rest of her life. Her husband died some years ago, though."

"Well . . . it's an hour later in New York. I guess I could call her in a couple of hours."

Leibovitz looked shocked. "You don't handle something like that over the phone, boy."

"You mean I should go to New York?"

"Is it so difficult? Would it take so much time out of your life? There and back in a day. Drive to Atlanta, get on a plane, you're there."

I tried to remember my hospital schedule, then realized with some embarrassment that I had taken the next three days off. After all, the man and woman who raised me had just died. I knew I'd need some time to clear up any final legal business, make arrangements about the estate and so on. But the simple fact was that all of that could wait a few days, if not months.

"What the hell?" I said. "Okay. I'd like to hear what she's been doing all these years. Maybe get her side of this story."

Leibovitz smiled. "I think you'll be glad you did."

In the end, I was glad. I flew into Newark on Monday, rented a car, and after a one-handed wrestling match with a cheap service-station map, navigated the rented Ford Tempo up to Westchester.

The house was smaller than I'd expected. Anna was supposedly a physician, after all, and she'd had the good fortune to practice medicine before the advent of so-called healthcare reform. Hell, she'd probably started practicing before they even established Medicaid.

I parked the Ford and walked up a flower-lined sidewalk right out of Fairplay, Georgia to the modest suburban house. I felt a little overdressed. I'd worn a nice suit in case the former Anna Kaas turned out to own the biggest palace in suburban New York. I pushed the bell twice, assuming—as I had learned to do in medical practice—that anyone over the age of sixty had some degree of hearing loss. I wondered if Anna would have a strong German accent.

When the door opened, I was struck dumb. I stood face to face with a mirror image of the woman from the photograph in my grandfather's box. There was only one difference. Anna's eyes had been dark. This woman's eyes were blue. She looked at me strangely, as if trying to decide whether or not I was dangerous. The Armani suit and gold Montblanc fountain pen finally tipped the scales in my favor.

"Can I help you?" she asked in a perfectly American voice.

I fished a Day-Timer notebook out of my inside coat pocket and took out the weathered photograph from my grandfather's box. I handed it to the woman. She looked at it for what seemed like a long time. Then she took my hand and pulled me inside.

She led me to a carpeted living room that held a sofa, two Queen Anne chairs, and a set of tall glass-fronted bookcases, which displayed a menagerie of porcelain figurines and heavy ornamental picture frames. The figurines looked like Hummels.

"Wait here," she instructed. "I'll only be a moment."

I walked over to the window and looked out at the well-kept lawn. Had Nurse Anna Kaas ever dreamed she would wind up here? I was still standing like that when I heard someone catch a breath.

"My God," said a deeper, almost rasping voice.

I turned. Standing in the foyer outside the living room was a woman of at least seventy-five, with silver hair and dark brown eyes. She leaned on the younger woman's arm for support. She stared at me for some moments, then said, "He's dead, isn't he?"

"Are you Doctor Anna Hastings?" I asked, though I knew she had to be. "Formerly Anna Kaas?"

"Is Mac dead?"

"Yes, ma'am. He died three days ago. It was an accident. A helicopter crash. My grandmother died with him."

The old woman nodded slowly, then stepped away from her support and walked across the carpet in measured steps. She stopped in front of me. I wanted to be polite, but my gaze kept wandering to the eyes of the younger woman, who was staring at me with a strange intensity.

Anna Hastings reached out and laid her hand against my cheek. "You could be him," she said softly. "I almost can't bear to look at you."

"She could be you," I said, nodding toward the young woman. Although, now that I had had time to study her, I saw subtle differences. The younger woman was more slender than Anna had ever been, and her cheekbones a bit higher.

"Katarina," said Anna Hastings. "My granddaughter."

I smiled at her. "I'm Mark McConnell. The third," I added quickly. "That never really seemed relevant, but now—"

"You would have finished your training by now, of course," Anna said. "You are a doctor?"

I nodded. "Emergency medicine."

She laughed softly at that. "Fighter-pilot mentality."

Her German accent was hardly noticeable. In fact, she probably spoke better English than I did.

"Sit down, sit down," the old woman insisted. "Katarina will make some coffee."

"Well, I really just came to . . . to give you the news."

"All the way from the back of beyond and already you want to leave? Sit down, Doctor."

It was on my way to the sofa that I noticed the picture. When I first looked at the shelves, I'd lost it among the others. Now it stood out like a beacon. It was black-and-white, with almost the same tint as the photo I had brought with me. It showed a man in his early thirties standing against a dark wooden beam. His intense countenance and lanky body could have been my own.

It was all so clear now. In the dark of that last night in the cottage, they had taken turns standing against the beam and taking each other's picture, probably thinking that their images on film would be all that survived. I felt a hard lump in my throat.

"I'd like to ask you some questions, if you don't mind," I said.

"Are you married, Doctor?" the old woman asked.

"What? Married? No."

"People wait too long nowadays. Katarina is the same."

"*Oma,*" her granddaughter said with embarrassment.

Anna Hastings laughed. "Too picky, too shy. No one is good enough. Go make us some coffee, girl."

Anna used one age-spotted hand to shoo me away from the shelves. "You go too, Doctor. Help her find the sugar. NutraSweet for her, of course. Go on, both of you."

"But I really do have some questions—"

The former Anna Kaas put her hand over her mouth. It was then that I saw the great effort it was taking to maintain her composure. "Your grandfather was a great man," she said. "A brave and a loyal man. What else does anyone need to know? There's plenty of time to talk about the past. Go make the coffee. Please."

Katarina took my hand and pulled me out of the room.

She led me into a spotless white kitchen, opened the refrigerator and took out a can of coffee. For some reason, I couldn't take my eyes off her. I told myself it was some kind of transference. That after hearing the story of the brave German nurse—who was actually the elderly lady in the next room—I had invested her granddaughter with her personality. But there was no denying the young woman's beauty, or the intelligence behind her bright eyes.

"I've never seen her that upset," Katarina said as she poured bottled water into the coffeemaker. "I think it might help her to talk to you. Even though she tries to pretend the past is dead, it haunts her. Were you planning to stay the night in New York? You have a hotel?"

"No. I'd really planned to fly back tonight."

"Tonight? But that's crazy. You can stay here with us—"

Suddenly she blushed, as if realizing she had overstepped some invisible line. "I'm sorry," she said. "I know how it is in medicine. I'm sure you've got to get back right away."

"Katarina," I said softly. "I'm not really sure why I came up here. I really don't have any plans at all."

She looked at me very openly then, directly into my eyes. "Call me Kat," she said. "That's what everyone calls me."

"Kat," I said, testing the name on my tongue. "Kat, I would really love to stay. If you have room, of course."

She smiled.

AFTERWORD

Black Cross is a novel of historical fiction. In certain instances,
I have taken small liberties with facts or time frames for dramatic purposes, but not in such a way as to distort essential
historical truths.

There was no concentration camp called Totenhausen in Mecklenburg. However, there were far too many camps like it throughout
Germany and Poland. The medical experiments described in the
book involving Dr. Clauberg are documented facts. Those involving
meningitis are fictional, but do not approach in horror and effect
some of the actual experiments carried out by the Nazis.

The Victoria Cross, Britain's highest military award, has been
awarded to only one non-British citizen: an "unknown American
warrior." So far as I know, there is no "secret list" as described in
Chapter One. The actual medal that would have been received by a
non-British civilian for the type of mission described in the book
would be the George Cross, which is relatively unknown to most
Americans.

Achnacarry Castle is a real place, and during the Second World
War produced some of the greatest unsung heroes in history. Colonel Charles Vaughan was the real C.O. of the Commando Depot
there, and much of the credit for the exploits of its graduates—
including the U.S. Army Rangers—goes to him. Sir Donald Walter
Cameron was the real Laird of Achnacarry during the war, and also
the father of the present laird, Sir Donald Hamish Cameron, who
served with distinction with the Lovat Scouts during WWII. I fic-
tionalized both Colonel Vaughan and the elder Sir Donald with the
utmost respect and admiration.

515

The nerve gases described in *Black Cross* were and are real. Tabun was discovered by the Germans in 1936; Sarin in 1938; and Soman in 1944. Sarin and Soman are still the most feared war gases in the world. The Nazis produced over 7,000 tons of Sarin by the end of the war. According to official accounts, Soman never reached the mass production stage; however, as a curtain of secrecy descended over all these captured compounds after the Nazi surrender, we cannot be certain that all facts are known.

I believe that Adolf Hitler, a man willing to destroy Germany rather than surrender, would have required powerful reasons to stay his hand from a weapon as potentially decisive as Sarin. I like to think that the Allies, particularly Winston Churchill, possessed the nerve and the guts to order a mission like the one described in *Black Cross*. A similar "suicide mission" was carried out by Norwegians— with the assistance of SOE—against a heavy water plant in Norway in 1943. This costly raid ensured that Adolf Hitler was denied nuclear weapons.

The Allied reaction—or lack thereof—to the news of what was occurring in the Nazi concentration camps remains one of the darkest chapters of WWII. It is expertly detailed in *Auschwitz and the Allies*, by Martin Gilbert.

All of us owe our freedom to men and women we shall never know. Some of their stories are told in: *Skis Against the Atom*, by Knut Haukelid; *The Holocaust* and *Churchill*, by Martin Gilbert; *Castle Commando*, by Donald Gilchrist; *Moon Squadron*, by Jerrard Tickell; *A Man Called Intrepid*, by William Stevenson; and *The Glory and the Dream*, by William Manchester.

Finally, I would ask young readers to realize that fifty years is not a long time.

The typeface used in this book is a version of Sabon, originally designed in the 1960s by Jan Tschichold (1902–1974) at the behest of a consortium of manufacturers of metal type. As one who began as an outspoken design revolutionary—calling for the elimination of serifs, scorning revivals of historic typefaces—Tschichold seemed an odd choice, but he met the challenge brilliantly: The typeface was to be based on the fonts of the sixteenth-century French typefounder Claude Garamond but five percent narrower; it had to be identical for three different processes, working around the quirks of each, such as linotype's inability to "kern" (allow one character into the space of another, the way the top of a lowercase f overhangs other letters). Aside from sabon, named for a sixteenth-century French punchcutter to avoid problems of attribution to garamond, Tschichold is best remembered as the designer of the Penguin paperbacks of the late 1940s.